HAND IN GL

DEAD WATER

DEATH AT THE DOLPHIN

Dame Ngaio Marsh was born in New Zealand in 1895 and died in February 1982. She wrote over 30 detective novels and many of her stories have theatrical settings, for Ngaio Marsh's real passion was the theatre. Both actress and producer, she almost single-handedly revived the New Zealand   public's interest in the theatre. It was for this work that she received what she called her 'damery' in 1966.

'The finest writer in the English language of the pure, classical puzzle whodunit. Among the crime queens, Ngaio Marsh stands out as an Empress.'   *The Sun*

'Ngaio Marsh transforms the detective story from a mere puzzle into a novel.'   *Daily Express*

'Her work is as nearly flawless as makes no odds. Character, plot, wit, good writing, and sound technique.'
Sunday Times

'She writes better than Christie!'   *New York Times*

'Brilliantly readable . . . first class detection.'   *Observer*

'Still, quite simply, the greatest exponent of the classical English detective story.'   *Daily Telegraph*

'Read just one of Ngaio Marsh's novels and you've got to read them all . . . '   *Daily Mail*

NGAIO MARSH

Hand in Glove

Dead Water

Death at the Dolphin

AND

The Cupid Mirror

HARPER

HARPER

an imprint of HarperCollins*Publishers*
77-85 Fulham Palace Road
Hammersmith, London W6 8JB
www.harpercollins.co.uk

This omnibus edition 2009

1

Hand in Glove first published in Great Britain by Collins 1962
Dead Water first published in Great Britain by Collins 1964
Death at the Dolphin first published in Great Britain by Collins 1967
The Cupid Mirror first published in Great Britain in
Death on the Air and Other Stories by HarperCollins*Publishers* 1995

Ngaio Marsh asserts the moral right to
be identified as the author of these works

Copyright © Ngaio Marsh Ltd 1962, 1963, 1966
The Cupid Mirror copyright © Ngaio Marsh (Jersey) Ltd 1989

ISBN 978 0 00 732876 5
Printed and bound in Great Britain by
Clays Ltd, St Ives plc

Mixed Sources
Product group from well-managed
forests and other controlled sources
www.fsc.org Cert no. SW-COC-1806
© 1996 Forest Stewardship Council

FSC is a non-profit international organisation established to promote the
responsible management of the world's forests. Products carrying the FSC
label are independently certified to assure consumers that they come
from forests that are managed to meet the social, economic and
ecological needs of present and future generations.

Find out more about HarperCollins and the environment at
www.harpercollins.co.uk/green

CONTENTS

Hand in Glove

for Jonathan Elsom

Contents

Cast of Characters

Alfred Belt	*Manservant to Mr Period*
Mrs Mitchell	*Cook to Mr Period*
Mr Percival Pyke Period	
Nicola Maitland-Mayne	
Desirée, Lady Bantling	*Now Mrs Bimbo Dodds, formerly Mrs Harold Cartell. Née Desirée Ormsbury*
Andrew Bantling	*Her son by her first marriage*
Bimbo Dodds	*Her third and present husband*
Mr Harold Cartell	*Her second husband*
Constance Cartell	*His sister*
Trudi	*Her maid*
Mary Ralston (Moppett)	*Her adopted niece*
Leonard Leiss	
George Copper	*Garage proprietor*
Mrs Nicholls	*Wife of Vicar of Ribblethorpe*
Superintendent Williams	*Little Codling constabulary*
Sergeant Raikes	*Little Codling constabulary*
A Foreman drainlayer	
Superintendent Roderick Alleyn	*CID New Scotland Yard*
Inspector Fox	*CID New Scotland Yard*
Detective-Sergeant Thompson	*CID New Scotland Yard*
Detective-Sergeant Bailey	*CID New Scotland Yard*
Sir James Curtiss	*Pathologist*
Dr Elekton, MD	

CHAPTER 1

Mr Pyke Period

While he waited for the water to boil, Alfred Belt stared absently at the kitchen calendar: *'With the compliments of The Little Codling Garage. Service with a smile. Geo. Copper'*. Below this legend was a coloured photograph of a kitten in a boot and below that the month of March. Alfred removed them and exposed a coloured photograph of a little girl smirking through apple blossom.

He warmed a silver teapot engraved on its belly with Mr Pyke Period's crest: a fish. He refolded the *Daily Press* and placed it on the breakfast tray. The toaster sprang open, the electric kettle shrieked. Alfred made tea, put the toast in a silver rack, transferred bacon and eggs from pan to crested entrée dish and carried the whole upstairs.

He tapped at his employer's door and entered. Mr Pyke Period, a silver-haired bachelor with a fresh complexion, stirred in his bed, gave a little snort, opened his large brown eyes, mumbled his lips, and blushed.

Alfred said: 'Good morning, sir.' He placed the tray and turned away in order that Mr Period could assume his teeth in privacy. He drew back the curtains. The village green looked fresh in the early light. Decorous groups of trees, already burgeoning, showed fragile against distant hills. Wood-smoke rose delicately from several chimneys and in Miss Cartell's house across the green, her Austrian maid shook a duster out of an upstairs window. In the field beyond, Miss Cartell's mare grazed peacefully.

'Good morning, Alfred,' Mr Period responded, now fully articulate.

Alfred drew back the curtains from the side window, exposing a small walled garden, a gardener's shed, a path and a gate into a lane.

Beyond the gate was a trench, bridged with planks and flanked by piled-up earth. Three labourers had assembled beside it.

'Those chaps still at it in the lane, sir,' said Alfred, returning to the bedside. He placed Mr Period's spectacles on his tray and poured his tea.

'Damn' tedious of them, I must say. However! Good God!' Mr Period mildly exclaimed. He had opened his paper and was reading the Obituary Notices. Alfred waited.

'Lord Ormsbury's gone,' Mr Period informed him.

'Gone, sir?'

'Died. Yesterday it seems. Motor accident. Terrible thing. Fifty-two, it gives here. One never knows. "Survived by his sister – "' He made a small sound of displeasure.

'That would be Desirée, Lady Bantling, sir, wouldn't it?' Alfred ventured, 'at Baynesholme?'

'Exactly, Alfred. Precisely. And what must these fellows do but call her "The Dowager". She hates it. Always has. And not even correct, if it comes to that. One would have expected the *Press* to know better.' He read on. A preoccupied look, indeed one might almost have said a look of pleasurable anticipation, settled about his rather babyish mouth.

Below, in the garden, a dog began to bark hysterically.

'Good God!' Mr Period said quietly and closed his eyes.

'I'll attend to her, sir.'

'I cannot for the life of me see – however!'

'Will there be anything further, sir?' Alfred asked.

'What? No. No, thank you. Miss Cartell for luncheon, you remember. And Miss Maitland-Mayne.'

'Certainly, sir. Arriving by the ten twenty. Will there be anything required in the library, sir?'

'I can't think of anything. She's bringing her own typewriter.' Mr Period looked over the top of his paper and appeared to come to a decision. 'Her grandfather,' he said, 'was General Maitland-Mayne. An old friend of mine.'

'Indeed, sir?'

'Ah – yes. Yes. *And* her father. Killed at Dunkirk. Great loss.'

A padded footfall was heard in the passage. A light tattoo sounded on the door and a voice, male but pitched rather high, called out, 'Bath's empty. For what it's worth.' The steps receded.

Mr Period repeated his sound of irritation.

'Have I or have I not,' he muttered, 'taken my bath in the evening for seven uncomfortable weeks?' He glanced at Alfred. 'Well, well,' he said. 'Thank you.'

'Thank you, sir,' Alfred rejoined and withdrew.

As he crossed the landing, he heard Mr Cartell singing in his bedroom. 'It won't answer,' Alfred thought, 'I never supposed it would,' and descended to the kitchen. Here he found Mrs Mitchell, the cook; a big and uninhibited woman. They exchanged routine observations, agreeing that spring really did seem to have come.

'All hotsey-totsey in the upper regions?' Mrs Mitchell asked.

'As well as can be expected, Mrs M.'

A shrill yelp modulating into a long drawn out howl sounded outside. 'That dog!' Mrs Mitchell said.

Alfred went to the back door and opened it. An enormous half-bred boxer hurled itself against his legs and rushed past him to the kitchen. 'Bitch!' Alfred said factually, but with feeling.

'Lay down! Get out of my kitchen! Shoo!' Mrs Mitchell cried confusedly.

'Here – Pixie!'

The boxer slavered, ogled and threshed its tail.

'Upstairs! Pixie! Up to your master.'

Alfred seized the bitch's collar and lugged it into the hall. A whistle sounded above. The animal barked joyously, flung itself up the stairs, skating and floundering as it went. Alfred sent a very raw observation after it and returned to the kitchen.

'It's too much,' he said. 'We never bargained for it. Never.'

'I don't mind a nice cat.'

'Exactly. And the damage it does!'

'Shocking. Your breakfast's ready, Mr Belt. New-laid egg.'

'Very nice,' Alfred said. He sat down to it, a neat man with quite an air about him, Mrs Mitchell considered. She watched him make an incisive stab at the egg. The empty shell splintered and collapsed. Mrs Mitchell, in a trembling voice, said: 'First of April, Mr B.,' and threw her apron over her face. He was so completely silent that for a moment she thought he must be annoyed. However, when she peeped round her apron, he shook his egg-spoon at her.

'You wait,' he threatened. 'You just wait, my lady. That's all.'

'To think of you falling for an old wheeze like that.'

'And I changed the calendar too.'

'Never mind. There's the genuine articles, look. Under your serviette.'

'Napkin,' Alfred said. He had been in Mr Period's service for ten years. 'I don't know if you're aware of the fact,' he added, taking the top off his egg, 'but April Fool's Day goes back to pagan times, Mrs Mitchell.'

'Fancy! With your attainments, I often wonder you don't look elsewhere for employment.'

'You might say I lack ambition.' Alfred paused, his spoon half-way to his mouth. 'The truth of the matter is,' he added, 'I like service. Given favourable circumstances, it suits me. And the circumstances here are – or were – very nice.'

A telephone rang distantly. 'I'll answer it,' Mrs Mitchell offered. 'You take your breakfast in peace.'

She went out. Alfred opened his second egg and his *Daily Mail* and was immersed in both when she returned.

'Miss Cartell,' she said.

'Oh?'

'Asking for her brother, "Oh," she says. "Mrs Mitchell!" she says, "just the person I wanted to have a word with!" You know her way. Bluff, but doing the gracious.'

Alfred nodded slightly.

'And she says, "I want you," she says, "before I say anything to my brother, to tell me, *absolutely* frankly," she says, "between you and me and the larder shelf, if you think the kweezeen would stand two more for lunch." Well!'

'To whom was she referring?'

'To that Miss Moppett and a friend. A gentleman friend, you may depend upon it. Well! Asking me! As far as the kweezeen is concerned, a nice curry can be stretched, as you know yourself, Mr Belt, to ridiculous lengths.'

'What did you say?'

'"I'm sure, miss," I says, just like that! Straight out! "My kitchen," I says, "has never been found wanting in a crisis," I says, and with that I switched her up to his room.'

'Mr Period,' Alfred said, 'will not be pleased.'

'You're telling me! Can't stand the young lady, to give her the benefit of the title, and I'm sure I don't blame him. Mr Cartell feels the same, you can tell. Well, I mean to say! She's no relation. Picked up nobody knows where and educated by a spinster sister to act like his niece, which call her as you may have remarked, Mr Belt, he will not. A bad girl, if ever I see one, and Miss Cartell will find it out one of these days, you mark my words.'

Alfred laid aside his paper and continued with his breakfast. 'It's the arrangement,' he said, following out his own thought, 'and you can't get away from it. Separate rooms with the joint use of the bathroom and meals to be shared, with the right of either party to invite guests.' He finished his tea. 'It doesn't answer,' he said. 'I never thought it would. We've been under our own steam too long for sharing. We're getting fussed. Looking forward to a nice day, with a letter of condolence to be written – Lady Bantling's brother, for your information, Mrs M., with whom she has not been on speaking terms these ten years or more. And a young lady coming in to help with the book, and now this has to happen. Pity.'

She went to the door and opened it slightly. 'Mr C.,' she said with a jerk of her head. 'Coming down.'

'His breakfast's in the dining-room,' said Alfred.

A light tattoo sounded on the door. It opened and Mr Cartell's face appeared: thin, anxious and tightly smiling. The dog, Pixie, was at his heels. Alfred and Mrs Mitchell stood up.

'Oh – ah – good morning, Mrs Mitchell. 'Morning, Alfred. Just to say that my sister telephoned to ask if we can manage two more. I hope it won't be too difficult, Mrs Mitchell, at such short notice.'

'I dare say we'll manage quite nicely, sir.'

'Shall we? Oh, excellent. Ah – I'll let Mr Period know. Good,' said Mr Cartell. He withdrew his head, shut the door and retired, whistling uncertainly, to the dining-room.

For the second time in half an hour Alfred repeated his leitmotiv. 'It won't answer,' he said. 'And I never thought it would.'

II

'Sawn-lee,' a hollow voice on the loudspeaker announced. 'Sawn-lee. The four carriages in the front portion of the train now arrived at number one platform will proceed to Rimble, Bornlee Green and

Little Codling. The rear portion will proceed to Forthampstead and Ribblethorpe. Please make sure you are in the correct part of the train. Sawn-lee. The four carriages – '

Nicola Maitland-Mayne heard this pronouncement with dismay. 'But I don't know,' she cried to her fellow passengers, 'which portion I'm in! *Is* this one of the first four carriages?'

'It's the fifth,' said the man in the corner. 'Next stop Forthampstead.'

'Oh, damn!' Nicola said cheerfully and hauled her typewriter and overcoat down from the rack. Someone opened the door for her. She plunged out, staggered along the platform and climbed into another carriage as the voice was saying: 'All seats, please, for Rimble, Bornlee Green and Little Codling.'

The first compartment was full and so was the second. She moved along the corridor, looked in at the third, and gave it up. A tall man, farther along the corridor said: 'There's plenty of room up at the end.'

'I'm second class.'

'I should risk it if I were you. You can always pay up if the guard comes along but he never does on this stretch, I promise you.'

'Oh, well,' Nicola said, 'I believe I will. Thank you.'

He opened the door of the first-class compartment. She went in and found nobody there. A bowler, an umbrella, and a *Times*, belonging, she supposed, to the young man himself, lay on one seat. She sat on the other. He shut the door and remained in the corridor with his back to her, smoking.

Nicola looked out of the window for a minute or two. Presently she remembered her unfinished crossword and took her own copy of *The Times* out of her overcoat pocket.

Eight across. 'Vehicle to be sick on or just get a ringing in the ears? (8).'

The train had roared through a cutting and was slowing down for Cabstock when she ejaculated: 'Oh, good lord! *Carillon*, of course, how stupid!' She looked up to find the young man smiling at her from the opposite seat.

'I stuck over that one, too,' he said.

'How far did you get?'

'All but five. Maddening.'

'So did I,' Nicola said.

'I wonder if they're the same ones. Shall I look?'

He picked up his paper. She noticed that under the nail of the first finger of his right hand there was a smear of scarlet.

Between them they continued the crossword. It is a matter of conjecture how many complete strangers have been brought into communication by this means. Rimble and Bornlee Green were passed before they filled in the last word.

'I should say,' the young man remarked as he folded up his *Times*, 'that we're in much the same class.'

'That may be true of crosswords, but it certainly isn't of railway carriages,' Nicola rejoined. 'Heavens, where are we?'

'Coming in to Codling. My station, what a bore!'

'It's mine, too,' Nicola exclaimed, standing up.

'No! Is it really? *Jolly* good,' said the young man. 'I'll be able to bluff you past the gate. Here we go. Are you putting your coat on? Give me that thing: what is it, a typewriter? Sorry about my unsuitable bowler, but I'm going to a cocktail party this evening. Where's me brolly? Come on.'

They were the only passengers to leave the train at Little Codling. The sun was shining and the smell of a country lane mingled with the disinfectant, cardboard and paste atmosphere of the station. Nicola was only mildly surprised to see her companion produce a second-class ticket.

'Joy-riding as usual, I suppose, Mr Bantling,' said the man at the gates.

Nicola gave up her ticket and they passed into the lane. Birds were fussing in the hedgerows and the air ran freshly. A dilapidated car waited outside with a mild-looking driver standing beside it.

'Hallo,' the young man said. 'There's the Bloodbath. It must be for you.'

'Do you think so? And why "Bloodbath"?'

'Well, they won't have sent it for me. Good morning, Mr Copper.'

'Good morning, sir. Would it be Miss Maitland-Mayne?' asked the car driver, touching his cap.

Nicola said it would and he opened the door. 'You'll take a lift, too, sir, I dare say. Mr Cartell asked me to look out for you.'

'What!' the young man exclaimed, staring at Nicola. 'Are *you*, too, bound for Ye Olde Bachelor's Lay-by?'

'I'm going to Mr Pyke Period's house. Could there be some mistake?'

'Not a bit of it. In we get.'

'Well, if you say so,' Nicola said and they got into the back of the car. It was started up with a good deal of commotion and they set off down the lane. 'What did you mean by "Bloodbath"?' Nicola repeated.

'You'll see. I'm going,' the young man shouted, 'to visit my step-father who is called Mr Harold Cartell. He shares Mr Pyke Period's house.'

'I'm going to type for Mr Pyke Period.'

'You cast a ray of hope over an otherwise unpropitious venture. Hold very nice and tight, please,' said the young man, imitating a bus conductor. They swung out of the lane, brought up short under the bonnet of a gigantic truck loaded with a crane and drain-pipes, and lost their engine. The truck driver blasted his horn. His mate leaned out of the cab.

'You got the death-wish, Jack?' he asked the driver.

The driver looked straight ahead of him and restarted his engine. Nicola saw that they had turned into the main street of a village and were headed for the green.

'Trembling in every limb, are you?' the young man asked her. 'Never mind; *now* you see what I meant by "Bloodbath".' He leant towards her. 'There is another rather grand taxi in the village,' he confided, 'but Pyke Period likes to stick to Mr Copper, because he's come down in the world.' He raised his voice. 'That was a damn' close-run thing, Mr Copper,' he shouted.

'Think they own the place, those chaps,' the driver rejoined. 'Putting the sewer up the side lane by Mr Period's house, and what for? Nobody wants it.'

He turned left at the green, pulled in at a short drive and stopped in front of a smallish Georgian house.

'Here we are,' said the young man.

He got out, extricated Nicola's typewriter and his own umbrella, and felt in his pocket. Although largish and exceptionally tall, he was expeditious and quick in all his movements.

'Nothing to pay, Mr Bantling,' said the driver. 'Mr Period gave the order.'

'Oh, well. One for the road anyway.'

'Very kind of you, but no need, I'm sure. All right, Miss Maitland-Mayne?'

'Quite, thank you,' said Nicola, who had alighted. The car lurched off uproariously. Looking to her right, Nicola could see the crane and the top of its truck over a quickset hedge. She heard the sound of male voices.

The front door had opened and a small dark man in an alpaca coat appeared.

'Good morning, Alfred,' her companion said. 'As you see, I've brought Miss Maitland-Mayne with me.'

'The gentlemen,' Alfred said, 'are expecting you both, sir.'

Pixie shot out of the house in a paroxysm of barking.

'Quiet,' said Alfred, menacing her.

She whined, crouched and then precipitated herself upon Nicola. She stood on her hind legs, slavering and grimacing and scraped at Nicola with her forepaws.

'Here, you!' said the young man indignantly. 'Paws off!'

He cuffed Pixie away and she made loud ambiguous noises.

'I'm sure I'm very sorry, miss,' said Alfred. 'It's said to be only its fun. This way, if you please, miss.'

Nicola found herself in a modest but elegantly proportioned hall. It looked like an advertisement from a glossy magazine. 'Small Georgian residence of character' and, apart from being Georgian, had no other character to speak of.

Alfred opened a door on the right. 'In the library, if you please, miss,' he said. 'Mr Period will be down immediately.'

Nicola walked in. The young man followed and put her typewriter on a table by a window.

'I can't help wondering,' he said, 'what you're going to do for P.P. After all, he'd never type his letters of condolence, would he?'

'What can you mean?'

'You'll see. Well, I suppose I'd better launch myself on my ill-fated mission. You might wish me luck.'

Something in his voice caught her attention. She looked up at him. His mouth was screwed dubiously sideways. 'It never does,' he said, 'to set one's heart on something, does it? Furiously, I mean.'

'Good heavens, what a thing to say! Of course, one must. Continuously. Expectation,' said Nicola grandly, 'is the springboard of achievement.'

'Rather a phoney slogan, I'm afraid.'

'I thought it neat.'

'I should like to confide in you. What a pity we won't meet over your nice curry. I'm lunching with my mamma who lives in the offing with her third husband.'

'How do you know it's going to be curry?'

'It often is.'

'Well,' Nicola said, 'I wish you luck.'

'Thank you very much.' He smiled at her. 'Good typing!'

'Good hunting! If you are hunting.'

He laid his finger against his nose, pulled a mysterious grimace and left her.

Nicola opened up her typewriter and a box of quarto paper and surveyed the library.

It looked out on the drive and the rose garden and it was like the hall in that it had distinction without personality. Over the fireplace hung a dismal little water-colour. Elsewhere on the walls were sporting prints, a painting of a bewhiskered ensign in the Brigade of Guards, pointing his sword at some lightning, and a faded photograph of several Edwardian minor royalties grouped in baleful conviviality about a picnic luncheon. In the darkest corner was a framed genealogical tree, sprouting labels, arms and mantling. There were bookcases with uniform editions, novels, and a copy of *Handley Cross*. Standing apart from the others, a *corps d'élite*, were Debrett, Burke, Kelly's and Who's Who. The desk itself was rich with photographs, framed in silver. Each bore witness to the conservative technique of the studio and the well-bred restraint of the sitter.

Through the side window, Nicola looked across Mr Period's rose garden, to a quickset hedge and an iron gate leading into a lane. Beyond this gate was a trench with planks laid across it, a heap of earth and her old friend the truck, from which, with the aid of the crane, the workmen were unloading drain-pipes.

Distantly and overhead, she heard male voices. Her acquaintance of the train (what had the driver called him?) and his step-father, Nicola supposed.

She was thinking of him with amusement when the door opened and Mr Pyke Period came in.

III

He was a tall, elderly man with a marked stoop, silver hair, large brown eyes and a small mouth. He was beautifully dressed with exactly the correct suggestion of well-worn scrupulously tended tweed.

He advanced upon Nicola with curved arm held rather high and bent at the wrist. The Foreign Office, or at the very least, Commonwealth Relations, was invoked.

'This is *really* kind of you,' said Mr Pyke Period, 'and awfully lucky for me.'

They shook hands.

'Now, do tell me,' Mr Period continued, 'because I'm the most inquisitive old party and I'm dying to know –you *are* Basil's daughter, *aren't* you?'

Nicola, astounded, said that she was.

'Basil Maitland-Mayne?' he gently insisted.

'Yes, but I don't make much of a to-do about the "Maitland",' said Nicola.

'Now, that's naughty of you. A splendid old family. These things matter.'

'It's such a mouthful.'

'Never *mind*! So you're dear old Basil's gel! I was sure of it. Such fun for me because, do you know, your grandfather was one of my very dear friends. A bit my senior, but he was one of those soldiers of the old school who never let you *feel* the gap in ages.'

Nicola, who remembered her grandfather as an arrogant, declamatory old egoist, managed to make a suitable rejoinder. Mr Period looked at her with his head on one side.

'Now,' he said gaily, 'I'm going to confess. Shall we sit down? Do you know, when I called on those perfectly splendid people to ask about typewriting and they gave me some names from their books, I positively leapt at yours. And do you know why?'

Nicola had her suspicions and they made her feel uncomfortable. But there was something about Mr Period – what was it? – something vulnerable and foolish, that aroused her compassion. She knew she was meant to smile and shake her head and she did both.

Mr Period said, sitting youthfully on the arm of a leather chair: 'It was because I felt that we would be working together on – dear me, too difficult! – on a common ground. Talking the same language.' He waited for a moment and then said cosily: 'And you now know *all* about me. I'm the most dreadful old anachronism – a Period Piece, in fact.'

As Nicola responded to this joke she couldn't help wondering how often Mr Period had made it.

He laughed delightedly with her. 'So, speaking as one snob to another,' he ended, 'I couldn't be more enchanted that you are *you*. Well, never mind! One's meant not to say such things in these egalitarian days.'

He had a conspiratorial way of biting his under-lip and lifting his shoulders: it was indescribably arch. 'But we mustn't be naughty,' said Mr Pyke Period.

Nicola said: 'They didn't really explain at the agency exactly what my job is to be.'

'Ah! Because they didn't exactly know. I was coming to that.'

It took him some time to come to it, though, because he would dodge about among innumerable parentheses. Finally, however, it emerged that he *was* writing a book. He had been approached by the head of a publishing firm.

'Wonderful,' Nicola said, 'actually to be *asked* by a publisher to write.'

He laughed. 'My dear child, I promise you it would never have come from *me*. Indeed, I thought he must be pulling my leg. But not at all. So in the end I madly consented and – and there we are, you know.'

'Your memoirs, perhaps?' Nicola ventured.

'No. No, although I must say – but no – You'll never guess!'

She felt that she never would and waited.

'It's – how can I explain? Don't laugh! It's just that in these extraordinary times there are all sorts of people popping up in places where one would least expect to find them: clever, successful people, we must admit, but *not*, as we old fogies used to say – "not quite-quite". And there they find themselves, in a milieu, where they really are, poor darlings, at a grievous loss.'

And there it was: Mr Pyke Period had been commissioned to write a book on etiquette. Nicola suspected that his publisher had displayed a remarkably shrewd judgement. The only book on etiquette she had ever read, a Victorian work unearthed in an attic by her brother, had been a favourite source for ribald quotation.'"It is a mark of ill-breeding in a lady,"' Nicola's brother would remind her, '"to look over her shoulder, still more behind her, when walking abroad."'

'"There should be no diminution of courteous observance,"' she would counter, '"in the family circle. A brother will always rise when his sister enters the drawing-room and open the door to her when she shows her intention of quitting it."'

'"While on the sister's part some slight acknowledgement of his action will be made: a smile or a quiet 'thank you' will indicate her awareness of the little attention."'

Almost as if he had read her thoughts, Mr Period was saying: 'Of course, one knows all about these delicious Victorian offerings – quite wonderful. And there *have* been contemporaries: poor Felicité Sankie-Bond, after their crash, don't you know. And one mustn't overlap with dear Nancy. Very diffy. In the meantime – '

In the meantime, it at last transpired, Nicola was to make a type-written draft of his notes and assemble them under their appropriate headings. These were: 'The Ball-dance', 'Trifles that Matter', 'The Small Dinner', 'The Partie Carrée', 'Addressing Our Letters & Betters', 'Awkwiddities', 'The Debutante – lunching and launching', 'Tips on Tipping'.

And bulkily, in a separate compartment, 'The Compleat Letter-Writer'.

She was soon to learn that letter-writing was a great matter with Mr Pyke Period.

He was, in fact, famous for his letters of condolence.

IV

They settled to work: Nicola at her table near the front French windows, Mr Period at his desk in the side one.

Her job was an exacting one. Mr Period evidently jotted down his thoughts, piecemeal, as they had come to him and it was often difficult to know where a passage precisely belonged. 'Never *fold* the napkin (there is no need, I feel sure, to put the unspeakable "serviette" in its place), but drop it lightly on the table.' Nicola listed this under 'Table Manners', and wondered if Mr Period would find the phrase 'refeened', a word he often used with humorous intent.

She looked up to find him in a trance, his pen suspended, his gaze rapt, a sheet of headed letter-paper under his hand. He caught her glance and said: 'A few lines to my dear Desirée Bantling. Soi-disant.

The Dowager, as the *Press* would call her. You saw Ormsbury had gone, I dare say?'

Nicola, who had no idea whether the Dowager Lady Bantling had been deserted or bereaved, said: 'No, I didn't see it.'

'Letters of condolence!' Mr Period sighed with a faint hint of complacency. 'How difficult they are!' He began to write again, quite rapidly, with sidelong references to his note-pad.

Upstairs a voice, clearly recognizable, shouted angrily: ' – and all I can say, you horrible little man, is I'm bloody sorry I ever asked you.' Someone came rapidly downstairs and crossed the hall. The front door slammed. Through her window, Nicola saw her travelling companion, scarlet in the face, stride down the drive, angrily swinging his bowler.

'He's forgotten his umbrella,' she thought.

'Oh, *dear*!' Mr Period murmured. 'An awkwiddity, I fear me. Andrew is in one of his rages. You know him, of course.'

'Not till this morning.'

'Andrew Bantling? My dear, he's the son of the very Lady Bantling we were talking about. Desirée you know. Ormsbury's sister. Bobo Bantling – Andrew's papa – was the first of her three husbands. The senior branch. Seventh Baron. Succeeded to the peerage – ' Here followed inevitably, one of Mr Period's classy genealogical digressions. 'My dear Nicola,' he went on, 'I hope, by the way, I *may* so far take advantage of a family friendship?'

'Please do.'

'Sweet of you. Well, my dear Nicola, you will have gathered that I don't vegetate all by myself in this house. No. I share. With an old friend who is called Harold Cartell. It's a new arrangement and I hope it's going to suit us both. Harold is Andrew's step-father and guardian. He is, by the way, a retired solicitor. I don't need to tell you about Andrew's *mum*,' Mr Period added, strangely adopting the current slang. 'She, poor darling, is almost *too* famous.'

'And she's called Desirée, Lady Bantling?'

'She naughtily sticks to the title in the teeth of the most surprising remarriage.'

'Then she's really Mrs Harold Cartell?'

'Not now. That hardly lasted any time. No. She's now Mrs Bimbo Dodds. Bantling. Cartell. Dodds. In that order.'

'Yes, of course,' Nicola said, remembering at last the singular fame of this lady.

'Yes. 'Nuff said,' Mr Period observed, wanly arch, 'under that heading. But Hal Cartell was Lord Bantling's solicitor and executor and is the trustee for Andrew's inheritance. I, by the way, am the other trustee and I do hope *that's* not going to be diffy. Well, now,' Mr Period went cosily on, 'on Bantling's death, Hal Cartell was also appointed Andrew's guardian. Desirée at that time, was going through a rather farouche phase and Andrew narrowly escaped being made a Ward-in-Chancery. Thus it was that Hal Cartell was thrown in the widow's path. She rather wolfed him up, don't you know? Black always suited her. But they were too dismally incompatible. However, Harold remained, nevertheless, Andrew's guardian and trustee for the estate. Andrew doesn't come into it until he's twenty-five: in six months' time, by the way. He's in the Brigade of Guards, as you'll have seen, but I gather he wants to leave in order to paint, which is so unexpected. Indeed, that *may* be this morning's problem. A *great* pity. *All* the Bantlings have been in the Brigade. And if he must paint, poor dear, why not as a hobby? What his father would have said – !' Mr Period waved his hands.

'But why isn't *he* Lord Bantling?'

'His father was a widower with one son when he married Desirée. That son of course, succeeded.'

'Oh, I see,' Nicola said politely. 'Of course.'

'You wonder why I go into all these begatteries, as I call them. Partly because they amuse me and partly because you will, I hope, be seeing quite a lot of my stodgy little household and, in so far as Hal Cartell is one of us, we – ah – we overlap. In fact,' Mr Period went on, looking vexed, 'we overlap at luncheon. Harold's sister, Connie Cartell, who is our neighbour, joins us. With – ah – with a protégée, a – soi-disant niece, adopted from goodness knows where. Her name is Mary Ralston and her nickname, an inappropriate one, is Moppett. I understand that she brings a friend with her. However! To return to Desirée. Desirée and her Bimbo spend a lot of time at the dower house, Baynesholme, which is only a mile or two away from us. I believe Andrew lunches there today. His mother was to pick him up here and I do hope he hasn't gone flouncing back to London: it would be too awkward and tiresome of him, poor boy.'

'Then Mrs Dodds – I mean Lady Bantling and Mr Cartell still – ?'

'Oh, lord, yes! They hob-nob occasionally. Desirée never bears grudges. She's a remarkable person. I dote on her but she *is* rather a law unto herself. For instance, one doesn't know in the very least how she'll react to the death of Ormsbury. Brother though he is. Better, I think, not to mention it when she comes, but simply to write – But there, I really mustn't bore you with all my dim little bits of gossip. To work, my child! To work!'

They returned to their respective tasks. Nicola had made some headway with the notes when she came upon one which was evidently a rough draft for a letter. 'My dear – ' it began, 'What can I say? Only that you have lost a wonderful' – here Mr Period had left a blank space – 'and I, a most valued and very dear old friend.' It continued in this vein with many erasures. Should she file it under 'The Compleat Letter-Writer'? Was it in fact intended as an exemplar?

She laid it before Mr Period.

'I'm not quite sure if this belongs.'

He looked at it and turned pink. 'No, no. Stupid of me. Thank you.'

He pushed it under his pad and folded the letter he had written, whistling under his breath. 'That's that,' he said, with rather forced airiness. 'Perhaps you will be kind enough to post it in the village.'

Nicola made a note of it and returned to her task. She became aware of suppressed nervousness in her employer. They went through the absurd pantomime of catching each other's eyes and pretending they had done nothing of the sort. This had occurred two or three times when Nicola said: 'I'm so sorry. I've got the awful trick of staring at people when I'm trying to concentrate.'

'My *dear* child! No! It is I who am at fault. In point of fact,' Mr Period went on with a faint simper, 'I've been asking myself if I dare confide a little problem.'

Not knowing what to say, Nicola said nothing. Mr Period, with an air of hardihood, continued. He waved his hand.

'It's nothing. Rather a bore, really. Just that the – ah – the publishers are going to do something quite handsome in the way of illustrations and they – don't laugh – they want my old mug for their frontispiece. A portrait rather than a photograph is thought to be appropriate and, I can't *imagine* why, they took it for granted one had been done, do you know? And one hasn't.'

'What a pity,' Nicola sympathized. 'So it will have to be a photograph.'

'Ah! Yes. That was my first thought. But then, you see – They made such a point of it – and I did just wonder – My friends, silly creatures, urge me to it. Just a line drawing. One doesn't know what to think.'

It was clear to Nicola that Mr Period died to have his portrait done and was prepared to pay highly for it. He mentioned several extremely fashionable artists and then said suddenly: 'It's naughty of dear Agatha Troy to be so diffy about who she does. She said something about not wanting to abandon bone for bacon, I think, when she refused – she actually *refused* to paint – '

Here Mr Period whispered an extremely potent name and stared with a sort of dismal triumph at Nicola. 'So she wouldn't dream of poor old me,' he cried. ''Nuff said!'

Nicola began to say: 'I wonder, though. She often – ' and hurriedly checked herself. She had been about to commit an indiscretion. Fortunately Mr Period's attention was diverted by the return of Andrew Bantling. He had reappeared in the drive, still walking fast and swinging his bowler, and with a fixed expression on his pleasantly bony face.

'He has come back,' Nicola said.

'Andrew? Oh, good. I wonder what for.'

In a moment they found out. The door opened and Andrew looked in.

'I'm sorry to interrupt,' he said loudly, 'but if it's not too troublesome, I wonder if I could have a word with you, P.P.?'

'My dear boy! But, of course.'

'It's not private from Nicola,' Andrew said. 'On the contrary. At the same time, I don't want to bore anybody.'

Mr Period said playfully: 'I myself have done nothing but bore poor Nicola. Shall we "withdraw to the withdrawing-room" and leave her in peace?'

'Oh. All right. Thank you. Sorry.' Andrew threw a distracted look at Nicola and opened the door.

Mr Period made her a little bow. 'You will excuse us, my dear?' he said and they went out.

Nicola worked on steadily and was only once interrupted. The door opened to admit a small, thin, querulous-looking gentleman who ejaculated: 'I beg your pardon. Damn!' and went out again. Mr Cartell, no doubt.

At eleven o'clock Alfred came in with sherry and biscuits and Mr Period's compliments. If she was in any difficulty would she be good enough to ring and Alfred would convey the message. Nicola was not in any difficulty, but while she enjoyed her sherry she found herself scribbling absent-mindedly.

'Good lord!' she thought. 'Why did I do that? A bit longer on this job and I'll be turning into a Pyke Period myself.'

Two hours went by. The house was very quiet. She was half-aware of small local activities: distant voices and movement, the rattle and throb of machinery in the lane. She thought from time to time of her employer. To which brand of snobbery, that overworked but always enthralling subject, did Mr Pyke Period belong? Was he simply a snob of the traditional school who dearly loves a lord? Was he himself a scion of ancient lineage; one of those old, uncelebrated families whose sole claim to distinction rests in their refusal to accept a title? No. That didn't quite fit Mr Period. It wasn't easy to imagine him refusing a title and yet –

Her attention was again diverted to the drive. Three persons approached the house, barked at and harassed by Pixie. A large, tweedy, middle-aged woman with a red face, a squashed hat and a walking-stick, was followed by a pale girl with fashionable coiffure and a young man who looked, Nicola thought, quite awful. These two lagged behind their elder who shouted and pointed with her stick in the direction of the excavations. Nicola could hear her voice, which sounded arrogant, and her gusts of boisterous laughter. While her back was turned, the girl quickly planted an extremely un-inhibited kiss on the young man's mouth.

'That,' thought Nicola, 'is a full-treatment job.'

Pixie floundered against the young man and he kicked her rapidly in the ribs. She emitted a howl and retired. The large woman looked round in concern but the young man was smiling damply. They moved round the corner of the house. Through the side window Nicola could see them inspecting the excavations. They returned to the drive.

Footsteps crossed the hall. Doors were opened. Mr Cartell appeared in the drive and was greeted by the lady who, Nicola saw, resembled him in a robust fashion. 'The sister,' Nicola said. 'Connie. And the adopted niece, Moppett, and the niece's frightful friend. I don't wonder Mr Period was put out.'

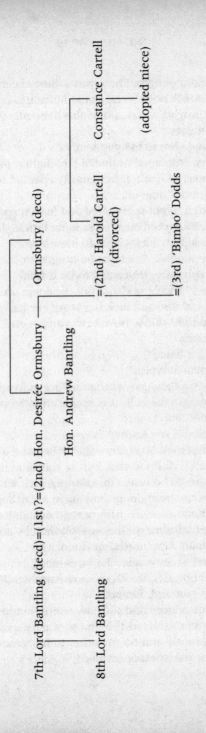

7th Lord Bantling (decd) = (1st) ? = (2nd) Hon. Desirée Ormsbury

Hon. Desirée Ormsbury (decd) = (2nd) Harold Cartell (divorced)
= (3rd) 'Bimbo' Dodds

Ormsbury (decd)

Harold Cartell ——— Constance Cartell

Constance Cartell (adopted niece)

Hon. Andrew Bantling

8th Lord Bantling

They moved out of sight. There was a burst of conversation in the hall, in which Mr Period's voice could be heard, and a withdrawal (into the 'withdrawing-room', no doubt). Presently Andrew Bantling came into the library.

'Hallo,' he said. 'I'm to bid you to drinks. I don't mind telling you it's a bum party. My bloody-minded step-father, to whom I'm not speaking, his bully of a sister, her ghastly adopted what-not and an unspeakable chum. Come on.'

'Do you think I might be excused and just creep in to lunch?'

'Not a hope. P.P. would be as cross as two sticks. He's telling them all about you and how lucky he is to have you.'

'I don't want a drink. I've been built up with sherry.'

'There's tomato juice. Do come. You'd better.'

'In that case – ' Nicola said and put the cover on her typewriter.

'That's right,' he said and took her arm. 'I've had such a stinker of a morning: you can't think. How have you got on?'

'I hope, all right.'

'Is he writing a book?'

'I'm a confidential typist.'

'My face can't get any redder than it's been already,' Andrew said and ushered her into the hall. 'Are you at all interested in painting?'

'Yes. You paint, don't you?'

'How the hell did you know?'

'Your first fingernail. And anyway, Mr Period told me.'

'Talk, talk, talk!' Andrew said, but he smiled at her. 'And what a sharp girl you are, to be sure. Oh, calamity, look who's here!'

Alfred was at the front door, showing in a startling lady with tangerine hair, enormous eyes, pale orange lips and a general air of good-humoured raffishness. She was followed by an unremarkable, cagey-looking man, very much her junior.

'Hallo, Mum!' Andrew said. 'Hallo, Bimbo.'

'Darling!' said Desirée Dodds or Lady Bantling. 'How lovely!'

'Hi,' said her husband, Bimbo.

Nicola was introduced and they all went into the drawing-room.

Here, Nicola encountered the group of persons with whom, on one hand disastrously and on the other to her greatest joy, she was about to become inextricably involved.

CHAPTER 2

Luncheon

Mr Pyke Period made much of Nicola. He took her round, introducing her to Mr Cartell and all over again to 'Lady Bantling' and Mr Dodds; to Miss Connie Cartell and, with a certain lack of enthusiasm, to the adopted niece, Mary or Moppett, and her friend, Mr Leonard Leiss.

Miss Cartell shouted: 'Been hearing all about you, ha, ha!'

Mr Cartell said: 'Afraid I disturbed you just now. Looking for P.P. So sorry.'

Moppett said: 'Hallo. I suppose you do shorthand? I tried but my squiggles looked like rude drawings. So I gave up.' Young Mr Leiss stared damply at Nicola and then shook hands: also damply. He was pallid and had large eyes, a full mouth and small chin. The sleeves of his violently checked jacket displayed an exotic amount of shirt-cuff and link. He smelt very strongly of hair oil. Apart from these features it would have been hard to say why he seemed untrustworthy.

Mr Cartell was probably by nature a dry and pedantic man. At the moment he was evidently much put out. Not surprising, Nicola thought, when one looked at the company: his step-son, with whom, presumably, he had just had a flaring row, his divorced wife and her husband, his noisy sister, her 'niece' whom he obviously disliked, and Mr Leiss. He dodged about, fussily attending to drinks.

'May Leonard fix mine, Uncle Hal?' Moppett asked. 'He knows my kind of wallop.'

Mr Period, overhearing her, momentarily closed his eyes and Mr Cartell saw him do it.

Miss Cartell shouted uneasily: 'The things these girls say, nowadays! Honestly!' and burst into her braying laugh. Nicola could see that she adored Moppett. Leonard adroitly mixed two treble Martinis.

Andrew had brought Nicola her tomato juice. He stayed beside her. They didn't say very much but she found herself glad of his company.

Meanwhile, Mr Period, who it appeared, had recently had a birthday, was given a present by Lady Bantling. It was a large brass paper-weight in the form of a fish rampant. He seemed to Nicola to be disproportionately enchanted with this trophy and presently she discovered why.

'Dearest Desirée,' he exclaimed. 'How wonderfully clever of you: my crest, you know! The form, the attitude, everything! Connie! Look! Hal, do look.'

The paper-weight was passed from hand to hand and Andrew was finally sent to put it on Mr Period's desk.

When he returned Moppett bore down upon him. 'Andrew!' she said. 'You must tell Leonard about painting. He knows quantities of potent dealers. Actually, he might be jolly useful to you. Come and talk to him.'

'I'm afraid I wouldn't know what to say, Moppett.'

'I'll tell you. Hi, Leonard! We want to talk to you.'

Leonard advanced with drinks. 'All right. All right,' he said. 'What about?'

'Which train are you going back by?' Andrew asked Nicola.

'I don't know.'

'When do you stop typing?'

'Four o'clock, I think.'

'There's a good train at twenty past. I'll pick you up. May I?'

His mother had joined them. 'We really ought to be going,' she said, smiling amiably at Nicola. 'Lunch is early today, Andrew, on account we're having a grand party tonight. You're staying for it, by the way.'

'I don't think I can.'

'I'm sure you can if you set your mind to it. We need you badly. I'd have warned you, but we only decided last night. It's an April Fool party: that makes the excuse. Bimbo's scarcely left the telephone since dawn.'

'We ought to go, darling,' said Bimbo over her shoulder.

'I know. Let's. Goodbye.' She held out her hand to Nicola. 'Are you coming lots of times to type for P.P.?'

'I think, fairly often.'

'Make him bring you to Baynesholme. We're off, Harold. Thank you for our nice drinks. Goodbye, P.P. Don't forget you're dining, will you?'

'How could I?'

'Not possibly.'

'It was – I wondered, dearest Desirée, if you'd perhaps rather – ? Still – I suppose – '

'My poorest sweet, what are you talking about,' said Lady Bantling and kissed him. She looked vaguely at Moppett and Leonard. 'Goodbye. Come along, boys.'

Andrew muttered to Nicola: 'I'll ring you up about the train.' He said goodbye, cordially to Mr Period and very coldly to his step-father.

Moppett said: 'I had something fairly important to ask you, you gorgeous Guardee, you.'

'How awful never to know what it was,' Andrew replied and with Bimbo, followed his mother out of the room.

Watching Desirée go, Nicola thought: 'Moppett would probably like to acquire that manner, but she never will. She hasn't got the style.'

Mr Period in a fluster, extended his hands. 'Desirée can't know!' he exclaimed. 'Neither can he or Andrew! How extraordinary!'

'Know what?' asked Miss Cartell.

'About Ormsbury. Her brother. It was in the paper.'

'If Desirée is giving one of her parties,' said Mr Cartell, 'she is not likely to put it off for her brother's demise. She hasn't heard of him since he went out to the antipodes, where I understand he's been drinking like a fish for the last twenty years.'

'Really, Hal!' Mr Period exclaimed.

Moppett and Leonard Leiss giggled and retired into a corner with their drinks.

Miss Cartell was launched on an account of some local activity, ' – so I said to the rector: "We all know damn' well what that means," and he said like *lightning*: "We may know but we don't let on." He's got quite a respectable sense of humour, that man.'

'Pause for laugh,' Moppett said very offensively.

Miss Cartell, who had in fact thrown back her head to laugh, blushed painfully and looked at her ward with such an air of baffled vulnerability, that Nicola, who had been thinking how patronizing and arrogant she was, felt sorry for her and furious with Moppett.

So, evidently, did Mr Period. 'My dear Mary,' he said. 'That was *not* the prettiest of remarks.'

'Quite so. Precisely,' Mr Cartell agreed. 'You should exercise more discipline, Connie.'

Leonard said: 'The only way with Moppett is to beat her like a carpet.'

'Care to try?' she asked him.

Alfred announced luncheon.

It was the most uncomfortable meal Nicola had ever eaten. The entire party was at cross purposes. Everybody appeared to be up to something indefinable.

Miss Cartell had bought a new car. Leonard spoke of it with languid approval. Moppett said they had seen a Scorpion for sale in George Copper's garage. Leonard spoke incomprehensibly of its merits.

'Matter of fact,' he said, 'I'd quite like to buy it. Trade in my own heap with him, of course.' He leant back in his chair and whistled quietly through his teeth.

'Shall we look at it again?' Moppett suggested, grandly.

'No harm in looking, is there?'

Nicola suddenly thought: 'That was a pre-planned bit of dialogue.'

Alfred came in with an envelope which he placed before Mr Period.

'What's this?' Mr Period asked pettishly. He peered through his eye-glass.

'From the rectory, sir. The person suggested it was immediate.'

'I do so dislike interruptions at luncheon,' Mr Period complained. ''Scuse, everybody?' he added playfully.

His guests made acquiescent noises. He read what appeared to be a very short letter and changed colour.

'No answer,' he said to Alfred. 'Or rather – say I'll call personally upon the rector.'

Alfred withdrew. Mr Period, after a fidgety interval and many glances at Mr Cartell, said: 'I'm very sorry, Hal, but I'm afraid your Pixie has created a parochial *crise*.'

Mr Cartell said: 'Oh, dear. What?'

'At the moment she, with some half dozen other – ah – boon companions, is rioting in the vicar's seed beds. There is a Mother's Union luncheon in progress, but none of them has succeeded in catching her. It couldn't be more awkward.'

Nicola had an uproarious vision of mothers thundering fruitlessly among rectorial flower-beds. Miss Cartell broke into one of her formidable gusts of laughter.

'You always were hopeless with dogs, Boysie,' she shouted. 'Why you keep that ghastly bitch!'

'She's extremely well bred, Connie. I've been advised to enter her for the parish dog show.'

'My God, who by? The rector?' Miss Cartell asked with a bellow of laughter.

'I have been advised,' Mr Cartell repeated stuffily.

'We'll have to have a freak class.'

'Are you entering your Pekinese?'

'They're very keen I should, so I might as well, I suppose. Hardly fair to the others but she'd be a draw, of course.'

'For people that like lap-dogs, no doubt.'

Mr Period intervened: 'I'm afraid you'll have to do something about it, Hal,' he said. 'Nobody else can control her.'

'Alfred can.'

'Alfred is otherwise engaged.'

'She's on heat, of course.'

'Really, Connie!'

Mr Cartell, pink in the face, rose disconsolately but at that moment there appeared in the garden, a dishevelled clergyman dragging the over-excited Pixie by her collar. They were watched sardonically by a group of workmen.

Mr Cartell hurried from the room and reappeared beyond the windows with Alfred.

'It's too much,' Mr Period said. 'Forgive me!' He too, left the room and joined the group in the garden.

Leonard and Moppett, making extremely uninhibited conversation, went to the window and stood there, clinging to each other in an ecstasy of enjoyment. They were observed by Mr Period and Mr Cartell. There followed a brief scene in which the rector, his Christian forbearance clearly exercised to its limit, received the apologies of both gentlemen, patted Mr Period, but not Mr Cartell, on the shoulder and took his leave. Alfred lugged Pixie, who squatted back on her haunches in protest, out of sight and the two gentlemen returned very evidently in high dudgeon with each other. Leonard and Moppett made little or no attempt to control their amusement.

'Well,' Mr Period said with desperate *savoir-faire*, 'what were we talking about?'

Moppett spluttered noisily. Connie Cartell said: 'You'll have to get rid of that mongrel, you know, Hal.' Her brother glared at her. 'You can't,' Connie added, 'make a silk purse out of a sow's ear.'

'I entirely agree,' Mr Cartell said, very nastily indeed, 'and have often said as much, I believe, to you.'

There was quite a dreadful silence, broken at last by Mr Period.

'Strange,' he observed, 'how, even in the animal kingdom, breeding makes itself felt.' And he was off, in a very big way, on his favourite topic. Inspired, perhaps, by what he would have called Pixie's lack of form, he went to immoderate lengths in praising this quality. He said, more than once, that he knew the barriers had been down for twenty years but nevertheless . . . On and on he went, all through the curry and well into the apple flan. He became, Nicola had regretfully to admit, more than a little ridiculous.

It was clear that Mr Cartell thought so. He himself grew more and more restive. Nicola guessed that he was fretted by divided loyalties and even more by the behaviour of Leonard Leiss who, having finished his lunch, continued to lean back in his chair and whistle softly through his teeth. Moppett asked him sardonically, how the chorus went. He raised his eyebrows and said: 'Oh, pardon me. I just can't seem to get that little number out of my system,' and smiled generally upon the table.

'Evidently,' said Mr Cartell.

Mr Period said he felt sure that he himself made far too much of the niceties of civilized behaviour and told them how his father had once caused him to leave the dining-room for using his fish-knife. Mr Cartell listened with mounting distaste.

Presently he wiped his lips, leant back in his chair and said: 'My dear P.P., that sort of thing is no doubt very well in its way, but surely one can make a little too much of it?'

'I happen to feel rather strongly about such matters,' Mr Period said with a small deprecating smile at Nicola.

Miss Cartell, who had been watching her adopted niece with anxious devotion, suddenly shouted: 'I always say that when people start fussing about family and all that, it's because they're a bit hairy round the heels themselves, ha, ha!'

She seemed to be completely unaware of the implications of her remark or its effect upon Mr Period.

'Well, really, Connie!' he said. 'I must say!'

'What's wrong?'

Mr Cartell gave a dry little laugh. 'After all,' he said, '"when Adam delved" you know.'

'"Dolve", I fancy, *not* "delved",' Mr Period corrected rather smugly. 'Oh, yes. The much-quoted Mr Ball who afterwards was hanged for his pains, wasn't he? "Who was then the gentleman?" The answer is, of course, "nobody". It takes several generations to evolve the genuine article, don't you agree?'

'I've known it to be effected in less than no time,' Mr Cartell said dryly. 'It's quite extraordinary to what lengths some people will go. I heard on unimpeachable authority of a man who forged his name in a parish register in order to establish descent from some ancient family or another.'

Miss Cartell laughed uproariously.

Mr Period dropped his fork into his pudding.

Leonard asked with interest: 'Was there any money in it?'

Moppett said: 'How was he found out? Tell us more.'

Mr Cartell said, 'There has never been a public exposure. And there's really no more to tell.'

Conversation then became desultory. Leonard muttered something to Moppett, who said: 'Would anybody mind if we were excused? Leonard's car is having something done to its guts and the chap in the garage seemed to be quite madly moronic. We were to see him again at two o'clock.'

'If you mean Copper,' Mr Period observed, 'I've always understood him to be a thoroughly dependable fellow.'

'He's a sort of half-pi, broken-down gent or something, isn't he?' Leonard asked casually.

'Jolly good man, George Copper,' Miss Cartell said.

'Certainly,' Mr Period faintly agreed. He was exceedingly pale.

'Oh,' Leonard said, stretching his arms easily, 'I think I can manage Mr George Copper quite successfully.' He glanced round the table. 'Smoking allowed?' he asked.

Miss Cartell swallowed her last fragment of cheese and her brother looked furious. Mr Period murmured: 'Since you are leaving us, why not?'

Leonard groped in his pockets. 'I've left mine in the car,' he said to Moppett. 'Hand over, Sexy, will you?'

Mr Period said: 'Please,' and offered his gold case. 'These are Turks,' he said. 'I'm so sorry if you don't like them. Old-fogishly, I can't get used to the others.'

'Makes a change,' Leonard said obligingly. He took a cigarette, looked at the case and remarked: 'That's nice.' It was extraordinary how off-key his lightest observations could sound.

'Do let me see,' Moppett asked and took the case.

'It was left me,' Mr Period said, 'by dear old Lady Barsington. An eighteenth-century card case. The jewelled clasp is said to be unique. There's an inscription, but it's very faint. If you take it to the light – '

Moppett took it to the window and Leonard joined her there. He began to hum and then to sketch in the words of his little number: '"If you mean what I think you mean, it's okay by me. Things aren't always what they seem. Okay by me."' Moppett gaily joined in.

Alfred came in to say that Mr Period was wanted on the telephone and he bustled out, after a pointedly formal apology.

Leonard strolled back to the table. He had evidently decided that some conventional apology was called for. '*So* sorry to break up the party,' he said winningly. 'But if it's all the same I think we'd better toddle.'

'By all means. Please,' said Mr Cartell.

'What P.P. and Uncle Hal will think of your manners, you two!' Miss Cartell said and laughed uneasily.

They got up. Moppett said goodbye to Mr Cartell quite civilly and was suddenly effusive in her thanks. Leonard followed her lead, but with an air of finding it only just worth while to do so.

'Be seeing you, ducks,' Moppett said in Cockney to Miss Cartell and they went out.

There followed a rather deadly little silence.

Mr Cartell addressed himself to his sister. 'My dear Connie,' he said, 'I should be failing in my duty if I didn't tell you I consider that young man to be an unspeakable bounder.'

Mr Period returned.

'Shall we have our coffee in the drawing-room?' he asked in the doorway.

Nicola would have dearly liked to excuse herself and go back to the study, but Mr Period took her gently by the arm and led her to the drawing-room. His fingers, she noticed, were trembling. 'I want,' he said, 'to show you a newly acquired treasure.'

Piloting her into a far corner, he unfolded a brown-paper parcel. It turned out to be a landscape in water-colour: the distant view of a manor house.

'It's charming,' Nicola said.

'Thought to be an unsigned Cotman, but the real interest for me is that it's my great-grandfather's house at Ribblethorpe. Destroyed, alas, by fire. I came across it in a second-hand shop. Wasn't that fun for me?'

Alfred took round the coffee tray. Nicola pretended she couldn't hear Mr Cartell and his sister arguing. As soon as Alfred had gone, Miss Cartell tackled her brother.

'I think you're jolly prejudiced, Boysie,' she said. 'It's the way they all talk nowadays. Moppett tells me he's brilliantly clever. Something in the City.'

'Too clever by half if you ask me. And what in the City?'

'I don't know exactly *what*. He's got rather a tragic sort of background, Moppett says. The father was killed in Bangkok and the mother's artistic.'

'You're a donkey, Connie. If I were you I should put a stop to the friendship. None of my business, of course. I am *not*,' Mr Cartell continued with some emphasis, 'Mary's uncle, despite the courtesy title she is good enough to bestow upon me.'

'You don't understand her.'

'I make no attempt to do so,' he replied in a fluster.

Nicola murmured: 'I think I ought to get back to my job.' She said goodbye to Miss Cartell.

'Typin', are you?' asked Miss Cartell. 'P.P. tells me you're Basil Maitland-Mayne's gel. Used to know your father. Hunted with him.'

'We all knew Basil,' Mr Period said with an attempt at geniality.

'I didn't,' Mr Cartell said crossly.

They glared at each other.

'You're very smart all of a sudden, P.P.,' Miss Cartell remarked. 'Private Secretary! You'll be telling us next that you're going to write a book.' She laughed uproariously. Nicola returned to the study.

II

Nicola had a ridiculously over-developed capacity for feeling sorry. She was sorry now for Mr Period, because he had been upset and had made a silly of himself: and for Miss Cartell, because she was boisterous and vulnerable and besotted with her terrible Moppett who treated her like dirt. She was sorry for Mr Cartell, because he had been balanced on a sort of tight-rope of irritability. He had been angry with his guests when they let him down and angry with Mr Period out of loyalty to his own sister.

Even Nicola was unable to feel sorry for either Moppett or Leonard.

She ordered herself back to work and was soon immersed in the niceties of polite behaviour. Every now and then she remembered Andrew Bantling and wondered what the row with his step-father had been about. She hoped she would meet him on the train though she supposed Lady Bantling would insist on him staying for the party.

She had worked solidly for about half an hour when her employer came in. He was still pale, but he smiled at her and tiptoed with playful caution to his desk.

'Pay no attention to me,' he whispered. 'I'm going to write another little note.'

He sat at his desk and applied himself to this task. Presently he began dismally to hum an erratic version of Leonard Leiss's song: 'If you mean what I think you mean, it's okay by me'. He made a petulant little sound. 'Now, why in the world,' he cried, 'should that distressingly vulgar catch come into my head? Nicola, my dear, what a perfectly dreadful young man! That you should be let in for that sort of party! Really!'

Nicola reassured him. By and by he sighed, so heavily that she couldn't help glancing at him. He had folded his letter and addressed an envelope and now sat with his head on his hand. 'Better wait a bit,' he muttered. 'Cool down.'

Nicola stopped typing and looked out of the window. Riding up the drive on a bicycle was a large policeman.

He dismounted, propped his machine against a tree trunk and removed his trouser clips. He then approached the house.

'There's a policeman outside.'

'What? Oh, really? Raikes, I suppose. Splendid fellow, old Raikes. I wonder what he wants. Tickets for a concert, I misdoubt me.'

Alfred came in. 'Sergeant Raikes, sir, would like to see you.'

'What's it all about, Alfred?'

'I don't know, I'm sure, sir. He says it's important.'

'All right. Show him in, if I must.'

'Thank you, sir.'

The impressive things about Sergeant Raikes were his size and his mildness. He was big, even for a policeman, and he was mild beyond belief. When Mr Period made him known to Nicola, he said: 'Good afternoon, miss,' in a loud but paddy voice and added that he hoped she would excuse them for a few minutes. Nicola took this as a polite dismissal and was about to conform, when Mr Period said that he wouldn't dream of it. She must go on typing and not let them bore her. Please. He insisted.

Poor Nicola, fully aware of Sergeant Raikes's wishes to the contrary, sat down again and banged away at her machine. She couldn't help hearing Mr Period's airy and inaccurate assurance that she was entirely in his confidence.

'Well,' Sergeant Raikes said, 'sir. In that case – '

'Sit down, Raikes.'

'Thank you, sir. I've dropped in to ask if you can help me in a small matter that has cropped up.'

'Ah, yes? More social activities, Raikes?'

'Not exactly, this time, sir. More of a routine item, really. I wonder if you'd mind telling me if a certain name is known to you – ' He lowered his voice.

'Leiss!' Mr Period shrilly ejaculated. 'Did you say *Leonard Leiss*?'

'That was the name. Yes.'

'I encountered him for the first time this morning.'

'Ah,' said Sergeant Raikes warmly. 'That makes everything much easier, sir. Thank you. For the first time. So you are not at all familiar with Mr Leiss?'

'Familiar!'

'Quite so, sir. And Mr Cartell?'

'Nor is Mr Cartell. Until this morning Mr Leiss was a complete stranger to both of us. He may be said to be one still.'

'Perhaps I could see Mr Cartell?'

'Look here, Raikes, what the deuce are you talking about? Nicola, my dear, pray stop typing, will you be so good? But don't go.'

Nicola stopped.

'Well, sir,' Sergeant Raikes said. 'The facts are as follows. George Copper happened to mention to me about half an hour ago, that he's selling a Scorpion sports model to a young gentleman called Leonard Leiss and he stated, further, that the customer had given your name and Mr Cartell's and Miss Cartell's as references.'

'Good God!'

'Now, sir, in the service there's a regular system by which all stations are kept informed about the activities of persons known to be operating in a manner contrary to the law or if not contrary, within the meaning of the Act, yet in a suspicious and questionable manner. You might describe them,' Sergeant Raikes said with a flash of imagery, 'as ripening fruit. Just about ready for the picking.'

'Raikes, what in heaven's name – Well. Go on.'

'The name of Leonard Sydney Leiss appears on the most recent list. Two previous convictions. Obtaining goods under false pretences. The *portrait-parlé* coincides. It's a confidential matter, Mr Period, but seeing that the young man gave your name with such assurance and seeing he was very warmly backed up by the young lady who is Miss Constance Cartell's adopted niece, I thought I would come and mention it, quietly. Particularly, sir, as there's a complication.'

Mr Period stared dismally at him. 'Complication?' he said.

'Well, sir, yes. You see, for some time Leiss has been working in collusion with a young female who – I'm very sorry, I'm sure, sir – but the description of this young female does tally rather closely with the general appearance of Miss Cartell's aforesaid adopted niece.'

There was a long silence. Then Mr Period said: 'This is all rather dreadful.'

'I take it, sir, you gave the young man no authority to use your name?'

'Merciful heavens, *no*.'

'Then perhaps we may just have a little chat with Mr Cartell?'

Mr Period rang the bell.

Mr Cartell behaved quite differently from Mr Period. He contracted into the shell of what Nicola supposed to be his professional manner as a solicitor. He looked pinched. Two isolated spots of colour appeared on his cheek-bones. Nicola thought he was very angry indeed.

'I am much obliged to you, Sergeant,' he said at last, 'for bringing this affair to my attention. You have acted very properly.'

'Thank you, sir.'

'Very properly. If I may suggest a course of action it will be this. I shall inform my sister of the undesirability of having any further communication with this person: and she will see that his acquaintance with Miss Mary Ralston is terminated. Copper, of course, must be advised at once and he may then, if he thinks it proper, decline any further negotiations.'

Sergeant Raikes opened his mouth, but Mr Cartell raised a finger and he shut it again.

'I need not add,' Mr Cartell said crisply, 'that no undertaking of any kind whatever was given by Mr Period or by myself. Permission was not asked, and would certainly have been declined, for the use of our names. It might be as well, might it not, if I were to telephone Copper at once and suggested that he rids himself of Leiss and the other car which he left, I understand, to be repaired at the garage. I shall then insist that Miss Ralston, who I imagine is there, returns at once. What's the *matter*, Raikes?'

'The matter,' Sergeant Raikes said warmly, 'is this, sir. George Copper can't be told not to make the sale and Miss Ralston can't be brought back to be warned.'

'My dear Raikes, why not?'

'Because George Copper has been fool enough to let young Leiss get away with it. And he *has* got away with it. With the sports car, sir, and the young lady inside it. And where they've gone, sir, is to use the expression, nobody's business.'

III

Who can form an objective view of events with which, however lightly, he has been personally involved? Not Nicola. When, after the climax, she tried to sort out her impressions of these events she found that in every detail they were coloured by her own preferences and sympathies.

At the moment, for instance, she was concerned to notice that, while Mr Period had suffered a shrewd blow to his passionate snobbery, Mr Cartell's reaction was more disingenuous and resourceful. And while Mr Period was fretful, Mr Cartell, she thought, was nipped with bitter anger.

He made a complicated noise in his throat and then said sharply: 'They must be traced, of course. Has Copper actually transacted the sale? Change of ownership and so on?'

'He's accepted Mr Leiss's car, which is a souped-up old bag of a job, George reckons, in part payment, and he's let Mr Leiss try out the Scorpion on the understanding that, if he likes it, the deal's on.'

'Then they will return to the garage?'

'They *ought* to,' Sergeant Raikes said with some emphasis. 'The point is, sir, *will* they? Likely enough, he'll drive straight back to London. He may sell the car before he's paid for it and trust to his connection here to get him out of the red if things become awkward. He's played that caper before and he may play it again.'

Mr Cartell said: 'May I, P.P.?' and reached for the telephone.

'If it's all the same with you gentlemen, I think I'll make the call,' Sergeant Raikes said unexpectedly.

Mr Cartell said: 'As you wish,' and moved away from the desk.

Mr Period began feeling, in an agitated way, in his pockets. He said fretfully: 'What have I done with my cigarettes?'

Nicola said: 'I think the case was left in the dining-room. I'll fetch it.'

As she hurried out she heard the telephone ring.

The dining-room table was cleared and the window open. The cigarette-case was nowhere to be seen. She was about to go in search of Alfred when he came in. He had not seen the case, he said. Nicola remembered very clearly that, as she stood back at the door for Miss Cartell, she had noticed it on the window-sill and she said as much to Alfred.

A shutter came down over Alfred's face.

'It wasn't there when I cleared, miss.'

Nicola said: 'Oh, well! I expect after all, Mr Period — ' and then remembered that Mr Period had left the dining-room to answer the telephone and had certainly not collected the cigarette-case when he briefly returned.

Alfred said: 'The window was on the latch as it is now, when I cleared, miss. I'd left it shut, as usual.'

Nicola looked at it. It was a casement window and was hooked open to the extent of some eight inches. Beyond it were the rose garden, the side gate and the excavations in the lane. As she stared out of it, a shovelful of earth was thrown up; derisively, she might almost have thought, by one of the workmen, invisible in the trench.

'Never mind,' she said. 'We'll find it. Don't worry.'

'I hope so, I'm sure, miss. It's a valuable object.'

'I know.'

They were staring doubtfully at each other when Mr Period came in looking exceedingly rattled.

'Nicola, my dear: Andrew Bantling on the telephone, for you. *Would* you mind taking it in the hall? We are *un peu occupé*, in the study. I'm so sorry.'

'Oh, dear!' Nicola said, 'so am I, that you've been bothered. Mr Period – your cigarette-case isn't in here, I'm afraid.'

'But I distinctly remember – ' Mr Period began. 'Well,' never mind. Your telephone call, child.'

Nicola went into the hall.

Andrew Bantling said: 'Oh, there you are at last! What goes on in the lay-by? P.P. sounded most peculiar.'

'He's awfully busy.'

'You're being discreet and trustworthy. Never mind, I shall gimlet it out of you on the train. You couldn't make the three thirty, I suppose?'

'Not possibly.'

'Then I shall simply have to lurk in the lane like a follower. There's nowhere for me to be in this district. Baynesholme has become uninhabitable on account – ' he lowered his voice and evidently put his mouth very close to the receiver, so that consonants popped and sibilants hissed in Nicola's eardrum.

'What did you say?'

'I said *the Moppett* and her *Leonard* have arrived in a smashing Scorpion under the pretence of wanting to see the family portraits. What's the matter?'

'I've got to go. Sorry. Goodbye,' Nicola said, and rushed to the library.

Mr Cartell and Mr Period broke off their conversation as she entered. Sergeant Raikes was dialling a number.

She said, 'I thought I should tell you at once. They're at Baynesholme. They've driven there in the Scorpion.'

Mr Cartell went into action.

'Raikes,' he said, 'tell Copper I want him here immediately in the car.'

'Which car, sir?' Raikes asked, startled, the receiver at his ear.

'The Bloodbath,' Mr Period said impatiently. 'What else? Really, Raikes!'

'He's to drive me to Baynesholme as fast as the thing will go. At once, Raikes.'

Sergeant Raikes began talking into the telephone.

'Be quick,' Mr Cartell said, 'and you'd better come too.'

' – yes, George,' said Sergeant Raikes into the telephone. 'That's correct. Now.'

'Come along, Raikes. My hat and coat!' Mr Cartell went out. '*Alfred!* My top-coat.'

'And you might ask them, Harold, while you're about it,' Mr Period quite shouted after him, 'what they did with my cigarette-case.'

'What?' the retreating voice asked.

'Lady Barsington's card case. Cigarettes.'

There was a shocked pause. Mr Cartell returned, half in and half out of an overcoat, and a tweed hat cocked over one eye.

'What do you mean, P.P.? Surely you don't suggest . . . '

'God knows! But ask them. Ask!'

IV

Desirée, Lady Bantling (ex-Cartell, factually Dodds), sat smiling to herself in her drawing-room. She smoked incessantly and listened to Moppett Ralston and Leonard Leiss and it would have been impossible for anyone to say what she thought of them. Her ravaged face, with its extravagant make-up, and her mop of orange hair made a flagrant statement against the green background of her chair. She was possibly not unamused.

Moppett was explaining how interested Leonard was in art and what a lot he knew about the great portrait painters.

'So I do hope,' Moppett was saying, 'you don't think it too boring and bold of us to ask if we may look. Leonard said you would, but I said we'd risk it and if we might just see the pictures and creep away again – ?'

'Yes, do,' Desirée said. 'They're all Bantling ancestors. Gentlemen in skin-tight breeches, and ladies with high foreheads and smashing bosoms. Andrew could tell you all about them, but he seems to have disappeared. I'm afraid I've got to help poor Bimbo make up pieces of poetry for a treasure hunt and in any case I don't know anything about them. I want my pictures to be modern and gay and, if possible, rude.'

'And of course, you're *so* right, Lady Bantling,' Leonard said eagerly. He leant forward with his head on one side sending little waves of hair-oil towards her. Desirée watched him and accepted everything he said without comment. When he had talked himself to an ingratiating standstill, she remarked that, after all, she didn't really think she was all that interested in painting.

'Andrew has done a portrait of me which I do quite fancy,' she said. 'I look like the third witch in *Macbeth* before she gave up trying to make the best of herself. Hallo, my darling, how's your Muse?'

Bimbo had come in. He threw an extremely cold glance at Leonard.

'My Muse,' he said, 'is bitching on me. You must help me, Desirée; there ought to be at least seven clues and it's more amusing if they rhyme.'

'Can we help?' Moppett suggested. 'Leonard's quite good at *really* improper ones. What are they for?'

'A treasure hunt,' he said, without looking at her.

'Treasure hunts are my vintage,' Desirée said. 'I thought it might be fun to revive them. So we're having one tonight.'

Moppett and Leonard cried out excitedly. 'But I'm *utterly* sold on them,' Moppett said. 'They're quite the gayest way of having parties. How exactly are you working it?' she asked Bimbo. He said shortly that they were doing it the usual way.

Desirée stood up. 'Bimbo's planting a bottle of champagne some-where and the leading-up clues will be dotted about the landscape. If you don't mind just going on your picture crawl under your own steam we'd better begin racking our brains for rhymes. Please do look wherever you like.' She held out her hand to Moppett. 'I'm sorry not to be more hospitable, but we are, as you see, in a taking-on. Goodbye.' She looked at Leonard. 'Goodbye.'

'My God!' Bimbo said. 'The food from Magnums! It'll be at the station.'

Moppett and Leonard stopped short and looked passionately concerned.

'Can't you pick it up,' Desirée asked, 'when you lay your trail of clues?'

'I can't start before we've done the clues, can I?'

'They're too busy to send anyone from the kitchen and they want the stuff. Madly. We'd better get the Bloodbath to collect it.'

'Look!' Moppett and Leonard said together and then gaily laughed at each other. '"Two minds with butter – "' Moppett quoted. 'But please – please do let us collect the things from Magnums. We'd adore to.'

Desirée said: 'Jolly kind, but the Bloodbath will do it.'

Bimbo much more emphatically added: 'Thank you, but we wouldn't dream of it.'

'But why not!' Moppett protested. 'Leonard's longing to drive that thing out there, aren't you, sweetie?'

'Of course. And, as a matter of fact,' Leonard said, 'I happen to know the Bloodbath – if that's George Copper's crate – is out of commission. It won't take us any time.'

'Do let us or we'll think,' Moppett urged engagingly, 'that we really are being hideously in the way. Please.'

'Well – ' Desirée said, not looking at her husband, 'if you really don't mind, it would, I must say, be the very thing.'

'Andrew!' Bimbo ejaculated. 'He'll do it. Where is he?'

'He's gone. Do you know, darling, I'm afraid we'd better accept the kind offer.'

'Of course!' Moppett cried. 'Come on, Face! Is there anything else to be picked up, while we're about it?'

Desirée said, with a faint twist in her voice: 'You think of every-thing, don't you. I'll talk to the kitchen.'

When she had gone, Bimbo said: 'Isn't that the Scorpion Copper had in his garage?'

'The identical job,' Leonard agreed, man-to-man. 'Not a bad little heap by and large, and the price is okay. Like to have a look at her, Mr Dodds? I'd appreciate your opinion.'

Bimbo, with an air of mingled distaste and curiosity, intimated that he would and the two men left Moppett in the drawing-room. Standing back from the French window, she watched them at the car; Leonard talking, Bimbo with his hands in his pockets. 'Trying,' thought Moppett, 'not to be interested, but he is interested. He's a car man. He's married her for his Bentley and his drinks and the grandeur and fun. She's old. She can't have all that much of what it takes. Or, by any chance, can she?'

A kind of contempt possessed her; a contempt for Desirée and Bimbo and anybody who was not like herself and Leonard. 'Living dangerously,' she thought, 'that's us.' She wondered if it would be advisable to ask Leonard not to say 'appreciated', 'okay', 'pardon me', and 'appro'. She herself didn't mind how he talked: she even enjoyed their rows when he would turn foul-mouthed, adder-like, and brutal. Still, if they *were* to crash the county – 'They'll have to ask us,' she thought, 'after this. They can't not. We've been clever as clever.'

She continued to peer slantwise through the window.

When Desirée returned, Moppett was looking with respect at a picture above the fireplace.

Desirée said there would be a parcel at the grocer's in Little Codling. 'Your quickest way to the station is to turn right, outside the gates,' she said. 'We couldn't be more obliged to you.'

She went out with Moppett to the car and when it had shot out of sight down the avenue, linked her arm in her husband's.

'Shockers,' she said, 'aren't they?'

'Honestly, darling, I can't think what you're about.'

'Can't you?'

'None of my business, of course,' he muttered. She looked at him with amusement.

'Don't you like them?' she asked.

'Like them!'

'I find myself quite amused by them,' she said and added indifferently, 'they do know what they want, at least.'

'It was perfectly obvious, from the moment they crashed their way in, that they were hell-bent on getting asked for tonight.'

'I know.'

'Are you going to pretend not to notice their hints?'

'Oh,' she said with a faint chuckle, 'I don't think so. I expect I'll ask them.'

Bimbo said: 'Of course I never interfere.'

'Of course,' she agreed. 'And how wise of you, isn't it?' He drew away from her. 'You don't usually sulk, either.'

'You let people impose on you.'

'Not,' she said gently, 'without realizing it,' and he reddened.

'That young man,' he said, 'is a monster. Did you *smell* him?'

'In point of fact he's got quite a share of what it takes.'

'You can't mean it!'

'Yes, I do. I never tell lies about sex, as such. I should think he's probably a bad hat, wouldn't you?'

'I would. As shifty as they make them.'

'P'raps he's a gangster and Moppett's his moll.'

'Highly probable,' he said angrily.

'I can't wait to hear Leonard being the life and soul of my party.'

'I promise you, if you do ask them, you'll regret it.'

'Should we hire a detective to keep an eye on the spoons?'

'At least you can come in and help me with the bloody poetry.'

'I think I shall ask them,' she said, in her rather hoarse voice. 'Don't you think it could be fun? Would you really not want it?'

'You know damn' well what I want,' he muttered, staring at her.

She raised her eyebrows. 'I forgot to tell you,' she said. 'Ormsbury's dead.'

'Your brother?'

'That's right. In Australia.'

'Ought you to – '

'I haven't seen him for thirty years and I never liked him. A horrid, dreary fellow.'

Bimbo said: 'Good God, who's this!'

'The Bloodbath,' Desirée said calmly. 'So it isn't out of commission. Bad luck for Leonard.'

It came slowly roaring and boiling up the long drive with George Copper at the wheel and Raikes beside him.

'Do you *see* who's in the back seat?' Desirée asked her husband. 'It's Harold.'

'It can't be.'

'But it is. His first visit since we had our final row and he shook my dust from his boots for ever. Perhaps he's going to claim me back from you after all these years.'

'What the hell *can* he want?'

'Actually I'm livid with him. He's being beastly to Andrew about that money. I shall pitch into him.'

'Why's he got Raikes? I'll never get my clues done,' Bimbo complained.

'You bolt indoors. I'll cope.'

Bimbo said: 'Fair enough,' and did so.

The car drew up with a jerk. Sergeant Raikes got out and opened the rear door for Mr Cartell, who was clearly flustered.

'Harold,' Desirée said, with amusement. 'How are you? I recognized your hat. Good afternoon, Mr Copper. Good afternoon, Mr Raikes.'

'I wonder,' Mr Cartell began as he removed his hat, 'if you could spare me a moment.'

'Why not? Come in.'

Bare-headed, baldish and perturbed, he followed her distrustfully into the house.

'What do *we* do?' Mr Copper asked Raikes.

'Wait. What else? The Scorpion's not here, George.'

'You don't say,' Mr Copper bitterly rejoined, looking round the open expanse of drive.

Raikes walked to the front of the Bloodbath and looked at the surface of the drive. He laid his hand pontifically on the bonnet and snatched it away with an oath.

'She's boiling,' Mr Copper observed.

'Ta for the information.'

'You would insist on the hurry. She can't take it.'

'All right. All right. I said I ought to come on the bike. Stay where you are, George.'

Mr Copper watched him with resentment. Doubled forward he cast about the drive.

'The Scorpion,' he said, 'drips her grease rather heavy, doesn't she?'

'That's right.'

'And she's shod on three feet with Griprich and on the off-hind with Startread. Correct?'

'Yes.'

'She's came,' Sergeant Raikes said, 'and went. Look for yourself.'

Mr Copper said: 'So what do we do? Roar after her with the siren screaming? If we had a siren.'

'We'll follow it up for you through the usual channels. Don't worry.'

'What'll I say to the owner? Tell me that. I'm selling her on commission, mind! I'm responsible!'

'No need to panic. They might come back.'

'More likely to be half-way to London with changed number-plates. Who started the panic, anyway. You, with your police records. *Come back!* Them!'

The front door opened and Mr Cartell appeared, white-faced, in the entrance.

'Oh – Raikes,' he said. 'I've a little further business to discuss indoors, but will join you in a moment. Will you stay where you are and deal with the car situation when they return?'

'Sir?'

'Yes,' said Mr Cartell. 'There's no immediate need for alarm. They are coming back.'

With a sharp look at both of them he returned indoors.

'There you are,' Sergeant Raikes said. 'What did I tell you? You leave this one to me.'

V

'What I can't see,' Desirée said, turning her enormous lack-lustre eyes upon her former husband, 'is why you've got yourself into such a state. Poor Mr Copper's been told that you and P.P. and Connie won't guarantee the sale. All he's got to do is take the car away from them.'

'If they return it,' Mr Cartell amended.

'I hope, Harold darling, you're not suggesting that they'll make a break for Epping Forest and go native on Magnums' smoked salmon. That really would be too tiresome. But I'm sure they won't. They're much too anxious to worm their way into my party.'

'You can't,' Mr Cartell said in a hurry, 'possibly allow that, of course.'

'So everybody keeps telling me.'

'My dear Desirée – '

'Harold, I want to tackle you about Andrew.'

Mr Cartell gave her one sharp glance and froze. 'Indeed,' he said.

'He tells me you won't let him have his money.'

'He will assume control of his inheritance at the appointed time, which is on the sixth of November next.'

'He did explain, didn't he, why he needs it now? About the Grantham Gallery being for sale and wanting to buy it?'

'He did. He also explained that he wishes to leave the Brigade in order to manage the gallery.'

'And go on with his own painting.'

'Precisely. I cannot agree to anticipating his inheritance for these purposes.'

'He's gone into it very carefully and he's not a baby or a fool. He's twenty-four and extremely level-headed.'

'In this matter, I cannot agree with you.'

'Bimbo's been into it, too. He's prepared to put up some of the cash and go in as a partner.'

'Indeed. I am surprised to learn he is in a position to do so.'

She actually changed colour at this. There was a short silence and then she said: 'Harold, I ask you very seriously to let Andrew have his inheritance.'

'I'm sorry.'

'You may remember,' she said, with no change of manner, 'that when I do fight, it's no holds barred.'

'In common with most – '

'Don't say "with most of my delightful sex", Harold.'

'One can always omit the adjective,' said Mr Cartell.

'Ah, well,' Desirée said pleasantly and stood up. 'I can see there's no future in sweet reasonableness. Are you enjoying life in P.P.'s stately cottage?'

Mr Cartell also rose. 'It's a satisfactory arrangement,' he said stiffly, 'for me: I trust for him.'

'He won't enjoy the Moppett-Leonard *crise*, will he? Poor P.P., such a darling as he is and such a God-almighty snob. Does he know?'

'Know what?' Mr Cartell asked unguardedly.

'About your niece and her burglar boyfriend?'

Mr Cartell turned scarlet and closed his eyes. 'She is NOT,' he said in the trembling voice of extreme exasperation, 'my niece.'

'How do you know? I've always thought Connie might have popped her away to simmer and then adopted her back, as you might say.'

'That is a preposterous and possibly an actionable statement, Desirée. The girl – Mary Ralston – came from an extremely reputable adoption centre.'

'Connie might have put her there.'

'If you will forgive me, I'll have a word with Raikes. I regret very much that I have troubled you.'

'P.P. is dining with us. He and I are going to have a cosy old chum's gossip before my treasure-hunt party arrives.'

Mr Cartell said: 'I am not susceptible to blackmail, Desirée. I shall not reconsider my decision about Andrew.'

'Look,' Desirée said. 'I fancy you know me well enough to realize that I'm not a sentimental woman.'

'That,' said Mr Cartell, 'I fully concede. A woman who gives a large party on the day her brother's death is announced – '

'My dear Hal, you know you looked upon Ormsbury as a social scourge and so did I. By and large, I'm not madly fond of other people. But I am fond of Andrew. He's my son and I like him very much indeed. You watch out for yourself, Harold. I'm on the warpath.'

A motor horn sounded distantly. They both turned to the windows.

'And here,' Desirée said, 'are your friends. I expect you want to go and meet them. Goodbye.'

When Mr Cartell had left her, she moved into the French window and, unlike Moppett, very openly watched the scene outside.

The Scorpion came up the drive at a great pace, but checked abruptly. Then it moved on at a more decorous speed and pulled up. Leonard and Moppett got out simultaneously. Sergeant Raikes advanced and so did they, all smiles and readiness, but with the faintest suggestion of self-consciousness, Desirée considered, in their joints. 'It's people's elbows,' she reflected, 'that give them away.'

They approached the group of three. Moppett, with girlish insouciance, linked her arm through Mr Cartell's causing him to become rigid with distaste. 'First blood to Moppett,' thought Desirée with relish.

Leonard listened to Sergeant Raikes with an expression that progressed from bonhomie through concern towards righteous astonishment. He bowed ironically and indicated the Scorpion.

Catching sight of Desirée, he shook his head slowly from side to side as if inviting her to share his bewilderment. He then removed two large packages from the Scorpion.

Desirée opened the French window and strolled down the steps towards them. Mr Cartell furiously disengaged himself from Moppett.

'I think,' he said, 'that we should get back, Raikes. If Copper drives the other car, you, I suppose – '

Sergeant Raikes glanced at Moppett and muttered something.

'Don't let *us* keep you,' Leonard said quickly and with excessive politeness. 'Please.'

They touched their hats to Desirée, mounted their respective cars and drove away, inexplicably at a disadvantage.

'Well!' Desirée asked cheerfully, 'did you find my tiresome food?'

Moppett and Leonard, all smiles, began to chatter and give way to each other.

Finally Moppett said: 'Dear Lady Bantling – yes. We've got it all, but, as you see, we ran into a muddle of sorts. Mr Copper's made a nonsense about the Scorpion and we've missed buying it.'

'Inefficient,' Leonard said. 'It appears somebody else had first refusal.'

'How very disappointing.'

'Isn't it!' Moppett agreed. 'Too sickening.' She gave a little scream and put her hand to her mouth. 'Leonard!' she cried. 'Fools that we are!'

'What, darling?'

'We ought to have gone back with them. Look at us! *Now*, what do we do?'

Leonard allowed the slightest possible gap to occur before he said: 'I'm afraid Mr George Copper will have to make a return trip in my car. Too bad!'

'What *will* you think of us?' Moppett asked Desirée.

'Oh,' she said lightly, 'the worst,' and they laughed with possibly a shade less conviction.

'At least,' Moppett said, 'we can bring the food in, can't we, and if we *might* ring up for *some* sort of transport.'

Bimbo came out of the house and fetched up short when he saw them. Desirée grinned at him.

'Why not stay?' she said very distinctly to Moppett. 'After fetching all our food, the least we can do is to ask you to eat it. Do stay.'

CHAPTER 3

Aftermath to a Party

Andrew put Nicola's overcoat on the seat and sat opposite her.

'The best thing about this train,' he said, 'is that it's nearly always empty. So you're returning to the fold tomorrow, are you?'

Nicola had said Mr Period had asked her to do so and that was why she had left her typewriter behind.

'But you're *not* returning to Little Codling tomorrow,' Andrew said, with the air of taking a plunge, 'you're returning tonight. At least, I hope so. Don't say another word. I've got an invitation for you.'

He produced it and gave it to her with an anxious smile.

It was from his mother and it said: 'Do come to my dotty party tonight. Andrew will bring you and we'll put you up. He'll explain all about it, but do come.'

Nicola stared at him in amazement.

'My mum,' he said, 'has taken a fancy to you. So, as is no doubt abundantly obvious, have I. Now don't go into a *brouhaha* and say you can't. Just say: "Thank you, Andrew. How sweet of your mum, I'd love to."'

'But *how* can I?'

'How?' Andrew said grandly. 'Anyhow. Why not?'

'I tell you what,' Nicola said. 'You've nagged at your mum to ask me.'

'I swear I haven't. She nagged at me and I said I would if you would.'

'There you are, you see.'

'No, I don't. And anyway, do stop carping and come. It's definitely not one of my mamma's more rococo parties. I wouldn't dream of taking you to one of them, of course.'

Nicola, who remembered hearing rumours of some of Lady
Bantling's parties, felt relieved.

'What I thought,' Andrew continued, 'I'll drop you wherever you
live and you can nip into your number one ceremonials and then I'll
pick up my dinner jacket and we'll dine somewhere and then we'll
drive down to Baynesholme.'

'What about the cocktail party you're all dressed up for?'

'Forget it, completely. Do come, Nicola. Will you?'

'Thank you, Andrew. How sweet of your mum to ask me. I'd
love to.'

'Thank you, Nicola.'

For the rest of the journey Andrew talked to Nicola about himself.
He said he wanted to paint more than anything else in life and that
he'd been having lessons and was 'meant to be not too bad'. He said
that if he could take the Grantham Gallery over, there was a studio
at the back where he could paint and manage the gallery at the same
time. Then he described his unproductive and bad-tempered meeting
that morning with his guardian and step-father, Mr Cartell.

'It was a snorter,' Andrew said thoughtfully. 'He treated the
whole thing as if it was a sort of adolescent whim. I'd brought down
all the figures for the turnover and he wouldn't look at them, damn
him. I gave him the names of jolly good people who would supply
an expert opinion and he wouldn't listen. All he would say was that
my father wouldn't have wanted me to resign my commission. What
the hell,' Andrew shouted and then pulled himself up. 'It's not so
much the practical side that infuriates me – I could, after all, I imagine,
borrow the money and insure my life or whatever one does. It's his
bloody pontificating philistinism. What I believe I most resented,' he
said, 'was having to talk about my painting. I said things that are
private to me and he came back at me with the sort of remarks that
made them sound phoney. Can you understand that?'

'I think I can. And I suppose in the end you began to wonder if,
after all, you were any good.'

'You do understand, don't you? Does everybody off-load their
difficulties on you, or – ? No,' Andrew said, 'I'd better not say that:
yet. Thank you, anyway, for listening.'

'Do you admire Agatha Troy's painting?'

He stared at her. 'Well, of course. Why?'

'I know her. She's married to Roderick Alleyn in the CID. I go there quite often. As a matter of fact I'm paying them a visit tomorrow evening.'

'What's she like? I know what she looks like. Lovely bones. Kind of gallant. Is she alarming?'

'Not at all. She's rather shy. She's jolly good about being interested in younger people's work,' Nicola added. She hesitated and then said: 'You may not care for the idea at all, but if you liked I could show her one of your things.'

He turned very red and Nicola wondered if she had offended him. He said at last, 'Do you know, I don't think I'd dare.'

'So Mr Cartell really has downed you, I see.'

'No, he hasn't, you low-cunning girl.'

'If you'd rather not I shan't take umbrage. On the other hand I'll be delighted if you say: "Thank you, Nicola. How sweet of you to ask me. I'd love to."'

Andrew grinned and for an appreciable interval was silent.

'You win,' he said at last. 'I'll say that same small thing.'

The rest of the journey passed quickly for both of them and in London they followed the plan proposed by Andrew.

At half past eight they were in his car on their way back into Kent. The night was warm for early April, the lights sailed past and there was a young moon in the sky. Nicola knew that she was beginning to fall in love.

II

'I tell you what, Mrs M.,' Alfred said as he prepared to set the dinner table. 'The weather in this household has deteriorated and the forecast is for atmospheric disturbances followed by severe storms.'

'Go on!' Mrs Mitchell said eagerly. 'How?'

'*How*, I don't know. If you ask me *why*, I can give a pretty good guess. For ten years, Mrs M., we've organized ourselves quietly and comfortably in the way that suits *us*. Everything very nice and going by clockwork. Nothing unexpected. Settled. No upsets of any kind whatsoever. Suits *us* and incidentally, I may say, suits you and me. *Now* what? What's the present situation? Look at today. We've had more upsets in this one day, Mrs M., than we've had to put up with in the total length of my service.'

Mrs Mitchell executed the toss of the head and upward turn of the eyes that had only one connotation.

'Him?' she suggested.

'Exactly. Him,' Alfred said. 'Mr Harold Cartell.'

'Good God, Mr Belt!' Mrs Mitchell exclaimed. 'Whatever's the matter?'

'The matter, Mrs M.?'

'The way you looked! Coo! Only for a sec but my word! Talk about old-fashioned.'

'You'd look old-fashioned yourself,' Alfred countered, 'if suggestions of the same nature were made to you.'

'By 'im?' she prompted, unguardedly.

'Correct. In reference to *our* cigarette-case. Which, as I mentioned earlier, was left by those two on the window-ledge and has disappeared. Well. As we noticed this afternoon, Mr Cartell went off in the Bloodbath with George Copper and Bert Raikes.'

'Very peculiar, yes.'

'Yes. All right. It now appears they went to Baynesholme.'

'To the Big House?'

'Exactly.'

'Well! To see her ladyship?'

'To see *them*. Those two. They'd gone there, if you please. Unasked, by all accounts.'

'Sauce!'

'What it was all about I have not yet gathered, but will from George Copper. The point is that when I take drinks to the library just now, they're at it hammer-and-tongs.'

'Our two gentlemen?'

'Who else? And so hot they don't stop when they see me. At least *he* doesn't. Mr C. He was saying he'd forgotten in the heat of the moment at Baynesholme to ask young Leiss and that Moppett about where they'd left the cigarette-case and Mr Period was saying the young lady, Miss Maitland-Mayne, saw it on the sill. And I was asked to say if it was there when I cleared and I said no. And I added that someone had opened the window.'

'Who?'

'Ah! You may well ask. So Mr Cartell says, in a great taking-on, that the chaps doing the sewage in Green Lane must have taken it and my gentleman says they're very decent chaps and he can't believe it. "Very well, then," says Mr C. very sharp and quite the lawyer, "perhaps Alfred would care to reconsider his statement." And the way he said it was sufficient! After that suggestion, Mrs M., I don't mind telling you it's him or me. Both of us this residence will not accommodate.'

'What did our gentleman say?'

'Ah! What would you expect? Came out very quiet and firm on my behalf. "I think," he said, "that Alfred has given us a perfectly clear picture and that there is no need to ask him to repeat it. Thank you, Alfred. I'm sorry to have troubled you." So, of course, I said, "Thank *you*, sir," with what I trust was the proper emphasis, and withdrew. But you can take it from me, there's serious trouble and deep feeling in more than one direction. Something was said at luncheon that was very ill-received by our gentleman. Said by Mr C. Speculation,' added Alfred, who had grown calmer and reverted to his normal habit of speech, 'speculation is unprofitable. Events will clarify.'

'Why Raikes, though?' she pondered.

'Ah! And I happened to ascertain from the chaps in the lane that Raikes brought Mr C. back in George Copper's Bloodbath and George himself turned up in that Scorpion he's got in his garage. And what's more, the rural mail-van gave those two a lift back. They've been invited to the Big House party tonight. They're dining and staying with Miss Cartell. They were very pleased with themselves, the mail-van driver said, but cagey in their manner.'

The kitchen door was ajar and Mr Cartell's voice sounded clearly from the hall.

'Very well,' he was saying. 'If that should prove to be the case I shall know how to act and I can assure you, P.P., that I shall act with the utmost vigour. I trust that you are satisfied.'

The front door slammed.

'Mercy on us!' Mrs Mitchell apostrophized. 'Now, what?' and added precipitantly: 'My bedroom window!'

She bolted from the kitchen and Alfred heard her thundering up the back stairs.

Presently she returned, flushed and fully informed.

'Across the green,' she reported, 'to Miss Cartell's.'

'And you may depend upon it, Mrs M.,' Alfred said, 'that the objective is Miss Moppett.'

III

Moppett had changed into the evening-dress she kept in her bedroom at Miss Cartell's house. It was geranium red, very décolleté and flagrantly becoming to her. She lay back in her chair, admiring her arms and glancing up from under her eyebrows at Mr Cartell.

'Auntie Con's at a Hunt Club committee do of sorts,' she said. 'She'll be in presently. Leonard's collecting his dinner-jacket off the bus.'

'I am glad,' Mr Cartell said, giving her one look and thereafter keeping his gaze on his own folded hands, 'of the opportunity to speak to you in private. I will be obliged if, as far as my sister is concerned, you treat our conversation as confidential. There is no need, at this juncture, to cause her unnecessary distress.'

'Dear me,' she murmured, 'you terrify me, Uncle Hal.'

'I will also be obliged if the assumption of a relationship which does not exist is discontinued.'

'Anything you say,' she agreed after a pause, 'Mr Cartell.'

'I have two matters to put before you. The first is this. The young man, Leonard Leiss, with whom you appear to have formed a close friendship, is known to the police. If he persists in his present habits it will only be a matter of time before he is in serious trouble and, if you continue in your association with him, you will undoubtedly become involved. To a criminal extent. I would prefer, naturally, to think you were unaware of his proclivities, but I must say that I am unable to do so.'

'I certainly am unaware of anything of the sort and I don't believe a word of it.'

'That,' Mr Cartell said, 'is nonsense.'

'I'm very sorry, but I'm afraid it's you that's talking nonsense. All this to-do because poor Leonard wants to buy a car and I simply mention to Copper that Auntie Con – I hope you don't mind if I go on calling her that – knows him and that you and P.P. might give him the okay. It was only a matter of form, anyway. Of course, if we'd thought you wouldn't like it we wouldn't have dreamt of doing it. I'm jolly sorry we did and Leonard is, too.'

Mr Cartell raised his eyes and looked at her. For a moment she boggled, but only for a moment. 'And I must say,' she said boldly, 'we both take a pretty poor view of you coming to Baynesholme and creating a scene. Not that it made any difference with Lady Bantling. She's asked us both for tonight in spite of whatever nonsense she may have been told about us,' Moppett announced and laughed rather shrilly.

He waited for a moment and then said: 'It would be idle to discuss this matter any further. I shall turn to my second point and put it very bluntly. What did you do with Mr Period's cigarette-case?'

Moppett recrossed her legs and waited much too long before she said: 'I don't know what you mean?'

'Precisely what I have said. You and Leiss examined it after luncheon. What did you do with it?'

'How dare you' – Moppett began – 'how *dare* you –' and Leonard came into the room.

When he saw Mr Cartell he fetched up short. 'Pardon me,' he said elegantly. 'Am I interrupting something?'

Moppett extended her arm towards him. 'Darling,' she said. 'I'm being badgered. Can you cope?'

He took her hand and sat on the arm of her chair. 'What goes on?' he asked. He was normally a white-faced young man: this characteristic at the moment was particularly noticeable.

'To be perfectly honest,' Moppett began, 'I haven't a clue. But it appears that we're meant to know where poor old P.P. puts his museum pieces.'

'Mr Period's cigarette-case has disappeared,' Mr Cartell said, addressing Leonard exclusively. 'You and Miss Ralston were the last persons known to handle it. You may care to make a statement as to what you did with it.'

Leonard said: '*Disappeared!* By Jove, that's too bad, isn't it?' His pale fingers closed tightly over Moppett's. 'Of *course*, we must help if we can. Yes, now – yes. I do remember. I left it on the window-ledge in the dining-room. You remember, sweetie, don't you?'

'Perfectly.'

'Was the window open or shut?'

'Oh,' Leonard said easily, 'open. Yes. Open.'

'Did you open it, Mr Leiss?'

'Me? What would I do that for? It *was* open.'

'It was shut,' Mr Cartell said, 'during luncheon.'

'Then I suppose the butler-chap – what's-'is-name – must have opened it.'

'No.'

'That,' Leonard remarked, smiling, 'is what he says.'

'It is what I say.'

'Then I'm afraid I don't much fancy the way you say it.' Leonard produced a silver case from his pocket, offered it to Moppett, helped himself and with great deliberation, lit both cigarettes. He snapped the case shut, smiled at Mr Cartell and returned it to his pocket. He inhaled deeply, breathed out the vapour and fanned it with his hand. He wore an emerald ring on his little finger. 'How about the sewer in the lane?' he asked. 'Anything in that?'

'They could not open the window from outside.'

'Perhaps it was opened for them.'

Mr Cartell stood up. 'Mr Leiss,' he said, 'I consider myself responsible to Mr Period for any visitors who, however unwelcome, come to his house under my aegis. Unless his case is returned within the next twelve hours, I shall call in the police.'

'You're quite an expert at that, aren't you?' Leonard remarked. He looked at the tip of his cigarette. 'One other thing,' he said. 'I resent the way you're handling this, Mr Cartell, and I know exactly what I can do about it.'

Mr Cartell observed him with a sort of astonished disgust. He addressed himself to Moppett. 'There's no point,' he said, 'in pursuing this conversation.'

A door banged, footsteps were heard in the hall together with an outbreak of yapping and long drawn-out whines. A loud, uninhibited voice shouted: 'Geddown! *Geddown*, you brute.' There followed a canine yelp and a renewed outbreak of yapping.

'*Quiet*, Li. Quiet sweetie. Who the hell let this blasted mongrel in! *Trudi!*'

'I have changed my mind,' Mr Cartell said. 'I shall speak to my sister.'

He went out and found her, clasping a frenzied Pekinese to her bosom, kicking Pixie and shouting at her Austrian house-parlourmaid.

'My God, Boysie,' she said when she saw her brother, 'are you dotty, bringing that thing in here. Take it out. Take it *out!*'

The Pekinese turned in her arms and bit her thumb.

Mr Cartell said with dignity: 'Come along, old girl, you're not wanted.' He withdrew Pixie to the garden, tied her to the gate-post and returned to the hall where he found his sister staunching her wound. The Pekinese had been removed.

'I am sorry, Constance. I apologize. Had I imagined – '

'Oh, come off it,' Miss Cartell rejoined. 'You're hopeless with animals and let's leave it at that. If you want to see me, come in here while I get some stuff on my thumb.'

He followed her into her 'den': a small room, crowded with photographs that she had long ago ceased to look at with the possible exception of those that recorded the progress of Moppett from infancy to her present dubious effulgence.

Miss Cartell rummaged in a drawer and found some cotton-wool which she applied to her thumb with stamp-paper and a heavy coating of some black and evil-smelling unguent.

'What is that revolting stuff?' asked her brother, taking out his handkerchief.

'I use it on my mare for girth-gall.'

'Really, Connie!'

'Really what? Now then, Boysie,' she said, 'what's up? I can see you're in one of your moods. Let's have a drink and hear all about it.'

'I don't want a drink, Connie.'

'Why not? I do,' she shouted, with her inevitable gust of laughter and opened a little cupboard. 'I've been having a go at the Hunt Club,' she added and embarked on a vigorous exposé of a kennel-maid. Mr Cartell suffered her to thrust a whisky-and-soda into his hand and listened to her with something like despair.

In the end he managed to get her to attend to him. He saw the expected and familiar look of obstinacy come into her face.

'I can't put it too strongly, Connie,' he said. 'The fellow's a bad lot and unless you put your foot down, the girl's going to be involved in serious trouble.'

But it was no use. She said, readily enough, that she would tackle Moppett, but almost at once she began to defend her and before long they had both lost their tempers and had become a middle-aged brother and sister furiously at odds.

'The trouble with you, Boysie, is that you've grown so damned selfish. I don't wonder Desirée got rid of you. All you think of is your own comfort. You've worked yourself up into a stink because you're dead scared P.P. will turn you out.'

'That's an insufferable construction to put on it. Naturally, I don't relish the thought – '

'There you are, you see.'

'Nonsense, Constance! Will you realize that you are entertaining a young man with a criminal record?'

'Moppett has told me all about him. She's taken him in hand and he's going as straight as a die.'

'You've made yourself responsible for Mary, you appear to be quite besotted on her and yet you can allow her to form a criminal association – '

'There's nothing like that about it. She's sorry for him.'

'She'll be sorry for herself before long.'

'Why?'

'This cigarette-case – '

'P.P.'ll find it somewhere. You've no right – '

'I have every right,' Mr Cartell cried, now quite beside himself with chagrin. 'And I tell you this, Connie. The girl is a bad girl. If you've any authority over her, you'd better use it. But in my opinion your sensible course would be to let her be brought to book and pay the consequences. She's got a record, Connie. You'll be well rid of her. And I promise you that unless this wretched cigarette-case is returned before tomorrow, I shall call in the police.'

'You wouldn't!'

'I shall. And the upshot no doubt will be gaol for the pair of them.'

'You miserable little pip-squeak, Boysie!'

'Very well,' Mr Cartell said and rose. 'That's my final word, Connie. Good evening to you.'

He strode from the hall into the garden where he fell over his dog. With some commotion, they effected an exit and returned, presumably, to Mr Period's house across the green.

IV

Desirée wore black for her April Fool's party. On any other woman of her age it would have been a disastrous dress but, by virtue of a sort of inner effrontery, she got away with it. Her neck, her bosom and that dismal little region, known, unprettily, as the armpit, were all so many statements of betrayal, but she triumphed over them and not so much took them in her own stride as obliged other people to take them in theirs. With her incredible hair brushed up into a kind of bonfire, her carefree make-up, her eyeglass, and her general air of raffishness, she belonged, as Mr Period mildly reflected, to Toulouse Lautrec rather than to any contemporary background.

They had dined. The party had assembled, made a great deal of noise and gone off in pairs by car to follow up the clues. Bimbo was driving round the terrain to keep observation, rescue any couple that had become unintentionally lost and whip in the deliberate stragglers. Everyone was to be in by midnight. Supper was set out in the ballroom and in the meantime Desirée and Mr Period sat over a fire in her boudoir enjoying coffee and brandy. It was, Mr Period noticed, Desirée's third brandy but she carried her drink with astonishing bravura. He nursed his own modest potion and cosily lamented his fate.

'Desirée, my dear,' he was saying, 'I really don't know what it is about you, but you have so got the gift of drawing one out. Here am I letting my back hair down in the naughtiest way and about poor old Hal, which is not at all the done thing, considering.'

'Why not?' she said propping her feet in their preposterously high heels above the fireplace. Mr Period, as she noticed with amusement, gazed tactfully at the flames. 'Why not? I found Harold plain hell to live with and I don't know why you should fare any better. Except that you're nicer than me and have probably got more patience.'

'It's the *little* things. *Every* morning to tap on one's door and say, "Bath's empty for what it's worth." *Every* day to clear his throat before he opens his paper and say he may as well know the worst. And his *dog*, Desirée! The noise!' Mr Period exclaimed, unconsciously plagiarizing. 'And the smell! And the destruction!'

'One of those mixed-up dogs that try to marry one's foot, I've noticed.'

Mr Period gave a little cough and murmured: 'Exactly. Moreover, every night, at one o'clock precisely, he takes it out of doors and it sets up the most hideous barking until, and indeed for some time after, he shuts it up. There have been complaints from all over the village. And now,' he added, throwing up his hands, 'this afternoon! This afternoon was *too* much.'

'But do tell me, P.P., what happened? With Moppett and her flash friend and the car? I've heard Harold's version, of course, but I'm having my own private war with him and was too angry to pay all that much attention.'

Mr Period told her the whole story.

'And I do feel, darling Desirée, that you should be warned. It's plain to be seen that this frightful person, the Leiss, is an out-and-out bad 'un. And indeed, for your ear alone, we most strongly suspect – ' Mr Period looked about him as if the boudoir concealed microphones and began to whisper the story of the cigarette-case.

'Oh, no!' Desirée said with relish. 'Actually a burglar! And is Moppett his con-girl, do you suppose?'

'I fear, only too probably. And, my dear, here you are, in the kindness of your heart, asking them to your wonderful party.'

'It wasn't kindness. It was to spite Harold. He won't give Andy his money. I can't tell you how livid it makes me.'

She looked rather fixedly at Mr Period. 'You're a trustee, P.P. Have you discussed it with Hal, or with Andrew?'

Mr Period said uncomfortably: 'Not really *discussed* it, my dear.'

'Don't tell me you disapprove, too!'

'No, no, no!' he said in a hurry. 'Not *disapprove*, exactly. It's just – leaving the Brigade and so on. For that *rather* outré world. Art . . . the Chelsea set . . . Not that Andrew . . . But there! 'Nuff said.'

'We're not going to quarrel over it, I hope?'

'My *dear*. Quarrel!'

'Well,' she said suddenly giving Mr Period a kiss. 'Let's talk about something more amusing.'

They embarked on a long gossip and Mr Period eased up. He was enjoying himself immensely, but he did not wish to stay until the return of the treasure-hunters. He looked at his watch, found it was eleven o'clock, and asked if he might telephone for the Bloodbath.

'No need,' Desirée said, 'my car's outside. I'd love to take you.
Don't fuss, P.P., I'd really like to. I can have a cast around the village
and see how the hunt's going. By the way, one of Bimbo's clues leads
to your sewage excavation. It says: "All your trouble and all your
pain will only land you down the drain." He's not very good at poetry,
poor sweet, but I thought that one of his neater efforts. Come on,
darling. I can see you're in a fever lest slick Len and his moll should
get back with the first prize before you make your getaway.'

They went out to her car. Mr Period was a little apprehensive
because of the amount of liqueur brandy Desirée had consumed but
she drove with perfect expertise and all the way to Little Codling
they talked about Mr Cartell. Presently they turned into Green Lane.
A red lantern marked the end of the open ditch. They passed an
elderly sports car parked in the rough grass on the opposite side.

'Andy,' said his mother, giving a long hoot on her horn. 'He's
going to fall in love with your secretary, I can see.'

'Already!' ejaculated Mr Period.

'Going to. Heavily, I fancy. I took to the girl, rather.'

'Charming! A *really* nice gel. I'm delighted with her.'

'P.P.,' Desirée said, as they drew near the house, 'there's something extra Harold's done to inflame you, isn't there?'

There was a silence.

'Don't tell me if you'd rather not, of course.'

'It's very painful to me. Something he said. One shouldn't,' Mr
Period added in a constrained and unnatural voice, 'let such things
upset one but – No, dearest Desirée, I shan't bore you with it. It was
nothing. I prefer to forget it.'

'Fair enough,' she said and pulled up.

Mr Period did not immediately get out of the car. He made
another little speech of thanks for his entertainment and then
with many hesitations and apologetic noises hinted obscurely at
bereavement.

'I haven't said anything, my dear,' he murmured, 'because I felt
you preferred *not*. But I wouldn't like you to think – but never mind,
I only wanted you to know – ' He waved his hands and was silent.

'Do you mean about Ormsbury?' she said in her direct way. Mr
Period made a small confirmatory sound. 'You didn't say anything,'
he added. 'So, of course – '

'There are some sorrows,' Desirée said and it was impossible to catch any overtones in her voice, 'that go too deep for words.'

Mr Period gave a little groan of sympathy, kissed her hand, and left her.

He went in by the side gate. She watched him, by the light of her headlamps, pick his way in a gingerly fashion over the planks that had been laid across the ditch. He was safely inside his house and Desirée was about to drive away when she caught sight of a figure in an upper window. She stopped her engine and got out of the car.

V

By midnight the winning pair had presented themselves with their prize, a magnum of champagne. They were inevitably, Moppett and Leonard, all smiles, but with a curious tendency to avoid looking at each other. Leonard was effulgent in the matter of cuff-links and lapels and his tie was large and plum-coloured. Bimbo looked upon him with loathing, gave them both drinks and put a jazz record on the machine. Leonard with ineffable grace extended his hands towards Desirée. 'May we?' he said and in a moment was dancing with her. He was a superb dancer. 'Much too good,' she said afterwards. 'Like the really expensive gigolos used to be. He smells like them too: it quite took me back. I adored it.'

Bimbo, sulking, was then obliged to dance with Moppett who made business-like passes at him. These exercises were interrupted by the arrival in straggling pairs of the rest of the treasure-hunters, Nicola and Andrew being the last to come in: looking radiantly pleased with themselves.

Desirée had a talent for parties. Sometimes they began presentably and ended outrageously, sometimes they were presentable almost all the time and sometimes they began, continued and ended outrageously. It was for the last sort that she had gained her notoriety. This one was, at the moment, both gay and decorous, possibly because Andrew had unexpectedly said he hoped it would be.

They were all dancing, and the time was a quarter past one, when a rumpus broke out on the drive. Bimbo was changing records, so the noise established itself readily; it was that of a multiple dog fight. Growls, yaps, full-blooded barking and strangulated cries of anguish mounted in a ragged crescendo.

Desirée said: 'A rival show, it seems,' and then, 'Bimbo! Ours! They must have got out!'

Bimbo swore, pulled back the curtains and went through French windows to the terrace, followed by Andrew, Desirée and most of the other men.

Nicola found herself on the terrace in a group composed of all the ladies and Leonard.

The combat was joined among parked cars at the head of the drive and was illuminated by lights from the house. All was confusion. Some six or seven contestants bit at each other in a central engagement, others rolled together under cars. One very large, isolated dog sat on its haunches howling dispassionately, and one could be discerned belting down the drive screaming its classic cry of 'pen-and-ink'.

Bimbo, Andrew and an advance guard went down into the arena and at first added greatly to the confusion. They shouted, swore, grabbed and kicked. Desirée suddenly joined them, was momentarily hidden, but emerged carrying an outraged poodle by the scruff of its neck. Servants ran out, offering hunting-crops and umbrellas. Expressions of human as well as canine anguish were now perceptible. Andrew detached himself, dragging two frenzied Aberdeens by their collars. They were Baynesholme dogs and were thrust with the poodle into a cloakroom where they got up a half-hearted row on their own account.

Bimbo now appeared carrying an air-gun. He waved the other men aside and presented his weapon at the central mélée. There was a mild explosion, followed by cries of distress and suddenly the arena had emptied and the night was plangent with the laments of rapidly retreating dogs.

Only one remained. Exhausted, gratified, infamous and complacent, her tongue lolling out of one side of her mouth, and her lead trailing from her collar, sat a boxer bitch: Mr Cartell's Pixie, the Helen of the engagement. When Bimbo approached her she gathered herself together and bit him.

VI

The next morning Connie Cartell woke slowly from a heavy sleep. She experienced that not unusual sensation during half-consciousness, in which the threat of something unpleasant anticipates the recollection of the thing itself. She lay, blinking and yawning for a second or two. She heard her Austrian maid stump along the passage and knock on a door.

'Damn!' Connie thought. 'I forgot to tell her not to disturb either of them.'

Then the full realization of all the horrors of the preceding evening came upon her.

She was not an imaginative woman, but it hadn't taken much imagination after her brother's visit to envisage what would happen to Moppett if Mr Period's cigarette-case was not discovered. Connie had tried to tackle Moppett and, as usual, had got nowhere at all. Moppett had merely remarked that P.P. and Mr Cartell had dirty minds. When Connie had broached the topic of Leonard Leiss and his reputation, Moppett had reminded her of Leonard's unhappy background and of how she, Moppett, was pledged to redeem him. She had assured Connie, with tears in her eyes and a great many caresses, that Leonard was indeed on the upward path. If Connie herself had had any experience at all of the Leiss milieu and any real inclination to cope with it, she might possibly have been able to bring a salutary point of view to bear on the situation. She might, it is not too preposterous to suppose, have been able to direct Moppett towards a different pattern of behaviour. But she had no experience and no real inclination. She only doted upon Moppett with the whole force of her unimaginative and uninformed being. She was in a foreign country and like many another woman of her class and kind, behaved stupidly, as a foreigner.

So she bathed and dressed and went down to breakfast in a sort of fog and ate large quantities of eggs, bacon and kidneys indifferently presented by her Austrian maid. She was still at her breakfast when she saw Alfred, in his alpaca jacket and the cloth cap he assumed for such occasions, crossing the green with an envelope in his hand.

In a moment he appeared before her.

'I beg pardon, miss,' Alfred said, laying the envelope on the table, 'for disturbing you, but Mr Period asked me to deliver this. No answer is required, I understand.' She thanked him and when he had withdrawn, opened the letter.

Silent minutes passed. Connie read and re-read the letter. Incredulity followed bewilderment and was replaced in turn by alarm. A feeling of horrid unreality possessed her and again she read the letter.

My dear: What can I say? Only that you have lost a devoted brother and I a very dear friend. I know so well, believe me so *very* well, what a grievous shock this has been for you and how bravely you will have taken it. If it is not an impertinence in an old fogey to do so, may I offer you these very simple lines written by my dear and so Victorian Duchess of Rampton? They are none the worse, I hope, for their unblushing sentimentality.

> *So must it be, dear heart, I'll not repine,*
> *For while I live the Memory is Mine.*

I should like to think that we know each other well enough for you to believe me when I say that I hope you won't dream of answering this all-too-inadequate attempt to tell you how sorry I am.

Yours sincerely,
Percival Pyke Period

The Austrian maid came in and found Connie still gazing at this letter.

'Trudi,' she said with an effort, 'I've had a shock.'

'*Bitte?*'

'It doesn't matter. I'm going out. I won't be long.'

And she went out. She crossed the green and tramped up Mr Pyke Period's drive to his front door.

The workmen were assembled in Green Lane.

Alfred opened the front door to her.

'Alfred,' she said, 'what's happened?'

'Happened, miss?'

'My brother. Is he – ?'

'Mr Cartell is not up yet, miss.'

She looked at him as if he had addressed her in an incomprehensible jargon.

'He's later than usual, miss,' Alfred said. 'Did you wish to speak to him?'

'Hall-o. Connie! Good morning to you.'

It was Mr Pyke Period, as fresh as paint, but perhaps not quite as rubicund as usual. His manner was over-effusive.

Connie said: 'P.P., for God's sake what is all this? Your letter?'

Mr Period glanced at Alfred, who withdrew. He then, after a moment's hesitation, took Connie's hand in both of his.

'Now, now!' he said. 'You mustn't let this upset you, my dear.'

'Are you mad!'

'Connie!' he faintly ejaculated. 'What do you mean? Do you – do you *know?*'

'I must sit down. I don't feel well.'

She did so. Mr Period, his fingers to his lips, eyed her with dismay. He was about to speak when a shrill female ejaculation broke out in the direction of the servants' quarters. It was followed by the rumble of men's voices. Alfred reappeared, very white in the face.

'Good God!' Mr Period said. 'What now?'

Alfred, standing behind Connie Cartell, looked his employer in the eyes and said: 'May I speak to you, sir?' He made a slight warning gesture and opened the library door.

'Forgive me, Connie. I won't be a moment.'

Mr Period went into the library followed by Alfred, who shut the door.

'Merciful heavens, Alfred, what's the matter with you! Why do you look at me like that?'

'Mr Cartell, sir,' Alfred moistened his lips. 'I, really, I scarcely know how to put it, sir. He's, he's – '

'What are you trying to tell me? What's happened?'

'There's been an accident, sir. The men have found him. He's – '

Alfred turned towards the library window. Through the open gate in the quickset hedge, the workmen could be seen grouped together, stooping.

'They found him,' Alfred said, 'not to put too fine a point on it, sir – in the ditch. I'm very sorry, I'm sure, sir, but I'm afraid he's dead.'

CHAPTER 4

Alleyn

'There you are,' said Superintendent Williams. 'That's the whole story and those are the local people involved. Or not involved, of course, as the case may be. Now, the way I looked at it was this. It was odds on we'd have to call you people in anyway, so why muck about ourselves and let the case go cold on you? I don't say we wouldn't have liked to go it alone, but we're too damned busy and a damn' sight too understaffed. So I rang the Yard as soon as it broke.'

'The procedure,' Alleyn said dryly, 'is as welcome as it's unusual. We couldn't be more obliged, could we, Fox?'

'Very helpful and clear-sighted, Super,' Inspector Fox agreed with great heartiness.

They were driving from the Little Codling constabulary to Green Lane. The time was ten o'clock. The village looked decorous and rather pretty in the spring sunshine. Miss Cartell's Austrian maid was shaking mats in the garden. The postman was going his rounds. Mr Period's house, as far as it could be seen from the road, showed no signs of disturbance. At first sight, the only hint of there being anything unusual toward, might have been given by a group of three labourers who stood near a crane truck at the corner, staring at their boots and talking to the driver. There was something guarded and uneasy in their manner. One of them looked angry.

A close observer might have noticed that in several houses round the green, people who stood back from their windows, were watching the car as it approached the lane. The postman checked his bicycle and with one foot on the ground, also watched. George Copper stood on the path outside his corner garage and was joined by two women, a youth and three small boys. They, too, were watching. The women's hands moved furtively across their mouths.

'The village has got on to it,' Superintendent Williams observed. 'Here we are, Alleyn.'

They turned into the lane. It had been cordoned off with a rope slung between iron stakes and a 'Detour' sign in front. The ditch began at some distance from the corner and was defined on its inner border by neatly heaped-up soil and on its outer by a row of heavy drain-pipes laid end to end. There was a gap in this row, opposite Mr Period's gate, and a single drain-pipe on the far side of the ditch.

One of the workmen made an opening for the car and it pulled up beyond the truck.

Two hundred yards away, by the side gate into Mr Period's garden, Sergeant Raikes waited self-consciously by a disorderly collection of planks, tools, a twelve-foot steel ladder, and an all too eloquent shape covered by a tarpaulin. Nearby, on the far side of the lane, was another car. Its occupant got out and advanced: a middle-aged, formally dressed man with well-kept hands.

'Doctor Elekton, our divisional surgeon,' Superintendent Williams said, and completed the introductions.

'Unpleasant business, this,' Dr Elekton said. 'Very unpleasant. I don't know what you're going to think.'

'Shall we have a look?'

'Yes, of course.'

'Bear a hand, Sergeant,' said Williams. 'Keep it screened from the green, we'd better.'

'I'll move my car across,' Dr Elekton said.

He did so. Raikes and Williams released the tarpaulin and presently raised it. Alleyn being particular in such details, he and Fox took their hats off and so, after a surprised glance at them, did Dr Elekton.

The body of Mr Cartell lay on its back, not tidily. It was wet with mud and water, and marked about the head with blood. The face, shrouded in a dark and glistening mask, was unrecognizable, the thin hair clotted and dirty. It was clothed in a dressing-gown, shirt and trousers, all of them stained and disordered. On the feet were black socks and red leather slippers. One hand was clenched about a clod of earth. Thin trickles of muddy water had oozed between the fingers.

Alleyn knelt beside it without touching it. He looked incongruous. Not his hands, his head, nor, for that matter, his clothes, suggested his occupation. If Mr Cartell had been a rare edition of any subject other than death, his body would have seemed a more appropriate object for Alleyn's fastidious consideration.

After a pause he replaced the tarpaulin, rose, and keeping on the hard surface of the lane, stared down into the drain.

'Well,' he said. 'And he was found below, there?' His very deep, clear voice struck loudly across the silence.

'Straight down from where they've put him. On his face. With the drain-pipe on top of him.'

'Yes. I see.'

'They thought he might be alive. So they got him out of it. They had a job,' said Superintendent Williams. 'Had to use the gear on the truck.'

'He was like this when you saw him, Doctor Elekton?'

'Yes. There are multiple injuries to the skull. I haven't made an extensive examination. My guess would be, it's just about held together by the scalp.'

'Can we have a word with the men?'

Raikes motioned them to come forward and they did so with every sign of reluctance. One, the tallest, carried a piece of rag and he wiped his hands on it continually, as if he had been doing so, unconsciously, for some time.

'Good morning,' Alleyn said. 'You've had an unpleasant job on your hands.'

The tall man nodded. One of his mates said: 'Terrible.'

'I want you, if you will, to tell me exactly what happened. When did you find him?'

Fox unobtrusively took out his note-book.

'When we come on the job. Eight o'clock or near after.'

'You saw him at once?'

'Not to say there and then, sir,' the tall man said. He was evidently the foreman. 'We had a word or two. Nutting out the day's work, like. Took off our coats. Farther along, back there, we was. You can see where the truck's parked. There.'

'Ah, yes. And then?'

'Then we moved up. And I see the planks are missing that we laid across the drain for a bridge. And one of the pipes gone. So I says:

"What the hell's all this? Who's been mucking round with them planks and the pipe?" That's correct, isn't it?' He appealed to the others.

'That's right,' they said.

'It's like I told you, Mr Raikes. We all told you.'

'All right, Bill,' Williams said easily. 'The superintendent just wants to hear for himself.'

'If you don't mind,' said Alleyn. 'To get a clear idea, you know. It's better at first hand.'

The foreman said: 'It's not all that pleasant, though, is it? And us chaps have got our responsibility to think of. We left the job like we ought to: everything in order. Planks set. Lamps lit. Everything safe. Now look!'

'Lamps? I saw some at the ends of the working. Was there one here?'

'A-course there was. To show the planks. That's the next thing we notice. It's gone. Matter of fact they're all laying in the drain now.'

'So they are,' Alleyn said. 'It's a thumping great drain you're digging here, by the way. What is it, a relief outfall sewer or something?'

This evidently made an impression. The foreman said that was exactly what it was and went into a professional exposition.

'She's deep,' he said, 'she's as deep as you'll come across anywhere. Fourteen-be-three she lays and very nasty soil to work, being wet and heavy. One in a thou' fall. All right. Leaving an open job you take precautions. Lamp. Planks. Notice given. The lot. Which is what we done, and done careful and according. And this is what we find. All right. We see something's wrong. All right. So I says: "And where's the bloody lamp?" and I walk up to the edge and look down. And then I seen.'

'Exactly what?'

The foreman ground the rag between his hands. 'First go off,' he said, 'I notice the pipe, laying down there with a lot of the soil, and then I notice an electric torch -it's there now.'

'It's the deceased's,' Williams said. 'His man recognized it, I thought best to leave it there.'

'Good. And then?' Alleyn asked the foreman.

'Well, I noticed all this, like, and – it's funny when you come to think of it – I'm just going to blow my top about this pipe, when I kind of realize I've been looking at something else. Sticking out, they was, at the end, half sunk in mud. His legs. It didn't seem real. Like

I said to the chaps: "Look, what's that?" Daft! Because I seen clear enough what it was.'

'I know.'

'So we get the truck and go down and clear the pipe and planks out of it. Had to use the crane. The planks are laying there now, where we left them. We slung the pipe up and off him and across to the far bank like. Then we seen more – all there was to see. Sunk, he was. Rammed down, you might say, by the weight. I knew, first go off, he was a goner. Well – the back of his head was enough. But – ' The foreman glared resentfully at Raikes. 'I don't give a b– what anyone tells me, you can't leave a thing like that. You got to see if there's anything to be done.'

Raikes made a non-committal noise and looked at Alleyn.

'I think you do, you know, Sergeant,' Alleyn said and the foreman, gratified, continued:

'So we got 'im out like you said, sir. It was a very nasty job, what with the depth and the wet and the state he was in. And once out – finish! Gone. No mistake about it. So we give the alarm in the house there and they take a fit of the horrors and fetch the doctor.'

'Good,' Alleyn said, 'couldn't be clearer. Now, look here. You can see pretty well where he was lying, although, of course, the impression has been trodden out a bit. Unavoidably. Now, the head was about there, I take it, so that he was not directly under the place where the planks had been laid, but at an angle to it. The feet beneath, the head out to the left. The left hand, now. Was it stretched out ahead of him? Like that? With the arm bent? Was the right arm extended – so?'

The foreman and his mates received this with grudging approval. One of the mates said: 'Dead right, innit?' and the other: 'Near enough.' The foreman blew a faint appreciative whistle.

'Well,' Alleyn said, 'he's clutching a clod of mud and you can see where the fingers dragged down the side of the ditch, can't you? All right. Was one plank – how? Half under him or what?'

'That's right, sir.'

Superintendent Williams said: 'You can see where the planks were placed all right, before they fell. Clear as mud, and mud's the word in this outfit. The ends near the gate were only just balanced on the edge. Look at the marks where they scraped down the side. Bound to give way as soon as he put his weight on them.'

The men broke into an angry expostulation. They'd never left them like that. They'd left them safe: overlapping the bank by a good six inches at each side; a firm bridge.

'Yes,' Alleyn said, 'you can see that, Williams. There are the old marks. Trodden down but there, undoubtedly.'

'Thank you, sir,' said the foreman pointedly.

'Now then, let's have a look at this lamp,' Alleyn suggested. Using the ladder, they retrieved it from its bed in the ditch, about two feet above the place where the body had lain. It was smothered in mud but unbroken. The men pointed out an iron stanchion from which it had been suspended. This was uprooted and lying near the edge of the drain.

'The lamp was lit when you knocked off yesterday, was it?'

'Same as the others and they was still burning, see, when we come on the job this morning.'

Alleyn murmured: 'Look at this, Fox.' He turned the lamp towards Fox who peered into it.

'Been turned right down,' he said under his breath. 'Hard down.'

'Take charge of it, will you?'

Alleyn rejoined the men. 'One more point,' he said. 'How did you leave the drain-pipe yesterday evening? Was it laid out in that gap, end to end with the others?'

'That's right,' they said.

'Immediately above the place where the body was found?'

'That's correct, sir.'

The foreman looked at his mates and then burst out again with some violence. 'And if anyone tries to tell you it could be moved be accident you can tell him he ought to get his head read. Them pipes is main sewer pipes. It takes a crane to shift them, the way we've left them, and only a lever will roll them in. Now! Try it out on one of the others if you don't believe me. Try it. That's all.'

'I believe you very readily,' Alleyn said. 'And I think that's all we need bother you about at the moment. We'll get out a written record of everything you've told us and ask you to call at the station and look it over. If it's in order, we'll want you to sign it. If it's not, you'll no doubt help us by putting it right. You've acted very properly throughout as I'm sure Mr Williams and Sergeant Raikes will be the first to agree.'

'There you are,' Williams said. 'No complaints.'

Huffily reassured, the men retired.

'The first thing I'd like to know, Bob,' Alleyn said, 'is what the devil's been going on round this dump? Look at it. You'd think the whole village had been holding May Day revels over it. Women in evening shoes, women in brogues. Men in heavy shoes, men in light shoes, and the whole damn' mess overtrodden, of course, by working boots. Most of it went on before the event, *all* of it except the boots, I fancy, but what the hell was it about?'

'Some sort of daft party,' Williams said. 'Cavorting through the village, they were. We've had complaints. It was up at the big house, Baynesholme Manor.'

'One of Lady Bantling's little frolics,' Dr Elekton observed dryly. 'It seems to have ended in a dog-fight. I was called out at two thirty to bandage her husband's hand. They'd broken up by then.'

'Can you be talking about Desirée, Lady Bantling?'

'That's the lady. The main object of the party was a treasure hunt, I understand.'

'A hideous curse on it,' Alleyn said heartily. 'We've about as much hope of disentangling anything useful in the way of footprints as you'd get in a wine press. How long did it go on?'

'The noise abated before I went to bed,' Dr Elekton said, 'which was at twelve. As I've mentioned, I was dragged out again.'

'Well, at least we'll be able to find out if the planks and lantern were untouched until then. In the meantime we'd better go through the hilarious farce of keeping our own boots off the area under investigation. What's this? Wait a jiffy.'

He was standing near the end of one of the drain-pipes. It lay across a slight depression that looked as if it had been scooped out. From this he drew a piece of blue letter-paper. Williams looked over his shoulder.

'Poetry,' Williams said disgustedly.

The two lines had been amateurishly typed. Alleyn read them aloud.

> 'If you don't know what to do
> Think it over in the loo.'

'Elegant, I must say!' Dr Elekton ejaculated.

'That'll be a clue, no doubt,' Fox said, and Alleyn gave it to him.

'I wish the rest of the job was as explicit,' he remarked.

'What,' Williams asked, 'do you make of it, Alleyn? Any chance of accident?'

'What do you think yourself?'

'I'd say, none.'

'And so would I. Take a look at it. The planks had been dragged forward until the ends were only just supported by the lip of the bank. There's one print, the deceased's by the look of it, on the original traces of the planks before they were moved. It suggests that he came through the gate, where the path is hard and hasn't taken an impression. I think he had his torch in his left hand. He stepped on the trace and then on the planks which gave under him. I should say he pitched forward as he fell, dropping his torch, and one of the planks pitched back, striking him in the face. That's guesswork, but I think Elekton, that when he's cleaned up, you'll find the nose is broken. As he was face down in the mud, the plank seems a possible explanation. All right. The lantern was suspended from an iron stanchion. The stanchion had been driven into the earth at an angle and overhung the edge between the displaced drain-pipe and its neighbour. And, by the way, it seems to have been jammed in twice: there's a second hole nearby. The lantern would be out of reach for him and he couldn't have grabbed it. How big is the dog?'

'What's that?' Williams asked, startled.

'Prints that have escaped the boots of the drain-layers, suggest a large dog.'

'Pixie,' said Sergeant Raikes who had been silent for a considerable time.

'Oh!' said Superintendent Williams disgustedly. 'Her.'

'It's a dirty great mongrel of a thing, Mr Alleyn,' Raikes offered. 'The deceased gentleman called it a boxer. He was in the habit of bringing it out here before he went to bed, which was at one o'clock, regular as clockwork. It's a noisy brute. There have been,' Raikes added, sounding a leitmotiv, 'complaints about Pixie.'

'Pixie,' Alleyn said, 'must be an athletic girl. She jumped the ditch. There *are* prints if you can sort them out. But have a look at Cartell's right hand, Elekton, would you?'

Dr Elekton did so. 'There's a certain amount of contusion,' he said, 'with ridges. And at the edges of the palm, well-defined grooves.'

'How about a leather leash, jerked tight?'

'It might well be.'

'Now the stanchion, Fox.'

Fox leaned over from his position on the hard surface of the lane. He carefully lifted and removed the stanchion. Handling it as if it was some fragile *objet d'art*, he said: 'There are traces, Mr Alleyn. Lateral rubbings. Something dragged tight and then pulled away might be the answer.'

'So it's at least possible that as Cartell dropped, Pixie jumped the drain. The lead jerked. Pixie got entangled with the stanchion, pulled it loose, freed herself from it and from the hand that had led her, and made off. The lantern fell in the drain. Might be. Where *is* Pixie, does anyone know?'

'Shall I inquire at the house?' Raikes asked.

'It can wait. All this is the most shameless conjecture, really.'

'To me,' Williams said, considering it, 'it seems likely enough.'

'It'll do to go on with. But it doesn't explain,' Alleyn said, 'why the wick in the lantern's been turned hard off, does it?'

'Is that a fact!' Raikes remarked, primly.

'This stanchion,' said Williams, who had been looking at it. 'Have you noticed the lower point? You'd expect it to come out of the soil clean or else dirty all round. But it's dirty on one side and sort of scraped clean on the other.'

'You'll go far in the glorious profession of your choice.'

'Come off it!' said Williams, who had done part of his training with Alleyn.

'Look at the ground where that great walloping pipe was laid out. That, at least, is not entirely obliterated by boots. See the scars in the earth on this side? Slanting hole with a scooped depression on the near side.'

'What of them?'

'Try it, Fox.'

Fox, who was holding the stanchion by its top, laid the pointed end delicately in one of the scars. 'Fits,' he said. 'There's your lever, I reckon.'

'If so the mud on one side was scraped off on the pipe. Wrap it up and lay it by. The flash and dabs boys will be here any moment now. We'll have to take casts, Br'er Fox.'

Dr Elekton said: 'What's all this about the stanchion?'

'We're wondering if it was used as a lever for the drain-pipe. We're not very likely to find anything on the pipe itself after the rough handling it's been given, but it's worth trying.'

He walked to the end of the drain, returned on the far side to the solitary pipe and squatted beside it. Presently he said: 'There *are* marks – scrapings – same distance apart, at a guess. I think we'll find they fill the bill.'

When he rejoined the others, he stood for a moment and surveyed the scene. A capful of wind blew down Green Lane, snatched at a corner of the tarpaulin and caused it to ripple very slightly as if Mr Cartell had stirred. Fox attended to it, tucking it under, with a macabre suggestion of cosiness.

Alleyn said: 'If ever it behoved us to keep open minds about a case it behoves us to do so over this one. My reading so far, may be worth damn all, but such as it is I'll make you a present of it. On the surface appearance, it looks to me as though this was a premeditated job and was carried out with the minimum of fancy work. Some time before Cartell tried to cross it, the plank bridge was pulled towards the road side of the drain until the farther ends rested on the extreme edge. The person who did this, then put out the light in the lantern and hid: very likely by lying down on the hard surface alongside one of the pipes. The victim came out with his dog on a leash. He stepped on the bridge which collapsed. He was struck in the face by a plank and stunned. The leash bit into his right hand before it was jerked free. The dog jumped the drain, possibly got itself mixed up with the iron stanchion and, if so, probably dislodged the lantern which fell into the drain. The concealed person came back, used the stanchion as a lever and rolled the drain-pipe into the drain. It fell fourteen feet on his victim and killed him. Ha – hallo! What's that!'

He leaned forward, peering into the ditch: 'This looks like something,' he sighed. 'Down, I fear, into the depths I go.'

'I will, sir,' Fox offered.

'You keep your great boots out of this,' Alleyn rejoined cheerfully.

He placed the foot of the steel ladder near the place where the body was found and climbed down it. The drain sweated dank water and smelt sour and disgusting. From where he stood, on the bottom rung, he pulled out his flashlight.

From above they saw him stoop and reach under the plank that rested against the wall.

When he came up he carried something wrapped in his handkerchief. He knelt and laid his improvised parcel on the ground.

'Look at this,' he said, and they gathered about him.

He unfolded his handkerchief.

On it lay a gold case, very beautifully worked. It had a jewelled clasp and was smeared with slime.

'His?' Williams said.

' – or somebody else's? I wonder.'

They stared at it in silence. Alleyn was about to wrap it again when they were startled by a loud, shocking and long-drawn-out howl.

About fifty yards away, sitting in the middle of the lane in an extremely dishevelled condition, with a leash dangling from her collar, was a half-bred boxer bitch, howling lamentably.

'Pixie,' said Raikes.

II

They met with difficulty when they tried to catch Pixie. If addressed, she writhed subserviently, threshed her tail, and whined. If approached, she sprang aside, ran a short distance in a craven manner, sat down again and began alternately to bark and howl.

The five men whistled, stalked, ran and cursed, all to no avail. 'She'll rouse the whole bloody village at this rate,' Superintendent Williams lamented and indeed several persons had collected beyond the cars at the road barrier.

Alleyn and Dr Elekton tried a scissors movement, Raikes and Williams an ill-conceived form of indirect strategy. Fox made himself hot and cross in a laughable attempt to jump upon Pixie's lead and all had come to nothing before they were aware of the presence of a small, exceedingly pale man in an alpaca jacket on the far side of Mr Period's gate. It was Alfred Belt.

How long he had been there it was impossible to say. He was standing quite still with his well-kept hands on the top of the gate and his gaze directed respectfully at Alleyn.

'If you will allow me, sir,' he said. 'I think I may be able to secure the dog.'

'For God's sake do,' Alleyn rejoined.

Alfred whistled. Pixie with a travesty of canine archness cocked her head on one side. 'Here, girl,' Alfred said disgustedly. 'Meat.' She loped round the top end of the drain and ran along the fence towards him. 'You bitch,' he said dispassionately as she fawned upon him.

Superintendent Williams, red with his exertions, formally introduced Alfred across the drain. Alfred said: 'Good morning, sir. Mr Period has asked me to present his compliments and to say that if there is anything you require he hopes you will call upon him.'

'Thank you,' Alleyn rejoined. 'I was going to. In about five minutes. Will you tell him?'

'Certainly, sir,' Alfred said and withdrew.

Alleyn said to Williams: 'When the flash and dabs lot turn up, ask them to cover the whole job, will you, Bob? Everything. I'll be in the house if I'm wanted. You know the story and can handle this end of it better than I. I'd be glad if you'd stay in.'

It was by virtue of such gestures as this that Alleyn maintained what are known as 'good relations' with the county forces. Williams said: 'Be pleased to,' and filled out his jacket.

Dr Elekton said: 'What about the body?'

'Could you arrange for it to be taken to the nearest mortuary? Sir James Curtis will do the PM and will be hoping to see you. He'll be here by midday.'

'I've laid on the ambulance. The mortuary's at Rimble.'

'Good. Either Fox or I will look you up at the station at noon. There's one other thing. What do you make of that?' He walked a few paces up the lane and pointed to a large damp patch on the surface. 'There was no rain last night and it's nothing to do with the digging. Looks rather as if a car with a leaky radiator had stood there. Might even have been filled up and overflowed. Damn' this hard surface. Yes, look. There's a bit of oil there too where the sump might well have dripped. Ah, well it may not amount to a row of beans. Ready, Fox? Let's go in through the side gate, shall we?'

They fetched a circuitous course round the drain and entered Mr Period's garden by the side gate. Near the house, Alleyn noticed a stand-pipe with a detached hose coiled up beside it and a nearby watering-can from which the rose had been removed.

'Take a look at this, Br'er Fox,' he said and indicated a series of indentations about the size of a sixpence leading to and from the stand-pipe.

'Yes,' Fox said. 'And the can's been moved and replaced.'

'That's right. And who, in this predominantly male household, gardens in stiletto heels? Ah, well! Come on.'

They walked round the house to the front door where Alfred formally admitted them.

'Mr Period is in the library, sir,' he said. 'May I take your coat?'

Fox, who, being an innocent snob, always enjoyed the treatment accorded to his senior officer on these occasions, placidly removed his own coat.

'What,' Alleyn asked Alfred, 'have you done with the dog?'

'Shut her up, sir, in the wood-shed. She ought never to have been let loose.'

'Quite so. Will you let me have her leash?'

'Sir?'

'The lead. Inspector Fox will pick it up. Will you, Fox? And join us in the library?'

Alfred inclined his head, straightened his arms, turned his closed hands outward from the wrists and preceded Alleyn to the library door.

'Mr Roderick Alleyn, sir,' he announced.

It was perhaps typical of him that he omitted the rank and inserted the Christian name. 'Because, after all, Mrs M.,' he expounded later on to his colleague, 'whatever opinions you and I may form on the subject, class is class and to be treated as such. *In* the Force he may be, and with distinction. *Of* it, he is not.'

Mrs Mitchell put this detestable point of view rather more grossly. 'The brother's a baronet,' she said. 'And childless, at that. I read it in the *News of the World*. "The Handsome Super", it was called. Fancy!'

Meanwhile Alleyn was closeted with Mr Pyke Period, who in a different key, piped the identical tune.

'My dear Alleyn,' he said. 'I can't tell you how relieved I am to see you. If anything could lessen the appalling nature of this calamity it would be the assurance that we are in your hands.' There followed, inevitably, the news that Mr Period was acquainted with Alleyn's brother and was also an ardent admirer of Alleyn's wife's paintings. 'She won't remember an old backwater buster like me,' he said, wanly arch, 'but I have had the pleasure of meeting her.'

All this was said hurriedly and with an air of great anxiety. Alleyn wondered if Mr Period's hand was normally as tremulous as it was this morning or his speech as breathless and uneven. As soon as Alleyn decently could do so, he got the conversation on a more formal basis.

He asked Mr Period how long Mr Cartell had been sharing the house and learned that it was seven weeks. Before that Mr Cartell had lived in London where he had been the senior partner of an extremely grand and vintage firm of solicitors, from which position he had retired upon his withdrawal into the country. The family, Mr Period said, came originally from Gloucestershire – Bloodstone Parva, in the Cotswolds. Having got as far as this he pulled himself up short and, unaccountably, showed great uneasiness.

Alleyn asked him when he had last seen Mr Cartell.

'Ah – yesterday evening. I dined out. At Baynesholme. Before the party.'

'The treasure hunt?'

'You've heard about it? Yes. I saw them start and then I came home. He was in his room, then, walking about and talking to that – his dog. Great heavens!' Mr Period suddenly exclaimed.

'What is it?'

'Desirée – his – Lady Bantling, you know! And Andrew! They must be told, I suppose. I wonder if Connie has thought of it – but no! No, she would hardly – My dear Alleyn, I beg your pardon, but it has only just struck me.' He explained confusedly, the connection between Baynesholme and Mr Cartell, and looked distractedly at his watch. 'They will be here at any moment. My secretary – a delightful gel – and Andrew who is to drive her. I suggested an eleven o'clock start as it was to be such a very late party.'

By dint of patient questioning, Alleyn got this sorted out. He noticed that Mr Period kept feeling in his pockets. Then, apparently recollecting himself, he would look about the room. He opened a cigarette-box and when he found it empty, ejaculated pettishly.

Alleyn said: 'I wonder if you'll let me give you a cigarette and smoke one myself: it's all wrong of course, for a policeman on duty – ' He produced his case.

'My *dear* Alleyn! Thank you. Do. Do. So will I. But I should have offered you one long ago, only with all this upset Alfred hasn't filled the boxes and – it's too tiresome – I've mislaid my case.'

'Really? Not lost, I hope.'

'I – I hope not,' he said hurriedly. 'It's all very unfortunate but never mind,' and again he showed great uneasiness.

'It's infuriating to lose a good case,' Alleyn remarked. 'I did myself, not long ago. It was a rather special and very old one and I regret it.'

'So is this,' Mr Period said abruptly. 'A card case.' He seemed to be in two minds whether to go on and then decided against it.

Alleyn said: 'When you saw Mr Cartell last evening was he his usual self? Nothing had happened to upset him at all?'

This question, also, produced a flurried reaction. 'Upset? Well – it depends upon what one means by "upset". He was certainly rather put out but it was nothing that could remotely be related – ' Mr Period fetched up short and appeared to summon all his resources. When he spoke again it was with very much more reserve and control. 'You would not,' he said, 'ask me a question of that sort, I think, unless you felt that this dreadful affair was not to be resolved by – by a simple explanation.'

'Oh,' Alleyn said lightly, 'we needn't put it as high as that, you know. If he was at all agitated or absent-minded, he might not be as careful as usual when he negotiated the bridge over the ditch. The dog – '

'Ah!' Mr Period exclaimed. 'The dog! Now, why on earth didn't one think of the dog before! It is – she – I assure you, Alleyn, a most powerful and undisciplined dog. At the moment, I am given to understand, particularly so. May she not have taken one of those great plunging leaps of hers, possibly across the drain and, dragged him into it? May she not have done that?'

'She seems, at least, to have taken a great, plunging leap.'

'There! You see?'

'She would also,' Alleyn said, 'have had to dislodge a walloping big drain-pipe and precipitate it into the ditch.'

Mr Period put his hands over his eyes. 'It's so horrible!' he said faintly. 'It's so unspeakably horrible.' And then, withdrawing his hands, 'But may she not have done precisely that very thing?'

'It's not very likely, I'm afraid.'

Mr Period stared at him. 'You don't think it was an accident,' he said. 'Don't bother to say anything. I can see you don't.'

'I'll be very glad if I find reason to change my opinion.'

'But why? Why not an accident? That dog, now: she *is* dangerous. I've told him so, over and over again.'

'There are certain appearances: things that don't quite tally. We must clear them up before we can come to any conclusion. There must, of course, be an inquest. And that is why,' Alleyn said cheerfully, 'I shall have to ask you any number of questions all of which will sound ridiculous and most of which, I dare say, will turn out to be just that and no more.'

It was at this juncture that Fox joined them, his excessively bland demeanour indicating, to Alleyn at least, that he had achieved his object and secured Pixie's leash. The interview continued. Fox, as usual, managed to settle himself behind the subject and to take notes quite openly and yet entirely unnoticed. He had a talent for this sort of thing.

Mr Period's conversation continued to be jumpy and disjointed, but gradually a fairly comprehensive picture of his ménage emerged. Alleyn heard of Cartell's sister who was, of course, deeply shocked. 'One of those red women who don't normally seem to feel anything except the heat,' Mr Period said oddly. 'Never wear gloves and look, don't you know, as if they never sit on anything but their hats or a shooting-stick. But I assure you she's dreadfully cut up, poor Connie.'

Alleyn felt that Mr Period had invented this definition of Miss Cartell long ago and was so much in the habit of letting fly with it that it had escaped him involuntarily.

'I mustn't be naughty,' he said unhappily. 'Poor Connie!' and looked exquisitely uncomfortable.

'Apart from Miss Cartell and Lady Bantling, who I suppose is in one sense a connection or an ex-connection, are there any near relations?'

'None that one would call near. It's an old family,' Mr Period said with a pale glance at his ruling passion, 'but going – going. Indeed, I fancy he and Connie are the last. Sad.'

Alleyn said: 'I'm afraid I shall have to ask you for an account of yesterday's activities. I really am very sorry to pester you like this when you've had such a shock, but there it is. "Duty, duty must be done."'

Mr Period brightened momentarily at this Gilbertian reference and even dismally hummed the tune, but the next second he was in the doldrums again. He worked backwards through the events of the previous day, starting with his own arrival in the lane, driven by Lady Bantling, at twenty past eleven. The plank bridge over the drain had supported him perfectly: the lamp was alight. As he approached the house he saw Mr Cartell at his bedroom window, which was wide open. Mr Cartell never, Mr Period explained, went to bed before one o'clock when he took Pixie out, but he often pottered about his room for hours before he retired. Alleyn thought he detected a note of petulance and also of extreme reticence.

'I think,' Mr Period said restlessly, 'that Hal must have heard me coming home. He was at his window. He seemed – ah – he seemed to be perfectly well.'

'Did you speak to him?'

'I – ah – I – ah – I did just call out something after I came upstairs. He replied. I don't remember – However!'

Mr Period himself, it transpired, had gone to bed, but not to sleep as the arrival and departure of treasure-hunters in the lane was disturbing. However, the last couple had gone before midnight and he had dozed off.

'Did you wake again?'

'That's what's so appalling to think of. I did. At one o'clock when he took Pixie out. She made the usual disturbance, barking and whining. I heard it. I'm afraid I cursed it. Then it stopped.'

'And did you go to sleep again?'

'Yes. Yes, I did. Yes.'

'Were you disturbed again?'

Mr Period opened his mouth and remained agape for some seconds and then said, 'No.'

'Sure?'

'Nobody disturbed me,' Mr Period said and looked perfectly wretched.

Alleyn took him back through the day. It was with reluctance that he was brought to admit that Mr Cartell had entertained his sister and two acquaintances to luncheon. As an afterthought he remarked that Lady Bantling and her son, Andrew Bantling, had been there for drinks.

'Who,' Alleyn asked, 'were the acquaintances?' and was told, sketchily, about Mary Ralston, Miss Cartell's ward, and her friend,

Leonard Leiss. At the Yard, Alleyn was often heard to lament the inadequacy of his memory, an affectation which was tolerantly indulged by his colleagues. His memory was in fact like any other senior detective-officer's, very highly trained, and in this instance it at once recalled the paragraph in the *Police Gazette* of some months ago in which the name and *portrait-parlé* of Leonard Leiss had appeared together with an account of his activities which were varied and dubious. He had started life in Bermondsey, shown some promise, achieved grammar-school status and come under the protection of a benevolent spinster whom he subsequently robbed and deserted. This episode was followed by an association with a flick-knife gang and an interval of luxury spent with a lady of greater wealth than discretion, and employment as a chauffeur with forged references. There had been two convictions. 'Passes himself off,' the *Police Gazette* had concluded 'as a person of superior social status.'

'Is Mr Leiss,' Alleyn asked, 'a young man of about twenty-seven? Dark, of pale complexion, rather too-smartly dressed and wearing a green ring on the signet finger?'

'Oh, dear!' Mr Period said helplessly. 'I suppose Raikes has told you. Yes. Alas, he is!'

After that it was not hard to induce a general lament upon the regrettability of Leonard. Although Sergeant Raikes had in fact not yet reported the affair of the Scorpion sports-car, Mr Period either took it for granted that he had done so or recognized the inevitability of coming round to it before long. He said enough for Alleyn to get a fair idea of what had happened. Leonard, Mr Period concluded, was a really rather dreadful young person whom it would be the greatest mistake to encourage.

'When I tell you, my dear fellow, that he leaned back in his chair at luncheon and positively whistled? Sang even! I promise! And the girl joined in! A terrible fellow! Poor Connie should have sent him packing at the first glance.'

'Mr Cartell thought so too, I dare say?'

'Oh, yes!' said Mr Period, waving it away. 'Yes, indeed. Oh, rather!'

'To your knowledge had he any enemies? That sounds melodramatic, but had he? Or, to put it another way, do you know of anyone to whom he might have done any damage if he had lived?'

There was a long pause. From the lane came the sound of a car in low gear. Alleyn could see through the window that a canvas screen had been erected. His colleagues, evidently, had arrived.

'I'm just trying to think,' said Mr Period. He turned sheet-white. 'Not in the sense you mean. No. Unless – but, no.'

'Unless?'

'You see, Alleyn, one does follow you. One does realize the implication.'

'Naturally,' Alleyn said. 'It's perfectly obvious, I'm sure. If a trap was laid for Mr Cartell last night, I should like to know if there's anyone who might have had some motive in laying it.'

'A booby-trap, for instance?' He stared at Alleyn, his rather prominent front teeth closed over his underlip. 'Of course I don't know what you've found. I – I – had to go out there and – and identify him, but frankly, it distressed me very much and I didn't notice – But, had, for instance, the planks over the ditch – had they been interfered with?'

'Yes,' said Alleyn.

'Oh, my God! I see. Well, then; might it not all have been meant for a joke? A very silly, dangerous one, but still no more than a booby-trap? Um? Some of those young people in the treasure hunt. Yes!' Mr Period ejaculated. 'Now, isn't that a possibility? Someone had moved the planks and poor Harold fell, you know, and perhaps he knocked himself out and then, while he was lying unconscious, may not a couple – they hunted in couples – have come along and – inadvertently dislodged the drain-pipe?'

'You try dislodging one of those pipes,' Alleyn said dryly. 'It could scarcely be done inadvertently, I think.'

'Then – then: even done deliberately out of sheer exuberance and not knowing he was there. A prank! One of those silly pranks. They were a high-spirited lot.'

'I wonder if you can give me their names?'

As most of them had come from the county, Mr Period was able to do this. He got up to twenty-four, said he thought that was all, and then boggled.

'Was there somebody else?'

'In point of fact – yes. By a piece of what I can only describe, I'm afraid, as sheer effrontery, the wretched Leiss and that tiresome gel, Mary Ralston, got themselves asked. Desirée is quite hopelessly good-natured. Now *he,*' Mr Period said quickly, 'in my opinion would certainly be capable of going too far – *capable de tout.* But I shouldn't say that. No. All the same, Alleyn, an accident resulting from some piece of comparatively innocent horse-play would not be as appalling as – as – '

'As murder?'

Mr Period flung up his hands. 'Alas!' he said. 'Yes. Of course, I've no real knowledge of how you go to work, but you've examined the ground no doubt. One reads of such astonishing deductions. Perhaps I shouldn't ask.'

'Why not?' Alleyn said amiably. 'The answer's regrettably simple. At the moment there are no deductions, only circumstances. And in point of fact there's nothing, as far as we've gone, to contradict your theory of a sort of double-barrelled piece of hooliganism. Somebody gets the enchanting idea of rearranging the planks. Somebody else gets the even more amusing idea of dislodging a main sewer pipe. The victim of the earlier *jeu d'esprit*, by an unfortunate coincidence, becomes the victim of the second.'

'Of course, if you put it like that – '

'Coincidences do happen with unbelievable frequency. I sometimes think they're the occupational hazards of police work. So far, for all we've seen, there's no reason to suppose that Mr Cartell has not been the victim of one of them. Unless,' Alleyn said, 'you count this.'

He had a very quick, dexterous way of using his hands. With the least possible amount of fuss he had produced, laid upon Mr Period's writing desk and lightly unfolded from his handkerchief, the gold case with a jewelled clasp. 'I'm afraid,' he said, 'I shall have to keep it for the time being. But can you identify it?'

Mr Period gave a startled ejaculation and got to his feet.

At the same moment there was a tap on the door which at once opened to admit a girl and a tall young man.

'I'm so sorry,' Nicola said, 'the front door was open and we thought – I'm awfully sorry.' She stopped short, catching sight of the gold case lying on the handkerchief. 'Oh,' she exclaimed. 'I *am* glad. Your lovely cigarette-case! You've found it!'

'Ah – yes,' Mr Period said with a little gasp. 'Yes. It – it would appear so.' He pulled himself together. 'Nicola, my dear,' he said, 'may I introduce – '

'But we've met!' Nicola cried. 'Often. Haven't we? I was talking about you only yesterday. Bless my soul,' she added gaily, 'who, to coin a phrase, would have thought of meeting you?'

'To coin another,' Alleyn said mildly, 'it's quite a coincidence, isn't it? Hallo, Nicola.'

III

'Put it like this,' Alleyn said. 'I don't say you'll ever have to, but suppose you were asked to swear on oath that the window was shut during the Pixie episode, would you do it?'

Nicola said: 'I'd have to, wouldn't I? Because it was.'

'Not a shadow of doubt?'

'Not one. Alfred will say the same.'

'I dare say.'

'I wish I knew what you were up to,' Nicola said, staring out into the garden.

'I? I'm on my job.'

'Yes, but are you peering into petty larceny or mucking into a – I'm sure I don't know why I'm trying to be facetious – into a murder? Or do they tie in together? Or what?'

'I don't know. No more than you do.'

'I suppose,' Nicola said with some penetration, 'you're not very pleased to find me here.'

'Not as enchanted as I would be to find you elsewhere.'

'It's funny. Because, before this blew up I was thinking of Troy. I'm coming in tomorrow evening and I wondered if I could bring a young man with me.'

'My dear child, she'll be delighted. Do I detect – ?'

'No!' Nicola said in a hurry. 'You don't detect anything. He paints.'

'Ah. Mr Andrew Bantling?'

'I suppose you spotted the paint under his fingernail.'

'So I did. It reminded me of my wife.'

'That sounds human, anyway.'

Alleyn said: 'Look here, Nicola, we'll have to keep all this on an aseptically impersonal basis, you know. I've got to look into a case that may well involve something that is generally called a serious charge. You, unfortunately may be a relevant witness. I wish it wasn't like that, but it is. Okay?'

'Do I have to call you Superintendent?'

'You needn't call me anything. Now, let's press on, shall we? I'm bringing Mr Fox in to take notes.'

'Lor!' Nicola looked at him for a moment and then said: 'Yes, okay. I won't be tiresome. I do see.'

'Of course you do.'

Fox came in and was introduced.

In great detail, Alleyn led her through the events of the past twenty-four hours and as he did so it seemed to Nicola that she grew physically colder. Her relationship with the Alleyns was something that she had taken for granted. Without realizing that she did so, she had depended upon them, as the young do with established friends, for a sort of anchorage. They were old enough to give her a feeling of security and young enough, she felt, to 'understand'. She had been free to turn up at their London house when she felt like it and was one of the few people that Alleyn's wife could endure in the studio when she was working. With Alleyn himself, Nicola had progressed by way of a schoolgirl crush, from which she soon managed to recover, into a solid affection. She called him 'Le Cid' shortened it into 'Cid' and by this time had forgotten the origin of the pun.

Now, here he was, CID in action, being friendly enough: considerate and impersonal, but, she had to face it, quietly panic-striking. She began to see him in headline terms. 'Superintendent Alleyn interviews society secretary.'

'Don't,' Alleyn's voice said, 'go fussing yourself with unnecessary complications. Be as objective as you can and it'll all pass off very quietly. Where had we got to? Ah, yes. You've arrived. You've started on your job. You're assisting at the pre-luncheon drinks party. This consists of Mr Cartell; his sister, Miss Constance Cartell; his former wife, the soi-disant Lady Bantling; her present husband, Mr Bimbo Dodds; her son by her first marriage, Mr Andrew Bantling; Miss Cartell's adopted niece or what-not, what's she called – Miss Mary or Moppett – what?'

'Ralston, I think.'

'That's right. And the Moppett's boyfriend, Mr Leonard Leiss. And, of course, Mr Period. So we have the piquant situation of a lady with two husbands, a young man with two step-fathers, and a brother and sister with a courtesy niece. How did the party go?'

'Not with a swing,' Nicola said.

'Because of the muddled relationships, would you say?'

'No. They seem to take those in their stride.'

'Because of what, then?'

'Well – Moppett and Leonard principally. Leonard really is a monster.'

'What sort? Beatnik? Smart Alec? Bounder? Straight-out cad? Or just plain nasty?'

'All except the beatnik. He's as clean as a whistle and smells dreadfully of lilies.'

'Not Period's cup of tea. Or, I should have thought, Cartell's.'

'Indeed, not. He and Moppett were self-invited. Or rather, I think Moppett had bludgeoned poor Miss Cartell into getting them there.'

'Why "poor"?'

'Did I say "poor"?' Nicola said, surprised at herself. 'I suppose, because I sort of felt she was vulnerable.'

'Go on.'

'Well – she's one of those clumsy women who sound arrogant but probably hoot and roar their way through life to cover up their shyness. I expect she's tried to compensate for her loneliness by pouring all her affection into Moppett . . . What a hope, poor darling!'

'Oh, wise young judge,' Alleyn murmured and Nicola wondered how much he was laughing at her.

'Can you remember,' he asked, 'any of the conversation?'

'At lunch it was about Pixie and Miss Cartell saying she was a mongrel and Mr Cartell turning huffy and about a car Leonard had seen in the local garage – I don't remember –'

'We know about the car. What else?'

'Well: about poor Mr Period's favourite thing: family grandeur and blue blood and *noblesse oblige*. I'm sure he didn't mean to have digs at Leonard and Moppett but it came over like that. And then Mr Cartell told a story about someone who cooked a baptismal record to pretend he was blue-blooded when he wasn't and that didn't exactly ring out like a peal of joybells although Leonard seemed quite interested. And then there was the Pixie episode and then the cigarette-case thing.' She elaborated on these themes.

'Plenty of incident throughout. What about the pre-luncheon party? Young Bantling, for instance? How did he fit in? Did he seem to get on quite well with his senior step-father?'

Nicola was aware of silence: the silence of Mr Period's drawing-room which had been given over to Alleyn. There was the alleged Cotman water-colour in its brown-paper wrappings. There were the unexceptionable chairs and curtains. Outside the windows was the drive, down which Andrew had walked so angrily, swinging his hat. And upstairs, somewhere, was dead Mr Cartell's room, where Andrew's voice had shouted yesterday morning.

'What's the matter?' Alleyn said.

'Nothing. He didn't stay to lunch. He lunched at Baynesholme.'

'But he came here, with you, from the station, didn't he?'

'Yes.'

'And stayed here until his mother and her husband called for him?'

'Yes. At least – '

'Yes?'

'He went out for a bit. I saw him go down the drive.'

'What did he do while he was here?'

'I think he saw Mr Cartell. Mr Cartell's his guardian and a trustee for his inheritance as well as his step-father. And Mr Period's the other trustee.'

'Did you gather that it was a business call?'

'Something of the sort. He talked to both of them.'

'About what, do you know?'

Could Nicola hear, or did she only feel, the thud of her heart?

'Do you know?' Alleyn repeated.

'Only roughly. He'd tell you himself.'

'You think he would?'

'Why not?'

'He told you about it?'

'A bit. But it was – it was sort of confidential. In a way.'

'Why are you frightened, Nicola?' Alleyn asked gently.

'I'm not. It's just that: well, the whole thing's rather a facer. What's happened. I suppose I've got a bit of a delayed shock or something.'

'Yes,' Alleyn said. 'It might, of course, be that.'

He rose and looked down at her from his immoderate height. 'As my maiden aunt said to her cat: "I can accept the urge and I can deal

with the outcome: what I cannot endure are these pointless preliminaries!" She ought to have been in the CID.'

'What am I supposed to make of that?'

'Don't have kittens before they're hatched. And for pity's sake
don't hedge or shuffle: that never did anybody any good. Least of all,
your young man.'

'He is *not* my young man. I only met him yesterday.'

'Even so quickly may one catch the plague. Did you stay here last
night?'

'No. I was at Baynesholme for a party.'

'Not Desirée Bantling's party!' Alleyn ejaculated.

'Yes, but it wasn't the sort you mean. It was a lovely party,' said
Nicola, looking mistily at him. She described it.

'Any unforeseen incidents?'

'Only Moppett and Leonard who practically gatecrashed. And
Pixie, of course.'

'What! What about Pixie?'

Nicola told him. 'Pixie,' she added, 'bit Bimbo. He had to go and
have his hand bandaged.'

'You wouldn't,' Alleyn asked, 'know what time it was when Pixie
staged this show?'

'Yes, I would,' Nicola said promptly and blushed. 'It was not much
after one o'clock.'

'How do you know?'

'We got back at half past twelve from the treasure hunt. It was not
more than half an hour after that.'

'We?'

'Andrew and I. We hunted in pairs.'

'I thought you said you all had to be in by midnight?'

'All right. Yes, we were meant to. But Andrew thought the treasure hunt was pretty tiresome so we talked instead. He told me about
his painting and somehow we didn't notice.'

Nicola looked squarely at Alleyn. 'It couldn't matter less,' she
said, 'but I would like to mention that I did *not* have a casual affair
with Andrew. We talked – and talked – '

Her voice faded on an indeterminate note. She was back at the end
of Mr Period's lane, in Andrew's draughty car, tucked up in Andrew's
old duffel coat that smelt of paint. The tips of their cigarettes glowed

and waned. Every now and then a treasure-hunter's car would go hooting past and they would see the occupants get out and poke about the drain-pipes and heaps of soil, flicking their torches and giggling. And Andrew talked – and didn't initiate any of the usual driver's seat techniques but was nevertheless very close to her. And the moon had gone down and the stars were bright and everything in the world seemed brand new and shining. She gave Alleyn the factual details of this experience.

'Do you remember,' he asked, 'how many cars stopped by the drain or who any of the people were?'

'Not really. They were all new to me: lots of Nigels and Michaels and Sarahs and Davids and Gileses.'

'You could see them fairly clearly?'

'Fairly. There was a hurricane lantern shining on two planks across the ditch and they all had torches.'

'Any of them walk across the planks?'

'I think most of them. But the clue was under one of the drain-pipes on the road side of the ditch. We'd see them find it and giggle over it and put it back and then go zooming off.'

'Anyone touch the planks? Look under the ends for the clue?'

'I don't think so.' Nicola hesitated and then said: 'I remember Leonard and Moppett. They were the last and they hadn't got a torch. He crossed the planks and stooped over as if he was looking in the ditch. I got the impression that they stared at us. There was something, I don't know what, kind of furtive about him. I can see him now,' Nicola said, surprised at the vivid memory. 'I think he had his hand inside his overcoat. The lamplight was on him. He turned his back to us. He stooped and straightened up. Then he recrossed the bridge and found the clue. They looked at it by the light of the lantern and he put it back and they drove away.'

'Was he wearing gloves?'

'Yes, he was. Light-coloured ones. Tight-fitting wash-leather I should think: a bit too svelte like everything else about Leonard.'

'Anything more?'

'No. At least – well, they didn't sort of talk and laugh like the others. I don't suppose any of this matters.'

'Don't you, indeed? And then, you good, observant child?'

'Well, Andrew said: "Funny how ghastly they look even at this distance!" And I said: "Like – !" No, it doesn't matter.'

'Like what?'

'"Like grand-opera assassins" was what I said but it was a silly remark. Actually, they looked more like sneak thieves but I can't tell you why. It's nothing.'

'And then?'

'Well, they were the last couple. You see, Andrew kept count, vaguely, because he thought it would be all right to continue our conversation as long as there were still hunters to come. But before them, Lady Bantling and Mr Period came past. She was driving him home. She stopped the car by the planks and I fancy she called out to a hunting couple that were just leaving. Mr Period got out and said good night with his hat off, looking rather touching, poor sweet, and crossed the planks and went in by his side gate. And she turned the car.' Nicola stopped.

'What is it?'

'Well, you see, I – I don't want – '

'All right. Don't bother to tell me. You're afraid of putting ideas into my head. How can I persuade you, Nicola, that it's only by a process of elimination that I can get anywhere with this case? Incidents that look as fishy as hell to you may well turn out to be the means of clearing the very character you're fussing about.'

'May they?'

'Now, look here. An old boy of, as far as we know, exemplary character, has been brutally and cunningly murdered. You think you can't bring yourself to say anything that might lead to an arrest and its possible consequences. I understand and sympathize. But, my poor girl, will you consider for a moment, the possible consequences of withholding information? They can be disastrous. They have led to terrible miscarriages of justice. You see, Nicola, the beastly truth is that if you are involved, however accidentally in a crime of this sort, you can't avoid responsibility.'

'I'm sorry. I suppose you're right. But in this instance – about Lady Bantling, I mean – it's nothing. It'll sound disproportionate.'

'So will lots of other things that turn out to be of no consequence. Come on. What happened? What did she do?'

Nicola, it transpired, had a gift for reportage. She gave a clear account of what had happened . . . Alleyn could see the car turn in the lane and stop. After a pause the driver got out, her flaming hair haloed momentarily in the light of the lantern as she crossed the planks, walking carefully in her high heels. She had gone through Mr Period's garden gate and disappeared. There had been a light in an upper window. Andrew Bantling had said: 'Hallo, what's my incalculable ma up to!' They had heard quite distinctly the spatter of pebbles against the upper window. A figure in a dark gown had opened it. 'Great grief!' Andrew had ejaculated. 'That's Harold! She's doing a balcony scene in reverse! She must be tight.'

And indeed, Lady Bantling had, surprisingly, quoted from the play. '"What light," she had shouted, "from yonder window breaks?"' and Mr Cartell had replied irritably, 'Good God, Desirée, what are you doing down there!'

Her next remark was in a lower tone and they had only caught the word 'warpath' to which he had rejoined: 'Utter nonsense!'

'And then,' Nicola told Alleyn, 'another light popped up and another window opened and Mr Period looked out. It was like a Punch and Judy show. He said something rather plaintive that sounded like: "Is anything the matter?" and Lady Bantling shouted: "Not a thing, go to bed, darling," and he said: "Well, really! How odd!" and pulled down his blind. And then Mr Cartell said something inaudible and Lady Bantling quite yelled: "Ha! Ha! You jolly well watch your step," and then *he* pulled *his* blind down and we saw her come out, cross the ditch, and get into the car. She drove past us and leant out of the driving window and said: "That was a tuppenny one. Don't be too late, darlings" and went on. And Andrew said he wished he knew what the hell she was up to and soon after that we went back to the party. Leonard and Moppett had already arrived.'

'Was Desirée Bantling, in fact, tight?'

'It's hard to say. She was perfectly in order afterwards and acted with the greatest expediency, I must say, in the Pixie affair. She's obviously,' Nicola said, 'a law unto herself.'

'I believe you. You've drifted into rather exotic and dubious waters, haven't you?'

'It was all right,' Nicola said quickly. 'And Andrew's not a bit exotic or dubious. He's a quiet character. Honestly. You'll see.'

'Yes,' Alleyn said. 'I'll see. Thank you, Nicola.' Upon which the door of Mr Period's drawing-room burst open and Andrew, scarlet in the face, stormed in.

'Look here!' he shouted, 'what the hell goes on? Are you grilling my girl?'

IV

Alleyn, with one eyebrow cocked at Nicola, was crisp with Andrew. Nicola herself, struggling between exasperation and a maddening tendency to giggle invited Andrew not to be an ass and he calmed down and presently apologized.

'I'm inclined to be quick-tempered,' he said with an air of self-discovery and an anxious glance at Nicola.

She cast her eyes up and, on Alleyn's suggestion, left Andrew with him and went to the study. There she found Mr Period in a dreadful state of perturbation, writing a letter.

'About poor old Hal,' he explained distractedly. 'To his partner. One scarcely knows what to say.'

He implored Nicola to stay and as she still had a mass of unassembled notes to attend to, she set to work on them in a strange condition of emotional uncertainty.

Alleyn had little difficulty with Andrew Bantling. He readily outlined his own problems, telling Alleyn about the Grantham Gallery and how Mr Cartell had refused to let him anticipate his inheritance. He also confirmed Nicola's account of their vigil in the car. 'You don't,' he said, 'want to take any notice of my mamma. She was probably a thought high. It would amuse her to bait Harold. She always does that sort of thing.'

'She was annoyed with him, I take it?'

'Well, of course she was. Livid. We both were.'

'Mr Bantling,' Alleyn said, 'your step-father has been murdered.'

'So I feared,' Andrew rejoined. 'Beastly, isn't it? I can't get used to the idea at all.'

'A trap was laid for him and when, literally, he fell into it, his murderer levered an eight-hundred-pound drain-pipe on him. It crushed his skull and drove him, face down, into the mud.'

The colour drained out of Andrew's cheeks. 'All right,' he said. 'You needn't go on. It's loathsome. It's too grotesque to think about.'

'I'm afraid we have to think about it. That's all for the moment. Thank you.'

'Well, yes. All right, I see. Thank you.' Andrew fidgeted with his tie and then said: 'Look; I dare say you think I'm being pretty callous about all this but the fact is I just can't assimilate it. It's so unreal and beastly.'

'Murder is beastly. Unfortunately it's not unreal.'

'So it seems. Is it in order for me to go up to London? I'm meant to be on guard tomorrow. As a matter of fact I had thought of going up on business.'

'Important business?'

'Well – to me. I wanted to ask them to give me a few days' grace over the gallery.' He stared at Alleyn. 'I suppose this will make a difference,' he said. 'I hadn't thought of that.'

'And now you have thought of it – ?'

'I don't know,' Andrew said slowly. 'It seems a bit low to think of it at all. I'd like to talk it over with Nicola. As a matter of fact – ' He looked sideways at Alleyn. 'I rather thought of coming back and then going up with her. After I've telephoned my mamma, I suppose. I can't imagine what she'll make of all this, I must say.'

'Where are you going to be on guard?'

'The Tower,' Andrew said dismally.

'All right. We'll get in touch if we want you.'

Leaving Andrew where he was, Alleyn had a discussion with Fox and Williams in Mr Period's garden and then checked the story of the cigarette-case with Alfred and then crossed the green to interview Miss Cartell.

She received him in her den. He found it a depressing room. Everything seemed to be the colour of mud. Faded snapshots of meets, of foxhounds and of other canines, covered the walls. On the desk, which was a shambles, were several framed photographs of a cagey-looking girl whom he supposed to be Moppett. The room smelt of dog, damp tweed and raw liver, this last being explained by a dish labelled 'Fido' in which a Pekinese was noisily snuffling. It broke off to bare its needle-like teeth at Alleyn and make the noise of a toy kettledrum.

Miss Cartell sat with her hands on her knees staring dolefully at him. Her left thumb was decorated with dirty, bloodstained cotton-wool and stamp-paper. She had evidently been crying.

'It's pretty ghastly,' she said. 'Poor old Boysie! I can't take it in. He was a bit of an old maid but a brother's a brother. We didn't see eye-to-eye over a lot of things, but still.'

Alleyn was visited by the fleeting wish that he could run into somebody who at least pretended to have liked Mr Cartell.

'When,' he asked her, 'did you last see him?'

'I don't know. Yes, I do. Last evening. He came over here with that ghastly bitch. It upset Li-chi. They're very highly strung animals, pekes. He's still nervous. Eat up, my poppet,' said Miss Cartell to the Pekinese. 'Lovely livvy!'

She poked her finger temptingly in the raw liver.

'Eat up,' she said and wiped her finger on the Pekinese. Alleyn noticed that her hand was unsteady.

'Was it just a casual, friendly visit?' he asked.

Miss Cartell's rather prominent blue eyes, slightly bloodshot, seemed to film over.

'He was taking the bitch for a walk,' she said, after a pause. 'Brought it into the house, like a fool, and of course, Li became hysterical and bit me, poor little chap. I've fixed it up with girth-gall stuff,' she added, 'it smells a bit, but it's good.'

'Did Mr Cartell meet anybody else during his call, do you remember?'

With a manner that was at once furtive and anxious she said: 'Not that I know. I mean, I didn't see anything.' She might have been a great elderly schoolgirl caught on the hop. 'He was here when I came in,' she added. 'I don't know who he'd seen.'

'Miss Cartell,' Alleyn said, 'I'm anxious to find out if your brother had any enemies. I expect that sounds rather melodramatic, but I'm afraid it's unavoidable. Is there, do you know, anyone who had cause, for any reason, however trivial, to dislike or fear him?'

She waited much too long before she said: 'No one in particular,' and then after a pause: 'he wasn't awfully popular, I suppose. I mean he didn't make friends with people all that easily.' She reached down her blunt ill-kept hand to the Pekinese and fondled it. 'He was a dry old stick,' she said. 'You know. Typical solicitor: I used to tell him he had ink instead of blood in his veins.'

She broke into one of her ungainly laughs and blew her nose on a man's handkerchief.

'There was a luncheon party,' Alleyn said, 'wasn't there? Yesterday, at Mr Pyke Period's house?'

Instead of answering him she suddenly blurted out: 'But I thought it was an accident! The way they told me. It sounded like an accident.'

'Who told you?'

'P.P.,' she said. 'Alfred told him and he told me. He made it sound like an accident.'

'The odds against,' Alleyn said, 'are considerable.'

'Why?'

Everything about her was dull; her face, her manner, her voice. He wondered if she was really attending to him.

'Because,' he said, 'accident would imply at least two lots of people behaving independently like dangerous hoodlums at the same spot with different objectives.'

'I don't follow that,' said Miss Cartell.

'Never mind, just tell me about the luncheon party. There were you and your adopted niece and Miss Nicola Maitland-Mayne and Mr Leonard Leiss. And, of course, your brother and Mr Period. Is that right?'

'That's right.'

'What did you talk about?'

Nicola had given him a pretty full account of the luncheon party. Miss Cartell was much less explicit. She described the Pixie incident with one or two dismal hoots of retrospective laughter and she dwelt, disjointedly, upon Mr Period's references to blue blood and polite behaviour. She was clearly very ill at ease.

'He's got a bee in his bonnet over that sort of thing,' she said. 'My brother ragged him about it and he got jolly ratty. You could see. Can't take a joke.'

'What sort of joke?' Alleyn ventured.

'Well – I dunno. Some story about a baptismal register in a vestry. I didn't listen.'

Alleyn asked her about the cigarette-case and she at once exhibited all the classic signs of a clumsy and unaccustomed liar. She changed colour, avoided his glance and again fondled the unenthusiastic Pekinese.

'I didn't notice anything about that,' she said. 'He'd *got* the case. I didn't know he'd lost it. He's an old fusspot anyway.' The colour started out in blotches on her flattish cheeks. 'He probably lost it himself,' she said. 'Muddling about.'

Alleyn said: 'Miss Cartell, I'm sorry to badger you when you've had such a shock, but I'm sure you want to get this wretched business cleared up, don't you?'

'Don't know,' she countered. 'Not if it's going to lead to a lot of unpleasantness. Won't bring poor old Boysie back, will it?'

Alleyn disregarded this. 'Your adopted niece and a friend of hers, called Mr Leiss, were at the luncheon, weren't they?'

'Yes,' she said, staring at him. She seemed to be in two minds whether to go on. Then she said: 'You don't want to pay any attention to what P.P. says about them. He's out of touch with the young. Expects them to behave like his generation; and a lot of pie-faced little humbugs *they* were, if you like.'

'Was there some talk of Mr Leiss buying a car?'

She bent over the dog. 'That's enough,' she said to it. 'You've had enough.' And then to Alleyn: 'It all petered out. He didn't buy it.'

The door opened and her Austrian maid came in with a letter.

'From Mr Period, please,' she said. 'The man left it.'

Miss Cartell seemed unwilling to take the letter. The maid put it on the desk at her elbow.

'All right, Trudi,' Miss Cartell mumbled. 'Thank you,' and the maid went out.

'Pay no attention to me,' Alleyn said.

'It'll wait.'

'Don't you think, perhaps, you should look at it?'

She opened the letter unhandily and as she read it turned white to the lips.

'What is it?' he asked, 'Miss Cartell, what's the matter?'

The letter was still quivering in her hands.

'He must be mad,' she said. 'Mad!'

'May I see it?'

She seemed to consider this but in an aimless sort of way as if she only gave him half her attention. When he took the sheet of paper from her fingers she suffered him to do so as if they were inanimate.

Alleyn read the letter.

'My dear: What can I say? Only that you have lost a devoted brother and I a very dear friend. I know so well, believe me so *very* well, what a shock this has been for you and how bravely you will have taken it. If it is not an impertinence in an old friend to do so, may I offer you these few simple lines written by my dear and so Victorian Duchess of Rampton? They are none the worse, I hope, for their unblushing sentimentality.

> *So it must be, dear heart, I'll not repine*
> *For while I live the Memory is Mine.*

I should like to think that we know each other well enough for you to believe me when I say that I hope you won't dream of answering this all-too-inadequate attempt to tell you how sorry I am.

Yours sincerely,
Percival Pyke Period

Alleyn folded the paper and looked at Miss Cartell. 'But why,' he said, 'do you say that? Why do you say he must be mad?'

She waited so long, gaping at him like a fish, that he thought she would never answer. Then she made a fumbling, inelegant gesture towards the letter.

'Because he must be,' she said. 'Because it's all happening twice. Because he's written it before. The lot. Just the same.'

'You mean – ? But when?'

'This morning,' Connie said and began rooting in the litter on her desk. 'Before breakfast. Before I knew.'

She drew in her breath with a whistling noise. 'Before anybody knew,' she said. 'Before they had found him.'

She stared at Alleyn, nodding her head and holding out a sheet of letter-paper.

'See for yourself,' she said miserably. 'Before they had found him.'

Alleyn looked at the two letters. Except in one small detail they were, indeed, exactly the same.

CHAPTER 5

Postscript to a Party

Connie raised no objections to his keeping the letters and with them both in his pocket he asked if he might see Miss Ralston and Mr Leiss. She said that they were still asleep in their rooms and added, with a slight hint of gratification, that they had attended the Baynesholme festivities.

'One of Desirée Bantling's dotty parties,' she said. 'They go on till all hours. Moppett left a note asking not to be roused.'

'It's now one o'clock,' Alleyn said, 'and I'm afraid I shall have to disturb Mr Leiss.'

He thought she was going to protest but at that moment the Pekinese set up a petulant demonstration, scratching at the door and raising a crescendo of imperative yaps.

'Clever boy!' Connie said distractedly. 'I'm coming!' She went to the door. 'I'll have to see to this,' she said. 'In the garden.'

'Of course,' Alleyn agreed. He followed them into the hall and saw them out through the front door. Once in the garden the Pekinese bolted for a newly raked flowerbed.

'Oh, no!' Connie ejaculated. 'After lunch,' she shouted as she hastened in pursuit of her pet. 'Come back later.'

The Pekinese tore round a corner of the house and she followed it.

Alleyn re-entered the house and went quickly upstairs.

On the landing he encountered Trudi, the maid, who showed him the visitors' rooms. They were on two sides of a passage.

'Mr Leiss?' Alleyn asked.

A glint of feminine awareness momentarily transfigured Trudi's not very expressive face.

'He is sleeping,' she said. 'I looked at him. He sleeps like a god.'

'We'll see what he wakes like,' Alleyn said, tipping her rather handsomely. 'Thank you, Trudi.'

He tapped smartly on the door and went in.

The room was masked from its entrance by an old-fashioned scrap screen. Behind this a languid, indefinably Cockney voice said: 'Come in.'

Mr Leiss was awake but Alleyn thought he saw what Trudi meant: the general effect was in Technicolor. The violet silk pyjama jacket was open, the torso was bronzed, smooth and rather shiny as well as hirsute. A platinum chain lay on the chest. The glistening hair was slightly disarranged and the large brown eyes were open. When they lighted on Alleyn they narrowed. There was a slight convulsive movement under the bedclothes. The room smelt dreadfully of some indefinable unguent.

'Mr Leiss?' Alleyn said. 'I'm sorry to disturb you. I am a police officer.'

A very old familiar look started up in Leonard's face: a look of impertinence, caginess, conceit and fear. It was there as if it had been jerked up from within and in a moment it was gone.

'I don't quite follow you,' Leonard said. Something had gone amiss with his voice. He cleared his throat and recovered. 'Is anything wrong?' he asked.

He raised himself on his elbow, plumped up his pillows and lay back on them. He reached out languidly for a cigarette-case and lighter on his bedside table. The ash-tray was already overloaded.

'How can I help you?' he said and lit a cigarette. He inhaled deeply and blew out a thin vapour.

'You can help me,' Alleyn said, 'by answering one or two questions about your movements since you arrived at Little Codling yesterday morning.'

Leonard raised his eyebrows and exhaled a drift of vapour. 'And just why,' he asked easily, 'should I do that small thing?'

'For reasons,' Alleyn said, 'that will explain themselves in due course. First of all, there's the matter of an attempted car purchase. You gave Mr Pyke Period and Mr Cartell and Miss Cartell as references.

They considered you had no authority to do so. I suggest,' Alleyn went on, 'that you don't offer the usual unconvincing explanations. They really won't do. Fortunately for the other persons involved, the deal collapsed and, apart from adding to your record, the incident has only one point of interest: it made Mr Cartell very angry.' He stopped and looked hard at Leonard. 'Didn't it?' he asked.

'Look,' Leonard drawled, 'do me a favour and get the hell out of this, will you?'

'Next,' Alleyn went on, 'there's the business of Mr Period's cigarette-case.'

It was obvious that Leonard was prepared for this. He went at once into an elaborate pantomime of turning up his eyes, wagging his head and waving his fingers.

'No, honestly,' he ejaculated. 'It's *too* much. Not again!'

'Oh?' Alleyn mildly remarked. 'Again? Who's been tackling you about Mr Period's cigarette-case? Mr Cartell?'

Leonard took his time. 'I don't,' he said at last, 'like your tone. I resent it in fact.' He looked at Alleyn through half-closed eyes and seemed to come to a decision. 'Pardon me,' he added, 'if I appear abrupt. As a matter of fact, we had a latish party up at Baynesholme. Quite a show. Her ladyship certainly knows how to turn it on.'

Alleyn caught himself wondering what on earth in charity and forbearance could be said for Leonard Leiss.

'Mr Cartell spoke to you about the cigarette-case,' he said, taking a sizeable chance, 'when he called here yesterday evening.'

'Who – ?' Leonard began and pulled himself together. 'Look,' he said, 'have you been talking to other people?'

'Oh, yes, several.'

'To him?' Leonard demanded. 'To Cartell?'

There was a long pause.

'No,' Alleyn said. 'Not to him.'

'Then who – ? Here!' Leonard ejaculated. 'There's something funny about all this. What is it?'

'I'll answer that one,' Alleyn said, 'when you tell me what you did with Mr Period's cigarette-case. Now don't,' he went on, raising a finger, 'say you don't know anything about it. I've seen the dining-room window. It can't be opened from the outside. It was shut during luncheon. You and Miss Ralston examined the case by the window and left it on the sill. No one else was near the window. When the man came in to clear, the window was open and the case had gone.'

'So he says.'

'So he says and I believe him.'

'Pardon me if I seem to be teaching you your job,' Leonard said, 'but if I was going to pinch this dreary old bit of tat, why would I open the window? Why not put it in my pocket there and then?'

'Because you would then quite obviously be the thief, Mr Leiss. If you or Miss Ralston left it on the sill and returned by way of the garden path – '

'How the hell – ' Leonard began, and then changed his mind. 'I don't accept that,' he said. 'I resent it, in fact.'

'Did you smoke any of Mr Period's cigarettes?'

'Only one, thank you very much. Turkish muck.'

'Did Miss Ralston?'

'Same story. Now, look,' Leonard began with a sort of spurious candour. 'There's such a thing as collusion, isn't there? We left this morsel of antiquity on the sill. All right. This man – Alfred What-have-you – opens the window. The workmen in the lane get the office from him and it's all as sweet as kiss your hand.'

'And would you suggest that we search the men in the lane?'

'Why not? Do no harm, would it?'

'We might even catch them handing the case round after elevenses?'

'That's right,' Leonard said coolly, 'you might at that. Or, they might have cached it on the spot. You can search this room, or me or my car or my girlfriend. Only too pleased. The innocent don't have anything to hide, do they?' asked Leonard.

'Nor do the guilty, when they've dumped the evidence.'

Leonard ran the tip of his tongue over his lips. 'Fair enough,' he said. 'So what?'

'Mr Leiss,' Alleyn said, 'the cigarette-case has been found.'

A second flickered past before Leonard, in a tone of righteous astonishment said: 'Found! Well, I ask you! Found! so why come at me? Where?'

'In my opinion, exactly where you dropped it. Down the drain.'

The door was thrust open. On the far side of the screen a feminine voice said: 'Sorry, darling, but you'll have to rouse up.' The door was shut. 'We *are* in a spot of bother,' the voice continued as its owner came round the screen. 'Old Cartell, dead as a doornail and down the drain.'

II

When Moppett saw Alleyn she clapped her hand to her mouth and eyed him over the top.

'I'm terribly sorry,' she said. 'Auntie C. thought you'd gone.'

She was a dishevelled figtire, half-saved by her youth and held together in a negligée that was as unfresh as it was elaborate. 'Isn't it frightful,' she said. 'Poor Uncle Hal! I can't believe it!'

Either she was less perturbed than Leonard or several times tougher. He had turned a very ill colour and had jerked cigarette ash across his chest.

'What the hell are you talking about?' he said.

'Didn't you *know?*' Moppett exclaimed and then to Alleyn, 'haven't you *told* him?'

'Miss Ralston,' Alleyn said, 'you have saved me the trouble. It is Miss Ralston, isn't it?'

'That's right. Sorry,' Moppett went on after a moment, 'if I'm interrupting something. I'll sweep myself out, shall I? See you, ducks,' she added in Cockney to Leonard.

'Don't go, if you please,' said Alleyn. 'You may be able to help us. Can you tell me where you and Mr Leiss lost Mr Period's cigarette-case?'

'No, she can't,' Leonard intervened. 'Because we didn't. We never had it. We don't know anything about it.'

Moppett opened her eyes very wide and her mouth slightly. She turned in fairly convincing bewilderment from Leonard to Alleyn.

'I don't understand,' she said. 'P.P.'s cigarette-case? Do you mean the old one he showed us when we lunched with him?'

'Yes,' Alleyn agreed. 'That's the one I mean.'

'Lenny, darling, what did happen to it, do you remember? I know! We left it on the window-sill. Didn't we? In the dining-room?'

'Okay. Okay. Like I've been telling the Chief God-almighty High Commissioner,' Leonard said and behind his alarm, his fluctuating style and his near-Americanisms, there flashed up an unrepentant barrow-boy. 'So, now it's been found. So what?'

'It's been found,' Alleyn said, 'in the open drain a few inches from Mr Cartell's body.'

Leonard seemed to retreat into himself. It was as if he shortened and compressed his defences.

'I don't know what you're talking about,' he said. He shot a glance at Moppett. 'That's a very nasty suggestion, isn't it? I don't get the picture.'

'The picture will emerge in due course. A minute or two ago,' Alleyn said, 'you told me I was welcome to search this room. Do you hold to that?'

Leonard went through the pantomime of inspecting his finger-nails but gave it up on finding his hands were unsteady.

'Naturally,' he murmured. 'Like I said. Nothing to hide.'

'Good. Please don't go, Miss Ralston,' Alleyn continued as Moppett showed some sign of doing so. 'I shan't be long.'

He had moved over to the wardrobe and opened the door when he felt a touch on his arm. He turned and there was Moppett, smelling of scent, hair and bed, gazing into his face unmistakably palpitating.

'I won't go, of course,' she said opening her eyes very wide, 'if you don't want me to but you *can* see, can't you, that I'm not actually dressed for the prevailing climate? It's a trifle chilly, this morning, isn't it?'

'I'm sure Mr Leiss will lend you his dressing-gown.'

It was a brocade and velvet affair and lay across the foot of the bed. She put it on.

'Give us a fag, ducks,' she said to Leonard.

'Help yourself.'

She reached for his case. 'It's not one of those – ?' she began and then stopped short. 'Fanks, ducks,' she said and lit a cigarette, lounging across the bed.

The room grew redolent of Virginian tobacco.

The wardrobe doors were lined with looking-glass. In them Alleyn caught a momentary glimpse of Moppett leaning urgently towards Leonard and of Leonard baring his teeth at her. He mouthed something and closed his hand over her wrist. The cigarette quivered between her fingers. Leonard turned his head as Alleyn moved the door and their images swung out of sight.

Alleyn's fingers slid into the pockets of Leonard's check suit, dinner-suit and camel-hair overcoat. They discovered three greasy combs, a pair of wash-leather gloves, a membership card from a Soho club called La Hacienda, a handkerchief, loose change, a pocket-book and finally, in the evening-trousers and the overcoat, the object of their search: strands of cigarette tobacco. He withdrew a thread and sniffed at it. Turkish. The hinges of Mr Period's case he had noticed, were a bit loose.

He came from behind the wardrobe door with the garments in question over his arm. Moppett, who now had her feet up, exclaimed with a fair show of gaiety: 'Look, Face, he's going to valet you.'

Alleyn said: 'I'd like to borrow these things for the moment. I'll give you a receipt, of course.'

'Like hell you will,' Leonard ejaculated.

'If you object, I can apply for a search-warrant.'

'Darling, don't be bloody-minded,' Moppett said. 'After all, what *does* it matter?'

'It's the principle of the thing,' Leonard mumbled through bleached lips. 'That's what I object to. People break in without a word of warning and start talking about bodies and – and – '

'And false pretences. And attempted fraud. And theft,' Alleyn put in. 'As you say, it's the principle of the thing. May I borrow these garments?'

'Okay. Okay. Okay.'

'Thank you.'

Alleyn laid the overcoat and dinner-suit across a chair and then went methodically through a suitcase and the drawers of a tallboy: there, wrapped in a sock he came upon a flick-knife. He turned with it in his hand, and found Leonard staring at him.

'This,' Alleyn said, 'is illegal. Where did you get it?'

'I picked it up,' Leonard said, 'in the street. Illegal, is it? Fancy.'

'I shall take care of it.'

Leonard whispered something to Moppett who laughed immoderately and said: 'Oh, lord!' in a manner that contrived to be disproportionately offensive.

Alleyn then sat at a small desk in a corner of the room. He removed Leonard's pocket-book from his dinner-jacket and examined the contents which embraced five pounds in notes and a photograph of Miss Ralston in the nude. They say that nothing shocks a police officer, but Alleyn found himself scandalized. He listed the contents of the pocket-book and wrote a receipt for them, which he handed, with the pocket-book to Leonard.

'I don't expect to be long over this,' he said. 'In the meantime I would like a word with you, if you please, Miss Ralston.'

'What for?' Leonard interposed quickly, and to Moppett: 'You don't have to talk to him.'

'Darling,' Moppett said. 'Manners! And I'll have you know I'm simply dying to talk to the . . . Inspector, is it? Or Super? I'm sure it's Super. Do we withdraw?'

She was stretched across the foot of the bed with her chin in her hands, 'a lost girl' Alleyn thought, adopting the Victorian phrase, 'if ever I saw one'.

He walked over to the window and was rewarded by the sight of Inspector Fox seated in a police car in Miss Cartell's drive. He looked up. Alleyn made a face at him and crooked a finger. Fox began to climb out of the car.

'If you don't mind,' Alleyn said to Moppett, 'we'll move into the passage.'

'Thrilled to oblige,' Moppett said. Drawing Leonard's gown tightly about her she walked round the screen and out of the door.

Alleyn turned to Leonard, 'I shall have to ask you,' he said, 'to stay here for the time being.'

'It's not convenient.'

'Nevertheless you will be well advised to stay. What is your address in London?'

'Seventy-six Castlereigh Walk, SW14. Though why . . .'

'If you return there,' Alleyn said, 'you will be kept under observation. Take your choice.'

He followed Moppett into the passage. He found her arranging her back against the wall and her cigarette in the corner of her mouth. Alleyn could hear Mr Fox's bass voice rumbling downstairs.

'What can I do for you, Super?' Moppett asked with the slight smile of the film underworldling.

'You can stop being an ass,' he rejoined tartly. 'I don't know why I waste time telling you this but if you don't, you may find yourself in serious trouble. Think that one out, if you can, and stop smirking

at me,' Alleyn said, rounding off what was possibly the most unprofessional speech of his career.

'Oi!' said Moppett, 'who's in a naughty rage?'

Alleyn heard Miss Cartell's edgeless voice directing Mr Fox upstairs.
He looked over the banister and saw her upturned face, blunt, red and
vulnerable. His distaste for Moppett was exacerbated. There she stood,
conceited, shifty and complacent as they come, without scruple or
compassion. And there, below stairs, was her guardian, wide open to
anything this detestable girl liked to hand out to her.

Fox could be heard saying in a comfortable voice: 'Thank you
very much, Miss Cartell. I'll find my own way.'

'More force?' Moppett remarked. 'Delicious!'

'This is Inspector Fox,' Alleyn said as his colleague appeared. He
handed Leonard's dinner-suit and overcoat to Fox. 'General routine
check,' he said, 'and I'd like you to witness something I'm going to
say to Miss Mary Ralston.'

'Good afternoon, Miss Ralston,' Fox said pleasantly. He hung
Leonard's garments over the banister and produced his note-book.
The half-smile did not leave Moppett's face but seemed rather, to
remain there by a sort of oversight.

'Understand this,' Alleyn continued, speaking to Moppett. 'We
are investigating a capital crime and I have, I believe, proof that last
night the cigarette-case in question was in the possession of that
unspeakable young man of yours. It was found by Mr Cartell's body
and Mr Cartell has been murdered.'

'Murdered!' she said, 'he *hasn't!*' And then she went very white
round the mouth. 'I can't believe you,' she said. 'People like him
don't get murdered. Why?'

'For one of the familiar motives,' Alleyn said. 'For knowing something damaging about someone else. Or threatening to take action
against somebody. Financial troubles. Might be anything.'

'Auntie Con said it was an accident.'

'I dare say she didn't want to upset you.'

'Bloody dumb of her!' Moppett said viciously.

'Obviously you don't feel the same concern for her. But if you did,
in the smallest degree, you would answer my questions truthfully. If
you've any sense, you'll do so for your own sake.'

'Why?'

'To save yourself from the suspicion of something much more serious than theft.'

She seemed to contract inside Leonard's dressing-gown. 'I don't know what you mean. I don't know anything about it.'

Alleyn thought: 'Are these two wretched young no-goods in the fatal line? Is that to be the stale, deadly familiar end?'

He said: 'If you stole the cigarette-case, or Mr Leiss stole it or you both stole it in collusion, and if, for one reason or another, you dropped it in the ditch last night, you will be well advised to say so.'

'How do I know that? You're trying to trap me.'

Alleyn said patiently: 'Believe me, I'm not concerned to trap the innocent. Nor, at the moment, am I primarily interested in theft.'

'Then you're trying to bribe me.'

This observation showing, as it did, a flash of perception, was infuriating.

'I can neither bribe nor threaten,' he said. 'But I can warn you and I do. You're in a position of great danger. You, personally. Do you know what happens to people who withhold evidence in a case of homicide? Do you know what happens to accessories before the fact, of such a crime? *Do you?*'

Her face crumpled suddenly, like a child's, and her enormous shallow eyes overflowed.

'All right,' she said. 'All right. I'll tell you. But it wasn't anything. You've got it all wrong. It was – '

'Well?'

'It was all a mistake,' Moppett whispered.

The bedroom door opened and Leonard came out in his purple pyjamas.

'You keep your great big, beautiful trap shut, honey,' he said. He stood behind Moppett, holding her arms. He really would, Alleyn had time to consider, do rather well in a certain type of film.

'Mr Leiss,' he said, 'will you be kind enough to take yourself out of this.'

But, even as he said it, he knew it was no good. With astonishing virtuosity Moppett, after a single ejaculation of pain and a terrified glance at Leonard, leant back against him, falling abruptly into the role of seductive accessory. The tears still stood in her eyes and her mouth twitched as his fingers bit into her arm. She contrived a smile.

'Don't worry, darling,' she said, rubbing her head against Leonard. 'I'm not saying a thing.'

'That's my girl,' said Leonard savagely.

III

'Not,' Mr Fox remarked as they drove away, 'the type of young people you'd expect to find in this environment.'

'Not county, you think?' Alleyn returned.

'Certainly not,' Fox said primly. 'Leiss, now. A bad type that. Wide boy. Only a matter of time before he's inside for a tidy stretch. But the young lady's a different story. Or ought to be,' Fox said, after a pause. 'Or ought to be,' he repeated heavily.

'The young lady,' Alleyn said tartly, 'is a young stinker. Look, Fox! There are threads of the Period cigarette tobacco in Leiss's pocket. Bob Williams'll lay on a vacuum cleaner, I dare say. Go through the pockets and return the unspeakable garments will you? And check his dabs from the oddments in the pockets. To my mind, there's no doubt they pinched the cigarette-case. Suppose Cartell or Period or both, cut up rough? What then?'

'Ah!' Fox said. 'Exactly. And suppose Mr Cartell threatened to go to the police and they set the trap for him and accidentally dropped the case in doing it?'

'All right. Suppose they did. Now as to their actions on the scene of the crime we've got that pleasant child, Nicola Maitland-Mayne, for a witness but she was in the throes of young love and may have missed one or two tricks. I'll check with her young man, although he was probably further gone than she. All right. I'll drop you at the station and return to the genteel assault on Mr Pyke Period. He'll have lunched by now. What about you?'

'Or you, Mr Alleyn, if it comes to that.'

'I think I'll press on, Br'er Fox. Get yourself a morsel of cheese and pickle at the pub and see if there's anything more to be extracted from that cagey little job, Alfred Belt.'

'As a matter of fact,' Fox confessed, 'Mr Belt and Mrs Mitchell the cook, who seems to be a very superior type of woman, suggested I should drop in for a snack later in the day. Mrs Mitchell went so far as to indicate she'd set something cold aside.'

'I might have known it,' Alleyn said. 'Meet you at the station at fiveish.' The car pulled up at Mr Pyke Period's gate and he got out, arranging for it to pick him up again in half an hour.

Mr Period received him fretfully in the drawing-room. He was evidently still much perturbed and kept shooting unhappy little glances out of the corners of his eyes. Alleyn could just hear the stutter of Nicola's typewriter in the study.

'I can't settle to anything. I couldn't eat my lunch. It's all too difficult and disturbing,' said Mr Period.

'And I'm afraid I'm not going to make it any easier,' Alleyn rejoined. He waited for a moment and decided to fire point-blank. 'Mr Period,' he said, 'will you tell me why you wrote two letters of condolence to Miss Cartell, why they are almost exactly the same and why the first was written and sent to her before either of you had been informed of her brother's death?'

There was nothing to be learnt from Mr Period's face. Shock, guilt, astonishment, lack of comprehension or mere deafness might have caused his jaw to drop and his eyes to glaze. When he did speak it was politely and conventionally. 'I beg your pardon? What did you say?'

Alleyn repeated his question. Mr Period seemed to think it over. After a considerable pause he said flatly: 'But I didn't.'

'You didn't what?'

'Write twice. The thing's ridiculous.'

Alleyn drew the two letters from his pocket and laid them before Mr Period who screwed his glass in his eye and stooped over them. When he straightened up, his face was the colour of beetroot. 'There has been a stupid mistake,' he said.

'I'm afraid I must ask you to explain it.'

'There's nothing to explain.'

'My dear Period!' Alleyn ejaculated.

'Nothing! My man must have made a nonsense.'

'Your man didn't, by some act of clairvoyance, anticipate a letter of condolence, and forge a copy and deliver it to a lady before anyone knew she was bereaved.'

'There's no need to be facetious,' said Mr Period.

'I couldn't agree with you more. It's an extremely serious matter.'

'Very well,' Mr Period said angrily. 'Very well! I ah – I – ah – I had occasion to write to Connie Cartell about something else. Something entirely different and extremely private.'

Astonishingly he broke into a crazy little laugh which seemed immediately to horrify him. He stared wildly at Alleyn. 'I – ah – I must have – ' He stopped short. Alleyn would have thought it impossible for him to become redder in the face but he now did so. 'The wrong letter,' he said, 'was put in the envelope. Obviously.'

'But that doesn't explain – Wait a bit!' Alleyn exclaimed. 'Come!' he said after a moment. 'Perhaps sense does begin to dawn after all. Tell me, and I promise I'll be as discreet as may be, has anybody else of your acquaintance been bereaved of a brother?'

Mr Period's eyeglass dropped with a click. 'In point of fact,' he said unhappily, 'yes.'

'When?'

'It was in yesterday's – ah! I heard of it yesterday.'

'And wrote?'

Mr Period inclined his head.

'And the letter was – ' Alleyn wondered how on earth his victim's discomfiture could be reduced and decided there was nothing much to be done about it. 'The letters were identical?' he suggested. 'After all, why not? One can't go on forever inventing consolatory phrases.'

Mr Period bowed and was silent. Alleyn hurried on. 'Do you mind giving me, in confidence, the name of the' – it was difficult to avoid a touch of grotesquery – 'the other bereaved sister?'

'Forgive me. I prefer not.'

Remembering there was always Nicola and the *Daily Press,* Alleyn didn't press the point.

'Perhaps,' he said, 'you wouldn't mind telling me what the missing letter was about: I mean, the one that you intended for Miss Cartell?'

'Again,' Mr Period said with miserable dignity, 'I regret.' He really looked as if he might cry.

'Presumably it has gone to the other bereaved sister? The wrong letter in the right envelope as it were.'

Mr Period momentarily closed his eyes as if overtaken by nausea and said nothing.

'You know,' Alleyn went on very gently, 'I have to ask about these things. If they're irrelevant to the case I can't tell you how completely and thankfully one puts them out of mind.'

'They are irrelevant,' Mr Period assured him with vehemence. 'Believe me, believe me, they *are*. *Entirely* irrelevant! My dear Alleyn – really – I promise you. There now!' Mr Period concluded with crackpot gaiety. ''Nuff said! Tell me, my dear fellow, you did have luncheon? I meant to suggest – but this frightful business puts everything out of one's head – *not*, I hope, at our rather baleful little pub?'

He babbled on distractedly. Alleyn listened in the hope of hearing something useful and this not being the case brought him up with a round turn.

He said: 'There's one other thing. I understand that Lady Bantling drove you home last night?'

Mr Period gaped at him. 'But of course,' he said at last. 'Dear Desirée! So kind! Of course! Why?'

'And I believe,' Alleyn plodded on, 'that after you had left her, she didn't at once return to Baynesholme but went into your garden and from there conducted a dialogue with Mr Cartell who was looking out of his bedroom window. Why didn't you tell me about this?'

'I don't – really, I don't know – '

'But I think you do. You looked through your own bedroom window and asked if anything was the matter.'

'And nothing was!' Mr Period ejaculated with a kind of pale triumph. 'Nothing! She said so! She said – '

'She said: "Nothing in the wide world. Go to bed, darling."'

'Precisely! So exuberant always!'

'Did you hear anything of the conversation?'

'Nothing!' Mr Period ejaculated. 'Nothing at all! But nothing! I simply heard their voices. And in my opinion she was just being naughty and teasing poor old Hal.'

As Mr Period could not be dislodged from this position Alleyn made his excuses and sought out Nicola in the study.

She was able to find a copy of yesterday's *Press*. He read through the obituary notices.

'Look here,' he said, 'your employer is in a great taking-on about his correspondence. Did you happen to notice what mail was ready to go out yesterday evening?'

'Yes,' Nicola said. 'Two letters.'

'Local addresses?'

'That's right,' she said uneasily.

'Mind telling me what they were?'

'Well – I mean . . .'

'All right. Were they to Miss Cartell and Desirée, Lady Bantling?'

'Why ask me,' Nicola said rather crossly, 'if you already know?'

'I was tricking you, my pretty one, oiled Hawkshaw the detective.'

'Ha-ha, very funny, I suppose,' Nicola sourly remarked.

'Well, only fairly funny.' Alleyn had wandered over to the corner of the room that bore Mr Period's illuminated genealogy. 'He seems woundily keen on begatteries,' he muttered. 'Look at all this. Hung up in a dark spot for modesty's sake, but framed and hung up, all the same. It's not an old one. Done at his cost, I'll be bound.'

'How do you know?'

'If you keep on asking "feed" questions you must expect to be handed the pay-off line. By the paper, gilt and paint.'

'Oh.'

'Where's Ribblethorpe?'

'Beyond Baynesholme, I think.'

'The Pyke family seems to have come from there.'

'So I've been told,' Nicola sighed, 'and at some length, poor lamb. He went on and on about it yesterday after luncheon. I think he was working something off.'

'Tell me again about the conversation at lunch.' Nicola did so and he thanked her. 'I must go,' he said.

'Where to?'

'Oh – up and down in the world seeking whom I may devour. See you later, no doubt.'

As he left the house Alleyn thought: 'That was all pretty bloody facetious, but the girl makes me feel young.' And as he got into the police car he added to himself: 'But so after all, does my wife. And that's what I call being happily married. To Baynesholme,' he added, to his driver. On the way there, he sat with his hat cocked forward, noticing that spring was advancing in the countryside and wondering what Desirée Ormsbury, as he remembered her, would look like after all these years.

'Pretty tough, I dare say, what with one thing and another,' he supposed, and when he was shown into her boudoir and she came forward to greet him, he found he had been right.

Desirée was wearing tight pants and an Italian shirt. The shirt was mostly orange and so were her hair and lipstick. Her make-up generally, was impressionistic rather than representational and her hands, quite desperately haggard.

But when she grinned at him there was the old raffish, disreputable charm he remembered so well and he thought: 'She's formidable, still.'

'It *is* you, then,' she said hoarsely. 'I wasn't sure if it was going to be you or your brother – George, was he? – who'd turned into a policeman.'

'I wonder at your remembering either of us.'

'I do, though. But of course, George turned into a baronet. You're Rory, the dashing one.'

'You appal me,' Alleyn said.

'You don't look all that different. I wish I could say as much for myself. Shall we have a drink?'

'Not me, thank you,' Alleyn said rather startled. He glanced at a clock: it was twenty to three.

'I've only just had lunch,' she explained. 'I thought brandy might be rather a thing. Where did you have lunch?' She looked at him. 'Wait a moment, will you? Sorry. I won't be long. Have a smoke.' She added over her shoulder as she walked away: 'I'm not trying to escape.'

Alleyn looked about him. It was a conventional country house boudoir with incongruous dabs of Desirée scattered about it in the form of 'dotty' bits of French porcelain and one astonishing picture of a nude sprouting green bay leaves and little flags.

There were photographs of Richard Bantling and a smooth-looking youngish man whom Alleyn supposed must be Desirée's third husband. It was a rather colourless photograph but he found himself looking at it with a sense of familiarity. He knew the wide-set eyes were grey rather than blue and that the mouth, when smiling, displayed almost perfect teeth. He knew he had heard the voice: a light baritone, lacking colour. He knew he had at some time encountered this man but he couldn't remember where or when.

'That's Bimbo,' said Desirée, returning. 'My third. We've been married a year.' She carried a loaded tray. 'I thought you were probably hungry,' she said, putting it on her desk. 'You needn't feel awkward,' she added. She strolled off and lit a cigarette. 'Do have it, for God's

sake, after all my trouble getting it. If I'm arrested, I promise I won't
split on you. Eat up.'

'Since you put it like that,' Alleyn rejoined, 'I shall, and very grate-
fully.' He sat down to chicken-aspic and salad, bread, butter, cheese,
a bottle of lager and something in an over-sized cocktail glass.

'Dry Martini,' Desirée said. She herself had a generously equipped
brandy glass. She picked up a magazine and disappeared into a sofa.
'Is that all right?'

By the smell he supposed it to be made up of nine parts gin to one
of french. He therefore tipped it quickly into a vase of flowers on the
desk and poured out the lager. The chicken-aspic was quite excellent.

'Andrew tells me,' Desirée said, 'that you seem to think Hal was
murdered.'

'Yes, I do.'

'It appears so unlikely, somehow. Unless somebody did it out of irritation. When we were married, I promise you I felt like it often
enough. Still, being rid of him I no longer do – or did. If you follow me.'

'Perfectly,' said Alleyn.

'Andrew says it's all about a kind of booby-trap, he thinks. Is that
right?'

'That's right.'

'I expected,' Desirée said after a pause, 'that it would be you asking
me the questions.'

'If you fill my mouth with delectable food, how can I?'

'Is it good? I didn't have any. I never fancy my lunch much except
for the drinks. *Was* Hal murdered? Honestly?'

'I think so.'

There was a longish silence and then she began to talk about people
they had both known and occasions when they had met. This went
on for some time. In her offhand way she managed to convey an
implicit familiarity. Presently she came up behind him. He could
smell her scent which was sharp and unfamiliar. He knew she was
trying to get him off-balance, to make him feel vulnerable, sitting
there eating and drinking. He also knew, as certainly as if she had
made the grossest of advances, that she was perfectly ready for an
unconventional interlude. He wondered where her Bimbo had
taken himself off to and if Andrew Bantling was in the house. He
continued sedately to eat and drink.

'My Bimbo,' she said as if he had spoken aloud, 'is having his bit of afternoon kip. We were latish last night. One of my parties. Quite a pure one, but I suppose you know about that.'

'Yes, it sounded a huge success,' Alleyn said politely. He laid down his knife and fork and got up. 'That was delicious,' he said. 'Thank you *very* much, jolly kind of you to think of it.'

'Not at all,' she murmured, coming at him with cigarettes and a lighter and an ineffable look.

'May we sit down?' Alleyn suggested and noticed that she took a chair facing a glare of uncompromising light: she was evidently one of those rare, ugly, provocative women who can't be bothered taking the usual precautions.

'I've got to ask you one or two pretty important questions,' Alleyn said. 'And the first is this. Have you by any chance had a letter from Mr Pyke Period? This morning, perhaps?'

She stared at him. 'Golly, yes! I'd forgotten all about it. He must be dotty, poor lamb. How did you know?'

Alleyn disregarded this question. 'Why dotty?' he asked.

'Judge for yourself.'

She put a hand on his shoulder, leant across him and pulled out a drawer in her desk, taking her time about it. 'Here it is,' she said and dropped a letter in front of him. 'Go on,' she said. 'Read it.'

It was written in Mr Period's old-fashioned hand, on his own letter-paper.

'My dear,' it read, 'Please don't think it too silly of me to be fussed about a little thing, but I can't help feeling that you might very naturally, have drawn a quite unwarrantable conclusion from the turn our conversation took today. It really is a little *too* much to have to defend one's own ancestry, but I care enough about such matters to feel I must assure you that mine goes back as far as I, or anyone else, might wish. I'm afraid Hal, poor dear, had developed a slight *thing* on the subject. But never mind! I don't! Forgive me for bothering you, but I know you will understand.

As ever,

P.P.P.'

'Have you any idea,' Alleyn said, 'what he's driving at?'

'Not a notion. He dined here last night and was normal.'

'Would you have expected another sort of letter from him?'

'Another sort? What sort? Oh! I see what you mean. About Ormsbury, poor brute? He's dead, you know.'

'Yes.'

'With P.P.'s passion for condolences it would have been more likely. You mean he's done the wrong thing? So, who was meant to have this one?'

'May I at all events keep it?'

'Do, if you want to.'

Alleyn pocketed the letter. 'I'd better say at once that you may have been the last person to speak to Harold Cartell, *not* excepting his murderer.'

She had a cigarette ready in her mouth and the flame from the lighter didn't waver until she drew on it.

'How do you make that out?' she asked easily. 'Oh, I know. Somebody's told you about the balcony scene. Who? Andrew, I suppose, or his girl. Or P.P., of course. He cut in on it from his window.'

'So you had a brace of Romeos in reverse?'

'Like hell I did. Both bald and me, if we face it, not quite the dewy job either.'

Alleyn found himself at once relishing this speech and knowing that she had intended him to have exactly that reaction.

'The dewy jobs,' he said, 'have their limitations.'

'Whereas for me,' Desirée said, suddenly overdoing it, 'the sky's the limit. Did you know that?'

He decided to disregard this and pressed on. 'Why,' he asked, 'having deposited Mr Period at his garden gate did you leave the car, cross the ditch and serenade Mr Cartell?'

'I saw him at his window and thought it would be fun.'

'What did you say?'

'I think I said: "But soft what light from yonder window breaks."'

'And after that?'

'I really don't remember. I pulled his leg a bit.'

'Did you tell him you were on the warpath?'

There was a fractional pause before she said: 'Well, I must say P.P. has sharp ears for an elderly gent. Yes, I did. It meant nothing.'

'And did you tell him to watch his step?'

'Why,' asked Desirée, 'don't we just let you tell me what I said and leave it at that?'

'Did you tackle him about that boy of yours?'

'All right,' she said, 'yes, I did!' And then: '*They* didn't tell you? Andy and the girl? Have you needled it out of them, you cunning fellow?'

'I'm afraid,' Alleyn prevaricated, 'they were too far up the lane and much too concerned with each other to be reliable witnesses.'

'So P.P. – ' She leant forward and touched him. 'Look,' she said, 'I honestly don't remember what I said to Hal. I'd had one or two little drinks and was a morsel high.' She waited for a moment and then, with a sharpness that she hadn't exhibited before, she said: 'If it was a booby-trap, I hadn't a chance to set it, had I? Not in full view of those two lovebirds.'

'Who told you about the booby-trap?'

'P.P. told Andy and Andy told me. And I drove straight here to Baynesholme arriving at twenty-five to twelve. The first couple got back soon afterwards. From then on I was under the closest imaginable observation. Isn't that what one calls a water-tight alibi?'

'I shall be glad,' Alleyn said, 'to have it confirmed. How do you know you got back at eleven thirty-five?'

'The clock in the hall. I was watching the time because of the treasure hunt.'

'Who won?'

'Need you ask! The Moppett and her bully. They probably cheated in some way.'

'Really? How do you suppose?'

'They heard us plotting about the clues in the afternoon. The last one led back to the loo tank in the downstairs cloakroom.'

'Here?'

'That's right. Most of the others guessed it but they were too late. Andrew and Nicola didn't even try, I imagine.'

'Any corroborative evidence, do you remember?'

'Of my alibi?'

'Of your alibi,' Alleyn agreed sedately.

'I don't know. I think I called out something to Bimbo. He might remember.'

'So he might. About last night's serenade to your second husband. Did you introduce the subject of your son's inheritance?'

She burst out laughing: she had a loud, formidable laugh like a female Duke of Wellington. 'Do you know,' she said, 'I believe I did. Something of the sort. Anything to get a rise.'

'He called on you yesterday afternoon, didn't he?'

'Oh, yes,' she said quickly. 'About Flash Len and a car. He was in a great taking-on, poor pet.'

'And on that occasion,' Alleyn persisted, 'did you introduce the subject of the inheritance?'

'Did we? Yes, so we did. I told Hal I thought he was behaving jolly shabbily which was no more than God's truth.'

'What was his reaction?'

'He was too fussed to take proper notice. He just fumed away about the car game. Your spies *have* been busy,' she added. 'Am I allowed to ask who told you? Wait a bit, though. It must have been Sergeant Raikes. What fun for him.'

'Why was Cartell so set against the picture gallery idea?'

'My dear, because he was what he was. Fuddy-duddy-plus. It's a bore, because he's Andy's guardian.'

'Any other trustees?'

'Yes. P.P.'

'What does he think?'

'He thinks Andy might grow a beard and turn beat, which he doesn't dig. Still, I can manage my P.P. Boo wouldn't have minded.'

'Boo?'

'Bantling. My first. Andy's papa. *You* knew Boo. Don't be so stuffy.'

Alleyn, who did in fact remember this singularly ineffectual peer, made no reply.

'*And*, I may add,' Lady Bantling said, apparently as an after-thought, 'Bimbo considered it a jolly good bet. And he's got a flair for that sort of thing, Bimbo has. As a matter of fact Bimbo offered – ' She broke off and seemed to cock an ear. Alleyn had already heard steps in the hall. 'Here, I do believe, he is!' Desirée exclaimed and called out loudly: 'Bimbo!'

'Hallo!' said a distant voice, rather crossly.

'Come in here, darling.'

The door opened and Bimbo Dodds came in. Alleyn now remembered where he had seen him.

IV

The recognition, Alleyn felt sure, was mutual though Bimbo gave no sign of this. They had last met on the occasion of a singularly disreputable turn-up in a small but esoteric night-club. There had been a stabbing, subsequent revelations involving a person of consequence and a general damping-down process ending in a scantily publicized conviction. Benedict Arthur Dodds, Alleyn recollected, had been one of a group of fashionable gentlemen who had an undercover financial interest in the club which had come to an abrupt and discreditable end and an almost immediate reincarnation under another name. Bimbo had appeared briefly in court, been stared at coldly by the magistrate, and was lucky to escape the headlines. At the time, Alleyn recollected, Bimbo was stated to be a declared bankrupt. It was before his marriage to Desirée.

She introduced them. Bimbo, who had the slightly mottled complexion of a man who has slept heavily in the afternoon, nodded warily and glanced at the tray. His right hand was neatly bandaged and he did not offer it to Alleyn.

'The Super and I, darling,' Desirée said, 'are boy-and-girl chums. He was starving and I've given him a snack. He's jolly famous nowadays, so isn't it nice to have him grilling us?'

'Oh, really?' said Bimbo. 'Ha-ha. Yes.'

'You must answer all his questions very carefully because it seems as if Hal was murdered. Imagine!'

Interpreting this speech to be in the nature of a general warning, Alleyn said: 'I wonder if I may have a word with you, Mr Dodds.' And to Desirée: 'Thank you so much for my delicious luncheon-without-prejudice.'

For a split second she looked irritated and then she said: 'Not a bit. Do I gather that you want to go into a huddle with my husband?'

'Just a word,' Alleyn said equably, 'if we may. Perhaps somewhere else – '

'Not at all. I'll go and snip the dead heads off roses except that there aren't any roses and it's the wrong time of the year.'

'Perhaps you could get on with your embroidery,' said Alleyn and had the satisfaction of seeing her blink.

'Suppose,' she suggested, 'that you adjourn to Bimbo's study. Why not?'

'Why not?' Bimbo echoed without cordiality.

As Alleyn passed her on his way out, she looked full in his face. It was impossible to interpret her expression, but he'd have taken a long bet that she was worried.

Bimbo's study turned out to be the usual sporting-print job with inherited classics on the shelves, together with one or two paperbacks, looking like Long Acre in its more dubious reaches. Bimbo, whose manner was huffy and remote, said: 'This is a very unpleasant sort of thing to happen.'

'Yes, isn't it?'

'Anything we can do, of course.'

'Thank you very much. There are one or two points,' Alleyn said without refurbishing the stock phrases, 'that I'd like to clear up. It's simply a matter of elimination, as I'm sure you'll understand.'

'Naturally,' said Bimbo.

'Well, then. You'll have heard that Mr Cartell's body was found in a trench that has been dug in Green Lane, the lane that runs past Mr Period's garden. Did you drive down Green Lane at any time last evening?'

'Ah – ' Bimbo said. 'Ah – let me think. Yes, I did. When going round the clues.'

He paused while Alleyn reflected that this was a fair enough description of his own preoccupation.

'The clues for the treasure hunt?' he said. 'When?'

'That's right. Oh, I don't know. About half past ten. Might be later. I simply drove over the territory to see how they were all getting on.'

'Yes, I see . . . Was there anybody in the lane?'

'Actually,' Bimbo said casually, 'I don't remember. Or do I? No, there wasn't.'

'Did you get out of the car?'

'Did I? I believe I did. Yes. I checked to make sure the last clue was still there.'

'"If you don't know what to do, think it over in the loo."'

'Quite. Was it still there this morning?' Bimbo asked sharply.

'When did you get back?'

'Here? I don't know exactly.'

'Before Lady Bantling, for instance?'

'Oh, yes. She drove old Period home. That was later. I mean, it was while I was out. I mean, we were both out, but I got home first.'

'You saw her come in?'

'I really don't remember that I actually saw her. I heard her, I think. I was looking round the ballroom to see everything was all right.'

'Any idea of the time?'

'I'm afraid I really wasn't keeping a stop-watch on our movements. It was before twelve because they were all meant to be back by midnight.'

'Yes, I see. And did you leave the house again?'

'I did not.'

'I believe there was some sort of dog-fight.'

'My God, yes! Oh, I see what you mean. I went out with the others to the terrace and dealt with it. That ghastly bitch – ' Here Bimbo made one or two extremely frank comments upon Pixie.

'She bit you, perhaps?'

'She certainly did,' Bimbo said, nursing his hand.

'Very professional bandage.'

'I had to get the doctor.'

'After the party?'

'That's right. I fixed it up myself at the time, but it came unstuck.'

'You tied it up?'

Bimbo stared at him. 'I did. I went to a bathroom, where there's a first-aid cupboard, and stuck a bandage on. Temporarily.'

'How long did this take you, do you know?'

'I don't know. How the hell should I?'

'Well – at a guess.'

'Quite a time. It kept oozing out, but in the end I fixed it. Quite a time really. I should think all of twenty minutes before I rejoined the party. Or more. Some bloody mongrel tore my trousers and I had to change.'

'Maddening for you,' Alleyn said sympathetically. 'Tell me: you are a member of the Hacienda Club?'

Bimbo went very still. Presently he said: 'I simply cannot conceive what that has to do with anything at issue.'

'It has, though,' Alleyn said cheerfully. 'I just wondered, you see, whether you'd ever run into Leonard Leiss at the Hacienda. His name's on their list.'

'I certainly have not,' Bimbo said. He moved away. Alleyn wondered if he was lying.

'I'm no longer a member and I've never seen Leiss to my knowledge,' Bimbo said, 'until yesterday. He got himself asked to our party. In my opinion he's the rock-bottom. A frightful person.'

'Right. So that settles that. Now, about the business of your step-son and the Grantham Galleries.'

He gave Bimbo time to register the surprise that this change in tactics produced. It was marked by a very slight widening of the eyes and recourse to a cigarette-case. Alleyn sometimes wondered how much the cigarette-smoking person scored over an abstainer when it came to police investigations. 'Oh, that!' Bimbo said. 'Yes, well, I must say I think it's quite a sound idea.'

'You talked it over with Bantling?'

'Yes, I did. We went into it pretty thoroughly. I'm all for it.'

'To the extent of taking shares in it yourself?'

Bimbo said airily: 'Even that. Other things being equal.'

'What other things?'

'Well – fuller inquiries and all that.'

'And the money of course?'

'Of course.'

'Have you got it?' Alleyn asked calmly.

'I must say!' Bimbo ejaculated.

'In police inquiries,' Alleyn said, 'no question is impertinent, I'm afraid.'

'And I'm afraid I disagree with you.'

'Would you mind telling me if you are still an undischarged bankrupt?'

'I mind very much, but the answer is no. The whole thing was cleared up a year ago.'

'That would be at the time of your marriage, I think?'

Bimbo turned scarlet and said not a word.

'Still,' Alleyn went on after a slight pause, 'I suppose the Grantham Gallery plan will go forward now, don't you?'

'I've no idea.'

'No reason why it shouldn't, one imagines, unless Mr Period, who's a trustee, objects.'

'In any case it doesn't arise.'

'No?'

'I mean it's got nothing to do with this ghastly business.'

'Oh, I see. Well, now,' Alleyn said briskly. 'I fancy that's about all. Except that I ought to ask you if there's anything in the wide world you can think of that could be of help to us.'

'Having no idea of the circumstances I can hardly be expected to oblige,' Bimbo said with a short laugh.

'Mr Cartell's body was found in the open drain outside Mr Period's house. He had been murdered. That,' Alleyn lied, 'is about all anyone knows.'

'How had he been murdered?'

'Hit on the head, it appears, and smothered.'

'Poor old devil,' said Bimbo. He stared absently at his cigarette. 'Look!' he said. 'Nobody likes to talk wildly about a thing like this. I mean it just won't do to put a wrong construction on what may be a perfectly insignificant detail, will it?'

'It's our job to forget insignificant details.'

'Yes, I know. Of course. All the same – '

'Mr Dodds, I really think I can promise you I won't go galloping down a false trail with blinkers over my eyes.'

Bimbo smiled. 'Okay,' he said. 'Fair enough. No doubt I'm behaving like the original Silly Suspect or something. It's just that, when it comes to the point, one doesn't exactly fancy trotting out something that may turn out to be – well – '

'Incriminating?'

'Well, exactly. Mind you, in principle, I'm for weighing in with the police. We belly-ache about them freely enough but we expect them to protect us. Of course everybody doesn't see it like that.'

'Not everybody.'

'No. And anyway with all the rot-gut that the long-haired gentry talk about understanding the thugs, it's up to the other people to show the flag.'

Disregarding a certain nausea in the region of his midriff, Alleyn said: 'Quite.'

Bimbo turned away to the window and seemed to be contemplating the landscape. Perhaps because of this, his voice had taken on a different perspective.

'Personally,' Alleyn heard him say, 'I'm in favour of capital punishment.'

Alleyn, who was one of an extremely small minority among his brother-officers, said: 'Ah, yes?'

'Anyway, that's nothing to do with the point at issue,' Bimbo said, turning back into the room. 'I don't know why I launched out like this.'

'We can forget it.'

'Yes, of course.'

'You were going to tell me – ?'

'Yes, I was. It's about this bloody fellow Leiss and his ghastly girl. They hung on to the bitter end of the party, of course. I've never seen anybody drink more or show it less, I'll say that for them. Well, the last car was leaving – except his bit of wreckage – and it was about two o'clock. I thought I'd give them the hint. I collected his revolting overcoat and went to hunt them out. I couldn't find them at first, but I finally ran them down in my study, here, where they had settled in with a bottle of my champagne. They were on the sofa with their backs to the door and didn't hear me come in. They were pretty well bogged down in an advanced necking party. He was talking. I heard the end of the sentence.' Bimbo stopped and frowned at his cigarette. 'Of course, it may not mean a damn' thing.' He looked at Alleyn who said nothing.

'Well, for what it's worth,' Bimbo went on. 'He said: "And that disposes of Mr Harold Cartell: for keeps." And she said something like: "When do you think they'll find it?" and he said: "In the morning, probably. Not windy are you? For Christ's sake, keep your head: we're in the clear."'

CHAPTER 6

Interlude

With this piece of reportage, spurious or not as the case might prove to be, it appeared that Bimbo had reached saturation point as a useful witness. He had nothing more to offer. After noticing that a good deal of unopened mail lay on the desk, including several bills and a letter from a solicitor, addressed to Benedict Arthur Dodds, Alleyn secured Bimbo's uneasy offer to sign a statement and took his leave.

'Please don't move,' Alleyn said politely, 'I can find my way out.' Before Bimbo could put himself in motion, Alleyn had gone out and shut the study door behind him.

In the hall, not altogether to his surprise, he found Desirée. She was, if anything, a little wilder in her general appearance and Alleyn wondered, if this was to be attributed to another tot of brandy. But, in all other respects she seemed to be more or less herself.

'Hallo,' she said. 'I've been waiting for you. There's a sort of *crise.'*

'What sort?'

'It may not be a *crise* at all, but I thought I'd better tell you. I really feel a bit awkward about it. I seem to have made a clanger, showing you P.P.'s funny letter. It wasn't meant for me.'

'Who was it meant for?'

'He wouldn't say. He's just rung up in a frightful taking-on, asking me to throw it on the fire and forget about it. He went on at great length, talking about his grand ancestors and I don't know what else.'

'You didn't tell him I'd seen the letter?'

Desirée looked fixedly at him. 'No,' she said. 'I didn't but I felt like a housemaid who's broken a cup. Poor P.P. What can it all be about? He is so fussed, you can't imagine.'

'Never mind,' Alleyn said, 'I dare say it's only his over-developed social sense.'

'Well, I know. All the same – ' She put her hand on his arm. 'Rory,' she said, 'if you don't awfully mind, *don't* tell him I gave you the letter. He'd think me such a *sweep.*'

At that moment Alleyn liked her very much. 'I won't tell him,' he said carefully, 'unless I have to. And, for your part, I'll be obliged if *you* don't tell him, either.'

'I'm not likely to am I? And, anyway, I don't quite see why the promises about this letter should all be on my side.'

'It may be important.'

'All right, but I can't think how. You've got it. Are you going to use it in some way?'

'Not if it's irrelevant.'

'I suppose it's no good asking you to give it back to me. No, I can see it's not.'

'It isn't, really, Desirée,' Alleyn said, using her name for the first time. 'Not till I make quite sure it's of no account. I'm sorry.'

'What a common sort of job you've got. I can't think how you do it.' She gave one of her harsh barks of laughter.

He looked at her for a moment. 'I expect that was a very clever thing to say,' he said. 'But I'm afraid it makes no difference. Goodbye. Thank you again for my lunch.'

When he was in the car he said: 'To Ribblethorpe. It's about five miles, I think. I want to go to the parish church.'

It was a pleasant drive through burgeoning lanes. There were snowdrops in the hedgerows and a general air of freshness and simplicity. Desirée's final observation stuck in his gullet.

Ribblethorpe was a tiny village. They drove past a row of cottages and a shop-post-office and came to a pleasant if not distinguished church with a big shabby parsonage beyond it.

Alleyn walked through the graveyard and very soon found a Victorian headstone to 'Frances Ann Patricia, infant daughter of Alfred Molyneux Piers Period Esquire and Lady Frances Mary Julia, his wife. She is not dead but sleepeth'. Reflecting on the ambiguity of the quotation, Alleyn moved away and had not long to search before he found carved armorial bearings exactly similar to those in Mr Period's study. These adorned the grave of Lord Percival Francis Pyke who died in 1701 and had conferred sundry and noble benefits upon this parish. The name recurred pretty regularly up and down the graveyard from Jacobean times onward. When he went into the church it was the same story. Armorial fish, brasses and tablets, all confirmed the eminence of innumerable Pykes.

Alleyn was in luck. The baptismal register was not locked away in the vestry but chained to a carved desk, hard by the font. In the chancel a lady wearing an apron and housemaid's gloves was polishing brasses. Her hat, an elderly toque, had been for greater ease, lifted up on her head, giving her a faint air of recklessness. He approached her.

'I wonder,' Alleyn said, 'if I may look in the baptismal register? I'm doing a bit of extremely amateurish research. I'll be very careful.'

'Oh, rather!' said the lady, jollily. 'Do. My husband's over at Ribblethorpe-Parva with the mothers or he'd help like a shot. I don't know if I – '

'Thank you so much but it's really quite a simple job,' Alleyn said hastily. 'Just a family thing, you know.'

'We haven't been here long: only three months, so we're not up to the antiquities.' The rector's wife, as Alleyn supposed she must be, gave a final buffet with her polisher, tossed her head at her work in a jocular manner, bobbed to the altar and made for the vestry. 'I'm Mrs Nicholls,' she said. 'My husband followed dear old Father Forsdyke. You'll find all the entries pretty erratic,' she added over her shoulder. 'Father Forsdyke was a saint but as vague as could be. Over ninety when he died, rest his soul.' She disappeared. Somehow, she reminded him of Connie Cartell.

The register was bound in vellum and bore the Royal Arms on its cover. Its pages were divided into columns headed 'When Baptized: Child's Christian Name: Parents' Names: Abode: Quality, Trade or Profession and By Whom Performed'. It had been opened in July 1874.

How old was Mr Pyke Period? Fifty-eight? Over sixty? Difficult to say. Alleyn started his search at the first entry in 1895. In that year the late Mr Forsdyke was already at the helm and although presumably not much over thirty, pretty far advanced in absence of mind. There was every sort of mistake and erasure, Mr Forsdyke madly representing himself by turns as Officiating Priest, Infant, Godmother, and in one entry as Abode. These slips were sometimes corrected by himself, sometimes by another person and sometimes not at all. In several places, the sponsors appeared under Quality, Trade or Profession, in others they were crammed in with the parents. In one respect, however, all was consistency. Where a male Pyke was in question the Quality was invariably Gentleman.

At the bottom of a particularly wild page in the year 1897, Alleyn found what he wanted. Here on the 7th of May (altered to the 5th) was baptized Frances Ann Patricia, daughter of Alfred Molyneux Piers Period and Lady Frances Mary Julia Period née Pyke, with a huddle of amended sponsors.

In another hand, crammed in under Frances Ann Patricia, a second infant had been entered: Percival Pyke. Brackets had been added, enclosing the word 'twins'.

It would seem that on the occasion of his baptism, Mr Pyke Period had fallen a victim to the rector's peculiarity and had been temporarily neglected for his twin sister who, Alleyn remembered from her headstone, had died in infancy.

He spent a long time over this additional entry, using a strong pocket lens. He would have been very glad to remove the page and give it the full laboratory treatment. As it was he could see that a fine-pointed steel nib had been used and he noted that such another nib was rusting in the pen on the desk which also carried an old-fashioned inkpot. The writing was in a copperplate style, without character and rather laborious.

Praying that Mrs Nicholls was engaged in further activities in the vestry, Alleyn slipped out to the car and took a small phial from his homicide kit. Back at the font and hearing Mrs Nicholls, who was an insecure mezzo, distantly proclaiming that she ploughed the fields and scattered, he let fall a drop from the phial on the relevant spot. The result was not as conclusive as the laboratory test would have been but he would have taken long odds that the addition had been made at a different time from the main entry. Trusting that if anybody looked at this page they would conclude that some sentimentalist had let fall a tear over the infant in question, Alleyn shut the register.

The rector's wife returned without her apron and with her hat adjusted. 'Any luck?' she asked.

'Thank you,' Alleyn said. 'Yes, I think so. I find these old registers quite fascinating. The same names recurring through the years: it gives one such a feeling of continuity: the quiet life of the country-side. You seem to have had a steady progression of Pykes.'

'One of the oldest families, *they* were,' said the rector's wife. 'Great people in their day by all accounts.'

'Have they disappeared?'

'Oh, yes. A long time ago. I think their manor house was burnt down in Victorian times and I suppose they moved away. At all events the family died out. There's a Mr Period over at Little Codling, who I believe was related, but I've been told he's the last. Rather sad.'

'Yes, indeed,' Alleyn said.

He thanked her again and said he was sorry to have bothered her.

'No bother to me,' she said. 'As a matter of fact we had someone else in, searching the register, a few weeks ago. A lawyer I think he was. Something to do with a client, I dare say.'

'Really? I wonder,' Alleyn improvised, 'if it was my cousin.' He summoned the memory of Mr Cartell, dreadfully blurred with mud. 'Elderly? Slight? Baldish, with a big nose? Rather pedantic old chap?'

'I believe he was. Yes, that exactly describes him. Fancy!'

'He's stolen a march on me,' Alleyn said. 'We're amusing our-selves hunting up the family curiosities.' He put something in the church maintenance box and took his leave. As he left the church a deafening rumpus in the lane announced the approach of an antique motor-car. It slowed down. The driver looked with great interest at Alleyn and the police car. He then accelerated and rattled off down the lane. It was Mr Copper in the Bloodbath.

II

'If there's one thing I fancy more than another, Mrs Mitchell,' said Inspector Fox laying down his knife and fork, 'it's a cut of cold lamb, potato salad and a taste of cucumber relish. If I may say so, your cucumber relish is something particular. I'm very much obliged to you. Delicious.'

'Welcome, I'm sure,' said Mrs Mitchell. 'I've got a nephew in the Force, Mr Fox, and from what he says it's the irregular meals that tells in the end. Worse than the feet even, my nephew says, and his are a treat, believe you me. Soft corns! Well! Like red-hot coals, my nephew says.'

Alfred cleared his throat. 'Occupational disabilities!' he generalized. 'They happen to the best of us, Mrs M.'

'That's right. Look at my varicose veins. I don't mean literally,' Mrs Mitchell added with a jolly laugh, in which Fox joined.

'Well, now,' he said, 'I mustn't stay here gossiping all the afternoon or I'll have the superintendent on my tracks.'

'Here we are, acting as pleasant as you please,' Mrs Mitchell observed, 'and all the while there's this wicked business hanging over our heads. You know? In a way I can't credit it.'

'Naturally enough, Mrs M.,' Alfred pointed out. 'Following as we do, the even tenor of our ways, the concept of violence is not easily assimilated. Mr Fox appreciates the point of view I feel sure.'

'Very understandable. I suppose,' Fox suggested, 'you might say the household has ticked over as comfortably as possible ever since the two gentlemen decided to join forces.'

There was a brief silence broken by Mrs Mitchell. 'In a manner of speaking, you might,' she concluded, 'although there have been – well – '

'Exterior influences,' Alfred said remotely.

'Well, exactly, Mr Belt.'

'Such as?' Fox suggested.

'Since you ask me, Mr Fox, such as the dog and the arrangement. And the connections,' Mrs Mitchell added.

'Miss Mary Ralston, for instance?'

'You took the words out of my mouth.'

'We mustn't,' Alfred intervened, 'give too strong an impression, Mrs M.'

'Well, I dare say we mustn't, but you have to face up to it. The dog is an animal of disgusting habits and that young lady's been nothing but a menace ever since the arrangement was agreed upon. You've said it yourself, Mr Belt, over and over again.'

'A bit wild, I take it,' Fox ventured.

'Blood,' Mrs Mitchell said sombrely, 'will tell. Out of an orphanage and why there, who knows?'

'As Mr Cartell himself realized,' Alfred said. 'I heard him make the observation last evening though he didn't frame it in those particular terms.'

'Last evening? Really? Cigarette, Mrs Mitchell?'

'Thank you, Mr Fox.' Alfred and Mrs Mitchell exchanged a glance. A bell rang.

'Excuse me,' Alfred said. 'The study.' He went out. Fox, gazing benignly upon Mrs Mitchell, wondered if he detected a certain easing-up in her manner.

'Mr Belt,' she said, 'is very much put about by all this. He don't show his feelings, but you can tell.'

'Very natural,' Fox said. 'So Mr Cartell didn't find himself altogether comfortable about Miss Ralston?' he hinted.

'It couldn't be expected he should take to her. A girl of that type calling him uncle, and all. As for *our* gentleman – well!'

'I can imagine,' Fox said cosily. 'Asking for trouble.' He beamed at her. 'So there were words?' he said. 'Well, bound to be, when you look at the situation but, I dare say, they didn't amount to much, the deceased gentleman being of such an easy-going nature, from all accounts.'

'I'm sure I don't know who gave you that idea, Inspector,' Mrs Mitchell said. 'I'd never have called him that, never. Real old bachelor and a lawyer into the bargain. Speak no ill, of course, but speak as you find, all the same. Take last evening. There was all this trouble over our gentleman's cigarette-case.'

Fox allowed her to tell him at great length about the cigarette-case.

' – so,' Mrs Mitchell said after some minutes, 'Mr Cartell goes over to the other house and by all accounts (though that Trudi, being a foreigner, can't make herself as clear as we would have wished) tackles Miss Moppett and as good as threatens her with the police. Hand back the case and give up her fancy-boy, or else. Accordin' to Trudi who dropped in last evening.'

Fox made clucky noises. Alfred returned to fetch his cap. 'Bloody dog's loose again,' he said angrily. 'Bit through her lead. Now, I'm told I've got to find her because of complaints in the village.'

'What will he do with her,' Mrs Mitchell wondered.

'I know what I'd do with her,' Alfred said viciously. 'I'd gas her. Well, if I don't see you again, Mr Fox – '

Fox remarked that he had no doubt that they would meet.

When Alfred had gone Mrs Mitchell said: 'Mr Belt feels strongly on the subject. I don't like to think of destroying the dog, I must say. I wonder if my sister would like her for the kiddies. Of course, with her out of the way and the other matter settled, it will seem more like old times.' She covered her mouth with her hand. 'That sounds terrible. Don't take me up wrong, Mr Fox, but we was all very comfortably situated before and therefore sorry to contemplate making a change.'

'Were you thinking of it? Giving notice?'

'Mr Belt was. Definitely. Though reluctant to do so, being he's stayed all his working life with our gentleman. However, he spoke to Mr Period on the subject and the outcome was promising.'

Mrs Mitchell enlarged upon this theme at some length. 'Which was a relief to all concerned,' she ended, 'seeing we are in other respects well situated, and the social background all that you could fancy. Tonight, for instance, there's the church social which we both attend regular and will in spite of everything. But after what passed between him and Mr Cartell over the missing article, nothing else could be expected. Mr Belt,' Mrs Mitchell added, 'is a man who doesn't forget. Not a thing of that sort. During the war,' she added obscurely, 'he was in the signalling.'

The back-door bell rang and Mrs Mitchell attended it. Fox could hear, but not distinguish, a conversation in which a male voice played the predominant part. He strolled to an advantageous position in time to hear Mrs Mitchell say: 'Fancy! I wonder why,' and to see a man in a shabby suit who said: 'Your guess is as good as mine. Well, I'll be on my way.'

Fox returned to his chair and Mrs Mitchell re-entered.

'Mr Copper from the garage,' she said. 'To inquire about the church social. He saw your superintendent coming out of Ribblethorpe church. I wonder why.'

Fox said Superintendent Alleyn was very interested in old buildings, and with the inner calm that characterized all his proceedings, took his leave and went to the Little Codling constabulary. Here he found Superintendent Williams with his wife's vacuum cleaner. 'Not the Yard job,' Williams said cheerfully, 'but it's got a baby nozzle and should do.'

They gave Leonard Leiss's dinner-suit and overcoat a very thorough going-over, extracting soil from the excavations and enough of Mr Period's Turkish cigarette tobacco to satisfy, as Fox put it, a blind juryman in a total eclipse.

They paid particular attention to Leonard's wash-leather gloves which were, as Nicola had suggested, on the dainty side.

'Soiled,' Williams pointed out, 'but he didn't lift any planks with those on his hands.' Fox wrote up his notes and in a reminiscent mood, drank several cups of strong tea with the superintendent and Sergeant Raikes who was then dispatched to return the garments to their owner.

At five o'clock Alleyn arrived in the police car and they all drove to the mortuary at Rimble. It was behind the police station and had rambling roses trained up its concrete walls. Here they found Sir James Curtis, the Home Office pathologist, far enough on with his autopsy on Harold Cartell's body to be able to confirm Alleyn's tentative diagnosis. The cranial injuries were consistent with a blow from the plank. The remaining multiple injuries were caused by the drain-pipe falling on the body and ramming it into the mud. The actual cause of death had been suffocation. Dr Elekton was about to leave and they all stood looking down at what was left of Mr Cartell. The face was now cleaned. A knowledgeable, faintly supercilious, expression lay about the mouth and brows.

In an adjoining shed, Williams had found temporary storage for the planks, the lantern and the crowbar. Here, Detective-Sergeants Thompson and Bailey were to be found, having taken further and more extensive photographs.

'I'm a bit of a camera-fiend myself and they've been using my dark-room,' said Williams. 'We're getting the workmen to bring the drain-pipe along in their crane-truck. Raikes'll come back with them and keep an eye on it, but these chaps of yours tell me they got what they wanted on the spot.'

Alleyn made the appropriate compliments which were genuine indeed. Williams was the sort of colleague that visiting superintendents yearn after and Alleyn told him so.

Bailey, a man of few words, great devotion and mulish disposition, indicated the two foot-planks which had been laid across packing cases, underside up.

'Hairs,' he said. 'Three. Consistent with deceased's.'

'Good.'

'There's another thing.' Bailey jerked his finger at a piece of microphotographic film and a print laid out under glass on an improvised bench. 'The print brings it up. Still wet, but you can make it out. Just.'

The planks were muddy where they had dug into the walls of the ditch, but at the edges and ten inches from the ends the microphotograph showed confused traces. Alleyn spent some time over them.

'Yes,' he said. 'Gloved hands. I don't mind betting. Big, heavy gloves.' He looked up at Bailey. 'It's a rough under-surface. If you can find as much leather as would go in the eye of a needle we're not home and dry but we may be in sight. Which way were they carried here?'

'Underside up,' Bailey said.

'Right. Well, you can but try.'

'I have, Mr Alleyn. Can again.'

'Do,' said Alleyn. He was going over the under-surface of the planks with his lens. 'Tweezers,' he said.

Bailey put a pair in his hand and fetched a sheet of paper.

'Have a go at these,' Alleyn said and dropped two minute specks on the paper. 'They may be damn' all but it looks as if they might have rubbed off the seam of a heavy glove. *Not* wash-leather by the way. Strong hide – and – look here.'

He had found another fragment. 'String,' he said. 'Heavy leather and string.'

'You got to have the eyes for it,' Detective-Sergeant Thompson said to nobody in particular.

During the brief silence that followed this pronouncement, the unmistakable racket of a souped-up engine made itself heard.

'That,' Mr Fox observed, 'sounds like young Mr Leiss's sports-car.'

'Stopping,' Williams observed.

'Come on, Fox,' Alleyn said. They went out to the gate. It was indeed Mr Leiss's sports-car but Mr Leiss was not at the wheel. The car screamed to a halt, leaving a trail of water from its radiator. Moppett, wearing a leather coat and jeans, leaned out of the driving window.

With allowances for her make-up which contrived to look both dirty and extreme, Alleyn would have thought she was pale. Her manner was less assured than it had been: indeed, she seemed to be in something of an emotional predicament.

'Oh, good,' she said. 'They told me you might be here. Sorry to bother you.'

'Not at all,' Alleyn said. Moppett's fingers, over-fleshed, sketchily nail-painted and stained with nicotine, moved restlessly on the driving wheel.

'It's like this,' she said. 'The local cop's just brought Lenny's things back: the overcoat and dinner-suit.'

'Yes?'

'Yes. Well, the thing is, his gloves are missing.'

Alleyn glanced at Fox.

'I beg your pardon, Miss Ralston,' Fox said, 'but I saw to the parcel myself. The gloves were returned. Cream wash-leather, size seven.'

'I don't mean those,' Moppett said. 'I mean his driving gloves. They're heavy leather ones with string backs. I ought to know. I gave them to him.'

III

'Suppose,' Alleyn suggested, 'you park your car and we get this sorted out.'

'I don't want to go in there,' Moppett said with a sidelong look at the mortuary. 'That's the dead-place, isn't it?'

'We'll use the station,' Alleyn said, and to that small yellow-wood office she was taken. The window was open. From a neighbouring garden came an insistent chatteration of bird-song and the smell of earth and violets. Fox shut a side door that led into the yard. Moppett sat down.

'Mind if I smoke?' she said.

Alleyn gave her a cigarette. She kept her hands in her pockets while he lit it. She then began to talk rapidly in a voice that was pitched above its natural level.

'I can't be long. Lennie thinks I'm dropping the car at the garage. It's sprung a leak,' she added unnecessarily, 'in the waterworks. He'd be livid if he knew I was here. He's livid, anyway, about the gloves. He swears they were in his overcoat pocket.'

Alleyn said: 'They were not there when we collected the coat. Did he have them last night, do you know?'

'He didn't wear them. He wore his other ones. He's jolly fussy about his gloves,' said Moppett. 'I tell him Freud would have had something to say about it. And now I suppose I'll get the rocket.'

'Why?'

'Well, because of yesterday afternoon. When we were at Baynesholme. We changed cars,' Moppett said without herself changing colour, 'and I collected his overcoat from the car he decided not to buy. He says the gloves were in the pocket of the coat.'

'What did you do with the coat?'

'That's just what I can't remember. We drove home to dine and change for the party and our things were still in the car. His overcoat and mine. I suppose I bunged the lot out while he went off to buy cigarettes.'

'You don't remember where you put the overcoat?'

'I should think I just dumped the lot. I usually do.'

'Mr Leiss's coat was in his wardrobe this morning.'

'That's right. Trudi put it there, I expect. She's got a letch for Lennie, that girl. Perhaps she pinched his gloves. And now I come to think of it,' Moppett said, 'I wouldn't mind betting she did.'

'Did you at any time wear the gloves yourself?'

After a longish silence Moppett said: 'That's funny. Lennie says I did. He says I pulled them on during the drive from London yesterday morning. I don't remember. I might or I might not. If I did I just don't know where I left them.'

'Did he wear his overcoat when you returned to Baynesholme for the party?'

'No,' Moppett said quickly. 'No, he didn't. It was rather warm.' She got to her feet. 'I ought to be going back,' she said. 'You don't have to tell Lennie I came, do you? He's a bit tricky about that sort of thing.'

'What sort of thing?'

'Well – you know.'

'I'm afraid I don't know.'

She watched him for a second or two: then, literally, she bared her teeth at him. It was exactly as if she had at the same time laid back her ears. 'You're lying,' she said. 'I know. You've found them and you're sticking to them. I know the sort of things you do.'

'That statement,' Alleyn said mildly, 'is utter nonsense and you will create an extremely bad impression if you persist in it. You have reported the loss of the gloves and the loss has been noted. Is there anything else you would like to discuss?'

'My God, no!' she said and walked out of the station. They heard her start up the car and go roaring off down the lane.

'Now what do we make of that little lot?' Fox asked.

'What we have to *do* is find the damn' gloves.'

'He'll have got rid of them. Or tried to. Or else she really has lost them and he's dead scared we'll pick them up. That'd be a good enough reason for him giving her the works.'

'Hold on, Br'er Fox. You're getting yourself wedded to a bit of hearsay evidence.'

'Am I?'

'We've only her word that he's giving her fits.'

'That's right,' Fox agreed in his rather heavy way. 'So we have.' He ruminated for a short time. 'Opportunity?' he said.

'They collared a bottle of their host's champagne and set themselves up in his study. He had to turf them out, I gather, at the tag-end of the party. And, by the way, he handed Leiss his overcoat, so that bit was a lie. I imagine they could have nipped off and back again without much trouble. It may interest you to learn, Br'er Fox, that when they were discovered by Bimbo Dodds, Mr Leiss was assuring his girlfriend that Mr Cartell was disposed of and she had no need to worry.'

'Good gracious.'

'Makes you fink, don't it?'

'When was this?'

'Dodds thinks it was about two a.m. He, by the way, is the B. A. Dodds who was mixed up in the Hacienda case and Leonard Leiss is a member of the Hacienda.'

'Fancy!'

'Of course he may have invented the whole story. Or mistaken the implication.'

'Two a.m. *About.* The only firm time we've got out of the whole lot,' Fox grumbled, 'is one a.m. According to everybody, the deceased always took the dog out at one. Mr Belt and Mrs Mitchell reckon he used to wait till he heard the church clock. The last car from the treasure hunt was back at Baynesholme by midnight. Yes,' Fox concluded sadly, 'it was an open field all right.'

'Did either Alfred or Mrs Mitchell hear anything?'

'Not a thing. They're both easy sleepers. Alfred,' Fox sighed, 'was thinking of turning in his job and she was thinking of following suit.'

'Why?'

'He reckons he couldn't take the new set-up. The bitch worried him. Not even clean, Mrs Mitchell says. And the deceased seems to have suggested that Alfred might have had something to do with the missing cigarette-case which, Mrs Mitchell says, Alfred took great exception to. They were both very upset because they've been there so long and didn't fancy a change at their time of life. Alfred went so far as to tell Mr Period that it was either them or Mr Cartell.'

'When did he do that, Mr Fox?'

'Last evening. Mr Period was horribly put out about it, Mrs Mitchell says. He made out life wouldn't be worth living without Alfred and her and he practically undertook to terminate Mr Cartell's tenancy. They'd never known him to be in such a taking-on. Quite frantic was the way she put it.'

'Indeed? I think he cooked the baptismal register, all right, Fox, and I think Mr Cartell rumbled it,' Alleyn said and described his visit to Ribblethorpe.

'Now, isn't that peculiar behaviour!' Fox exclaimed. 'A gentleman going to those lengths to make out he's something he is not. You'd hardly credit it.'

'You'd better, because I've a strong hunch that this case may well turn about Mr Period's obsession. And it is an obsession, Br'er Fox. He's been living in a world of fantasy and it's in danger of exploding over his head.'

'Lor'!' Fox remarked comfortably.

'When you retire in fifty years' time,' Alleyn said with an affectionate glance at his colleague, 'you must write a monograph on "Snobs you have Known". It's a fruitful field and it has yet to be exhausted. Shall I tell you what I think might be the Period story?'

'I'd be obliged,' said Fox.

'Well, then. A perfectly respectable upper-middle-class origin. A natural inclination for grandeur and a pathologically sensitive nose for class distinctions. Money, from whatever source, at an early enough age to provide the suitable setting. Employment that brings him in touch with the sort of people he wants, God save the mark, to cultivate. And all this, Br'er Fox, in, let us say, the twenties, when class distinctions were comparatively unjolted. It would be during this period – what a name he's got to be sure! – that a fantasy began to solidify. He became used to the sort of people he had admired, felt himself to be one of them, scarcely remembered his natural back-ground and began to think of himself as one of the nobs. The need for justification nagged at him. He's got this unusual name. Somebody said: "By the way, are you any relation of the Period who married one of the Ribblethorpe Pykes?" and he let it be thought he was. So he began to look into the Ribblethorpe Pykes and Periods and found that both sides have died out. It would be about now that "Pyke" was adopted as a second name – not hyphenated but always used. He may have done it by deed poll. That, of course, can be checked. And – well, there you are. I dare say that by now he'd persuaded himself he was all he claimed to be and was happily established in his own fairy-tale until Cartell, by some chance, was led to do a little private investigation and, being exasperated beyond measure, blew the gaff at yesterday's luncheon party. And if that,' Alleyn concluded, 'is not an excursion into the hateful realms of surmise and conjecture, I don't know *what* it is.'

'Silly,' Fox said, 'if true. But it makes you feel sorry for him.'

'Does it? Yes, I suppose it does.'

'Well, it does me,' Fox said uneasily. 'What's the next move, Mr Alleyn?'

'We'll have to try to find those blasted gloves.'

'Where do we start?'

'Ask yourself. We're told by the unspeakable Moppett that she wore them when they drove from London to Little Codling. They might have been dropped at Miss Cartell's, Mr Period's or Baynesholme. They might be in the pocket of the Scorpion. They might have been burnt or buried. All we know is that it's odds-on the planks were shifted, with homicidal intent, by someone who was probably wearing leather and string gloves and that Leonard Leiss, according to his fancy-girl, is raising merry hell because he's lost such a pair. So, press on, Br'er Fox. Press on.'

'Where do we begin?'

'The obvious place is Miss Cartell's. The Moppett says she dumped their overcoats there and that the gloves were in Leiss's pocket. I don't want Miss Cartell to think we're hounding her treasured ward, because if she does think that, she's perfectly capable of collaborating with Leiss or the Moppett herself or Lord knows who, out of pure protective hennery. She's a fool of a woman, Lord help her. I tell you what, Fox. You do your well-known stuff with Trudi and make it jolly careful. Then try your hand with the Period household which evidently, as far as the staff is concerned, has been nicely softened up by you.'

'They're going out this evening,' Fox said. 'Church social. They'll be in great demand, I dare say.'

'Damn! All right, we'd better let them go. And, if that fails we'll have to ask at Baynesholme. What's the matter?'

Fox was looking puffy: a sure sign in that officer, of embarrassment.

'Well, Mr Alleyn,' he said, 'I was just thinking.'

'Thinking what?'

'Well, there's one aspect of the case which of course you've considered so I'm sure there's no need to mention it. But since you ask me, there's the other young couple, Mr Bantling and Miss Maitland-Mayne.'

'I know. They were canoodling in the lane until after the last couple went back to Baynesholme and might therefore have done the job. So they might, Br'er Fox. So, indubitably they might.'

'It'll be nice to clear them up.'

'Your ideas about what would be nice vary between a watertight capital charge and cold lamb with cucumber relish. But it would be nice, I agree.'

'You may say, you see, that as far as the young man is concerned, somebody else's defending counsel, with his back to the wall, could talk about motive.'

'You may, indeed.'

'Mind, as far as the young lady's concerned, the idea's ridiculous. I think you said they met for the first time yesterday morning.'

'I did. And apparently took to each other at first sight. But, I promise you, you're right. As far as the young lady is concerned I really do believe the idea's ridiculous. As for Master Andrew

Bantling, he's a conventionally dressed chap. I can't think that his rig was topped off by a pair of string-backed hacking gloves. All right,' Alleyn said, raising a finger. 'Could he by some means have got hold of Leiss's gloves? When? At Baynesholme? There, or at Mr Period's? Very well! So he drove his newly acquired girlfriend to the lane, confided his troubles to her, put on Leiss's gloves and asked her to wait a bit while he rearranged the planks.'

'Well, there you are!' Fox exclaimed. 'Exactly. Ridiculous!' He nodded once or twice and then said: 'Where is he? Not that it matters.'

Alleyn looked at his watch.

'I should think,' he said, 'he's on the main London highway with Nicola Maitland-Mayne. God bless my soul!' he ejaculated.

'What's up, Mr Alleyn?'

'Do you know, I believe she's taking him to show one of his paintings to Troy. Tonight. She asked me if I thought Troy would mind. This was before the case had developed. I don't mind betting she sticks to it.'

In this supposition he was entirely right.

IV

'She's not a Scorpion,' Andrew remarked as he negotiated a conservative overtake, 'but she goes, bless her tiny little horse-power. It feels to me, Nicola, that we have been taking this trip together much more often than twice. Are you ever called "Nicky"?'

'Sometimes.'

'I don't really take to abbreviations, but I shall think about it. Better than "Cola" which sounds like a commercial.'

'I am never called "Cola".'

'That's right. One must draw the line somewhere, must not one?'

Conscious of an immense and illogical wave of happiness, Nicola looked at him. Why should his not singularly distinguished profile be so pleasing to her? Was it the line of the jaw about which she seemed to remember lady-novelists make a great to-do? Or his mouth, which she supposed should be called generous: it was certainly amusing.

'What's the matter?' he asked.

'Nothing. Why?'

'You were looking at me,' Andrew said, keeping a steady eye on the road.

'Sorry.'

'Not at all. Dear Nicola.'

'Don't go too fast.'

'I'm not. She won't do more than fifty. Oh, I beg your pardon. I see what you mean. All right, I won't. But my aim, as I thought I had indicated, is not an immediate, snappy little affair, with no bones broken. Far from it.'

'I see.'

'Tell me, if you don't mind, what do you think of *my people*. No holds barred. It's not an idle question.'

'I like your mamma.'

'So do I, but of course, one ought to point out her legend which I expect you're familiar with, anyway. Most of it's fairly true. She's an outrageous woman, really.'

'But kind. I set great store by kindness.'

'Well, yes. As long as she doesn't get stuck into a feud with somebody. She's generous and you can talk to her about anything. You may get a cockeyed reaction but it'll be intelligent. I dote on her.'

'Are you like her?'

'I expect so, but less eccentric in my habits. I'm of a retiring disposition, compared to her, and spend most of my spare time painting which makes me unsociable. I know I don't look like it, but I'm a serious painter.'

'Well, of course. Are you very modern? All intellect, paint droppings and rude shapes?'

'Not really. You'll have to see.'

'By the way the Cid says Troy would be delighted if we'd call. To show her your work.'

'The Cid?'

'Superintendent Alleyn, CID. Just my girlish fun.'

'I can take it if he can,' Andrew said kindly. 'But you know, I doubt really, if I dare show her anything. Suppose she should find it tedious and sterile?'

'She will certainly say so.'

'That's what I feared. She takes pupils, doesn't she? Very grand ones with genius dripping out of their beards?'

'That's right. Would you like her to take you?'

'Lord, lord!' Andrew said, 'what a notion!'

'If it's not a question in bad taste, will you be able to get the Grantham Gallery now, like you hoped?'

'I wanted to talk to you about that. I think I might, you know. I don't imagine P.P. will raise the same objections. I talked to him about it yesterday morning.'

Remembering what Mr Period had said about these plans, Nicola asked Andrew if he didn't think there would be some difficulty.

'Oh, I don't, really. He talked a lot of guff about tradition and so on but I'm sure he'll be reasonable. He's different from Hal. *He* was just being bloody-minded because I wanted to leave the Brigade and because he was bloody-minded anyway, poor old Hal. All the same, I wish I hadn't parted from him, breathing hell-fury. Seeing what's happened. He wasn't such a bad old stinker,' Andrew reflected. 'Better than Bimbo, anyway. What, by the way, did you think of Bimbo?'

'Well – '

'Come on. Honestly.'

'There wasn't anything to think. Just a rather negative, fashionable, ambiguous sort of person.'

'I simply can't imagine what persuaded my mamma to marry him. Well, I suppose I can, really.' Andrew hit his closed fist once upon the driving-wheel. 'Still, don't let's talk about that.'

He drove on for some minutes in silence while Nicola tried to sort out her desperate misgivings. 'Andrew,' she said at last and because he answered: 'What, dear?' so gently, and with such an old-fashioned air, found herself at a complete disadvantage.

'Look,' she said, 'have you thought – I know it's fantastic – but have you – ?'

'All right,' Andrew said. 'I know. Have I thought that Hal's death is a material advantage to me and that your Cid probably knows it? Yes, I have. Strangely enough, it doesn't alarm me. Nicola, it's not fair to wish all this business on you. Here I am, doing nothing but talk about me and setting myself up as an insufferable egoist, no doubt. Am I boring you very much?'

'No,' Nicola said truthfully. 'You're not doing that. You're talking about yourself which is the usual thing.'

'My God!' Andrew ejaculated. 'How very chastening.'

'This time it's a bit different.'

'Is it? How much?'

'No,' Nicola said. 'Don't let's rush our fences. We only met yesterday morning. Everything's being precipitated like one of those boring chemical experiments. Don't let's pay too much attention.'

'Just as you like,' he said huffily. 'I was going to ask if you'd dine with me. Is that too precipitate?'

'I expect it is, really, but I'd like to. Thank you, Andrew. I have a motive.'

'And what the hell is that?'

'I did mention it before. I'm going to visit Troy Alleyn this evening and I wondered if you'd come with me and show her a picture. Like I told you, the Cid says she'd be delighted.'

Andrew was silent for a moment and then burst out laughing. 'Well, I must say!' he ejaculated. 'As one of the suspects in a murder charge – yes, I am, Nicola. You can't escape it – I'm being invited to pay a social call on the chief cop's wife. How dotty can you get!'

'Well, why not?'

'Will he be there? No, I suppose not. He'll be lying flat on his stomach in Green Lane looking for my boot-prints.'

'So it's a date?'

'It's a date.'

'Then, shall we collect your pictures? I live quite close to the Alleyns. Could you make do with an omelet in my flat?'

'Do you share it with two other nice girls?'

'No.'

'Then I'd love to.'

Nicola's flat was a converted studio off the Brompton Road. It was large and airy and extremely uncluttered. The walls were white and the curtain and chairs yellow. A workmanlike desk stood against the north window and a pot of yellow tulips on the table. There was only one picture, hung above the fireplace. Andrew went straight to it.

'Gosh!' he said, 'it's a Troy. And it's you.'

'It was for my twenty-first birthday, last year. Wasn't it wonderful of her?'

There was a long silence. 'Wonderful,' Andrew said. 'Wonderful.'
And she left him to look at it while she rang Troy Alleyn and then
set to work in her kitchen.

They had cold soup, an omelet, white wine, cheese and salad and
their meal was extremely successful. They both behaved in an exemplary manner and if their inclination to depart from this standard
crackled in the air all round them, they contrived to disregard it.
They talked and talked and were happy.

'It's almost nine o'clock,' Nicola said. 'We mustn't be too late at
Troy's. She'll be delighted to see you, by the way.'

'Will she?'

'Why did you leave your pictures in the car?'

'I don't know. Well, yes, I do, but it doesn't matter. Wouldn't it be
nice to stay here?'

'Come on,' Nicola said firmly.

When they had shut the door behind them, Andrew took her
hands in his, thanked her for his entertainment and kissed her lightly
on the cheek.

'Here we go,' he said.

They collected the canvases from the car and walked to the
Alleyns' house which was at the end of a blind street near
Montpelier Square. It was such a natural and familiar thing for
Nicola to take this evening walk that her anxieties left her and by the
time they reached their destination and Troy herself opened the door
to them, she felt nothing but pleasure in their expedition.

Troy was wearing the black trousers and smock that meant she
had been working. Her shortish dark hair capped a spare head and
fell in a single lock across her forehead. Andrew stood to attention
and carried his canvases as if they were something rather disgraceful
that had been found in the guardroom.

'I'm in the studio,' Troy said. 'Shall we go there, it's a better light.'

Andrew fell himself in and followed them.

There was a large charcoal drawing on the easel in Troy's studio.
A woman with a cat. On the table where Troy had been working
were other drawings under a strong lamp.

Andrew said: 'Mrs Alleyn, it's terribly kind of you to let me come.'

'Why?' Troy said cheerfully. 'You're going to show me some
work, aren't you?'

'Oh, God!' Andrew said. 'So Nicola tells me.'

Troy looked at him in a friendly manner and began to talk about the subject of the drawing, saying how paintable and silly she was, always changing her hair and coming in the wrong clothes, and that the drawing was a study for a full-scale portrait. Andrew eased up a little.

Nicola said: 'There are one or two things to explain.'

'Not as many as you may think. Rory rang up an hour ago from Little Codling.'

'Did he tell you about Andrew's step-father?'

'Yes, he did. I expect,' Troy said to Andrew, 'it seems unreal as well as dreadful, doesn't it?'

'In a way it does. We – I didn't see much of him. I mean – '

'Andrew,' Nicola said, 'insists that the Cid has got him down among the suspects.'

'Well, it's not for me to say,' Troy replied, 'but I didn't think it sounded like that. Let's have a look at your things.'

She took her drawing off the easel and put it against the wall. Andrew dropped all his paintings on the floor with a sudden crash. 'I'm frightfully sorry,' he said.

'Come on,' Troy said. 'I'm not a dentist. Put it on the easel.'

The first painting was a still-life: tulips on a window-sill in a red goblet with roof-tops beyond them.

'Hal-lo!' Troy said and sat down in front of it.

Nicola wished she knew a great deal more about painting. She could see it was incisive, freely done and lively, with a feeling for light and colour. She realized that she would have liked it very much if she had come across it somewhere else. It didn't look at all amateurish.

'Yes, well of course,' Troy said and it was clear that she meant: 'Of course you're a painter and you were right to show me this.' She went on talking to Andrew asking him about his palette and the conditions under which he worked. Then she saw his next canvas which was a portrait. Desirée's flaming hair and cadaverous eyes leapt out of a flowery background. She had sat in a glare of sunlight and the treatment was far from being conventional.

'My mum,' Andrew said.

'You had fun with the colour, didn't you? Don't you find the eye-round-the-corner hell to manage in a three-quarter head? This one hasn't quite come off, has it? Look, it's that dab of pink that hits up. Now, let's see the next one.'

The next and last one was a male torso uncompromisingly set against a white wall. It had been painted with exhaustive attention to anatomy. 'Heavens!' Troy ejaculated, 'you've practically skinned the man.' She looked at it for some time and then said: 'Well, what are you going to do about this? Would you like to work here once a week?'

After that Andrew was able to talk to her and did so with such evident delight that Nicola actually detected in herself a twinge of something that astonished her and gave an edge to her extreme happiness.

It was not until much later, when Troy had produced lager, and they were telling her about the Grantham Gallery project, that Nicola remembered Mr Period.

'I think,' she told Troy, 'you're going to be approached by my new boss. He's writing a book on etiquette and his publishers want a drawing of him. He's rather shy about asking because you turned down one of his lordly chums. You know him, don't you? Mr Pyke Period?'

'Yes, of course I do. He crops up at all the private views that he thinks are smart occasions. I'll be blowed if I'll draw him.'

'I was afraid that might be your reaction.'

'Well,' Troy said, 'there's no denying he really is a complete old phoney. Do you know he once commissioned a pupil of mine to do a painting from some print he'd picked up, of a Georgian guardee making faces at a thunderstorm. He said it was one of his ancestors and so it may have been, but after a lot of beating about the bush he made it quite clear that he wanted this job faked to look like an eighteenth-century portrait. My pupil was practically on the breadline at the time and I'm afraid the thing was done.'

'Oh, dear!' Nicola sighed. 'I know. It's there, in the library, I think. He's like that but he's rather an old sweetie-pie, all the same. Isn't he, Andrew?'

'Nicola,' said Andrew, 'I dare say he is. But he's a terrible old donkey. And yet – I don't know. Is P.P. just plain silly? I doubt it. I rather think there's an element of low cunning.'

'Childish, not low,' Nicola insisted, but Andrew was looking at her with such a degree of affectionate attention that she was extremely flustered.

'Well,' Andrew said. 'Never mind, anyway, about P.P.'

'I can't help it. He was so miserable all the afternoon. You know: trying to forge ahead with his tips on U-necessities, as he inevitably calls them, and then falling into wretched little trances. He really was in a bad state. Everything seemed to upset him.'

'What sorts of things?' Troy asked. 'Have some more lager?'

'No, thank you. Well, he kept singing in an extremely dismal manner. And then he would stop and turn sheet white. He muttered something about: "No, no, I mustn't. Better forget it," and looked absolutely terrified.'

'How very odd,' Andrew said. 'What was his song?'

'I don't remember – yes, I do!' Nicola ejaculated. 'Of course, I do! Because he'd done the same sort of thing yesterday, after lunch: hummed it and then been cross with himself. But it was different today. He seemed quite shattered.'

'And the song?'

'It was the pop-song that ghastly Leonard kept whistling through his teeth at luncheon. He even sang a bit of it when they were look-ing at the cigarette-case: 'If you mean what I think you mean: it's okay by me. Things aren't always what they seem. It's okay by me."

'Not exactly a "Period Piece".'

'It was all very rum.'

'Did you happen to mention it to Rory?' Troy asked.

'No. I haven't seen him since it happened. And anyway, why should I?'

'No reason at all, I dare say.'

'Look,' Nicola said quickly, 'however foolish he may be, Mr Period is quite incapable of the smallest degree of hanky-panky – ' She stopped short and the now familiar jolt of indefinable panic revisited her. 'Serious hanky-panky, I mean,' she amended.

'Good lord, no!' Andrew said. 'Of course he is. Incapable, I mean.'

Nicola stood up. 'It's a quarter to twelve,' she said. 'We must go, Andrew. Poor Troy!'

The telephone rang and Troy answered it. The voice at the other end said quite distinctly: 'Darling?'

'Hallo,' Troy said. 'Still at it?'

'Very much so. Is Nicola with you?'

'Yes,' Troy said. 'She and Andrew Bantling.'

'Could I have a word with her?'

'Here you are.'

Troy held out the receiver and Nicola took it feeling her heart thud stupidly against her ribs.

'Hallo, Cid,' she said.

'Hallo, Nicola. There's something that's cropped up here that you might just possibly be able to give me a line about. After I left you today, did you discuss our conversation with anybody?'

'Well, yes,' she said. 'With Andrew.'

'Anyone else? Now don't go jumping to conclusions, there's a good child, but did Mr Period want to know if you told me anything about his luncheon party?'

Nicola swallowed. 'Yes, he did. But it was only, poor lamb, because he hates the idea of your hearing about the digs Mr Cartell made at his snob-values. He was terribly keen to know if I'd told you anything about the baptismal register story.'

'And you said you had told me?'

'Well, I had to when he asked me point-blank. I made as little of it as I could.'

'Yes. I see. One other thing and it's important, Nicola. Do you, by any chance, know anything that would connect Mr Period with a popular song?'

'A song! Not – not – '

'Something about "Okay by me".'

CHAPTER 7

Pixie

It had been five past eleven when Alleyn was summoned to the telephone. He and Fox having struck a blank in respect of the gloves, had been mulling over their notes in the Codling pub, when the landlord, avid with curiosity, summoned him.

'It's a call for you, sir,' he said. 'Local. I didn't catch the name. There's no one in the bar parlour, if that suits you.'

Alleyn took the call in the bar parlour.

He said: 'Alleyn here. Hallo?'

Mr Pyke Period, unmistakable and agitated, answered. 'Alleyn? Thank God! I'm so sorry to disturb you at this unconscionable hour. Do forgive me. The thing is there's something I feel I ought to tell – '

The voice stopped. Alleyn heard a bump, followed by a soft, heavier noise and then by silence. He waited for a moment or two. There was a faint definite click and, again silence. He rang and got the engaged signal. He hung up and turned to find Fox at his side.

'Come on,' he said. 'I'll tell you on the way.'

When they were clear of the pub he broke into a run with Fox, heavy and capable, on his heels.

'Period,' Alleyn said, 'and it looks damn' fishy. Stopped dead in full cry. Characteristic noises.'

The pub was in a side street that led into the green at Mr Period's end of it. There was nobody about and their footsteps sounded loud on the paving-stones. Connie Cartell's Pekinese was yapping somewhere on the far side of the green. Distantly, from the parish schoolroom, came the sound of communal singing.

Only one room in Mr Period's house was lit and that was the library. Stepping as quietly as the gravelled drive would permit, they moved towards the French windows. Bay trees stood on either side of the glass doors which were almost but not quite shut.

Alleyn looked across the table Nicola had used, past her shrouded typewriter and stacked papers. Beyond, to his right, and against the window in the side wall, was Mr Period's desk. His shaded lamp, as if it had been switched on by a stage-manager, cast down a pool of light on that restricted area, giving it an immense theatricality. The telephone receiver dangled from the desk and Mr Period's right arm hung beside it. His body was tipped forward in his chair and his face lay among his papers. The hair was ruffled like a baby's and from his temple a ribbon of blood had run down the cheekbone to the nostril.

'Doctor,' Alleyn said. 'What's-his-name. Elekton.'

Fox said: 'Better use the other phone.' He replaced the receiver very gingerly and went into the hall.

Mr Period was not dead. When Alleyn bent over him, he could hear his breathing – a faint snoring sound. The pulse was barely perceptible.

Fox came back. 'On his way,' he said. 'Will I search outside?'

'Right. We'd better not move him. I'll do the house.'

It was perfectly quiet and empty of living persons. Alleyn went from room to room, opening and shutting doors, receiving the indefinable smells of long-inhabited places, listening, looking and finding nothing. Mrs Mitchell's room smelt stuffily of hairpins and Alfred Belt's of boot polish. Mr Period's bedroom smelt of hair lotion and floor polish and Mr Cartell's of blankets and soap. Nothing was out of place anywhere in Mr Period's house. Alleyn returned to the library as Fox came in.

'Nothing,' Fox said. 'Nobody, anywhere.'

'There's the instrument,' Alleyn said.

It was the bronze paper-weight in the form of a fish that Desirée had given Mr Period. It lay on the carpet close to his dangling hand.

'I'll get our chaps,' Fox said. 'They're in the pub. Here's the doctor.'

Dr Elekton came in looking as if his professional manner had been fully extended.

'What now, for God's sake?' he said and went straight to his patient. Alleyn watched him make his examination which did not take long.

'All right,' he said. 'On the face of it he's severely concussed. I don't think there's any extensive cranial injury but we'll have to wait. Half an inch either way and it'd have been a different matter. We'd better get him out of this. Where's this man of his. Alfred?'

'At a church social,' said Alleyn. 'We could get a mattress. Or what about the sofa in the drawing-room?'

'All right. Better than manhandling him all over the shop.'

Fox and Alleyn carried Mr Period into the drawing-room and propped him up on the sofa, Dr Elekton supporting his head.

'Will he speak?' Alleyn asked Dr Elekton.

'Might or might not. Your guess is as good as mine. There's nothing we can do at the moment. He may have to go to hospital. I'd better get a nurse. What's the story, if there is a story?'

'Somebody chucked a bronze paper-weight at him. You'd better look at it. Don't touch it unless you have to. Fox will show you. I'm staying here. I'll let you know if there's a change.'

'Attempted murder?' Dr Elekton said, making a mouthful of it.

'I think so.'

'For God's sake!' Dr Elekton repeated. He and Fox went out of the room. Alleyn drew up a chair and watched Mr Period.

His eyes were not quite closed and his breathing, though still markedly stertorous, seemed to be more regular. Alleyn heard Dr Elekton at the telephone.

The door-bell rang. The other chaps, he thought. Fox would cope.

Mr Period's eyes opened and looked, squintingly at nothing.

'You're all right,' Alleyn said, leaning towards him.

Dr Elekton came back. 'It's the paper-weight sure enough,' he said. 'Trace of blood on the edge.' He went to the sofa and took Mr Period's hand in his.

'Don't worry,' he said. 'You're all right.'

The flaccid lips parted. After an indeterminate noise a whisper drifted through them: *'It was that song.'*

'Song? What song?'

'He's deeply concussed, Alleyn.'

'What song?'

'Should have told Alleyn. Whistling. Such awfully bad form. Luncheon.'

'What song?'

'*Couldn't – out of my head,*' Mr Period whispered plaintively. '*So silly. "Okay by me". So, of course. Recognized. At once.*' The sound faded and for a moment or two the lips remained parted. Then Mr Period's voice uncannily articulate said quite clearly: '*May I speak to Superintendent Alleyn?*'

'Yes,' Alleyn said, holding up a warning hand. 'Alleyn speaking.'

'*Just to tell you. Whistling. Recognized it. Last night. In the lane. Very wrong of me not to – Divided loyalties*' There was a longish silence. Alleyn and Elekton stared absently at each other. '*"Okay by me",*' the voice sighed. '*So vulgar.*'

The eyes closed again.

'This may go on for hours, Alleyn.'

'How much will he remember, when he comes round?'

'Everything probably, up to the moment he was knocked out. Unless there's a serious injury to the brain.' Dr Elekton was stooping over his patient. 'Still bleeding a bit. I'll have to put in a couple of stitches. Where's my bag?' He went out. Fox was talking to the men in the hall. 'We'll seal the library and cover the area outside the window.'

'Do we search?' asked somebody. Williams, Alleyn decided.

'Better talk to the chief.'

Fox and Williams came in with Dr Elekton who opened his professional bag.

'Just steady his head, will you?' he asked Alleyn.

Holding Mr Period's head between his hands, Alleyn said to Fox and Williams: 'It looks as if the thing was thrown at him by somebody standing between the table and the French windows while he was ringing me up. I heard the receiver knock against the desk as it fell and I heard a click that might well have been made by the windows being pulled to. You're not likely to find anything on the drive. It's as dry as a bone and in any case the French doors are probably used continually. Whoever made the attack, had time to effect a clean getaway before we came trundling in, but I think the best line we can take is to keep watch in case he's still hiding in the garden – Raikes and Thompson can do that – and Fox, you rouse up Miss Cartell's household. Somebody will have to stay here in case he speaks again. Bob, would you do that?'

'Right,' said Superintendent Williams.

'I've got a call to London.'

To London?' Williams ejaculated.

'It may give us a line. Fox, I'll join you at Miss Cartell's. Okay?'

'Okay, Mr Alleyn.'

'And Bailey had better have a go at the paper-weight. I think it was probably on the table near the French windows. There are various piles of stacked papers, all but one weighed down. And one of the ashtrays has got two lipsticked butts in it. Miss Ralston and Leiss smoke Mainsails, Lady Bantling smokes Cafards and Mr Period, Turkish. Ask him to look. Gloves!' Alleyn ejaculated. 'If we could find those damn' gloves. Not that they are likely to have anything to do with this party but we've a glove-conscious homicide on our hands, I fancy. All right . . . Let's get cracking.'

And it was at this juncture – at a quarter to midnight – that he talked on the telephone to Nicola Maitland-Mayne.

Then he rejoined Elekton in the drawing-room.

'Has he said anything else?'

'No.'

'Look here, Elekton, can you stick it here with Williams for a bit? We're fully extended, we can't risk the chance of missing anything he may say and Williams will be glad of a witness. Somebody will relieve you as soon as possible.'

'Yes, of course.'

'Write it down, Bob, if he does speak. I'm much obliged to you both.'

He was about to go when a sound, fainter than anything they had heard, came from the sofa. It wavered tenuously for a second or two and petered out. Mr Period, from whatever region he at present inhabited, had been singing.

II

As Alleyn was about to leave the house, Detective-Sergeant Bailey presented himself.

'There's a small thing,' he said.

'What small thing?'

'There's nothing for us on the gravel outside the French windows, Mr Alleyn, but I reckon there's something on the carpet.'

'What?'

'Traces of ash. Scuffed into the carpet, I reckon, by one of those pin-point heels.'

'Good man,' Alleyn said. 'Carry on.' He let himself out and walked down the drive.

It was a dark night, overcast and rather sultry. As he approached the gates he became aware of a very slight movement in a patch of extremely black shadows cast by a group of trees. He stopped dead. Was it Thompson or Raikes, on to something and keeping doggo or was it – ? He listened again and there was a rustle and the sound of heavy breathing. At this moment a spot of torchlight danced about the drive and Sergeant Raikes himself appeared from the opposite direction, having apparently crossed the lawn and emerged through Mr Period's shrubs. He shone his light in Alleyn's face and said: 'Oh, beg pardon, sir. There's nothing to be seen, sir, anywhere. Except dog prints. Two kinds.'

Alleyn gestured silently towards the shadows. 'Eh?' said Raikes. 'What?' And then comprehensively: 'Cor!'

There being no point after this in attempting any further conceal-ment Alleyn said: 'Look out, you ass,' and switched on his own torchlight, aiming it at the shadows.

'On your toes now,' he said and advanced, Raikes with him.

He walked past a lowish thicket of evergreens, pointed his light into the depths beyond and illuminated Alfred Belt with Mrs Mitchell, transfixed in his arms.

'I'm sure I beg your pardon, sir,' said Alfred.

Mrs Mitchell said: 'Oh, dear; what a coincidence! What will the gentlemen be thinking,' and tittered.

'What we'll be thinking,' Alleyn said, 'depends to a certain extent on what you'll be saying. Come out.'

Alfred looked at his arms as if they didn't belong to him, released Mrs Mitchell and advanced to the drive. 'I should have thought, sir,' he said with restraint, 'that the circumstance was self-explanatory.'

'We didn't return by the side gate,' Mrs Mitchell offered, 'on account of my not fancying it after what has taken place.'

'A very natural feminine reaction, sir, if I may say so.'

'We were returning,' said Mrs Mitchell, 'from the church social.'

'Mrs Mitchell has been presented with the long-service Girls' Friendly Award. Richly deserved. I was offering my congratulations.'

'Jolly good,' Alleyn said. 'May I offer mine?'

'Thank you very much, I'm sure. It's a teapot,' Mrs Mitchell said, exhibiting her trophy.

'And of course, a testimonial,' Alfred amended.

'Splendid. And you have spent the evening together?'

'Not to say together, sir. Mrs Mitchell as befitted the occasion, occupied the rostrum. I am merely her escort,' said Alfred.

'The whole thing,' Alleyn confessed, 'fits together like a jigsaw puzzle. What are you going to do next?'

'Next, sir?'

'Next.'

'Well, sir. As it's something of an event, I hope to persuade Mrs Mitchell to join me in a nightcap after which we will retire,' Alfred said with some emphasis, 'to our respective accommodations.'

'Dog permitting,' Mrs Mitchell said abruptly.

'Dog?'

'Pixie, sir. She is still at large. There may be disturbances.'

'Alfred,' Alleyn said, 'when did you leave Mr Period?'

'Leave him, sir?'

'Tonight?'

'After I had served coffee, sir, which was at eight thirty.'

'Do you know if he was expecting a telephone call?'

'Not that I was aware,' Alfred said. 'He didn't mention it. Is anything the matter, sir, with Mr Period?'

'Yes,' Alleyn said, 'there is. He has been the victim of a murderous assault and is severely concussed.'

'Oh, my Gawd!' Mrs Mitchell ejaculated and clapped a hand over her mouth.

'My gentleman? Where is he? Here,' Alfred said loudly, 'let me go in!'

'By all means. You will find Doctor Elekton there and Superintendent Williams. Report to them, will you?'

'Certainly, sir,' said Alfred.

'One other thing. When did you empty the ash-trays in the library?'

'After dinner, sir . . . As usual.'

'Splendid. Thank you.'

'Thank you, sir,' Alfred said automatically.

Alleyn saw them go in and himself crossed the green to Miss Cartell's house. A belated couple closely entwined, was making its way home, presumably from the social. Otherwise all was quiet.

He found Fox in Miss Cartell's drawing-room with the household rounded up before him. On these occasions Fox always reminded Alleyn of a dependable sheep-dog.

Connie herself was lashed into a dull purple robe, beneath the hem of which appeared the decent evidence of a sensible nightgown and a pair of extremely grubby slippers. Leonard Leiss was in trousers and shirt and Moppett in the negligée she had worn that morning. She was made up. Her pale lipstick had been smudged and her hair was dishevelled. She looked both sulky and frightened. Trudi, in a casque of hair curlers, but still fully dressed, seemed to be transfixed by astonishment.

Connie said: 'Look here, this is all pretty ghastly, isn't it? How is he?'

'He's not conscious.'

'Yes, but I mean, how *bad* is it?'

Alleyn said they were not sure how bad it was.

'Well, but what happened?' Connie persisted, looking resentfully at Mr Fox. 'We don't know anything. Turfing everybody out of bed and asking all these questions.'

'Oh, do pipe down, Auntie,' Moppett ejaculated with some violence. 'It's perfectly obvious what it's all about.'

'It's not obvious to me.'

'Fancy!' Leonard remarked offensively.

Fox said with forbearance: 'Well, now, Mr Alleyn, we're getting on slowly. I've tried to explain the necessity, as a purely routine affair, for checking up these good people's whereabouts.'

'Certainly.'

'Yes. Well, it seems Miss Cartell has been at home this evening, apart from an interval when she took her little dog into the garden – '

'That's right,' Connie interrupted indignantly. 'And if it wasn't for that damned bitch, I'd have been in my bed an hour ago. And where's my Li? That's what I want to know. He's a valuable dog and if anything's happened to him, chasing after that mongrel, I'll hold you responsible.' She wrung her hands distractedly.

'The little dog,' Fox explained, 'has gone off for a romp.'

Moppett laughed shrilly.

'What happened exactly?'

'I'll tell you what happened,' Connie shouted. 'I was going to bed and he asked for outies. He'd already had them once, so I might have known, but he kept on asking. So I took him down. No sooner were we in the garden than I saw that brute and so did he. She went floundering off and he was out of my arms and after her before I could stop him. I'm a bit clumsy because of my thumb. Otherwise,' she added proudly, 'he wouldn't have made it.'

'Miss Cartell,' Fox explained, 'was in the garden calling the little dog when I arrived.'

'There'll have to be an organized search,' Connie blustered. 'That's all. An organized search. I'm jolly sorry about P.P. but I can't help it.'

'How long ago did this happen?'

'Did what happen?'

'The Pekinese business.'

'How the hell should I know!' Connie said rudely. 'I seem to have been out there for hours. All over the village in this kit. Look at my feet! Nobody about, luckily. Not that I care. God knows where he's got to.'

'What time did you go to bed?'

'I haven't been to bed.'

'Well, when did you get ready to go to bed?'

'I don't know. Yes, I do. About nine o'clock.'

'Early!' Alleyn remarked.

'I wanted to watch the telly. I like to be comfortable,' said Connie.

'And did you watch your telly?'

'Started to, but it was a lot of guff about delinquent teenagers. I went to sleep. Li woke me. That's when he asked for outies.'

'Well,' Alleyn said, 'we progress.'

'If you've finished with me – '

'I'll have to ask you to wait a minute or two longer.'

'My God!' Connie said and threw up her hands.

Alleyn turned to Moppett and Leonard.

'And neither of you, I gather, joined in the search.'

Leonard stretched himself elaborately. 'Afraid not,' he said. 'I understood it to be a routine party.'

'I shouted up to you,' Connie pointed out resentfully.

'So sorry,' Moppett said. 'I was in my bath.'

'You haven't washed your face,' Alleyn observed.

'I don't clean my face in my bath.'

'But you bathed?'

'Yes.'

'When? For how long?'

'I don't know when and I like to take my time.'

'Fox?' Alleyn said. 'Will you look in the bathroom?' Fox made for the door.

'All right,' Moppett said breathlessly. 'I didn't have a bath. I was going to and I heard all the rumpus and auntie shrieking for Li and I went to Lennie's room and said ought we to do anything and we got talking and then your friend Mr Fox came and hauled us down here.'

'And earlier? Before you thought of taking a bath?'

'We were talking.'

'Where?'

'In my room.'

Connie looked at her with a sort of despair. 'Really, you two,' she said like an automaton. 'What Mr Alleyn will think!' She looked anxiously at him. 'I can vouch for them,' she said. 'They were both in. All the evening. I'd swear it.'

'You were asleep with the television on, Miss Cartell.'

'I'd have known if anyone went out. I always do. It was only a cat-nap. They always bang the door. Anyway I heard them talking and laughing upstairs.'

'Can you help us, Trudi?' Alleyn asked.

'I do not know what is all happen,' said Trudi. 'I am at the priest's hall where is a party. I sing. *Schuhplatter* dancing also I do.'

'That'd send them,' said Leonard and laughed.

'I return at half past eleven o'clock and I make my hair.'

'Did you help in the search?'

'Please?'

'Did you help look for the little dog?'

'Ach! Yes. I hear the screech of Miss Cartell who is saying "Come Li, come Li," and I go.'

'There you are!' Connie cried out with a sort of gloomy triumph about nothing in particular.

Leonard murmured: 'You're wasting your time, chum.'

Alleyn said: 'I should like to know if there were any personal telephone calls during the day, Miss Cartell. Apart from routine domestic ones.'

Connie stared at him distractedly. 'I don't know,' she said. 'No. I don't think so. No. Not for me.'

'For anyone else? Outgoing or incoming calls? Mr Leiss?'

'I had a call to London,' Leonard said. 'I had to put off an urgent business engagement. Thanks to your keeping me here.'

'It was a jolly long call,' Connie said, obviously with thoughts of the bill.

'Who was it made to, if you please?'

'Fellow at my club,' Leonard said grandly.

'The Hacienda?'

Leonard darted a venomous glance at him, leant back in his chair and looked at the ceiling.

'And that was the only call?' Alleyn continued.

'Far as I know,' said Connie.

'Any messages?'

'Messages?'

'Notes? Word of mouth?'

'Not that I know,' Connie said wearily.

'Please?' Trudi asked. 'Message? Yes?'

'I was asking if anyone brought a letter, a written note, or a message.'

'No, they didn't,' Moppett loudly interrupted.

'But, yes, miss. For you. By Mr Belt.'

'All right. *All* right,' Leonard drawled. 'She can't remember every damn' thing. It didn't amount to a row of beans – '

'One moment,' Alleyn said, raising a finger. Leonard subsided. 'So Belt brought you a message from Mr Period. When, Miss Ralston?'

'I don't know.'

'After tea,' Trudi said.

'What was the message?'

'I didn't pay much attention. I don't remember,' said Moppett.

'You don't have to talk,' Leonard said. 'Shut up.' He began to whistle under his breath. Moppett nudged his foot and he stopped abruptly.

'What,' Alleyn asked, 'is that tune? Is it "Okay by me"?'

'No idea, I'm afraid,' Leonard said. Moppett looked deadly sick.

'Have you had the leak in the radiator mended?'

Moppett made a strange little noise in her throat.

'Miss Ralston,' Alleyn said, 'did you whistle late last night when you were near Mr Period's garden gate?'

There was a kind of stoppage in the room as if a film had been halted at a specific point. Moppett said: 'You must be dotty. What do you mean – in the lane?'

'Like I told you. You don't have to say one single thing. Just keep your little trap shut, Baby,' said Leonard.

'Moppett!' Connie cried out. 'Don't. Don't say anything, darling.'

Moppett hurled herself at her guardian and clawed her like a terrified kitten. 'Auntie Con!' she sobbed. 'Don't let him! Auntie Con! I'm sorry. I don't know anything. I haven't done anything. Auntie Con!'

Connie enfolded her with a gesture that for all its clumsiness had something classic about it. She turned her head and looked at Alleyn with desperation. 'My ward,' she said, 'hasn't anything to tell you. Don't frighten her.'

The front-door bell sounded loudly.

'I answer?' Trudi asked composedly.

'If you please,' Alleyn said.

Leonard got up and walked away. Connie's large, uncomely hand, patted Moppett as if she was a dog. Voices sounded in the hall and an exclamation from Trudi.

'My God!' Connie exclaimed, 'what now!'

'Don't let them come,' Moppett said. 'Who is it? Don't let them come.'

Connie put her aside. After a venomous and terrified look at Alleyn, Moppett joined Leonard at the far end of the room, noisily blowing her nose.

A strangulated yapping broke out and an unmistakable voice said: 'Shut up, you little ass,' and then, apparently to Trudi: 'Well, just for a moment.'

Desirée Bantling came in, followed by her husband. She was dressed in green and mink and carried the dishevelled and panting Pekinese. 'Hallo, Connie,' she said. 'Look what we've found!'

Connie made a plunge at her and gathered the dog into her arms in much the same way as she had taken Moppett.

'Hallo, Rory,' said Desirée, 'still at it? Good evening,' she added in the direction of Fox, Moppett and Leonard.

Bimbo said: 'We picked him up out there having a high old time with the boxer bitch.'

'She took another bite at poor Bimbo,' Desirée said. 'Same hand
and all. It's becoming quite a thing with her. Show them, darling.'

Bimbo, who had his left hand in his overcoat pocket said: 'Do
shut up about it, darling.'

'He's rather touchy on the subject,' Desirée explained. 'I can't
think why.'

'You bad boy,' Connie said. The Pekinese licked her face excitedly.

'So, knowing you'd be in a fever we roped him in. I fear she's
seduced him, Connie,' said Desirée.

'Is nature,' Trudi observed. She was standing inside the door.

'And there,' Desirée remarked with a grin, 'you have the matter
in a nutshell.' She gave a comprehensive glance round the room.
'We're not staying,' she said, 'having had a pretty lethal evening . . .
Sorry to interrupt. Come along, darling.'

Alleyn said: 'Just a minute, if you don't mind.'

She looked at him in her leisurely, unconcerned way. 'What,
again?' she remarked and sat down.

'Where exactly did you find the dog?'

With Pixie, it appeared, on the green. It had taken Desirée and
Bimbo some time to catch Li and they must have looked, she said,
pretty silly, if there'd been anyone to see them. She fitted a cigarette
into a holder. Her beautiful gloves were dirty.

'Where had you come from?'

'My dears, we'd been dining near Bornlee Green. A dim general
and his wife and pretty heavy weather, by and large, we made of it.'

'Rather late for a dinner party.'

'With bridge afterwards, darling.'

'I see. Tell me,' Alleyn said, 'have you seen or heard anything of
Pyke Period since I left Baynesholme this afternoon?'

'No,' said Bimbo at once. 'Why?'

Alleyn turned to Desirée who raised her eyebrows at him. 'And
you?' he asked her.

'I ran in for a moment on our way to Bornlee Green. There was
something I wanted to tell him. Bimbo waited in the car.'

'Was it something about the letter we discussed just before I left
Baynesholme?'

'Actually, yes.' She gave him a half smile. 'Sorry,' she said. 'I
changed my mind. I told him.'

'I don't know what anybody's talking about,' Connie grumbled. She looked anxiously at Moppett, who had got herself under control and, with Leonard, stayed at the far end of the room, avidly listening. 'You're not alone in that, Auntie,' said Moppett.

Bimbo said, loudly: 'Look here, I don't know if anybody agrees with me but I'm getting very bored with the turn this affair is taking. We're being asked all sorts of personal questions without the smallest reason being given and I don't feel inclined to take much more of it.'

'Hear, hear,' said Leonard. Bimbo glanced at him with profound distaste.

'I fear, my darling,' Desirée said, 'you will have to lump it. Our finer feelings are not of much account, I fancy.'

'All the same, I want to know. What's this about P.P.? Why the hell shouldn't you call in to see him! We might be living in a police state,' he blustered, looking sideways at Alleyn.

'Mr Dodds,' Alleyn said, 'any visit to Mr Period during the last few hours is perfectly relevant since, at about eleven o'clock this evening, somebody attempted to murder him.'

There are not so very many ways in which people react to news of this sort. They may cry out in what appears to be astonishment, they may turn red or white and look ambiguous, or they may simply sit and gape. Bimbo and Desirée followed this last pattern.

After a moment Desirée exclaimed: 'P.P.? Not true!' and, at the same time, Bimbo said: 'Not possible!'

'On the contrary,' said Alleyn, 'possible and unfortunately true.'

'Attempted to *murder* him,' Bimbo echoed. 'How? Why?'

'With a brass paper-weight. Possibly,' Alleyn said, turning to Desirée, 'because you told him that I'd got the letter he sent by mistake to you.'

III

Looking at Desirée, Alleyn thought: 'But I won't get any change out of you, my girl. If I've given you a jolt you're not going to let anyone know it.'

'That seems very far-fetched,' she said composedly.

'Here!' Connie intervened. 'Did you get a funny letter too, Desirée. Here – what is all this?'

'I'm afraid I don't believe you,' Desirée said to Alleyn.

'You've no right to make an accusation of that sort,' Bimbo cried out. 'Making out people are responsible for murderous attacks and not giving the smallest explanation. What evidence have you got – ?'

'Since the damage has been done,' Alleyn said, 'I'm prepared to put a certain amount of the evidence before you.'

'Damn' big of you, I must say! Though why it should concern Desirée – '

Alleyn said: 'Directly or indirectly you are all concerned.' He waited for a moment. Nobody said anything and he went on.

'It's too much to expect that each one of you will answer any questions fully or even truthfully, but it's my duty to ask you to do so.'

'Why shouldn't we?' Connie protested. 'I don't see why you've got to say a thing like that. Boysie always said that in murder trials the guilty have nothing to fear. He always said that. I mean the innocent,' she added distractedly. 'You know what I mean.'

'How right he was. Very well, shall we start with that premise in mind? Now. Yesterday at luncheon, Mr Cartell told a story about a man who cooked a baptismal register in order to establish blood-relationship with a certain family. Those of you who were there may have thought that Mr Period seemed to be very much put out by this anecdote. Would you agree?'

Connie said bluntly: 'I thought P.P.'s behaviour was jolly peculiar. I thought he'd got his knife into Boysie about something.'

Moppett, who seemed to have regained her composure, said: 'If you ask me, P.P. was terrified Uncle Hal would tell the whole story. He looked murder at him. Not that I mean anything by that.'

'In any case,' Alleyn continued, 'Mr Period was disturbed by the incident. He wrote a short and rather ambiguous letter to Miss Cartell, suggesting that his ancestry did, in fact, go back as far as anyone who bothered about such things might wish, and asking her to forgive him for pursuing the matter. At the same time he wrote a letter of condolence to Lady Bantling. Unfortunately he transferred the envelopes.'

'How bad is he?' Desirée asked suddenly.

Alleyn told her how bad Mr Period seemed to be and she said: 'We can take him if it'd help.'

Bimbo started to say something and stopped.

'Now this misfortune with the letter,' Alleyn plodded on, 'threw him into a fever. On the one hand he had appeared to condole with Miss Cartell for a loss that had not yet been discovered, and, on the other, he had sent Lady Bantling a letter that he would give the world to withdraw, since, once it got into my hands, I might follow it up. As long as this letter remained undisclosed, Mr Period remained unwilling to make any statement that might lead to an arrest for the murder of Mr Cartell. He was afraid; first, that he might bring disaster upon an innocent person, and second, that anything he said might lead to an examination of his own activities and Mr Cartell's veiled allusions to them. All this,' he added, 'supposes him, for the moment, to be innocent of the murder.'

'Of course he is,' Desirée muttered impatiently. 'Good lord! P.P.!'

'You don't know,' Bimbo intervened with a sharp look at her. 'If he'd go to those lengths, he might go the whole hog.'

'Murder Hal, to save his own face! Honestly, darling!'

'You don't know,' Bimbo repeated obstinately. 'He might.'

'Assume for the moment,' Alleyn said, 'that he didn't, but that he was in possession of evidence that might well throw suspicion on someone else. Assume that his motive in not laying this information was made up of consideration for an old friend and fear of the consequences to himself. He learns that I have been told of yesterday's luncheon party, and also that I have been given the letter that was occasioned by the conversation at the party. It's more than possible that he heard on the village grapevine, that I visited Ribblethorpe church this afternoon. So the gaff, he thinks, is as good as blown. With a certain bit of evidence weighing on his conscience, he sends his man here with a note asking you, Miss Ralston, to visit him. Wanting to keep the encounter private, he suggests a late hour. After a good deal of discussion with Mr Leiss, no doubt, you decide to fall in with this plan. You do, in fact, cross the green at about ten forty-five and visit Mr Period in his library.'

'You're only guessing,' Moppett said. 'You don't know.'

'You enter the library by the French windows. During the interview you smoke. You drop ash on the carpet and grind it in with your heel. You leave two butts of Mainsail cigarettes in the ash-tray. Mr Period tells you he heard someone whistling in the lane very late last night and that he recognized the tune. You and Mr Leiss knew your way about the garden, I believe. To support this theory, we have the theft of Mr Period's cigarette-case – '

'I never,' Leonard interrupted, 'heard anything so fantastic. You don't know what you're talking about.'

' – which you, Mr Leiss, left on the sill, having opened the window with this theft in mind. Subsequently, it may be, the case became too hot and you threw it in the drain, hoping it would be supposed that Mr Period had lost it there, or that the workmen had stolen and dumped it. Alternatively, you might have dropped it, inadvertently, when you altered the planks in order to bring about Mr Cartell's death.'

He waited for a moment. An all too familiar look of conceit and insolence appeared in Leonard. He stretched out his legs, leant back in his chair and stared through half-closed eyes at the opposite wall. A shadow trembled on his shirt and he kept his hands in his pockets.

Connie said: 'It's not true: none of it's true.'

Moppett repeated: 'Not true,' in a whisper.

'As to what actually took place at this interview,' Alleyn went on, 'Mr Period will no doubt be willing to talk about it, when he recovers. My guess would be that he tackled Miss Ralston pretty firmly, told her what he suspected and said that if she could give him an adequate explanation he would, for Miss Cartell's sake, go no further. She may have admitted she was the whistler he heard from his window and said that she had come into his garden on the way home from the party to get water for Mr Leiss's car radiator which had sprung a leak. I think this explanation is true.'

Moppett cried out: 'Of course it's true. I did. I got the water and I put the bloody can back. I remembered having seen it under the tap.'

'After lunch, when you took Mr Period's cigarette-case off the sill?'

'Fantastic!' Leonard repeated. 'That's all. Fantastic!'

'Very well,' Alleyn said. 'Let it remain in the realms of fantasy. The facts are sufficiently abundant and we may add to them. What time was it when you fetched the watering-can?'

'After two,' she said with a sidelong glance at Bimbo. 'We left Baynesholme at two.'

'And did you cross the ditch by the planks?'

'No,' she said at once. 'They weren't there. I went round by the hedge.' She gaped at Alleyn. 'Does that mean –?'

'It means among other things, that if you'd told me this before, you would have gone some way towards clearing yourself.'

'But – had it happened? Was he – ?'

'If you're telling the truth, Mr Cartell's body was lying in the ditch.'

'My God!' Moppett said quietly.

'To return to your call, tonight, on Mr Period. Whatever the culmination of the interview, something prompted him to ring me up. The call went through and I answered it. As he was speaking someone threw a brass paper-weight at his head.'

'I didn't,' Moppett said. 'I swear I didn't. I went straight out. I didn't do a thing. I didn't touch him. Auntie Con! I didn't. *I didn't.*'

'Of course you didn't, my lamb,' Connie said with the naked tenderness that characterized all her responses to her ward. 'Never mind. Of course you didn't.'

'If it's in order,' Desirée said, 'I'd like to ask something.'

'Of course.'

'Are we meant to think that whoever threw the fish, laid the trap for Hal?'

'A fish?' Leonard asked, with an insufferable air of innocence. 'But has anyone said anything about a fish?'

Desirée disregarded him. She said to Alleyn: 'I ought to know. I gave it to P.P. yesterday morning. He's dotty about pikes and this thing looked like one. He put it in the library. Could I have an answer to my question?'

'I think the murderer and the paper-weight-thrower are one and the same person.'

'Good,' said Desirée. 'That lets us out, Bimbo.'

'I'm glad to hear it,' Bimbo said with a short laugh. 'Why?'

'Well, because neither of us has the slightest motive for hurling anything at P.P.'

'Isn't he one of the trustees for Andrew Bantling's estate?' Leonard asked of nobody in particular.

She turned her head and looked very steadily at him. 'Certainly,' she said. 'What of it?'

'I was just wondering, Lady Bantling. You might have discussed business with Mr Period when you called on him this evening?'

Bimbo said angrily: 'I'm afraid I fail entirely to see why you should wonder anything of the sort or how you can possibly know the smallest thing about it.'

'Yes, but I do as it happens. I heard you talking things over with your dashing step-son at the party.'

'Good God!' Bimbo said, and turned up his eyes.

Desirée said to Alleyn: 'I told you. I called to own up that I'd given you his letter. I felt shabby about it and wanted to get it off my chest.'

'What's his attitude about the Grantham Gallery proposal, do you know?'

'Oh,' Desirée said easily, 'he waffles.'

'He'll be all right,' Bimbo said.

'Just a moment,' Leonard intervened. He still lay back in his chair and looked at the ceiling but there was a new edge in his voice. 'If you're talking about this proposition to buy an art gallery,' he said, 'I happen to know P.P. was all against it.'

Bimbo said: 'You met Mr Period for the first time when you got yourself asked to lunch in his house: I fail to see how that gives you any insight into his views on anything.'

'You don't,' Leonard observed, 'have to know people all their lives to find out some of the bits and pieces. The same might apply to you, chum. How about that affair over a certain club?'

'You bloody little pip-squeak – '

'All right, darling,' Desirée said easily. 'Pipe down. It couldn't matter less.'

'Not when you marry money, it couldn't,' Leonard agreed offensively.

Bimbo strode down the room towards him: 'By God, if the police don't do something about you, I will.'

Fox rose from obscurity. 'Now, then, sir,' he said blandly. 'We mustn't get too hot, must we?'

'Get out of my way.'

Leonard was on his feet. Moppett snatched his arm. He jabbed at her with his elbow, side-stepped, and backed down the room, his hand in his jacket pocket. Alleyn took him from behind by the arms.

'You've forgotten,' he said. 'I've got your knife.'

Leonard uttered an elaborate obscenity and at the same time Fox, with the greatest economy, caused Bimbo to drop backwards into the nearest chair. 'That's right, sir,' he said. 'We don't want to get too warm. It wouldn't look well, in the circumstances, would it?'

Bimbo swore at him. 'I demand,' he said, pointing a bandaged hand at Alleyn, 'I demand an explanation. You're keeping us here without authority. You're listening to a lot of bloody, damaging, malicious lies. If you suspect one of us, I demand to know who and why. Now then!'

'Fair enough,' said Desirée. 'You stick out for your rights, duckie. All the same,' she added, looking Alleyn full in the face, 'I don't believe he knows. He's letting us cut up rough and hoping something will come out of it. Aren't you, Rory?'

She was inviting Alleyn, as he very well knew, to acknowledge, however slightly, that he and she spoke the same language: that alone, of all this assembly, they could understand each other without elaboration. He released the now quiescent Leonard and answered her directly.

'No,' he said. 'It isn't quite like that. It's true that I believe I know who murdered Harold Cartell. I believe that there is only one of you who fills the bill. Naturally I'm looking for all the corroborative evidence I can find.'

'I demand – ' Bimbo reiterated, but his wife cut him short.

'All right, darling,' she said. 'So you've told us. You demand an explanation and I rather fancy you're going to get it. So do pipe down.' She returned to Alleyn. 'Are you going to tell us,' she asked, 'that we all had red-hot motives for getting rid of Hal? Because I feel sure we had.'

'Contrary to popular belief,' he said, 'the police are concerned less with motive than with opportunity and behaviour. But, yes. As it happens you all had motives of a sort. Yours, for instance, could be thought to come under the heading of maternal love.'

'Could it, indeed?' said Desirée.

'By God – !' Bimbo shouted, but Alleyn cut him short.

'And you,' he said, 'wanted to invest in this project that Cartell wouldn't countenance. Judging from the unopened bills on your desk and your past history, this could be a formidable motive.'

'And that,' Leonard observed, smirking at Bimbo, 'takes the silly grin off your face, Jack, doesn't it.'

'Whereas,' Alleyn continued, 'you, Mr Leiss, and Miss Ralston, were directly threatened both by Mr Cartell and, I think, Mr Period, with criminal proceedings which would almost certainly land you in gaol.'

'No!' Connie ejaculated.

'A threat,' Alleyn said, 'that may be said to provide your motive as well, I'm afraid, Miss Cartell. As for Alfred Belt and Mrs Mitchell, who are not present, they were both greatly concerned to end Mr Cartell's tenancy which they found intolerable. Murder has been done for less.'

It was not pleasant, he thought, to see the veiled eagerness with which they welcomed this departure. Leonard actually said: 'Well, of course. Now you're talking,' and Moppett flicked the tip of her tongue over her lips.

'But I repeat,' Alleyn went on, 'that it is circumstance, opportunity and behaviour that must concern us. Opportunity, after a fashion, you all had. Miss Ralston and Mr Leiss were on the premises late that night. They had stolen the cigarette-case and the case was found by the body. The trap was laid by somebody wearing leather and string gloves and Mr Leiss had lost such a pair of gloves.'

Leonard and Moppett began to talk together but Alleyn held up his hand and they stopped dead.

'Their behaviour, however, doesn't make sense. If they were planning to murder Mr Cartell they would hardly have publicized their actions by singing and whistling under Mr Period's window.'

Moppett gave a strangulated sob, presumably of relief.

'Lady Bantling had opportunity and she knew the lie of the land. She could have set the trap but it's obvious she didn't do so as she was seen by Mr Bantling and Miss Maitland-Mayne, returning, across the planks, to her car. She, too, had publicized her visit by serenading Mr Cartell from the garden. Her behaviour does not commend itself as that of an obsessive, maternal murderess.'

'Too kind of you to say so,' Desirée murmured.

'Moreover, I fancy she is very well aware that her son could anticipate his inheritance by borrowing upon his expectations and insuring his life as security for the loan. This reduces her motive to one of mere exasperation and the same may be said of Mr Bantling himself.'

'And of me,' said Bimbo quickly.

Alleyn said: 'In your case there might well be something we haven't yet winkled out. Which is what I mean about the secondary importance of motive. However, I was coming to you. You had ample opportunity. You retired to a bathroom where you tell me you spent a long time bandaging your hand. You could equally well have spent it driving back to the ditch and arranging the trap. No, please don't interrupt. I know you were bitten. That proves nothing. You may also remember that you took Mr Leiss's overcoat to him. Were his gloves in the pocket?'

'How the hell do I know! I didn't pick his ghastly pockets,' said Bimbo, turning very white.

'A statement that at the moment can't be checked. All the same, there's this to be said for you: if you are both telling the truth about your movements this evening, you are unlikely to have chucked the paper-weight at Mr Period's head. Although,' Alleyn said very coolly, 'the amorous dog-chase might well have led you into Mr Period's garden.'

'It might have,' Desirée remarked, 'but in point of fact it didn't. Bimbo was never out of my sight.'

'If that is so,' Alleyn said, 'it leads us to an inescapable conclusion.'

He waited, and across the stillness of the room there floated small, inconsequent sounds: the whisper of Fox's pencil and his rather heavy breathing, the faint rasp of Moppett's fingernails on the arms of her chair and from somewhere within the house a scarcely perceptible mechanical throb.

'There remains,' Alleyn said, 'just one person to whom opportunity, behaviour and motive all point, inescapably. This person presents certain characteristics: a knowledge of Mr Cartell's movements, the assurance that at one o'clock the Baynesholme guests would have long ago left the scene, and access to Mr Leiss's gloves. So much for opportunity. Behaviour. There are certain reactions. Everybody knows about Mr Period's propensity for writing letters of condolence; he's famous for them. Now, suppose one of you gets a Period letter, couched in rather ambiguous terms but commiserating with you on the loss of somebody whom you saw fighting-fit the previous evening. What would you think? Either that he was dotty or that he had sent you the wrong letter. You might get an initial shock, but a few moments thought would reassure you. You would not, having gone to find out what it was all about and encountered a bewildered Mr Period, turn deadly white and almost faint. But if you had murdered the supposed subject of the letter, how would you react? Suppose you had awakened in the morning with the remembrance of your deed festering in your mind and then been presented with this letter. Suppose, finally, that when you were being interviewed by the police, a second letter arrived, couched in exactly the same phrases. Wouldn't that seem like a nightmare? Wouldn't it seem as if Mr Period knew what you'd done and was torturing you with his knowledge? What would you do then?'

Connie Cartell had risen to her feet. She made an extraordinary gesture with her weather-chapped bandaged hand.

'You can't prove it,' she said. 'You haven't got the gloves.'

At that moment a loud and confused rumpus broke out in the garden. There was a cry of frustration and a yelp of pain. The Pekinese leapt from Connie's embrace.

A body crashed against the French windows. They burst open to admit Pixie, immensely overwrought and carrying some object in her mouth. She was closely followed by Alfred Belt.

Alleyn shouted: 'Shut those windows.' Alfred did so and stood in front of them, panting noisily.

With an expertise borne of their early training, Alleyn and Fox seized, respectively, Pixie and Li. Alleyn thrust his thumbs into the corners of Pixie's slavering mouth.

Her plaything dropped to the floor. Alfred, gasping for breath, stammered: 'In the garden, sir. Here. Ran her to earth. Digging.'

Moppett cried out: 'Lennie! Lennie! Look! They're your gloves!'

Alleyn said to Bimbo: 'Catch hold of this dog.'

'I'll be damned if I do.'

'I do her,' said Trudi.

She dragged Pixie from the room.

Alleyn stooped to retrieve the gloves. He unrolled them. The leather in the palms had been torn and fragments of string hung loose from the knitted backs. The thumb of the left hand glove was discoloured with blood. He began to turn it inside out. As he did so, Connie Cartell screamed.

It was a shocking sound, scarcely less animal than the canine outcry that had preceded it. Her mouth remained open and for a moment she looked like a mask for a Fury. Then she plunged forward and when Fox seized her, screamed again.

The lining of the thumb showed a fragment of blackened and blood-stained cotton-wool and smelt quite distinctly of the black ointment used for girth-gall.

CHAPTER 8

Period Piece

Mr Pyke Period reclined on his library sofa, nibbling calves'-foot jelly and giving audience to Alleyn, Nicola and Andrew. He had just prevailed upon Dr Elekton to allow him downstairs. Wan though he was, he might nevertheless have been suspected of enjoying himself.

'It's so utterly dreadful,' he said. 'One *cannot* believe it. Connie! One knows, of course, that she has the reputation of a thruster in the hunting field, but I've always thought of her as just another of those fatiguing women who shout and laugh. Rather stupid, in fact.'

'She is,' Alleyn conceded, 'a very stupid woman. But she has the cunning of her stupidity, I'm afraid.'

'And all for that wretched girl! I fear,' Mr Period said, 'that I may have precipitated matters, I mean, by suggesting that the girl should come and see me. The thing was, my dear fellow, I woke on that dreadful night and I heard that tune being whistled somewhere outside. And voices: hers and that appalling young man's. And when you described what must have been done, I thought they were responsible.'

'But,' Alleyn pointed out, 'you decided not to tell me about this?'

Mr Period changed colour. 'Yes – for a number of reasons. You see – if it had only been intended as a trick – the consequences – so terrible for Connie. Oh, dear – *Connie!* And then I must confess – '

'You couldn't face the publicity?'

'No,' Mr Period whispered. 'No – I couldn't. Very wrong of me. There – there was a personal matter – ' He stopped and waved his hands.

178

'I know about the baptismal register,' Alleyn said gently.

Mr Period turned scarlet but said nothing.

Alleyn looked at Andrew and Nicola: 'Perhaps,' he suggested, 'I might just have a word – '

'Yes, of course,' they both said and made for the door.

'No!' Mr Period quite shouted. They turned. His face was still red and his eyes were screwed up as if he expected a blow. 'No!' he repeated. 'Don't go! I am resigned. If I have to dree my weird I may as well dree it now. My nanny,' Mr Period explained with a travesty of his family preoccupation, 'was a Highlander. I prefer, I repeat, that you should remain. Nicola: you lunched here, you heard the conversation? About – about the baptismal register? You remember?'

'Well, yes.'

''Nuff said. But I felt sure that Hal was going to tell Connie and Connie would tell the girl and – and if I — indeed, when I saw her, the girl threatened – '

'Little beast,' Nicola said heartily.

'Worse than that! I gathered they were prepared to use blackmail. And then, dear Desirée came in that evening and said, Alleyn, she'd given you that *unfortunate* letter so – '

'So you felt you had nothing to lose?'

'Quite! Quite!'

'So you told the girl that unless she could explain their presence in the lane you would report it to the police.'

'Yes. I said I felt it my duty to speak, in case innocent people should be suspected. It was then she threatened to use – to make public – however! She was so impertinent and so brazen I lost my temper. I said I would ring you up at once. I quite shouted it after her as she went away. And then, you know, I *did* ring up and — and then I don't know what happened.'

Alleyn said: 'What happened was this. Constance Cartell, on the hunt for her Pekinese, came into your garden. She probably caught a glimpse of her ward coming out by the French windows. She heard your final threat. She was terribly suspicious, indeed terrified, of you.'

'Of Mr Period,' Nicola exclaimed. 'But why?'

'Because of the identical letters of condolence. She thought he suspected her. She had let me see the second letter, hoping to anticipate anything he might tell me by throwing suspicion on him.'

'But how dreadful of her!' Mr Period faintly exclaimed.

'She heard you shout that you were going to ring me up. You had your back to the window as you telephoned. The paper-weight was on the table, near to hand. In an ecstasy of rage and of fear for herself and her ward, she threw it at you and bolted. Everything she has done has been out of the unreasoning depths of her passion for that wretched girl. Her brother had threatened to bring a charge of theft against Mary, so Connie picked up Leiss's gloves from wherever they had been dumped in her hall and laid the trap for him. Afterwards, because the gloves were torn and stained with the stuff she put on her thumb, she buried them in her rubbish heap, which was due to be lit next day. She didn't wear gloves when she threw the paper-weight. Her prints were there, quite clearly, along with several others.'

'But – ' Nicola began and then said: 'Yes. Of course.'

'Of course – why?'

'I was just remembering. They would be, anyway, because Mr Period handed it round before lunch.'

'I wonder if she's thought of that,' said Alleyn.

He went over to Mr Period. 'You've had a horrid time of it,' he said, 'and I can't say the sequel will be anything but very deeply distressing, but as far as your private affairs are concerned, I don't think they will come into the case at all.'

Mr Period tried once or twice to speak. At last he said: 'You are very kind. Too kind. I'm most grateful.'

Alleyn shook his hand and left him. Nicola and Andrew saw him out.

Nicola said: 'I've often tried to imagine what you were like in action. Now, I know. It's a bit sobering.'

'I've been wondering,' Andrew said. 'Did you ever suspect me?'

'You?' Alleyn looked at the pair of them and grinned. 'You didn't, it appeared, leave Nicola for long enough. And I'm damned if I go any further with this recital. Goodbye to you both.' He went a few paces down the drive and turned. 'By the way,' he said. 'I've been talking to Troy. She seems to think you're an acquisition as a pupil. I've seldom heard her so enthusiastic. Congratulations.'

He waved his hand and left them.

Nicola looked at Andrew. 'Congratulations,' she said.

'Darling!' Andrew began excitedly, but she backed away from him, 'No! Not now! Not yet. Let's wait. I must get back to Mr Period,' said Nicola in a flurry.

'I love you,' said Andrew. 'Isn't it astonishing?'

'It's heaven,' Nicola cried and ran into the house.

Mr Period was looking pensive and had the air of a man who has made up his mind.

'Nicola, my love,' he said, still in a slightly invalidish voice, 'it's just occurred to me that I really should explain about that business. In case there is any misunderstanding. The old rector at Ribblethorpe was a dear old boy but a *leetle* eccentric. He christened me, you know. But would you believe it, he forgot to put my name in the register? I was a twin. He became so ga-ga, poor darling, that I'm afraid that when I discovered the omission, I was very naughty and took things into my own hands. It seemed the simplest way out,' Mr Period said, looking Nicola very straight in the eye. He gave a little titter. 'But we won't put it in the book.'

'No?'

'No,' said Mr Period firmly. ''Nuff said.'

Dead Water

for Alister and Doris McIntosh with love

Contents

Cast of Characters

Wally Trehern	*Of Fisherman's Bay, Portcarrow Island*
Jenny Williams	*School-mistress*
Mrs Trehern	*Wally's mother*
James Trehern	*Her husband*
Dr Maine	*Of the Portcarrow Convalescent Home*
The Rev. Mr Adrian Carstairs	*Rector of Portcarrow*
Mrs Carstairs	*His wife*
Major Keith Barrimore	*Landlord of The Boy-and-Lobster*
Mrs Barrimore	*His wife*
Patrick Ferrier	*Her son*
Miss Elspeth Cost	*A shopkeeper*
Kenneth Joyce	*A journalist*
Mrs Thorpe	*A patient*
Miss Emily Pride	*Suzerain of the Island*
Mr Ives Nankivell	*Mayor of Portcarrow*
Superintendent Coombe	*Portcarrow Constabulary*
Sergeant Pender	*Portcarrow Constabulary*
PC Carey	*Portcarrow Constabulary*
PC Pomeroy	*Portcarrow Constabulary*
Superintendent Roderick Alleyn	*CID Scotland Yard*
Troy Alleyn	*His wife*
Detective-Inspector Fox	*Scotland Yard*
Detective-Sergeant Bailey	*Scotland Yard*
Detective-Sergeant Thompson	*Scotland Yard*
Sir James Curtis	*Home Office Pathologist*
Cissy Pollock	*Telephonist*
Trethaway	*A father*

CHAPTER 1

Prelude

A boy stumbled up the hillside, half-blinded by tears. He fell and, for a time, choked and sobbed as he lay in the sun but presently blundered on. A lark sang overhead. Farther up the hill he could hear the multiple chatter of running water. The children down by the jetty still chanted after him:

> *Warty-hog, warty-hog*
> *Put your puddies in the bog*
> *Warty Walter, Warty Walter*
> *Wash your warties in the water.*

The spring was near the top. It began as a bubbling pool, cascaded into a miniature waterfall, dived under pebbles, earth and bracken and at last, loquacious and preoccupied, swirled mysteriously underground and was lost. Above the pool stood a boulder, flanked by briars and fern, and above that the brow of the hill and the sun in a clear sky.

He squatted near the waterfall. His legs ached and a spasm jolted his chest. He gasped for breath, beat his hands on the ground and looked at them. Warty-hog. Warts clustered all over his fingers like those black things that covered the legs of the jetty. Two of them bled where he'd cut them. The other kids were told not to touch him.

He thrust his hands under the cold pressure of the cascade. It beat and stung and numbed them, but he screwed up his blubbered eyes and forced them to stay there. Water spurted icily up his arms and into his face.

'Don't cry.'

He opened his eyes directly into the sun or would have done so if she hadn't stood between: tall and greenish, above the big stone and rimmed about with light like something on the telly so that he couldn't see her properly.

'Why are you crying?'

He ducked his head, and stared like an animal that couldn't make up its mind to bolt. He gave a loud, detached sob and left his hands under the water.

'What's the matter? Are you hurt? Tell me.'

'Me 'ands.'

'Show me.'

He shook his head and stared.

'Show me your hands.'

'They'm mucky.'

'The water will clean them.'

'No, t'won't, then.'

'Show me.'

He withdrew them. Between clusters of warts his skin had puckered and turned the colour of dead fish. He broke into a loud wail. His nose and eyes ran salt into his open mouth.

From down below a voice, small and distant, halfheartedly chanted: 'Warty Walter. Warty Walter. Stick your warties in the water.' Somebody shouted: 'Aw *come* on.' They were going away.

He held out his desecrated hands towards her as if in explanation. Her voice floated down on the sound of the waterfall.

'Put them under again. If you believe: they will be clean.'

'Uh?'

'They will be clean. Say it. Say 'Please take away my warts.' Shut your eyes and do as I tell you. Say it again when you go to bed. Remember. Do it.'

He did as she told him. The sound of the cascade grew very loud in his ears. Blobs of light swam across his eyeballs. He heard his own voice very far away, and then nothing. Ice-cold water was bumping his face on drowned pebbles.

When he lifted his head up there was no one between him and the sun.

He sat there letting himself dry and thinking of nothing in particular until the sun went down behind the hill. Then, feeling cold, he
returned to the waterfront and his home in the bay.

II

For about twenty-four hours after the event, the affair of Wally
Trehern's warts made very little impression on the Island. His parents
were slugabeds: the father under the excuse that he was engaged in
night-fishing and the mother without any excuse at all unless it
could be found in the gin bottle. They were not a credit to the Island.
Wally, who slept in his clothes, got up at his usual time, and went
out to the pump for a wash. He did this because somehow or another
his new teacher had fixed the idea in his head and he followed it out
with the sort of behaviourism that can be established in a domestic
animal. He was still little better than half-awake when he saw what
had happened.

Nobody knows what goes on in the mind of a child: least of all in a
mind like Wally Trehern's where the process of thought was so sluggish
as to be no more than a reflex of simple emotions: pleasure, fear or
pride.

He seemed to be feeling proud when he shambled up to his
teacher and, before all the school, held out his hands.

'Why – !' she said. 'Why – why – *Wally!*' She took both his hands
in hers and looked and pressed and looked again. 'I can't believe it,'
she said. 'It's not true.'

'Be'ant mucky,' he said. 'All gone,' and burst out laughing.

The school was on the mainland but the news about Wally
Trehern's warts returned with him and his teacher to the Island. The
Island was incorrectly named: it was merely a rocky blob of land at
the end of an extremely brief, narrow and low-lying causeway
which disappeared at full tide and whenever the seas along that
coast ran high. The Island was thus no more than an extension of
the tiny fishing village of Portcarrow and yet the handful of people
who lived on it were accorded a separate identity as if centuries of
tidal gestures had given them an indefinable status. In those parts

they talked of 'islanders' and 'villagers' making a distinction where none really existed.

The Portcarrow school-mistress was Miss Jenny Williams, a young New Zealander who was doing post graduate research in England, and had taken this temporary job to enrich her experience and augment her bursary. She lodged on the Island at The Boy-and-Lobster, a small Jacobean pub, and wrote home enthusiastically about its inconveniences. She was a glowing, russet-coloured girl and looked her best that afternoon, striding across the causeway with the wind snapping at her hair and moulding her summer dress into the explicit simplicity of a shift. Behind her ran, stumbled and tacked poor Wally, who gave from time to time a squawking cry not unlike that of a seagull.

When they arrived on the Island she told him she would like to see his mother. They turned right at the jetty, round a point and into Fisherman's Bay. The Treherns lived in the least prepossessing of a group of cottages. Jenny could feel nothing but dismay at its smell and that of Mrs Trehern who sat on the doorstep and made ambiguous sounds of greeting.

'She'm sozzled,' said Wally, and indeed, it was so.

Jenny said: 'Wally: would you be very kind and see if you can find me a shell to keep. A pink one.' She had to repeat this carefully and was not helped by Mrs Trehern suddenly roaring out that if he didn't do what his teacher said she'd have the hide off of him.

Wally sank his head between his shoulders, shuffled down to the foreshore and disappeared behind a boat.

'Mrs Trehern,' Jenny said, 'I do hope you don't mind me coming: I just felt I must say how terribly glad I am about Wally's warts and – and – I did want to ask about how it's happened. I mean,' she went on, growing flurried, 'it's so extraordinary. Since yesterday. I mean – well – it's – *Isn't it?*'

Mrs Trehern was smiling broadly. She jerked her head and asked Jenny if she would take a little something.

'No, thank you.' She waited for a moment and then said: 'Mrs Trehern, haven't you noticed? Wally's hands? Haven't you seen?'

'Takes fits,' said Mrs Trehern. 'Our Wally!' she added with an air of profundity. After several false starts she rose and turned into the house. 'You come on in,' she shouted bossily. 'Come on.'

Jenny was spared this ordeal by the arrival of Mr Trehern who lumbered up from the foreshore where she fancied he had been sitting behind his boat. He was followed at a distance by Wally.

James Trehern was a dark, fat man with pale eyes, a slack mouth and a manner that was both suspicious and placatory. He hired out himself and his boat to visitors, fished and did odd jobs about the village and the Island.

He leered uncertainly at Jenny and said it was an uncommon brave afternoon and he hoped she was feeling pretty clever herself. Jenny at once embarked on the disappearance of the warts and found that Trehern had just become aware of it. Wally had shown him his hands.

'Isn't it amazing, Mr Trehern?'

'Proper flabbergasting,' he agreed without enthusiasm.

'When did it happen exactly, do you know? Was it yesterday, after school? Or when? Was it – sudden? – I mean his hands were in such a state, weren't they? I've asked him, of course, and he says – he says it's because of a lady. And something about washing his hands in the spring up there. I'm sorry to pester you like this but I felt I just *had* to know.'

It was obvious that he thought she was making an unnecessary to-do about the whole affair, but he stared at her with a sort of covert intensity that was extremely disagreeable. A gust of wind snatched at her dress and she tried to pin it between her knees. Trehern's mouth widened. Mrs Trehern advanced uncertainly from the interior.

Jenny said quickly: 'Well, never mind, anyway. It's grand that they've gone, isn't it? I mustn't keep you. Good evening.'

Mrs Trehern made an ambiguous sound and extended her clenched hand. 'See yurr,' she said. She opened her hand. A cascade of soft black shells dropped on the step.

'Them's our Wally's,' she said. 'In 'is bed.'

'All gone,' said Wally.

He had come up from the foreshore. When Jenny turned to him, he offered her a real shell. It was broken and discoloured but it was pink. Jenny knelt down to take it. 'Thank you very much,' she said. 'That's just what I wanted.'

It seemed awful to go away and leave him there. When she looked back he waved to her.

III

That evening in the private tap at The Boy-and-Lobster Wally Trehern's warts were the principal topic of conversation. It was a fine evening and low-tide fell at eight o'clock. In addition to the regular Islanders, there were patrons who had strolled across the causeway from the village: Dr Maine of the Portcarrow Convalescent Home; the Rector, the Rev. Mr Adrian Carstairs, who liked to show, as was no more than the case, that he was human; and a visitor to the village, a large pale young man with a restless manner and a general air of being on the look-out for something. He was having a drink with Patrick Ferrier, the step-son of the landlord, down from Oxford for the long vacation. Patrick was an engaging fellow with a sensitive mouth, pleasant manners and a quick eye which dwelt pretty often upon Jenny Williams. There was only one other woman in the private beside Jenny. This was Miss Elspeth Cost, a lady with vague hair and a tentative smile who, like Jenny, was staying at The Boy-and-Lobster and was understood to have a shop somewhere and to be interested in handicrafts and the drama.

The landlord, Major Keith Barrimore, stationed between two bars, served both the public and the private taps: the former being used exclusively by local fishermen. Major Barrimore was well-set-up and of florid complexion. He shouted rather than spoke, had any amount of professional bonhomie and harmonized perfectly with his background of horse-brasses, bottles, glasses, tankards and sporting prints. He wore a check coat, a yellow waistcoat and a signet ring and kept his hair very smooth.

'Look at it whichever way you choose,' Miss Cost said, 'it's astounding. Poor little fellow! To think!'

'Very dramatic,' said Patrick Ferrier, smiling at Jenny.

'Well it was,' she said. 'Just that.'

'One *hears* of these cases,' said the restless young man, 'Gipsies and charms and so on.'

'Yes, I know one does,' Jenny said. 'One *hears* of them but I've never met one before. And who, for heaven's sake, was the green lady?'

There was a brief silence.

'Ah,' said Miss Cost. 'Now that *is* the really rather wonderful part. The green lady!' She tipped her head to one side and looked at the rector. 'M-m – ?' she invited.

'Poor Wally!' Mr Carstairs rejoined. 'All a fairytale, I daresay. It's a sad case.'

'The cure isn't a fairytale,' Jenny pointed out.

'No, no, no. Surely not. Surely not,' he said in a hurry.

'A *fairytale*. I wonder. Still pixies in these yurr parts, Rector, d'y'm reckon?' asked Miss Cost essaying a roughish burr.

Everyone looked extremely uncomfortable.

'All in the poor kid's imagination, I should have thought,' said Major Barrimore and poured himself a double Scotch. 'Still: damn' good show, anyway.'

'What's the medical opinion?' Patrick asked.

'Don't ask me!' Dr Maine ejaculated, throwing up his beautifully kept hands. 'There is no medical opinion as far as I know.' But seeing perhaps that they all expected more than this from him, he went on half-impatiently. 'You do, of course, hear of these cases. They're quite well-established. I've heard of an eminent skin-specialist who actually mugged up an incantation or spell or what have-you and used it on his patients with marked success.'

'There! You see!' Miss Cost cried out, gently clapping her hands. She became mysterious. 'You wait!' she said. 'You jolly well wait!'

Dr Maine glanced at her distastefully.

'The cause of warts is not known,' he said. 'Probably viral. The boy's an epileptic,' he added. '*Petit mal.*'

'Would that predispose him to this sort of cure?' Patrick asked.

'Might,' Dr Maine said shortly. 'Might predispose him to the right kind of suggestibility.' Without looking at the Rector, he added: 'There's one feature that sticks out all through the literature of reputed cures by some allegedly supernatural agency. The authentic cases have emotional or nervous connotations.'

'Not all, surely,' the Rector suggested.

Dr Maine shot a glance at him. 'I shouldn't talk,' he said. 'I really know nothing about such matters. The other half, if you please.'

Jenny thought: 'The Rector feels he ought to nip in and speak up for miracles and he doesn't like to because he doesn't want to be parsonic. How tricky it is for them! Dr Maine's the same, in his way. He doesn't like talking shop for fear of showing off. English reticence,' thought Jenny, resolving to make the point in her next letter home. 'Incorrigible amateurs.'

The restless young man suddenly said: 'The next round's on me,' and astonished everybody.

'Handsome offer!' said Major Barrimore. 'Thank you, sir.'

'Tell me,' said the young man expansively and at large. 'Where is this spring or pool or whatever it is?'

Patrick explained. 'Up the hill above the jetty.'

'And the kid's story is that some lady in green told him to wash his hands in it? And the warts fell off in the night. Is that it?'

'As far as I could make out,' Jenny agreed. 'He's not at all eloquent, poor Wally.'

'Wally Trehern, did you say? Local boy?'

'That's right.'

'Were they bad? The warts?'

'Frightful.'

'Mightn't have been just kind of ripe to fall off? Coincidence?'

'Most unlikely, I'd have thought,' said Jenny.

'I see,' said the young man, weighing it up. 'Well, what's everybody having? Same again, all round?'

Everybody murmured assent and Major Barrimore began to pour the drinks.

Jenny said: 'I could show you a photograph.'

'No? Could you, though? I'd very much like to see it. I'd be very interested, indeed. Would you?'

She ran up to her room to get it: a colour-slide of the infant-class with Wally in the foreground, his hands dangling. She put it in the viewer and returned to the bar. The young man looked at it intently, whistling to himself. 'Quite a thing,' he said. 'Quite something. Nice sharp picture, too.'

Everybody wanted to look at it. While they were handing it about, the door from the house opened and Mrs Barrimore came in.

She was a beautiful woman, very fine-drawn with an exquisite head of which the bone-structure was so delicate and the eyes so quiet in expression that the mouth seemed like a vivid accident. It was as if an artist, having started out to paint an ascetic, had changed his mind and laid down the lips of a voluptuary.

With a sort of awkward grace that suggested shyness, she moved into the bar, smiling tentatively at nobody in particular. Dr Maine looked quickly at her and stood up. The Rector gave her good-evening and the restless young man offered her a drink. Her husband, without consulting her, poured a glass of lager.

'Hallo, Mum. We've all been talking about Wally's warts,' Patrick said.

Mrs Barrimore sat down by Miss Cost. 'Have you?' she said. 'Isn't it strange? I can't get over it.' Her voice was charming: light and very clear. She had the faintest hesitation in her speech and a trick of winding her fingers together. Her son brought her drink to her and she thanked the restless young man rather awkwardly for it. Jenny, who liked her very much, wondered, not for the first time, if her position at The Boy-and-Lobster was distasteful to her and exactly why she seemed so alien to it.

Her entrance brought a little silence in its wake. Dr Maine turned his glass round and round and stared at the contents. Presently Miss Cost broke out in fresh spate of enthusiasm.

'. . . Now, you may all laugh as loud as you please,' she cried with a reckless air. '*I* shan't mind. I daresay there's some clever answer explaining it all away or you can, if you choose, call it coincidence. But I don't care. I'm going to say my little say.' She held up her glass of port in a dashing manner and gained their reluctant attention. 'I'm an asthmatic!' she declared vaingloriously. 'Since I came here, I've had my usual go, regular as clockwork, every evening at half past eight. I daresay some of you have heard me sneezing and wheezing away in my corner. Very well. Now! This evening, when I'd heard about Wally, I walked up to the spring and while I sat there, it came into my mind. Quite suddenly. '*I wonder.*' And I dipped my fingers in the waterfall – ' She shut her eyes, raised her brows and smiled. The port slopped over on her hand. She replaced the glass. 'I wished my wee wish,' she continued. 'And I sat up there, feeling ever so light and unburdened, and then I came down.' She pointed dramatically to the bar clock. 'Look at the time!' she exulted. 'Five past ten!' She slapped her chest. 'Clear as a bell! And I *know*, I just *know* it's happened. To ME.'

There was a dead silence during which, Jenny thought, everyone listened nervously for asthmatic manifestations from Miss Cost's chest. There were none.

'Miss Cost,' said Patrick Ferrier at last. 'How perfectly splendid!' There were general ambiguous murmurs of congratulation. Major

Barrimore, looking as if he would like to exchange a wink with somebody, added: 'Long may it last!' They were all rather taken aback by the fervency with which she ejaculated. 'Amen! Yes, indeed. Amen!' The Rector looked extremely uncomfortable. Dr Maine asked Miss Cost if she'd seen any green ladies while she was about it.

'N-n-o!' she said and darted a very unfriendly glance at him.

'You sound as if you're not sure of that, Miss Cost.'

'My eyes were closed,' she said quickly.

'I see,' said Dr Maine.

The restless young man who had been biting at his nails said loudly: 'Look!' and having engaged their general attention, declared himself. 'Look!' he repeated, 'I'd better come clean and explain at once that I take a – well, a professional interest in all this. On holiday: but a news-hound's job's never done, is it? It seems to me there's quite a story here. I'm sure my paper would want our readers to hear about it. The London *Sun* and I'm Kenneth Joyce. "K.J.'s Column." You know? "What's The Answer?" Now, what do you all say? Just a news item. Nothing spectacular.'

'O, *no!*' Mrs Barrimore ejaculated and then added: 'I'm sorry. It's simply that I really do so dislike that sort of thing.'

'Couldn't agree more,' said Dr Maine. For a second they looked at each other.

'I really think,' the Rector said, '*not*. I'm afraid I dislike it too, Mr Joyce.'

'So do I,' Jenny said.

'*Do* you?' asked Mr Joyce. 'I'm sorry about that. I was going to ask if you'd lend me this picture. It'd blow up quite nicely. My paper would pay – '

'No,' said Jenny.

'Golly, how fierce!' said Mr Joyce, pretending to shrink. He looked about him. 'Now *why* not?' he asked.

Major Barrimore said: 'I don't know why not. I can't say I see anything wrong with it. The thing's happened, hasn't it, and it's damned interesting. Why shouldn't people hear about it?'

'O, I *do* agree,' cried Miss Cost. 'I'm sorry but I *do* so agree with the Major. When the papers are full of such dreadful things *shouldn't* we welcome a lovely, lovely true story like Wally's. O, yes!'

Patrick said to Mr Joyce: 'Well, at least you declared yourself,' and grinned at him.

'He wanted Jenny's photograph,' said Mrs Barrimore quietly. 'So he had to.'

They looked at her with astonishment. 'Well, honestly, Mama!' Patrick ejaculated. 'What a very crisp remark!'

'An extremely cogent remark,' said Dr Maine.

'I don't think so,' Major Barrimore said loudly and Jenny was aware of an antagonism that had nothing to do with the matter under discussion.

'But, of course I had to,' Mr Joyce conceded with a wide gesture and an air of candour. 'You're dead right. I *did* want the photograph. All the same, it's a matter of professional etiquette, you know. My paper doesn't believe in pulling fast ones. That's not *The Sun's* policy, at all. In proof of which I shall retire gracefully upon a divided house.'

He carried his drink over to Miss Cost and sat beside her. Mrs Barrimore got up and moved away. Dr Maine took her empty glass and put it on the bar.

There was an uncomfortable silence, induced perhaps by the general recollection that they had all drunk at Mr Joyce's expense and a suspicion that his hospitality had not been offered entirely without motive.

Mrs Barrimore said: 'Good night, everybody,' and went out.

Patrick moved over to Jenny. 'I'm going fishing in the morning if it's fine,' he said. 'Seeing it's a Saturday, would it amuse you to come? It's a small, filthy boat and I don't expect to catch anything.'

'What time?'

'Dawn. Or soon after. Say half past four.'

'Crikey! Well, yes, I'd love to if I can wake myself up.'

'I'll scratch on your door like one of the Sun King's courtiers. Which door is it? Frightening, if I scratched on Miss Cost's!'

Jenny told him. 'Look at Miss Cost now,' she said. 'She's having a whale of a time with Mr Joyce.'

'He's getting a story from her.'

'O, no!'

'O, yes! And tomorrow, betimes, he'll be hunting up Wally and his unspeakable parents. With a camera.'

'He won't!'

'Of course he will. If they're sober they'll be enchanted. Watch out for K.J.'s "What's The Answer" column in *The Sun.*'

'I do think the gutter-press in this country's the rock bottom.'

'Don't you have a gutter-press in New Zealand?'

'Not as low.'

'Well done, you. All the same, I don't see why K.J.'s idea strikes you as being so very low. No sex. No drugs. No crime. It's as clean as a whistle, like Wally's hands.' He was looking rather intently into Jenny's face. 'Sorry,' he said. 'You didn't like that, either, did you?'

'It's just – I don't know, or yes, I think I do. Wally's so vulnerable. I mean, he's been jeered at and cowed by the other children. He's been puzzled and lonely and now he's a comparatively happy little creature. Quite a hero, in a way. He's not attractive: his sort aren't, as a rule, but I've got an affection for him. Whatever's happened ought to be private to him.'

'But he won't take it in, will he? All the ballyhoo, if there *is* any ballyhoo? He may even vaguely enjoy it.'

'I don't want him to. All right,' Jenny said crossly, 'I'm being bloody-minded. Forget it. P'raps it won't happen.'

'I think you may depend upon it,' Patrick rejoined. 'It will.'

And, in the event, he turned out to be right.

IV

WHAT'S THE ANSWER?

Do You Believe in Fairies?

Wally Trehern does. Small boy of Portcarrow Island had crop of warts that made life a misery.

Other Kids Shunned Him Because of his Disfigurement. So Wally washed his hands in the Pixie Falls and – you've guessed it.

This is what they looked like before.

And here they are now.

Wally, seen above with parents, by Pixie Falls, says mysterious green lady 'told me to wash them off'.

Parents say no other treatment given.

Miss Elspeth Cost (inset) cured of chronic asthma?
Local doctor declines comment.
(Full story on Page 9.)

Dr Maine read the full story, gave an ambiguous ejaculation and started on his morning round.

The Convalescent Home was a very small one: six single rooms for patients, and living quarters for two nurses and for Dr Maine who was a widower. A veranda at the back of the house looked across a large garden and an adjacent field towards the sea and the Island.

At present he had four patients, all convalescent. One of them, an elderly lady, was already up and taking the air on the veranda. He noticed that she, like the others, had been reading *The Sun*.

'Well, Mrs Thorpe,' he said, bending over her, 'this is a step forward, isn't it? If you go on behaving nicely we'll soon have you taking that little drive.'

Mrs Thorpe wanly smiled and nodded. 'So unspoiled,' she said waving a hand at the prospect. 'Not many places left like it. No horrid trippers.'

He sat down beside her, laid his fingers on her pulse and looked at his watch. 'This is becoming pure routine,' he said cheerfully.

It was obvious that Mrs Thorpe had a great deal more to say. She scarcely waited for him to snap his watch shut before she began.

'Dr Maine, *have* you seen *The Sun*?'

'Very clearly. We're in for a lovely day.'

She made a little dab at him. 'Don't be provoking! You know what I mean. The paper. *Our* news! The *Island!*'

'Oh that. Yes, I saw that.'

'Now, *what* do you think? Candidly. Do tell me.'

He answered her as he had answered Patrick Ferrier. One heard of such cases. Medically there could be no comment.

'But you don't pooh-pooh?'

No, no. He didn't altogether do that. And now he really must –

As he moved away she said thoughtfully, 'My little nephew is dreadfully afflicted. They *are* such an eyesore, aren't they? And infectious, it's thought. One can't help wondering – '

His other patients were full of the news. One of them had a first cousin who suffered abominably from chronic asthma.

Miss Cost read it over and over again: especially the bit on page nine where it said what a martyr she'd been and how she had perfect faith in the waters. She didn't remember calling them the Pixie Falls but now she came to think of it, the name was pretty. She wished she'd had time to do her hair before Mr Joyce's friend had taken the snapshot and it would have been nicer if her mouth had been quite shut. But still. At low tide she strolled over to the newsagent's shop in the village. All their copies of *The Sun*, unfortunately, had been sold. There had been quite a demand. Miss Cost looked with a professional and disparaging eye at the shop. Nothing really at all in the way of souvenirs and the postcards were very limited. She bought three of the Island and covered the available space with fine writing. Her friend with arthritic hands would be interested.

V

Major Barrimore finished his coffee and replaced the cup with a slightly unsteady hand. His immaculately shaven jaws wore their morning purple tinge and his eyes were dull.

'Hasn't been long about it,' he said, referring to his copy of *The Sun*. 'Don't waste much time, these paper wallahs. Only happened day-before-yesterday.'

He looked at his wife. 'Well. Haven't you read it? 'he asked.

'I looked at it.'

'I don't know what's got into you. Why've you got your knife into this reporter chap? Decent enough fellah of his type.'

'Yes, I expect he is.'

'It'll create a lot of interest. Enormous circulation. Bring people in, I wouldn't wonder. Quite a bit about The Boy-and-Lobster.' She didn't answer and he suddenly shouted at her. 'Damn it, Margaret, you're about as cheerful as a dead fish. You'd think there'd been a death on the Island instead of a cure. God knows we could do with some extra custom.'

'I'm sorry, Keith. I know.'

He turned his paper to the racing page. 'Where's that son of yours?' he said presently.

'He and Jenny Williams were going to row round as usual to South Bay.'

'Getting very thick, aren't they?'

'Not alarmingly so. She's a dear girl.'

'If you can stomach the accent.'

'Hers is not so very strong do you think?'

'P'raps not. She's a fine strapping filly, I will say. Damn' good legs. Oughtn't he to be swotting?'

'He's working quite hard, really.'

'Of course *you'd* say so.' He lit a cigarette and returned to the racing notes. The telephone rang.

'I will,' said Mrs Barrimore.

She picked up the receiver. 'Boy-and-Lobster. Yes. Yes.' There was a loud crackle and she said to her husband, 'It's from London.'

'If it's Mrs Winterbottom,' said her husband, referring to his suzerain. 'I'm out.'

After a moment or two the call came through. 'Yes,' she said. 'Certainly. Yes, we can. A single room? May I have your name?'

There were two other long-distance calls during the day. By the end of the week the five rooms at The Boy-and-Lobster were all engaged.

A correspondence had got underway in *The Sun* on the subject of faith-healing and unexplained cures. On Friday there were inquiries from a regular television programme.

The school holidays had started and Jenny Williams had come to the end of her job at Portcarrow.

VI

While the Barrimores were engaged in their breakfast discussion, the Rector and Mrs Carstairs were occupied with the same topic. The tone of their conversation was, however, dissimilar.

'There!' Mr Carstairs said, smacking *The Sun* as it lay by his plate. 'There! Wretched creature! He's gone and done it!'

' 'T, yes, so he has. I saw. Now for the butcher,' said Mrs Carstairs who was worrying through the monthly bills.

'No, Dulcie, but it's too much. I'm furious,' said the Rector uncertainly. 'I'm livid.'

'Are you? Why? Because of the vulgarity or what? And *what*,' Mrs Carstairs continued, 'does Nankivell mean by saying "2 lbs bst fil." when we never order fillet let alone best? Stewing steak at the utmost. He must be mad.'

'It's not only the vulgarity, Dulcie. It's the effect on the village.'

'What effect? And threepence ha'penny is twelve, two, four. It doesn't even begin to make sense.'

'It's not that I don't rejoice for the boy. I do. I rejoice like anything and remember it in my prayers.'

'Of course you do,' said his wife.

'That's my whole point. One should be grateful and not jump to conclusions.'

'I shall speak to Nankivell. What conclusions?'

'Some ass,' said the Rector, 'has put it into the Treherns' heads that – O dear! – that there's been a – a – '

'Miracle?'

'Don't! One shouldn't. It's not a word to be bandied about. And they are bandying it about, those two.'

'So much for Nankivell and his rawhide,' she said, turning to the next bill. 'No, dear, I'm sure it's not. All the same it *is* rather wonderful.'

'So are all recoveries. Witnesses to God's mercy, my love.'

'Were the Treherns drunk?'

'Yes,' he said shortly. 'As owls. The Romans know how to deal with these things. Much more talk and we'll be in need of a devil's advocate.'

'Don't fuss,' said Mrs Carstairs, 'I expect it'll all simmer down.'

'I hae me doots,' her husband darkly rejoined. 'Yes, Dulcie. I hae me doots.'

VII

'How big is the Island?' Jenny asked, turning on her face to brown her back.

'Teeny. Not more than fourteen acres, I should think.'

'Who does it belong to?'

'To an elderly lady called Mrs Fanny Winterbottom who is the widow of a hairpin king. He changed over to bobby-pins at the right moment and became a millionaire. The Island might be called his Folly.'

'Pub and all?'

'Pub and all. My mother,' Patrick said, 'has shares in the pub. She took it on when my step-father was axed out of the Army.'

'It's Heaven: the Island. Not too pretty. This bay might almost be at home. I'll be sorry to go.'

'Do you get homesick, Jenny?'

'A bit. Sometimes. I miss the mountains and the way people think. All the same, it's fun trying to get tuned-in. At first, I was all prickles and antipodean prejudice, belly-aching away about living-conditions like the Treherns' cottage and hidebound attitudes and so on. But now – ' she squinted up at Patrick. 'It's funny,' she said, 'but I resent that rotten thing in the paper much more than you do and it's not only because of Wally. It's a kind of insult to the Island.'

'It made me quite cross too, you know.'

'English understatement. Typical example of.'

He gave her a light smack on the seat.

'When I think,' Jenny continued, working herself into a rage, 'of how that brute winkled the school group out of the Treherns and when I think how he had the damned impertinence to put a ring round *me* – '

' "Red-headed Jennifer Williams says warts were frightful",' Patrick quoted.

'How he dared!'

'It's not red, actually. In the sun it's copper. No, gold almost.'

'Never you mind what it is. O Patrick – '

'Don't say "Ow Pettruck".'

'Shut up.'

'Well, you asked me to stop you. And it is my name.'

'All right. Ae-oh, Pe-ah-trick, then.'

'What?'

'Do you suppose it might lead to a ghastly invasion? People smothered in warts and whistling with asthma bearing down from all points of the compass?'

'Charabancs.'

'A Giffte Shoppe.'

'Wire-netting round the spring.'

'And a bob to get in.'

'It's a daunting picture,' Patrick said. He picked up a stone and hurled it into the English Channel. 'I suppose,' he muttered, 'it would be profitable.'

'No doubt.' Jenny turned to look at him and sat up. 'Oh, no doubt,' she repeated. 'If that's a consideration.'

'My dear, virtuous Jenny, of course it's a consideration. I don't know whether, in your idyllic antipodes, you've come across the problem of constant hardupness. If you haven't I can assure you it's not much cop.'

'Well, but I have. And, Patrick, I'm sorry. I didn't know.'

'I'll forgive you. I'll go further and tell you that unless things look up a bit at The Boy-and-Lobster or, alternatively, unless my stepfather can be moved to close his account with his bookmaker and keep his hands off the whisky bottle you'll be outstaying us on the Island.'

'Patrick!'

'I'm afraid so. And the gentlemen of the Inns of Court will be able to offer their dinners to some more worthy candidate. I shan't eat them. I shall come down from Oxford and sell plastic combs from door to door. Will you buy one for your red-gold hair?' Patrick began to throw stones as fast as he could pick them up. 'It's not only that,' he said presently. 'It's my Mama. She's in a pretty dim situation, anyway, but here, at least, she's – ' He stood up. 'Well, Jenny,' he said. 'There's a sample of the English reticence that strikes you as being so comical.' He walked down to the boat and hauled it an unnecessary inch or two up the beach.

Jenny felt helpless. She watched him and thought that he made a pleasing figure against the sea as he tugged back in the classic posture of controlled energy.

'What am I to say to him?' she wondered. 'And does it matter what I say?'

He took their luncheon basket out of the boat and returned to her.

'Sorry about all that,' he said. 'Shall we bathe before the tide changes and then eat? Come on.'

She followed him down to the sea and lost her sensation of inadequacy as she battled against the incoming tide. They swam, together and apart, until they were tired and then returned to the beach and had their luncheon. Patrick was well-mannered and attentive and asked her a great many questions about New Zealand and the job she hoped to get, teaching English in Paris. It was not until they had decided to row back to their own side of the Island and he had shipped his oars, that he returned to the subject that waited, Jenny felt sure, at the back of both their minds.

'There's the brow of the hill,' he said. 'Just above our beach. And below it on the far side, is the spring. Did you notice that Miss Cost, in her interview, talked about the Pixie Falls?'

'I did. With nausea.'

He rowed round the point into Fisherman's Bay.

'Sentiment and expediency,' he said, 'are uneasy bedfellows. But, of course, it doesn't arise. It's quite safe to strike an attitude and say you'd rather sell plastic combs than see the prostitution of the place you love. There won't be any upsurge of an affluent society on Portcarrow Island. It will stay like this – as we both admire it, Jenny. Only we shan't be here to see. Two years from now and everybody will have forgotten about Wally Trehern's warts.'

He could scarcely have been more at fault. Before two years had passed everybody in Great Britain who could read a newspaper knew all about Wally Trehern's warts and because of them the Island had been transformed.

CHAPTER 2

Miss Emily

'The trouble with my family,' said Miss Emily Pride, speaking in exquisite French and transferring her gaze from Alleyn to some distant object, 'is that they go too far.'

Her voice was pitched on the high didactic note she liked to employ for sustained narrative. The sound of it carried Alleyn back through time on a wave of nostalgia. Here he had sat, in this very room that was so much less changed than he or Miss Emily. Here, a candidate for the Diplomatic Service, he had pounded away at French irregular verbs and listened to entrancing scandals of the days when Miss Emily's papa had been chaplain at our embassy in Paris. How old could she be now? Eighty? He pulled himself together and gave her his full attention.

'My sister, Fanny Winterbottom,' Miss Emily announced, 'was not free from this fault. I recall an informal entertainment at our embassy in which she was invited to take part. It was a burlesque. Fanny was grotesquely attired and carried a vegetable bouquet. She was not without talent of a farouche sort and made something of a hit. *Verb. sap.*: as you shall hear. Inflamed by success she improvised a short equivocal speech at the end of which she flung her bouquet at H.E. It struck him in the diaphragm and might well have led to an incident.'

Miss Emily recalled her distant gaze and focused it upon Alleyn. 'We are none of us free from this wild strain,' she said, 'but in my sister Fanny its manifestations were extreme. I cannot help but think there is a connection.'

'Miss Emily, I don't quite see what you mean.'

'Then you are duller than your early promise led me to expect. Let me elaborate.' This had always been an ominous threat with Miss Emily. She resumed her narrative style.

'My sister Fanny,' she said, 'married. A Mr George Winterbottom who was profitably engaged in Trade. So much for him. He died, leaving her a childless widow with a more than respectable fortune. Included in her inheritance was the soi-disant island which I mentioned in my letter.'

'Portcarrow?'

'Precisely. You cannot be unaware of recent events on this otherwise characterless promontory.'

'No, indeed.'

'In that case I shall *not* elaborate. Suffice it to remind you that within the last two years there has arisen, fructified and flourished, a cult of which I entirely disapprove and which is the cause of my present concern and of my calling upon your advice.'

She paused. 'Anything I can do, of course – ' Alleyn said.

'Thank you. Your accent has deteriorated. To continue. Fanny, intemperate as ever, encouraged her tenants in their wart-claims. She visited the Island, interviewed the child in question, and, having at the time an infected outbreak on her thumb, plunged it in the spring whose extreme coldness possibly caused it to burst. It was no doubt ripe to do so but Fanny darted about talking of miracles. There were other cases of an equally hysterical character. The thing had caught on and my sister exploited it. The inn was enlarged, the spring was enclosed, advertisements appeared in the papers. A shop was erected on the Island. The residents, I understand, are making money hand-over-fist.'

'I should imagine so.'

'Very well. My sister Fanny (at the age of 87), has died. I have inherited her estates. I need hardly tell you that I refuse to countenance this unseemly charade, still less to profit by it.'

'You propose to sell the place?'

'Certainly not. Do,' said Miss Emily sharply, 'pull yourself together, Roderique. This is not what I expect of you.'

'I beg your pardon, Miss Emily.'

She waved her hand. 'To sell would be to profit by its spurious fame and allow this nonsense full play. No, I intend to restore the

Island to its former state. I have instructed my solicitors to acquaint the persons concerned.'

'I see,' said Alleyn. He got up and stood looking down at his old tutoress. How completely Miss Emily had taken on the character of a certain type of elderly Frenchwoman. Her black clothes seemed to disclaim, clear-sightedly, all pretence to allure. Her complexion was grey: her jewellery of jet and gold. She wore a general air of disassociated fustiness. Her composure was absolute. The setting was perfectly consonant with the person: pieces of buhl; formal, upholstered, and therefore dingy, chairs; yellowing photographs, among which his own young, thin face stared back at him, and an unalterable arrangement of dyed pampas plumes in an elaborate vase. For Miss Emily, her room was absolutely *comme-il-faut*. Yes, after all, she must be –

'At the age of eighty-three,' she said, with uncanny prescience, 'I am not to be moved. If that is in your mind, Roderique.'

'I'm much too frightened of you, Miss Emily, to attempt any such task.'

'Ah, no!' she said in English. 'Don't say that! I hope not.'

He kissed her dry little hand as she had taught him to do. 'Well,' he said, 'tell me more about it. What *is* your plan?'

Miss Emily reverted to the French language. 'In effect, as I have told you, to restore the *status quo*. Ultimately I shall remove the enclosure, shut the shop and issue a general announcement disclaiming and exposing the entire affair.'

Alleyn said: 'I've never been able to make up my mind about these matters. The cure of warts by apparently irrational means is too well-established to be questioned. And even when you admit the vast number of failures, there *is* a pretty substantial case to be made out for certain types of faith-healing. Or so I understand. I can't help wondering why you are so very fierce about it all, Miss Emily. If you are repelled by the inevitable vulgarities, of course – '

'As, of course, I am. Still more, by the exploitation of the spring as a business concern. But most of all by personal experience of a case that failed: a very dear friend who suffered from a malignancy and who was absolutely – but I assure you, *absolutely* – persuaded it would be cured by such means. The utter cruelty of her disillusionment, her incredulity, her agonized disappointment and her death: these made a bitter impression upon me. I would sooner die myself,'

Miss Emily said with the utmost vigour, 'than profit in the smallest degree from such another tragedy.'

There was a brief silence. 'Yes,' Alleyn said. 'That does, indeed, explain your attitude.'

'But not my reason for soliciting your help. I must tell you that I have written to Major Barrimore who is the incumbent of the inn, and informed him of my decision. I have announced my intention of visiting the Island to see that this decision is carried out. And, since she will no doubt wish to provide for herself, I have also written to the proprietress of the shop, a Miss Elspeth Cost. I have given her three months' notice, unless she chooses to maintain the place as a normal establishment and refrain from exploiting the spring or mounting a preposterous anniversary festival which, I am informed, she has put in hand and which has been widely advertised in the Press.'

'Major Barrimore and Miss Cost must have been startled by your letters.'

'So much so, perhaps, that they have lost the power of communication. I wrote a week ago. There has been no *formal* acknowledgment.'

She said this with such a meaning air that he felt he was expected to take it up. 'Has there been an informal one? 'he ventured.

'Judge for yourself,' said Miss Emily, crisply.

She went to her desk, and returned with several sheets of paper which she handed to him.

Alleyn glanced at the first, paused, and then laid them all in a row on an occasional table. There were five. 'Hell!' he thought, 'this means a go with Miss Emily.' They were in the familiar form of newsprint pasted on ruled paper which had been wrenched from an exercise book. The first presented an account of several cures effected by the springs and was headed with unintentional ambiguity, 'Pixie Falls Again.' It was, he recognized, from the London *Sun*. Underneath the cutting was an irregularly assembled sentence of separated words, all in newsprint.

'Do not Attempt THREAT to close you are WARNED.' The second read, simply: 'DANGER keep OUT,' the third, 'Desecration will be prevented all costs,' the fourth: 'Residents are prepared interference will prove FATAL,' and the last, in one strip, 'DEATH OF ELDERLY WOMAN' with a piecemeal addendum 'this could be you.'

'Well,' Alleyn said, 'that's a pretty collection, I must say. When did they come?'

'One by one, over the last five days. The first must have been posted immediately after the arrival of my letter.'

'Have you kept the envelopes?'

'Yes. The postmark is Portcarrow.'

'May I see them?'

She produced them: five cheap envelopes. The address had been built up from newsprint.

'Will you let me keep these? And the letters?'

'Certainly.'

'Any idea who sent them?' he asked.

'None.'

'Who has your address?'

'The landlord. Major Barrimore.'

'It's an easy one to assemble from any paper. Thirty-seven Forecast Street. Wait a moment though. This one wasn't built up piece-meal. It's all in one. I don't recognize the type.'

'Possibly a local paper. At the time of my inheritance.'

'Yes. Almost certainly.'

He asked her for a larger envelope and put the collection into it.

'When do you plan to go to Portcarrow?'

'On Monday,' said Miss Emily composedly. 'Without fail.'

Alleyn thought for a moment and then sat down and took her hand in his. 'Now, my dear Miss Emily,' he said. 'Please do listen to what I'm going to say – in English, if you don't mind.'

'Naturally, I shall listen carefully since I have invited your professional opinion. As to speaking in English – very well, if you prefer it. *Enfin, en ce moment, on ne donne pas une leçon de français.*'

'No. One gives, if you'll forgive me, a lesson in sensible behaviour. Now, I don't suggest for a minute that these messages mean, literally, what they seem to threaten. Possibly they are simply intended to put you off and if they fail to do that, you may hear no more about it. On the other hand they do suggest that you have an enemy at Portcarrow. If you go there you will invite unpleasant reactions.'

'I am perfectly well aware of that. Obviously. And,' said Miss Emily on a rising note, 'if this person imagines that I am to be frightened off – '

'Now, wait a bit. There's no real need for you to go, is there? The whole thing can be done, and done efficiently, by your solicitors. It would be a – a dignified and reasonable way of settling.'

'Until I have seen for myself what goes on in the Island I cannot give explicit instructions.'

'But you can. You can get a report.'

'That,' said Miss Emily, 'would not be satisfactory.'

He could have shaken her.

'Have you,' he asked, 'shown these things to your solicitors.'

'I have not.'

'I'm sure they would give you the same advice.'

'I should not take it.'

'Suppose this person means to do exactly what the messages threaten? Offer violence? It might well be, you know.'

'That is precisely why I have sought your advice. I am aware that I should take steps to protect myself. What are they? I am not,' Miss Emily said, 'proficient in the use of small-arms and I understand that, in any case, one requires a permit. No doubt in your position, you could obtain one and might possibly be so very kind as to give me a little instruction.'

'I shall not fiddle a small-arms permit for you and nor shall I teach you to be quick on the draw. The suggestion is ridiculous.'

'There are, perhaps, other precautions,' she conceded, 'such as walking down the centre of the road, remaining indoors after dark and making no assignations at unfrequented rendezvous.'

Alleyn contemplated his old instructress. Was there or was there not a remote twinkle in that dead-pan eye?

'I think,' he said, 'you are making a nonsense of me.'

'Who's being ridiculous now?' asked Miss Emily tartly.

He stood up. 'All right,' he said. 'As a police officer it's my duty to tell you that I think it extremely unwise for you to go to Portcarrow. As a grateful, elderly, ex-pupil, I assure you that I shall be extremely fussed about you if you're obstinate enough to persist in your plan. Dear Miss Emily,' said Alleyn, with a change of tone, 'do, for the love of Mike, pipe down and stay where you are.'

'You would have been successful,' she said, 'if you had continued in the Corps Diplomatique. I have never comprehended why you elected to change.'

'Obviously, I've had no success in this instance.'

'No. I shall go. But I am infinitely obliged to you, Roderique.'

'I suppose this must be put down to the wild strain in your blood.'

'Possibly.' Indicating that the audience was concluded, she rose and reverted to French. 'You will give my fondest salutations to your wife and son?'

'Thank you. Troy sent all sorts of messages to you.'

'You appear to be a little fatigued. When is your vacation?'

'When I can snatch it. I hope, quite soon,' Alleyn said and was at once alarmed by a look of low cunning in Miss Emily. 'Please *don't* go,' he begged her.

She placed her hand in the correct position to be kissed. '*Au revoir*,' she said, '*et mille remerciements.*'

'*Mes hommages, madame,*' said Alleyn crossly. With the profoundest misgivings he took his leave of Miss Emily.

II

It was nine o'clock in the evening when the London train reached Dunlowman where one changed for the Portcarrow bus. On alighting, Jenny was confronted by several posters depicting a fanciful Green Lady across whose image was superimposed a large notice advertising 'The Festival of the Spring.' She had not recovered from this shock when she received a second one in the person of Patrick Ferrier. There he was, looking much the same after nearly two years, edging his way through the crowd, quite a largish one, that moved towards the barrier. 'Jenny!' he called. 'Hi! I've come to meet you.'

'But it's miles and miles!' Jenny cried, delighted to see him.

'A bagatelle. Hold on. Here I come.'

He reached her and seized her suitcases. 'This *is* fun,' he said. 'I'm so glad.'

Outside the station a number of people had collected under a sign that read 'Portcarrow Bus.' Jenny watched them as she waited for Patrick to fetch his car. They looked, she thought, a singularly mixed bunch and yet there was something about them – what was it? – that gave them an exclusive air, as if they belonged to some rather outlandish sect. The bus drew up and as these people began to climb in, she saw that among them there was a girl wearing a steel brace on her leg. Further along the queue a man with an emaciated face and terrible eyes quietly waited his turn. There was a plain, heavy youth with a bandaged ear and a woman who laughed repeatedly, it seemed without cause, and drew no response from her companion, an older woman, who kept her hand under the other's forearm and looked ahead. They filed into the bus and although there were no other outward signs of the element that united them, Jenny knew what it was.

Patrick drove up in a two-seater. He put her luggage into a boot that was about a quarter of the size of the bonnet and in a moment they had shot away down the street.

'This is very handsome of you, Patrick,' Jenny said. 'And what a car!'

'Isn't she pleasant?'

'New, I imagine.'

'Yes. To celebrate. I'm eating my dinners, after all, Jenny. Do you remember?'

'Of course. I do congratulate you.'

'You may not be so polite when you see how it's been achieved, however. Your wildest fantasies could scarcely match the present reality of the Island.'

'I did see the English papers in Paris and your letters were fairly explicit.'

'Nevertheless you're in for a shock, I promise you.'

'I expect I can take it.'

'Actually, I rather wondered if we ought to ask you.'

'It was sweet of your mama and I'm delighted to come. Patrick, it's wonderful to be back in England. When I saw the Battersea power-station, I cried. For sheer pleasure.'

'You'll probably roar like a bull when you see Portcarrow and not for pleasure, either. You haven't lost your susceptibility for places, I see. By the way,' Patrick said after a pause, 'you've arrived for a crisis.'

'What sort of crisis?'

'In the person of an old, old angry lady called Miss Emily Pride, who has inherited the Island from her sister (Winterbottom, deceased). She shares your views about exploiting the spring. You ought to get on like houses on fire.'

'What's she going to do?'

'Shut up shop unless the combined efforts of interested parties can steer her off. Everybody's in a frightful taking-on about it. She arrives on Monday, breathing restoration and fury.'

'Like a wicked fairy godmother?'

'Very like. Probably flourishing a black umbrella and emitting sparks. She's flying into a pretty solid wall of opposition. Of course,' Patrick said abruptly, 'the whole thing has been fantastic. For some reason the initial story caught on. It was the silly season and the papers, as you may remember, played it up. Wally's warts became big news. That led to the first lot of casual visitors. Mrs Winterbottom's men of business began to make interested noises and the gold-rush, to coin a phrase, set in. Since then it's never looked back.'

They had passed through the suburbs of Dunlowman and were driving along a road that ran out towards the coast.

'It was nice getting your occasional letters,' Patrick said, presently. 'Operative word "occasional".'

'And yours.'

'I'm glad you haven't succumbed to the urge for black satin and menacing jewellery that seems to overtake so many girls who get jobs in France. But there's a change, all the same.'

'You're not going to suggest I've got a phoney foreign accent?'

'No, indeed. You've got no accent at all.'

'And that, no doubt, makes the change. I expect having to speak French has cured it.'

'You must converse with Miss Pride. She is, or was, before she succeeded to the Winterbottom riches, a terrifically high-powered coach for chaps entering the Foreign Service. She's got a network of little spokes all round her mouth from making those exacting noises that are required by the language.'

'You've seen her, then?'

'Once. She visited with her sister about a year ago and left in a rage.'

'I suppose,' Jenny said after a pause, 'this is really very serious, this crisis?'

'It's hell,' he rejoined with surprising violence.

Jenny asked about Wally Trehern and was told that he had become a menace. 'He doesn't know where he is but he knows he's the star-turn,' Patrick said. 'People make little pilgrimages to the cottage which has been tarted up in a sort of Peggotty-style *Kitsch*. Seaweed round the door almost, and a boat in a bottle. Mrs Trehern keeps herself to herself and the gin bottle but Trehern is a new man. He exudes a kind of honest-tar sanctity and sells Wally to the pilgrims.'

'You appal me.'

'I thought you'd better know the worst. What's more, there's an Anniversary Festival next Saturday, organized by Miss Cost. A choral procession to the Spring and Wally, dressed up like a wee fisher lad, reciting doggerel if he can remember it, poor little devil.'

'Don't!' Jenny exclaimed. 'Not true!'

'True, I'm afraid.'

'But Patrick – about the cures? The people that come? What happens?'

Patrick waited for a moment. He then said in a voice that held no overtones of irony: 'I suppose, you know, it's what always happens in these cases. Failure after failure until one thinks the whole thing is an infamous racket and is bitterly ashamed of having any part of it. And then, for no apparent reason, one, perhaps two, perhaps a few more, people do exactly what the others have done but go away without their warts or their migraine or their asthma or their chronic diarrhoea. Their gratitude and sheer exuberance! You can't think what it's like, Jenny. So then, of course, one diddles oneself – or is it diddling? – into imagining these cases wipe out all the others and all the ballyhoo, and my fees and this car, and Miss Cost's Giffte Shoppe. She really has called it that, you know. She sold her former establishment and set up another on the Island. She sells tiny plastic models of the Green Lady and pamphlets she's written herself, as well as handwoven jerkins and other novelties that I haven't the face to enumerate. Are you sorry you came?'

'I don't think so. And your mother? What does she think?'

'Who knows?' Patrick said, simply. 'She has a gift for detachment, my mama.'

'And Dr Maine?'

'Why he?' Patrick said sharply, and then: 'Sorry: Why not? Bob Maine's nursing home is now quite large and invariably full.'

Feeling she had blundered, Jenny said: 'And the Rector? How on earth has he reacted?'

'With doctrinal *léger de main*. No official recognition on the one hand. Proper acknowledgments in the right quarter on the other. Jolly sensible of him, in my view.'

Presently they swept up the downs that lie behind the coastline, turned into a steep lane and were, suddenly, on the cliffs above Portcarrow.

The first thing that Jenny noticed was a red neon sign, glaring up through the dusk: 'Boy-and-Lobster.' The tide was almost full and the sign was shiftingly reflected in dark water. Next, she saw that a string of coloured lights connected the Island with the village and that the village itself must now extend along the foreshore for some distance. Lamps and windows, following the convolutions of bay and headland, suggested a necklace that had been carelessly thrown down on some night-blue material. She supposed that in a way the effect must be called pretty. There was a number of cars parked along the cliffs with people making love in them or merely staring out to sea. A large, prefabricated, multiple garage had been built at the roadside. There was also a café.

'There you have it,' Patrick said. 'We may as well take the plunge.'

They did so literally, down a precipitous and narrow descent. That at least had not changed and nor at first sight had the village itself. There was the old post-office-shop and, farther along, the Portcarrow Arms with a new coat of paint. 'This is now referred to as the Old Part,' said Patrick. 'Elsewhere there's a rash of boarding establishments and a multiple store. Trehern, by the way is Ye Ancient Ferryman. I'll put you down with your suitcase at the jetty, dig him out of the pub and park the car. OK?'

There was nobody about down by the jetty. The high tide slapped quietly against wet pylons and whispered and dragged along the foreshore. The dank smell of it was pleasant and familiar. Jenny looked across the narrow gap to the Island. There was a lamp now, at the landing and a group of men stood by it. Their voices sounded clear and tranquil. She saw that the coloured lights were strung on metal poles mounted in concrete, round whose bases sea-water eddied and slopped, only just covering the causeway.

Patrick returned and with him Trehern who was effusive in salutations and wore a peaked cap with 'Boy-and-Lobster' on it.

'There's a motor launch,' Patrick said, pointing to it. 'For the peak hours. But we'll row over, shall we?' He led the way down the jetty to where a smart dinghy was tied up. She was called, inevitably, *The Pixie*.

'There were lots of people in the bus,' said Jenny.

'I expect so,' he rejoined, helping her into the dinghy. 'For the Festival, you know.'

'Ar, the por souls!' Trehern ejaculated. 'May the Heavenly Powers bring them release from their afflictions.'

'Cast off,' said Patrick.

The gurgle of water and rhythmic clunk of oars in their rowlocks carried Jenny back to the days when she and Patrick used to visit their little bay.

'It's a warm, still night, isn't it?' she said.

'Isn't it?' Patrick agreed. He was beside her in the stern. He slipped his arm round her. 'Do you know,' he said in her ear, 'it's extraordinarily pleasant to see you again.'

Jenny could smell the Harris tweed of his coat. She glanced at him. He was staring straight ahead. It was very dark but she fancied he was smiling.

She felt that she must ask Trehern about Wally and did so.

'He be pretty clever, Miss, thank you. You'll see a powerful change in our little lad, no doubt, him having been the innocent means of joy and thanksgiving to them as seeked for it.'

Jenny could find nothing better to say than: 'Yes, indeed.'

'Not that he be puffed-up by his exclusive state, however,' Trehern added. 'Meek as a mouse but all-glorious within. That's our Wally.'

Patrick gave Jenny a violent squeeze.

They pulled into the jetty and went ashore. Trehern begged Jenny to visit her late pupil at the cottage and wished them an unctuous good night.

Jenny looked about her. Within the sphere of light cast by the wharf lamp, appeared a shop-window which had been injected into an existing cottage front. It was crowded with small indistinguishable objects. 'Yes,' Patrick said. 'That's Miss Cost. Don't dwell on it.'

It was not until they had climbed the steps, which had been widened and re-graded and came face-to-face with The Boy-and-Lobster that the full extent of the alterations could be seen. The old pub had been smartened but not altered. At either end of it, however, there now projected large two-storied wings which completely dwarfed the original structure. There was a new and important entrance and a 'lounge' into which undrawn curtains admitted a view of quite an assemblage of guests, some reading, others playing cards or writing letters. In the background was a ping-pong table and beyond that, a bar.

Patrick said, 'There you have it.'

They were about to turn away when someone came out of the main entrance and moved uncertainly towards them. He was dressed in a sort of Victorian smock over long trousers and there was a jellybag cap on his head. He had grown much taller. Jenny didn't recognize him at first but as he shambled into a patch of light she saw his face.

'Costume,' Patrick said, 'by Maison Cost.'

'Wally!' she cried. 'It's Wally.'

He gave her a sly look and knuckled his forehead. ' 'Evening, 'evening,' he said. His voice was still unbroken. He held out his hands. 'I'm Wally,' he said. 'Look. All gone.'

'Wally, do you remember me? Miss Williams? Do you?'

His mouth widened in a grin. 'No,' he said.

'Your teacher.'

'One lady gave me five bob, she done. One lady done.'

'You mustn't ask for tips,' Patrick said.

Wally laughed. 'I never,' he said and looked at Jenny. 'You come and see me. At Wally's place.'

'Are you at school, still?'

'At school. I'm in the fustivell.' He showed her his hands again, gave one of his old squawks and suddenly ran off.

'Never mind,' Patrick said. 'Come along. Never mind, Jenny.'

He took her in by the old door, now marked Private, and here everything was familiar. 'The visitors don't use this,' he said. 'There's an office and reception desk in the new building. You're *en famille*, Jenny. We've put you in my room. I hope you don't mind.'

'But what about you?'

'I'm all right. There's an emergency bolt-hole.'

'Jenny!' said Mrs Barrimore, coming into the little hall. 'How lovely!'

She was much more smartly dressed than she used to be and looked, Jenny thought, very beautiful. They kissed warmly. 'I'm so glad,' Mrs Barrimore said. 'I'm so very glad.'

Her hand trembled on Jenny's arm and, inexplicably, there was a blur of tears in her eyes. Jenny was astounded.

'Patrick will show you where you are and there's supper in the old dining-room. I – I'm busy at the moment. There's a sort of meeting. Patrick will explain,' she said hurriedly. 'I hope I shan't be long. You can't think how pleased we are, can she, Patrick?'

'She hasn't an inkling,' he said. 'I forgot about the emergency meeting, Jenny. It's to discuss strategy and Miss Pride. How's it going, Mama?'

'I don't know. Not very well. I don't know.'

She hesitated, winding her fingers together in the old way. Patrick gave her a kiss. 'Don't give it a thought,' he said. 'What is it they say in Jenny's antipodes? "She'll be right"? She'll be right, Mama, never you fear.'

But when his mother had left them, Jenny thought for a moment he looked very troubled.

III

In the old bar-parlour Major Barrimore with Miss Pride's letter in his hand and his double-Scotch on the chimneypiece, stood on the hearthrug and surveyed his meeting. It consisted of the Rector, Dr Maine, Miss Cost and Mr Ives Nankivell, who was the newly-created Mayor of Portcarrow, and also its leading butcher. He was an undersized man with a look of perpetual astonishment.

'No,' Major Barrimore was saying, 'apart from yourselves I haven't told anyone. Fewer people know about it, the better. Hope you all agree.'

'From the tone of her letter,' Dr Maine said, 'the whole village'll know by this time next week.'

'Wicked!' Miss Cost cried out in a trembling voice, 'that's what she must be. A wicked woman. Or mad,' she added, as an afterthought. 'Both, I expect.'

The men received this uneasily.

'How, may I inquire, Major, did you frame your reply?' the Mayor asked.

'Took a few days to decide,' said Major Barrimore, 'and sent a wire. "Accommodation reserved will be glad to discuss matter outlined in your letter".'

'Very proper.'

'Thing is, as I said when I told you about it: we ought to arrive at some sort of agreement among ourselves. She gives your names, as the people she wants to see. Well, we've all had a week to think it over. What's our line going to be? Better be consistent, hadn't we?'

'But can we be consistent?' the Rector asked. 'I think you all know my views. I've never attempted to disguise them. In the pulpit or anywhere else.'

'But you don't,' said Miss Cost, who alone had heard the Rector from the pulpit, 'you *don't* deny the truth of the cures, now *do* you?'

'No,' he said. 'I thank God for them but I deplore the – excessive publicity.'

'Naow, naow, naow,' said the Mayor excitedly. 'Didn't we ought to take a wider view? Didn't we ought to think of the community as a whole? In my opinion, sir, the remarkable properties of our Spring has brought nothing but good to Portcarrow: nothing but good. And didn't the public at large ought to be made aware of the benefits we offer? I say it did and it ought which is what it has and should continue to be.'

'Jolly good, Mr Mayor,' said Barrimore. 'Hear, hear!'

'Hear!' said Miss Cost.

'Would she sell?' Dr Maine asked suddenly.

'I don't think she would, Bob.'

'Ah well, naow,' said the Mayor, 'Naow! Suppose – and mind, gentlemen, I speak unofficially. Private – But, suppose she would. There might be a possibility that the borough itself would be interested. As a spec – ' He caught himself up and looked sideways at the Rector. 'As a civic duty. Or maybe a select group of right-minded residents – '

Dr Maine said dryly: 'They'd find themselves competing in pretty hot company, I fancy. If the Island came on the open market.'

'Which it won't,' said Major Barrimore. 'If I'm any judge. She's hell-bent on wrecking the whole show.'

Mr Nankivell allowed himself a speculative grin. 'Happen she don't know the value, however,' he insinuated.

'Perhaps she's concerned with other values,' the Rector murmured.

At this point Mrs Barrimore returned.

'Don't move,' she said and sat down in a chair near the door. 'I don't know if I'm still – ?'

Mr Nankivell embarked on a gallantry but Barrimore cut across it. 'You'd better listen, Margaret,' he said, with a restless glance at his wife. 'After all, she may talk to you.'

'Surely, surely!' the Mayor exclaimed. 'The ladies understand each other in a fashion that's above the heads of us mere chaps, be'ant it, Miss Cost?'

Miss Cost said: 'I'm sure I don't know,' and looked very fixedly at Mrs Barrimore.

'We don't seem to be getting anywhere,' Dr Maine observed.

The Mayor cleared his throat. 'This be'ant what you'd call a formal committee,' he began, 'but if it was and if I was in occupation of the chair, I'd move we took the temper of the meeting.'

'Very good,' Barrimore said. 'Excellent suggestion. I propose His Worship be elected chairman. Those in favour?' The others muttered a disjointed assent and the Mayor expanded. He suggested that what they really had to discover was how each of them proposed to respond to Miss Pride's onslaught. He invited them to speak in turn, beginning with the Rector who repeated that they all knew his views and that he would abide by them.

'Does that mean,' Major Barrimore demanded, 'that if she says she's going to issue a public repudiation of the Spring, remove the enclosure and stop the festival, you'd come down on her side?'

'I shouldn't try to dissuade her.'

The Mayor made an explosive ejaculation and turned on him: 'If you'll pardon my frankness, Mr Carstairs,' he began, 'I'd be obliged if you'd tell the company what you reckon would have happened to your Church Restoration Fund if Portcarrow hadn't benefited by the Spring to the extent it has done. Where'd you've got the money to repair your tower? You *wouldn't* have got it, no, nor anything like it.'

Mr Carstairs's normally sallow face reddened painfully. 'No,' he said, 'I don't suppose we should.'

'Hah!' said Miss Cost, 'there you are!'

'I'm a Methodist myself,' said the Mayor in triumph.

'Quite so,' Mr Carstairs agreed.

'Put it this way. Will you egg the woman on, sir, in her foolish notions. Will you do that?'

'No. It's a matter for her own conscience.'

The Mayor, Major Barrimore and Miss Cost all began to expostu-late. Dr Maine said with repressed impatience: 'I really don't think there's any future in pressing the point.'

'Nor do I,' said Mrs Barrimore unexpectedly.

Miss Cost, acidly smiling, looked from her to Dr Maine and then, fixedly, at Major Barrimore.

'Very good, Doctor,' Mr Nankivell said. 'What about yourself, then?'

Dr Maine stared distastefully at his own hands and said: 'Paradoxically, I find myself in some sort of agreement with the Rector. I, too, haven't disguised my views. I have an open mind about these cases. I have neither encouraged nor discouraged my patients to make use of the Spring. When there has been apparent benefit I have said nothing to undermine anyone's faith in its permanency. I am neutral.'

'And from that impregnable position,' Major Barrimore observed, 'you've added a dozen rooms to your bloody nursing home. Beg pardon, Rector.'

'Keith!'

Major Barrimore turned on his wife. 'Well, Margaret?' he demanded. 'What's *your* objection?'

Miss Cost gave a shrill laugh.

Before Mrs Barrimore could answer, Dr Maine said very coolly, 'You're perfectly right. I have benefited like all the rest of you. But as far as my practice is concerned, I believe Miss Pride's activities will make very little difference, in the long run. Either to it or to the pop-ular appeal of the Spring. Sick people who are predisposed to the idea, will still think they know better. Or hope they know better,' he added. 'Which is, I suppose, much the same thing.'

'That's all damn' fine but it won't be the same thing to the com-munity at large,' Barrimore angrily pointed out. 'Tom, Dick and Harry and their friends and relations, swarming all over the place. The Island, a tripper's shambles, and the Press making a laughing-stock of the whole affair.' He emptied his glass.

'And the Festival!' Miss Cost wailed. 'The Festival! All our devotion! The response! The disappointment. The humiliation!' She waved her hands. A thought struck her. 'And Wally! He has actually memorized! After weeks of patient endeavour, he has memorized his little verses. Only this afternoon. One trivial slip. The choir is *utterly* committed.'

'I'll be bound!' said Mr Nankivell heartily. 'A credit to all concerned and a great source of gratification to the borough if looked at
in the proper spirit. We'm all waiting on the doctor, however,' he
added. 'Now, Doctor, what is it to be? What'll you say to the lady?'

'Exactly what I said two minutes ago to you,' Dr Maine snapped.
'I'll give my opinion if she wants it. I don't mind pointing out to her
that the thing will probably go on after a fashion, whatever she does.'

'I suppose that's something,' said the Mayor gloomily. 'Though
not much, with an elderly female so deadly set on destruction.'

'I,' Miss Cost intervened hotly, 'shall not mince my words. I shall
tell her – No,' she amended with control. 'I shall plead with her. I
shall appeal to the nobler side. Let us hope that there is one. Let us
hope so.'

'I second that from the chair,' said Mr Nankivell. 'Though with
reservations prejudicial to an optimistic view. Major?'

'What'll I do? I'll try and reason with her. Give her a straight picture of the incontrovertible cures. If the man of science,' Major
Barrimore said with a furious look at Dr Maine, 'would come off his
high horse and back me up, I might get her to listen. As it is – ' he
passed his palm over his hair and gave a half-smile, 'I'll do what I
can with the lady. I want another drink. Anyone join me?'

The Mayor and, after a little persuasion, Miss Cost, joined him. He
made towards the old private bar. As he opened the door, he admitted sounds of voices and of people crossing the flagstones to the
main entrance.

Patrick looked in. 'Sorry to interrupt,' he said to his mother. 'The
bus load's arrived.'

She got up quickly. 'I must go,' she said. 'I'm sorry.'

His step-father said: 'Damn! All right.' And to the others. 'I won't
be long. Pat, look after the drinks, here, will you? Two double
Scotches and a glass of the sweet port.'

He went out followed by his wife and Patrick and could be heard
welcoming his guests. 'Good evening! Good evening to you! Now,
come along in. You must all be exhausted. Awfully glad to see you – '

His voice faded.

There was a brief silence.

'Yes,' said the Mayor. 'Yes. Be-the-way, we didn't get round to
axing the lady's view, did we? Mrs Barrimore?'

For some reason they all looked extremely uncomfortable.
Miss Cost gave a shrill laugh.

IV

' " – and I'd take it as a personal favour",' Alleyn dictated, ' "if
you could spare a man to keep an eye on the Island when Miss
Pride arrives there. Very likely nothing will come of these communications but, as we all know, they can lead to trouble. I
ought to warn you that Miss Pride, though eighty-three, is in
vigorous possession of all her faculties and if she drops to it that
you've got her under observation, she may cut up rough. No
doubt, like all the rest of us, you're under-staffed and won't
thank me for putting you to this trouble. If your chap does
notice anything out of the way, I would be very glad to hear of
it. Unless a job blows up to stop me, I'm grabbing an overdue
week's leave from tomorrow and will be at the above address.
    ' " Again – sorry to be a nuisance,
            Yours sincerely,"

'All right. Got the name? Superintendent A. F. Coombe,
Divisional HQ, wherever it is – at Portcarrow itself, I fancy. Get it off
straight away, will you?'

When the letter had gone he looked at his watch. Five minutes
past midnight. His desk was cleared and his files closed. The calendar showed Monday. He flipped it over. 'I should have written
before,' he thought. 'My letter will arrive with Miss Emily.' He was
ready to leave, but, for some reason, dawdled there, too tired, suddenly, to make a move. After a vague moment or two he lit his pipe,
looked round his room and walked down the long corridor and the
stairs, wishing the PC on duty at the doors good night.

It was his only superstition. 'By the pricking of my thumbs.'

As he drove away down the Embankment he thought: 'Damned
if I don't ring that Super up in the morning: be damned if I don't.'

CHAPTER 3

Threats

Miss Emily arrived at noon on Monday. She had stayed overnight in Dorset and was as fresh as paint. It was agreeable to be able to command a chauffeur-driven car and the man was not unintelligent.

When they drew up at Portcarrow jetty she gave him a well-considered tip, asked his name and told him she would desire, particularly, that he should be deputed for the return journey.

She then alighted, observed by a small gang of wharf loiterers.

A personable young man came forward to meet her.

'Miss Pride? I'm Patrick Ferrier. I hope you had a good journey.'

Miss Emily was well-disposed towards the young and, she had good reason to believe, a competent judge of them. She inspected Patrick and received him with composure. He introduced a tall, glowing girl who came forward, rather shyly, to shake hands. Miss Emily had less experience of girls but she liked the look of this one and was gracious.

'The causeway is negotiable,' Patrick said, 'but we thought you'd prefer the launch.'

'It is immaterial,' she rejoined. 'The launch, let it be.'

Patrick and the chauffeur handed her down the steps. Trehern stowed away her luggage and was profuse in cap-touching. They shoved-off from the jetty, still watched by idlers among whom, conspicuous in his uniform, was a police sergeant. ' 'Morning, Pender!' Patrick called cheerfully as he caught sight of him.

In a motor launch, the trip across was ludicrously brief but even so Miss Emily, bolt upright in the stern, made it portentous. The sun shone and against it she displayed her open umbrella as if it were a piece of ceremonial plumage. Her black kid gloves gripped the handle centrally and her handbag, enormous and vice-like in its security, was placed between her feet. She looked, Patrick afterwards suggested, like some Burmese female deity. 'We should have arranged to have had her carried, shoulder-high, over the causeway,' he said.

Major Barrimore, with a porter in attendance, awaited her on the jetty. He resembled, Jenny thought, an illustration from an Edwardian sporting journal. 'Well-tubbed' was the expression. His rather prominent eyes were a little bloodshot. He had to sustain the difficult interval that spanned approach and arrival and decide when to begin smiling and making appropriate gestures. Miss Emily gave him no help. Jenny and Patrick observed him with misgivings. 'Good morning!' he shouted, gaily bowing, as they drew alongside. Miss Emily slightly raised and lowered her umbrella.

'That's right, Trehern. Easy does it. Careful, man,' Major Barrimore chattered. 'Heave me that line. Splendid!' He dropped the loop over a bollard and hovered, anxiously solicitous, with extended arm. 'Welcome! Welcome!' he cried.

'Good morning, Major Barrimore,' Miss Emily said. 'Thank you. I can manage perfectly.' Disregarding Trehern's outstretched hand, she looked fixedly at him. 'Are you the father?' she asked.

Trehern removed his cap and grinned with all his might. 'That I be, ma-am,' he said. 'If you be thinking of our Wally, ma-am, that I be, and mortal proud to own up to him.'

'I shall see you, if you please,' said Miss Emily, 'later.' For a second or two everyone was motionless.

She shook hands with her host.

'This *is* nice,' he assured her. 'And what a day we've produced for you! Now, about these steps of ours. Bit stiff, I'm afraid. May I – ?'

'No, thank you. I shall be sustained in my ascent,' said Miss Emily, fixing Miss Cost's shop and then the hotel façade in her gaze, 'by the prospect.'

She led the way up the steps.

' 'Jove!' the Major exclaimed when they arrived at the top. 'You're too good for me, Miss Pride. Wonderful going! Wonderful!'

She looked briefly at him. 'My habits,' she said, 'are abstemious. A little wine or cognac only. I have never been a smoker.'

'Jolly good! Jolly good!' he applauded. Jenny began to feel acutely sorry for him.

Margaret Barrimore waited in the main entrance. She greeted Miss Emily with no marked increase in her usual diffidence. 'I hope you had a pleasant journey,' she said. 'Would you like to have luncheon upstairs? There's a small sitting-room we've kept for you. Otherwise, the dining-room is here.' Miss Emily settled for the dining-room but wished to see her apartment first. Mrs Barrimore took her up. Her husband, Patrick and Jenny stood in the hall below and had nothing to say to each other. The Major, out of forgetfulness, it seemed, was still madly beaming. He caught his step-son's eye, uttered an expletive and without further comment, made for the bar.

Miss Emily, when she had lunched, took her customary siesta. She removed her dress and shoes, loosened her stays, put on a grey cotton peignoir and lay on the bed. There were several illustrated brochures to hand and she examined them. One contained a rather elaborate account of the original cure. It displayed a fanciful drawing of the Green Lady, photographs of the Spring, of Wally Trehern and a number of people passing through a sort of turnpike. A second gave a long list of subsequent healings with names and personal tributes. Miss Emily counted them up. Nine warts, five asthmas (including Miss Cost), three arthritics, two migraines and two chronic diarrhoeas (anonymous). 'And many many more who have experienced relief and improvement,' the brochure added. A folder advertised the coming Festival and, inset, Elspeth Cost's Giffte Shoppe. There was also a whimsical map of the Island with boats, fish, nets and pixies and, of course, a Green Lady.

Miss Emily studied the map and noted that it showed a direct route from The Boy-and-Lobster to the Spring.

A more business-like leaflet caught her attention.

THE TIDES AT PORTCARROW

The tides running between the village and the island show considerable variation in clock times. Roughly speaking, the water reaches its peak level twice in 24 hours and its lowest level at times which are about midway between those of high water. High and dead water times may vary from day to day with a lag of about 1-1 3/4 hours in 24 hours. Thus if high water falls at noon on Sunday it may occur somewhere between 1 and 2.45 p.m. on Monday afternoon. About a fortnight may elapse before the cycle is completed and high water again falls between noon and 1.45 on Sunday.

Visitors will usually find the causeway is negotiable for 2 hours before and after low water. The hotel launch and dinghies are always available and all the jetties reach into deep water at low tide.

Expected times for high tide and dead water will be posted up daily at the Reception Desk in the main entrance.

Miss Emily studied this information for some minutes. She then consulted the whimsical map.

At five o'clock she caused tea to be brought to her. Half an hour later, she dressed and descended, umbrella in hand, to the vestibule.

The hall-porter was on duty. When he saw Miss Emily he pressed a bell-push on his desk and rose with a serviceable smirk. 'Can I help you, madam?' he asked.

'In so far as I require admission to the enclosure, I believe you may. I understand that entry is effected by means of some plaque or token,' said Miss Emily.

He opened a drawer and extracted a metal disc. 'I shall require,' she said, 'seven,' and laid two half-crowns and a florin on the desk. The hall-porter completed the number.

'No, no, no!' Major Barrimore expostulated, bouncing out from the interior. 'We can't allow this. Nonsense!' He waved the hall-porter away. 'See that a dozen of these things are sent up to Miss Pride's suite,' he said and bent gallantly over his guest. 'I'm so sorry! Ridiculous!'

'You are very good,' she rejoined, 'but I prefer to pay.' She opened her reticule, swept the discs into it and shut it with a formidable snap. 'Thank you,' she said dismissing the hall-porter. She prepared to leave.

'I don't approve,' Major Barrimore began, 'I – really, it's very naughty of you. Now, may I – as it's your first visit since – may I just show you the easiest way?'

'I have, I think, discovered it from the literature provided and need not trespass upon your time, Major Barrimore. I am very much obliged to you.' Something in her manner, or perhaps a covert glance from his employer, had caused the hall-porter to disappear. 'In respect of my letter,' Miss Emily said, with a direct look at the Major, 'I would suggest that we postpone any discussion until I have made myself fully conversant with prevailing conditions on my property. I hope this arrangement is convenient?'

'Anything!' he cried. 'Naturally. Anything! But I do hope – '

'Thank you,' said Miss Emily and left him.

The footpath from the hotel to the Spring followed, at an even level, the contour of an intervening slope. It was wide and well-surfaced and, as she had read in one of the brochures, amply provided for the passage of a wheeled chair. She walked along it at a steady pace, looking down as she did so at Fisherman's Bay, the cottages, the narrow strip of water and a not very distant prospect of the village. A mellow light lay across the hillside; there was a prevailing scent of sea and of bracken. A lark sang overhead. It was very much the same sort of afternoon as that upon which, two years ago, Wally Trehern had blundered up the hillside to the Spring. Over the course he had so blindly taken there was now a well-defined, tar-sealed, and tact-fully graded route which converged with Miss Emily's footpath at the entrance to the Spring.

The Spring itself, its pool, its modest waterfall and the bouldered slope above it, were now enclosed by a high wire-netting fence. There were one or two rustic benches outside this barricade. Entrance was effected through a turnpike of tall netted flanges which could be operated by the insertion into a slot-machine of one of the discs with which Miss Emily was provided.

She did not immediately make use of it. There were people at the Spring. An emaciated man whose tragic face had arrested Jenny Williams's attention at the bus stop and a young woman with a baby. The man knelt by the fall and seemed only by an effort to sustain his thin hands against the pressure of the water. His head was downbent. He rose, and, without looking at them, walked by the mother and child to a one-way exit from the enclosure. As he passed Miss Emily his gaze met hers and his mouth hesitated in a smile. Miss Emily inclined her head and they said 'Good evening' simultaneously. 'I have great hopes,' the man said rather faintly. He lifted his hat and moved away downhill.

The young woman, in her turn, had knelt by the fall. She had bared the head of her baby and held her cupped hand above it. A trickle of water glittered briefly. Miss Emily sat down abruptly on a bench and shut her eyes.

When she opened them again, the young woman with the baby was coming towards her.

'Are you all right?' she asked. 'Can I help you? Do you want to go in?'

'I am not ill,' Miss Emily said and added, 'thank you, my dear.'

'Oh, excuse me. I'm sorry. That's all right, then.'

'Your baby. Has your baby – ?'

'Well, yes. It's a sort of deficiency, the doctor says. He just doesn't seem to thrive. But there've been such wonderful reports – you can't get away from it, can you? So I've got great hopes.'

She lingered on for a moment and then smiled and nodded and went away.

'Great hopes!' Miss Emily muttered. '*Ah, Mon Dieu!* Great hopes indeed.'

She pulled herself together and extracted a nickel disc from her bag. There was a notice by the turnstile saying that arrangements could be made at the hotel for stretcher cases to be admitted. Miss Emily let herself in and inspected the terrain. The freshet gurgled in and out of its pool. The waterfall prattled. She looked towards the brow of the hill. The sun shone full in her eyes and dazzled them. She walked round to a ledge above the Spring and found a flat rock upon which she seated herself. Behind her was a bank, and, above that, the boulder and bracken where Wally's green lady was generally supposed to have appeared. Miss Emily opened her umbrella and composed herself.

She presented a curious figure, motionless, canopied and black and did indeed resemble, as Patrick had suggested, some outlandish presiding deity, whether benign or inimical must be a matter of conjecture. During her vigil seven persons visited the Spring and were evidently much taken aback by Miss Emily.

She remained on her perch until the sun went down behind the hill and, there being no more pilgrims to observe, descended and made her way downhill to Fisherman's Bay, and thence, round the point, to Miss Cost's shop. On her way she overtook the village police sergeant who seemed to be loitering. Miss Emily gave him good evening.

II

It was now a quarter to seven. The shop was open and, when Miss Emily went in, deserted. There was a bell on the counter but she did not ring it. She examined the welter of objects for sale. They were as Patrick had described them to Jenny: fanciful reconstructions in plastic of the Spring, the waterfall and 'Wally's Cottage'; badly print-ed rhyme-sheets; booklets, calendars and postcards all of which covered much the same ground. Predominant amongst all these wares, cropping up everywhere, in print and in plastic, smirking, even, in the form of doll and cut-out, was the Green Lady. The treatment was consistent – a verdigris-coloured garment, long yellow hair, upraised hand and a star on the head. There was a kind of madness in the prolific insistence of this effigy. Jostling each other in a corner were the products of Miss Cost's handloom; scarves, jerkins and cloaks of which the prevailing colours were sad blue and mauve. Miss Emily turned from them with a shudder of incredulity.

A door from the interior opened and Miss Cost entered on a wave of cottage-pie and wearing one of her own jerkins.

'I thought I heard – ' she began and then she recognized her visitor. 'Ae-oh!' she said. 'Good evening. Hem!'

'Miss Cost, I believe. May I have a dozen threepenny stamps, if you please.'

When these had been purchased Miss Emily said: 'There is possi-bly no need for me to introduce myself. My name is Pride. I am your landlord.'

'So I understand,' said Miss Cost. 'Quite.'

'You are no doubt aware of my purpose in visiting the Island but I think perhaps I should make my position clear.'

Miss Emily made her position very clear indeed. If Miss Cost wished to renew her lease of the shop in three months' time, it could only be on condition that any object which directly or indirectly advertised the Spring was withdrawn from sale.

Miss Cost listened to this with a fixed stare and a clasp-knife smile. When it was over she said that she hoped Miss Pride would not think it out of place if she, Miss Cost, mentioned that her little stock of fairings had been highly praised in discriminating quarters and had given pleasure to thousands. Especially, she added, to the kiddies.

Miss Emily said she could well believe it but that was not the point at issue.

Miss Cost said that each little novelty had been conceived in a spirit of reverence.

Miss Emily did not dispute the conception. The distribution, however, was a matter of commercial enterprise, was it not?

At this juncture a customer came in and bought a plastic Green Lady.

When she had gone, Miss Cost said she hoped that Miss Pride entertained no doubts about the efficacy of the cures.

'If I do,' said Miss Emily, 'it is of no moment. It is the commercial exploitation that concerns us. That, I cannot tolerate.' She examined Miss Cost for a second or two and her manner changed slightly. 'I do not question your faith in the curative properties of the Spring,' she said. 'I do not suggest, I assure you, that in exploiting public credulity, you do so consciously and cynically.'

'I should hope not!' Miss Cost burst out. 'I! I! My asthma – ! I, who am a living witness! Ae-oh!'

'Quite so. Moreover, when the Island has been restored to its former condition, I shall not prevent access to the Spring any more than I shall allow extravagant claims to be canvassed. It will not be closed to the public. Quite on the contrary.'

'They will ruin it! The vandalism! The outrages! Even now with every precaution. The desecration!'

'That can be attended to.'

'Fairy ground,' Miss Cost suddenly announced, 'is holy ground.'

'I am unable to determine whether you adopt a pagan or a Christian attitude,' said Miss Emily. She indicated a rhyme-sheet which was clothes-pegged to a line above the counter.

> Ye olde wayes, *it read*, were wise old wayes
> (Iron and water, earthe and stone)
> Ye Hidden Folke of antient dayes
> Ye Greene Companions' Runic Layes
> Wrought Magick with a Bone.
>
> Ye plashing Falles ther Secrette holde.
> (Iron and water, earthe and stone)

On us as on those menne of olde
Their mighte of healing is Bestowed
And wonders still are showne.

O, thruste your handes beneath the rille
(Iron and water, earthe and stone)
And itte will washe awaye your ille
With neweborn cheere your bodie fille
That antient Truth bee knowne.

'Who,' asked Miss Emily, fixing her gaze upon Miss Cost, 'is the author of this doggerel?'

'It is unsigned,' she said loudly. 'These old rhymes – '

'The spelling is spurious and the paper contemporary. Does it express your own views, Miss Cost?'

'Yes,' said Miss Cost, shutting her eyes. 'It does. A thousand times, yes.'

'So I imagined. Well, now,' Miss Emily briskly continued, 'you know mine. Take time to consider. There is one other matter.'

Her black kid forefinger indicated a leaflet advertising the Festival. 'This,' she said.

A spate of passionate defiance broke from Miss Cost. Her voice was pitched high and she stared at some object beyond Miss Emily's left shoulder. 'You can't stop us!' she cried. 'You can't! You can't prevent people walking up a hill. You can't prevent them singing. I've made inquiries. We're not causing a disturbance and it's all authorized by the Mayor. He's part of it. Ask him! Ask the Mayor'! Ask the Mayor. We've got hundreds and hundreds of people coming and you can't stop them. You can't. *You can't!*'

Her voice cracked and she drew breath. Her hands moved to her chest.

Into the silence that followed there crept a very small and eerie sound: a faint, rhythmic squeak. It came from Miss Cost.

Miss Emily heard it. After a moment she said, with compassion: 'I am sorry. I shall leave you. I shall not attempt to prevent your Festival. It must be the last but I shall not prevent it.'

As she prepared to leave, Miss Cost, now struggling for breath, gasped after her.

'You wicked woman! This is your doing.' She beat her chest. 'You'll suffer for it. More than I do. Mark my words! You'll suffer.'

Miss Emily turned to look at her. She sat on a stool behind the counter. Her head nodded backwards and forwards with her laboured breathing.

'Is there anything I can do?' Miss Emily asked. 'You have an attack – '

'I haven't! *I haven't! Go away*. Wicked woman! Go away.'

Miss Emily, greatly perturbed, left the shop. As she turned up from the jetty, a boy shambled out of the shadows, stared at her for a moment, gave a whooping cry and ran up the steps. It was Wally Trehern.

The encounter with Miss Cost had tired her. She was upset. It had, of course, been a long day and there were still those steps to be climbed. There was a bench half-way up and she decided to rest there for a few minutes before making the final ascent. Perhaps she would ask for an early dinner in her room and go to bed afterwards. It would never do to let herself get overdone. She took the steps slowly, using her umbrella as a staff and was rather glad when she reached the bench. It was a relief to sit there and observe the foreshore, the causeway and the village.

Down below, at the end of the jetty, a group of fishermen stood talking. The police-sergeant, she noticed, had joined them. They seemed to be looking up at her. 'I daresay it's got about,' she thought, 'who I am and all the rest of it. Bah!'

She stayed on until she was refreshed. The evening had begun to close in and she was in the lee of the hill. There was a slight coolness in the air. She prepared, after the manner of old people, to rise.

At that moment she was struck between the shoulder blades, on the back of her neck and head and on her arm. Stones fell with a rattle at her feet. Above and behind her there was a scuffling sound of retreat and of laughter.

She got up, scarcely knowing what she did. She supposed afterwards that she must have cried out. The next thing that happened was that the sergeant was running heavily uphill towards her.

'Hold hard, now, ma'am,' he was saying. 'Be you hurt, then?'

'No. Stones. From above. Go and look.'

He peered at her for a moment and then scrambled up the sharp rise behind the bench. He slithered and skidded, sending down a cascade of earth. Miss Emily sank back on the bench. She drew her glove off and touched her neck with a trembling hand. It was wet.

The sergeant floundered about overhead. Unexpectedly two of the fishermen had arrived and, more surprisingly still, the tall bronze girl. What was her name?

'Miss Pride,' she was saying, 'you're hurt. What happened?' She knelt down by Miss Emily and took her hands.

The men were talking excitedly and presently the sergeant was there again, swearing and breathing hard.

'Too late,' he was saying. 'Missed 'im.'

Miss Emily's head began to clear a little.

'I am perfectly well,' she said rather faintly and more to herself than to the others. 'It is nothing.'

'You've been hurt. Your neck!' Jenny said, also in French. 'Let me look.'

'You are too kind,' Miss Emily murmured. She suffered her neck to be examined. 'Your accent,' she added more firmly, 'is passable though not entirely *d'une femme du monde*. Where did you learn?'

'In Paris,' said Jenny. 'There's a cut in your neck, Miss Pride. It isn't very deep but I'm going to bind it up. Mr Pender, could I borrow your handkerchief? And I'll make a pad of mine. Clean, luckily.'

While Miss Emily suffered these ministrations the men muttered together. There was a scrape of boots on the steps and a third fisherman came down from above. It was Trehern. He stopped short. 'Hey!' he ejaculated. 'What's amiss, then?'

'Lady's been hurt, poor dear,' one of the men said.

'Hurt!' Trehern exclaimed. 'How? Why, if it be'ant Miss Pride. Hurt! What way?'

'Where would you be from then, Jim?' Sergeant Pender asked.

'Up to pub as usual, George,' he said. 'Where else?' A characteristic parcel protruded from his overcoat pocket. 'Happen she took a fall? Them steps be treacherous going for females well-gone into the terrors of antiquity.'

'Did you leave the pub this instant-moment?'

'Surely. Why?'

'Did you notice anybody up-along, off of the steps, like? In the rough?'

'Are you after them courting couples again, George Pender?'

'No,' said Mr Pender shortly. 'I be'ant.'

'I did *not* fall,' said Miss Emily loudly. She rose to her feet and confronted Trehern. 'I was struck,' she said.

'Lord forbid, ma'am! Who'd take a fancy to do a crazy job like that?'

Jenny said to Pender: 'I think we ought to get Miss Pride home.'

'So we should, then. Now, ma'am,' said Pender with an air of authority, 'you'm not going to walk up them steps, if you please, so if you've no objection us chaps'll manage you, same as if we was bringing you ashore in a rough sea.'

'I assure you, officer – '

'Very likely, ma'am, and you with the heart of a lion as all can see, but there'd be no kind of sense in it. Now then, souls. Hup!'

And before she knew what had happened, Miss Emily was sitting on a chair of woollen-clad arms with her own arms neatly disposed by Mr Pender round a pair of slightly fishy shoulders and her face in close association with those of her bearers.

'Pretty as a picture,' Pender said. 'Heave away, chaps. Stand aside, if you please, Jim.'

'My umbrella.'

'I've got it,' said Jenny. 'And your bag.'

When they reached the top Miss Emily said: 'I am extremely obliged. If you will allow me, officer, I would greatly prefer it if I might enter in the normal manner. I am perfectly able to do so and it will be less conspicuous.' And to Jenny: 'Please ask them to put me down.'

'I think she'll be all right,' Jenny said.

'Very good, ma'am,' said Pender. 'Set 'er down, chaps. That's clever. Gentle as a lamb.'

They stood round Miss Emily, and grinned bashfully at her.

'You have been very kind,' she said. 'I hope you will be my guests though it will be wiser perhaps, if I do not give myself the pleasure of joining you. I will leave instructions. Thank you very much.'

She took her umbrella and handbag from Jenny, bowed to her escort and walked quite fast towards the entrance. Jenny followed her. On the way they passed Wally Trehern.

Patrick was in the vestibule. Miss Emily inclined her head to him and made for the stairs. Her handbag was bloody and conspicuous. Jenny collected her room key from the desk.

'What on earth – ?' Patrick said coming up to her.

'Get Dr Maine, could you? Up to her room. And Patrick – there are two fishermen and Mr Pender outside. She wants them to have drinks on her. Can you fix it? I'll explain later.'

'Good lord! Yes, all right.'

Jenny overtook Miss Emily on the landing. She was shaky and, without comment, accepted an arm. When they had reached her room she sat on her bed and looked at Jenny with an expression of triumph.

'I am not surprised,' she said. 'It was to be expected, my dear,' and fainted.

III

'Well,' said Dr Maine, smiling into Miss Emily's face, 'there's no great damage done. I think you'll recover.'

'I have already done so.'

'Yes, I daresay, but I suggest you go slow for a day or two, you know. You've had a bit of shock. How old are you?'

'I'm eighty-three and four months.'

'Good God!'

'Ours is a robust family, Dr Maine. My sister, Fanny Winterbottom, whom I daresay you have met, would be alive today if she had not, in one of her extravagant moods, taken an excursion in a speedboat.'

'Did it capsize?' Jenny was startled into asking.

'Not at all. But the excitement was too much and the consequent depression exposed her to an epidemic of Asiatic influenza. From which she died. It was quite unnecessary and the indirect cause of my present embarrassment.'

There was a short silence. Jenny saw Dr Maine's eyebrows go up.

'Really?' he said. 'Well, now, I don't think we should have any more conversation tonight. Some hot milk with a little whisky or brandy, if you like it, and a couple of aspirins. I'll look in tomorrow.'

'You do not, I notice, suggest that I bathe my injuries in the Spring.'

'No,' he said, and they exchanged a smile.

'I had intended to call upon you tomorrow with reference to my proposals. Have you heard of them?'

'I have. But I'm not going to discuss them with you tonight.'

'Do you object? To my proposals?'

'No. Good night, Miss Pride. Please don't get up until I've seen you.'

'And yet they would not, I imagine, be to your advantage.'

There was a tap on the door and Mrs Barrimore came in. 'Miss Pride,' she said. 'I'm so sorry. I've just heard. I've come to see if there's anything – ' she looked at Dr Maine.

'Miss Pride's quite comfortable,' he said. 'Jenny's going to settle her down. I think we'll leave her in charge, shall we?'

He waited while Mrs Barrimore said another word or two, and then followed her out of the room. He shut the door and they moved down the passage.

'Bob,' she said, 'what is it? What happened? Has she been attacked?'

'Probably some lout from the village.'

'You don't think – ?'

'No.' He looked at her. 'Don't worry,' he said. 'Don't worry so, Margaret.'

'I can't help it. Did you see Keith?'

'Yes. He's overdone it tonight. Flat out in the old bar parlour. I'll get him up to bed.'

'Does Patrick know?'

'I've no idea.'

'He wasn't flat out an hour ago. He was in the ugly stages. He – he – was talking so wildly. What he'd do to her – to Miss Pride. You know?'

'My dear girl, he was plastered. Don't get silly ideas into your head, now, will you? Promise?'

'All right,' she said. 'Yes. All right.'

'Good night,' he said and left her there with her fingers against her lips.

IV

On the next day, Tuesday, Miss Emily kept to her room, where in the afternoon she received in turn, Mr Nankivell (the Mayor of Portcarrow), Dr Maine and the Rev. Mr Carstairs. On Wednesday she called at

Wally's Cottage. On Thursday she revisited the Spring, mounted to her observation post and remained there, under her umbrella, for a considerable time, conscientiously observed by Sergeant Pender to whom she had taken a fancy, and by numerous visitors as well as several of the local characters, including Miss Cost, Wally Trehern and his father.

On Friday she followed the same routine, escaping a trip-wire which had been laid across her ascent to the ledge and removed by Mr Pender two minutes before she appeared on the scene.

An hour later, this circumstance having been reported to him, Superintendent Alfred Coombe rang up Roderick Alleyn at his holiday address.

V

Alleyn was mowing his host's tennis court when his wife hailed him from the terrace. He switched the machine off.

'Telephone,' she shouted. 'Long distance.'

'Damnation!' he said and returned to the house.

'Where's it from, darling?'

'Portcarrow. District Headquarters. That'll be Miss Emily, won't it?'

'Inevitably, I fear.'

'Might it only be to say there's nothing to report?' Troy asked doubtfully.

'*Most* unlikely.'

He answered the call, heard what Coombe had to say about the stone-throwing and turned his thumb down for Troy's information.

'Mind you,' Coombe said, 'it might have been some damned Ted larking about. Not that we've had trouble of that sort on the Island. But she's raised a lot of feeling locally. Seeing what you've told us, I thought I ought to let you know.'

'Yes, of course. And you've talked to Miss Pride?'

'I have,' said Coombe with some emphasis. 'She's a firm old lady, isn't she?'

'Gibraltar is as butter compared to her.'

'What say?'

'I said: Yes, she is.'

'I asked her to let me know what her plans might be for the rest of the day. I didn't get much change out of her. The doctor persuaded her to stay put on Tuesday but ever since she's been up and about, worse luck. She's taken to sitting on this shelf above the Spring and looking at the visitors. Some of them don't like it.'

'I bet they don't.'

'The thing is, with this Festival coming along tomorrow the place is filling up and we're going to be fully extended. I mean, keeping observation, as you know, takes one man all his time.'

'Of course. Can you get reinforcements?'

'Not easily. But I don't think it'll come to that. I don't reckon it's warranted. I reckon she'll watch her step after this. But she's tricky. You've got to face it: she is tricky.'

'I'm sorry to have landed you with this, Coombe.'

'Well, I'd rather know. I'm glad you did. After all she's in my district – and if anything did happen – '

'*Has* there been anything else?'

'That's why I'm ringing. My chap, Pender, found a trip-wire stretched across the place where she climbs up to her perch. He was hanging about waiting for her to turn up and noticed it. Workman-like job. Couple of iron pegs and a length of fine clothes-line. Could have been nasty. There's a five foot drop to the pond. And rocks.'

'Did you tell her?'

'Yes. She said she'd have spotted it for herself.'

'When was this?'

'This morning. About an hour ago.'

'Damn.'

'Quite so.'

'Does she suspect anyone?'

'Well, yes. She reckons it's a certain lady. Yes, Mr Mayor. Good morning, sir. I won't keep you a moment.'

'Has your Mayor just walked in?'

'That's right.'

'Did you by any chance, mean the shop-keeper? Miss Cost, is it?'

'That's right.'

'I'll ring up Miss Pride. I suppose she knocks off for lunch, does she? Comes off her perch? '

'That's right. Quite so.'

'What's the number of the pub?'

'Portcarrow 1212.'

'You'll keep in touch?'

'That'll be quite all right, sir. We'll do that for you.'

'Thank you,' Alleyn said. 'No matter what they say I've got great faith in the police. Goodbye.'

He heard Coombe give a chuckle and hung up.

'O, Rory!' his wife said. 'Not again? Not this time? It's been such fun, our holiday.'

'I'm going to talk to her. Come here to me and keep your fingers crossed. She's hell when she's roused. Come here.'

He kept his arm round her while he waited for the call to go through. When at last Miss Emily spoke from her room at the Boy-and-Lobster, Troy could hear her quite clearly though she had some difficulty in understanding since Miss Emily spoke in French. So did Alleyn.

'Miss Emily, how are you getting on?'

'Perfectly well, I thank you, Roderique.'

'Have there been unpleasantnesses of the sort that were threatened?'

'Nothing of moment. Do not disarrange yourself on my account.'

'You have been hurt.'

'It was superficial.'

'You might well have been hurt again.'

'I think not.'

'Miss Emily, I must ask you to leave the Island.'

'In effect: you have spoken to the good Superintendent Coombe. It was kind but it was not necessary. I shall not leave the Island.'

'Your behaviour is, I'm afraid, both foolish and inconsiderate.'

'Indeed? Explain yourself.'

'You are giving a great deal of anxiety and trouble to other people. You are being silly, Miss Emily.'

'That,' said Miss Emily distinctly, 'was an improper observation.'

'Unfortunately not. If you persist I shall feel myself obliged to intervene.'

'Do you mean, my friend,' said Miss Emily with evident amusement, 'that you will have me arrested?'

'I wish I could. I wish I could put you under protective custody.'

'I am already protected by the local officer who is, for example, a man of intelligence. His name is Pender.'

'Miss Emily, if you persist you will force me to leave my wife.'

'That is nonsense.'

'Will you give me your word of honour that you will not leave the hotel unaccompanied?'

'Very well,' said Miss Emily after a pause. 'Understood.'

'And that you will not sit alone on a shelf? Or anywhere? At any time?'

'There is no room for a second occupant on the shelf.'

'There must be room somewhere. Another shelf. Somewhere.'

'It would not be convenient.'

'Nor is it convenient for me to leave my wife and come traipsing down to your beastly Island.'

'I beg that you will do no such thing. I assure you – ' Her voice stopped short. He would have thought that the call had been cut off if he hadn't quite distinctly heard Miss Emily catch her breath in a sharp gasp. Something had fallen.

'Miss Emily!' he said. 'Hallo! Hallo! Miss Emily!'

'Very well,' her voice said. 'I can hear you. Perfectly.'

'What happened?'

'I was interrupted.'

'Something's wrong. What is it?'

'No, no. It is nothing. I knocked a book over. Roderique, I beg that you do not break your holiday. It would be rather ridiculous. It would displease me extremely, you understand. I assure you that I will do nothing foolish. Goodbye, my dear boy.'

She replaced the receiver.

Alleyn sat with his arm still round his wife. 'Something happened,' he said. 'She sounded frightened. I swear she was frightened. Damn and blast Miss Emily for a pigheaded old effigy. What the hell does she think she's up to!'

'Darling: she promised to be sensible. She doesn't want you to go. Does she, now?'

'She was frightened,' he repeated. 'And she wouldn't say why.'

At the same moment Miss Emily with her hand pressed to her heart was staring at the object she had exposed when she had knocked the telephone directory on its side.

This object was a crude plastic image of a Green Lady. A piece of ruled paper had been jammed down over the head and on it was pasted a single word of newsprint.

'Death.'

VI

Miss Emily surveyed the assembled company.

There were not enough chairs for them all in her sitting-room. Margaret Barrimore, the Rector and the Mayor were seated. Jenny and Patrick sat on the arms of Mrs Barrimore's chair. Major Barrimore, Superintendent Coombe and Dr Maine formed a rather ill-assorted group of standees.

'That then,' said Miss Emily, 'is the situation. I have declared my purpose. I have been threatened. Two attempts have been made upon me. Finally, this object – ' she waved her hand in the direction of the Green Lady which, with its unlovely label still about its neck, simpered at the company ' – this object has been placed in my room by someone who evidently obtained possession of the key.'

'Now, my dear Miss Pride,' Barrimore said. 'I do assure you that I shall make the fullest possible investigation. Whoever perpetrated this ridiculous – ' Miss Emily raised her hand. He goggled at her, brushed up his moustache and was silent.

'I have asked you to meet me here,' she continued exactly as if she had not been interrupted, 'in order to make it known, first, that I am not of course, to be diverted by threats of any sort. I shall take the action I have already outlined. I have particularly invited you, Mr Mayor, and the Rector and Dr Maine because you are persons of authority in Portcarrow and also because each of you will be affected in some measure by my decision. As perhaps more directly, will Major Barrimore and his family. I regret that Miss Cost finds she is unable to come. I have met each of you independently since I arrived and I hope you are all convinced that I am not to be shaken in my intention.'

Mr Nankivell made an unhappy noise.

'My second object in trespassing upon your time is this. I wish, with the assistance of Superintendent Coombe, to arrive at the identity of the person who left this figurine, with its offensive label, on my desk. It is presumably the person who is responsible for the two attempts to inflict injury. It was – I believe "planted" is the correct expression – while I was at luncheon. My apartment was locked. My key was on its hook on a board in the office. It is possible to remove it without troubling the attendant and without attracting attention. That is what must have been done, and done by a person who was aware of my room number. Unless, indeed, this outrage was performed by somebody who is in possession of, or has access to, a duplicate or master key.' She turned with splendid complacency to Superintendent Coombe. 'That is my contention,' said Miss Emily. 'Perhaps you, Mr Coombe, will be good enough to continue the investigation.'

An invitation of this sort rested well outside the range of Superintendent Coombe's experience. Under the circumstances, he met the challenge with good sense and discretion. He kept his head.

'Well, now,' he said. 'Miss Pride, Mr Mayor and ladies and gentlemen, I'm sure we're all agreed that this state of affairs won't do. Look at it whatever way you like, it reflects no credit on the village or the Island.'

'Yurr-yurr,' said the Mayor who was clearly fretted by the minor role for which he seemed to be cast. 'Speak your mind, Alfred. Go ahead.'

'So I will, then. Now. As regards the stone-throwing and the trip-wire incidents. Inquiries have been put in hand. So far, from information received, I have nothing to report. As regards this latest incident: in the ordinary course of events, it having been reported to the police, routine inquiries would be undertaken. That would be the normal procedure.'

'It has been reported,' said Miss Emily. 'And I have invited you to proceed.'

'The method, if you will pardon me, Miss Pride, has *not* been normal. It is not usual to call a meeting on such an occasion.'

'Evidently I have not made myself clear. I have called the meeting in order that the persons who could have effected an entry into this room by the means I have indicated, may be given an opportunity of clearing themselves.'

This pronouncement had a marked but varied effect upon her audience. Patrick Ferrier's eyebrows shot up and he glanced at Jenny who made a startled grimace. Mrs Barrimore leant forward in her chair and looked, apparently with fear, at her husband. He, in his turn, had become purple in the face. The Mayor's habitual expression of astonishment was a caricature of itself. Dr Maine scrutinized Miss Emily as if she were a test case for something. The Rector ran his hands through his hair and said: 'Oh, but surely!'

Superintendent Coombe, with an air of abstraction, stared in front of him. He then produced his notebook and contemplated it as if he wondered where it had sprung from.

'Now, *just* a *minute!*' he said.

'I must add,' said Miss Emily, 'that Miss Jenny Williams may at once be cleared. She very kindly called for me, assisted me downstairs and to my knowledge remained in the dining-room throughout luncheon, returning to my table to perform the same kind office. Do you wish to record this?'

He opened his mouth, shut it again and actually made a note.

'It will perhaps assist the inquiry if I add that Major Barrimore did not come into the dining-room at all, that Mrs Barrimore left it five minutes before I did and that Mr Patrick Ferrier was late in arriving there. They will no doubt wish to elaborate.'

'By God!' Major Barrimore burst out. 'I'll be damned if I do! By God, I'll – '

'No, Keith! Please!' said his wife.

'You shut up, Margaret.'

'I suggest,' Patrick said, 'that on the whole it might be better if *you* did.'

'Patrick!' said the Rector. 'No, old boy.'

Superintendent Coombe came to a decision.

'I'll ask you all for your attention, if you please,' he said, and was successful in getting it. 'I don't say this is the way I'd have dealt with the situation,' he continued, 'if it had been left to me. It hasn't. Miss Pride has set about the affair in her own style and has put me in the position where I haven't much choice but to take up the inquiry on her lines. I don't say it's a desirable way of going about the affair and I'd have been just as pleased if she'd have had a little chat with me first. She hasn't and that's that. I think it'll be better for all concerned if we get the whole thing settled and done with by taking routine statements from everybody. I hope you're agreeable.'

Patrick said quickly: 'Of course. Much the best way.' He stood up. 'I was late for lunch,' he said, 'because I was having a drink with George Pender in the bar. I went direct from the bar to the dining-room. I didn't go near the office. What about you, Mama?'

Mrs Barrimore twisted her fingers together and looked up at her son. She answered him as if it were a matter private to them both. 'Do you mean, what did I do when I left the dining-room? Yes, I see. I – I went into the hall. There was a crowd of people from the bus. Some of them asked about – oh, the usual things. One of them seemed – very unwell – and I took her into the lounge to sit down. Then I went across to the old house. And – '

Dr Maine said: 'I met Mrs Barrimore as she came in. I was in the old house. I'd called to have a word with her about Miss Pride. To learn if she was,' he glanced at her, 'if she was behaving herself,' he said dryly. 'I went into the old bar-parlour. Major Barrimore was there. I spoke to him for a minute or two and then had a snack lunch in the new bar. I then visited a patient who is staying in the hotel and at two-thirty I called on Miss Pride. I found her busy at the telephone summoning this meeting. At her request I have attended it.'

He had spoken rapidly. Mr Coombe said, 'Just a minute if you please, Doctor,' and they were all silent while he completed his notes. 'Yes,' he said at last. 'Well, now. That leaves His Worship, doesn't it and – '

'I must say,' Mr Nankivell interrupted, 'and say it I do and will, I did not anticipate when called upon at a busy and inconvenient time, to be axed to clear myself of participation in a damn' fool childish prank. Further, I take leave to put on record that I look upon the demand made upon me as one unbecoming to the office I have the honour to hold. Having said which, I'll thank you to make a note of it, Alf Coombe. I state further that during the first part of the period in question I was in the Mayoral Chambers at the execution of my duties from which I moved to the back office of my butchery attending to my own business which is more than can be said of persons who shall for purposes of this discussion, remain nameless.'

Mr Coombe made a short note: 'In his Butchery,' and turned to the Rector.

'I've been trying to think,' said Mr Carstairs. 'I'm not at all good at times and places, I fear, and it's been a busy day. Let me see. O, yes. I visited the cottages this morning. Actually, the main object was to call on that wretched Mrs Trehern. Things have been very much amiss, there. It's a sad case. And one or two other folk on the Island. I don't know when I walked back but I believe I was late for lunch. My wife, I daresay, could tell you.'

'Did you come up to The Boy-and-Lobster, sir?'

'Did I? Yes, I did. As a matter of fact, Miss Pride, I intended to call on you to see if you were quite recovered, but the main entrance was crowded and I saw that luncheon had begun so – I didn't, you see.'

'You went home, sir?' asked the Superintendent.

'Yes. Late.'

Mr Coombe shut his notebook. 'All right,' he said, 'so far as it goes. Now, in the normal course of procedure these statements would be followed up and follow them up I shall which takes time. So unless anyone has anything further to add – Yes, Miss Pride?'

'I merely observe, Superintendent, that I shall be glad to support you in your investigations. And to that end,' she added, in the absence of any sign of enthusiasm, 'I shall announce at once, that I have arrived at my own conclusion. There is, I consider, only one individual to whom these outrages may be attributed and that person, I firmly believe, is – '

The telephone rang.

It was at Miss Emily's elbow. She said 'T'ch!' and picked it up. 'Yes? Are you there?' she asked.

A treble voice, audible to everybody in the room asked:

'Be that Miss Emily Pride?'

'Speaking.'

'You leave us be, Miss Emily Pride, or the Lady will get you. You'll be dead as a stone, Miss Emily Pride.'

'Who is that?'

The telephone clicked and began to give the dialling sound.

Patrick said: 'That was a child's voice. It must have been – '

'No,' said Miss Emily. 'I think not. I have an acute ear for phonetics. It was an assumed accent. And it was not a child. It was the voice of Miss Elspeth Cost.'

CHAPTER 4

Fiasco

The persons taking part in the Festival celebrations assembled at four
o'clock on Saturday at the foot of the hill in Fisherman's Bay. There
was a company of little girls wearing green cheesecloth dresses and
stars in their hair, about a dozen larger girls, similarly attired, and a
few small boys in green cotton smocks. In the rear of this collection
came Wally Trehern, also smocked, with his hair sleeked down and
a bewildered expression on his face. His hands were noticeably
clean. The Mayor and City Councillors and other local dignitaries
were yet to come.

Miss Cost marshalled and re-marshalled her troupe. She wore a
mop cap and a hand-woven cloak of the prevailing green over a full
skirt and an emerald velveteen bodice. The afternoon was sultry and
her nose and eyebrows glittered. She carried a camera and a sheaf of
papers clipped to a board and exhibited signs of emotional stress.

Thunderous clouds were massed in the north-west and everybody
eyed them with distrust. Not a breath of air stirred. An ominous, hot,
stillness prevailed.

The enclosure was packed. An overflow of spectators had climbed
the hill above the Spring and sat or lay in the blinding heat. The
route from the foreshore to the Spring – 'Wally's Way,' in the
programme – was lined with spectators. Seats in the enclosure were
provided for the ailing and for the official party and other persons of
importance. These included the Barrimores, Jenny, Dr Maine and the
Carstairs. The Rector, preserving his detachment, had declined any
official part in the ceremony. 'Though I must say,' he confided to his

wife, 'it sounds innocuous enough, in a way, from what I've heard.
I'm afraid Miss Cost's verse is really pretty dreadful, poor dear.'

'Tell me the moment you see Miss Pride.'

'I can't help hoping that in the event we shan't see her at all.'

'I suppose that chair by Mrs Barrimore is reserved for her.'

'Let us hope she occupies it and doesn't return to her original
plan. She would look *too* out of place on the ledge.'

'It would put Wally off his poetry, I have no doubt,' Mrs Carstairs
agreed.

'Not only that, but I understand they use it in their pageant or
whatever it is.'

'Then it would be very inconsiderate if she insisted.'

'Mind you, Dulcie, I maintain that in principle she is right.'

'Yes, dear, I'm sure you do,' said Mrs Carstairs. She gave a little
sigh and may have been thinking that things had been a good deal
easier over the last two years.

Patrick said to Jenny: 'Did you see her before we left?'

'Yes. She's agreed not to sit on the ledge.'

'How did you do it, you clever girl?'

'I told her I thought it would be unbecoming and that the children
would giggle and the gentlemen look at her legs.'

'Do you suppose she'll cut up rough at any stage?'

'I've no idea. Listen.'

'What?'

'Wasn't that thunder?'

'I wouldn't be surprised. Look, there's Coombe coming in now.
Who's that with him, I wonder. The tall chap.'

'Jolly good-looking,' said Jenny.

'Jolly good tailor, anyway.'

'P'raps it's one of Miss Pride's smart chums. She's got masses, it
appears, nearly all diplomats of the first water, she told me.'

'There's the band. It must have been the big drum you heard, not
thunder.'

'It was thunder,' said Jenny.

The band debouched from the village towards the jetty. It was a
small combination entirely dominated by the drum. Behind it walked
Mr Nankivell in full regalia, supported by his Council. They embarked
in the large motor launch, manned by Trehern, who was got up as a

sort of wherryman. The band filled a small fleet of attendant dinghies and continued to play with determination if a trifle wildly throughout the short passage. Miss Cost could be seen darting up and down the length of her procession, taking photographs.

A union of the two elements was achieved and soon they ascended the hill. The children sang. The band attempted a diminuendo.

'Through the night of doubt and sorrow.'

'Now, why *that!*' the Rector exclaimed. 'You see? No, Dulcie, it's too much!'

'Look, dear. Do look. There she is.'

Miss Emily had approached by the path from the hotel. She inserted her disc, entered the enclosure and advanced to her seat just before the procession arrived. Major Barrimore stood up to welcome her, looking furious.

A double gate, normally locked and only used to admit stretcher cases, was now opened. The procession marched in and disposed itself in a predestined order.

It is doubtful if any of the official party paid much attention to the Mayor's inaugural address. They were all too busy furtively keeping an eye on Miss Emily. She sat bolt upright with her hands clasped over the handle of her furled umbrella and she stared at Mr Nankivell.

'. . . and so, Ladies and Gentlemen, I have great pleasure in declaring the First – the *First* Festival of Portcarrow Island Springs, O–PEN.'

He sat down to a patter of applause through which Miss Cost advanced to a position near the little waterfall. Wally stood behind her. A microphone had been set up but she neglected to use it consistently. When she did speak into it, it seized upon her words and loud-speakers savagely flung them upon the heavy air. When she turned aside she changed into a voiceless puppet that opened and shut its mouth, cast up its eyes and waved its arms. The Mayor, nodding and smiling, pointed repeatedly to the microphone but Miss Cost did not observe him.

' – One Wonderful Afternoon – little Boy – so Sorrowful – who can tell? – Ancient Wisdom – Running Water – ' Evidently she approached her climax but all was lost until she turned sharply and the loud-speakers bellowed 'All Gone.'

The words reverberated about the hillside in a very desolate fashion – 'all gone – all gone – ' Miss Cost was bowing and ineffably smiling. She added something that was completely inaudible and, with an arch look at her audience, turned to Wally and found he had vanished. He was extricated from the rear of the choir where he had retired to sit down on some seepage from the Spring.

Miss Cost led him forward. The back of his smock was slimy and green. Unfortunately she did not place him before the microphone but for the first time herself directly confronted it.

'Now, Wally, *now*,' roared the loud-speakers. ' *"Once upon a Summer's day."* Go *on*, dear.'

At first, little of Wally's recitation was lost since he required constant prompting which Miss Cost, unwittingly, fed into the microphone. At the second stanza, however, the Mayor advanced upon her and in his turn was broadcast. 'Shift over,' the loud-speakers' advised. 'Come 'ere, you silly lad.' The Mayor, quick to perceive his error, backed away.

'O *dear!*' cried Miss Cost, publicly, and effected the change.

'Got it right this time!' said Major Barrimore loudly and gave a snort of laughter. Miss Cost evidently heard him. She threw him a furious glance.

Wally's recitation continued.

'Be not froightened sayed the Loidy . . . '

'This is killing me,' Jenny whispered.

'Shut up, for pity's sake. O, God!' Patrick muttered. 'What now? What's he saying now?'

'Shut up.'

Mrs Carstairs turned and shook her head at them. They moaned together in agony.

Wally came to an unexpected stop and walked away.

The audience, relieved, burst into sustained applause.

Miss Emily remained immovable.

The choir, accompanied by tentative grunts from the band, began to sing. Wally, recaptured, squatted beside the waterfall, looked cheerfully about him, and pushed his hands under the stream.

'This will be the inexplicable dumb show,' Patrick said.

'Look! O, look!'

From behind a boulder above the Spring emerged a large girl dressed in green cheesecloth. She was a blonde and the most had been made of her hair which was crowned by a tinsel star. From her left hand depended a long string of glittering beads, symbolic, clearly, of Water. Her right hand was raised. The gesture, inappropriately, was accompanied by a really formidable roll of thunder. The sun was now overcast and the heavens were black.

Wally looked up at the newcomer, gave one of his strange cries, pointed to her and laughed uproariously.

'Thus,' sang the choir, 'the Magic Spell was wroughten
Thus the little lad was healed – '

The Green Lady executed some weaving movements with her left hand. A sudden clap of thunder startled her. The string of beads fell on the ledge below. She looked helplessly after it and continued her pantomime. The choir sang on and began a concerted movement. They flanked the Spring and formed up in set groups, kneeling and pointing out the green girl to the audience. Miss Cost propelled Wally towards the ledge. It was the dénouement.

The applause had scarcely died away when Miss Emily rose and approached the microphone.

'Mr Mayor,' she began, 'ladies and gentlemen. I wish to protest – '

Major Barrimore had risen to his feet with an oath. At the same moment there was a blinding flash of lightning, followed immediately by a stentorian thunder-clap, a deluge of rain, and a shout of uncontrollable laughter from Dr Maine.

II

The stampede was immediate. Crowds poured out of the enclosure and down to the foreshore. The launch filled. There were clamorous shouts for dinghies. The younger element ran round the point of the bay, made for the hotel causeway and splashed precariously across it. The Boy-and-Lobster contingent took to the path that led directly to the hotel. It was a holocaust. Miss Cost, wildly at large among her drenched and disorganized troupe, was heard to scream: 'It's a judgment.' Unmindful they swept past her. She was deserted. Her velvet bodice leaked green dye into her blouse. Green rivulets ran down her arms. Her hair was plastered like seaweed against her face. The text of the play fell from her hand, and lay, disregarded, in the mud.

Mrs Barrimore held a brief exchange with Miss Emily who had opened her umbrella and from beneath it, steadily regarded Superintendent Coombe's late companion. She waved her hostess aside. Mrs Barrimore took to her heels, followed by her husband and Dr Maine. She outdistanced them, fled the enclosure, ran like a gazelle along the path to The Boy-and-Lobster and disappeared.

Major Barrimore and Dr Maine, who was still laughing, made after her. They were confronted at the gate by Miss Cost.

It was an ugly and grotesque encounter. She pushed her wet face towards them and her jaw trembled as if she had a rigor. She looked from one to the other. '*You,*' she stuttered. '*You!* Both of you. Animals. Now wait! Now, wait and see!'

Major Barrimore said: 'Look here, Elspeth,' and Dr Maine said: 'My dear Miss Cost!'

She broke into uncertain laughter and mouthed at them.

'Oh, for God's sake!' Barrimore said. She whispered something and he turned on his heel and left her. He was scarlet in the face.

'Miss Cost,' Maine said, 'you'd better go home. You're overwrought and I'm sorry if I – '

'You *will* be sorry,' she said. 'All of you. Mark my words.'

He hesitated for a moment. She made an uncouth and ridiculous gesture and he, too, left her.

Miss Emily was motionless under her umbrella. Miss Cost made for her, stumbling on the muddy slope. 'Wicked, *wicked* woman,' she said. 'You will be punished.'

'My poor creature – ' Miss Emily began but Miss Cost screamed at her, turned aside and floundered down the path. She passed through the gates into Wally's Way and after a precipitant descent, was lost among those of her adherents who were clustered round the jetty.

Jenny and Patrick had set off after the others but, on looking back, saw Miss Emily alone in the downpour. At Jenny's suggestion they returned and she approached Miss Emily. 'Miss Pride,' she said. 'Let's go back. Come with us. You'll be drenched.'

'Thank you, dear child, I have my umbrella,' said Miss Emily. She was still staring across the Spring at Superintendent Coombe's late

companion who now advanced towards her. 'Please don't wait for
me,' she said. 'I have an escort.'

Jenny hesitated. 'I insist,' said Miss Emily impatiently. Patrick
took Jenny's arm. 'Come on,' he said. 'We're not needed.' They
hunched their shoulders and ran like hares.

Alleyn crossed the enclosure. 'Good evening, Miss Emily,' he said.
'Shall we go?'

On the way to The Boy-and-Lobster he held her umbrella over
her. 'I am sufficiently protected by my waterproof and overshoes,'
she said. 'The forecast was for rain. Pray, let us share the umbrella.'
She took his arm. The path was now deserted.

They hardly spoke. Rain drummed down on the umbrella in a
pentateuchal deluge. Earth and sea were loud with its onslaught and
the hillside smelt of devouring grass and soil. Miss Emily, in her
goloshes, was insecure. Alleyn closed his hand round her thin old
arm and was filled with a sort of infuriated pity.

The entrance to the hotel was deserted except for the man on
duty who stared curiously at them. Miss Emily drew her key from
her reticule. 'I prefer,' she said loudly, 'to retain possession. Will you
come up? I have a so-called suite.'

She left Alleyn in her sitting-room with injunctions to turn on the
heater and dry himself while she retired to change.

He looked about him. The plastic Green Lady, still wearing its
infamous legend round its neck, had been placed defiantly in a glass
fronted wall cupboard. He looked closely at it without touching it. A
stack of London telephone directories stood near the instrument on
the writing desk.

Miss Emily called from her bedroom. 'You will find cognac and
soda-water in the small cupboard. Help yourself, I beg you. And me.
Cognac, *simplement*.' She sounded quite gay. Alleyn poured two double
brandies.

'Don't wait for me,' Miss Emily shouted. 'Drink at once. Remove
and dry your shoes. Have you engaged the heater?'

He did everything she commanded and felt that he was putting
himself at a disadvantage.

When Miss Emily reappeared, having changed her skirt, shoes
and stockings, she looked both complacent and stimulated. It
occurred to Alleyn that she got a sort of respectable kick out of

entertaining him so dashingly in her suite. She sat in an armchair and jauntily accepted her brandy.

'First of all, you must understand that I am extremely angry with you,' she said. She was almost coquettish. 'Ah – ah-ah! And now you have the self-conscious air?' She shook her finger at him.

'I may look sheepish,' he rejoined, 'but I assure you I'm in a devil of a temper. You are outrageous, Miss Emily.'

'When did you leave and how is your dear Troy?'

'At seven o'clock this morning and my dear Troy is furious.'

'Ah, no!' She leaned forward and tapped his hand. 'You should not have come, my friend. I am perfectly able to look after myself. It was kind but it was not necessary.'

'What were you going to say to that crowd if you hadn't been cut off by a cloud-burst? No, don't tell me. I know. You must be mad, Miss Emily.'

'On the contrary, I assure you. And why have you come, Roderique? As you see, I have taken no harm.'

'I want to know, among other matters, the full story of that object over there. The obscene woman with the label.'

Miss Emily gave him a lively account of it.

'And where, precisely, was it planted?'

'Behind one of the London telephone directories which had been placed on its edge, supported by the others.'

'And you knocked the book over while you were speaking to me?'

'That is correct. Revealing the figurine.'

He was silent for some time. 'And you were frightened,' Alleyn said at last.

'It was a shock. I may have been disconcerted. It was too childish a trick to alarm me for more than a moment.'

'Do you mind if I take possession of this object?'

'Not at all.'

'Has anybody but you touched it, do you know?'

'I think not. Excepting of course the culprit.'

He wrapped it carefully, first in a sheet of writing-paper from the desk and then in his handkerchief. He put it in his pocket.

'Well,' he said. 'Let's see what we can make of all this nonsense.'

He took her through the events of the last five days and found her account tallied with Superintendent Coombe's.

When she had finished he got up and stood over her.

'Now look,' he said. 'None of these events can be dismissed as childish. The stones might have caused a serious injury. The trip-wire almost certainly would have done so. The first threats that you got in London have been followed up. You've had two other warnings – the figurine and the telephone call. They will be followed up, too. Coombe tells me you suspect Miss Cost. Why?'

'I recognized her voice. You know my ear for the speaking voice, I think.'

'Yes.'

'On Monday, I interviewed her in her shop. She was in an extremity of anger. This brought on an attack of asthma and that in its turn added to her chagrin.'

Alleyn asked her if she thought Miss Cost had dogged her to the steps, swarmed up the hill and thrown stones at her, asthma notwithstanding.

'No,' said Miss Emily coolly. 'I think that unfortunate child threw the stones. I encountered him after I had left the shop and again outside the hotel. I have no doubt he did it: possibly at his father's instigation who was incited in the first instance, I daresay, by that ass Cost. The woman is a fool and a fanatic. She is also, I think, a little mad. You saw how she comported herself after that fiasco.'

'Yes, I did. All right. Now, I want your solemn promise that on no condition will you leave your rooms again this evening. You are to dine and breakfast up here. I shall call for you at ten o'clock and I shall drive you back to London or, if you prefer it, put you on the train. There are no two ways about it, Miss Emily. That is what you will do.'

'I *will not* be cowed by these threats. I *will not*.'

'Then I shall be obliged to take you into protective custody and you won't much fancy that, I promise you,' Alleyn said and hoped it sounded convincing.

Miss Emily's eyes filled with angry tears.

'Roderique – to me? To your old *institutrice?*'

'Yes, Miss Emily.' He bent down and gave her a kiss: the first he had ever ventured upon. 'To my old *institutrice,*' he said. 'I shall set a great strapping policewoman over you and if that doesn't answer, I shall lock you up, Miss Emily.'

Miss Emily dabbed her eyes.

'Very well,' she said. 'I don't believe you, of course, but very well.'

Alleyn put on his shoes.

'Where are you staying?' she asked.

'Coombe's giving me a bed. The pubs are full. I must go. It's seven o'clock.'

'You will dine with me, perhaps?'

'I don't think – ' He stopped. 'On second thoughts,' he said, 'I should be delighted. Thank you *very* much.'

'Are you going to "taste" my wine?' she asked, ironically.

'And I might do that, too,' he said.

III

He left her at nine.

She had settled for the eleven o'clock train from Dunlowman in the morning. He had arranged to book a seat for her and drive her to the station. He had also telephoned her *bonne-à-tout-faire* as she called the pugnacious Cockney who, in spite of Miss Emily's newly acquired riches, served her still. He saw that the outside doors to her apartment could be locked and made certain that, on his departure, she would lock them. He bade her good night and went downstairs, wondering how big a fuss he might be making over nothing in particular.

Major Barrimore was in the office smelling very strongly of whisky, smoking a large cigar and poring uncertainly over a copy of *The Racing Supplement*. Alleyn approached him.

'Major Barrimore? Miss Pride has asked me to tell you she will be leaving at ten in the morning and would like coffee and toast in her room at eight o'clock.'

'Would she, by God!' said the Major thickly and appeared to pull himself together. 'Sorry,' he said. 'Yes, of course. I'll lay it on.'

'Thank you.'

Alleyn had turned away when the Major, slurring his words a little but evidently under a tight rein, said: 'Afraid the lady hasn't altogether enjoyed her visit.'

'No?'

'No. Afraid not. But if she's been – ' he swayed very slightly and leant on the desk. 'Hope she hasn't been giving us a bad chit,' he said. 'Dunno who I'm talking to, acourse. Have the advantage of me, there.'

'I'm a police officer,' Alleyn said. 'Superintendent Alleyn, CID.'

'Good God! She's called in the Yard!'

'No. I'm an old friend of Miss Pride's. The visit was unofficial.'

Major Barrimore leant across the desk with an uncertain leer. 'I say,' he said, 'what is all this? You're no damned copper, old boy. You can't gemme t' b'lieve that. I know my drill. 'F y'ask me – more like a bloody guardee. What?'

Patrick and Jenny came into the hall from the old house.

'I think I'll just run up, first, and see how Miss Pride is,' Jenny was saying.

'Must you?'

'She's all right,' Major Barrimore said loudly. 'She's under police protection. Ask this man. M' – I – introduce Miss Jenny Williams and my step-son? Superintendent, or so he tells me . . . Sorry, I forget your name, sir.'

'Alleyn.'

They murmured at each other. Patrick said to his step-father: 'I'll take the office if you'd like to knock off.'

'The clerk fellah's on in ten minutes. What d'you mean? I'm all right.'

'Yes, of course.'

Alleyn said to Jenny: 'Miss Pride was thinking about a bath and bed when I left her.'

'She's going. In the morning,' said the Major, and laughed.

'Going!' Jenny and Patrick exclaimed together. 'Miss Pride!'

'Yes,' Alleyn said. 'It seems a sensible move. I wonder if you can tell me whether the causeway's negotiable and if not, whether there'll be a ferryman on tap.'

'It'll be negotiable,' Patrick said, 'but not very pleasant. Jenny and I are going down. We'll row you across, sir. It won't take ten minutes.'

'That's very civil of you. Are you sure?'

'Perfectly. We'd thought of taking the boat out anyway.'

'Then in that case – ' Alleyn turned to Major Barrimore. 'Good night, sir.'

'G'night,' he said. When they had moved away he called after Alleyn. 'If you put her up to it, you've done us a damn' good turn. Have a drink on it, won't you?'

'Thank you very much but I really must be off. Good night.'

They went out of doors. The sky had cleared and was alive with stars. The air was rain-washed and fresh.

As they walked down the steps Patrick said abruptly: 'I'm afraid my step-father was not exactly in his best form.'

'No doubt he's been rather highly tried.'

'No doubt,' said Patrick shortly.

'You were at the Festival, weren't you?' Jenny asked. 'With Mr Coombe?'

'I was, yes.'

'You don't have to be polite about it,' Patrick said. 'The burning question is whether it was as funny as it was embarrassing. I can't really make up my mind.'

'I suppose it depends upon how far one's sympathies were engaged.'

They had reached the half-way bench. Alleyn halted for a moment and glanced up the dark slope above it.

'Yes,' Jenny said. 'That was where she was.'

'You arrived on the scene, I think, didn't you? Miss Emily said you were a great help. What *did* happen exactly?'

Jenny told him how she had come down the steps, heard the patter of stones, Miss Emily's cry, and a high-pitched laugh. She described how she found Miss Emily with the cut on her neck. 'Very much shaken,' said Jenny, 'but full of fight.'

'A high-pitched laugh?' Alleyn repeated.

'Well, really more of a sort of squawk like – 'Jenny stopped short. 'Just an odd sort of noise,' she said.

'Like Wally Trehern, for instance?'

'Why do you say that?'

'He gave a sort of squawk this afternoon when that regrettable green girl appeared.'

'Did he?'

'You taught him at school, didn't you?'

'How very well informed you are, Mr Alleyn,' said Patrick airily.

'Coombe happened to mention it.'

'Look,' Jenny said, 'your visit isn't really unofficial, is it?'

'To tell you the truth,' Alleyn said, 'I'm damned if I know. Shall we move on?'

On the way across, Jenny said she supposed Alleyn must be worried on Miss Pride's account and he rejoined cheerfully that he was worried to hell. After all, he said, one didn't exactly relish one's favourite old girl being used as a cockshy. Patrick, involuntarily, it seemed, said that she really had rather turned herself into one, hadn't she? 'Sitting on her ledge under that umbrella, you know, and admonishing the pilgrims. It made everyone feel so shy.'

'*Did* she admonish them?'

'Well, I understand she said she hoped they'd enjoy a recovery but they oughtn't to build on it. They found it very off-putting.'

Jenny said: 'Will an effort be made to discover who's behind all these tricks?'

'That's entirely over to Superintendent Coombe.'

'Matter of protocol?' Patrick suggested.

'Exactly.'

The dinghy slid into deep shadow and bumped softly against the jetty. 'Well,' Alleyn said. 'I'm very much obliged to you both. Good night.'

'I can't imagine why it should be so,' Jenny said, 'but Miss Pride's rather turned into my favourite old girl, too.'

'Isn't it extraordinary? She doesn't present any of the classic features. She is not faded or pretty nor as far as I've noticed does she smell of lavender. She's by no means gentle or sweet, and doesn't exude salty common-sense. She is, without a shadow of doubt, a pig-headed, arrogant old thing.' He rose and steadied himself by the jetty steps. 'Do you subscribe to the Wally-gingered-up-by-Miss Cost theory?' he asked.

'It's as good as any other,' Patrick said. 'I suppose.'

'There's only one thing against it,' Jenny said. 'I don't believe Wally would ever deliberately hurt anyone. And he's a *very* bad shot.'

Alleyn stepped ashore.

'I expect,' said Patrick's voice quietly from the shadowed boat, 'you'll be relieved to get her away.'

'Yes,' he said. 'I shall. Good night.'

As he walked down the jetty he heard the dip of Patrick's oars and the diminishing murmur of their voices.

He found Superintendent Coombe's cottage and his host waiting for him. They had a glass of beer and a talk and turned in. Alleyn thought he would telephone his wife in the morning and went fast to sleep.

IV

He was wakened at seven by a downpour of rain. He got up, bathed and found breakfast in preparation. Mr Coombe, a widower, did for himself.

'Bit of a storm again,' he said, 'but it's clearing fast. You'll have a pleasant run.'

He went into his kitchen from whence, presently, the splendid smell of panfrying bacon arose. Alleyn stood at the parlour window and looked down on a deserted front, gleaming mud-flats and the exposed spine of the causeway.

'Nobody about,' he said.

'It's clearing,' Coombe's voice said above the sizzle of bacon. 'The local people think the weather's apt to change at low tide. Nothing in it.'

'It's flat out, now.'

'Yes,' Coombe said. 'Dead water.'

And by the time breakfast was over, so was the rain. Alleyn rang up his wife and said he'd be back for dinner. He put his suitcase in his car and as it was still too early to collect Miss Emily, decided, it being low tide, to walk over the causeway up Wally's Way and thence by footpath to the hotel. He had an inclination to visit the Spring again. Coombe, who intended to fish, said he'd come as far as the jetty. Alleyn drove there and left him with the car. The return trip with Miss Emily and her luggage, would be by water.

When he reached the Island, the bell for nine o'clock service was ringing in Mr Carstairs's church, back on the mainland.

Wally's Way was littered with evidence of yesterday's crowds: ice-cream wrappers, cigarette cartons and an occasional bottle. He wondered whose job it was to clear up.

It was a steep pull but he took it at a fair clip and the bell was still ringing when he reached the top.

He walked towards the enclosure and looked through the netting at the Spring.

On the shelf above it, open, and lying on its side was a large black umbrella.

It was one of those moments without time that strike at body and mind together with a single blow. He looked at the welling pool below the shelf. A black shape, half-inflated, pulsed and moved with the action of the Spring. Its wet surface glittered in the sun.

The bell had stopped and a lark sang furiously overhead.

He had to get through the turnstile.

The slot machine was enclosed in a wire cage, with a padlock which was open. He had no disc.

For a second or two, he thought of using a rock, if he could find one, or hurling his weight against the netted door, but he looked at the slot mechanism and with fingers that might have been handling ice, searched his pockets. A half-crown? No. A florin? As he pushed it down, he saw a printed notice that had been tied to the netting: 'Warning,' it was headed, and was signed: 'Emily Pride.' The florin jammed. He picked up a stone, hit it home and wrenched at the handle. There was a click and he was through and running to the Spring.

She was lying face-down in the pool, only A few inches below the water, her head almost at the lip of the waterfall.

Her sparse hair, swept forward, rippled and eddied in the stream. The gash in her scalp had stopped bleeding and gaped flaccidly.

Before he had moved the body over on its back he knew whose face would be upturned towards his own. It was Elspeth Cost's.

CHAPTER 5

Holiday Task

When he had made certain, beyond all shadow of a doubt, that there was nothing to be done, he ran out of the enclosure and a few yards along the footpath. Down below, on the far side of the causeway he saw Coombe, in his shirtsleeves, with his pipe in his mouth, fishing off the end of the jetty. He looked up, saw Alleyn, waved and then straightened. Alleyn beckoned urgently and signalled that they would meet at the top of the hotel steps. Coombe, seeing him run, himself broke into a lope, back down the jetty and across the causeway. He was breathing hard when he got to the top of the steps. When Alleyn had told him, he swore incredulously.

'I'll go into the hotel and get one of those bloody discs,' Alleyn said. 'I had to lock the gate, of course. And I'll have to get a message to Miss Pride. I'll catch you up. Who's your div. surgeon?'

'Maine.'

'Right.'

There was no one in the office. He went in, tried the drawers, found the right one, and helped himself to half a dozen discs. He looked at the switchboard, plugged in the connection and lifted the receiver. He noticed with a kind of astonishment that his hand was unsteady. It seemed an eternity before Miss Emily answered.

He said: 'Miss Emily? Roderick. I'm terribly sorry but there's been an accident and I'm wanted here. It's serious. Will it be a great bore if we delay your leaving? I'll come back later and explain.'

'By all means,' Miss Emily's voice said crisply. 'I shall adjust. Don't disarrange yourself on my account!'

'You admirable woman,' he said and hung up.

He had just got back on the lawful side of the desk when the hall-porter appeared, wiping his mouth. Alleyn said: 'Can you get Dr Maine quickly? There's been an accident. D'you know his number?'

The porter consulted a list and, staring at Alleyn, dialled it.

'What is it, then?' he asked. 'Accident? Dearrr, dearr!'

While he waited for the call to come through, Alleyn saw that a notice, similar to the one that had been tied to the enclosure, was now displayed in the letter rack. 'Warning.' And signed 'Emily Pride.' He had started to read it when the telephone quacked. The porter established the connection and handed him the receiver.

Alleyn said: 'Dr Maine? Speaking? This is a police call. I'm ringing for Superintendent Coombe. Superintendent Alleyn. There's been a serious accident at the Spring. Can you come at once?'

'At the *Spring?*'

'Yes. You'll need an ambulance.'

'What is it?'

'Asphyxia following cranial injury.'

'Fatal?'

'Yes.'

'I'll be there.'

'Thank you.'

He hung up. The porter was agog. Alleyn produced a ten-shilling note. 'Look here,' he said. 'can you keep quiet about this? I don't want people to collect. Be a good chap, will you, and get Sergeant Pender on the telephone. Ask him to come to the Spring. Say the message is from Mr Coombe. Will you do that? And don't talk.'

He slid the note across the desk and left.

As he returned by the footpath, he saw a car drive along the fore-shore to the causeway. A man with a black bag in his hand got out.

Coombe, waiting by the gate, was peering into the enclosure.

'I may have broken the slot-machine,' Alleyn said. But it worked and they went through.

He had dragged the body on to the verge of the pool and masked it, as well as he could, by the open umbrella.

Coombe said: 'Be damned, when I saw that brolly, if I didn't think I'd misheard you and it was the other old – Miss Pride.'

'I know.'

'How long ago, d'you reckon?'

'I should have thought about an hour. We'll see what the doctor thinks. He's on his way. Look at this, Coombe.'

The neck was rigid. He had to raise the body by the shoulders before exposing the back of the head.

'Well, well,' said Coombe. 'Just fancy that, now. Knocked out, fell forward into the pool and drowned. That the story?'

'Looks like it, doesn't it? And, see here.'

Alleyn lifted a fold of the dripping skirt. He exposed Miss Cost's right hand, bleached and wrinkled. It was rigidly clenched about a long string of glittering beads.

'Cor!' said Coombe.

'The place is one solid welter of footprints but I think you can pick hers: leading up to the shelf. The girl dropped the beads yesterday from above, I remember. They dangled over this ledge, half in the pool. In the stampede nobody rescued them.'

'And she came back? To fetch them?'

'It's a possibility, wouldn't you think? There's her handbag on the shelf.'

Coombe opened it. 'Prayer-book and purse,' he said.

'When's the first service?'

'Seven, I think.'

'There's another at nine. She was either going to church or had been there. That puts it at somewhere before seven for the first service. Or round about eight-forty-five if she had attended it or was going to the later one. When did it stop raining? About eight-thirty, I think. If those are her prints, they've been rained into and she'd got her umbrella open. Take a look at it.'

There was a ragged split in the wet cover which was old and partly perished. Alleyn displayed the inside. It was stained round the split and not with rainwater. He pointed a long finger. 'That's one of her hairs,' he said. 'There was a piece of rock in the pool. I fished it out and left it on the ledge. It looked as if it hadn't been there long and I think you'll find it fits.'

He fetched it and put it down by the body. 'Any visual traces have been washed away,' he said. 'You'll want to keep these exhibits intact, won't you?'

'You bet I will,' said Coombe.

There was a sound of footsteps and a metallic rattle. They turned and saw Dr Maine letting himself in at the turnstile. Coombe went down to meet him.

'What's it all about?' he asked. ' 'Morning, Coombe.'

'See for yourself, Doctor.'

They joined Alleyn who was introduced. 'Mr Alleyn made the discovery,' said Coombe and added: 'Rather a coincidence.'

Dr Maine, looking startled, said: 'Very much so.'

Alleyn said: 'I'm on a visit. Quite unofficial. Coombe's your man.'

'I wondered if you'd been produced out of a hat,' said Dr Maine. He looked towards the Spring. The umbrella, still open, masked the upper part of the body. 'Good God!' he ejaculated. 'So it *has* happened after all!'

Coombe caught Alleyn's eye and said nothing. He moved quickly to the body and exposed the face. Dr Maine stood stock-still. '*Cost!*' he said. 'Old *Cost*! Never!'

'That's right, Doctor.'

Dr Maine wasted no more words. He made his examination. Miss Cost's eyes were half-open and so was her mouth. There were flecks of foam about the lips and the tongue was clenched between the teeth. Alleyn had never become completely accustomed to murder. This grotesque shell, seconds before its destruction, had been the proper and appropriate expression of a living woman. Whether here, singly, or multiplied to the monstrous litter of a battlefield, or strewn idiotically about the wake of a nuclear explosion, or dangling with a white cap over a cyanosed, tongue-protruding mask; the destruction of one human being by another was the unique offence. It was the final outrage.

Dr Maine lowered the stiffened body on its back. He looked up at Alleyn. 'Where was she?'

'Face down and half-submerged. I got her out in case there was a chance but obviously there was none.'

'Any sign of rigor?'

'Yes.'

'It's well on its way now,' said Dr Maine.

'There's the back of the head, Doctor,' said Coombe. 'There's that too.'

Dr Maine turned the body and looked closely at the head. 'Where's the instrument?' he said. 'Found it?'

Alleyn said: 'I think so.'

Dr Maine glanced at him. 'May I see it?'

Alleyn gave it to him. It was an irregular jagged piece of rock about the size of a pineapple. Dr Maine turned it in his hands and stooped over the head. 'Fits,' he said.

'What's the verdict then, Doctor?' Coombe asked.

'There'll have to be a PM. of course. On the face of it: stunned and drowned.' He looked at Alleyn. 'Or, as you would say: "asphyxia following cranial injury".'

'I was attempting to fox the hotel porter.'

'I see. Good idea.'

'And when would it have taken place?' Coombe insisted.

'Again, you'll have to wait before you get a definite answer to that one. Not less than an hour ago, I'd have thought. Possibly much longer.'

He stood up and wiped his hands on his handkerchief.

'Do you know,' he said, 'I saw her. I saw her: it must have been about seven o'clock. Outside the church with Mrs Carstairs. She was going in to early service. I'd got a confinement on the Island and was walking down to the foreshore. Good lord!' said Dr Maine. 'I saw her.'

'That's a help, Doctor,' said Coombe. 'We were wondering about church. Now, that means she couldn't have got over here until eight at the earliest, wouldn't you say?'

'I should say so. Certainly. Rather later if anything.'

'And Mr Alleyn found her at nine. I suppose you didn't notice anyone about the cottages or anything of the sort, Doctor?'

'Not a soul. It was pouring heavens-hard. Wait a moment though.'

'Yes?'

He turned to Alleyn. 'I've got my own launch and jetty, and there's another jetty straight opposite on the foreshore by the cottages. I took the launch across. Well, the baby being duly delivered, I returned by the same means and I do remember that when I'd started up the engine and cast off, I saw that fantastic kid – Wally Trehern – dodging about on the road up to the Spring.'

'Did you watch him?' Coombe asked.

'Good lord, no. I turned the launch and had my back to the Island.'

'When would that be, now, Doctor?'

'The child was born at 7.30. Soon after that.'

'Yes. Well. Thanks,' said Coombe, glancing rather self-conscious-ly at Alleyn. 'Now: any ideas about *how* it happened?'

'On what's before us, I'd say that if this bit of rock *is* the instru-ment, it struck the head from above. Wait a minute.'

He climbed to the higher level above the shelf and Coombe followed him.

Alleyn was keeping a tight rein on himself. It was Coombe's case and Alleyn was a sort of accident on the scene. He thought of Patrick Ferrier's ironical remark: 'Matter of protocol' and silently watched the two men as they scrambled up through bracken to the top level.

Dr Maine said: 'There are rocks lying about up here. And yes – But this is your pigeon, Coombe. You'd better take a look.'

Coombe joined him.

'There's where it came from,' said Maine, 'behind the boulder. You can see where it was prised up.'

Coombe at last said, 'We'd better keep off the area, Doctor.' He looked down at Alleyn: 'It's clear enough.'

'Any prints?'

'A real mess. People from above must have swarmed all over it when the rain came. Pity.'

'Yes,' Alleyn said. 'Pity.'

The other two men came down.

'Well,' Dr Maine said. 'That's that. The ambulance should be here by now. Glad you suggested it. We'll have to get her across. How's the tide?' He went through the exit gates and along the footpath to a point from where he could see the causeway.

Alleyn said to Coombe: 'I asked the porter to get on to Pender and say you'd want him. I hope that was in order.'

'Thanks very much.'

'I suppose you'll need a statement from me, won't you?'

Coombe scraped his jaw. 'Sounds silly, doesn't it?' he said. 'Well, yes, I suppose I will.' He had been looking sideways at Alleyn, off and on, for some time.

'Look,' he said abruptly. 'There's one thing that's pretty obvious about this affair, isn't there? Here's a case where a Yard man with a top reputation is first on the scene and you might say, starts up the investigation. Look at it what way you like, it'd be pretty silly if I just said: "thanks, chum" and let it go at that. Wouldn't it now? I don't mind admitting I felt it was silly, just now, with you standing by, tactful as you please and leaving it all to me.'

'Absolute rot,' Alleyn said. 'Come off it.'

'No, I mean it. And, anyway,' Coombe added on a different note, 'I haven't got the staff.' It was a familiar plaint.

'My dear chap,' Alleyn said, 'I'm meant to be on what's laughingly called a holiday. Take a statement for pity's sake, and let me off. I'll remove Miss Pride and leave you with a fair field. You'll do well. "Coombe's Big Case".' He knew, of course, that this would be no good.

'You'll remove Miss Pride, eh?' said Coombe. 'And what say Miss Pride's the key figure, still? *You* know what I'm driving at. It's sticking out a mile. Say I'm hiding up there behind that boulder. Say I hear someone directly below and take a look-see. Say I see the top of an open umbrella and a pair of female feet, which is what I've been waiting for. Who do I reckon's under that umbrella? Not Miss Elspeth Cost. Not her. O, dear me no!' said Coombe in a sort of gloomy triumph. 'I say: "That's the job," and I bloody well let fly! But I bring down the wrong bird. I get – '

'All right, all right,' Alleyn said exasperated by the long build-up. 'And you say: "Absurd mistake. Silly old me! *I* thought you were Miss Emily Pride".'

II

The upshot, as he very well knew it would be, was an understanding that Coombe would get in touch with his Chief Constable and then with the Yard.

Coombe insisted on telling Dr Maine that he hoped Alleyn would take charge of the case. The ambulance men arrived with Pender and for the second time in twenty-four hours, Miss Cost went in procession along Wally's Way.

Alleyn and Coombe stayed behind to look over the territory again. Coombe had a spring-tape in his pocket and they took preliminary measurements and decided to get the areas covered in case of rain. He showed Alleyn where the trip-wire had been laid: through dense bracken on the way up to the shelf. Pender had caught a glint of it in the sunshine and had been sharp enough to investigate.

They completed their arrangements. The handbag, the string of beads and the umbrella were to be dropped at the police-station by Pender who was then to return with extra help if he could get it. The piece of rock would be sent with the body to the nearest mortuary which was at Dunlowman.

When they were outside the gates, Alleyn drew Coombe's attention to the new notice, tied securely to the wire-netting.

'Did you see this?'

It had been printed by a London firm.

WARNING

Notice is given that the owner of this property wishes to disassociate herself from any claims that have been made, in any manner whatsoever, for the curative properties of the spring. She gives further notice that the present enclosure is to be removed. Any proceedings of any nature whatsoever that are designed to publicize the above claims will be discontinued. The property will be restored, as far as possible, to conditions that obtained two years ago and steps will be taken to maintain it in a decent and orderly condition.

(Signed) *Emily Pride*

'When the hell was this put up?' Coombe ejaculated. 'It wasn't there yesterday. There'd have been no end of a taking-on.'

'Perhaps this morning. It's been rained on. More than that. It's muddied. As if it had lain face-downwards on the ground. Look. Glove marks. No finger-prints, though.'

'P'raps she dropped it.'

'Perhaps,' Alleyn said. 'There's another on display in the hotel letter-rack. It wasn't there last night.'

'Put them there herself? Miss Pride?'

'I'm afraid so.'

'There you are!' Coombe said excitedly. 'She came along the foot-path. Somebody spotted her, streaked up Wally's Way, got in ahead and hid behind the boulder. She hung up her notice and went back to the pub. Miss Cost arrives by the other route, goes in, picks up her beads and Bob's your uncle.'

'Is he, though?' Alleyn muttered, more to himself than to Coombe. 'She promised me she wouldn't leave the pub. I'll have to talk to Miss Emily.' He looked at Coombe. 'This is going to be tricky,' he said. 'If your theory's the right one, and at this stage it looks healthy enough, do we assume that the stone-chucker, wire-stretcher, composite letter-writer, dumper of green lady and telephonist are one and the same person and that this person is also the murderer of Miss Cost?'

'That's what I reckon. I know you oughtn't to get stuck on a theory. I know that. But unless we find something that cuts dead across it – '

'You'll find that all right,' Alleyn said. 'Miss Pride, you may remember, is convinced that the ringer-up was Miss Cost.'

Coombe thought this over and then said, well, all right, he knew that, but Miss Pride might be mistaken. Alleyn said Miss Pride had as sharp a perception for the human voice as was possible for the human ear. 'She's an expert,' he said. 'If I wanted an expert witness in phonetics I'd put Miss Pride in the box.'

'Well, all right, if you tell me so. So where does that get us? Does she reckon Miss Cost was behind *all* the attacks?'

'I think so.'

'Conspiracy, like?'

'Sort of.'

Coombe stared ahead of him for a moment or two. 'So where does *that* get us?' he repeated.

'For my part,' Alleyn said, 'it gets me rather quicker than I fancy, to Wally Trehern and his papa.'

Coombe said with some satisfaction that this, at any rate, made sense. If Wally had been gingered up to make the attacks, who more likely than Wally to mistake Miss Cost for Miss Pride and drop the rock on the umbrella?

'Could Wally rig a trip-wire? You said it was a workman-like job.'

'His old man could,' said Coombe.

'Which certainly makes sense. What about this padlocked cage over the slot-machine? Is it ever used?'

Coombe made an exasperated noise. 'That was her doing,' he said. 'She used to make a great to-do about courting couples. Very hot, she used to get: always lodging complaints and saying we ought to do something about it. Disgusting. Desecration and all that. Well, what could I do? Put Pender on the job all day and half the night, dodging about the rocks? It couldn't be avoided and I told her so. We put this cage over to pacify her.'

'Is it never locked?'

'It's supposed to be operated by the hotel at eight o'clock, morning and evening. In the summer that is. But a lot of their customers like to stroll along to the Spring of a summer's evening. Accordingly, it is not kept up very consistently.'

'We'd better get the key. I'll fix it now,' Alleyn said and snapped the padlock. It was on a short length of chain: not long enough, he noticed, to admit a hand into the cage.

On the way back to the hotel they planned out the rest of the day. Coombe would ring the Yard from the station. Alleyn in the meantime would start inquiries at the hotel. They would meet in an hour's time. It was now half past ten.

They had rounded the first spur along the path and come up with an overhanging outcrop of rock, when Alleyn stopped.

'Half a minute,' he said.

'What's up?'

Alleyn moved to the edge of the path and stooped. He picked something up and walked gingerly round behind the rock. 'Come over here,' he called. 'Keep wide of those prints, though.'

Coombe looked down and then followed him.

'There's a bit of shelter here,' Alleyn said. 'Look.'

The footprints were well defined on the soft ground, and, in the lee of the outcrop, fairly dry. 'Good, well-made boots,' he said. 'And I don't think the owner was here so very long ago. Here's where he waited and there, a little gift for the industrious officer, Coombe, is his cigar ash.' He opened his hand. A scarlet paper ring lay on the palm. 'Very good make,' he said. 'The Major smokes them. Sells them, too, no doubt, so what have you? Come on.'

They continued on their way.

As soon as Alleyn went into The Boy-and-Lobster he realized that wind of the catastrophe was abroad. People stood about in groups with a covert, anxious air. The porter saw him and came forward.

'I'm very sorry, sir. It be'ant none of my doing. I kept it close as a trap. But the ambulance was seen and the stretcher party and there you are. I said I supposed it was somebody took ill at the cottages but there was Sergeant Pender, sir, and us – I mean, they – be all wondering why it's a police matter.'

Alleyn said ambiguously that he understood. 'It'd be a good idea,' he suggested, 'if you put up a notice that the Spring will be closed today.'

'The Major'll have to be axed about that, sir.'

'Very well. Where is he?'

'He'll be in the old house, sir. He be'ant showed up round hereabouts.'

'I'll find him. Would you ring Miss Pride's rooms and say I hope to call on her within the next half-hour? Mr Alleyn.'

He went out and in again by the old pub door. There was nobody to be seen but he heard voices in what he thought was probably the ex-bar-parlour and tapped on the door. It was opened by Patrick Ferrier.

'Hallo. Good morning, sir,' said Patrick and then: 'Something's wrong, isn't it?'

'Yes,' Alleyn said. 'Very wrong. May I see your step-father?'

'Well – yes, of course. Will you come in?'

They were all seated in the parlour – Mrs Barrimore, Jenny Williams and the Major who looked very much the worse for wear but assumed a convincing enough air of authority, and asked Alleyn what he could do for him.

Alleyn told them in a few words what had happened. Margaret Barrimore turned white and said nothing. Jenny and Patrick exclaimed together: '*Miss Cost!* Not Miss *Cost!*'

Major Barrimore said incredulously: 'Hit on the head and drowned? Hit with what?'

'A piece of rock, we think. From above.'

'You mean it was an accident? Brought down by the rains, what?'

'I think not.'

'Mr Alleyn means she was murdered, Keith,' said his wife. It was the first time she had spoken.

'Be damned to that!' said the Major furiously. 'Murdered! Old Cost! Why?'

Patrick gave a sharp ejaculation. 'Well!' his step-father barked at him, 'what's the matter with you?'

'Did you say, sir, that she was under an umbrella?'

'Yes,' Alleyn said and thought: 'This is going to be everybody's big inspiration.'

He listened to Patrick as he presented the theory of mistaken identity.

Jenny said: 'Does Miss Pride know?'

'Not yet.'

'It'll be a shock for her,' said Jenny. 'When will you tell her?'

'As soon as I've left you.' He looked round at them. 'As a matter of form,' he said. 'I must ask you all where you were between half past seven and nine this morning. You will understand, won't you – '

'That it's purely a matter of routine,' Patrick said. 'Sorry. I couldn't help it. Yes, we do understand.'

Mrs Barrimore, Jenny and Patrick had got up and bathed in turn, round about eight o'clock. Mrs Barrimore did not breakfast in the public dining-room but had toast and coffee by herself in the old kitchen which had been converted into a kitchen-living-room. Jenny had breakfasted at about nine and Patrick a few minutes later. After breakfast they had gone out of doors for a few minutes, surveyed the weather and decided to stay in and do a crossword together. Major Barrimore, it appeared, slept in and didn't get up until half past nine. He had two cups of coffee but no breakfast.

All these movements would have to be checked but at the moment there was more immediate business. Alleyn asked Major Barrimore to put up a notice that the Spring was closed.

He at once objected. Did Alleyn realize that there were people from all over the country – from overseas, even – who had come with the express purpose of visiting the Spring? Did he realize that it was out of the question coolly to send them about their business: some of them, he'd have Alleyn know, in damned bad shape?

Alleyn said that the Spring could probably be reopened in two day's time.

'*Two days*, my dear fellah, *two days!* You don't know what you're talking about. I've got one draft going out tonight and a new detachment coming in tomorrow. Where the hell d'you suppose I'm going to put them? Hey?'

Alleyn said it was no doubt extremely inconvenient.

'Inconvenient! It's outrageous.'

'So,' Alleyn suggested, 'is murder.'

'I've no proof of where you get your authority and I'll have you know I won't act without it. I refuse point blank,' shouted the Major. 'And categorically,' he added as if that clinched the matter.

'The authority,' Alleyn said, 'is Scotland Yard and I'm very sorry, but you really can't refuse, you know. Either you decide to frame an announcement in your own words and get it out at once or I shall be obliged to issue a police notice. In any case that will be done at the Spring itself. It would be better, as I'm sure you must agree, if intending visitors were stopped here rather than at the gates.'

'Of course it would,' said Patrick impatiently.

'Yes, Keith. Please,' said Mrs Barrimore.

'When I want your suggestions, Margaret, I'll ask for them.'

Patrick looked at his step-father with disgust. He said to Alleyn: 'With respect, sir, I suggest that my mother and Jenny leave us to settle this point.'

Mrs Barrimore at once rose.

'May we?' she asked. Jenny said: 'Yes, please, may we?'

'Yes, of course,' said Alleyn, and to Patrick, 'Let the court be cleared of ladies, by all means, Mr Ferrier.'

Patrick gave him a look and turned pink. All the same, Alleyn thought, there was an air of authority about him. The wig was beginning to sprout and would probably become this young man rather well.

'Here. Wait a bit,' said the Major. He spread his hands. 'All right. *All right*,' he said. 'Have it your own way.' He turned on his wife. 'You're supposed to be good at this sort of rot, Margaret. Get out a notice and make it tactful. Say that owing to an accident in the area – no, my God, that sounds bloody awful. Owing to unforeseen circumstances – I don't know. *I* don't know. Say what you like. Talk to them. But get it *done.*' Alleyn could cheerfully have knocked him down.

Mrs Barrimore and Jenny went out.

Patrick, who had turned very white, said: 'I think it will be much better if we help Mr Alleyn as far as we're able. He wants to get on with his work, I'm sure. The facts will have to become known sooner or later. We'll do no good by adopting delaying tactics.'

Major Barrimore contemplated his step-son with an unattractive smile. 'Charming!' he said. 'Now, I know exactly how I should behave, don't I?' He appeared to undergo a change of mood and illustrated it by executing a wide gesture and then burying his face in his hands. 'I'm sorry,' he said and his voice was muffled. 'Give me a moment.'

Patrick turned his back and walked over to the window. The Major looked up. His eyes were bloodshot and his expression dolorous. 'Bad show,' he said. 'Apologize. Not myself. Truth of the matter is, I got a bit plastered last night and this has hit me rather hard.' He stood up and made a great business of straightening his shoulders and blowing his nose. 'As you were,' he said bravely. 'Take my orders from you. What's the drill?'

'Really, there isn't any at the moment,' Alleyn said cheerfully. 'If you can persuade your guests not to collect round the enclosure or use the path to it we'll be very grateful. As soon as possible we'll get the approaches cordoned off and that will settle the matter, won't it? And now, if you'll excuse me – '

He was about to go when Major Barrimore said: 'Quite so. Talk to the troops, what? Well – sooner the better.' He put his hand on Alleyn's arm. 'Sorry, old boy,' he said gruffly. 'Sure you understand.'

He frowned, came to attention and marched out.

'Not true,' Patrick said to the window. 'Just not true.'

Alleyn said: 'Never mind,' and left him.

When he re-entered the main buildings he found Major Barrimore the centre of a group of guests who showed every sign of disgruntlement tempered with avid curiosity. He was in tremendous form. 'Now, I know you're going to be perfectly splendid about this,' he was saying. 'It's an awful disappointment to all of us and it calls for that good old British spirit of tolerance and understanding. Take it on the chin and look as if you liked it, what? And you can take it from me – ' He was still in full cry as Alleyn walked up the stairs and went to call on Miss Emily.

III

She was of course dressed for travel. Her luggage, as he saw through the open door, was ready. She was wearing her toque.

He told her what had happened. Miss Emily's sallow complexion whitened. She looked very fixedly at him and did not interrupt.

'Roderique,' she said when he had finished. 'This is my doing. I am responsible.'

'Now, my dearest Miss Emily – '

'No. Please. Let me look squarely at the catastrophe. This foolish woman has been mistaken for me. There is no doubt in my mind at all. It declares itself. If I had obeyed the intention and not the mere letter of the undertaking I gave you, this would not have occurred.'

'You went to the Spring this morning with your notice?'

'Yes. I had, if you recollect, promised you not to leave my apartment again last night and to breakfast in my apartment this morning. A loophole presented itself.'

In spite of Miss Emily's distress there was more than a hint of low cunning in the sidelong glance she gave him. 'I went out,' she said. 'I placed my manifesto. I returned. I took my *petit déjeuner* in my room.'

'When did you go out?'

'At half past seven.'

'It was raining?'

'Heavily.'

'Did you meet anybody? Or see anybody?'

'I met nobody,' said Miss Emily. 'I *saw* that wretched child. Walter Trehern. He was on the roadway that leads from the cottages up to the Spring. It has, I believe, been called – ' She closed her eyes. 'Wally's Way. He was half-way up the hill.'

'Did he see you?'

'He did. He uttered some sort of gibberish, gave an uncouth cry and waved his arms.'

'Did he see you leave?'

'I think not. When I had affixed my manifesto and faced about, he had already disappeared. Possibly he was hiding.'

'And you didn't, of course, see Miss Cost.'

'No!'

'You didn't see her umbrella on your ledge above the pool? As you were tying up your notice?'

'Certainly not. I looked in that direction. It was not there.'

'And that would be at about twenty to eight. It wouldn't, I think, take you more than ten minutes to walk there, from the pub?'

'No. It was five minutes to eight when I re-entered the hotel.'

'Did you drop the notice, face down in the mud?'

'Certainly not. Why?'

'It's no matter. Miss Emily: please try to remember if you saw anybody at all on the village side of the causeway or indeed anywhere. Any activity round the jetty, for instance, or on the bay or in the cottages? Then, or at any time during your expedition.'

'Certainly not.'

'And on your return journey?'

'The rain was driving in from the direction of the village. My umbrella was therefore inclined to meet it.'

'Yes. I see.'

A silence fell between them. Alleyn walked over to the window. It looked down on a small garden at the back of the old pub. As he stood there, absently staring, someone came into the garden from below. It was Mrs Barrimore. She had a shallow basket over her arm and carried a pair of secateurs. She walked over to a clump of Michaelmas daisies and began to cut them, and her movement was so unco-ordinated and wild that the flowers fell to the ground. She made as if to retrieve them, dropped her secateurs and then the basket. Her hands went to her face and for a time she crouched there, quite motionless. She then rose and walked aimlessly and hurriedly about the paths, turning and returning as if the garden were a prison yard. Her fingers twisted together. They might have been encumbered with rings of which she tried fruitlessly to rid them.

'That,' said Miss Emily's voice, 'is a very unhappy creature.'

She had joined Alleyn without attracting his notice.

'Why?' he asked. 'What's the matter with her?'

'No doubt her animal of a husband ill-treats her.'

'She's a beautiful woman,' Alleyn said. He found himself quoting from – surely? – an inappropriate source. ' "What is it she does now? Look how she rubs her hands" ' and Miss Emily replied at once: ' "It is an accustomed action with her, to seem thus washing her hands".'

'Good heavens!' Alleyn ejaculated. 'What do we think we're talking about!'

Margaret Barrimore raised her head and instinctively they both drew back. Alleyn walked away from the window and then, with a glance at Miss Emily, turned back to it.

'She has controlled herself,' said Miss Emily. 'She is gathering her flowers. She is a woman of character, that one.'

In a short time Mrs Barrimore had filled her basket and returned to the house.

'Was she very friendly,' he asked, 'with Miss Cost?'

'No. I believe, on the contrary, that there was a certain animosity. On Cost's part. Not, as far as I could see, upon Mrs Barrimore's. Cost,' said Miss Emily, 'was, I judged, a spiteful woman. It is a not unusual phenomenon among spinsters of Cost's years and class. I am glad to say I was not conscious, at her age, of any such emotion. My sister Fanny, in her extravagant fashion, used to say I was devoid of the mating instinct. It may have been so.'

'Were you never in love, Miss Emily?'

'That,' said Miss Emily, 'is an entirely different matter.'

'Is it?'

'In any case it is neither here nor there. What do you wish me to do, Roderique? Am I to remain in this place?' She examined him. 'I think you are disturbed upon this point,' she said.

Alleyn thought: 'She's sharp enough to see I'm worried about her and yet she can't see why. Or can she?'

He said: 'It's a difficult decision. If you go back to London I'm afraid I shall be obliged to keep in touch and bother you with questions and you may have to return. There will be an inquest, of course. I don't know if you will be called. You may be.'

'With whom does the decision rest?'

'Primarily, with the police.'

'With you, then?'

'Yes. It rests upon our report. Usually the witnesses called at an inquest are the persons who found the body; me, in this instance, together with the investigating officers, the pathologist and anyone who saw or spoke to the deceased shortly before the event. Or anyone else who the police believe can throw light on the circumstances. Do you think,' he asked, 'you can do that?'

Miss Emily looked disconcerted. It was the first time, he thought, that he had ever seen her at a loss.

'No,' she said. 'I think not.'

'Miss Emily, do you believe that Wally Trehern came back after you had left the enclosure, saw Miss Cost under her umbrella, crept up to the boulder by a roundabout way (there's plenty of cover) and threw down the rock, thinking he threw it on you?'

'How could that be? How could he get in? The enclosure was locked.'

'He may have had a disc, you know.'

'What would be done to him?'

'Nothing very dreadful. He would probably be sent to an institution.'

She moved about the room with an air of indecision that reminded him, disturbingly, of Mrs Barrimore. 'I can only repeat,' she said at last, 'what I know. I saw him. He cried out and then hid himself. That is all.'

'I think we may ask you to speak of that at the inquest.'

'And in the meantime?'

'In the meantime, perhaps we should compromise. There is, I'm told, a reasonably good hotel in the hills outside Dunlowman. If I can arrange for you to stay there, will you do so? The inquest may be held at Dunlowman. It would be less of a fuss for you than returning from London.'

'It's inadvisable for me to remain here?'

'Very inadvisable.'

'So be it,' said Miss Emily. His relief was tempered by a great uneasiness. He had never known her so tractable before.

'I'll telephone the hotel,' he said. 'And Troy, if I may,' he added with a sigh.

'Had I taken your advice and remained in London, this would not have happened.'

He was hunting through the telephone book. 'That,' he said, 'is a prime example of utterly fruitless speculation. I am surprised at you, Miss Emily.' He dialled the number. The Manor Court Hotel would have a suite vacant at five o'clock the next day. There would also be a small single room. There had been cancellations. He booked the suite. 'You can go over in the morning,' he said, 'and lunch there. It's the best we can do. Will you stay indoors today, please?'

'I have given up this room.'

'I don't think there will be any difficulty.'

'People are leaving?'

'I daresay some will do so.'

'O,' she said, 'I am so troubled, my dear. I am so troubled.'

This, more than anything else she had said, being completely out of character, moved and disturbed him. He sat her down and because she looked unsettled and alien in her travelling toque, carefully removed it. 'There,' he said, 'and I haven't disturbed the coiffure. Now, you look more like my favourite old girl.'

'That is no way to address me,' said Miss Emily. 'You forget yourself.' He unbuttoned her gloves and drew them off. 'Should I blow in them?' he asked. 'Or would that be *du dernier bourgeois?*'

He saw with dismay that she was fighting back tears.

There was a tap at the door. Jenny Williams opened it and looked in. 'Are you receiving?' she asked and then saw Alleyn. 'Sorry,' she said. 'I'll come back later.'

'Come in,' Alleyn said. 'She may, mayn't she, Miss Emily?'

'By all means. Come in, Jennifer.'

Jenny gave Alleyn a look. He said: 'We've been discussing appropriate action to be taken by Miss Emily,' and told her what he had arranged.

Jenny said: 'Can't the hotel take her today?' And then hurried on: 'Wouldn't you like to be shot of the Island as soon as possible, Miss Pride? It's been a horrid business, hasn't it?'

'I'm afraid they've nothing until tomorrow,' Alleyn said.

'Well then, wouldn't London be better, after all? It's so anti-climaxy to gird up one's loins and then ungird them. Miss Pride, if you'd at all like me to, I'd love to go with you for the train journey.'

'You are extremely kind, dear child. Will you excuse me for a moment. I have left my handkerchief in my bedroom, I think.'

Jenny, about to fetch it, caught Alleyn's eye and stopped short. Alleyn opened the door for Miss Emily and shut it again.

He said quickly: 'What's happened? Talk?'

'She mustn't go out. Can't we get her away? Yes. Talk. Beastly, unheard-of, *filthy* talk. She mustn't know. God!' said Jenny, 'how I hate *people*.'

'She's staying indoors all day.'

'Has she any idea what they'll be saying?'

'I don't know. She's upset. She's gone in there to blow her nose and pull herself together. Look. Would you go with her to Dunlowman? It'll only be a few days. As a job?'

'Yes, of course. Job be blowed.'

'Well, as her guest. She wouldn't hear of anything else.'

'All right. If she wants me. She might easily not.'

'Go out on a pretence message for me and come back in five minutes. I'll fix it.'

'OK.'

'You're a darling, Miss Williams.'

Jenny pulled a grimace and went out.

When Miss Emily returned she was in complete control of herself. Alleyn said Jenny had gone down to leave a note for him at the office. He said he'd had an idea. Jenny, he understood from Miss Emily, herself was hard up and had to take holiday jobs to enable her to stay in England. Why not offer her one as companion for as long as the stay in Dunlowman lasted?

'She would not wish it. She is the guest of the Barrimores and the young man is greatly attached.'

'I think she feels she'd like to get away,' Alleyn lied. 'She said as much to me.'

'In that case,' Miss Emily hesitated. 'In that case I – I shall make the suggestion. Tactfully, of course. I confess it – it would be a comfort.' And she added firmly: 'I am feeling old.'

It was the most devastating remark he had ever heard from Miss Emily.

CHAPTER 6

Green Lady

When he arrived downstairs it was to find Major Barrimore and the office clerk dealing with a group of disgruntled visitors who were relinquishing their rooms. The Major appeared to hang on to his professional aplomb with some difficulty. Alleyn waited and had time to read a notice that was prominently displayed and announced the temporary closing of the Spring owing to unforeseen circumstances.

Major Barrimore made his final bow, stared balefully after the last guest and saw Alleyn. He spread his hands. 'My God,' he said.

'I'm very sorry.'

'Bloody people!' said the Major in unconscious agreement with Jenny. 'God, how I hate bloody people.'

'I'm sure you do.'

'They'll all go! The lot! They'll cackle away among themselves and want their money back and change their minds and jibber and jabber and in the bloody upshot, they'll be off. The whole bloody boiling of them. And the next thing: a new draft! Waltzing in and waltzing out again. What the – ' His language grew more fanciful; he sweated extremely. A lady with a cross face swept out of the lounge and up the stairs. He bowed to her distractedly. 'That's right, madam,' he whispered after her. 'That's the drill. Talk to your husband and pack your bags and take your chronic eczema to hell out of it.' He smiled dreadfully at Alleyn. 'And what can I do for *you*?' he demanded.

'I hardly dare ask you for a room.'

'You can have the whole pub. Bring the whole Yard.'

Alleyn offered what words of comfort he could muster. Major Barrimore received them with a moody sneer but presently became calmer. 'I'm not blaming you,' he said. 'You're doing your duty. Fine service, the police. Always said so. Thought of it myself when I left my regiment. Took on this damned poodlefaking instead. Well, there you are.'

He booked Alleyn in and even accepted, with gloomy resignation, the news that Miss Emily would like to delay her departure for another night.

As Alleyn was about to go he said: 'Could you sell me a good cigar? I've left mine behind and I can't make do with a pipe.'

'Certainly. What do you smoke?'

'Las Casas, if you have them.'

'No can do. At least – well, as a matter of fact, I do get them in for myself, old boy. I'm a bit short. Look here – let you have three, if you like. Show there's no ill-feeling. But not a word to the troops. If you want more, these things are smokable.'

Alleyn said: 'Very nice of you but I'm not going to cut you short. Let me have one Las Casas and I'll take a box of these others.'

He bought the cigars.

The Major had moved to the flap end of the counter. Alleyn dropped his change and picked it up. The boots, he thought, looked very much as if they'd fit. They were wet round the welts and flecked with mud.

He took his leave of the Major.

When he got outside the hotel he compared the cigar band with the one he had picked up and found them to be identical.

Coombe was waiting for him. Alleyn said: 'We'd better get the path cordoned off as soon as possible. Where's Pender?'

'At the Spring. Your chaps are on their way. Just made the one good train. They should be here by five. I've laid on cars at Dunlowman. And I've raised another couple of men. They're to report here. What's the idea, cordoning the path?'

'It's that outcrop,' Alleyn said and told him about the Major's cigars. 'Of course,' he said, 'there may be a guest who smokes his own Las Casas and who went out in a downpour at the crack of dawn to hide behind a rock, but it doesn't seem likely. We may have to take casts and get hold of his boots.'

'The Major! I *see!*'

'It may well turn out to be just one of those damn' fool things. But *he* said he got up late.'

'It'd fit. In a way, it'd fit.'

'At this stage,' Alleyn said. 'Nothing fits. We collect. That's all.'

'Well, I know that,' Coombe said quickly. He had just been warned against the axiomatic sin of forming a theory too soon. 'Here are these chaps now,' he said.

Two policemen were walking over the causeway.

Alleyn said: 'Look, Coombe. I think our next step had better be the boy. Dr Maine saw him and so did Miss Pride. Could you set your men to patrol the path and then join me at Trehern's cottage?'

'There may be a mob of visitors there. It's a big attraction.'

'Hell! Hold on. Wait a bit, would you?'

Alleyn had seen Jenny Williams coming out of the old pub. She wore an orange-coloured bathing dress and a short white coat and looked as if she had had twice her fair share of sunshine.

He joined her. 'It's all fixed with Miss Emily,' she said, 'I'm a lady's companion as from tomorrow morning. In the meantime, Patrick and I are thinking of a bathe.'

'I don't know what we'd have done without you. And loath as I am to put anything between you and the English Channel, I have got another favour to ask.'

'Now, what is all this?'

'You know young Trehern, don't you? You taught him? Do you get on well with him?'

'He didn't remember me at first. I think he does now. They've done their best to turn him into a horror but – yes – I can't help having a – I suppose it's a sort of compassion,' said Jenny.

'I expect it is,' Alleyn agreed. He told her he was going to see Wally and that he'd heard she understood the boy and got more response from him than most people. Would she come down to the cottage and help with the interview?

Jenny looked very straight at him and said: 'Not if it means you want me to get Wally to say something that may harm him.'

Alleyn said: 'I don't know what he will say. I don't in the least know whether he is in any way involved in Miss Cost's death. Suppose he was. Suppose he killed her, believing her to be Miss

Emily. Would you want him to be left alone to attack the next old lady who happened to annoy him? Think.'

She asked him, as Miss Emily had asked him, what would be done with Wally if he was found to be guilty. He gave her the same answer: nothing very dreadful. Wally might be sent to an appropriate institution. It would be a matter for authorized psychiatrists. 'And they do have successes in these days, you know. On the other hand, Wally may have nothing whatever to do with the case. But I must find out. Murder,' Alleyn said abruptly, 'is always abominable. It's hideous and outlandish. Even when the impulse is understandable and the motive overpowering, it is still a terrible, unique offence. As the law stands, its method of dealing with homicide is, as I think, open to the gravest criticism. But for all that, the destruction of a human being remains what it is: the last outrage.'

He was to wonder after the case had ended, why on earth he had spoken as he did.

Jenny stared out, looking at nothing. 'You must be an unusual kind of cop,' she said. And then: 'OK. I'll tell Patrick and put on a skirt. I won't be long.'

The extra constables had arrived and were being briefed by Coombe. They were to patrol the path and stop people climbing about the hills above the enclosure. One of them would be stationed near the outcrop.

Jenny reappeared wearing a white skirt over her bathing dress.

'Patrick,' she said, 'is in a slight sulk. I asked him to pick me up at the cottage.'

'My fault, of course. I'm sorry.'

'He'll get over it,' she said cheerfully.

They went down the hotel steps. Jenny moved ahead. She walked very quickly past Miss Cost's shop, not looking at it. A group of visitors stared in at the window. The door was open and there were customers inside.

Coombe said: 'The girl that helps is carrying on.'

'Yes. All right. Has she been told not to destroy anything – papers – rubbish – anything?'

'Well, yes. I mean, I said: just serve the customers and attend to the telephone calls. It's a sub-station for the Island. One of the last in the country.'

'I think the shop would be better shut, Coombe. We can't assume anything at this stage. We'll have to go through her papers. I suppose the calls can't be operated through the central station?'

'Not a chance.'

'Who is this assistant?'

'Cissy Pollock. She was that green girl affair in the show. Pretty dim type, is Cissy.'

'Friendly with Miss Cost?'

'Thick as thieves, both being hell-bent on the Festival.'

'Look. Could you wait until the shop clears and then lock up? We'll have to put somebody on the board or simply tell the subscribers that the Island service is out of order.'

'The Major'll go mad. Couldn't we shut the shop and leave Cissy on the switchboard?'

'I honestly don't think we should. It's probably a completely barren precaution but at this stage – '

' "We must not",' Coombe said, ' "allow ourselves to form a hard-and-fast theory to the prejudice of routine investigation." I know. But I wouldn't mind taking a bet on it that Miss Cost's got nothing to do with this case.'

'Except in so far as she happens to be the body?'

'You know what I mean. All right: she fixed the earlier jobs. All right: she may have got at that kid and set him on to Miss Pride. In a way, you might say she organized her own murder.'

'Yes,' Alleyn said. 'You might indeed. It may well be that she did.' He glanced at his colleague. 'Look,' he said. 'Pender will be coming back this way any time now, won't he? I suggest you put him in the shop just to see Miss Cissy Thing doesn't exceed her duty. He can keep observation in the background and leave you free to lend a hand in developments at Wally's joint or whatever it's called. I'll be damned glad of your company.'

'All right,' Coombe said. 'If you say so.'

This, Alleyn thought, is going to be tricky.

'Come on,' he said and put his hand on Coombe's shoulder. 'It's a hell of a bind but, as the gallant Major would say, it *is* the drill.'

'That's right,' said Superintendent Coombe. 'I know that. See you later, then.'

Alleyn left him at the shop.

Jenny was waiting down by the seafront. They turned left,
walked round the arm of the bay, and arrived at the group of fishermen's dwellings. Boats pulled up on the foreshore, a ramshackle
jetty and the cottages themselves, tucked into the hillside, all fell,
predictably, into a conventional arrangement.

'In a moment,' said Jenny, 'you will be confronted by Wally's
Cottage, but *not* as I remember it. It used to be squalid and dirty and
it stank to high heaven. Mrs Trehern is far gone in gin and Trehern,
as you may know, is unspeakable. But somehow or another the
exhibit has been evolved: very largely through the efforts of Miss
Cost egged on – well – '

'By whom? By Major Barrimore?'

'Not entirely,' Jenny said quickly. 'By the Mayor, who is called Mr
Nankivell, and his councillors and anybody in Portcarrow who is
meant to be civic-minded. And principally, I'm afraid, by Mrs Fanny
Winterbottom and her financial advisors. Or so Patrick says. So, of
course, does your Miss Emily. It's all kept up by the estate. There's a
guild or something that looks after the garden and supervises the
interior. Miss Emily calls the whole thing "*complètement en toc*". There
you are,' said Jenny as they came face-to-face with their destination.
'That's Wally's Cottage, that is.'

It was, indeed, dauntingly pretty. Hollyhocks, daisies, foxgloves
and antirrhinums flanked a cobbled path: honeysuckle framed the
door. Fishing-nets of astonishing cleanliness festooned the fence.
Beside the gate, in gothic lettering, hung a legend: 'Wally's Cottage.
Admission 1/-. West-country Cream-Teas, Ices.'

'There's an annex at the back,' explained Jenny. 'The teas are run
by a neighbour, Mrs Trehern not being up to it. The Golden Record's
in the parlour with other exhibits.'

'The Golden Record?'

'Of cures,' said Jenny shortly.

'Will Wally be on tap?'

'I should think so. And his papa, unless he's ferrying. There are
not nearly as many visitors as I'd expected. O!' exclaimed Jenny
stopping short. 'I suppose – will that be because of what's happened?
Yes, of course it will.'

'We'll go in,' Alleyn said, producing the entrance money.

Trehern was at the receipt of custom.

He leered ingratiatingly at Jenny and gave Alleyn a glance in which truculence, subservience and fear were unattractively mingled. Wally stood behind his father. When Alleyn looked at him he grinned and held out his hands.

Jenny said: 'Good morning, Mr Trehern. I've brought Mr Alleyn to have a look round. Hallo, Wally.'

Wally moved towards her: 'You come and see me,' he said. 'You come to school. One day soon.' He took her hand and nodded at her.

'Look at that, now!' Trehern ejaculated. 'You was always the favourite, miss. Nobody to touch Miss Williams for our poor little chap, is there, then, Wal?'

There were three visitors in the parlour. They moved from one exhibit to another, listened, and looked furtively at Jenny.

Alleyn asked Wally if he ever went fishing. He shook his head contemptuously and, with that repetitive, so obviously conditioned, gesture, again exhibited his hands. A trained animal, Alleyn thought with distaste. He moved away and opened the Golden Record which was everything that might be expected of it: like a visitors' book at a restaurant in which satisfied clients are invited to record their approval. He noted the dates where cures were said to have been effected and moved on.

The tourists left with an air of having had their money's-worth by a narrow margin.

Alleyn said: 'Mr Trehern, I am a police officer and have been asked to take charge of investigations into the death of Miss Elspeth Cost. I'd like to have a few words with Wally, if I may. Nothing to upset him. We just wondered if he could help us.'

Trehern opened and shut his hands as if he felt for some object to hold on by. 'I don't rightly know about that,' he said. 'My little lad be'ant like other little lads, mister. He'm powerful easy put out. Lives in a world of his own, and not to be looked to if it's straight-out facts that's required. No hand at facts, be you, Wal? Tell you the truth, I doubt he's took in this terrible business of Miss Cost.'

'She'm dead,' Wally shouted. 'She'm stoned dead.' And he gave one of his odd cries. Trehern looked very put out.

'Poor Miss Cost,' Jenny said gently.

'Poor Miss Cost,' Wally repeated cheerfully. Struck by some association of ideas he suddenly recited: '*Be not froightened sayed the loidy*

Ended now is all your woe,' and stopped as incontinently as he had begun.

Alleyn said: 'Ah! That's your piece you said yesterday, isn't it?' He clapped Wally on the shoulders. 'Hallo, young fellow, you've been out in the rain! You're as wet as a shag. That's the way to get rheumatism.'

Trehern glowered upon his son. 'Where you been?' he asked.

'Nowheres.'

'You been mucking round they boats. Can't keep him away from they boats,' he said ingratiatingly. 'Real fisherman's lad, our Wal. Be'ant you, Wal?'

'I dunno,' Wally said nervously.

'Come and show me these things,' Alleyn suggested. Wally at once began to escort him round the room. It was difficult to determine how far below normal he was. He had something to say about each regrettable exhibit and what he said was always, however uncouth, applicable. Even if it was parrot-talk, Alleyn thought, it at least proved that Wally could connect the appropriate remark with the appointed object.

Jenny stayed for a minute or two, talking to Trehern who presently said something of which Alleyn only caught the tone of the voice. This was unmistakable. He turned quickly, saw that she was disconcerted and angry and called out: 'How do you feel about tea and a bun? Wally: do you like ice-cream?'

Wally at once took Jenny's hand and began to drag her to a door marked Teas at the end of the room.

There was nobody else in the tea-room. An elderly woman, whom Jenny addressed by name, took their order.

'Was he being offensive, that type in there?' Alleyn asked in French.

'Yes.'

'I'm sorry.'

'It doesn't matter in the least,' Jenny said. 'What sort of tea do you like? Strong?'

'Weak and no milk.' Alleyn contemplated Wally whose face was already daubed with ice-cream. He ate with passionate, almost trembling, concentration.

'It was raining this morning, wasn't it, Wally?'

He nodded slightly.

'Were you out in the rain?'

Wally laughed and blew ice-cream across the table.

'Wally, don't,' Jenny said. 'Eat it properly, old boy. You were out in the rain, weren't you? Your shoes are muddy.'

'So I wor, then. I don't mind the rain, do I?'

'No,' Jenny said and added rather sadly: 'You're a big boy now.'

'I don't suppose,' Alleyn suggested, 'there was anybody else out in that storm was there? I bet there wasn't.'

'Was there, Wally? Out in the rain?'

'There wur! *There wur!*' he shouted and banged the table.

'All right. All right. Who was it?'

Wally thrust his tongue into the cornet. 'There wur,' he said.

'This is heavy work,' Alleyn observed mildly.

Jenny asked the same question and Wally at once said: 'I seen 'er. I seen the old b . . . *Yah*!'

'Who do you mean? Who did you see?'

He flourished his right arm: the gesture was as uncoordinated and wild as a puppet's, but it was not to be mistaken. He made as if to throw something. Jenny caught back an exclamation.

'Who did you see? Was it – ' Jenny looked at Alleyn who nodded. 'Was it Miss Pride?'

'*Pridey-Pridey bang on the bell*
 Smash and bash 'er and send 'er to hell.'

'*Wally!* who taught you that?'

'The kids,' he said promptly, and began again: '*Pridey-Pridey –* '

'Stop. Don't do that, Wally. Be quiet.' She said to Alleyn: 'It's true, I heard them, yesterday evening.'

Wally pushed the last of the cornet into his mouth. 'I want another,' he said indistinctly.

Coombe had come in from the parlour. Wally's back was towards him. Alleyn gave a warning signal and Coombe stayed where he was. Trehern loomed up behind him, smirking and curious. Coombe turned and jerked his thumb. Trehern hesitated and Coombe shut the door in his face.

'More,' said Wally.

'You may have another,' Alleyn said, before Jenny could protest. 'Tell me what happened when you were out in the rain this morning.'

He lowered his head and glowered. 'Another one. More,' he said.

'Where was Miss Pride?'

'Up along.'

'By the gate?'

'By the gate,' he repeated like an echo.

'Did you see her go away?'

'She come back.'

Jenny's hand went to her lips.

Alleyn said: 'Did Miss Pride come back?'

He nodded.

'Along the path? When?'

'She came back,' Wally shouted irritably. 'Back!'

'A long time afterwards?'

'Long time.'

'And went into the Spring? She went through the gate and into the Spring? Is that right?'

'It's *my* Spring. She be'ant allowed up to my Spring.'

He again made his wild throwing gesture. 'Get out!' he bawled.

'Did you throw a rock at Miss Pride? Like that?'

Wally turned his head from side to side. 'You dunno what I done,' he said. 'I ain't telling.'

'Tell Miss Williams.'

'No, I won't, then.'

'Did you throw stones, Wally?' Jenny asked. 'One evening? Did you?'

He looked doubtfully at her and then said: 'Where's my dad?'

'In there. Wally, tell me.'

He leant his smeared face towards her and she stooped her head. Alleyn heard him whisper: 'It's a secret.'

'What is?'

'They stones. Like my dad said.'

'Is the rock a secret, too?'

He pulled back from her. 'I dunno nothing about no rock,' he said vacantly. 'I want another.'

'Was Miss Cost at the Spring?' Alleyn asked.

Wally scowled at him.

'Wally,' Jenny said, taking his hand, 'did you see Miss Cost? In the rain? This morning? Was Miss Cost at the Spring?'

'At the fustyvell.'

'Yes, at the festival. Was she at the Spring this morning too? In the rain?'

'This is getting positively fugal,' Alleyn muttered.

'This morning,' Jenny repeated.

'Not this morning. At the fustyvell,' said Wally. 'I want another one.'

'In a minute,' Alleyn said. 'Soon. Did you see a man this morning in a motor-boat?' And, by a sort of compulsion, he added: 'In the rain?'

'My dad's got the biggest launch.'

'Not your dad's launch. Another man in another launch. Dr Maine. Do you know Dr Maine?'

'Doctor,' said Wally vacantly.

'Yes. Did you see him?'

'I dunno.'

Alleyn said to Jenny: 'Maine noticed him at about half past seven.' He waited for a moment and then pressed on: 'Wally: where were you when you saw the lady at the Spring? Where were you?'

Wally pushed his forefinger round and round the table, leaving a greasy trail on the plastic surface. He did this with exaggerated violence and apparently no interest.

'You couldn't get in, could you?' Alleyn suggested. 'You couldn't get through the gates.'

With his left hand, Wally groped under his smock. He produced a number of entrance discs, let them fall on the table and shoved them about with violent jabs from his forefinger. They clattered to the floor.

'Did you go into the Spring this morning?'

He began to make a high whimpering sound.

'It's no good,' Jenny said. 'When he starts that it's no good. He'll get violent. He may have an attack. Really, you mustn't. *Really*. I promise, you mustn't.'

'Very well,' Alleyn said. 'I'll get him his ice-cream.'

'Never mind, Wally, it's all right,' Jenny said. 'It's all right now. Isn't it?'

He looked at her doubtfully and then, with that too familiar gesture, reached his hands out towards her.

'O don't!' Jenny whispered. 'O Wally, *don't* show me your hands.'

II

When Wally had absorbed his second ice-cream they left the tea-room by a door that, as it turned out, led into the back garden.

Coombe said: 'We've come the wrong way,' but Alleyn was looking at a display of greyish undergarments hung out to dry. A woman of unkempt appearance was in the yard. She stared at them with bleared disfavour.

'Private,' she said and pointed to a dividing fence. 'You'm trespassing.'

'I'm sorry, Mrs Trehern,' Jenny said. 'We made a mistake.'

Trehern had come out through a back door. 'Get in, woman,' he said. 'Get in.' He took his wife by her arm and shoved her back into the house. 'There's the gate,' he said to Alleyn. 'Over yon.'

Alleyn had wandered to the clothes-line. A surplus length dangled from the pole. It had been recently cut.

'I wonder,' he said, 'if you could spare me a yard of this. The bumper-bar on my car's loose.'

'Be'ant none to spare. Us needs it. Rotten anyways and no good to you. There's the gate.'

'Thank you,' Alleyn said and they went out.

'Was it the same as the trip-wire?' he asked Coombe.

'Certainly was: but I reckon they all use it.'

'It's old but it's been newly cut. Have you kept the trip-wire?'

'Yes.'

'How was it fastened?'

'With iron pegs. They use them when they dry out their nets.'

'Well, let's move on, shall we?'

Patrick was sitting in a dinghy alongside the jetty, looking aloof and disinterested. Wally made up to a new pair of sightseers.

'That was very nice of you,' Alleyn said to Jenny. 'And I'm more than obliged.'

'I hated it. Mr Alleyn, he really isn't responsible. You can see what he's like.'

'Do you think he threw the stones at Miss Emily the other night?'

She said, very unhappily: 'Yes.'

'So do I.'

'But nothing else. I'm sure: nothing more than that.'

'You may be right. I'd be very grateful, by the way, if you'd keep the whole affair under your hat. Will you do that?'

'Yes,' she said slowly. 'All right. Yes, of course, if you say so.'

'Thank you *very* much. One other thing. Have you any idea who the Green Lady could have been?'

Jenny looked startled. 'No, I haven't. Somehow or another I've sort of forgotten to wonder. She may not have been real at all.'

'What did he say about her?'

'Only that she was very pretty and her hair shone in the sun. And that she said his warts would be all gone.'

'Nothing else?'

'No – nothing.'

'Has he got that sort of imagination – to invent her?'

Jenny said slowly: 'I don't think he has.'

'I don't think so either.'

'Not only that,' Jenny said. 'He's an extraordinarily truthful little boy. He never tells lies – never.'

'That's an extremely valuable piece of information,' Alleyn said. 'Now go and placate your young man.'

'I'll be blowed if I do. He can jolly well come off it,' she rejoined but Alleyn thought she was not altogether displeased with Patrick. He watched her climb down into the dinghy. It ducked and bobbed towards the far point of the bay. She looked up and waved to him. Her tawny hair, shone in the bright sunshine.

'That's a pleasing young lady,' said Coombe. 'What did you make of the lad?'

'We're not much further on, are we?'

'Aren't we, though? He as good as said he threw the stones that evening and what's more he has good as let on his dad had told him to keep his mouth shut.'

'Yes. Yes, it looked like that, didn't it?'

'Well, then?'

'He wouldn't say anything about the rock. He says he saw Miss Pride leave and return. The figure that returned may have been Miss Cost.'

'Ah!' said Coombe with satisfaction.

'Dr Maine, you remember, noticed Wally dodging about the road up to the Spring soon after half past seven. Miss Pride saw him at much the same time. Miss Pride got back to the pub at five to eight. She didn't encounter Miss Cost. Say the seven o'clock service ended about ten to eight – we'll have to find out about that – it would mean that Miss Cost would get to the causeway – when?'

'About eight.'

'Just after Miss Pride had gone indoors. And to the Spring?'

'Say a quarter past.'

'And I found her body at ten past nine.'

Coombe said: 'The kid would have had time between seven-thirty and eight-fifteen, to let himself into the enclosure and take cover behind that boulder. Before she came.'

'Why should he do that? He thought Miss Pride had gone. He saw her go. Why should he anticipate her return?'

'Just one of his silly notions.'

'Yes,' Alleyn said. 'One of his silly notions. Put that boy in the witness-box and we'd look as silly as he does. If he's at the end of this case, Coombe, we'll only get a conviction on factual evidence, not on anything the poor little devil says. Unmistakable prints of his boots behind the boulder, for instance.'

'You saw the ground. A mess.' Coombe reddened. 'I suppose I slipped up there. We were *on* the place before I thought.'

'It's so easy,' Alleyn said, saving his face for him. 'Happens to the best of us.'

'It was all churned up, wasn't it? Almost as if – ?'

'Yes?'

'Now I come to think of it, almost as if, before the doctor and I went up, someone had kind of scuffled it.'

'Yes. Behind the boulder and the trace of the rock. There was a flat bit of stone, did you notice, lying near the bank. Muddy edge. It might have been used to obliterate prints.'

'I suppose,' Coombe said, 'in a quiet type of division like this, you get a bit rusty. I could kick myself. At my time of life!'

'It may not amount to much. After all, we can isolate your prints and Dr Maine's from the rest.'

'Well, yes. Yes, you can do that, all right. But still!'

Alleyn looked at his watch. It was just on noon. He suggested that they return to the mainland and call on the rectory. The tide was coming in and they crossed the channel by dinghy. There was

Alleyn's car by the jetty with his luggage in it. If things had gone according to plan, he would have been half-way to Troy by now.

They left it where it stood. The rectory was a five minutes' walk along the front. It stood between a small and charming Norman church and Dr Maine's Convalescent Home: a pleasant late-Georgian house with the look, common to parsonages, of being exposed to more than its fair share of hard usage.

'It was a poorish parish, this,' Coombe said, 'but with the turn things have taken over the last two years, it's in better shape. The stipend's gone up for one thing. A lot of people that reckon they've benefited by the Spring, make donations. It'd surprise you to know the amounts that are put into the restoration-fund boxes. I'm people's warden,' he added, 'should have been there myself at ten-thirty for the family service. The Rector'll be back home by now. It's his busy day, of course.'

They found Mrs Carstairs briskly weeding. She wore a green linen dress and her hair, faded yellow, made an energetic sort of halo round her head. Her church-going hat, plastic raincoat, gloves and prayer-book were scattered in a surrealistic arrangement along the border. When Alleyn was introduced she shook hands briskly and said she supposed he'd come about this dreadful business and wanted to see her husband who was, of course, appalled.

'He's in the study,' she said to Coombe. 'Those accounts from the dry-rot people are *all* wrong again, Mr Coombe, and the Mayor suggests a combined memorial service but we don't *quite* think – however.'

'I'd really like a word with *you*, if I may,' Alleyn said. 'We're trying to trace Miss Cost's movements early this morning.'

'*O dear*! Yes. Well, of *course*.'

She confirmed Dr Maine's account. Miss Cost had attended the first celebration at seven o'clock and they had met at the gate. 'She was in a great fuss, poor thing, because of my necklace.'

'Your necklace?'

'Yes. It's really rather a nice old one. Pinchbeck and paste but long and quite good. I lent with reluctance but she was so keen to have it because of the glitter and then, of course, what must her great Cissy do but drop it at the first thunder-clap and in the stampede, nobody remembered. I said we'd retrieve it after church or why not let Cissy go? But no: she made a great to-do, *poor* Miss Cost (when one *thinks)* and insisted that she would go herself. She was rather an *on-goer*: conversationally, if you know what I mean: on and on and I wanted to go into church and say my prayers and it was pouring. So then she saw Dr Maine and she was curious to know if it was Mrs Trethaway's twins, though of course in the event it *wasn't* twins, (that was all nonsense) so I'm afraid I left her to tackle him as she clearly died to do. And after church I saw her streak off through the rain before anyone could offer. Isn't it *dreadful?*' Mrs Carstairs asked energetically. 'Well, *isn't* it? Adrian! Can you spare a moment, dear?'

'Coming.'

The Rector, wearing his cassock, emerged through french windows. He said how extraordinary it was that Alleyn should have been at Portcarrow, added that they were lucky to have him and then became doubtful and solemn. 'One finds it hard to believe,' he said. 'One, is appalled.'

Alleyn asked him when the first service ended and he said at about a quarter to eight. 'I'd expected a large congregation. There are so many visitors. But the downpour, no doubt, kept a lot of folk away and there were only six communicants. The nine o'clock was crowded.'

Alleyn wondered absently why clergymen were so prone to call people 'folk' and asked Mr Carstairs if he knew Miss Cost very well. He seemed disturbed and said: well, yes, in so far as she was a member of his congregation. He glanced at his wife and added: 'Our friendship with Miss Cost was perhaps rather limited by our views on the Spring. I could not sympathize or, indeed, approve of her, as I thought, rather extravagant claims. I thought them woolly,' said the Rector. 'Woolly and vulgar.' He expounded, carefully, his own attitude which, in its anxious compromise, declared, Alleyn thought, its orthodoxy.

'And you saw her,' he asked, 'after the service?'

They said simultaneously that they did.

'I'm one of those parsons who come out to the porch and see folk off,' the Rector explained. 'But Miss Cost was on her way when I got there. Going down the path. Something about my wife's necklace. Wasn't it, Dulcie?'

'Yes, dear. I told Mr Alleyn.'

Coombe said: 'The necklace has been recovered and will be returned in due course, Mrs Carstairs.'

'O, dear!' she said. 'Will it? I – I don't think – '

'Never mind, dear,' said her husband.

Alleyn asked if anybody from the Island had been at the first service. Nobody, it appeared. There were several at the nine o'clock.

'The Barrimores, for instance?'

No, not the Barrimores.

There was a silence through which the non-attendance of the Barrimores was somehow established as a normal state-of-affairs.

'Although,' Mrs Carstairs said, in extenuation of a criticism that no one had voiced, 'Margaret used to come *quite* regularly at one time, Adrian. Before Wally's Warts, you remember?'

'Not that there's any connection, Dulcie.'

'Of course not, dear. And Patrick and *nice* Jenny Williams have been to evensong, we must remember.'

'So we must,' her husband agreed.

'Poor things. They'll all be terribly upset no doubt,' Mrs Carstairs said to Alleyn. 'Such a shock for everyone.'

Alleyn said carefully: 'Appalling. And apart from everything else a great worry for Barrimore, one imagines. After all, it won't do his business any good, this sort of catastrophe.'

They looked uncomfortable and faintly shocked. 'Well – ' they both said and stopped short.

'At least,' Alleyn said casually, 'I suppose The Boy-and-Lobster *is* his affair, isn't it?'

'It's the property of the estate,' Coombe said. 'Miss Pride's the landlord. But I have heard they put everything they'd got into it.'

'*She* did,' Mrs Carstairs said firmly. 'It was Margaret Barrimore's money, wasn't it, Adrian?'

'My dear, I don't know. In any case – '

'Yes, dear. Of course,' said Mrs Carstairs, turning pink. She glanced distractedly at the knees of her linen dress. 'O, look!' she said. 'Now, I shall have to change. It was that henbane that did it. What a disgrace I am. Sunday and everything.'

'You melt into your background, my dear,' the Rector observed. 'Like a wood-nymph,' he added, with an air of recklessness.

'Adrian, you are awful,' said Mrs Carstairs automatically. It was clear that he was in love with her.

Alleyn said: 'So there would be a gap of about an hour and a quarter between the first and second services?'

'This morning, yes,' said the Rector. 'Because of the rain, you see, and the small attendance at seven.'

'How do you manage?' Alleyn asked Mrs Carstairs. 'Breakfast must be quite a problem.'

'Oh, there's usually time to boil an egg before nine. This morning, as you see, we had over an hour. At least,' she corrected herself. '*You* didn't, did you, dear? Adrian had to make a visit: poor old Mr Thomas,' she said to Coombe. 'Going, I'm afraid.'

'So you were alone after all. When did you hear of the tragedy, Mrs Carstairs?'

'Before matins. Half past ten. Several people had seen the – well, the ambulance and the stretcher, you know. And Adrian met Sergeant Pender and – and there it was.'

'Is it true?' the Rector asked abruptly. 'Was it – deliberate? Pender said – I mean?'

'I'm afraid so.'

'How very dreadful,' he said. 'How appallingly dreadful.'

'I know,' Alleyn agreed. 'A woman, it appears, with no enemies. It's incomprehensible.'

Coombe cleared his throat. The Carstairses glanced at each other quickly and as quickly looked away.

'Unless, I suppose,' Alleyn said, 'you count Miss Pride?'

'There, I'm afraid,' the Rector said, and Alleyn wondered if he'd caught an overtone of relief, 'there, it was all on Miss Cost's side, poor soul.'

'You might say,' his wife added, 'that Miss Pride had the whip-hand.'

'Dulcie!'

'Well, Adrian, you know what I mean.'

'It's quite beside the point,' said the Rector with authority.

A telephone rang in the house. He excused himself and went indoors.

'There was nothing, I suppose, in her day-to-day life to make people dislike her,' Alleyn said. 'She seems, as far as I can make out, to have been a perfectly harmless obsessive.'

Mrs Carstairs began to pick up her scattered belongings, rather as if she was giving herself time to consider. When she straightened up, with her arms full, she was quite red in the face.

'She wasn't always perfectly kind,' she said.

'Ah! Which of us is?'

'Yes, I know. You're quite right. Of course,' she agreed in a hurry.

'Did she make mischief?' he asked lightly.

'She tried. My husband – Naturally, we paid no attention. My husband feels very strongly about that sort of thing. He calls it a cardinal sin. He preaches *very* strongly against. *Always*,' Mrs Carstairs looked squarely at Alleyn. 'I'm offending, myself, to tell you this. I can't think what came over me. You must have a – have a talent for catching people off guard.'

He said wryly: 'You make my job sound very unappetizing. Mrs Carstairs, I won't bother you much longer. One more question and we're off. Have you any idea who played those ugly tricks on Miss Pride? If you have, I do hope you will tell me.'

She seemed, he thought, to be relieved. She said at once: 'I've always considered she was behind them. Miss Cost.'

'Behind them? You thought she encouraged someone else to take the active part?'

'Yes.'

'Wally Trehern?'

'Perhaps.'

'And was that what you were thinking of when you said Miss Cost was not always kind?'

'O no!' she ejaculated and stopped short. 'Please don't ask me any more questions, Mr Alleyn. I shall not answer them, if you do.'

'Very well,' he said. He thanked her and went away, followed, uncomfortably, by Coombe.

They lunched at the village pub. The whole place was alive with trippers. The sun glared down, the air was degraded by transistors and the ground by litter. Groups of sightseers in holiday garments crowded the foreshore, eating, drinking and pointing out the Island to each other. The tide was full. The hotel launch and a number of dinghies plied to and fro and their occupants stared up at the enclosure. It was obvious that the murder of Miss Cost was now common knowledge.

The enclosure itself was not fully visible from the village, being masked by an arm of Fisherman's Bay, but two constables could be seen on the upper pathway. Visitors returning from the Island told each other and anybody that cared to listen, that you couldn't get anywhere near the Spring. 'There's nothing to see,' they said. 'The coppers have got it locked up. You wouldn't know.'

When they had eaten a flaccid lunch they called on the nearest JP and picked up a search-warrant for Wally's Cottage. They went on to the station where Alleyn collected a short piece of the trip-wire. It was agreed that he would return to The Boy-and-Lobster. Coombe was to remain at the station, relieving his one spare constable, until the Yard men arrived. He would then telephone Alleyn at The Boy-and-Lobster. Pender would remain on duty at Miss Cost's shop.

Coombe said: 'It's an unusual business, this. You finding the body and then this gap before your chaps come in.'

'I hope you'll still be on tap, but I do realize it's taking more time than you can spare.'

'Well, you know how it is.' He waited for a moment and then said: 'I appreciate your reluctance to form a theory too soon. I mean, it's what we all know. You can't. But as I'm pulling out I can't help saying it looks a sure thing to me. Here's this dopey kid as good as letting on he pitched in with the stones. There's more than a hint that his old man was behind it and a damn' good indication that he set the trip-wire. The kid says Miss Pride came back and there's every likelihood he mistook Miss Cost for her. I reckon he'd let himself into the enclosure and was up by the boulder. He looked down and saw the umbrella below and let fly at it. I mean: well, it hangs together, doesn't it?'

'Who do you think planted the figurine in Miss Pride's sitting-room and sent her the anonymous message and rang her up?'

'Well, *she* reckons Miss Cost.'

'So Miss Cost's death was the end product of the whole series? Laid on, you might say, by herself?'

'In a sense. Yes.'

'Has it struck you at all,' Alleyn asked, 'that there's one feature of the whole story about which nobody seems to show the slightest curiosity?'

'I can't say it has.'

Alleyn took from his pocket the figurine that he had wrapped in paper and in his handkerchief. He opened it up and, holding it very gingerly, stood it on Coombe's desk. The single word, Death, gummed to a sheet of paper, was still fixed in position.

'Nobody,' Alleyn said, 'as far as I can gather, has ever asked themselves who was the original Green Lady.'

III

'That piece of paper,' Alleyn said, 'is not the kind used for the original messages. It's the same make as this other piece which is a bit of The Boy-and-Lobster letter paper. The word 'Death' is not in a type that is used in your local rag. I can't be sure but I think it's from a London sporting paper called *The Racing Supplement*. The printer's ink, as you see, is a bluish black and the type's distinctive. Was Miss Cost a racing fan?'

'Her?' Coombe said. 'Don't be funny.'

'The Major is. He takes *The Racing Supplement*.'

'Does he, by gum!'

'Yes. Have you got a dabs-kit handy?'

'Nothing very flash, but, yes: we've got the doings.'

Alleyn produced his box of cigars. He opened this up.

'There ought to be good impressions inside the lid. Bailey can give it the full works, if necessary, but we'll take a fly at it, shall we?'

Coombe got out his insufflator and a lens. They developed a good set of prints on the lid and turned to the paper impaled over the figurine's head.

After a minute or two Alleyn gave a satisfied grunt.

'Fair enough,' he said. 'The index and thumb prints are as good as you'd ask. I think I'll call on the gallant Major.'

He left Coombe still poring lovingly over the exhibits, walked down to his car, collected his suitcases and crossed by the hotel launch to the Island. Trehern was in charge. His manner unattractively combined truculence with servility.

It was now two o'clock.

The Major, it presently transpired, was in the habit of taking a siesta.

'He got used to it in India,' Mrs Barrimore said. 'People do.'

Alleyn had run into her at the door of the old pub. She was perfectly composed and remote in her manner: a beautiful woman who could not, he thought, ever be completely unaware of the effect she made. It was inescapable. She must, over and over again, have seen it reflected in the eyes of men who looked at, and at once recognized, her. She was immensely attractive.

He said: 'Perhaps, in the meantime, I may have a word with you?'

'Very well. In the parlour, if you like. The children are out, just now.'

'The children?'

'Jenny and Patrick. I should have said "the young" I expect. Will you come in.'

He could hardly recognize the woman he had seen in her garden, veering this way and that like a rudderless ship and unable to control her hands. She sat perfectly still and allowed him to look at her while she kept her own gaze on her quietly, interlaced fingers.

He supposed she must have had a hand in the transformation of the old bar-parlour into a private living-room: if so she could have taken little interest in the process. Apart from the introduction of a few unexceptionable easy-chairs, one or two photographs, a non-committal assembly of books and a vase of the flowers she had so mishandled in the garden, it must be much as it was two years ago: an impersonal room.

Alleyn began by following the beaten paths of routine investigation. He tried to establish some corroboration of her alibi, though he did not give it this name, for the period covered by Miss Emily's visit to the enclosure up to the probable time of Miss Cost's death. There was none to be had. Nobody had visited the kitchen-dining-room while she drank her coffee and ate her toast. The servants were all busy in the main building. Jenny and Patrick had breakfasted in the public dining-room, her husband was presumably asleep. Alleyn gathered that they occupied separate rooms. She had no idea how long this solitary meal had lasted. When it was over she had attended to one or two jobs, interviewed the kitchen staff and then gone up to her room and changed from a housecoat to a day dress. When she came downstairs again she had found the young people in the parlour. Alleyn had arrived soon afterwards.

'And for the rest of the morning,' he asked casually, 'did you go out at all?'

'No farther than the garden,' she said after a fractional pause. 'I went into the garden for a time.'

'To cut flowers?' he suggested, looking at those in the room.

She lifted her eyes to his for a moment. 'Yes,' she said, 'to cut flowers. I do the flowers on Sunday as a rule: it takes quite a time. Jenny helped me,' she added as an afterthought.

'In the garden?'

Again the brief look at him, this time perhaps, fractionally less controlled. 'No. Not in the garden. In the house. Afterwards.'

'So you were alone in the garden?'

She said quickly with the slight hesitation he had noticed before in her speech: 'Yes. Alone. Why d-do you keep on about the garden? What interest can it have for you? It was after – afterwards. Long afterwards.'

'Yes, of course. Did the news distress you very much, Mrs Barrimore?'

The full, unbridled mouth so much at variance with the rest of her face, moved as if to speak, but, as in a badly-synchronized sound-film, her voice failed. Then she said: 'Naturally. It's a terrible thing to have happened, isn't it?'

'You were fond of Miss Cost?'

Something in her look reminded him, fantastically, of the strange veiling of a bird's eyes. Hers were heavy-lidded and she had closed them for a second. 'Not particularly,' she said. 'We had nothing – ' She stopped, unaccountably.

'Nothing in common?'

She nodded. Her hands moved but she looked at them and refolded them in her lap.

'Had she made enemies?'

'I don't know of any,' she said at once as if she had anticipated the question. 'I know very little about her.'

Alleyn asked her if she subscribed to the theory of mistaken identity and she said that she did. She was emphatic about this and seemed relieved when he spoke of it. She was, she said, forced to think that it might have been Wally.

'Excited, originally, by Miss Cost herself?'

'I think it's possible. She was – It doesn't matter.'

'Inclined to be vindictive?'

She didn't answer.

'I'm afraid,' Alleyn said, 'that in these cases one can't always avoid speaking ill of the dead. I did rather gather from something in Mrs Carstairs' manner – '

'Dulcie Carstairs!' she exclaimed, spontaneously and with animation. 'She never says anything unkind about anybody.'

'I'm sure she doesn't. It was just that – well, I thought she was rather desperately determined not to do so in this case.'

She gave him a faint smile. It transfigured her face.

'Dear Dulcie,' she murmured.

'She and the Rector are horrified, of course. They struck me as being such a completely unworldly pair, those two.'

'Did they? You were right. They are.'

'I mean – not only about Miss Cost but about the whole business of the Spring being more or less discredited by the present owner. The events of the last two years must have made a great difference to them, I suppose.'

'Yes,' she said. 'Enormous.'

'Were they very hard up before?'

'O yes. It was a dreadfully poor parish. The stipend was the least that's given, I believe, and they'd no private means. We were all so sorry about it. Their clothes! She's nice-looking but she needs careful dressing,' said Mrs Barrimore with all the unconscious arrogance of a woman who would look lovely in a sack. 'Of course everyone did what they could. I don't think she ever bought anything for herself.'

'She looked quite nice this morning, I thought.'

'Did she?' For the first time, Margaret Barrimore spoke as if there was some kind of rapprochement between them. 'I thought men never noticed women's clothes,' she said.

'Do you bet me I can't tell you what you wore yesterday at the Spring?'

'Well?'

'A white linen dress with a square neck and a leather belt. Brown Italian shoes with large buckles. Brown suede gloves. A wide string-coloured straw hat with a brown velvet ribbon. A brown leather bag. No jewellery.'

'You win,' said Mrs Barrimore. 'You don't look like the sort of man who notices but I suppose it's part of your training and I shouldn't feel flattered. Or should I?'

'I would like you to feel flattered. And now I'm going to ruin my success by telling you that Mrs Carstairs, too, wore a linen dress, this morning.' He described it. She listened to this talk about clothes as if it was a serious matter.

'White?' she asked.

'No. Green.'

'O yes. That one.'

'Was it originally yours?'

'If it's the one I think it is, yes.'

'When did you give it to her?'

'I don't in the least remember.'

'Well: as long as two years ago?'

'Really, I've no idea.'

'Try.'

'But I *don't* remember. One doesn't remember. I've given her odd things from time to time. You make me feel as if I'm parading – as if I'm making a lot of it. As if it was charity. Or patronage. It was nothing. Women do those sorts of things.'

'I wouldn't press it if I didn't think it might be relevant.'

'How can it be of the slightest interest?'

'A green dress? If she had it two years ago? Think.'

She was on her feet with a quick controlled movement.

'But that's nonsense! You mean – Wally?'

'Yes. I do. The Green Lady.'

'But – most people have always thought he imagined her. And even if he didn't – there are lots of green dresses in the summer-time.'

'Of course. What I'm trying to find out is whether this was one of them. Is there nothing that would call to mind when you gave it to her?'

She waited for a moment, looking down at her hands.

'Nothing. It was over a year ago, I'm sure.' She turned aside. 'Even if I could remember, which I can't, I don't think I would want to tell you. It can't have any bearing on this ghastly business – how could it? – and suppose you're right, it's private to Dulcie Carstairs.'

'Perhaps she'd remember.'

'I don't believe it. I don't for a moment believe she would think of playing a – a fantastic trick like that. It's not like her. She was never the Green Lady.'

'I haven't suggested she was, you know.' Alleyn walked over to her. She lifted her head and looked at him. Her face was ashen.

'Come,' he said, 'don't let us fence any more. You were the Green Lady, weren't you?'

CHAPTER 7

The Yard

He wondered if she would deny it and what he could say if she did. Very little. His assumption had been based largely on a hunch and he liked to tell himself that he didn't believe in hunches. He knew that she was deeply shocked. Her white face and the movement of her hands gave her away completely but she was, as Miss Emily had remarked, a woman of character.

She said: 'I have been very stupid. You may, I suppose, congratulate yourself. What gave you the idea?'

'I happened to notice your expression when that monstrous girl walked out from behind the boulder. You looked angry. But, more than that, I've been told Wally sticks to it that his Green Lady was tall and very beautiful. Naturally, I thought of you.'

A door slammed upstairs. Someone, a man, cleared his throat raucously.

She twisted her hands into his. Her face was a mask of terror. 'Mr Alleyn, promise me, for God's sake, promise me you won't speak about this to my husband. It won't help you to discuss it with him. I swear it won't. You don't know what would happen if you did.'

'Does he not know?'

She tried to speak but only looked at him in terror.

'He *does* know?'

'It makes no difference. He would be – he would be angry. That you knew.'

'Why should he mind so much? You said what you said, I expect, impulsively. And it worked. Next morning the boy's hands were clean. You couldn't undo your little miracle.'

'No, no, no, you don't understand. It's not that. It's – O God, he's coming down. O God, how can I make you? What shall I do! Please, please.'

'If it's possible I shall say nothing.' He held her hands firmly for a moment until they stopped writhing in his. 'Don't be frightened,' he said and let her go. 'He'd better not see you like this. Where does that door lead to? The kitchen?' He opened it. 'There you are. Quickly.'

In a moment she was gone.

Major Barrimore came heavily downstairs. He yawned, crossed the little hall and went into the old private bar. The slide between it and the parlour was still there. Alleyn heard the clink of glass. A mid-afternoon drinker; he thought and wondered if the habit was long-established. He picked up his suitcase, went quietly into the hall and out at the front door. He then noisily returned.

'Anyone at home?' he called.

After an interval, the door of the private opened and Barrimore came out, dabbing at his mouth with a freshly-laundered handker-chief and an unsteady hand. He was, as usual, impeccably turned-out. His face was puffy and empurpled and his manner sombre.

'Hallo,' he said. 'You.'

'I'm on my way to sign in,' Alleyn said cheerfully. 'Can you spare me a few minutes? Routine, as usual. One's never done with it.'

Barrimore stared dully at him and then opened the door of the parlour. 'In here,' he said.

Margaret Barrimore had left the faintest recollection of her scent behind her but this was soon lost in the Major's blended aura of Scotch-cigar-and-hair-lotion.

'Well,' he said. 'What's it, this time? Made any arrests?'

'Not yet.'

'Everybody nattering about the boy, I s'ppose. You'd think they'd all got their knife into the poor kid.'

'You don't agree?'

'I don't. He's too damn' simple, f'one thing. No harm in him, f'r'nother. You get to know 'bout chap's character in a regiment. Always pick the bad 'uns. He's not.'

'Have you any theories yourself?'

The Major predictably said: 'No names, no pack drill.'

'Quite. But I'd be glad of your opinion.'

'You wouldn't, old boy. You'd hate it.'

Now, Alleyn thought, this is it. I know what this is going to be. 'I?' he said, 'why?'

'Heard what they're saying in the village?'

'No. What are they saying?'

'I don't necessarily agree, you know. Still: they hated each other's guts, those two. Face it.'

'Which two?'

'The females. Beg pardon: the ladies. Miss P. and Miss C. And she was *there*, old boy. Can't get away from it. She was on the spot. Hanging up her bloody notice.'

'*How do you know?*' Alleyn said and was delighted to speak savagely.

'Here! Steady! Steady, the Buffs!'

'The path has been closed. No one has been allowed near the enclosure. How do you know Miss Pride was there? How do you know she hung up her notice?'

'By God, sir – '

'I'll tell you. You were there yourself.'

The blood had run into patches in the Major's jowls. 'You must be mad,' he said.

'You were on the path. You took shelter behind an outcrop of stone by the last bend. After Miss Pride had left and returned to the hotel, you came out and went to the enclosure.'

He was taking chances again, but, looking at that outfaced blinking man, he knew he was justified.

'You read the notice, lost your temper and threw it into the mud. The important thing is that you were there. If you want to deny it you are, of course, at perfect liberty to do so.'

Barrimore drew his brows together and went through a parody of brushing his moustache. He then said: 'Mind if I get a drink?'

'You'd better not, but I can't stop you.'

'You're perfectly right,' said the Major. He went out. Alleyn heard him go into the private and pushed back the slide. The Major was pouring himself a Scotch. He saw Alleyn and said: 'Can I persuade you? No. S'pose not. Not the drill.'

'Come back,' Alleyn said.

He swallowed his whisky neat and returned.

'Better,' he said. 'Needed it.' He sat down. 'There's a reasonable explanation,' he said.

'Good. Let's have it.'

'I followed her.'

'Who? Miss Pride?'

'That's right. Now, look at it this way. I wake. Boiled owl. Want a drink of water. Very well. I get up. Raining cassandogs. All v'y fine. Look outer th'window. Cassandogs. And there *she* is with her bloody great brolly, falling herself in, down below. Left wheel and into the path. What's a man going to do? Coupler aspirins and into some togs. Trench coat. Hat. Boots. See what I mean? You can't trust her an inch. Where was I?'

'Following Miss Pride along the path to the enclosure.'

'Certainly. She'd gained on me. All right. Strategy of indirect approach. Keep under cover. Which I did. Just like you said, old boy. Perfectly correct. Don't fire till you see the whites of their eyes.' He leered at Alleyn.

'Do you mean that you confronted her?'

'Me! No, thank you!'

'You mean you kept under cover until she'd gone past you on her way back to the hotel.'

'What I said. Or did I?'

'Then you went to the enclosure?'

'Nasherally.'

'You read the notice and threw it aside?'

' 'Course.'

'And then? What did you do?'

'Came back.'

'Did you see Wally Trehern?'

The Major stared. 'I did not.'

'Did you meet anyone?'

A vein started out on Barrimore's forehead. Suddenly, he looked venomous.

'Not a soul,' he said loudly.

'Did you see anyone?'

'No?'

'You met Miss Cost. You must have done so. She was on the path a few minutes after Miss Pride got back. You either met her at the enclosure itself or on the path. Which was it?'

'I didn't see her. I didn't meet her.'

'Will you sign a statement to that effect?'

'I'll be damned if I do.' Whether through shock or by an astonishing effort of will, he had apparently got himself under control. 'I'll see you in hell first,' he said.

'And that's your last word?'

'Not quite.' He got up and confronted Alleyn, staring into his face. 'If there's any more of this,' he said. 'I'll ring up the Yard and tell your O.C. you're a prejudiced and therefore an untrustworthy officer. I'll have you court-martialled, by God! Or whatever they do in your show.'

'I really think you'd better not,' Alleyn said mildly.

'No? I'll tell them what's no more than the case: you're suppressing evidence against an old woman who seems to be a very particular friend. No accounting for taste.'

'Major Barrimore,' Alleyn said. 'You will not persuade me to knock your tongue down your throat but you'd do yourself less harm if you bit it off.'

'I know what I'm talking about: You can't get away from it. Ever since she came here she's had her knife into poor old Cost. Accusing her of writing letters. Chucking stones. Telephone messages. Planting ornaments.'

'Yes,' Alleyn said. 'Miss Pride was wrong there, wasn't she? Miss Cost didn't put the Green Lady in Miss Pride's room. You did.'

Barrimore's jaw dropped.

'Well,' Alleyn said. 'Do you deny it? I shouldn't if I were you. It's smothered in your finger-prints and so's the paper round its neck.'

'You're lying. You're bluffiing.'

'If you prefer to think so. There's been a conspiracy between you, against Miss Pride, hasn't there? You and Miss Cost, with the Treherns in the background? You were trying to scare her off. Miss Cost started it with threatening messages pieced together from the local paper. You liked the idea and carried on with the word 'Death' cut out of your *Racing Supplement* and stuck round the neck of the image. You didn't have to ask Miss Cost for one. They're for sale in your pub.'

'Get to hell out of here. *Get out.*'

Alleyn picked up his suitcase. 'That's all for the present. I shall ask you to repeat this conversation before a witness. In the meantime, I suggest that you keep off the whisky and think about the amount of damage you've done to yourself. If you change your mind about any of your statements I'm prepared to listen to you. You will see to it, if you please, that Miss Pride is treated with perfect civility during the few hours she is most unfortunately obliged to remain here as your guest.'

He had got as far as the door when the Major said: 'Hold on. Wait a bit.'

'Well?'

'Daresay I went too far. Not myself. Fellah shouldn't lose his temper, should he? What!'

'On the contrary,' said Alleyn, 'the exhibition was remarkably instructive.' And went out.

II

'And after all that,' he thought, 'I suppose I should grandly cancel my room and throw myself on Coombe's hospitality again. I won't though. It's too damned easy and it's probably exactly what Barrimore hopes I'll do.'

He collected his key at the office and went up to his room. It was now a quarter past three. Miss Emily would still be having her siesta. In an hour and forty-five minutes, Detective-Inspector Fox, Detective-Sergeant Bailey and Detective-Sergeant Thompson would arrive. Curtis, the pathologist, would be driving to Dunlowman under his own steam. Coombe had arranged for Dr Maine to meet him there. The nearest mortuary was at Dunlowman. Alleyn would be damned glad to see them all.

He unpacked his suitcase and began to write his notes on hotel paper. It was the first time he'd ever embarked on a case without his regulation kit and he felt uncomfortable and amateurish. He began to wonder if, after all, he should hand over to Fox or somebody else. Triumph for the gallant Major, he thought.

For a minute or two he indulged in what he knew to be fantasy. Was it, in the smallest degree, remotely possible that Miss Emily, inflamed by Miss Cost's activities, could have seen her approaching, bolted into the enclosure, hidden behind the boulder and under a sudden access of exasperation, hurled a rock at Miss Cost's umbrella? It was not. But supposing for a moment that it was? What would Miss Emily then have done? Watched Miss Cost as she drowned in the pool; as her hair streamed out over the fall; as her dress inflated and deflated in the eddying stream? Taken another bit of rock, and scraped out her own footprints and walked back to The Boy-and-Lobster? And, where, all that time, was the Major? What became of his admission that he tore down the notice and threw it away? Suppose there was an arrest and a trial and defending council used Miss Emily as a counterblast? Could her innocence be established? Only, as things stood, by the careful presentation of the Major's evidence and the Major thought, or pretended to think, she was guilty. And, in any case, the Major was a chronic alcoholic.

He got up and moved restlessly about the room. A silly, innocuous print of anemones in a mug, had been hung above the bed. He could have wrenched it down and chucked it, with as much fury as had presumably inspired the Major, into the wastepaper basket.

There must have been an encounter between Barrimore and Miss Cost. He had seen Emily pass and repass, had come out of concealment and gone to the enclosure. By that time Miss Cost was approaching. Why, when he saw her, should he again take cover, and where? No: they must have met. What, then, did they say to each other in the pouring rain? Did she tell him she was going to retrieve the necklace? Or did he, having seen her approaching, let himself into the enclosure and hide behind the boulder? But why? And where, all this time, was Wally? Dr Maine and Miss Emily had both seen him, soon after half past seven. He had shouted at Miss Emily and then ducked out of sight. The whole damned case seemed to be littered with people that continually dodged in and out of concealment. What about Trehern? Out and about in the landscape with the rest of them? Inciting his son to throw rocks at a supposed Miss Emily? Dr Maine had not noticed him but that proved nothing.

Next, and he faced this conundrum with distaste, what about Mrs Barrimore alias the Green Lady? Did she fit in anywhere or had he merely stumbled down an odd, irrelevant by-way? But why was she so frightened at the thought of her husband being told of her masquerade? The Green Lady episode had brought Barrimore nothing but material gain. Wouldn't he simply have ordered her to shut up about it and if anything, relished the whole story? She had seemed to suggest that the fact of Alleyn himself being aware of it would be the infuriating factor. And why had she been so distressed when she was alone in the garden? At that stage there was no question of her identity with the Green Lady being discovered.

Finally, of course, was Miss Cost murdered, as it were, in her own person, or because she was mistaken for Miss Emily?

The answer to that one must depend largely upon motive and motive is one of the secondary elements in police investigation. The old tag jog-trotted through his mind. *'Quis? Quid? Ubi? Quibus auxilis? Cur? Quomodo? Quando?'* Which might be rendered: 'Who did the deed? What was it? Where was it done? With what? Why was it done? And how done? When was it done?' The lot!

He completed his notes and read them through. The times were pretty well established. The weapon. The method. The state of the body. The place – no measurements yet, beyond the rough ones he and Coombe had made on the spot. Bailey would attend to all that. The place? He had described it in detail. The boulder? – between the boulder and the hill behind it, was a little depression, screened by bracken and soft with grass. A 'good spot for courting couples,' as Coombes had remarked, 'when it wasn't raining.' The ledge –

He was still poring over his notes when the telephone rang. Mr Nankivell, the Mayor of Portcarrow, would like to see him.

'Ask him to come up,' Alleyn said and put his notes in the drawer of the desk.

Mr Nankivell was in a fine taking-on. His manner suggested a bothering confusion of civic dignity, awareness of Alleyn's reputation and furtive curiosity. There was another element, too. As the interview developed, so did his air of being someone who has information to impart and can't quite make up his mind to divulge it. Mr Nankivell, for all his *opéra bouffe* façade, struck Alleyn as being a pretty shrewd fellow.

'This horrible affair,' he said, 'has taken place at a very regrettable juncture, Superintendent Alleyn. This, sir, is the height of our season. Portcarrow is in the public eye. It has become a desirable resort. We'll have the Press down upon us and the type of information

they'll put out will not conduce to the general benefit of our
community. A lot of damaging clap-trap is what we may expect from
those chaps and we may as well face up to it.'

'When does the local paper come out?'

'Tuesday,' said the Mayor gloomily. 'But they've got their system.
Thick as thieves with London – agents, as you might say. They'll
have handed it on.'

'Yes,' Alleyn said. 'I expect they will.'

'Well, there now!' Mr Nankivell said waving his arm. 'There yarr!
A terrible misfortunate thing to overtake us.'

Alleyn said: 'Have you formed any opinion yourself, Mr Mayor?'

'So I have, then. Dozens. And each more objectionable than the
last. The stuff that's being circulated already by parties that ought to
know better! Now, I understand, sir, and I hope you'll overlook my
mentioning it, that Miss Pride is personally known to you.'

With a sick feeling of weariness Alleyn said: 'Yes. She's an old
friend.' And before Mr Nankivell could go any further he added: 'I'm
aware of the sort of thing that is being said about Miss Pride. I can
assure you that, as the case has developed, it is clearly impossible that
she could have been involved.'

'Is that so? Is that the case?' said Mr Nankivell. 'Glad to hear it,
I'm sure.' He did not seem profoundly relieved, however. 'And
then,' he said, 'there's another view. There's a notion that the one
lady was took for the other! Now, there's a very upsetting kind of a
fancy to get hold of. When you think of the feeling there's been and
them that's subscribed to it.'

'Yourself among them?' Alleyn said lightly. 'Ridiculous, when
you put it like that, isn't it?'

'I should danged well hope it is ridiculous,' he said violently and
at once produced his own alibi. 'Little though I ever thought to be
put in the way of making such a demeaning statement,' he added
angrily. 'However. Being a Sunday, Mrs Nankivell and I did not
raise up until nine o'clock and was brought our cup of tea at eight
by the girl that does for us. The first I hear of this ghastly affair is at
ten-thirty when Mrs Nankivell and I attended chapel and then it
was no more than a lot of chatter about an accident and George
Pender, looking very big, by all accounts, and saying he'd nothing
to add to the information. When we come out it's all over the

village. I should of been informed at the outset but I wasn't. Very bad.'

Alleyn did his best to calm him.

'I'm very grateful to you for calling,' he said. 'I was going to ring up and ask if you could spare me a moment this afternoon but I wouldn't have dreamt of suggesting you took the trouble to come over. I really must apologize.'

'No need, I'm sure,' said Mr Nankivell, mollified.

'Now, I wonder, if, in confidence, Mr Mayor, you can help me at all. You see, I know nothing about Miss Cost and it's always a great help to get some sort of background. For instance, what was she like? She was, I take it, about forty to forty-five years old and, of course, unmarried. Can you add anything to that? A man in your position is usually a very sound judge of character, I've always found.'

'Ah!' said the Mayor, smoothing the back of his head. 'It's an advantage, of course. Something that grows on you with experience, you might say.'

'Exactly. Handling people and getting to know them. Now, between two mere males, how would you sum up Miss Elspeth Cost?'

Mr Nankivell raised his brows and stared upon vacancy. A slow, knowing smile developed. He wiped it away with his fingers but it crept back.

'A proper old maiden, to be sure,' he said.

'Really?'

'Not that she was what you'd call ancient: forty-five, as you rightly judged and a tricksy time of life for females, which is a well-established phenomenon, I believe.'

'Yes, indeed. You don't know,' Alleyn said cautiously, 'what may turn up.'

'God's truth, if you never utter another word,' said Mr Nankivell with surprising fervour. He eased back in his chair, caught Alleyn's eye and chuckled. 'The trouble I've had along of that lady's crankiness,' he confided, 'you'd never credit.'

Alleyn said 'Tch!'

'Ah! With some it takes the form of religious activities. Others go all out for dumb animals. Mrs Nankivell herself, although a very

level-headed lady, worked it off in cats which have in the course of
nature simmered down to two. Neuters, both. But with Miss Cost,
not to put too fine a point on it, with Miss Cost, it was a matter of
her female urges.'

'Sex?'

'She spotted it everywhere,' Mr Nankivell exclaimed. 'Up hill and
down dell, particularly the latter. Did I know what went on in the
bay of an evening? Was I aware of the opportunities afforded by
open dinghies? Didn't we ought to install more lights along the
front? And when it came to the hills round about the Spring she was
a tiger. Alf Coombe got it. The Rector got it, the doctor got it and I
came in for it, hot and strong, continuous. She was a masterpiece.'

Alleyn ventured a sympathetic laugh.

'You may say so, but beyond a joke nevertheless. And that's not
the whole story. The truth of the matter is, and I tell you this, sir, in
the strictest confidence, the silly female was – dear me, how can I
put it? – she was chewed-up by the very fury she come down so
hard upon. Now, that's a fact and well-known to all and sundry. She
was a manhunter, was poor Elspeth Cost. In her quiet, mousy sort of
fashion, she raged to and fro seeking whom she might devour.
Which was not many.'

'Any success?'

The Mayor, to Alleyn's infinite regret, pulled himself up. 'Well,
now,' he said. 'That'd be talking. That'd be exceeding, sir.'

'I can assure you that if it has no bearing on the case, I shall forget
it. I'm sure, Mr Mayor, you would prefer me to discuss these, quite
possibly irrelevant matters with you, rather than make widespread
inquiries through the village. We both know, don't we, that local
gossip can be disastrously unreliable?'

Mr Nankivell thought this over. 'True as fate,' he said at last.
'Though I'm in no position myself to speak as to facts and don't
fancy giving an impression that may mislead you. I don't fancy that,
at all.'

This seemed to Alleyn to be an honest scruple and he said warmly:
'I think I can promise you that I shan't jump to conclusions.'

The Mayor looked at him. 'Very good,' he said. He appeared to be
struck with a sudden thought. 'I can tell you this much,' he continued with a short laugh. 'The Rector handled her with ease, being

well-versed in middle-aged maidens. And she had no luck with me and the doctor. Hot after him, she was, and drawing attention and scorn upon herself right and left. But we kept her at bay, poor wretch, and in the end she whipped round against us with as mighty a fury as she'd let loose on the pursuit. Very spiteful. Same with the Major.'

'What!' Alleyn ejaculated. 'Major Barrimore!'

Mr Nankivell looked extremely embarrassed. 'That remark,' he said, 'slipped out. All gossip, I daresay, and better forgotten, the whole lot of it. Put about by the Ladies' Guild upon which Mrs Nankivell sits, *ex officio*, and, as she herself remarked, not to be depended upon.'

'But what is it that the Ladies' Guild alleges? That Miss Cost set her bonnet at Major Barrimore and he repelled her advances?'

'Not azackly,' said the Mayor. His manner strangely suggested a proper reticence undermined by an urge to communicate something that would startle his hearer.

'Come on, Mr Mayor,' Alleyn said. 'Let's have it, whatever it is. Otherwise you'll get me jumping to a most improper conclusion.'

'Go on, then,' invited Mr Nankivell, with hardihood, 'Jump!'

'You're not going to tell me that Miss Cost is supposed to have had an affair with Major Barrimore?'

'Aren't I? I am, then. And a proper, high-powered, blazing set to at that. While it lasted,' said Mr Nankivell.

III

Having taken his final hurdle, Mr Nankivell galloped freely down the straight. The informant, it appeared, was Miss Cissy Pollock, yesterday's Green Lady and Miss Cost's assistant and confidante. To her, Miss Cost was supposed to have opened her heart. Miss Pollock, in her turn, had retailed the story, under a vow of strictest secrecy, to the girlfriend of her bosom whose mother, a close associate of Mrs Nankivell, was an unbridled gossip. You might as well, the Mayor said, have handed the whole lot over to the Town Crier and have done with it. The affair was reputed to have been of short duration and to have taken place at the time of Miss Cost's first visit to the Island. There was dark talk of an

equivocal nature about visits paid by Major Barrimore' to an unspecified rival in Dunlowman. He was, Mr Nankivell remarked, a full-
blooded man.

With the memory of Miss Cost's face, as Alleyn had seen it that
morning made hideous by death, this unlovely story took on a
grotesque and appalling character. Mr Nankivell himself seemed to
sense something of this reaction: he became uneasy and Alleyn had
to assure him, all over again, that it was most unlikely that the matter
would turn out to be relevant and that supposing it was, Mr
Nankivell's name would not appear as everything he had said came
under the heading of hearsay and would be inadmissible as
evidence. This comforted him and he took his leave with the air of a
man who, however, distasteful the task, has done his duty.

When he had gone, Alleyn got his notes out again and added a
fairly lengthy paragraph. He then lit his pipe and walked over to the
window.

It looked down on the causeway, the landing jetty and the roof of
Miss Cost's shop. Across the channel, in the village, trippers still dappled the foreshore. There were several boats out in the calm waters
and among them, pulling towards the Island, he saw Patrick's dinghy
with Jenny Williams in the stern. She sat bolt upright and seemed to
be looking anywhere but at her companion. He was rowing with
exaggerated vigour, head down and shoulders hunched. Even at that
distance, he looked as if he was in a temper. As they approached the
jetty, Jenny turned towards him and evidently spoke. He lifted his
head, seemed to stare at her and then back-paddled into a clear
patch of water and half-shipped his oars. The tide was going out and
carried them very slowly towards the point of Fisherman's Bay. They
were talking now. Jenny made a quick repressed gesture and shook
her head.

'Lovers' quarrel,' Alleyn thought. 'Damned awkward in a boat.
He won't get anywhere, I daresay.'

'You won't get anywhere,' Jenny was saying in a grand voice, 'by
sulking.'

'I am *not* sulking.'

'Then you're giving a superb imitation of it. As the day's been
such a failure why don't we pull in and bring it to an inglorious conclusion?'

'All right,' he said but made no effort to do so.

'Patrick.'

'What?'

'Couldn't you just mention what's upset your applecart? It'd be better than huffing and puffing behind a thundercloud.'

'You're not so marvellously forthcoming yourself.'

'Well, what am I meant to do? Crash down on my knees in the bilge water and apologize for I don't know what?'

'You do know what.'

'O lord!' Jenny pushed her fingers through her dazzling hair, looked at him and began to giggle. 'Isn't this *silly*?' she said.

The shadow of a grin lurked about Patrick's mouth and was suppressed. 'Extremely silly,' he said. 'I apologize for being a figure of fun.'

'Look,' Jenny said. 'Which is it? Me going off with Mr Alleyn to see Wally? Me being late for our date? Or me going to Dunlowman with Miss Emily tomorrow? Or the lot? Come on.'

'You're at perfect liberty to take stewed tea and filthy cream buns with anybody you like for as long as you like. It was evidently all very private and confidential and far be me from it – I mean it from me – to muscle in where I'm not wanted.'

'But I *told* you. He asked me not to talk about it.'

Patrick inclined, huffily. 'So I understand,' he said.

'Patrick! I'm sorry, but I do find that I respect Mr Alleyn. I'm *anti* a lot of things that I suppose you might say he seems to stand for, although I'm not so sure, even, of that. He strikes me as being – well – far from reactionary,' said young Jenny.

'I'm sure he's a paragon of enlightenment.'

She wondered how it would go if she said: 'Let's face it, you're jealous,' and very wisely decided against any such gambit. She looked at Patrick: at his shock of black hair, at his arms and the split in his open shirt where the sunburn stopped and at his intelligent, pig-headed face. She thought: 'He's a stranger and yet he's so very familiar.' She leant forward and put her hand on his bony knee.

'Don't be unhappy,' she said. 'What is it?'

'Good God!' he said. 'Can you put it out of your mind so easily! It's Miss Cost, with her skull cracked. It's Miss Cost, face down in our wonderful Spring. It's your pin-up detective, inching his way into our lives. Do you suppose I enjoy the prospect of – ' He stopped short. 'I happen,' he said, 'to be rather attached to my mother.'

Jenny said quickly: 'Patrick – yes, of course you are. But – '

'You must know damned well what I mean.'

'All right. But surely it's beside the point. Mr Alleyn can't think – '

'Can't he?' His eyes slid away from her. 'She was a poisonous woman,' he said.

A silence fell between them and suddenly Jenny shivered: unexpectedly as if some invisible hand had shaken her.

'What's the matter?' he said irritably. 'Are you cold?'

He looked at her miserably and doubtfully.

Jenny thought: 'I don't know him. I'm lost.' And at once was caught up in a wave of compassion.

'Don't let's go on snarling,' she said. 'Let's go home and sort ourselves out. It's clouded over and I'm getting rather cold.'

He said: 'I don't blame you for wanting to get away from this mess. What a party to have let you in for! It's better you should go to Dunlowman.'

'Now *that*,' said Jenny, 'is really unfair and you know it, darling.'

He glowered at her. 'You don't say that as a rule. Everyone says "darling" but you don't.'

'That's right. I'm saying it now for a change. Darling.'

He covered her hand with his. 'I'm sorry,' he said. 'I am really sorry. Darling Jenny.'

From his bedroom window Alleyn watched and thought: 'He'll lose his oar.'

It slipped through the rowlock. Patrick became active with the other oar. The dinghy bobbed and turned about. They both reached dangerously overboard. Through the open window Alleyn faintly caught the sound of their laughter.

'That's done the trick,' he thought. The telephone rang and he answered it.

'Fox here, sir,' said a familiar placid voice. 'Speaking from Portcarrow station.'

'You sound like the breath of spring.'

'I didn't quite catch what you said.'

'It doesn't matter. Have you brought my homicide kit?'

'Yes.'

'Then come, Birdie, come.'

Mr Fox replaced the receiver and said to Superintendent Coombe and the Yard party: 'We're to go over. He's worried.'

'He sounded as if he was acting the goat or something,' said Coombe.

'That's right,' said Fox. 'Worried. Come on, you chaps.'

Detective-Sergeants Bailey and Thompson, carrying their kit, accompanied him to the Island. Coombe showed them the way, saw them off and returned to his office.

They walked in single file over the causeway. Alleyn saw them from his window, picked up his raincoat and went down the steps to meet them. They had attracted a considerable amount of attention.

'Quite a picturesque spot,' said Mr Fox. 'Popular, too, by the looks of it. What's the story, Mr Alleyn?'

'I'll tell you on the way, Br'er Fox.'

They had their suitcases with them. Alleyn gave a likely-looking boy five shillings to take them up to the hotel. Numbers of small boys had collected and were shaping up to accompany them. 'Move along,' said Mr Fox majestically. 'Shove along, now. Right away. Clear out of it.'

They backed off.

'You'm Yard men, be'ant you, mister?'said the largest of the boys.

'That's right,' Alleyn said. 'Push off or we'll be after you.'

They broke into peals of derisive but gratified laughter and scattered. One of them started a sort of chant but the others told him to shut up.

Alleyn took his own kit from Fox and suggested that they all walked round the arm of Fisherman's Bay and up by Wally's route to the enclosure. On the way he gave them a résumé of the case.

'Complicated,' Mr Fox remarked when Alleyn had finished. 'Quite a puzzle.'

'And that's throwing roses at it.'

'Which do you favour, Mr Alleyn? Mistaken identity or dead on the target?'

'I don't want to influence you – not that I flatter myself I can – at the outset. The popular theory with Coombe is the first. To support it this wretched boy says he saw Miss Pride arrive, leave and return. She herself saw *him*. Down on the road we're coming to in a minute. So did Dr Maine. Now the second figure, of course, must have been Miss Cost not Miss Pride. But between the departure of Miss Pride and the arrival of Miss Cost, Barrimore went to the gates and chucked away the notice. Who replaced it? The murderer? Presumably. And when did Wally let himself into the enclosure? If he did? It must have been before Miss Cost appeared or she would have seen him. So we've got to suppose that for some reason Wally *did* go in and *did* hide behind the boulder, after Miss Pride had left, and avoiding Barrimore who didn't see him. I don't like it. It may be remotely possible but I don't like it. And I'm certain he wouldn't replace the notice. He hasn't got the gumption. Anyway the time-table barely allows all this.'

'He'd hardly mistake the deceased for Miss Pride, silly and all as he may be, if he got anything like a fair look at her.'

'Exactly, Br'er Fox. As for the galloping Major: he swims round in an alcoholic trance. Never completely drunk. Hardly ever sober. And reputed, incredibly enough, to have had a brief fling with Miss Cost at about the same time as Wally's warts vanished. He is thought to have proved fickle and to have aroused her classic fury. She also set her bonnet, unsuccessfully, it seems, at the doctor, the Rector and the Mayor. Barrimore's got a most beautiful and alluring wife who is said to be bullied by him. She showed signs of acute distress after she heard the news. She's the original Green Lady. It's all in the notes: you can have a nice cosy read any time you fancy.'

'Thanks.'

'That's Wally's Cottage. We are about to climb Wally's Way and that is Wally's mama, another alcoholic, by the by, leering over the back fence. His father is ferryman at high-tide and general showman in between. The whole boiling of them, the Barrimores, the parson, the doctor, the Major, the Treherns, Miss Cost herself, with pretty well everybody else in the community, stood to lose by Miss Pride's operations. Apart from arousing the cornered fury of a hunted male, it's difficult to discover a motive for Miss Cost's murder. Good evening, Mrs Trehern,' Alleyn shouted and lifted his hat.

'Yoo-hoo!' Mrs Trehern wildly returned, clinging to her back fence. 'Lock 'er up. Bloody murderess.'

'Who's she mean?' asked Fox.

'Miss Pride.'

'Bless my soul! *Quelle galère!*' Fox added, cautiously.

'You must meet Miss Pride, Br'er Fox, she's a top authority on French as she should be spoke.'

'Ah!' said Fox, 'To be properly taught from the word go! That's the thing. What does she think of the gramophone method?'

'Not much.'

'That's what I was afraid of,' said Fox with a heavy sigh.

Mrs Trehern gave a screech, not unlike one of her son's and tacked into the cottage. Alleyn went over to the fence and looked into the back garden. The clothes-line had been removed.

They climbed up Wally's Way to the enclosure. One of Coombe's men was standing a little way along the hotel path.

Alleyn said to Bailey: 'The whole area was trampled over when the rain came down. From below, up to the boulder, it's thick broken bracken and you won't get results, I'm afraid. On the shelf above the pool where the deceased was crouched, leaning forward, you'll find her prints superimposed over others. Above that, behind the boulder, is the area where our man, woman or child is thought to have hidden. There's a clear indication of the place where the rock was prised up and signs that some effort was made to scrape out the footprints. All this, on top of the mess left by the crowd. And to add to your joy, Superintendent Coombe and Dr Maine were up there this morning. Their prints ought to be fairly easy to cut out. The Super was wearing his regulation issue and the doctor's are ripple-soled. Thompson, give us a complete coverage, will you? And we'll need casts, Bailey. Better take them as soon as possible.' He looked up at the sky. Heavy clouds were rolling in from the north-west and a fresh wind had sprung up. The sea was no longer calm. 'Anyone notice the forecast?'

'Yes,' said Fox. 'Gales and heavy rain before morning.'

'Damn.'

He produced Coombe's key for the wire cage which had been locked over the slot machine.

'Notice this, Br'er Fox, would you? It was installed at Miss Cost's insistence to baffle courting couples after dark, and not often used. I think it might be instructive. Only Coombe and The Boy-and-Lobster had keys. You can get out of the enclosure by the other gate, which is on a spring and is self-locking on the inside. You could go in by this turnstile and, if you used a length of string, pull the padlock, on the slack of its chain, round to the netting and lock yourself in.'

'Any reason to think it's been done?'

'Only this: there's a fragment of frayed string, caught in the groove of the wire. Get a shot of it, Thompson, will you, before we take possession.'

Thompson set up his camera. Alleyn unlocked the cage. He gave each of the others a disc and, in turn, they let themselves in. The shelf and the area above it, round the boulder, had been covered with tarpaulins. 'Laid on by Coombe's chaps,' Alleyn said. 'He's done a good job, never mind his great boots.' He stood there for a moment and watched the movement of the welling pool, the sliding lip of water, its glassy fall and perpetual disappearance. Its voices, consulting together, filled the air with their colloquy.

'Well,' Alleyn said. 'Here you are, Bailey. We'll leave you to it. I'd better have a word with the local PCs. Here are my notes, Fox. Have a look at them for what they're worth.'

Mr Fox drew out his spectacle case and seated himself in the lee of the hillside. Bailey, a man of few words, at once began work and in a minute or two, Thompson joined him. Alleyn returned to the gates and let himself out. He stood with his back to the enclosure where Miss Emily had hung her notice. He looked down Wally's Way to the spot where Wally himself had waved and shouted at her and, beyond that, to the back of the Treherns' cottage and the jetty in Fisherman's Bay. He was very still for a moment. Then he called to Fox who joined him.

'Do you see what I see?' he asked.

Fox placidly related what he saw.

'Thank you,' Alleyn said. 'Bear it in mind, Br'er Fox, when you digest those notes. I'm going along to that blasted outcrop.' He did so and was met by the constable on duty. The wind was now very strong and much colder. Clouds, inky dark and blown ragged at their edges, drove swiftly in from the sea which had turned steely and was whipped into broken corrugations. The pleasure boats, all heading inshore, danced and bucketed as they came. Portcarrow front was deserted and a procession of cars crawled up the road to the downlands. The hotel launch was discharging a load of people for whom a bus waited by the village jetty. 'There goes the Major's drink-cheque,' thought Alleyn.

' 'Evening,' he said to the constable. 'This doesn't look too promising, does it? What are we in for?'

'A dirty spell, sir, by all tokens. When she bears in sudden and hard like this from the nor'west there's only one way of it. Rain, high seas and a gale.'

'Keep the trippers off, at least. Have you had much trouble?'

'A lot of foolish inquiries, sir, and swarms of they nippers from down along.'

'Where's your mate? Round the point there?'

'Yes, sir. Nobody's come past the point, though there was plenty that tried. Sick ones and all.'

'Anyone you knew?'

'Two of the maids from The Boy-and-Lobster, sir, giggling and screeching after their silly fashion. The Major came. One of his visitors had dropped a ring, they reckoned, behind that rock, and he wanted to search for it. Us two chaps took a look but it warn't thereabouts. We kept off the ground, sir. So did he, though not best pleased to be said by us.'

'Good for you. Sergeant Bailey will deal with it in a minute and we'll get some pictures. Did Major Barrimore leave any prints, did you notice?'

'So he did, then, and us reckons they'm the dead spit-identicals for the ones that's there already.'

'You use your eyes, I see, in this division. What's your name?'

'Carey, sir.'

'I'll come along with you.'

They went to the outcrop where Carey's mate, PC Pomeroy, kept a chilly watch. Alleyn was shown the Major's footprints where he had pushed forward to the soft verge. He measured them and made a detailed comparison with those behind the outcrop.

'Good as gold,' he said. 'We'll get casts. You've done well, both of you.'

They said: 'Thank you, sir,' in unison and glanced at each other. Alleyn asked if they could raise another tarpaulin for the area and Pomeroy said he'd go down to Fisherman's Bay and borrow one.

They returned with him to the enclosure and found Fox in argument with James Trehern who was wearing an oilskin coat and looked like a lifeboat hero who had run off the rails. His face was scarlet and his manner both cringing and truculent.

'I left my launch in charge of my mate,' he was saying, 'to come up yurr and get a fair answer to a fair question which is what the hell's going on in these parts? I got my good name to stand by, mister, and my good name's being called in question. Now.'

Fox, who had his notebook in his palm said: 'We'll just get this good name and your address, if you please, and then find out what seems to be the trouble.'

'Well, Mr Trehern,' Alleyn said, 'what *is* the trouble?'

Pomeroy gave Trehern a disfavouring look and set off down the road. Trehern pulled at the peak of his cap and adopted a whining tone. 'Not to say, sir,' he said to Alleyn, 'as how I'm out to interfere with the deadly powers of the law. Us be lawful chaps in this locality and never a breath of anything to the contrary has blowed in our direction. Deny that if you've got the face to, Bill Carey!' he added turning on that officer.

'Address yourself,' Carey said stuffily, 'to them that's axing you. Shall I return to my point, sir?'

'Yes, do, thank you, Carey,' Alleyn said and received a salute followed by a smart turn. Carey tramped off along the path.

'Now,' Alleyn said to Trehern. 'Give Inspector Fox your name and address and we'll hear what you've got to say.'

He complied with an ill grace. 'I've no call to be took down in writing,' he said.

'I thought you were lodging a complaint. Didn't you, Mr Fox?'

'So I understood, sir. *Are* you?' Fox asked Trehern, and looked placidly at him over the top of his spectacles. 'We may as well know, one way or the other, while we're about it.'

'Just for the record,' Alleyn agreed.

'Not to say a complaint,' Trehern temporized. 'Don't put words into my mouth, souls. No call for that.'

'We wouldn't dream of it,' Fox rejoined. 'Take your time.'

After an uneasy silence, Trehern broke into a long, disjointed plaint. People, he said, were talking. Wally, he inferred, had been taken aside and seduced with ice-cream. Anybody would tell them that what the poor little lad said was not to be relied upon since he was as innocent as a babe unborn and was only out to please all and sundry, such being his guileless nature. They let him ramble on disconsolately until he ran out of material. Fox took notes throughout.

Alleyn said: 'Mr Trehern, we meant to call on you this evening but you've anticipated us. We want to search your house and have a warrant to do so. If it suits you we'll come down with you, now.'

Trehern ran the tip of his tongue round his mouth and looked frightened. 'What's that for?' he demanded. 'What's wrong with my property? I be'ant got nothing but what's lawful and right and free for all to see.'

'In that case you can have no objection.'

'It's a matter of principle, see?'

'Quite so.'

Trehern was staring through the wire enclosure at the Spring where Bailey and Thompson had begun to pack up their gear. 'Yurr!' he said. 'What's that! What be they chaps doing up there? Be they looking fur footprints?'

'Yes.'

'They won't find our Wal's then! They won't find his'n. Doan't 'ee tell me they will, mister. I know better.'

'He was there yesterday.'

'Not up to thicky shelf, he warn't. Not up to the top neither.'

'How do you know it matters where he may have been? Do you know how Miss Cost was killed?'

Trehern gaped at him.

'Well,' Alleyn said, 'do you feel inclined to tell us, Mr Trehern?'

He said confusedly that everyone was talking about stones being thrown.

'Ah,' Alleyn said. 'You're thinking of the night you encouraged Wally to throw stones at Miss Pride, aren't you?'

Trehern actually ducked his head as if he himself was some sort of target. 'What's the lad been telling you?' he demanded. 'He's silly. He'll say anything.'

Alleyn said: 'We'll leave it for the moment and go down to the house.'

He called through the gate for Bailey and Thompson to follow and led the way down. Trehern looked at his back and opened and shut his hands.

'Will you move along, Mr Trehern?' Fox invited him. 'After you.'

Trehern walked between them down to his cottage.

There were no visitors. The nets were half blown off the fence. The hollyhocks along the front path bent and sprang back in the wind, and the sign rattled.

Trehern stopped inside the gate. 'I want to see thick. I want to see the writing.'

Alleyn showed him the warrant. He examined it with a great show of caution and then turned to the door.

Alleyn said: 'One moment.'

'Well? What then?'

'It will save a great deal of time and trouble if you will let us see the thing we're most interested in. Where have you put the clothes-line?'

'I don't have to do nothing,' he said, showing the whites of his eyes. 'You can't force me.'

'Certainly not. It's your choice.' He looked at Fox. 'Will you take the outhouses? We can go round this way.'

He led the way round to the backyard.

Fox said pleasantly: 'This'll be the shed where you keep all your gear, won't it? I'll just take a look round, if you please.'

It was crammed with a litter of old nets, broken oars, sacking, boxes, tools and a stack of empty gin bottles. Alleyn glanced in and then left it to Fox. There was a hen coop at the far end of the yard with a rubbish heap nearby that looked as if it had been recently disturbed.

'Give me that fork, would you, Fox?' he said and walked down the path with it. Trehern started to follow him and then stood motionless. The first of the rain drove hard on their backs.

The clothes-line had been neatly coiled and buried under the rubbish. Alleyn uncovered it in a matter of seconds.

'Shall we get under shelter?' he said and walked back past Trehern to the shed. He wondered, for a moment, if Trehern would strike out at him but he fumbled with his oilskin coat and stayed where he was.

'All right, Fox,' Alleyn said. 'First time lucky. Here we are.'

He gave Fox the coil and took from his pocket the piece of trip-wire from Coombe's office. They held the ends together. 'That's it,' said Fox.

Alleyn looked at Trehern. 'Will you come here for a moment?' he asked.

He thought Trehern was going to refuse. He stood there with his head lowered and gave no sign. Then he came slowly forward, lashed now, by the rain; a black shining figure.

'I am not going to arrest you at this juncture,' Alleyn said, 'but I think it right to warn you that you are in a serious position. It is quite certain that the wire which, two days ago, was stretched across the way up to the shelf above the Spring, has been cut from this line. Photography and accurate measurements of the strands will prove it. Is there anything you want to say?'

Trehern's jaw worked convulsively as if he were chewing gum. He made a hoarse indeterminate sound in his throat: like a nervous dog, Alleyn thought. At last he said: 'Who-sumdever done them tricks was having no more than a bit of fun. Boy-fashion. No harm in it.'

'You think not?'

'If it was my Wal, I'll have the hide off of him.'

'I shouldn't go in for any more violence if I were you, Mr Trehern. And Wally didn't rig the trip-wire. It was done by a man who knows how to use his hands and it was done with a length of your clothes-line which you've tried to conceal. Will you make a statement about that? You are not compelled to do so. You must use your own judgment.'

'A statement! And be took down in writing? Not such a damned fool. Lookie-yurr! What's these silly larks to do with Elspeth Cost? It's her that's laying cold, be'ant it? Not t'other old besom.'

'Of course,' Alleyn said, swallowing the epithet. After all, he'd thrown one or two himself, at Miss Emily. 'So you don't think,' he said, 'that Miss Cost was mistaken for Miss Pride?'

'I do not, mister. Contrariwise. I reckon one female done it on t'other.'

'What were *you* doing at half past seven this morning?'

'Asleep in my bed.'

'When did you wake?'

'How do I know when I woke? Hold on, though.'

'Yes?'

'Yes, b'God!' Trehern said slowly. 'Give a chap time to think, will you? I disremembered but it's come back, like. I heered the lad, bang-ing and hooting about the place. Woke me up, did young Wal, and I hollered out to him to shut his noise. He takes them fits of screeching. Por lil' chap.' Trehern added with a belated show of parental concern. 'Gawd knows why, but he does. I look at the clock and it's five past eight. I rouse up my old woman which is a masterpiece of a job she being a mortal heavy slumberer, and tell 'er to wet a pot of tea. Nothing come of it. She sunk back in her beastly oblivyan. So I uprose myself and put the kettle on and took a look at the weather which were mucky.'

'Was Wally still in the house?'

'So 'e were, then, singing to hisself after his simple fashion and setting in a corner.'

'Did you see anybody about when you looked out of doors?'

Trehern peered sidelong at him. He waited for a moment and then said: 'I seed the doctor, in 'is launch. Putting out across the gap to go home, he was, having seen Bessy Trethaway, over the way, yurr, come to light with another in this sinful vale of tears.'

'Is your clock right?'

'Good as gold,' he said quickly. 'Can't go wrong.'

'Can I see it?'

He looked as if he might refuse but in the end, lurched into the house, followed by Fox, and returned with a battered alarm clock. Alleyn checked it by his watch.

'Six minutes slow,' he said.

Trehern burst out angrily: 'I don't have no call for clocks! I'm a seafaring chap and read the time of day off of the face of nature. Sky and tides is good enough for me and my mates in the bay'll bear me out. Six minutes fast or six minutes slow by thicky clock's no matter to me. I looked outer my winder and it wur dead water and dead water come when I said it come and if that there por female was sent to make the best of 'erself before 'er Maker when I looked outer my winder she died at dead water and that's an end of it.'

'Trehern,' Alleyn said, 'what are you going to make of this? Mrs Trethaway's baby was born at seven-thirty and Dr Maine left in his launch about ten minutes later. You're a full half hour out in your times.'

There was a long silence.

'Well?' Alleyn said. 'Any comment?'

He broke into a stream of oaths and disjointed expostulations. Did they call him a liar? Nobody called Jim Trehern a liar and got away with it. If they weren't going to believe him why did they ask? There was talk against him in the bay. Jealousy seemed to be implied. His anger modulated through resentfulness and fear into his familiar occupational whine. Finally he said that a man could make mistakes, couldn't he? When Alleyn asked if he meant that he'd mistaken the time, Trehern said he didn't want his words taken out of his mouth and used against him. He could scarcely have made a more dubious showing. He was joined briefly by his spouse who emerged from the interior, stood blinking in the back doorway, and was peremptorily ordered back by her husband. Inside the cottage, actors could be heard, galloping about on horses and shouting 'C'm' on. Let's go,' to each other. Wally, Alleyn supposed, was enjoying television.

Trehern suddenly bawled out: 'You boy! Wal! Come yurr! Come out of it when you're bid!'

Wally shambled into the back porch, saw Alleyn and smiled widely.

'Come on!' his father said and took him by the arm. Wally began to whimper.

'Now then. Tell truth and shame the devil. You been chucking rocks?'

'No. No, I be'ant.'

'No, and better not. Speak up and tell these yurr gents. Swear if you hope you won't get half-skinned for a liar as you never chucked no rocks at nobody.'

'I never chucked no rocks only stones,' Wally said, trembling. 'Like you said to.'

'That'll do!' his father said ferociously. 'Get in.' Wally bolted.

Alleyn said: 'You'd better watch your step with that boy. Do you thrash him?'

'Never raise a hand to him, mister. Just a manner of speaking. He don't understand nothing different. Never had no mother-love, poor kid: I have to pour out sufficient for both and a heavy job it is.'

'You may find yourself describing it to the welfare officer, one of these days.'

'Them bastards!'

'Now, look here, Trehern, you heard what the boy said. "No rocks only stones, like you said to." Hadn't you better make the best of that statement and admit he threw stones at Miss Pride and you knew it. Think it out.'

Trehern made a half-turn, knocked his boot against an old tin and kicked it savagely to the far end of the yard. This, apparently, made up his mind for him.

'If I say he done it in one of his foolish turns meaning no harm and acting the goat – all right – I don't deny it and I don't axcuse it. But I do deny and will, and you won't shift me an inch, he never heaved no rock at Elspeth Cost. I'll take my Bible oath on it and may I be struck dead if I lie.'

'How can you be so sure? Miss Pride saw the boy in the lane at about twenty to eight. So did Dr Maine. You weren't there. Or were you?'

'I was not. *By God I was not*, and I'll lay anyone cold that says different. And how can I be so sure?' He advanced upon Alleyn and thrust his face towards him. His unshaven jowls glittered with rain-drops. 'I'll tell you flat how I can be so sure. That boy never told a lie in his life, mister. He'm too simple. Ax anybody. Ax his teacher. Ax parson. Ax his mates. He'm a truth-speaking lad, por little sod, and for better or worse, the truth's all you'll ever get out of our Wal.'

Alleyn heard Jenny Williams's voice: 'He's an extraordinarily truthful little boy. He never tells lies – never.' He looked at Trehern and said: 'All right. We'll let it go at that, for the moment. Good evening to you.'

As they walked round the side of the house Trehern shouted after them: 'What about the female of the speeches? Pride? Pride has to take a fall, don't she?'

There was a wild scream of laughter from Mrs Trehern and a door banged.

'That will do to go on with,' Alleyn said to Fox, and aped Wally's serial: 'C'm' on. Let's go.'

CHAPTER 8

The Shop

They found Bailey and Thompson outside, locked in their mackintoshes with an air of customary usage and with their gear stowed inside waterproof covers. Rain cascaded from their hat brims.

'We'll go back to the pub,' Alleyn said. 'In a minute.'

The Trethaways' cottage was across the lane from the Treherns'. Alleyn knocked at the back door and was invited in by the proud father: an enormous grinning fellow. The latest addition was screaming very lustily in the bedroom. Her father apologized for this drawback to conversation.

' 'Er be a lil' maid, 'er be,' he said, 'and letting fly with 'er vocal powers according.'

They stood by the kitchen window which looked up the lane towards the Spring. Seeing this, Alleyn asked him if he'd happened to notice Wally in the lane at about the time the baby was born or soon after and was given the reasonable answer that Mr Trethaway's attention was on other matters. The baby had indeed been born at seven-thirty and Dr Maine had in fact left very soon afterwards.

Alleyn congratulated Trethaway, shook his hand, rejoined his colleagues and told them what he'd gleaned.

'So why does Trehern say he saw the doctor leave at about five past eight?' Fox asked. 'There's usually only one reason for that sort of lie, isn't there? Trying to rig the time, so that you look as if you couldn't have been on the spot. That's the normal caper.'

'So it is then,' Alleyn agreed with a reasonable imitation of the local voice. 'But there are loose ends here. Or are there?'

'Well yes,' Fox said. 'In a way.'

'Bailey: what did you get? Any fisherman's boots superimposed on the general mess? Or boy's boots? I couldn't find any.'

'Nothing like that, Mr Alleyn. But as you said yourself, this flat slice of stone's been used to cut out recent prints. We've picked up enough to settle that point,' Bailey said grudgingly, 'not much else. The only nice jobs are the ones left after this morning's rain by a set of regulation tens and another of brogues or gentleman's country shoes, size nine-and-a-half ripple soles and in good repair.'

'I know. The Super and the doctor.'

'That's right, sir, from what you've mentioned.'

'What about the stuff near the outcrop and behind it?'

'What you thought, Mr Alleyn. They match. Hand-sewn, officer's type. Ten-and-a-half but custom-made. Worn but well-kept.'

'In a sense you might be describing the owner. Did you tell Carey he could go off duty?'

'Yes, sir. There seemed no call for him to stay. We've got all the casts and photographs we want. I used salt in the plaster, seeing how the weather was shaping. It was OK. Nice results.'

'Good. It's getting rougher. Look at that sea.'

In the channel between Island and village, the tide now rolled and broke in a confusion of foam and jetting spray. Out at sea there were white horses everywhere. The horizon was dark and broken. The causeway was lashed by breakers that struck, rose, fell across it and withdrew, leaving it momentarily exposed and blackly glinting in what remained of the daylight. The hotel launch bucketed and rolled at the jetty. A man in oilskins was mounting extra fenders. Above the general roar of sea and rain, the thud of the launch's starboard side against the legs of the jetty could be clearly heard.

Light shone dimly behind the windows of Miss Cost's Giffte Shoppe.

'PC Pender's locked up in there with Miss Cissy Pollock on the switchboard,' Alleyn muttered. 'I'll just have a word with him.' He tapped on the door. After a moment, it was opened a crack and Mr Pender said: 'Be'ant no manner of use pestering – ' and then saw Alleyn. 'Beg pardon, sir, I'm sure,' he said. 'Thought you was one of they damned kids come back.' He flung open the door. Alleyn called to Fox and the others and they went in.

The shop smelt fustily of cardboard, wool and gum. In the postal section, Miss Cissy Pollock bulged at a switchboard: all eyes and teeth when she saw the visitors.

Pender said that a call had come through for Alleyn from Dunlowman. 'Sir James Curtis, it were, sir,' he said with reverence. Curtis was the Home Office pathologist. 'Wishful to speak with you. I intercepted the call, sir, and informed the station and The Boy-and-Lobster.'

'Where was he?'

'Dunlowman mortuary, sir, along with the body and the doctor. I've got the number.'

'Aw, dear!' Miss Pollock exclaimed. 'Be'ant it shocking though!' She had removed her headphones.

Alleyn asked if she could put him through. She engaged to do so and directed him to an instrument in a cubbyhole.

The mortuary attendant answered and said Sir James was just leaving but he'd try to catch him. He could be heard pounding off down a concrete passage. In a minute or two the great man spoke.

'Hullo, Rory, where the devil have you been? I've done this job for you. Want the report?'

'Please.'

It was straightforward enough. Death by drowning following insensibility caused by a blow on the head. The piece of rock was undoubtedly the instrument. Contents of stomach, Sir James briskly continued, showed that she'd had a cup of tea and a biscuit about an hour and three-quarters before she died. On Dr Maine's evidence he would agree that she had probably been dead about an hour when Alleyn found her. Sir James had another case more or less on the way back to London and would like to get off before he himself was drowned. Would Alleyn let him know about the inquest? Dr Maine would tell him anything else he wanted to hear and was now on his way back to Portcarrow. 'I'm told you're on an island,' said Sir James, merrily. 'You'll be likely to stay there if the weather report's to be trusted. What book will you choose if you can only have one?'

'*The Gentle Art of Making Enemies,*' said Alleyn and hung up.

He told Pender that he and Fox would return after dinner and asked him what he himself would do for a meal. Pender said that there was a cut loaf and some butter and ham in Miss Cost's refrigerator and would it be going too far if he and Cissy made sandwiches? There was also some cheese and pickle. They could, he said, be replaced.

'You can't beat a cheese and pickle sandwich,' Fox observed, 'if the cheese is tasty.'

Alleyn said that under the circumstances he felt Pender might proceed on the lines indicated and left him looking relieved.

They climbed the hotel steps, staggering against the gale, and entered The Boy-and-Lobster. It was now five minutes to eight.

Alleyn asked the reception clerk if he could find rooms for his three colleagues and learnt that the guests had dwindled to thirty. All incoming trains and buses had been met at Dunlowman and intending visitors told about the situation. Accommodation had been organized with various establishments over a distance of fifteen miles and, in view of the weather forecast and the closure of the Spring, most of the travellers had elected, as the clerk put it, to stay away. 'We can be cut off,' he said, 'if it's really bad. It doesn't often happen but if this goes on, it might.' The guests in residence had all come by car and were now at dinner.

Alleyn left the others to collect their suitcases and arranged to meet them in the dining-room. He went to his own room, effected a quick change and called on Miss Emily who was four doors away.

She was finishing her dinner. She sat bolt upright, peeling grapes. A flask of red wine was before her and a book was at her elbow with a knife laid across to keep it open. She was perfectly composed.

'I've only looked in for a moment,' he said. 'We're running late. How are you, Miss Emily? Bored to sobs, I'm afraid.'

'Good evening, Roderique. No, I am not unduly bored, though I have missed taking my walk.'

'It's no weather for walking, I assure you. How are they treating you?'

'This morning the chambermaid's manner was equivocal and at luncheon I found the waiter impertinent. Tonight, however, there is a marked change. It appears that I am, or was, suspected of murder,' said Miss Emily.

'What makes you think so?'

'Before taking my siesta I ventured out on the balcony. There was a group of children on the steps leading to the hotel. When they saw me they began to chant. I will not trouble you with the words. The intention was inescapable.'

'Little animals.'

'Oh, perfectly. It was of no moment.'

There was a tap on the door and a waiter came in.

'Thank you,' said Miss Emily. 'You may clear.'

Alleyn watched the man for a moment and then said:

'I'd like a word with you, if you please.'

'With me, sir?'

'Yes. I am a Superintendent of Scotland Yard, in charge of investigations into the death of Miss Elspeth Cost. I think perhaps the staff of the hotel should be informed that this lady is associated with me in the case and may be regarded as an expert. Do you understand?'

'Yes, sir. Certainly, sir. I'm sure I hope madam has no complaints, sir.'

'I hope so, too. She hasn't made any but I shall do so if any more idiotic nonsense is circulated. You may say so to anybody that is interested.'

'Thank you, sir,' said the waiter and withdrew.

'*Chose remarquable!*' said Miss Emily. 'So now, it appears I am a detectrice.'

'It'll be all over the hotel in five minutes and Portcarrow will have it by morning. About your transport to Dunlowman – '

'Do not trouble yourself. The young man – Patrick – has offered to drive us,' Miss Emily said with an air of amusement.

'I see. It may be pretty rough going across to the village, if this weather persists.'

'No matter.'

'Before I go, would you mind very much if we went over one incident: the few minutes, round about twenty to eight, when you hung your notice by the Spring?'

'Certainly,' Miss Emily said. She repeated her story. She had seen Wally down on the road. He had whooped, chanted, waved his arms and afterwards disappeared. She had seen nobody else and had returned to the hotel with her umbrella between herself and the prospect.

'Yes,' he said. 'I know. I just wanted to hear it again. Thank you, Miss Emily. You don't ask me how the case progresses, I notice.'

'You would tell me, no doubt, if you wished to do so.'

'Well,' he said. 'I always think it's unlucky to talk at this stage: but it does progress.'

'Good. Go and have your dinner. If you are not too fatigued I should be glad if you would call upon me later in the evening.'

'When do you retire?'

'Not early. I find I am restless,' said Miss Emily.

They fell silent. The wind made a sudden onslaught on her windows. 'Perhaps it is the storm,' she said.

'I'll see if there's a light under your door. *Au revoir*, then, Miss Emily.'

'*Au revoir*, my dear Roderique. Enjoy, if that is not too extravagant a word, your dinner. The dressed crab is not bad. *The filet mignon*, on the other hand, is contemptible.'

She waved her hand and he left her.

Fox, Bailey and Thompson were already in the dining-room. Alleyn had been given a table to himself. As there was not room at theirs, he took it, but joined them for a minute or two before he did so.

Everyone else had gone except Jenny and Patrick who sat at the family table, nursing balloon glasses. They had an air of subdued celebration and as often as they looked at each other, broke into smiles. When Jenny saw Alleyn, she waggled her fingers at him.

Alleyn said: 'Afraid it's a case of pressing on, chaps. We'll meet in the hall, afterwards, and go down to the shop. Have you ordered drinks?'

'Not so far, Mr Alleyn.'

'Well, have them with me. What shall it be? Waiter!'

They settled for beer. Alleyn went to his own table and was fawned upon by Miss Emily's waiter. Jenny and Patrick passed by and Jenny paused to say: 'We're going to try and whip up a bit of *joie de vivre* in the lounge, like they do in ships. Patrick's thought up a guessing game. Come and help.'

'I'd love to,' Alleyn said, 'but I'm on a guessing game of my own, bad luck to it.' He looked at Patrick. 'I hear you've offered to do the driving tomorrow. Very civil of you. Miss Emily's looking forward to it.'

'It's going to be a rough crossing if this keeps up.'

'I know.'

'Will she mind?'

'Not she. At the age of sixty, she was a queen-pin in the *Resistance* and hasn't noticed the passage of time. Get her to tell you how she dressed up a couple of kiwis as nuns.'

'Honestly!' Jenny exclaimed.

'It's quite a story.'

The waiter came up to say that Dr Maine had arrived and was asking for him.

'Right,' Alleyn said. 'I'll come.'

'In the writing-room, sir.'

It was a small deserted place off the entrance hall. Dr Maine had removed his mackintosh and hung it over the back of a chair. He was shaking the rain off his hat when Alleyn came in. 'What a night!' he said. 'I thought I wouldn't make it.'

'How did you cross?'

'In my launch. Damned if I know how she'll take it going back. The causeway's impossible. Sir James thought you'd like to see me and I had to come over, anyway, to a patient.'

Alleyn said: 'I'm glad to see you. Not so much about the PM! Curtis made that clear enough. I wanted to check up one or two points. Have a drink, won't you?'

'I certainly will. Thank you.'

Alleyn found a bell-push. 'I hope you won't mind if I don't join you,' he said. 'I've had my allowance and I've got a night's work ahead of me.'

'I suppose you get used to it – like a GP.'

'Very much so, I imagine. What'll you have?'

Dr Maine had a whisky and soda. 'I thought I'd take a look at Miss Pride while I'm here,' he said. 'She's recovered, of course, but she had quite a nasty cut in her neck. I suppose I mustn't ask about the police view of that episode. Or doesn't it arise?'

'I don't see why you shouldn't. It arises in a sort of secondary way, if only to be dismissed. What do you think?'

'On the face of it, Wally Trehern. Inspired by his father, I daresay. It's Miss Pride's contention and I think she may well be right.'

'I think so, too. Does it tie up with the general pattern of behaviour – from your point of view?'

'Oh yes. Very characteristic. He gets over-excited and wildish. Sometimes this sort of behaviour is followed up by an attack of *petit mal*. Not always, but it's quite often the pattern.'

'Can't anything be done for the boy?'

'Not much, I'm afraid. When they start these attacks in early childhood. it's a poorish prospect. He should lead a quiet, regular life.

It may well be that his home background and all the nonsense of producing him as a showpiece, is bad for him. I'm not at all sure,' Dr Maine said, 'that I shouldn't have taken his case up with the child-welfare people but there's been no marked deterioration and I've hesitated. Now, well – now, one wonders.'

'One wonders – *what* exactly?'

'A, if he shouldn't, in any case, be removed to a suitable institution and B, whether he's responsible for heaving that rock at Miss Cost.'

'If he did heave it, it must have been about half an hour after you saw him doing his stuff on Wally's Way.'

'I know. Sir James puts the death at about eight o'clock, give and take twenty minutes. I wish I'd watched the boy more closely but of course there was no reason to do so. I was swinging the launch round.'

'And it *was* about seven-forty, wasn't it?'

'About that, yes. Within a couple of minutes, I should say.'

'You didn't happen to notice Miss Pride? She was in the offing too, and saw Wally.'

'*Was* she, by George! No, I didn't see her. The top of the wheel-house would cut off my view, I fancy.'

'What *exactly* was Wally doing? Sorry to nag on about it, but Miss Pride may have missed some little pointer. We need one badly enough, Lord knows.'

'He was jumping about with his back towards me. He waved his arms and did a sort of throwing gesture. Now that you tell me Miss Pride *was* up by the gates, I should think his antics were directed at her. I seem to remember that the last thing I saw him do was to take a run uphill. But it was all quite momentary, you know.'

'His father says Wally was in the house at five past eight.'

Dr Maine considered this. 'It would still be possible,' he said. 'There's time, isn't there?'

'On the face of it – yes. Trehern also says that at five past eight or soon afterwards, he saw you leave in your launch.'

'Does he, indeed! He lies like a flat-fish,' said Dr Maine. He looked thoughtfully at Alleyn. 'Now, I wonder just why,' he said thoughtfully. 'I wonder.'

'So do I, I assure you.' They stared meditatively at each other. Alleyn said: 'Who do you think was the original Green Lady?'

Dr Maine was normally of a sallow complexion but now a painful red blotted his lean face and transfigured it. 'I have never considered the matter,' he said. 'I have no idea. It's always been supposed that he imagined the whole thing.'

'It was Mrs Barrimore.'

'You can have no imaginable reason for thinking so,' he said angrily.

'I've the best possible reason,' said Alleyn. 'Believe me. Every possible reason.'

'Do you mean that Mrs Barrimore herself told you this?'

'Virtually, yes. I am not,' Alleyn said, 'trying to equivocate. I asked her and she said she supposed she must congratulate me.'

Dr Maine put his glass down and walked about the room with his hands in his pockets. Alleyn thought he was giving himself time. Presently he said: 'I can't for the life of me, make out why you concern yourself with this. Surely it's quite beside the point.'

'I do so because I don't understand it. Or am not sure that I understand it. If it turns out to be irrelevant I shall make no more of it. What I don't understand, to be precise, is why Mrs Barrimore should be so distressed at the discovery.'

'But, good God, man, of course she's distressed! Look here. Suppose – I admit nothing – but suppose she came across that wretched kid, blubbing his eyes out because he'd been baited about his warts. Suppose she saw him trying to wash them off and on the spur of the moment, remembering the history of wart-cures, she made him believe they would clear up if he thought they would. Very well. The boy goes home and they do. Before we know – she knows – where she is, the whole thing blows up into a highly publicized nine-days-wonder. She can't make up her mind to disabuse the boy or disillusion the people that follow him. It gets out of hand. The longer she hesitates, the harder it gets.'

'Yes,' Alleyn said. 'I know. That all makes sense and is perfectly understandable.'

'Very well, then!' he said impatiently.

'She was overwhelmingly anxious that I shouldn't tell her husband.'

'I daresay,' Dr Maine said shortly. 'He's not a suitable subject for confidences.'

'Did she tell you? All right,' Alleyn said answering the extremely dark look Dr Maine gave him. 'I know I'm being impertinent. I've got to be.'

'I am her doctor. She consulted me about it. I advised her to say nothing.'

'Yes?'

'The thing was working. Off and on, as always happens in these emotional – these faith-cures, if you like – there are authentic cases. With people whose troubles had a nervous connotation, the publicizing of this perfectly innocent deception would have been harmful.'

'Asthma, for one?'

'Possibly.'

'Miss Cost, for instance?'

'If you like.'

'Was Miss Cost a patient of yours?'

'She was. She had moles that needed attention; she came into my nursing home and I removed them. About a year ago, it would be.'

'I wish you'd tell me what she was like.'

'Look here, Alleyn, I really do not see that the accident of my being called out to examine the body requires me to disregard my professional obligations. I do *not* discuss my patients alive or dead, with any layman.'

Alleyn said mildly: 'His Worship the Mayor seems to think she was a near-nymphomaniac.'

Dr Maine snorted.

'Well, was she?'

'All right. All right. She was a bloody nuisance, like many another frustrated spinster. Will that do?'

'Nicely, thank you. Do you imagine she ever suspected the truth about the Green Lady?'

'I have not the remotest idea but I should think it most unlikely. She, of all people! Look at that damn' farce of a show yesterday. Look at her shop! Green Ladies by the gross. If you want my opinion on the case which I don't suppose you do – '

'On the contrary I was going to ask for it.'

'Then, I think the boy did it, and I hope that, for his sake, it will go no further than finding that he's irresponsible and chucked the rock aimlessly or at least with no idea of the actual damage it would do. He can then be removed from his parents, who are no good to him anyway, and given proper care and attention. If I'm asked for an opinion at the inquest that will be it.'

'Tidy. Straightforward. Obvious.'

'And you don't believe it?'

'I would like to believe it,' said Alleyn.

'I need hardly say I'd be interested to know your objections.'

'You may say they're more or less mechanical. No,' Alleyn said correcting himself. 'That's not quite it, either. We'll just have to press on and see how we go. And press on I must, by the same token. My chaps'll be waiting for me.'

'You're going out?'

'Yes. Routine, you know. Routine.'

'You'll be half-drowned.'

'It's not far. Only to the shop. By the way, did you know we're moving Miss Pride in the morning? She's going to the Manor Park Hotel outside Dunlowman.'

'But why? Isn't she comfortable here?'

'It's not particularly comfortable to be suspected of homicide.'

'But – oh, good *lord!*' he exclaimed disgustedly.

'The village louts shout doggerel at her and the servants have been unpleasant. I don't want her to be subjected to any more Portcarrow humour in the form of practical jokes.'

'There's no chance of that, surely. Or don't you think Miss Cost inspired that lot?'

'I think she inspired them, all right, but they might be continued in her permanent absence; the habit having been formed and Miss Pride's unpopularity having increased.'

'Absolute idiocy!' he said angrily.

'I think, as a matter of fact, I've probably stopped the rot but it's better for her to get away from the place.'

'You know, I very much doubt if the channel will be negotiable in the morning. This looks like being the worst storm we've had for years. In any case it'll be devilishly awkward getting her aboard the launch. We don't want a broken leg.'

'Of course not. We'll simply have to wait and see what the day brings forth. If you're going to visit her, you might warn her about the possibility, will you?'

'Yes, certainly.'

They were silent for a moment. A sudden onslaught of the gale
beat against The Boy-and-Lobster and screamed in the chimney.
'Well, good night,' Alleyn said.

He had got as far as the door when Dr Maine said: 'There *is* one
thing you perhaps ought to know about Elspeth Cost.'

'Yes?'

'She lived in a world of fantasy. Again, with women of her temperament, condition and age, it's a not unusual state of affairs, but
with her its manifestations were extreme.'

'Was she in consequence a liar?'

'Oh yes,' he said. 'It follows on the condition. You may say she
couldn't help it.'

'Thank you for telling me,' Alleyn said.

'It may not arise.'

'You never know. Good night, then, Maine.'

II

When they were outside and the hotel doors had shut behind them,
they were engulfed in a world of turbulence: a complex uproar into
which they moved, leaning forward, with their heads down. They
slipped on concrete steps, bumped into each other and then hung on
by an iron rail and moved down crabwise towards the sea. Below
them, riding-lights on the hotel launch tipped, rose, sank and shuddered. A single street lamp near the jetty was struck across by continuous diagonals of rain. On the far side, black masses heaved and broke
against the front, obscured and revealed dimly-lit windows and flung
their crests high above the glittering terrace. As the three men came to
the foot of the steps they were stung and lashed by driven spume.

Miss Cost's shop window glowed faintly beyond the rain. When
they reached it they had to bang on the door and yell at Pender
before he heard them above the general clamour. It opened a crack.
'Easy on, souls,' Pender shouted, 'or she'll blow in.' He admitted
them, one by one, with his shoulder to the door.

The interior fug had become enriched by a paraffin heater that
reeked in Miss Cissy Pollock's corner and by Pender who breathed

out pickled onions. Miss Pollock, herself a little bleary-eyed now, but ever-smiling, still presided at the switchboard.

'Wicked night,' Pender observed bolting the door.

'You must be pretty well fed up, both of you,' Alleyn said.

'No, sir, no. We be tolerably clever, thank you. Cissy showed me how her switchboard works. A simple enough matter to the male intelligence, it turned out to be, and I took a turn at it while she had a nap. She come back like a lion refreshed and I followed her example. Matter of fact, sir, I was still dozing when you hammered at the door, wasn't I, Ciss? She can't hear with they contraptions on her head. A simple pattern of a female, she is, sir, as you'll find out for yourself, if you see fit to interrogate her, but rather pleased than otherwise to remain.' He beamed upon Miss Pollock who giggled.

Fox gravely contemplated Sergeant Pender. He was a stickler for procedure.

Alleyn introduced Pender to his colleagues. They took off their coats and hats and he laid down a plan of action. They were to make a systematic examination of the premises.

'We're not looking for anything specific,' he said. 'I'd like to find out how she stood, financially. Correspondence, if any. It would be lovely if she kept a diary and if there's a dump of old newspapers, they'll have to be gone over carefully. Look for any cuts. Bailey, you'd better pick up a decent set of prints if you can find them. Cashbox – tooth-glass – she had false teeth – take your pick. Thompson, will you handle the shelves in here? You might work the back premises and the bedroom, Fox. I'll start on the parlour.'

He approached Cissy Pollock who removed her headphones and simpered.

'You must have known Miss Cost very well,' he began. 'How long have you been here with her, Miss Pollock?'

A matter of a year and up, it appeared. Ever since the shop was made a post office. Miss Cost had sold her former establishment at Dunlowman and had converted a cottage into the premises as they now stood. She had arranged for a wholesale firm to provide the Green Ladies, which she herself painted, and for a regional printer to reproduce the rhyme-sheets. Cissy talked quite readily of these activities and Miss Cost emerged from her narrative as an experienced businesswoman. 'She were proper sharp,' Cissy said appreciatively.

When Alleyn spoke of yesterday's Festival she relapsed briefly into giggles but this seemed to be a token manifestation, obligatory upon the star-performer. Miss Cost had inaugurated a Drama Circle of which the Festival had been the first-fruit and Cissy herself, the leading light. He edged cautiously towards the less public aspects of Miss Cost's life and character. Had she many close friends? None that Cissy knew of though she did send Christmas cards. She hardly got any herself, outside local ones.

'So you were her best friend, then?'

'Aw well,' said Cissy and shuffled her feet.

'What about gentlemen friends?'

This produced a renewed attack of giggles. After a great deal of trouble he elicited the now familiar story of advance and frustration. Miss Cost had warned Cissy repeatedly of the gentlemen and had evidently dropped a good many dark hints about improper overtures made to herself. Cissy was not pretty and was no longer very young. He thought that, between them, they had probably indulged in continuous fantasy and the idea rather appalled him. On Major Barrimore's name being introduced in a roundabout fashion, she became uncomfortable and said, under pressure, that Miss Cost was proper set against him, and that he'd treated her bad. She would say nothing more under this heading. She remembered Miss Cost's visit to the hospital. It appeared that she had tried the Spring for her moles but without success. Alleyn ventured to ask if Miss Cost liked Dr Maine. Cissy, with a sudden burst of candour, said she fair worshipped him.

'Ah!' said Sergeant Pender who had listened to all this with the liveliest attention. 'So, she did then, and hunted the poor chap merciless, didn't she, Ciss?'

'Aw, you do be awful, George Pender,' said Cissy, with spirit.

'Couldn't help herself, no doubt, and not to be blamed for it,' he conceded.

Alleyn again asked Cissy if Miss Cost had any close women friends. Mrs Carstairs? Or Mrs Barrimore, for instance?

Cissy made a prim face that was also, in some indefinable way, furtive. 'She weren't terrible struck on Mrs Barrimore,' she said. 'She didn't hold with her.'

'Oh? Why was that, do you suppose?'

'She reckoned she were sly,' said Cissy and was not to be drawn any further.

'Did Miss Cost keep a diary, do you know?' Alleyn asked, and as Cissy looked blank, he added: 'A book. A record of day-to-day happenings?'

Cissy said Miss Cost was always writing in a book of an evening but kept it away careful-like, she didn't know where. Asked if she had noticed any change in Miss Cost's behaviour over the last three weeks, Cissy gaped at Alleyn for a second or two and then said Miss Cost had been kind of funny.

'In what way, funny?'

'Laughing,' said Cissy. 'She took fits to laugh, suddenlike. I never see nothing to make her.'

'As if she was – what? Amused? Excited?'

'Axcited. Powerful pleased too. Sly-like.'

'Did you happen to notice if she sent any letters to London?'

Miss Cost had on several occasions put her own letters in the mailbag but Cissy hadn't got a look at them. Evidently, Alleyn decided, Miss Cost's manner had intrigued her assistant. It was on these occasions that Miss Cost laughed.

At this juncture, Cissy was required at the switchboard. Alleyn asked Pender to follow him into the back room. He shut the door and said he thought the time had come for Miss Pollock to return to her home. She lived on the Island, it appeared, in one of the Fisherman's Bay cottages. Alleyn suggested that Pender had better see her to her door as the storm was so bad. They could be shown how to work the switchboard during his absence.

When they had gone, Alleyn retired to the parlour and began operations upon Miss Cost's desk which, on first inspection, appeared to be a monument to the dimmest kind of disorder. Bills, dockets, trade-leaflets and business communications were jumbled together in ill-running drawers and overcrowded pigeon-holes. He sorted them into heaps and secured them with rubber bands.

He called out to Fox, who was in the kitchen: 'As far as I can make out she was doing very nicely indeed, thank you. There's a crack-pot sort of day-book. No outstanding debts and an extremely healthy bank statement. We'll get at her financial position through the income-tax people, of course. What've you got?'

'Nothing to rave about,' Fox said.

'Newspapers?'

'Not yet. It's a coal range, though.'

'Damn.'

They worked on in silence. Bailey reported a good set of impressions from a tumbler by the bed and Thompson, relieved of the switchboard, photographed them. Fox put on his mackintosh and retired with a torch to an outhouse, admitting, briefly, the cold and uproar of the storm. After an interval he returned, bland with success, and bearing a coal-grimed, wet, crumpled and scorched fragment of newsprint.

'This might be something,' he said and laid it out for Alleyn's inspection.

It was part of a sheet from the local paper from which a narrow strip had been cleanly excised. The remainder of a headline read: ' – to Well-known Beauty Spot' and underneath: 'The Natural Amenities Association. At a meeting held at Dunlowman on Wednesday it was resolved to lodge a protest at the threat to Hatcherds Common where it is proposed to build – '

'That's it, I'm sure,' Alleyn said. 'Same type. The original messages are in my desk, blast it, but one of them reads "Threat" (in these capitals) "to close You are warned": a good enough indication that she was responsible. Any more?'

'No. This was in the ash-bin. Fallen into the grate, most likely, when she burnt the lot. I don't think there's anything else but I'll take another look by daylight. She's got a bit of a darkroom rigged up out there. Quite well-equipped, too, by the look of it.'

'Has she now? Like to take a slant at it, Thompson?'

Thompson went out and presently returned to say it was indeed a handy little job of a place and he wouldn't mind using it. 'I've got that stuff we shot up at the Spring,' he said. 'How about it, sir?'

'I don't see why not. Away you go. Good. Fox, you might penetrate to the bedchamber. I can't find her blasted diary anywhere.'

Fox retired to the bedroom. Pender came back and said it was rougher than ever out of doors and he didn't see himself getting back to the village. Would it be all right if he spent the rest of the night on Miss Cost's bed? 'When vacant, in a manner of speaking,' he added, being aware of Fox's activities. He emerged from a pitchpine wardrobe, obviously scandalized by Sergeant Pender's unconventional approach, but Alleyn said he saw nothing against the suggestion and set Pender to tend the switchboard and help Thompson.

He returned to his own job. The parlour was a sort of unfinished echo of the front shop. Rows of plastic ladies, awaiting coats of green, yellow and pink paint, smirked blankly from the shelves. There were stacks of rhyme-sheets and stationery and piles of jerkins, still to be sewn up the sides. Through the open door he could see the kitchen table with a jug and sugar-basin and a dirty cup with a sodden crust in its saucer. Miss Cost would have washed them up, no doubt, if she had returned from early service and not gone walking through the rain to her death.

In a large envelope he came across a number of photographs. A group of village maidens, Cissy prominent among them, with their arms upraised in what was clearly intended for corybantic ecstasy. Wally, showing his hands. Wally with his mouth open. Miss Cost herself, in a looking-glass with her thumb on the camera trigger and smiling dreadfully. Several snapshots, obviously taken in the grounds of the nursing home, with Dr Maine caught in moments of reluctance shading into irritation. Views of the Spring and one of a dark foreign-looking lady with an intense expression.

He heard Fox pull a heavy piece of furniture across the wooden floor and then give an ejaculation.

'Anything?' Alleyn asked.

'Might be. Behind the bed-head. A locked cupboard. Solid, mortise job. Now, where'd she have stowed the key?'

'Not in her bag. Where do spinsters hide keys?'

'I'll try the chest of drawers for a start,' said Fox.

'You jolly well do. A favourite cache. Association of ideas. Freud would have something to say about it.'

Drawers were wrenched open, one after another.

'By gum!' Fox presently exclaimed. 'You're right, Mr Alleyn. Two keys. Here we are.'

'Where?'

'Wrapped up in her combs.'

'In the absence of a chastity belt, no doubt.'

'What's that, Mr Alleyn?'

'No matter. Either of them fit?'

'Hold on. The thing's down by the skirting board. Yes. Yes, I do believe – here we are.'

A lock clicked.

'Well?'

'Two cash boxes, so far,' Fox said, his voice strangely muffled.

Alleyn walked into the bedroom and was confronted by his colleague's stern, up-ended beneath an illuminated legend which read:

> 'Jog on, jog on the footpath way
> And merrily hent the stile-a.'

This was supported by a bookshelf on which the works of Algernon Blackwood and Dennis Wheatley predominated.

Fox was on his knees with his head to the floor and his arm in a cupboard. He extracted two japanned boxes and put them on the unmade bed, across which lay a rumpled nightgown embroidered with lazy daisies.

'The small key's the job for both,' he said. 'There you are, sir.'

The first box contained rolled bundles of bank notes and a well-filled cashbag; the second, a number of papers. Alleyn began to examine them. The top sheet was a carbon copy with a perforated edge. It showed, in type, a list of dates and times covering the past twelve months.

The Spring.	15th August	8.15 p.m.
	21st "	8.20 "
	29th "	8.30 "

There were twenty entries. Two, placed apart from the others, and dated the preceding year, were heavily underlined. '22nd July, 5 p.m.' and '30th September, 8.45.'

'From a duplicating book in her desk,' Alleyn said, 'a page has been cut out. It'll be the top copy of this one.'

'Typewritten,' Fox commented.

'There's a decrepit machine in the parlour. We'll check but I think this'll be it.'

'Do the dates mean anything to you, Mr Alleyn?'

'The underlined item does. Year before last. July 22nd 5 p.m. That's the date and time of the Wally's Warts affair. Yesterday was the second anniversary.'

'Would the others be notes of later cures? Was any record kept?'

'Not to begin with. There is now. The book's on view at Wally's Cottage. We can check, but I don't think that's the answer. The dates are too closely bunched. They give – let's see; they give three entries for August of last year, one for September, and then nothing until 27th April of this year. Then a regular sequence over the last three months up to – yes, by George! – up to a fortnight ago. What do you make of it, Br'er Fox? Any ideas?'

'Only that they're all within licensing hours. Very nice bitter, they serve up at The Boy-and-Lobster. It wouldn't go down too badly. Warm in here, isn't it?'

Alleyn looked thoughtfully at him. 'You're perfectly right,' he said. He went into the shop. 'Pender,' he called out, 'who's the bartender in the evenings at The Boy-and-Lobster?'

'In the old days, sir, it were always the Major hisself. Since these yurr princely extensions, however, there be a barmaid in the main premises and the Major serves in a little wee fancy kind of a place behind the lounge.'

'Always?'

'When he'm capable,' said Pender dryly, 'which is pretty well always. He'm a masterpiece for holding his liquor.'

Pender returned to the shop. 'There's one other thing,' Alleyn said to Fox. 'The actual times she's got here grow later as the days grow longer.'

'So they do,' Fox said. 'That's right. So they do.'

'Well: let it simmer. What's next? Exhibit two.'

It was an envelope containing an exposed piece of film and a single print. Alleyn was about to lay the print on Miss Cost's pillow. This bore the impress of her head and a single grey hair. He looked at it briefly, turned aside, and dropped the print on her dressing-table. Fox joined him.

It was a dull, indifferent snapshot: a tangle of bracken, a downward slope of broken ground and the top of a large boulder. In the foreground out of focus was the image of wire-netting.

'Above the Spring,' Alleyn said. 'Taken from the hillside. Look here, Fox.'

Fox adjusted his spectacles. 'Feet,' he said. 'Two pairs. Courting couple.'

'Very much so. Miss Cost's anathema. I'm afraid Miss Cost begins to emerge as a progressively unattractive character.'

'Shutter-peeping,' said Fox. 'You don't get it so often among women.'

Alleyn turned it over. Neatly written across the back was the current year and '17th June. 7.30 p.m.'

'Last month,' Alleyn said. 'Bailey!' he called out. 'Here, a minute, would you?' Bailey came in. 'Take a look at this. Use a lens. I want you to tell me if you think the man's shoes in this shot might tally with anything you saw at the Spring. It's a tall order, I know.'

Bailey put the snapshot under a lamp and bent over it. Presently he said: 'Can I have a word with Thompson, sir?' Sergeant Thompson was summoned from outer darkness. 'How would this blow up?' Bailey asked him.

'Here's the neg.'

'It's a shocking neg,' Thompson said, and added grudgingly, 'she's got an enlarger.'

Alleyn said: 'On the face of it, do you think there's any hope of a correspondence, Bailey?'

Bailey, still using his lens said: 'Can't really say, sir. The casts are in my room at the pub.'

'What about you, Thompson? Got your shots of the prints?'

'They're in the dish now.'

'Well, take this out and see what you make of it. Have you found her camera?'

'Yes. Lovely job,' Thompson said. 'You wouldn't have expected it. Very fast.' He named the make with reverence.

'Pender,' Alleyn said, re-entering the shop. 'Do you know anything about Miss Cost's camera?'

Pender shook his head and then did what actors call a double-take. 'Yes, I do, though,' he said. 'It was give her in gratitude by a foreign lady that was cured of a terrible bad rash. She was a patient up to hospital and Miss Cost talked her into the Spring.'

'I see. Thompson, would it get results round about seven-thirty on a summer evening?'

'Certainly would. Better than this affair, if properly handled.'

'All right. See what you can do.'

Bailey and Thompson went away and Alleyn rejoined Fox in the bedroom.

'Fox,' Alleyn said distastefully, 'I don't know whose feet the male pair may prove to be but I'm damn' sure I've recognized the female's.'

'Really, Mr Alleyn?'

'Yes. Very good buckskin shoes with very good buckles. She wore them to the Festival. I'm afraid it's Mrs Barrimore.'

'Fancy!' said Fox, after a pause, and he added with his air of simplicity: 'Well, then, it's to be hoped the others turn out to be the Major's.'

III

There were no other papers and no diary in either of the boxes.

'Did you reach to the end of the cupboard?' Alleyn asked Fox.

'No, I didn't. It's uncommonly deep. Extends through the wall and under the counter in the shop,' Fox grumbled.

'Let me try.'

Alleyn lay on the bedroom floor and reached his long arm into the cupboard. His fingers touched something – a book. 'She must have used her brolly to fish it out,' he grunted. 'Hold on. There are two of them – no, three. Here they come: I think – yes. Yes. Br'er Fox. This is *it*.'

They were large commercial diaries and were held together with a rubber band. He took them into the parlour and laid them out on Miss Cost's desk. When he opened the first he found page after page covered in Miss Cost's small skeleton handwriting. He read an entry at random:

'. . . sweet spot, so quaint and *unspoilt*. Sure I shall like it. One feels the *tug* of earth and sea. The "pub" (!) is *really* genuine and goes back to smuggling days. Kept by a *gentleman*. Major B. I take my noggin "of an evening" in the taproom and listen to the wonderful "burr" in the talk of the fisherfolk. All v. friendly . . . Major B. kept looking at me. I know your sort, sez I. Nothing to object to, *really*. Just an awareness. The wife is rather peculiar: I am not altogether taken. A *man's* woman in every sense of the word, I'm afraid. He doesn't pay her v. much attention.'

Alleyn read on for a minute or two. 'It would take a day to get through it,' he said. 'This is her first visit to the Island. Two years ago.'

'Interesting?'

'Excruciating. Where's that list of dates?'

Fox put it on the desk.

Alleyn turned the pages of the diary. References to Major B., later
K., though veiled in unbelievable euphemisms, became more and
more explicit. In this respect alone, Alleyn thought, the gallant
Major had a lot to answer for. He turned back to the entry for the
day after Wally's cure. It was ecstatic.

'I have always,' wrote Miss Cost, 'believed in fairies. The old
magic of water and the spoken rune! The Green Lady! He *saw* her,
this little lad *saw* her and obeyed her behest. Something *led* me to
this Island.' She ran on in this vein for the whole of the entry. Alleyn
read it with a sensation of exasperated compassion. The entry itself
was nothing to his purpose. But across it, heavily inked, Miss Cost
on some later occasion had put down an enormous mark of interro-
gation and, beside this, had added a note: '30th Sept. 8.45.'

This was the second of the two underlined dates on the paper. He
turned it up in the diary.

'I am shocked and horrified and *sickened* by what I have seen this
evening. My hand shakes. I can hardly bring myself to write it down.
I *knew*, from the moment I first set eyes on her, that she was unwor-
thy of him. One *always* knows. Shall not tell K. It would serve him
right if I did. All these months and he never guessed. But I won't tell
him. Not yet. Not unless – But I must *write* it. Only so can I rid myself
of the horror. I was sitting on the hill below the Spring, thinking so
happily of all my plans and so glad I have settled for the shop and
ordered my lovely Green Ladies. I was *feeling* the magic of the water.
(Blessed, blessed water. *No* asthma, now, for *four* weeks.) And then I
heard them. Behind the boulder, laughing. I shrank down in the
bracken. And then *she* came out from behind the boulder in her
green dress and stood above the pool. She raised her arms. I could
hear the man laughing still but I couldn't see him. I *knew*. I *knew*. The
wicked desecration of it! But I won't believe it. I'll put it out of my
mind forever. She was mocking – pretending. I *won't* think anything
else. She went back to him. I waited. And then, suddenly, I couldn't
bear it any longer. I came back here . . .'

Alleyn, looking increasingly grim, went over the entries for the
whole list; throughout two summers, Miss Cost had hunted her

evening quarry with obsessive devotion and had recorded the fruits
of the chase as if in some antic game-book – time, place and circumstances. On each occasion that she spied upon her victims, she had
found the enclosure padlocked and had taken up a point of vantage
on the hillside. At no stage did she give the names of the lovers but
their identity was inescapable. 'Mrs Barrimore and Dr Maine,'
Alleyn said. 'To hell with this case!'

'Awkward,' observed Fox.

'My dear old Fox, it's dynamite. And it fits,' Alleyn said, staring
disconsolately at his colleague. 'The devil of it is, it fits.'

He began to read the entries for the past month. Dr Maine, Miss
Cost weirdly concluded, was not to blame. He was a victim, caught in
the toils, unable to free himself and therefore unable to follow his
nobler inclination towards Miss Cost herself. Interlarded with furious
attacks upon Miss Emily and covert allusions to the anonymous messages, were notes on the Festival, a savage comment on Miss Emily's
visit to the shop and a distracted reference to the attack of asthma that
followed it. 'The dark forces of evil that emanate from this woman'
were held responsible. There followed a number of cryptic asides: –

('Trehern agrees. It's *right*. I *know* it's right.')

' "It is the Cause, it is the Cause, my soul",' Alleyn muttered, disconsolately. 'The old, phoney argument.'

Fox, who had been reading over his shoulder, said: 'It'd be a
peculiar thing if she'd worked Trehern up to doing the job and then
got herself mistaken for the intended victim.'

'It sounds very neat, Br'er Fox, but in point of fact, it's lousy with
loose ends. I can't take it. Just let's go through the other statements
now.'

They did this and Fox sighed over the result. 'I suppose so,' he
said and added, 'I like things to be neat and they so seldom are.'

'You're a concealed classicist,' Alleyn said. 'We'd better go back to
this ghastly diary. Read on.'

They had arrived at the final week. Rehearsals for the Festival.
Animadversions upon Miss Emily. The incident of the Green Lady
on Miss Emily's desk. 'He did it. K. I'm certain. And I'm *glad*, glad.
She no doubt, suspects *me*. I refused to go. She finds she can't order
me about. To sit in that room with *her* and the two she has ruined!
Never.'

Alleyn turned a page and there, facing them, was the last entry Miss Cost was to make in her journal.

'Yesterday evening,' Alleyn said. 'After the debacle at the Spring.'

The thunderstorm, he was not surprised to find, was treated as a judgment. Nemesis, in the person of one of Miss Cost's ambiguous deities, had decided to touch-up the unbelievers with six of the cosmic best. Among these offenders Miss Emily was clearly included but it emerged that she was not the principal object of Miss Cost's spleen. 'Laugh at your peril,' she ominously wrote, 'at the Great Ones.' And, as if stung by this observation she continued, in a splutter of disjointed venom, to threaten some unnamed persons. 'At last,' she wrote. 'After the agony of months, the cruelty and now, the final insult, *at last* I shall speak. I shall face both of them with the facts. I shall tell *her* what was between us. And I shall show that other one how I know. He – both – all of them shall suffer. I'll drag their names through the papers. Now. Tonight. I am determined. It is the end.'

'And so it was,' Fox said, looking up over his spectacles. 'Poor thing. Very sad, really, these cases. Do you see your way through all this, Mr Alleyn?'

'I think I do, Br'er Fox. I'm afraid I do. And I'll tell you why.'

He had scarcely begun, when Bailey, moving rather more quickly than he was wont, came through from the shop.

'Someone for you, sir. A Miss Williams. She says it's urgent.'

Alleyn went to the telephone.

Jenny sounded as if it was very urgent indeed.

'Mr Alleyn? Thank God! Please come up here, quickly. Please do. Miss Emily's rooms. I can't say anything else.' Alleyn heard a muffled ejaculation. A man shouted distantly and a woman screamed. There was the faint but unmistakable crash of broken glass . . . 'Please come,' said Jenny.

'At once,' Alleyn said. And to Fox: 'Leave Pender on the board and you others follow as quick as you can. Room 35 to the right of the stairhead on the first floor.'

Before they had time to answer he was out of the shop and had plunged, head down, into the storm outside.

CHAPTER 9

Storm

It was not raining now but the night was filled with so vast an uproar that there was no room for any perception but that of noise: the clamour of wind and irregular thud and crash of a monstrous tide. It broke over the foreshore and made hissing assaults on the foot of the steps. Alleyn went up them at a sort of shambling run, bent double and feeling his way with his hands. When he reached the last flight and came into range of the hotel windows, his heart pounded like a ram and his throat was dry. He beat across the platform and went in by the main entrance. The night porter was reading behind his desk. He looked up in astonishment at Alleyn who had not waited to put on his mackintosh.

'Did you get caught, sir?'

'I took shelter,' Alleyn said. 'Good night.'

He made for the stairs and when he was out of sight, waited for a moment or two to recover his wind. Then he went up to the first floor.

The passage had the vacant look of all hotel corridors at night. A wireless blared invisibly. When he moved forward he realized the noise was coming from Miss Emily's room. A brass band was playing 'Colonel Bogey.'

He knocked on the door and was not answered. He opened it and went in.

It was as if a tableau had been organized for his benefit; as if he had been sent out of the room while the figures arranged themselves to their best effect. Miss Emily stood on the hearthrug very pale and grand, with Jenny in support. Margaret Barrimore, with her hands to her mouth, was inside the door on his left. He had narrowly missed striking her with it when he came in. The three men had pride of place. Major Barrimore stood centre with his legs straddled and blood running from his nose into his gaping mouth. Dr Maine faced him and frowned at a cut across the knuckles of his own well-kept doctor's hand. Patrick, dishevelled, stood between them, like a referee who had just stopped a fight. The wireless bellowed remorselessly. There was a scatter of broken glass in the fireplace.

They all turned their heads and looked at Alleyn. They might have been asking him to guess the word of their charade.

'Can we switch that thing off?' he asked.

Jenny did so. The silence was deafening.

'I did it to drown the shouting,' she said.

'Miss Emily,' Alleyn said. 'Will you sit down?' She did so.

'It might be as well,' he suggested, 'if everyone did.'

Dr Maine made an impatient noise and walked over to the window. Barrimore sucked his moustache, tasted blood and got out his handkerchief. He was swaying on his feet. Alleyn pushed a chair under him and he collapsed on it. His eyes were out of focus and he reeked of whisky. Mrs Barrimore moved towards Dr Maine. Jenny sat on an arm of Miss Emily's chair and Patrick on the edge of the table.

'And now,' Alleyn said, 'what has happened?'

For a second or two nobody spoke and then Jenny said: 'I asked you to come so I suppose I'd better explain.'

'You better hold your tongue,' Barrimore mumbled through his bloodied handkerchief.

'That'll do,' said Patrick dangerously.

Alleyn said to Jenny, 'Will you, then?'

'If I can. All right. I'd come in to say good night to Miss Emily. Patrick was waiting for me downstairs, I think. Weren't you?'

He nodded.

'Miss Emily and I were talking. I was just going to say good night when – when Mrs Barrimore came in.'

'Jenny – no! No!' Margaret Barrimore whispered.

'Don't stop her,' Miss Emily said quietly, 'it's better not to. I am sure of it.'

'Patrick?' Jenny appealed to him.

He hesitated, stared at his mother and then said, 'You'd better go on, I think. Just the facts, Jenny.'

'Very well. Mrs Barrimore was distressed and – I think – frightened. She didn't say why. She looked ill. She asked if she could stay with us for a little while and Miss Emily said yes. We didn't talk very much. Nothing that could matter.'

Margaret Barrimore said rapidly: 'Miss Pride was extremely kind. I wasn't feeling well. I haven't been well lately. I had a giddy turn: I was near her room. That's why I went in.'

Dr Maine said: 'As Mrs Barrimore's doctor I must insist that she's not troubled by any questioning. It's true that she is unwell.' He jerked a chair forward and touched her arm. 'Sit down, Margaret,' he said gently and she obeyed him.

' "*As Mrs Barrimore's doctor*",' her husband quoted and gave a whinnying laugh. 'That's wonderful! That's a superb remark.'

'Will you go on, please?'

'OK. Yes. Well, that lasted quite a long time – just the three of us here. And then Dr Maine came in to see Miss Pride. He examined the cut on her neck and he told us it would probably be too rough for us to cross the channel tomorrow. He and Mrs Barrimore were saying good night when Major Barrimore came in.'

So far Jenny had spoken very steadily but she faltered now, and looked at Miss Emily. 'It's – it's then that – that things began to happen. I – '

Miss Emily with perfect composure, said: 'In effect, my dear Roderique, there was a scene. Major Barrimore made certain accusations. Dr Maine intervened. A climax was reached and blows were exchanged. I suggested, aside to Jenny, that she solicit your aid. The fracas continued. A glass was broken. Mrs Barrimore screamed and Mr Patrick arrived upon the scene. He was unsuccessful and, after a renewal of belligerency, Major Barrimore fell to the floor. The actual fighting came to a stop but the noise was considerable. It was at this juncture that the wireless was introduced. You entered shortly afterwards.'

'Does everybody agree to this?'

There was no answer.

'I take it that you do.'

Dr Maine said: 'Will you also take it that whatever happened has not the remotest shade of bearing upon your case? It was an entirely private matter and should remain so.' He looked at Patrick and, with disgust, at Major Barrimore. 'I imagine you agree,' he said.

'Certainly,' Patrick said shortly.

Alleyn produced his stock comment on this argument. 'If it turns out that there's no connection, I assure you I shall be glad to forget it. In the meantime, I'm afraid I must make certain.'

There was a tap at the door. He answered it. Fox, Bailey and Thompson had arrived. Alleyn asked Fox to come in and the others to wait.

'Inspector Fox,' he said, 'is with me on this case.'

'Good evening, ladies and gentlemen,' Fox said.

They observed him warily. Miss Emily said: 'Good evening, Mr Fox. I have heard a great deal about you.'

'Have you, ma'am?' he rejoined. 'Nothing to my discredit, I hope.' And to Alleyn: 'Sorry to interrupt, sir.'

Alleyn gave him a brief summary of the situation and returned to the matter in hand. 'I'm afraid I must ask you to tell me what it was that triggered off this business,' he said. 'What were Major Barrimore's accusations?'

Nobody answered. 'Will you tell me, Miss Emily?'

Miss Emily said: 'I cannot. I am sorry. I – I find myself unable to elaborate upon what I have already said.' She looked at Alleyn in distress. 'You must not ask me,' she said.

'Never mind.' He glanced at the others. 'Am I to know?' he asked and, after a moment, 'Very well. Let us make a different approach. I shall tell you instead, what we have been doing. We have, as some of you know, been at Miss Cost's shop. We have searched the shop and the living quarters behind it. I think I should tell you that we have found Miss Cost's diary. It is a long, exhaustive, and in many places, relevant document. It may be put in evidence.'

Margaret Barrimore gave a low cry.

'The final entry was made last night. In it she suggests that as a result of some undefined insult she is going to make public certain matters which are not specifically set out in that part of the diary but will not, I think, be difficult to arrive at when the whole document is reviewed. It may be that after she made this last entry, she wrote a letter to the Press. If so, it will be in the mailbag.'

'Has it gone out yet?' Patrick asked sharply.

'I haven't inquired,' Alleyn said coolly.

'It must be stopped.'

'We don't usually intercept Her Majesty's mail.'

Barrimore said thickly: 'You can bloody well intercept this one.'

'Nonsense,' said Dr Maine crisply.

'By God, sir, I won't take that from you. By God!' Barrimore began, trying to get to his feet.

'Sit down,' Alleyn said. 'Do you want to be taken in charge for assault? Pull yourself together.'

Barrimore sank back. He looked at his handkerchief, now drenched with blood. His face was bedabbled and his nose still ran with it. 'Gimme 'nother,' he muttered.

'A towel, perhaps,' Miss Emily suggested. Jenny fetched one from the bathroom.

'He'd better lie down,' Dr Maine said impatiently.

'I'll be damned if I do,' said the Major.

'To continue,' Alleyn said, 'the facts that emerge from the diary and from the investigations are these. We now know the identity of the Green Lady. Miss Cost found it out for herself on 30th September of last year. She saw the impersonator repeating her initial perform-ance for a concealed audience of one. She afterwards discovered who this other was. You will stay where you are, if you please, Major Barrimore. Miss Cost was unwilling to believe this evidence. She began, however, to spy upon the two persons involved. On 17th June of this year she took a photograph at the Spring.'

Dr Maine said: 'I can't allow this,' and Patrick said: 'No, for God's sake!'

'I would avoid it if I could,' Alleyn said. 'Mrs Barrimore, would you rather wait in the next room? Miss Williams will go with you, I'm sure.'

'Yes, darling,' Jenny said quickly. 'Do.'

'O no,' she said. 'Not now. Not now.'

'It would be better,' Patrick said.

'It would be better, Margaret,' Dr Maine repeated.

'No.'

There was a brief silence. An emphatic gust of wind battered at the window. The lights flickered, dimmed and came up again.

Alleyn's hearers were momentarily united in a new uneasiness. When he spoke again, they shifted their attention back to him with an air of confusion.

'Miss Cost,' he was saying, 'kept her secret to herself. It became, I think, an obsession. It's clear from other passages in her diary that some time before this discovery, she had conceived an antagonism for Major Barrimore. The phrases she uses suggest that it arose from the reaction commonly attributed to a woman scorned.'

Margaret Barrimore turned her head and for the first time looked at her husband. Her expression, one of profound astonishment, was reflected in her son's face and Dr Maine's.

'There is no doubt, I think,' Alleyn said. 'That during her first visit to the Island their relationship, however brief, had been of the sort to give rise to the later reaction.'

'Is this true?' Dr Maine demanded of Barrimore.

He had the towel clapped to his face. Over the top of it his eyes, prominent and dazed, narrowed as if he were smiling. He said nothing.

'Miss Cost, as I said just now, kept her knowledge to herself. Later, it appears, she transferred her attention to Doctor Maine and was unsuccessful. It's a painful and distressing story and I shan't dwell on it except to say that up to yesterday's tragedy we have the picture of a neurotic who has discovered that the man upon whom her fantasy is now concentrated, is deeply attached to the wife of the man with whom she herself had a brief affair that ended in humiliation. She also knows that this wife impersonated the Green Lady in the original episode. These elements are so bound up together, that if she makes mischief, as her demon urges her to do, she will be obliged to expose the truth about the Green Lady and that would be disastrous. Add to this, the proposal to end all publicity and official recognition of the Spring and you get some idea, perhaps, of the emotional turmoil that she suffered and that declares itself in this unhappy diary.'

'You do, indeed,' said Miss Emily abruptly and added: 'One has much to answer for, I perceive. I have much to answer for. Go on.'

'In opposing the new plans for the Spring, Miss Cost may have let off a head of emotional steam. She sent anonymous messages to Miss Pride. She was drawn into the companionship of the general front made against Miss Pride's intentions. I think there is little doubt that she conspired with Trehern and egged-on ill feeling in the village. She had received attention. She had her Festival in hand. She was somebody. It was, I daresay, all rather exciting and gratifying. Wouldn't you think so?' he asked Dr Maine.

'I'm not a psychiatrist,' he said. 'But, yes. You may be right.'

'Now this was the picture,' Alleyn went on, 'up to the time of the Festival. But when she came to write the final entry in her diary, which was last night, something had happened: something that revived all her sense of injury and spite, something that led her to write: 'Both – all of them – shall suffer. I'll drag their names through the papers. Now. Tonight. I am determined. It is the end'.'

Another formidable onslaught roared down upon The Boy-and-Lobster and again the lights wavered and recovered.

'She doesn't say, and we can't tell, positively, what inflamed her. I am inclined to think that it might be put down to aesthetic humiliation.'

'What!' Patrick ejaculated.

'Yes. One has to remember that all the first-night agonies that beset a professional director are also visited upon the most ludicrously inefficient amateur. Miss Cost had produced a show and exposed it to an audience. However bad the show, she still had to undergo the classic ordeal. The reaction among some of the onlookers didn't escape her notice.'

'O dear!' Jenny said. 'O *dear!*'

'But this is all speculation and a policeman is not allowed to speculate,' Alleyn said. 'Let us get back to hard facts, if we can. Here are some of them. Miss Cost attended early service this morning and afterwards walked to the Spring to collect a necklace. It was in her hand when we found her. We know, positively, that she encountered and spoke to three people: Mrs Carstairs and Dr Maine before church; Major Barrimore afterwards.'

'Suppose I deny that?' Barrimore said thickly.

'I can't, of course, make any threats or offer any persuasion. You might, on consideration, think it wiser, after all, to agree that you met and tell me what passed between you. Major Barrimore,' Alleyn explained generally, 'has already admitted that he was spying upon Miss Pride who had gone to the enclosure to put up a notice which he afterwards removed.'

Miss Emily gave a sharp ejaculation.

'It was later replaced.' Alleyn turned to Barrimore and stood over him. 'Shall I tell you what I think happened? I think hard words passed between you and Miss Cost and that she was stung into telling you her secret. I think you parted from her in a rage and that when you came back to the hotel this morning, you bullied your wife. You had better understand at once, that your wife has not told me this. Finally, I believe that Miss Cost may even have threatened to reveal your former relationship with herself. She suggests in her diary that she has some such intention. Now. Have you anything to say to all this?'

Patrick said: 'You had better say nothing.' He walked over to his mother and put his arm about her shoulders.

'I didn't do it,' Barrimore said. 'I didn't kill her.'

'Is that all?'

'Yes.'

'Very well. I shall move on,' Alleyn said and spoke generally. 'Among her papers we have found a typewritten list of dates. It is a carbon copy. The top copy is missing. Miss Cost had fallen into the habit of sending anonymous letters. As we know only too well, this habit grows by indulgence. It is possible, having regard for the dates in question, that this document has been brought to the notice of the person most likely to be disturbed by it. Possibly with a print of the photograph. Now, this individual has, in one crucial respect, given a false statement as to time and circumstance and because of that – '

There was a tap at the door. Fox opened it. A voice in the passage shouted: 'I can't wait quiet-like, mister. I got to see 'im.' It was Trehern.

Fox said: 'Now then, what's all this?' And began to move out. Trehern plunged at him, head down and was taken in a half-nelson. Bailey appeared in the doorway. 'You lay your hands off of me,' Trehern whined. 'You got nothing against me.'

'Outside,' said Fox.

Trehern struggling, looked wildly round the assembled company and fixed on Alleyn. 'I got something to tell you, mister,' he said. 'I got something to put before all of you. I got to speak out.'

'All right, Fox,' Alleyn said and nodded to Bailey, who went out and shut the door. Fox relaxed his hold. 'Well, Trehern, what is it?'

Trehern wiped the back of his hand across his mouth and blinked. 'I been thinking,' he said.

'Yes?'

'I been thinking things over. Ever since you come at me up to my house and acted like you done and made out what you made out which is not the case. I be'ant a quick-brained chap, mister, but the light has broke and I see me way clear, I got to speak and speak public.'

'Very well. What do you want to say?'

'Don't you rush me now, mister. What I got to say is a mortal serious matter and I need to take my time.'

'Nobody's rushing you.'

'No, nor they better not,' he said. His manner was half truculent, half cringing. 'It concerns this yurr half-hour in time what was the matter which you flung in my teeth. So fur so good. Now. This yurr lady,' he ducked his head at Miss Emily, 'tells you she seen my lil' chap in the road round about twenty to eight on this yurr fatal morning. Right?'

'Certainly,' said Miss Pride.

'Much obliged. And I says, so she might of then, for all I know to the contrariwise me being asleep in my bed. And I says I uprose at five past eight. Correct?'

'That's what you said, yes.'

'And God's truth if I never speak another word. And my lil' chap was then to home in my house. Right. Now then. Furthermore to that, you says the doctor saw him at that same blessed time, twenty to eight, which statement agrees with the lady.'

'Yes.'

'Yes. And you says, don't rush me, you says the doctor was in his launch at that mortal moment.'

Alleyn glanced at Maine: 'Agreed?' he asked.

'Yes. I saw Wally from the launch.'

Trehern moved over to Dr Maine. 'That's a bloody lie, Doctor,' he said.' Axcusing the expression. I face you out with it, man to man. I seen you, Doctor, clear as I see you now, moving out in thicky launch of yourn at five to ten bloody minutes past eight and by God, I reckon you'm not telling lies for the fun of it. I reckon as how you got half an hour on your conscience, Doctor Maine, and if the law doesn't face you out with it I'm the chap to do the law's job for it.'

'I have already discussed the point with Superintendent Alleyn,' Maine said, looking at Trehern with profound distaste. 'Your story is quite unsupported.'

'Is it?' Trehern said. 'Is it, then? That's where you're dead wrong. You mind me. And you t'other ladies and gents and you, mister.' He turned back to Alleyn. 'After you shifted off this evening, I took to thinking. And I remembered. I remembered our young Wal come up when I was looking out of my winder and I remembered he said in his por simple fashion: "Thick's doctor's launch, be'ant she?" You ax him, mister. You face him up with it and he'll tell you.'

'No doubt!' said Maine. He looked at Alleyn. 'I imagine you accept my statement,' he said.

'I haven't said so,' Alleyn replied. 'I didn't say so at the time, if you remember.'

'By God, Alleyn!' he said angrily and controlled himself. 'This fellow's as shifty as they come. You must see it. And the boy! Of what value is the boy's statement if you get one from him. He's probably been thrashed into learning what he's got to say.'

'I never raised a hand – ' Trehern began but Alleyn stopped him.

'I was coming to this point,' he said, 'when we were interrupted. It may as well be brought out by this means as any other. There are factors, apart from those I've already discussed, of which Trehern knows nothing. They may be said to support his story.' He glanced at Miss Emily. 'I shall put them to you presently but I assure you they are cogent. In the meantime, Dr Maine, if you have any independent support for your own version of your movements, you might like to say what it is. I must warn you – '

'*Stop.*'

Margaret Barrimore had moved out into the room. Her hands writhed together, as they had done when he saw her in the garden, but she had an air of authority and was, he thought, in command of herself.

She said: 'Please don't go on, Mr Alleyn. There's something that I see I must tell you.'

'Margaret!' Dr Maine said sharply.

'No,' she said. 'No. Don't try to stop me. If you do I shall insist on seeing Mr Alleyn alone. But I'd rather say it here. In front of you all. After all, everybody knows now, don't they? We needn't pretend any more. Let me go on.'

'Go on, Mrs Barrimore,' Alleyn said.

'It's true,' she said. 'He didn't leave the bay in his launch at half past seven or whenever it was. He came to the hotel to see me. I said I had breakfast alone. I wasn't alone. He was there. Miss Cost had told him she was going to expose – everything. She told him when they met outside the church so he came to see me and ask me to go away with him. He wanted us to make a clean break before it all came out. He asked me to meet him in the village tonight. We were to go to London and then abroad. It was all very hurried. Only a few minutes. We heard somebody coming. I asked him to let me think, to give me a breathing space. So he went away. I suppose he went back to the bay.'

She walked over to Maine and put her hand on his arm. 'I couldn't let you go on,' she said. 'It's all the same now. It doesn't matter, Bob. It doesn't matter. We'll be together.'

'Margaret, my dear,' said Dr Maine.

There was a long silence. Fox cleared his throat.

Alleyn turned to Trehern.

'And what have you to say to that?' he asked.

Trehern was gaping at Mrs Barrimore. He seemed to be lost in some kind of trance.

'I'll be going,' he said at last. 'I'll be getting back along.' He turned and made for the door. Fox stepped in front of it.

Barrimore had got to his feet. His face, bedabbled with blood, was an appalling sight.

'Then it's true,' he said very quietly. 'She told me. She stood there, grinning and jibbering. She said she'd make me a public laughing stock. And when I said she could go to hell she – d'you know what she did? – she spat at me. And I – I – '

His voice was obliterated by a renewed onslaught of the gale: heavier than any that had preceded it. A confused rumpus broke out. Some metal object, a dustbin perhaps, racketed past the house and vanished in a diminishing series of irregular clashes, as if it bumped down the steps. There was a second monstrous buffet. Somebody, Margaret Barrimore, Alleyn thought, cried out, and at the same moment the lights failed altogether.

The dark was absolute and the noise intense. Alleyn was struck violently on the shoulder and cannoned into something solid and damp: Fox. As he recovered, he was hit again and putting out his hand, felt the edge of the door.

He yelled to Fox: 'Come on!' and snatching at the door, dived into the passage. There, too, it was completely dark. But less noisy. He thought he could make out the thud of running feet on carpet. Fox was behind him. A flashlight danced on a wall. 'Give it me,' Alleyn said. He grabbed it and it displayed for an instant the face of Sergeant Bailey. 'Out of my way,' he said. 'Come on, you two. Fox – get Coombe.'

He ran to the stairhead and flashed his torch downwards. For a split second it caught the top of a head. He went downstairs in a con-trolled plunge, using the torch, and arrived in the entrance hall as the front door crashed. His flashlight discovered, momentarily, the startled face of the night porter who said: 'Here, what's the matter?' and disappeared, open-mouthed.

The door was still swinging. He caught it and was once more engulfed in the storm.

It was raining again, heavily. The force of the gale was such that he leant against it and drove his way towards the steps in combat with it. Two other lights, Bailey's and Thompson's, he supposed, dodged eccentrically across the slanting downpour. He lost them when he reached the steps and found the iron rail. But there was yet another lancet of broken light beneath him. As Alleyn went down after it, he was conscious only of noise and idiot violence. He slipped, fell and recovered. At one moment, he was hurled against the rail.

'These bloody steps,' he thought. 'These bloody steps.' When he reached the bottom flight he saw his quarry, a dark, foreshortened, anonymous figure, veer through the dull light from Miss Cost's shop window. 'Pender's got a candle or a torch,' Alleyn thought.

The other's torch was still going: a thin erratic blade. 'Towards the jetty,' Alleyn thought. 'He's making for the jetty.' And down there were the riding lights of the hotel launch, jaucing in the dark.

Here at last, the end of the steps. Now he was in seawater, sometimes over his feet. The roar of the channel was all-obliterating. The gale flat-tened his lips and filled his eyes with tears. When he made the jetty, he had to double-up and grope with his left hand, keeping the right, with Fox's torch still alive, held out in front: he was whipped by the sea.

He had gained ground. The other was moving on again, doubled up, like Alleyn himself, and still using a torch. There were no more than thirty feet between them. The riding-lights danced near at hand and shuddered when the launch banged against the jetty.

The figure was poised: it waited for the right moment. A torch-light swung through the rain and Alleyn found himself squinting into the direct beam. He ducked and moved on, half-dazzled but aware that the launch rose and the figure leapt to meet it. Alleyn struggled forward, took his chance, and jumped.

He had landed aft, among the passengers' benches; had fallen across one of them and struck his head on another. He hung there, while the launch bucketed under him and then he fell between the benches and lay on the heaving deck, fighting for breath and help-less. His torch had gone and he was in the dark. There must have been a brief rent in the night sky because a company of stars careened across his vision, wheeled and returned. The deck tilted again and he saw the hotel windows, glowing. They curtsied and tipped. 'The power's on,' he thought, and a sudden deadly sinking blotted everything out. When he opened his eyes he thought with astonishment: 'I was out.' Then he heard the engine and felt the judder of a propeller racing above water. He laid hold of a bench and dragged himself to his knees. He could see his opponent, faintly haloed by light from the wheelhouse, back towards him, wrestling with the wheel itself. A great sea broke over them. The windows along Portcarrow front lurched up and dived out of sight again.

Alleyn began to crawl down the gangway between rows of fixed seats, clinging to them as he went. His feet slithered. He fell sideways and propping himself up, managed to drag off his shoes and socks. His head cleared and ached excruciatingly. The launch was now in mid-channel, taking the seas full on her beam and rolling monstrously. He thought 'she'll never make it,' and tried to remember where the lifebelts should be.

Did that other, fighting there with the wheel, know he was aboard? How had the launch been cast off? Were the mooring-lines freed from their cleats and was she now without them? Or had they been loosed from the bollards while he was unconscious? What should he do? 'Keep observation!' he thought sourly. An exquisite jab of pain shot through his eyeballs.

The launch keeled over and took in a solid weight of sea. He thought: 'Well, this is it,' and was engulfed. The iron legs of the bench bit into his hands. He hung on, almost vertical, and felt the water drag at him like an octopus. It was disgusting. The deck

kicked. They wallowed for a suspended moment and then, shudder-
ing, recovered and rose. The first thing he saw was the back of the
helmsman. Something rolled against his chest: he unclenched his
left hand and felt for it. The torch.

Street lamps along the front came alive and seemed dramatically
near at hand. At the same time the engine was cut. He struggled to
his feet and moved forward. He was close now, to the figure at the
wheel. There was the jetty. Their course had shifted and the launch
pitched violently. His left hand knocked against the back of a seat
and a beam of light shot out from the torch and found the figure at
the wheel. It turned.

Maine and Alleyn looked into each other's faces.

Maine lurched out of the wheelhouse. The launch lifted prodi-
giously, tilted, and dived, nose down. Alleyn was blinded by a deluge
of salt water. When he could see again, Maine was on the port gun-
wale. For a fraction of time he was poised, a gigantic figure against the
shore lights. Then he flexed his knees and leapt overboard.

The launch went about and crashed into the jetty. The last thing
he heard was somebody yelling high above him.

II

He was climbing down innumerable flights of stairs. They were
impossibly steep – perpendicular – but he had to go down. They
tipped and he fell outwards and looked into an abyss laced with
flashlights. He lost his hold, dropped into nothing, and was on the
stairs again, climbing, climbing. Somebody was making comfortable
noises. He looked into a face.

'Fox,' he said, with immense satisfaction.

'There now!' said Inspector Fox.

Alleyn went to sleep.

When he woke, it was to find Troy nearby. Her hand was against
his face. 'So there you are,' he said.

'Hallo,' said Troy and kissed him.

The wall beyond her was dappled with sunshine and looked
familiar. He puzzled over it for a time and because he wanted to lay

his face closer to her hand, turned his head and was stabbed through the temples.

'Don't move,' Troy said. 'You've taken an awful bash.'

'I see.'

'You've been concussed and all.'

'How long?'

'About thirty-four hours.'

'This is Coombe's cottage.'

'That's right, but you're meant not to talk.'

'Ridiculous,' he said and dozed off again.

Troy slid her hand carefully from under his bristled jaw and crept out of the room.

Superintendent Coombe was in his parlour with Sir James Curtis and Fox. 'He woke again,' Troy said to Curtis, 'just for a moment.'

'Say anything?'

'Yes. He's – ' her voice trembled. 'He's all right.'

'Of course he's all right. I'll take a look at him.'

She returned with him to the bedroom and stood by the window while Curtis stooped over his patient. It was a brilliant morning. The channel was dappled with sequins. The tide was low and three people walked over the causeway: an elderly woman, a young man and a girl. Five boats ducked and bobbed in Fisherman's Bay. The hotel launch was still jammed in the understructure of the jetty and looked inconsequent and unreal, suspended above its natural element. A complete write-off, it was thought.

'You're doing fine,' Curtis said.

'Where's Troy?'

'Here, darling.'

'Good. What happened?'

'You were knocked out,' Curtis said. 'Coombe and two other chaps managed to fish you up.'

'Coombe?'

'Fox rang him from the hotel as soon as you'd set off on your wild goose chase. They were on the jetty.'

'Oh yes. Yelling. Where's Fox?'

'You'd better keep quiet for a bit, Rory. Everything's all right. Plenty of time.'

'I want to see Fox, Curtis.'

'Very well, but only for one moment.'

Troy fetched him.

'This is more like it now,' Fox said.

'Have you found him?'

'We have, yes. Yesterday evening, at low tide.'

'Where?'

'About four miles along the coast.'

'It was deliberate, Fox.'

'So I understand. Coombe saw it.'

'Yes, well now, that's quite enough,' said Curtis.

Fox stepped back.

'Wait a minute,' Alleyn said. 'Anything on him? Fox? Anything on him?'

'All right. Tell him.'

'Yes, Mr Alleyn, there was. Very sodden. Pulp almost, but you can make it out. The top copy of that list and the photograph.'

'Ah!' Alleyn said. 'She gave them to him. I thought as much.'

He caught his breath and then closed his eyes.

'That's right,' Curtis said. 'You go to sleep again.'

III

'My sister, Fanny Winterbottom,' said Miss Emily, two days later, 'once remarked with characteristic extravagance (nay, on occasion, vulgarity), that, wherever I went, I kicked up as much dust as a dancing dervish. The observation was inspired more by fortuitous alliteration than by any degree of accuracy. If, however, she were alive to-day, she would doubtless consider herself justified. I have made disastrous mischief in Portcarrow.'

'My dear Miss Emily, aren't you, yourself, falling into Mrs Winterbottom's weakness for exaggeration? Miss Cost's murder had nothing to do with your decision on the future of the Spring.'

'But it *had*,' said Miss Emily, smacking her gloved hand on the arm of Superintendent Coombe's rustic seat. 'Let us have logic. If I had not persisted with my decision, her nervous system, to say nothing of her emotions (at all times unstable), would not have been exacerbated to such a degree that she would have behaved as she did.'

'How do you know?' Alleyn asked. 'She might have cut up rough on some other provocation. She had her evidence. The possession of a dangerous instrument is, in itself, a danger. Even if you had never visited the Island, Miss Emily, Barrimore and Maine would still have laughed at the Festival.'

'She would have been less disturbed by their laughter,' said Miss Emily. She looked fixedly at Alleyn. 'I am tiring you, no doubt,' she said. 'I must go. Those kind children are waiting in the motor. I merely called to say *au revoir*, my dear Roderique.'

'You are not tiring me in the least and your escort can wait. I imagine they are very happy to do so. It's no good, Miss Emily. I know you're eaten up with curiosity.'

'Not curiosity. A natural dislike of unexplained detail.'

'I couldn't sympathize more. Which details?'

'No doubt you are always asked when you first began to suspect the criminal. When did you first begin to suspect Dr Maine?'

'When you told me that, at about twenty to eight, you saw nobody but Wally on the road down to Fisherman's Bay.'

'And I should have seen Dr Maine?'

'You should have seen him pulling out from the bay jetty in his launch. And then Trehern, quite readily, said he saw the doctor leaving in his launch about five past eight. Why should he lie about the time he left? And what, as Trehern pointed out, did he do in the half-hour that elapsed?'

'Did you not believe that poor woman when she accounted for the half-hour?'

'Not for a second. If he had been with her she would have said so when I first interviewed her. He has a patient in the hotel and she could have quite easily given that as a reason and would have wanted to provide him with an alibi. Did you notice his look of astonishment when she cut in? Did you notice how she stopped him before he could say anything? No, I didn't believe her and I think he knew I didn't.'

'And that, you consider, was why he ran away?'

'Partly that, perhaps. He may have felt,' Alleyn said, 'quite suddenly, that he couldn't take it. He may have had his moment of truth. Imagine it, Miss Emily. The blinding realization that must come to a killer: the thing that forces so many of them to give themselves up or to bolt or to commit suicide. Suppose we had believed her and they had gone away together. For the rest of his life he would have been tied to the woman he loved by the most appalling obligation it's possible to imagine.'

'Yes,' she said. 'He was a proud man, I think. You are right. Pray go on.'

'Maine had spoken to Miss Cost outside the church. She was telling Mrs Carstairs she would go to the Spring after the service and collect the necklace that had been left on the shelf. She ran after Maine and Mrs Carstairs went into church. We don't know what passed between them but I think she may, poor creature, have made some final advance and been rebuffed. She must have armed herself with her horrid little snapshot and list of dates and been carrying them about in her bag, planning to call on him, precipitate a final scene and then confront him with her evidence. In any case she forced them on him and very likely told him she was going to give the whole story to the Press.'

'Did she – ?'

'Yes. It was in the mailbag.'

'You said, I think, that you did not normally intercept Her Majesty's mail.'

'I believe I did,' said Alleyn blandly. 'Nor do we. Normally.'

'Go on.'

'He knew she was going to the Spring. He was no doubt on the lookout as he washed his hands at the sink in the Trethaways' cottage. He saw Wally. He probably saw you pin up your notice. He saw Barrimore tear it down and go away. He went up and let himself in. He had admittance discs and used one when we sent for him. He hid behind the boulder and waited for Miss Cost. He knew of course that there were loose rocks up there. He was extremely familiar with the terrain.'

'Ah, yes.'

'When it was over he scraped away his footprints. Later on, when we were there, he was very quick to get up to the higher level and walk over it. Any prints that might be left would thus appear to be innocuous. Then he went back in his launch at ten minutes past eight and waited to be sent for to examine the body.'

'It gives me an unpleasant *frisson* when I remember that he also examined mine,' said Miss Emily. 'A cool, resourceful man. I rather liked him.'

'So did I,' Alleyn said. 'I liked him. He intended us, of course, to follow up the idea of mistaken identity but he was too clever to push it overmuch. If we hadn't discovered that you visited the Spring, he would have said he'd seen you. As it was he let us find out for ourselves. He hoped Wally would be thought to have done it and would have given evidence of his irresponsibility and seen him bestowed in a suitable institution, which, as he very truly observed, might be the best thing for him, after all.'

'I shall do something about that boy,' said Miss Emily. 'There must be special schools. I shall attend to it.' She looked curiously at Alleyn. 'What would you have done if the lights had not failed, or if you had caught up with him?'

'Routine procedure, Miss Emily. Asked him to come to Coombe's office and make a statement. I doubt if we had a case against him. Too much conjecture. I hoped, by laying so much of the case open, to induce a confession. Once the Wally theory was dismissed, I think Maine would have not allowed Barrimore or anyone else, to be arrested. But I'm glad it turned out as it did.'

Fox came through the gate into Coombe's garden.

'*Bon jour, Mademoiselle*,' he said laboriously. '*J'espère que vous êtes en bonne santé ce matin.*'

Miss Emily winced. 'Mr Fox,' she said in slow but exquisite French. 'You are, I am sure, a very busy man, but if you can spare an hour twice a week, I think I might be able to give you some assistance with your conversation. I should be delighted to do so.'

Fox asked her if she would be good enough to repeat her statement and as she did so, blushed to the roots of his hair.

'*Mademoiselle*,' he said, '*c'est bonne*, no blast – *pardon* – *bien aimable de vous* – I mean – *de votre part*. Would you really? I can't think of anything I'd like better.'

'*Alors, c'est entendu*,' said Miss Emily.

IV

Patrick and Jenny sat in his car down by the waterfront. Miss Emily's luggage and Jenny's and Patrick's suitcases were roped into the open boot. Miss Emily had settled to spend a few days at the Manor Park

Hotel and had invited them both to be her guests. Patrick felt he should stay with his mother but she was urgent for him to go.

'It made me feel terribly inadequate,' he said. 'As if somehow I must have failed her. And yet, you know, I thought we got on awfully well together, always. I'm fond of my mama.'

'Of course you are. And she adores you. I expect it's just that she wants to be by herself until – well, until the first ghastly shock's over.'

'By herself? With him there?'

'He's not behaving badly, Patrick. Is he?'

'No. Oddly enough, no.' He looked thoughtfully at Jenny. 'I knew about Bob Maine,' he said. 'Of course I did. I've never been able to make out why I didn't like it. Not for conventional reasons. If you say Œdipus Complex I shall be furious.'

'I won't say it then.'

'The thing is, I suppose, one doesn't like one's mama being a *femme fatale*. And she is, a bit, you know. I'm so sorry for her,' he said violently, 'that it makes me angry. Why should that be? I really don't understand it at all.'

'Do you know, I think it's impossible for us to take the idea of older people being in love. It's all wrong, I expect, and I daresay it's the arrogance of youth or something.'

'You may be right. Jenny, I do love you with all my heart. Could we get married, do you think?'

'I don't see anything against it,' said Jenny.

After a longish interval, Jenny said: 'Miss Emily's taking her time, isn't she? Shall we walk up to the cottage and say goodbye to that remarkable man?'

'Well – if you like.'

'Come on.'

They strolled along the seafront, holding hands. A boy was sitting on the edge of the terrace, idly throwing pebbles into the channel.

It was Wally.

As they came up he turned and, when he saw them, held out his hands.

'All gone,' he said.

Death at the Dolphin

For Edmund Cork in gratitude and with affection

Contents

Cast of Characters

A clerk
Peregrine Jay   *Playwright and Theatre Director*
Henry Jobbins   *Caretaker*
Mr Vassily Conducis
His Chauffeur
Mawson   *His manservant*
Jeremy Jones   *Designer*
Mr Greenslade   *Solicitor to Mr Conducis*
An Expert on Historic Costume
Winter Morris   *Manager, Dolphin Theatre*
Marcus Knight   *'Shakespeare' in Peregrine's play*
Destiny Meade   *'The Dark Lady' in Peregrine's play*
W. Hartly Grove   *'The Rival' in Peregrine's play*
Gertrude Bracey   *'Ann Hathaway' in Peregrine's play*
Emily Dunne   *'Joan Hart' in Peregrine's play*
Charles Random   *'Dr Hall' in Peregrine's play*
Trevor Vere   *'Hamnet' in Peregrine's play*
Mrs Blewitt   *Trevor's mother*
Hawkins   *A Security Officer*
A Police Sergeant
Divisional-Superintendent Gibson
PC Grantley
A Divisional Surgeon
Superintendent Roderick Alleyn CID
Inspector Fox CID
Detective Sergeant Thompson CID
Detective Sergeant Bailey CID
Mrs Guzman   *An American millionairess*

CHAPTER 1

Mr Conducis

'Dolphin?' the clerk repeated. 'Dolphin. Well, yerse. We hold the keys. Were you wanting to view?'

'If I might, I was,' Peregrine Jay mumbled, wondering why such conversations should always be conducted in the past tense. 'I mean,' he added boldly, 'I did and I still do. I want to view, if you please.'

The clerk made a little face that might have been a sneer or an occupational tic. He glanced at Peregrine, who supposed his appearance was not glossy enough to make him a likely prospect.

'It *is* for sale, I believe?' Peregrine said.

'Oh, it's for *sale*, all right.' The clerk agreed contemptuously. He re-examined some document that he had on his desk.

'May I view?'

'*Now*?'

'If it's possible.'

'Well – I don't know, really, if we've anybody free at the moment,' said the clerk and frowned at the rain streaming dirtily down the windows of his office.

Peregrine said, 'Look. The Dolphin is an old theatre. I am a man of the theatre. Here is my card. If you care to telephone my agents or the management of my current production at The Unicorn they will tell you that I am honest, sober and industrious, a bloody good director and playwright and possessed of whatever further attributes may move you to lend me the keys of The Dolphin for an hour. I would like,' he said, 'to view it.'

The clerk's face became inscrutable. 'Oh, quite,' he muttered and edged Peregrine's card across his desk, looking sideways at it as if it might scuttle. He retired within himself and seemed to arrive at a guarded conclusion.

'Yerse. Well, OK, Mr er. It's not usually done but we try to oblige.' He turned to a dirty-white board where keys hung like black tufts on a piece of disreputable ermine.

'Dolphin,' said the clerk, 'Aeo, yerse. Here we are.' He unhooked a bunch of keys and pushed them across the desk. 'You may find them a bit hard to turn,' he said. 'We don't keep *on* oiling the locks. There aren't all that many inquiries.' He made what seemed to be a kind of joke. 'It's quite a time since the blitz,' he said.

'Quarter of a century,' said Peregrine, taking the keys.

'That's right. What a spectacle! I was a kid. Know your way I suppose, Mr – er – Jay?'

'Thank you, yes.'

'Thank *you*, sir,' said the clerk suddenly plumping for deference, but establishing at the same time his utter disbelief in Peregrine as a client. 'Terrible weather. You *will* return the keys?'

'Indubitably,' said Peregrine, aping, he knew not why, Mr Robertson Hare.

He had got as far as the door when the clerk said: 'Oh, be-the-way, Mr – er – Jay. You *will* watch how you go. Underfoot. On stage particularly. There was considerable damage.'

'Thank you. I'll be careful.'

'The hole *was* covered over but that was some time ago. Like a well,' the clerk added, worrying his first finger. 'Something of the sort. Just watch it.'

'I will.'

'I – er – I don't answer for what you'll find,' the clerk said. 'Tramps get in, you know. They *will* do it. One died a year or so back.'

'Oh.'

'Not that it's likely to happen twice.'

'I hope not.'

'Well, *we* couldn't help it,' the clerk said crossly. 'I don't know how they effect an entrance, really. Broken window or something. You can't be expected to attend to everything.'

'No,' Peregrine agreed and let himself out.

Rain drove up Wharfingers Lane in a slanting wall. It shot off the pavement, pattering against doors and windows and hit Peregrine's umbrella so hard that he thought it would split. He lowered it in front of him and below its scalloped and beaded margin saw, as if at rise of curtain in a cinema, the Thames, rain-pocked and choppy on its ebb-tide.

There were not a great many people about. Vans passed him grinding uphill in low gear. The buildings were ambiguous: warehouses? Wharfingers offices? Farther down he saw the blue lamp of a River Police Station. He passed a doorway with a neat legend: 'Port of London Authority' and another with old-fashioned lettering 'Camperdown and Carboys Rivercraft Company. Demurrage. Wharfage. Inquiries.'

The lane turned sharply to the left; it now ran parallel with the river. He lifted his umbrella. Up it went, like a curtain, on The Dolphin. At that moment, abruptly, there was no more rain.

There was even sunshine. It washed thinly across the stagehouse of The Dolphin and picked it out for Peregrine's avid attention. There it stood: high, square and unbecoming, the object of his greed and deep desire. Intervening buildings hid the rest of the theatre except for the wrought-iron ornament at the top of a tower. He hurried on until, on his left, he came to a pub called The Wharfinger's Friend and then the bomb site and then, fully displayed, the wounded Dolphin itself.

On a fine day, Peregrine thought, a hundred years ago, watermen and bargees, ship's chandlers, business gents, deep-water sailors from foreign parts and riverside riffraff looked up and saw The Dolphin. They saw its flag snapping and admired its caryatids touched up on the ringlets and nipples with tasteful gilt. Mr Adolphus Ruby, your very own Mr Ruby, stood here in Wharfingers Lane with his thumbs in his armholes, his cigar at one angle and his hat at the other and feasted his pop eyes on his very own palace of refined and original entertainment. 'Oh, Oh!' thought Peregrine, 'and here I stand but not, alas, in Mr Ruby's lacquered high-lows. And the caryatids have the emptiest look in their blank eyes for me.'

They were still there, though, two on each side of the portico. They finished at their waists, petering out with grimy discretion in pastry-cook's scrolls. They supported with their sooty heads and arms a lovely wrought-iron balcony and although there were occasional gaps in their plaster foliations they were still in pretty good trim. Peregrine's doting fancy cleaned the soot from upper surfaces. It restored, too, the elegant sign: supported above the portico by two prancing cetaceous mammals, and regilded its lettering: 'The Dolphin Theatre'.

For a minute or two he looked at it from the far side of the lane. The sun shone brightly now. River, shipping and wet roofs reflected it and the cobblestones in front of the theatre began to send up a thin vapour. A sweep of seagulls broke into atmospheric background noises and a barge honked.

Peregrine crossed the wet little street and entered the portico.

It was stuck over with old bills including the agents' notice which had evidently been there for a very long time and was torn and discoloured. 'This Valuable Commercial Site', it said.

'In that case,' Peregrine wondered, 'why hasn't it been sold? Why had no forward-looking commercial enterprise snapped up the Valuable Site and sent the Dolphin Theatre crashing about its own ears?'

There were other moribund bills. 'Sensational!' one of them proclaimed but the remainder was gone and it was anybody's guess what sensation it had once recommended. 'Go home – ' was chalked across one of the doors but somebody had rubbed out the rest of the legend and substituted graffiti of a more or less predictable kind. It was all very dismal.

But as Peregrine approached the doors he found, on the frontage itself high up and well protected, the tatter of a playbill. It was the kind of thing that patrons of the Players Theatre cherish and Kensington Art shops turn into lampshades.

THE BEGGAR GIRL'S WEDDING
In response to
Overwhelming Solicitation!! –
Mr Adolphus Ruby
Presents
A Return Performa –

The rest was gone.

When, Peregrine speculated, could this overwhelming solicitation have moved Mr Ruby? In the eighties? He knew that Mr Ruby had

lived to within ten years of the turn of the century and in his
heyday had bought, altered, restored and embellished The Dolphin,
adding his plaster and jute caryatids, his swags, his supporting
marine mammals and cornucopia, his touches of gilt and lolly-pink
to the older and more modest elegance of wrought iron and un-
molested surfaces. When did he make all these changes? Did he, upon
his decline, sell The Dolphin and, if so, to whom? It was reputed to
have been in use at the outbreak of the Second World War as a rag-
dealer's storehouse.

Who was the ground landlord now?

He confronted the main entrance and its great mortice lock for
which he had no trouble in selecting the appropriate key. It was big
enough to have hung at the girdle of one of Mr Ruby's very own
stage-gaolers. The key went home and engaged but refused to turn.
Why had Peregrine not asked the clerk to lend him an oil-can? He
struggled for some time and a voice at his back said:

'Got it all on yer own, mate, aincher?'

Peregrine turned to discover a man wearing a peaked cap like a
waterman's and a shiny blue suit. He was a middle-aged man with a
high colour, blue eyes and a look of cheeky equability.

'You want a touch of the old free-in-one,' he said. He had a gritty
hoarseness in his voice. Peregrine gaped at him. 'Oil, mate.
Loobrication,' the man explained.

'Oh. Yes, indeed, I know I do.'

'What's the story, anyway? Casing the joint?'

'I want to look at it,' Peregrine grunted. 'Ah, damn, I'd better try
the stage-door.'

'Let's take a butcher's.'

Peregrine stood back and the man stooped. He tried the key,
delicately at first and then with force. 'Not a hope,' he wheezed. ''Alf
a mo'.'

He walked away, crossed the street and disappeared between two
low buildings and down a narrow passageway that seemed to lead to
the river.

'Damnation!' Peregrine thought, 'he's taken the key!'

Two gigantic lorries with canvas-covered loads roared down
Wharfingers Lane and past the theatre. The great locked doors shook
and rattled and a flake of plaster fell on Peregrine's hand. 'It's dying

slowly,' he thought in a panic. 'The Dolphin is being shaken to death.'

When the second lorry had gone by there was the man again with a tin and a feather in one hand and the key in the other. He re-crossed the street and came through the portico.

'I'm very much obliged to you,' Peregrine said.

'No trouble, yer Royal 'Ighness,' said the man. He oiled the lock and after a little manipulation turned the key. 'Kiss yer 'and,' he said. Then he pulled back the knob. The tongue inside the lock shifted with a loud clunk. He pushed the door and it moved a little. 'Sweet as a nut,' said the man, and stepped away. 'Well, dooty calls as the bloke said on 'is way to the gallers.'

'Wait a bit – ' Peregrine said, 'you must have a drink on me. Here.' He pushed three half crowns into the man's hand.

'Never say no to that one, Mister. Fanks. Jolly good luck.'

Peregrine longed to open the door but thought the man, who was evidently a curious fellow, might attach himself. He wanted to be alone in The Dolphin.

'Your job's somewhere round about here?' he asked.

'Dahn Carboy Stairs. Phipps Bros. Drugs and that. Jobbins is the name. Caretaker, uster be a lighterman but it done no good to me chubes. Well, so long, sir. Hope you give yerself a treat among them spooks. Best of British luck.'

'Goodbye, and thank you.'

The door opened with a protracted groan and Peregrine entered The Dolphin.

II

The windows were unshuttered and though masked by dirt, let enough light into the foyer for him to see it quite distinctly. It was surprisingly big. Two flights of stairs with the prettiest wrought-iron balustrades curved up into darkness. At the back and deep in shadow, passages led off on either side giving entrance no doubt to boxes and orchestra stalls. The pit entrance must be from somewhere outside.

On Peregrine's right stood a very rococo box-office, introduced, he felt sure, by Mr Ruby. A brace of consequential plaster putti hovered upside down with fat-faced insouciance above the grille and must have looked in their prime as if they were counting the doorsales. A fibre-plaster bust of Shakespeare on a tortuous pedestal lurked in the shadows. The filthy walls were elegantly panelled and he thought must have originally been painted pink and gilded.

There was nothing between Peregrine and the topmost ceiling. The circle landing, again with a wrought-iron balustrade, reached less than half-way across the well. He stared up into darkness and fancied he could distinguish a chandelier. The stench was frightful: rats, rot, general dirt and, he thought, an unspeakable aftermath of the hobos that the clerk had talked about. But how lovely it must have been in its early Victorian elegance and even with Mr Ruby's preposterous additions. And how surprisingly undamaged it seemed to be.

He turned to the right-hand flight of stairs and found two notices. 'Dress Circle' and 'To the Paris Bar'. The signwriter had added pointing hands with frills round their wrists. Upstairs first, or into the stalls? Up.

He passed by grimed and flaking panels, noticing the graceful airiness of plaster ornament that separated them. He trailed a finger on the iron balustrade but withdrew it quickly at the thick touch of occulted dust. Here was the circle foyer. The double flight of stairs actually came out on either side of a balcony landing that projected beyond the main landing and formed the roof of a portico over the lower foyer. Flights of three shallow steps led up from three sides of this 'half-landing' to the top level. The entire structure was supported by very elegant iron pillars.

It was much darker up there and he could only just make out the Paris Bar. The shelves were visible but the counter had gone. A nice piece of mahogany it may have been – something to sell or steal. Carpet lay underfoot in moth-eaten tatters and the remains of curtains hung before the windows. These must be unbroken because the sound of the world outside was so very faint. Boarded up, perhaps. It was extraordinary how quiet it was, how stale, how stifling, how dead.

'*Not a mouse stirring*' he thought and at that moment heard a rapid patter. Something scuttled across his foot. Peregrine was astonished to find himself jolted by a violent shudder. He stamped with both feet and was at once half-stifled by the frightful cloud of dust he raised.

He approached the Paris Bar. A man without a face came out of the shadows and moved towards him.

'Euh!' Peregrine said in his throat. He stopped and so did the man. He could not have told how many heart thuds passed before he saw it was himself.

The bar was backed by a sheet of looking-glass.

Peregrine had recently given up smoking. If he had now had access to a cigarette he would have devoured it. Instead, he whistled and the sound in that muffled place was so lacking in resonance, so dull, that he fell silent and crossed the foyer to the nearest door into the auditorium. There were two, one on each side of the sunken half-landing. He passed into the circle.

The first impression was dramatic. He had forgotten about the bomb damage. A long shaft of sunlight from a gap in the roof of the stage-house took him by surprise. It produced the effect of a wartime blitz drawing in charcoal and, like a spotlight, found its mark on the empty stage. There, in a pool of mild sunlight, stood a broken chair still waiting, Peregrine thought, for one of Mr Ruby's very own actors. Behind the chair lay a black patch that looked as if a paint pot had been upset on the stage. It took Peregrine a moment or two to realize that this must be the hole the clerk had talked about. It was difficult to see it distinctly through the shaft of light.

Against this one note of brilliance the rest of the house looked black. It was in the classic horseshoe form and must have seated, Peregrine thought, about five hundred. He saw that the chairs had little iron trimmings above their plushy backs and that there were four boxes. A loop of fringe dangled from the top of the proscenium and this was all that could be seen of the curtain.

Peregrine moved round the circle and entered the O.P. box, which stank. He backed out of it, opened a door in the circle wall and found an iron stair leading to the stage.

He climbed down. Even these iron steps were muffled with dust but they gave out a half-choked clang as if he were soft-pedalling them.

Now, he was onstage, as a man of the theatre should be, and at once he felt much easier; exhilarated even, as if some kind of authority had passed to him by right of entry. He peered through the shaft of sunshine which he saw was dense with motes that floated,

danced and veered in response to his own movement. He walked
into it, stood by the broken chair and faced the auditorium. Quite
dazzled and bemused by the strange tricks of light he saw the front
of the house as something insubstantial and could easily people it
with Mr Ruby's patrons. Beavers, bonnets, ulsters, shawls. A flutter
of programmes. Rows of pale discs that were faces. 'O, wonderful!'
Peregrine thought and in order to embrace it all took a pace backwards.

III

To fall without warning, even by the height of a single step, is disturbing. To fall as he did now, by his height and the length of his
arms into cold, stinking water, is monstrous, nightmarish, like a
small death. For a moment he only knew that he had been physically insulted. He stared into the shaft of light with its madly jerking
molecules, felt wood slip under his gloved fingers and tightened his
grip. At the same time he was disgustingly invaded, saturated up to
the collarbone in icy stagnant water. He hung at arm's length.

'O God!' Peregrine thought, 'why aren't I a bloody Bond? Why
can't I make my bloody arms hitch me up? O God, don't let me
drown in this unspeakable muck. O God, let me keep my head.'

Well, of course, he thought, his hands and arms didn't have to
support his entire weight. Eleven stone. He was buoyed up by whatever he had fallen into. What? A dressing-room turned into a well
for surface water? Better not speculate. Better explore. He moved his
legs and dreadful ambiguous waves lapped up to his chin. He could
find nothing firm with his feet. He thought: How long can I hang on
like this? And a line of words floated in: 'How long will a man lie i'
the earth ere he rot?'

What *should* he do? Perhaps a frog-like upward thing? Try it and
at least gain a better finger hold? He tried it: he kicked at the water,
pulled and clawed at the stage. For a moment he thought he had
gained but his palms slid back, scraping on the edge and sucking at
his soaked gloves. He was again suspended. The clerk? If he could
hang on, would the clerk send someone to find out why he hadn't
returned the keys? When? *When?* Why in God's name had he shaken

off the man with the oil can from Phipps Bros? Jobbins. Suppose he
were to yell? Was there indeed a broken window where tramps
crept in? He took a deep breath and being thus inflated, rose a little
in the water. He yelled.

'Hallo! Hallo! Jobbins!'

His voice was silly and uncannily stifled. Deflated, he sank to his
former disgusting level.

He had disturbed more than water when he tried his leap. An
anonymous soft object bobbed against his chin. The stench was outrageous. I can't, he thought, I can't stay like this. Already his fingers
had grown cold and his arms were racked. Presently – soon – he
would no longer feel the edge, he would only feel pain and his fingers would slip away. And what then? Float on his back in this
unspeakable water and gradually freeze? He concentrated on his
hands, tipping his head back to look up the length of his stretched
arms at them. The details of his predicament now declared themselves: the pull on his pectoral muscles, on his biceps and forearms
and the terrible strain on his gloved fingers. The creeping obscenity
of the water. He hung on for some incalculable age and realized that
he was coming to a crisis when his body would no longer be control-
lable. Something must be done. Now. Another attempt? If there
were anything solid to push against. Suppose, after all, his feet were
only a few inches from the bottom? But what bottom? The floor of
a dressing-room? An understage passage? A boxed-in trap? He
stretched his feet and touched nothing. The water rose to his mouth.
He flexed his legs, kicked, hauled on the edge and bobbed upwards.
The auditorium appeared. If he could get his elbows on the edge. No.

But at the moment when the confusion of circle and stalls shot up
before his eyes, he had heard a sound that he recognized, a protracted
groan, and at the penultimate second, he had seen – what? A splinter
of light? And heard? Somebody cough.

'Hi!' Peregrine shouted. 'Here! Quick! Help!'

He sank and hung again by his fingers. But someone was coming
through the house. Muffled steps on the rags of carpet.

'Here! Come here, will you? On stage.'

The steps halted.

'Look here! I say! Look, for God's sake come up. I've fallen through
the stage. I'll drown. Why don't you answer, whoever you are?'

The footsteps started again. A door opened nearby. Pass-door in the prompt side box, he thought. Steps up. Now: crossing the stage. Now.

'Who are you?' Peregrine said. 'Look out. Look out for the hole. *Look out for my hands. I've got gloves on. Don't tread on my hands.* Help me out of this. But look out. And say something.'

He flung his head back and stared into the shaft of light. Hands covered his hands and then closed about his wrists. At the same time heavy shoulders and a head wearing a hat came as a black silhouette between him and the light. He stared into a face he could not distinguish.

'It doesn't need much,' he chattered. 'If you could just give me a heave I can do it.'

The head was withdrawn. The hands changed their grip. At last the man spoke.

'Very well,' said a voice. 'Now.'

He gave his last frog leap, was heaved up, was sprawled across the edge and had crawled back on the stage to the feet of the man. He saw beautiful shoes, sharp trouser ends and the edge of a fine overcoat. He was shivering from head to foot.

'Thank you,' he said. 'I couldn't be more grateful. My God, how I stink.'

He got to his feet.

The man was, he thought, about sixty years old. Peregrine could see his face now. It was extremely pale. He wore a bowler hat and was impeccably dressed.

'You are Mr Peregrine Jay, I think,' said the man. His voice was toneless, educated and negative.

'Yes – I – I?'

'The people at the estate agents told me. You should have a bath and change. My car is outside.'

'I can't get into anyone's car in this state. I'm very sorry, sir,' Peregrine said. His teeth were going like castanets. 'You're awfully kind but – '

'Wait a moment. Or no. Come to the front of the theatre.'

In answer to a gesture, Peregrine walked through the pass-door down into the house and was followed. Stagnant water squelched and spurted in his shoes. They went through a box and along a passage and came into the foyer. 'Please stay here. I shall only be a moment,' said his rescuer.

He went into the portico leaving the door open. Out in Wharfingers Lane Peregrine saw a Daimler with a chauffeur. He began to jump and thrash his arms. Water splashed out of him and clouds of dust settled upon his drenched clothes. The man returned with the chauffeur who carried a fur rug and a heavy mackintosh.

'I suggest you strip and put this on and wrap the rug round you,' the man said. He stretched out his arms as if he were actually thinking of laying hands on Peregrine. He seemed to be suspended between attraction and repulsion. He looked, it struck Peregrine, as if he were making some kind of appeal. 'Let me – ' he said.

'But, sir, you can't. I'm disgusting.'

'Please.'

'No, no – really.'

The man walked away. His hands were clasped behind him. Peregrine saw, with a kind of fuddled astonishment, that they were trembling. 'My God!' Peregrine thought, 'this is a morning and a half. I'd better get out of this one pretty smartly but how the hell – '

'Let me give you a hand, sir,' said the chauffeur to Peregrine. 'You're that cold, aren't you?'

'I can manage. If only I could wash.'

'Never mind, sir. That's the idea. Leave them there, sir. I'll attend to them. Better keep your shoes on, hadn't you? The coat'll be a bit of help and the rug's warm. Ready, sir?'

'If I could just have a taxi, I wouldn't be such an infernal nuisance.'

His rescuer turned and looked, not fully at him but at his shoulder. 'I beg you to come,' he said.

Greatly worried by the extravagance of the phrase Peregrine said no more.

The chauffeur went ahead quickly and opened the doors of the car. Peregrine saw that newspaper had been spread over the floor and back seat.

'Please go,' his rescuer said, 'I'll follow.'

Peregrine shambled across the portico and jumped in at the back. The lining of the mackintosh stuck to his body. He hitched the rug around him and tried to clench his chattering jaw.

A boy's voice in the street called, 'Hey, look! Look at that bloke!'
The caretaker from Phipps Bros had appeared at the top of his alley
and stared into the car. One or two people stopped and pointed him
out to each other.

As his master crossed the portico the chauffeur locked the theatre
doors. Holding Peregrine's unspeakable clothes at arm's length he
put them in the boot of the car and got into the driver's seat. In
another moment they were moving up Wharfingers Lane.

His rescuer did not turn his head or speak. Peregrine waited for a
moment or two and then, controlling his voice with some success, said:

'I'm giving you far too much trouble.'

'No.'

'If – if you would be so very kind as to drop me at The Unicorn
Theatre I think I could – '

Still without turning his head the man said with extreme formal-
ity, 'I really do beg that you will allow me to – ' he stopped for an
unaccountably long time and then said loudly, '– to rescue you. I
mean to take you to my house and set you right. I shall be most
upset otherwise. Dreadfully upset.'

Now he turned and Peregrine had never seen an odder look in
anyone's face. It was an expression almost, he thought, of despair.

'I am responsible,' said his extraordinary host. 'Unless you allow
me to make amends I shall – I shall feel – very guilty.'

'*Responsible?* But – '

'It will not take very long I hope. Drury Place.'

'Oh lord!' Peregrine thought, 'what poshery.' He wondered, suddenly, if perhaps the all too obvious explanation was the wrong
one and if his rescuer was a slightly demented gentleman and the
chauffeur his keeper.

'I really don't see, sir – ' he began but an inaudible conversation
was taking place in the front seat.

'Certainly, sir,' said the chauffeur and drew up outside the estate
agents. He pulled the keys out of his pocket as he entered. The clerk's
face appeared looking anxiously and crossly over the painted lower
pane of his window. He disappeared and in a moment came running
out and round to the passenger's side.

'Well, sir,' he obsequiously gabbled, 'I'm sure I'm very sorry this
has occurred. Very regrettable, I'm sure. But as I was saying to your

driver, sir, I did warn the viewer.' He had not yet looked at Peregrine but he did so now, resentfully. 'I warned you,' he said.

'Yes, yes,' Peregrine said. 'You did.'

'Yes, well, thank you. But I'm sure – '

'That will do. There has been gross negligence. Good morning.' The voice was so changed, so brutally icy that Peregrine stared and the clerk drew back as if he'd been stung. They moved off.

The car's heating system built up. By the time they had crossed the river Peregrine was a little less cold and beginning to feel drowsy. His host offered no further remarks. Once when Peregrine happened to look at the rear-vision glass on the passenger's side he found he was being observed, apparently with extreme distaste. Or no. Almost with fear. He looked away quickly but out of the tail of his eye saw a gloved hand change the angle of the glass.

'Oh well,' he thought bemusedly, 'I'm bigger and younger than he is. I suppose I can look after myself but how tricky it all is. Take away a man's clothes, after all, and you make a monkey of him. What sort of public image will I present, fleeing down Park Lane in a gent's mack and a fur rug, both the property of my pursuer?'

They were in Park Lane now and soon turned off into a side street and thence into the cul-de-sac called Drury Place. The car pulled up. The chauffeur got out and rang the bell of No.7. As he returned to the car, the house door was opened by a manservant.

Peregrine's host said in a comparatively cheerful voice: 'Not far to go. Up the steps and straight in.'

The chauffeur opened the door. 'Now, sir,' he said, 'shan't be long, shall we?'

There really was nothing else for it. Three impeccable men, an errand boy and a tightly encased lady carrying a little dog, walked down the footpath.

Peregrine got out and instead of bolting into the house, made an entrance of it. He ascended the steps with deliberation leaving a trail of filthy footprints behind him and dragging his fur rug like a ceremonial train. The manservant stood aside.

'Thank you,' Peregrine said grandly. 'I have fallen, as you see, into dirty water.'

'Quite so, sir.'

'Up to my neck.'

'Very unfortunate, sir.'

'For all concerned,' said Peregrine.

His host had arrived.

'First of all, of course, a bath,' he was saying, 'and something to defeat that shivering, Mawson?'

'Certainly, sir.'

'And then come and see me.'

'Very good, sir.'

The man went upstairs. Peregrine's host was now behaving in so normal a manner that he began to wonder if he himself had perhaps been bemused by his hideous experience. There was some talk of the efficacy of Epsom salts in a hot bath and of coffee laced with rum. Peregrine listened in a trance.

'Do forgive me for bossing you about like this. You must be feeling ghastly and really, I *do* blame myself.'

'By *why*?'

'Yes, Mawson?'

'If the gentleman will walk up, sir.'

'Quite so. Quite so. Good.'

Peregrine walked up and was shown into a steaming and aromatic bathroom.

'I thought pine, sir, would be appropriate,' said Mawson. 'I hope the temperature is as you like it. May I suggest a long, hot soak, sir?'

'You may indeed,' said Peregrine warmly.

'Perhaps I may take your rug and coat. And shoes,' said Mawson with an involuntary change of voice. 'You will find a bath wrap on the rail and a hot rum and lemon within easy reach. If you would be good enough to ring, sir, when you are ready.'

'Ready for what?'

'To dress, sir.'

It seemed a waste of time to say: 'In what?' so Peregrine merely said 'Thank you' and Mawson said 'Thank you' and withdrew.

It was rapture beyond compare in the bath. Essence of pine. A lovely longhandled brush. Pine-smelling soap. And the hot rum and lemon. He left off shivering, soaped himself all over, including his head, scrubbed himself scarlet, submerged completely, rose, drank and tried to take a responsible view of the situation. In this he failed. Too much had occurred. He realized after a time that he was becoming light-headed and without at all fancying the idea took a hard-hitting cold shower. This restored him. Rough-dried and wrapped in a towelling bathrobe he rang the bell. He felt wonderful.

Mawson came and Peregrine said he would like to telephone for some clothes though when he thought about it he didn't quite know where he would ring. Jeremy Jones with whom he shared a flat would certainly be out and it wasn't the morning for their charlady. The Unicorn Theatre? *Somebody* would be there, of course, but who?

Mawson showed him to a bedroom where there was a telephone.

There were also clothes laid out on the bed. 'I think they are approximately your size, sir. It is hoped that you will have no objection to making use of them in the meantime,' said Mawson.

'Yes, but look here – '

'It will be much appreciated if you make use of them. Will there be anything else, sir?'

'I – honestly – I – '

'Mr Conducis sends his compliments, sir, and hopes you will join him in the library.'

Peregrine's jaw dropped.

'Thank you, sir,' said Mawson neatly and withdrew.

Conducis? *Conducis!* It was as if Mawson had said 'Mr Onassis'. Could this possibly be Mr Vassily Conducis? The more Peregrine thought about it the more he decided that it could. But what in the wide world would Mr Vassily Conducis be up to in a derelict theatre on the South Bank at half past ten in the morning when he ought to have been abominably lolling on his yacht in the Aegean? And what was *he*, Peregrine, up to in Mr Conducis's house which (it now dawned upon him) was on a scale of insolently quiet grandeur such as he had never expected to encounter outside the sort of book which, in any case, he never read.

Peregrine looked round the room and felt he ought to curl his lip at it. After all he *did* read his *New Statesman*. He then looked at the clothes on the bed and found them to be on an equal footing with what, being a man of the theatre, he thought of as the décor. Absently, he picked up a gayish tie that was laid out beside a heavy silk shirt. 'Charvet' said the label. Where had he read of Charvet?

'I don't want any part of this,' he thought. He sat on the bed and dialled several numbers without success. The theatre didn't answer.

He put on the clothes and saw that though they were conservative in style he looked startlingly presentable in them. Even the shoes fitted.

He rehearsed a short speech and went downstairs where he found Mawson waiting for him.

He said: 'Did you say: Mr Conducis?'

'Yes, sir, Mr Vassily Conducis. Will you step this way, sir?'

Mr Conducis stood in front of his library fire and Peregrine wondered how on earth he had failed to recognize a face that had been so widely publicized with, it was reported, such determined opposition from its owner. Mr Conducis had an olive, indeed a swarthy complexion and unexpectedly pale eyes. These were merely facial adjuncts and might, Peregrine afterwards thought, have been mass produced for all the speculation they inspired. The mouth, however, was disturbing, being, or so Peregrine thought, both ruthless and vulnerable. The chin was heavy. Mr Conducis had curly black hair going predictably grey at the temples. He looked, by and large, enormously expensive.

'Come in,' he said. 'Yes. Come in.' His voice was a light tenor. Was there a faintly foreign inflection? A slight lisp, perhaps.

As Peregrine approached, Mr Conducis looked fixedly at his guest's hands.

'You are well?' he asked. 'Recovered?'

'Yes, indeed. I can't thank you enough, sir. As for – well, as for lending me these things – I really do feel – !'

'Do they fit?'

'Yes. Very well.'

'That is all that is necessary.'

'Except that after all they *are* yours,' Peregrine said and tried a light laugh in order not to sound pompous.

'I have told you. I am responsible. You might – ' Mr Conducis's voice faded but his lips soundlessly completed the sentence: ' – have been drowned.'

'But honestly, sir!' Peregrine launched himself on his little speech. 'You've saved my life, you know. I would have just hung on by my fingers until they gave out and then – and then – well, finally and disgustingly drowned as you say.'

Almost soundlessly Mr Conducis said: 'I should have blamed myself.'

'But why on earth! For a hole in The Dolphin stage?'

'It is my property.'

'Oh,' Peregrine ejaculated before he could stop himself, 'how splendid!'

'Why do you say that?'

'I mean: how splendid to own it. It's such an adorable little playhouse.'

Mr Conducis looked at him without expression. 'Indeed?' he said. 'Splendid? Adorable? You make a study of theatres, perhaps?'

'Not really. I mean I'm not an expert. Good lord, no! But I earn my living in theatres and I am enormously attracted by old ones.'

'Yes. Will you join me in a drink?' Mr Conducis said in his wooden manner. 'I am sure you will.' He moved to a tray on a sidetable.

'Your man has already given me a very strong and wonderfully restoring hot rum and lemon.'

'I am sure that you will have another. The ingredients are here.'

'A very small one, please,' Peregrine said. There was a singing sensation in his veins and a slight thrumming in his ears but he still felt wonderful. Mr Conducis busied himself at the tray. He returned with a steaming and aromatic tumbler for Peregrine and something that he had poured out of a jug for himself. Could it be barley water?

'Shall we sit down,' he suggested. When they had done so he gave Peregrine a hurried, blank glance and said: 'You wonder why I was at the theatre, perhaps. There is some question of demolishing it and building on the site. An idea that I have been turning over for some time. I wanted to refresh my memory. The agents told my man you were there.' He put two fingers in a waistcoat pocket and Peregrine saw his own card had been withdrawn. It looked incredibly grubby.

'You – you're going to pull it down?' he said and heard a horribly false jauntiness in his own unsteady voice. He took a pull at his rum. It was extremely strong.

'You dislike the proposal,' Mr Conducis observed, making it a statement rather than a question. 'Have you any reason other than a general interest in such buildings?'

If Peregrine had been absolutely sober and dressed in his own clothes it is probable that he would have mumbled something ineffectual and somehow or another made an exit from Mr Conducis's house and from all further congress with its owner. He was a little removed however from his surroundings and the garments in which he found himself.

He began to talk excitedly. He talked about The Dolphin and about how it must have looked after Mr Adolphus Ruby had gloriously tarted it up. He described how, before he fell into the well, he had imagined the house: clean, sparkling with lights from chandeliers, full, warm, buzzing and expectant. He said that it was the last of its kind and so well designed with such a surprisingly large stage that it would be possible to mount big productions there.

He forgot about Mr Conducis and also about not drinking any more rum. He talked widely and distractedly.

'Think what a thing it would be,' Peregrine cried, 'to do a season of Shakespeare's comedies! Imagine *Love's Labour's* there. Perhaps one could have a barge – Yes. *The Grey Dolphin* – and people could take water to go to the play. When the play was about to begin we would run up a flag with a terribly intelligent dolphin on it. And we'd do them quickly and lightly and with elegance and O!' cried Peregrine, 'and with that little catch in the breath that never, *never* comes in the same way with any other playwright.'

He was now walking about Mr Conducis's library. He saw, without seeing, the tooled spines of collected editions and a picture that he would remember afterwards with astonishment. He waved his arms. He shouted.

'There never was such a plan,' shouted Peregrine. 'Never in all London since Burbage moved the first theatre from Shoreditch to Southwark.' He found himself near his drink and tossed it off. 'And not too fancy,' he said, 'mind you. Not twee. God, no! Not a pastiche either. Just a good theatre doing the job it was meant to do. And doing the stuff that doesn't belong to any bloody Method or Movement or Trend or Period or what-have-you. Mind that.'

'You refer to Shakespeare again?' said Mr Conducis's voice. 'If I follow you.'

'Of course I do!' Peregrine suddenly became fully aware of Mr Conducis. 'Oh dear!' he said.

'Is something the matter?'

'I'm afraid I'm a bit tight, sir. Not *really* tight but a bit uninhibited. I'm awfully sorry. I think perhaps I'd better take myself off and I'll return all these things you've so kindly lent me. I'll return them as soon as possible, of course. So, if you'll forgive me – '

'What do you do in the theatre?'

'I direct plays and I've written two.'

'I know nothing of the theatre,' Mr Conducis said heavily. 'You are reasonably successful?'

'Well, sir, yes. I think so. It's a jungle, of course. I'm not at all affluent but I make out. I've had as much work as I could cope with over the last three months and I think my mana's going up. I hope so. Goodbye, sir.'

He held out his hand. Mr Conducis, with an expression that really might have been described as one of horror, backed away from it.

'Before you go,' he said, 'I have something that may be of interest to you. You can spare a moment?'

'Of course.'

'It is in this room,' Mr Conducis muttered and went to a bureau that must, Peregrine thought, be of fabulous distinction. He followed his host and watched him pull out a silky, exquisitely inlaid, drawer.

'How lovely that is,' he said.

'Lovely?' Mr Conducis echoed as he had echoed before. 'You mean the bureau? Yes? It was found for me. I understand nothing of such matters. That is not what I wished to show you. Will you look at this? Shall we move to a table?'

He had taken from the drawer a very small wooden Victorian hand-desk, extremely shabby, much stained, and Peregrine thought, of no particular distinction. A child's possession perhaps. He laid it on a table under a window and motioned to a chair beside it. Peregrine now felt as if he was playing a part in somebody else's dream. 'But I'm all right,' he thought. 'I'm not really drunk. I'm in that pitiable but enviable condition when all things seem to work together for good.'

He sat before the table and Mr Conducis, standing well away from him, opened the little desk, pressed inside with his white, flat thumb and revealed a false bottom. It was a commonplace device and Peregrine wondered if he was meant to exclaim at it. He saw that in the exposed cavity there was a packet no bigger than a half-herring and much the same shape. It was wrapped in discoloured yellow-brown silk and tied with a morsel of tarnished ribbon. Mr Conducis had a paper knife in his hand. 'Everything he possesses,' Peregrine thought, 'is on museum-piece level. It's stifling.' His host used the paper knife as a sort of server, lifting the little silk packet out on its blade and, as it were, helping Peregrine to it like a waiter.

It slid from the blade and with it, falling to one side, a discoloured card upon which it had lain. Peregrine, whose vision had turned swimmy, saw that this card was a menu and bore a date some six years past. The heading: 'The Steam Yacht Kalliope. Off Villefranche. Gala Dinner' floated tipsily into view with a flamboyant and illegible signature that was sprawled across it above a dozen others. A short white hand swiftly covered and then removed the card.

'That is nothing,' Mr Conducis said. 'It is of no consequence.' He went to the fire. A bluish flame sprang up and turned red. Mr Conducis returned.

'It is the packet that may be of interest. Will you open it?' he said.

Peregrine pulled gingerly at the ribbon ends and turned back the silk wrapping.

He had exposed a glove.

A child's glove. Stained as if by water it was the colour of old parchment and finely wrinkled like an old, old face. It had been elegantly embroidered with tiny roses in gold and scarlet. A gold tassel, now blackened and partly unravelled, was attached to the tapered gauntlet. It was the most heartrending object Peregrine had ever seen.

Underneath it lay two pieces of folded paper, very much discoloured.

'Will you read the papers?' Mr Conducis invited. He had returned to the fireplace.

Peregrine felt an extraordinary delicacy in touching the glove. 'Cheverel,' he thought. 'It's a cheverel glove. Has it gone brittle with age?' No. To his fingertip it was flaccid: uncannily so as if it had only just died. He slipped the papers out from beneath it. They had split along the folds and were foxed and faded. He opened the larger with great care and it lay broken before him. He pulled himself together and managed to read it.

This little glove and accompanying note were given to my Great-Great-Grandmother by her Beft Friend: a Mifs Or Mrs J. Hart. My dear Grandmother always infifted that it had belonged to the poet. N. B. mark infide gauntlet.

M. E. 23 April 1830

The accompanying note was no more than a slip of paper. The writing on it was much faded and so extraordinarily crabbed and tortuous that he thought at first it must be hieroglyphic and that he therefore would never make it out. Then it seemed to him that there was something almost familiar about it. And then, gradually, words began to emerge. Everything was quiet. He heard the fire settle. Someone crossed the room above the library. He heard his own heart thud.

He read:

Mayde by my father for my sonne on his XI birthedy and never worne butte ync

Peregrine sat in a kind of trance and looked at the little glove and the documents. Mr Conducis had left the paper knife on the table. Peregrine slid the ivory tip into the gauntlet and very slowly lifted and turned it. There was the mark, in the same crabbed hand. 'H.S.'

' – But where – ' Peregrine heard his own voice saying, ' – where did it come from? Whose is it?'

'It is mine,' Mr Conducis said and his voice seemed to come from a great distance. 'Naturally.'

'But – where did you find it?'

A long silence.

'At sea.'

'At sea?'

'During a voyage six years ago. I bought it.'

Peregrine looked at his host. How pale Mr Conducis was and how odd was his manner!

He said: 'The box – it is some kind of portable writing desk – was a family possession. The former owner did not discover the false bottom until – ' He stopped.

'Until – ?' Peregrine said.

'Until shortly before he died.'

Peregrine said: 'Has it been shown to an authority?'

'No. I should, no doubt, get an opinion from some museum or perhaps from Sotheby's.'

His manner was so completely negative, so toneless that Peregrine wondered if by any extraordinary chance he did not understand the full implication. He was wondering how, without offence, he could find out when Mr Conducis continued.

'I have not looked it all up but I understand the age of the boy at the time of his death is consistent with the evidence and that the grandfather was in fact a glover.'

'Yes.'

'And the initials inside the gauntlet do in fact correspond with the child's initials.'

'Yes. Hamnet Shakespeare.'

'Quite so,' said Mr Conducis.

CHAPTER 2

Mr Greenslade

'I know that,' Peregrine said. 'You don't need to keep on at it, Jer. I know there's always been a Bardic racket and that since the quarto-centenary it's probably been stepped up. I *know* about the tarting-up of old portraits with dome foreheads and the fake signatures and "stol'n and surreptitious copies" and phoney "discovered" documents and all that carry-on. I *know* the overwhelming odds are against this glove being anything but a fake. I merely ask you to accept that with the things lying there in front of me, I was knocked all of a heap.'

'Not only by them, I understand. You were half-drowned, half-drunk, dressed up in a millionaire's clobber and not knowing whether the owner was making a queer pass at you or not.'

'I'm almost certain, not.'

'His behaviour, on your own account, seems to have been, to say the least of it, strange.'

'Bloody strange but not, I have decided, queer.'

'Well, you're the judge,' said Jeremy Jones. He bent over his work-table and made a delicate slit down a piece of thin cardboard. He was building a set to scale for a theatre-club production of *Venice Preserved*. After a moment he laid aside his razor-blade, and looked up at Peregrine. 'Could you make a drawing of it?' he said.

'I can try.'

Peregrine tried. He remembered the glove very clearly indeed and produced a reasonable sketch.

'It *looks* OK,' Jeremy said. 'Late sixteenth century. Elaborate in the right way. Tabbed. Embroidered. Tapering to the wrist. And the leather?'

'Oh, fine as fine. Yellow and soft and wrinkled and old, old, old.'

'It may be an Elizabethan or Jacobean glove but the letter could be a forgery.'

'But why? Nobody's tried to cash in on it.'

'You don't know. You don't know anything. Who was this chum Conducis bought it from?'

'He didn't say.'

'And who was M.E. whose dear grandma insisted it had belonged to the poet?'

'Why ask me? You might remember that the great-*great*-grandmother was left it by a Mrs J. Hart. And that Joan Hart – '

'Née Shakespeare, was left wearing-apparel by her brother. Yes. The sort of corroborative details any good faker would cock up. But, of course, the whole thing should be tackled by experts.'

'I told you: I said so. I said: wouldn't he take it to the V. and A. And he gave me one of his weird looks; furtive, scared, blank – I don't know how you'd describe them – and shut up like a clam.'

'Suspicious in itself!' Jeremy grinned at his friend and then said: '"*I would I had been there*".'

'Well, at that, "*it would have much amazed you*".'

'"*Very like. Very like*" What do we know about Conducis?'

'I can't remember with any accuracy,' Peregrine said. 'He's an all-time-high for money, isn't he? There was a piece in one of the Sunday supplements some time back. About how he loathes publicity and does a Garbo and leaves Mr Gulbenkian wondering what it was that passed him. And how he doesn't join in any of the joy and is thought to be a fabulous anonymous philanthropist. A Russian mum, I think it said, and an Anglo-Rumanian papa.'

'Where does he get his pelf?'

'I don't remember. Isn't it always oil? "Mystery Midas" it was headed and there was a photograph of him looking livid and trying to dodge the camera on the steps of his bank and a story about how the photographer made his kill. I read it at the dentist's.'

'Unmarried?'

'I think so.'

'How did you part company?'

'He just walked out of the room. Then his man came in and said the car was waiting to bring me home. He gave me back my revolting, stinking pocket book and said my clothes had gone to the cleaner and were thought to be beyond salvation. I said something about Mr Conducis and the man said Mr Conducis was taking a call from New York and would "quite understand". Upon which hint, off I slunk. I'd better write a sort of bread-and-butter, hadn't I?'

'I expect so. And he owns The Dolphin and is going to pull it down and put up, one supposes, another waffle-iron on the South Bank?'

'He's "turning over the idea" in his mind.'

'May it choke him,' said Jeremy Jones.

'Jer,' Peregrine said. 'You *must* go and look at it. It'll slay you. Wrought iron. Cherubs. Caryatids. A wonderful sort of potpourri of early and mid-Vic and designed by an angel. O God, God when I think of what could be done with it.'

'And this ghastly old Croesus – '

'I know. I know.'

And they stared at each other with the companionable indignation and despair of two young men whose unfulfilled enthusiasms coincide.

They had been at the same drama school together and had both decided that they were inclined by temperament, interest and ability to production rather than performance in the theatre. Jeremy finally settled for design and Peregrine for direction. They had worked together and apart in weekly and fortnightly repertory and had progressed to more distinguished provincial theatres and thence, precariously, to London. Each was now tolerably well-known as a coming man and both were occasionally subjected to nerve-racking *longueurs* of unemployment. At the present juncture Peregrine had just brought to an auspicious opening the current production at The Unicorn and had seen his own first play through a trial run out of London. Jeremy was contemplating a décor for a masque which he would submit to an international competition for theatrical design.

He had recently bought a partnership in a small shop in Walton Street where they sold what he described as: 'Very superior tatt. Jacobean purses, stomachers and the odd cod-piece.' He was a fanatic on authenticity and had begun to acquire a reputation as an expert.

Jeremy and Peregrine had spent most of what they had saved on leasing and furnishing their studio flat and had got closer than was comfortable to a financial crisis. Jeremy had recently become separated from a blonde lady of uncertain temper: a disentanglement that was rather a relief to Peregrine who had been obliged to adjust to her unpredictable descents upon their flat.

Peregrine himself had brought to uneventful dissolution an affair with an actress who had luckily discovered in herself the same degree of boredom that he, for his part, had hesitated to disclose. They had broken up with the minimum of ill-feeling on either part and he was, at the moment, heartfree and glad of it.

Peregrine was dark, tall and rather mischievous in appearance. Jeremy was of medium stature, reddish in complexion and fairly truculent. Behind a prim demeanour he concealed an amorous inclination. They were of the same age: twenty-seven. Their flat occupied the top storey of a converted warehouse on Thames-side east of Blackfriars. It was from their studio window about a week ago, that Peregrine, idly exploring the South Bank through a pair of fieldglasses, had spotted the stage-house of The Dolphin, recognized it for what it was and hunted it down. He now walked over to the window.

'I can just see it,' he said. 'There it is. I spent the most hideous half-hour of my life, so far, inside that theatre. I ought to hate the sight of it but, by God, I yearn after it as I've never yearned after anything ever before. You know if Conducis does pull it down I honestly don't believe I'll be able to stay here and see it happen.'

'Shall we wait upon him and crash down on our knees before him crying, "Oh, sir, please sir, spare The Dolphin, pray do, sir".'

'I can tell you exactly what the reaction would be. He'd back away as if we smelt and say in that deadpan voice of his that he knew nothing of such matters.'

'I wonder what it would cost.'

'To restore it? Hundreds of thousands no doubt,' Peregrine said gloomily. 'I wonder if National Theatre has so much as thought of it. Or *somebody*. Isn't there a society that preserves Ancient Monuments?'

'Yes. But "I know nothing of such matters",' mocked Jeremy. He turned back to his model. With a degree of regret to which wild horses wouldn't have persuaded him to confess, Peregrine began packing Mr Conducis's suit. It was a dark charcoal tweed and had been made by a princely tailor. He had washed and ironed the socks, undergarments and

shirt that he had worn for about forty minutes and had taken a box that
Jeremy was hoarding to make up the parcel.

'I'll get a messenger to deliver it,' he said.

'Why on earth?'

'I don't know. Too bloody shy to go myself.'

'You'd only have to hand it over to the gilded lackey.'

'I'd feel an ass.'

'You're mad,' said Jeremy briefly.

'I don't want to go back there. It was all so rum. Rather wonderful, of course, but in a way rather sinister. Like some wish-fulfilment
novel.'

'The wide-eyed young dramatist and the kindly recluse.'

'I don't think Conducis is kindly but I will allow and must admit
I was wide-eyed over the glove. You know what?'

'What?'

'It's given me an idea.'

'Has it, now? Idea for what?'

'A play. I don't want to discuss it.'

'One must never discuss too soon, of course,' Jeremy agreed.
'That way abortion lies.'

'You have your points.'

In the silence that followed they both heard the metallic clap of
the letter box downstairs.

'Post,' said Jeremy.

'Won't be anything for us.'

'Bills.'

'I don't count them. I daren't,' said Peregrine.

'There might be a letter from Mr Conducis offering to adopt you.'

'Heh, heh, heh.'

'Do go and see,' Jeremy said. 'I find you rather oppressive when
you're clucky. The run downstairs will do you good.'

Peregrine wandered twice round the room and absently out at
the door. He went slowly down their decrepit staircase and fished in
their letter box. There were three bills (two, he saw, for himself), a
circular and a typed letter.

'Peregrine Jay, Esq. By Hand.'

For some reason that he could not have defined, he didn't open
the letter. He went out-of-doors and walked along their uneventful

street until he came to a gap through which one could look across
the river to Southwark. He remembered afterwards that his bitch-
muse as he liked to call her was winding her claws in his hair. He
stared unseeing at a warehouse that from here partly obscured The
Dolphin: Phipps Bros, perhaps, where the man with the oil-can –
Jobbins – worked. A wind off the river whipped his hair back.
Somewhere downstream a hooting set up. Why, he wondered idly,
do river-craft set up gaggles of hooting all at once? His right hand
was in his jacket pocket and his fingers played with the letter.

With an odd sensation of taking some prodigious step he suddenly pulled it out of his pocket and opened it.

Five minutes later Jeremy heard their front door slam and
Peregrine come plunging up the stairs. He arrived, white-faced and
apparently without the power of speech.

'What now, for pity's sake,' Jeremy asked. 'Has Conducis tried to
kidnap you?'

Peregrine thrust a sheet of letter paper into his hand.

'Go on,' he said. 'Bloody read it, will you. Go on.'

Dear Sir, *Jeremy read*. I am directed by Mr V. M. G. Conducis to
inform you that he has given some consideration to the matter of
The Dolphin Theatre, Wharfingers Lane, which he had occasion
to discuss with you this morning. Mr Conducis would be interested to have the matter examined in greater detail. He suggests,
therefore, that to this end you call at the office of Consolidated
Oils, Pty Ltd, and speak to Mr S. Greenslade who has been fully
informed of the subject in question. I enclose for your conven-
ience a card with the address and a note of introduction.

I have ventured to make an appointment for you with Mr
Greenslade for 11.30 tomorrow (Wednesday). If this is not a
convenient time perhaps you will be good enough to telephone Mr Greenslade's secretary before 5.30 this evening.

Mr Conducis asks me to beg that you will not trouble yourself to return the things he was glad to be able to offer after
your most disagreeable accident for which, as he no doubt
explained, he feels a deep sense of responsibility. He under-
stands that your own clothes have been irretrievably spoilt and
hopes that you will allow him to make what he feels is a most

inadequate gesture by way of compensation. The clothes, by
the way, have not been worn. If, however, you would prefer
it, he hopes that you will allow him to replace your loss in a
more conventional manner.

Mr Conducis will not himself take a direct part in any developments that may arise in respect of The Dolphin and does not
wish at any juncture to be approached in the matter. Mr
Greenslade has full authority to negotiate for him at all levels.

With Compliments,

I am,

Yours truly,

M. SMYTHIMAN
(Private Secretary to Mr Conducis)

'Not true,' Jeremy said, looking over the tops of his spectacles.

'True. Apparently. As far as it goes.'

Jeremy read it again. 'Well,' he said, 'at least he doesn't want you
to approach him. We've done him wrong, there.'

'He doesn't want to set eyes on me, thank God.'

'Were you passionately eloquent, my poor Peregrine?'

'It looks as if I must have been, doesn't it? I was plastered, of
course.'

'I have a notion,' Jeremy said with inconsequence, 'that he was
once wrecked at sea.'

'Who?'

'Conducis, you dolt. Who but? In his yacht.'

'Was his yacht called *Kalliope*?'

'I rather think so. I'm sure it went down.'

'Perhaps my predicament reminded him of the experience.'

'You know,' Jeremy said, 'I can't really imagine why we're making
such a thing of this. After all, what's happened? You look at a derelict
theatre. You fall into a fetid well from which you are extricated by the
owner who is a multi-millionaire. You urge in your simple way the
graces and excellence of the theatre. He wonders if, before he pulls it
down, it might just be worth getting another opinion. He turns you over
to one of his myrmidons. Where's the need for all the agitation?'

'I wonder if I should like M. Smythiman if I met him and if I shall
take against S. Greenslade at first sight. Or he against me, of course.'

'What the hell does that matter? You place far too much importance upon personal relationships. Look at the fatuous way you go
on about your women. And then suspecting poor Mr Conducis of
improper intentions when he never wants to look upon your like
again!'

'Do you suggest that I accept his gorgeous apparel?' Peregrine
asked on an incredulous note.

'Certainly, I do. It would be rude and ungenerous and rather vulgar to return it with a po-faced note. The old boy wants to give you
his brand new clobber because you mucked up your own in his dirty
great well. You should take it and not slap him back as if he'd tried
to tip you.'

'If you had seen him you would not call him an old boy. He is the
uncosiest human being I have ever encountered.'

'Be that as it may, you'd better posh yourself up and wait upon
S. Greenslade on the stroke of 11.30.'

Peregrine said, after a pause, 'I shall do so, of course. He says
nothing about the letter and glove, you observe.'

'Nothing.'

'I shall urge S. Greenslade to get it vetted at the V. and A.'

'You jolly well do.'

'Yes, I will. Well, Jer, as you say, why make a thing? If by some
wild, rapturous falling-out of chance, I could do anything to save the
life of The Dolphin I would count myself amply rewarded. But it
will, of course, only be a rum little interlude and, in the meantime,
here's the latest batch of bills.'

'At least,' Jeremy said, 'there won't be a new one from your tai-
lors for some time to come.'

II

Mr S. Greenslade was bald, pale, well-dressed and unremarkable.
His office was quietly sumptuous and he was reached through a hin-
terland of equally conservative but impressive approaches. He now
sat, with a file under his hand, a distinguished painting behind him,
and before him, Peregrine, summoning all the techniques of the
theatre in order to achieve relaxation.

'Mr Jay,' Mr Greenslade said, 'you appreciate, of course, the fact that your meeting yesterday with Mr Conducis has led to this appointment.'

'I suppose so. Yes.'

'Quite. I have here a digest, as it were, of a – shall I say a suggestion you made to Mr Conducis as he recollects it. Here it is.'

Mr Greenslade put on his spectacles and read from the paper before him.

'Mr Jay proposed that The Dolphin Theatre should be restored to its former condition and that a company should be established there performing Shakespeare and other plays of a high cultural quality. Mr Jay suggested that The Dolphin is a building of some cultural worth and that, historically speaking, it is of considerable interest.'

Mr Greenslade looked up at Peregrine. 'That was, in fact, your suggestion?'

'Yes. Yes. It was. Except that I hate the word culture.'

'Mr Jay, I don't know if you are at all informed about Mr Conducis's interests.'

'I – no – I only know he's – he's –'

'Extremely wealthy and something of a recluse?' Mr Greenslade suggested with a slight, practised smile.

'Yes.'

'Yes.' Mr Greenslade removed his spectacles and placed them delicately in the centre of his writing pad. Peregrine thought he must be going to make some profound revelation about his principal. Instead he merely said: 'Quite' again and after a dignified silence asked Peregrine if he would be good enough to tell him something about himself. His schooling, for example, and later career. He was extremely calm in making this request.

Peregrine said he had been born and educated in New Zealand, had come to England on a drama bursary and had remained there.

'I am aware, of course, of your success in the theatrical field,' said Mr Greenslade and Peregrine supposed that he had been making some kind of confidential inquiries.

'Mr Jay,' said Mr Greenslade, 'I am instructed to make you an offer. It is, you may think, a little precipitant. Mr Conducis is prepared to consider the rehabilitation of the theatre, subject, of course, to favourable opinions from an architect and from building authorities and to the granting of necessary permits. He will finance this under-taking. On one condition.' Mr Greenslade paused.

'On one condition?' Peregrine repeated in a voice that cracked like an adolescent's.

'Exactly. It is this. That you yourself will undertake the working management of The Dolphin. Mr Conducis offers you, upon terms to be arrived at, the post of organizing the running of the theatre, plan-ning its artistic policy, engaging the company and directing the pro-ductions. You would be given a free hand to do this within certain limits of expenditure which would be set down in this contract. I shall be glad to hear what your reactions are to this, at its present stage, necessarily tentative proposal.'

Peregrine suppressed a frightening inclination towards giving himself over to maniac laughter. He looked for a moment into Mr Greenslade's shrewd and well-insulated face and he said:

'It would be ridiculous of me to pretend that I am anything but astonished and delighted.'

'Are you?' Mr Greenslade rejoined. 'Good. In that case I shall proceed with the preliminary investigations. I, by the way, am the solicitor for a number of Mr Conducis's interests. If and when it comes to drawing up contracts I presume I should negotiate with your agents?'

'Yes. They are –'

'Thank you,' said Mr Greenslade, 'Messrs Slade and Opinger, I believe?'

'Yes,' said Peregrine, wondering if at any stage of his tipsy rhap-sody he had mentioned them to Mr Conducis and rather concluding that he hadn't.

'There is one other matter.' Mr Greenslade opened a drawer in his desk and with an uncanny re-enacting of his principal's gestures on the previous morning, withdrew from it the small Victorian writing desk. 'You are already familiar with the contents, I understand, and expressed some anxiety about their aunthenticity.'

'I said I wished they could be shown to an expert.'

'Quite. Mr Conducis has taken your point, Mr Jay, and wonders if you yourself would be so obliging as to act for him in this respect.'

Peregrine, in a kind of trance, said: 'Are the glove and documents insured?'

'They are covered by a general policy but they have not been specifically insured since their value is unknown.'

'I feel the responsibility would be –'

'I appreciate your hesitation and I may say I put the point to Mr Conducis. He still wishes me to ask you to undertake this mission.'

There was a short silence.

'Sir,' said Peregrine, 'why is Mr Conducis doing all this? Why is he giving me at least the chance of undertaking such fantastically responsible jobs? What possible motive can he have? I hope,' Peregrine continued with a forthrightness that became him very well, 'that I'm not such an ass as to suppose I can have made an impression in the least degree commensurable with the proposals you've put before me and I – I – ' He felt himself reddening and ran out of words. Mr Greenslade had watched him, he thought, with renewed attention. He now lifted his spectacles with both hands, held them poised daintily over his blotter and said, apparently to them:

'A reasonable query.'

'Well – I hope so.'

'And one which I am unable to answer.'

'Oh?'

'Yes. I will,' said Mr Greenslade, evenly, 'be frank with you, Mr Jay. I am at a loss to know why Mr Conducis is taking this action. If, however, I have interpreted your misgivings correctly I can assure you they are misplaced.' Suddenly, almost dramatically, Mr Greenslade became human, good-tempered and coarse. 'He's not that way inclined,' he said and laid down his spectacles.

'I'm extremely glad to hear it.'

'You will undertake the commission?'

'Yes, I will.'

'Splendid.'

III

The expert folded his hands and leant back in his chair.

'Well,' he said, 'I think we may say with certainty this is a glove of late sixteenth- or early seventeenth-century workmanship. It has, at some time, been exposed to saltwater but not extensively. One might surmise that it was protected. The little desk is very much stained. Upon the letters H.S. inside the gauntlet I am unable to give an authoritative opinion but could, of course, obtain one. As for these two, really rather startling documents: they can be examined and submitted to a number of tests – infra red, spectography and so on – not in my province, you know. If they've been concocted it will certainly be discovered.'

'Would you tell me how I can get the full treatment for them?'

'Oh, I think we could arrange that, you know. But we would want written permission from the owner, full insurance and so on. You've told me nothing, so far, of the history, have you?'

'No,' Peregrine said. 'But I will. With this proviso, if you don't mind: the owner, or rather his solicitor on his behalf, has given me permission to disclose his name to you on your undertaking to keep it to yourself until you have come to a conclusion about these things. He has a – an almost morbid dread of publicity which you'll understand, I think, when you learn who he is.'

The expert looked very steadily at Peregrine. After a considerable silence he said: 'Very well. I am prepared to treat the matter confidentially as far as your principal's name is concerned.'

'He is Mr Vassily Conducis.'

'Good God.'

'Quite,' said Peregrine, doing a Greenslade. 'I shall now tell you as much as is known of the history. Here goes.'

And he did in considerable detail.

The expert listened in a startled manner.

'Really, very odd,' he said when Peregrine had finished.

'I assure you I'm not making it up.'

'No, no. I'm sure. I've heard of Conducis, of course. Who hasn't? You do realize what a – what a really flabbergasting thing this would be if it turned out to be genuine?'

'I can think of nothing else. I mean: there they lie – a child's glove and a letter asking one to suppose that on a summer's morning in the year 1596 a master-craftsman of Stratford made a pair of gloves and gave them to his grandson who wore them for a day and then –'

'Grief filled the room up of an absent child?'

'Yes. And a long time afterwards – twenty years – the father made his Will – I wonder he didn't chuck in a ghastly pun – Will's Will – don't you? And he left his apparel to his sister Joan Hart. And for her information wrote that note there. I mean – *his* hand moved across that bit of paper. If it's genuine. And then two centuries go by and somebody called E. M. puts the glove and paper in a Victorian desk with the information that her great-great-grandmother had them from J. Hart and her grandmother insisted they were the Poet's. It *could* have *been* Joan Hart. She died in 1664.'

'I shouldn't build on it,' the expert said drily.

'Of course not.'

'Has Mr Conducis said anything about their value? I mean – even if there's only a remote chance they will be worth – well, I can't begin to say what their monetary value might be but I know what *we'd* feel about it, here.'

Peregrine and the expert eyed each other for a moment or two. 'I suppose,' Peregrine said, 'he's thought of that but I must say he's behaved pretty casually over it.'

'Well, *we* shan't,' said the expert. 'I'll give you your receipt and ask you to stay and see the things safely stowed.'

He stooped for a moment over the little, dead wrinkled glove. 'If it were true!' he murmured.

'I know, I know,' Peregrine cried. 'It's frightening to think what would happen. The avid attention, the passionate greed for possession.'

'There's been murder done for less,' said the expert lightly.

IV

Five weeks later Peregrine, looking rather white about the gills and brownish under the eyes, wrote the last word of his play and underneath it: 'Curtain.' That night he read it to Jeremy who thought well of it.

There had been no word from Mr Greenslade. The stage-house of The Dolphin could still be seen on Bankside. Jeremy had asked at the estate agents for permission to view and had been told that the theatre was no longer in their hands and they believed had been withdrawn from the market. Their manner was stuffy.

From time to time the two young men talked about The Dolphin but a veil of unreality seemed to have fallen between Peregrine and his strange interlude: so much so that he sometimes almost felt as if he had invented it.

In an interim report on the glove and documents, the museum had said that preliminary tests had given no evidence of spurious inks or paper and so far nothing inconsistent with their supposed antiquity had been discovered. An expert on the handwriting of ancient documents, at present in America, would be consulted on his return. If his report was favourable, Peregrine gathered, a conference of authorities would be called.

'Well,' Jeremy said, 'they haven't laughed it out of court, evidently.'

'Evidently.'

'You'll send the report to the man Greenslade?'

'Yes, of course.'

Jeremy put his freckled hand on Peregrine's manuscript.

'What about opening at The Dolphin this time next year with *The Glove*, a new play by Peregrine Jay?'

'Gatcha!'

'Well – why not? For the hell of it,' Jeremy said, 'let's do a shadow casting. Come on.'

'I have.'

'Give us a look.'

Peregrine produced a battered sheet of paper, covered in his irregular handwriting.

'Listen,' he said. 'I know what would be said. That it's been done before. Clemence Dane for one. And more than that: it'd be a standing target for wonderful cracks at synthetic Bardery. The very sight of the cast. Ann Hathaway and all that lot. You know? It'd be held to stink. Sunk before it started.'

'I for one don't find any derry-down tatt in the dialogue.'

'Yes: but to cast "Shakespeare". What gall!'

'*He* did that sort of thing. You might as well say: "Oo-er! To cast Henry VIII!" Come on: who *would* you cast for Shakespeare?'

'It sticks out a mile, doesn't it?'

'Elizabethan Angry, really, isn't he? Lonely. Chancy. Tricky. Bright as the sun. A Pegasus in the Hathaway stable? Enormously over-sexed and looking like the Grafton portrait. In which I entirely believe.'

'And I. All right. Who looks and plays like that?'

'Oh God!' Jeremy said, reading the casting list.

'Yes,' Peregrine rejoined. 'What I said. It sticks out a mile.'

'Marcus Knight, my God.'

'Of course. He *is* the Grafton portrait and as for fire! Think of his Hotspur. And Harry Five. And the Mercutio. And, by heaven, his Hamlet. Remember the Peer Gynt?'

'What's his age?'

'Whatever it is he doesn't show it. He can look like a stripling.'

'He'd cost the earth.'

'This is only mock-up, anyway.'

'Has he ever been known to get through a production without creating a procession of dirty big rows?'

'Never.'

'Custombuilt to wreck the morale of any given company?'

'That's Marco.'

'Remember the occasion when he broke off and told latecomers after the interval to sit down or get the hell out of it?'

'Vividly.'

'And when the rest of the cast threw in their parts as one man?'

'I directed the fiasco.'

'He's said to be more than usually explosive just now on account of no knighthood last batch.'

'He is, I understand, apoplectic, under that heading.'

'Well,' said Jeremy, 'it's your play. I see you've settled for rolling the lovely boy and the seduced fair friend and "Mr W. H." all up in one character.'

'So I have.'

'How you dared!' Jeremy muttered.

'There have been madder notions over the centuries.'

'True enough. It adds up to a damn' good part. How do you see him?'

'Very blond. Very male. Very impertinent.'

'W. Hartly Grove?'

'Might be. Type casting.'

'Isn't he held to be a bad citizen?'

'Bit of a nuisance.'

'What about your Dark Lady? The Rosaline? Destiny Meade, I see you've got here.'

'I rather thought: Destiny. She's cement from the eyes up but she gives a great impression of smouldering depths and really inexhaustible sex. She can produce what's called for in any department as long as it's put to her in basic English and very slowly. And she lives, by the way, with Marco.'

'That might or might not be handy. And Ann H.?'

'Oh, any sound unsympathetic actress with good attack,' Peregrine said.

'Like Gertie Bracey?'

'Yes.'

'Joan Hart's a nice bit. I tell you who'd be good as Joan. Emily Dunne. You know? She's been helping in our shop. You liked her in that TV show. She did some very nice Celias and Nerissas and Hermias at Stratford. Prick her down on your list.'

'I shall. "*See, with a blot I damn her*".'

'The others seem to present no difficulty but the spirit sinks at an infant phenomenon.'

'He dies before the end of Act I.'

'Not a moment too soon. I am greatly perturbed by the vision of some stunted teenager acting its pants off.'

'It'll be called Gary, of course.'

'Or Trevor.'

'Never mind.'

'Would you give me the designing of the show?'

'Don't be a bloody ass.'

'It'd be fun,' Jeremy said grinning at him, 'face it: it *would be* fun.'

'Don't worry, it won't happen. I have an instinct and I know it won't. None of it: the glove, the theatre, the play. It's all a sort of miasma. It won't happen.'

Their post box slapped.

'There you are. Fate knocking at the door,' said Jeremy.

'I don't even wonder if it might be, now,' Peregrine said. 'However, out of sheer kindness I'll get the letters.'

He went downstairs, collected the mail and found nothing for himself. He climbed up again slowly. As he opened the door, he said: 'As I foretold you. No joy. All over. Like an insubstantial pageant faded. The mail is as dull as ditchwater and all for you. Oh, sorry!'

Jeremy was talking on the telephone.

He said: 'Here he is, now. Would you wait a second?'

He held out the receiver with one hand over the mouthpiece.

'Mr Greenslade,' he said, 'wishes to speak to you. Ducky – this is it.'

CHAPTER 3

Party

'A year ago,' Peregrine thought, 'I stood in this very spot on a February morning. The sun came out and gilded the stage tower of the injured Dolphin and I lusted after it. I thought of Adolphus Ruby and wished I was like him possessed. And here I am again, as the Lord's my judge, a little jumped-up Cinderella-man in Mr Ruby's varnished boots.'

He looked at the restored caryatids, the bouncing cetaceans and their golden legend, and the immaculate white frontage and elegance of ironwork and he adored them all.

He thought: 'Whatever happens, this is, so far, the best time of my life. Whatever happens I'll look back at today, for instance, and say: "Oh *that* was the morning when I knew what's meant by bliss".'

While he stood there the man from Phipps Bros came out of Phipps Passage.

'Morning, guvnor,' he said.

'Good morning, Jobbins.'

'Looks a treat, dunnit?'

'Lovely.'

'Ah. Different. From what it was when you took the plunge.'

'Yes: indeed.'

'Yes. You wouldn't be looking for a watchman, I suppose? Now she's near finished-like? Night or day. Any time?'

'I expect we *shall* want someone. Why? Do you know of a good man?'

'Self-praise, no recommendation's what they say, ainnit?'

'Do you mean you'd take it on?'

'Not to deceive yer, guvnor, that *was* the idea. Dahn the Passage in our place, it's too damp, for me chubes, see? Something chronic. I got good references, guvnor. Plenty'd speak up for me. 'Ow's it strike yer? Wiv a sickening thud or favourable?'

'Why,' said Peregrine. 'Favourably, I believe.'

'Will you bear me in mind, then?'

'I'll do that thing,' said Peregrine.

'Gor' bless yer, guv,' said Jobbins and retired down Phipps Passage.

Peregrine crossed the lane and entered the portico of his theatre. He looked at the framed notice:

DOLPHIN THEATRE

REOPENING SHORTLY

UNDER NEW MANAGEMENT

It hung immediately under the tatter of a Victorian playbill that he had seen on his first remarkable visit.

THE BEGGAR GIRL'S WEDDING

In response to

Overwhelming Solicitation!! –

Mr Adolphus Ruby

When the painters cleaned and resurfaced the façade, Peregrine had made them work all round that precarious fragment without touching it. 'It shall stay here,' he had said to Jeremy Jones, 'as long as I do.'

He opened the front doors. They had new locks and the doors themselves had been stripped and scraped and restored to their original dignity.

The foyer was alive. It was being painted, gilded, polished and furbished. There were men on scaffolds, on long ladders, on pendant platforms. A great chandelier lay in a sparkling heap on the floor. The two fat cherubim, washed and garnished, beamed upside-down into the resuscitated box-office.

Peregrine said good morning to the workmen and mounted the gently curving stairs.

There was still a flower-engraved looking-glass behind the bar but now he advanced towards himself across shining mahogany, framed by brass. The bar was all golden syrup and molasses in colour. 'Plain, serviceable, no tatt,' Peregrine muttered.

The renovations had been completed up here and soon a carpet would be laid. He and Jeremy and the young decorator had settled in the end for the classic crimson, white and gilt and the panelling blossomed, Peregrine thought, with the glorious vulgarity of a damask rose. He crossed the foyer to a door inscribed 'Management' and went in.

The Dolphin was under the control of 'Dolphin Theatres Incorporated'. This was a subsidiary of Consolidated Oils. It had been created, broadly speaking, by Mr Greenslade, to encompass the development of the Dolphin project. Behind his new desk in the office sat Mr Winter Morris, an extremely able theatrical business manager. He had been wooed into the service by Mr Greenslade upon Peregrine's suggestion, after a number of interviews and, he felt sure, exhaustive inquiries. Throughout these preliminaries, Mr Conducis had remained, as it were, the merest effluvium: far from noxious and so potent that a kind of plushy assurance seemed to permeate the last detail of renaissance in The Dolphin. Mr Morris had now under his hand an entire scheme for promotion, presentation and maintenance embracing contracts with actors, designers, costumiers, front of house staff, stage crew and press agents and the delicate manipulation of such elements as might be propitious to the general mana of the enterprise.

He was a short, pale and restless man with rich curly hair, who, in what little private life belonged to him, collected bric-à-brac.

'Good morning, Winty.'

'Perry,' said Mr Morris as a defensive statement rather than a greeting.

'Any joy?'

Mr Morris lolled his head from side to side.

'Before I forget. Do we want a caretaker, watchman, day or night, stage-door-keeper or any other lowly bod about the house?'

'We shall in a couple of days.'

Peregrine told him about Mr Jobbins.

'All right,' said Mr Morris. 'If the references are good. Now, it's my turn. Are you full cast?'

'Not quite. I'm hovering.'

'What do you think of Harry Grove?'

'As an actor?'

'Yes.'

'As an actor I think a lot of him.'

'Just as well. You've got him.'

'Winty, what the hell do you mean?'

'A directive, dear boy: or what amounts to it. From Head Office.'

'About *W. Hartly Grove?*'

'You'll probably find something in your mail.'

Peregrine went to his desk. He was now very familiar with the looks of Mr Greenslade's communications and hurriedly extracted the latest from the pile.

Dear Peregrine Jay,

Your preliminaries seem to be going forward smoothly and according to plan. We are all very happy with the general shaping and development of the original project and are satisfied that the decision to open with your own play is a sound one, especially in view of your current success at The Unicorn. This is merely an informal note to bring to your notice Mr W. Hartly Grove, an actor, as you will of course know, of repute and experience. Mr Conducis personally will be very pleased if you give favourable attention to Mr Grove when forming your company.

With kind regards,
Yours sincerely,
STANLEY GREENSLADE

When Peregrine read this note he was visited by a sense of misgiving so acute as to be quite disproportionate to its cause. In no profession are personal introductions and dear-boy-manship more busily exploited than in the theatre. For an actor to get the ear of the casting authority through an introduction to *régisseur* or management is a commonplace manoeuvre. For a second or two, Peregrine wondered with dismay if he could possibly be moved by jealousy and if the power so strangely, so inexplicably put into his hands had perhaps already sown a detestable seed of corruption. But no, he thought, on consideration and he turned to Morris to find the latter watching him with a half-smile.

'I don't like this,' Peregrine said.

'So I see, dear boy. May one know why?'

'Of course. I don't like W. Hartly Grove's reputation. I try to be madly impervious to gossip in the theatre and I don't know that I believe what they say about Harry Grove.'

'What do they say?'

'Vaguely shady behaviour. I've directed him once and knew him before that. He taught voice production at my drama school and disappeared over a weekend. Undefined scandal. Most women find him attractive, I believe. I can't say,' Peregrine added, rumpling up his hair, 'that he did anything specifically objectionable in the latter production and I must allow that personally I found him an amusing fellow. But apart from the two women in the company nobody liked him. *They* said *they* didn't but you could see them eyeing him and knowing he eyed them.'

'This,' said Morris, raising a letter that lay on his desk, 'is practically an order. I suppose yours is, too.'

'Yes, blast it.'

'You've been given a fabulously free hand up to now, Perry. No business of mine, of course, dear boy, but frankly I've never seen anything like it. General management, director, author – the lot. Staggering.'

'I hope,' Peregrine said with a very direct look at his manager, 'staggering though it may be, I got it on my reputation as a director and playwright. I believe I did. There is no other conceivable explanation, Winty.'

'No, no, old boy, of course not,' said Winter Morris in a hurry.

'As for W. Hartly Grove, I suppose I can't jib. As a matter of fact he would be well cast as Mr W. H. It's his sort of thing. But I don't like it. My God,' Peregrine said, 'haven't I stuck my neck out far enough with Marcus Knight in the lead and liable to throw an average of three dirty great temperaments per rehearsal? What have I done to deserve Harry Grove as a bonus?'

'The Great Star's shaping up for trouble already. He's calling me twice a day to make difficulties over his contract.'

'Who's winning?'

'I am,' said Winter Morris. 'So far.'

'Good for you.'

'I'm getting sick of it,' Morris said. 'Matter-of-fact it's on my desk now.' He lifted a sheet of blotting paper and riffled the pages of the typewritten document he exposed. 'Still,' he said, 'he's signed and he can't get past that one. We almost had to provide an extra page for it. Take a gander.'

The enormous and completely illegible signature did indeed occupy a surprising area. Peregrine glanced at it and then looked more closely.

'I've seen that before,' he said. 'It looks like a cyclone.'

'Once seen never forgotten.'

'I've seen it,' Peregrine said, 'recently. *Where*, I wonder.'

Winter Morris looked bored.

'Did he sign your autograph book?' he asked bitterly.

'It was somewhere unexpected. Ah, well. Never mind. The fun will start with the first rehearsal. He'll want me to rewrite his part, of course, adding great hunks of ham and corn and any amount of fat. It's tricky enough as it is. Strictly speaking a playwright shouldn't direct his own stuff. He's too tender with it. But it's been done before and by the Lord I mean to do it again. Marco or no Marco. He looks like the Grafton portrait of Shakespeare. He's got the voice of an angel and colossal prestige. He's a brilliant actor and this is a part he can play. It'll be a ding-dong go which of us wins but by heaven I'm game if he is.'

'Fair enough,' said Morris. 'Live for ever, dear boy. Live for ever.'

They settled at their respective desks. Presently Peregrine's buzzer rang and a young woman provided by the management and secreted in an auxiliary cubby-hole said: 'Victoria and Albert for you, Mr Jay.'

Peregrine refrained from saying: 'Always available to Her Majesty and the Prince Consort.' He was too apprehensive. He said: 'Oh yes. Right. Thank you,' and was put into communication with the expert.

'Mr Jay,' the expert said, 'is this a convenient time for you to speak?'

'Certainly.'

'I thought it best to have a word with you. We will, of course, write formally with full reports for you to hand to your principal but

I felt – really,' said the expert and his voice, Peregrine noticed with mounting excitement, was trembling, 'really, it is the most remarkable thing. I – well, to be brief with you, the writing in question has been exhaustively examined. It has been compared by three experts with the known signatures and they find enough coincidence to give the strongest presumption of identical authorship. They are perfectly satisfied as to the age of the cheverel and the writing materials and that apart from salt-water stains there has been no subsequent interference. In fact, my dear Mr Jay, incredible as one might think it, the glove and the document actually seem to be what they purport to be.'

Peregrine said: 'I've always felt this would happen and now I can't believe it.'

'The question is: what is to be done with them?'

'You will keep them for the time being?'

'We are prepared to do so. We would very much like,' said the expert and Peregrine caught the wraith of a chuckle in the receiver, 'to keep them altogether. However! I think my principals will, after consultation, make an approach to – er – the owner. Through you, of course and – I imagine this would be the correct proceeding – Mr Greenslade.'

'Yes. And – no publicity?'

'Good God, no!' the expert ejaculated quite shrilly. 'I should hope not. Imagine!' There was a long pause. 'Have you any idea,' the expert said, 'whether he will contemplate selling?'

'No more than you have.'

'No. I see. Well: you will have the reports and a full statement from us within the next week. I – must confess – I – I have rung you up simply because I – in short – I am as you obviously are, a *dévoté*.'

'I've written a play about the glove,' Peregrine said impulsively. 'We're opening here with it.'

'Really? A play,' said the expert and his voice flattened.

'It isn't cheek!' Peregrine shouted into the telephone. 'In its way it's a tribute. A play! Yes, a play.'

'Oh, please! Of course. Of course.'

'Well, thank you for telling me.'

'No, no.'

'Goodbye.'

'What? Oh, yes. Of course. Goodbye.'

Peregrine put down the receiver and found Winter Morris staring at him.

'You'll have to know about this, Winty,' he said. 'But as you heard – no publicity. It concerns the Great Person so that's for sure. Further it must not go.'

'All right. If you say so: not an inch.'

'Top secret?'

'Top secret as you say. Word of honour.'

So Peregrine told him. When he had finished, Morris ran his white fingers through his black curls and lamented. 'But listen, but listen, listen, listen. What material! What a talking line! The play's *about* it. Listen: it's *called The Glove.* We've *got* it. Greatest Shakespeare relic of all time. The *Dolphin* Glove. American offers. Letters to the papers: "Keep the Dolphin Glove in Shakespeare's England." "New fabulous offer for Dolphin Glove!' Public subscriptions. The lot! Ah Perry, cherub, dear *dear* Perry. All this lovely publicity and we should keep it secret!'

'It's no good going on like that.'

'How do you expect me to go on? The Great Person must be handled over this one. He must be seen. He must be made to work. What makes him work? You've seen him. Look: he's a financial wizard: he *knows*. He knows what's good business. Listen: if this was handled right and we broke the whole story at the psychological moment: you know, *with* the publicity: the right kind of class publicity . . . Look – '

'Do pipe down,' Peregrine said.

'Ah! Ah! Ah!'

'I'll tell you what my guess is, Winty. He'll take it all back to his iron bosom and lock it away in his Louis-the-Somethingth bureau and that's the last any of us will ever see of young Hamnet Shakespeare's cheverel glove.'

In this assumption, however, Peregrine was entirely mistaken.

II

'*But that's all one,*' Marcus Knight read in his beautiful voice. '*Put it away somewhere. I shall not look at it again. Put it away.*'

He laid his copy of Peregrine's play down and the six remaining members of the company followed his example. A little slap of type-scripts ran round the table.

'Thank you,' Peregrine said. 'That was a great help to me. It was well read.'

He looked round the table. Destiny Meade's enormous black eyes were fixed on him with the determined adulation of some mixed-up and sexy medieval saint. This meant, as he knew, nothing. Catching his eye, she raised her fingers to her lips and then in slow motion, extended them to him.

'Darling Perry,' she murmured in her celebrated hoarse voice, 'what can we say? It's all too much. Too much.' She made an appeal-ing helpless little gesture to the company at large. They responded with suitable if ambiguous noises.

'My dear Peregrine,' Marcus Knight said (and Peregrine thought: 'his voice is like no other actor's'). 'I like it. I see great possibilities. I saw them as soon as I read the play. Naturally, that was why I accepted the role. My opinion, I promise you, is unchanged. I look forward with interest to creating this part.' Royalty could not have been more gracious.

'I'm so glad, Marco,' Peregrine said.

Trevor Vere whose age, professionally, was eleven, winked abom-inably across the table at Miss Emily Dunne who disregarded him. She did not try to catch Peregrine's eye and seemed to be disregard-ful of her companions. He thought that perhaps she really had been moved.

W. Hartly Grove leant back in his chair with some elegance. His fingers tapped the typescript. His knuckles, Peregrine absently noted, were like those of a Regency prizefighter. His eyebrows were raised and a faint smile hung about his mouth. He was a blond man, very comely, with light blue eyes, set far apart, and an indefinable expres-sion of impertinence. 'I think it's fabulous,' he said. 'And I like my Mr W.H.'

Gertrude Bracey, patting her hair and settling her shoulders said: 'I *am* right, aren't I, Perry? Ann Hathaway *shouldn't be* played unsympathetically. I mean: definitely not a bitch?'

Peregrine thought: 'Trouble with this one: I foresee trouble.'

He said cautiously: 'She's had a raw deal, of course.'

Charles Random said: 'I wonder what Joan Hart did with the gloves?' and gave Peregrine a shock.

'But there weren't any gloves, *really*,' Destiny Meade said, 'were there, darling? Or were there? Is it historical?'

'No, no, love,' Charles Random said. 'I was talking inside the play. Or out of wishful thinking. I'm sorry.'

Marcus Knight gave him a look that said it was not usual for secondary parts to offer gratuitous observations round the conference table. Random, who was a very pale young man, reddened. He was to play Dr Hall in the first act.

'I see,' Destiny said. 'So I mean there weren't *really* any gloves? In Stratford or anywhere real?'

Peregrine looked at her and marvelled. She was lovely beyond compare and as simple as a sheep. The planes of her face might have been carved by an angel. Her eyes were wells of beauty. Her mouth, when it broke into a smile, would turn a man's heart over and although she was possessed of more than her fair share of common sense, professional cunning and instinctive technique, her brain took one idea at a time and reduced each to the comprehensive level of a baby. If she were to walk out on any given stage and stand in the least advantageous place on it in a contemptible lack of light and with nothing to say, she would draw all eyes. At this very moment, fully aware of her basic foolishness, Marcus Knight, W. Hartly Grove and, Peregrine observed with dismay, Jeremy Jones, all stared at her with the solemn awareness that was her habitual tribute while Gertrude Bracey looked at her with something very like impotent fury.

The moment had come when Peregrine must launch himself into one of those pre-production pep-talks upon which a company sets a certain amount of store. More, however, was expected of him, now, than the usual helping of: 'We're all going to love this so let's get cracking' sort of thing. For once he felt a full validity in his own words when he clasped his hands over his play and said:

'This is a great occasion for me.' He waited for a second and then, abandoning everything he had so carefully planned, went on. 'It's a great occasion for me because it marks the rebirth of an entrancing playhouse: something I'd longed for and dreamed of and never, never thought to see. And then: to be given the job I have been given of shaping the policy and directing the productions and – as a final and incredible *bon-bouche* – the invitation to open with my own play – I do hope you'll believe me when I say all this makes me feel not only immensely proud but extremely surprised and – although it's not a common or even appropriate emotion in a director-playwright – very humble.

'It might have been more politic to behave as if I took it all as a matter of course and no more than my due, but I'd rather, at the outset, and probably for the last time, say that I can't get over my good fortune. I'm not the first dramatist to have a bash at the man from Warwickshire and I'm sure I won't be the last. In this piece I've – well you've seen, I hope, what I've tried to do. Show the sort of combustion that built up in that unique personality: the terrifying sensuality that lies beyond the utterly unsentimental lyricism: gild-ed flies under daisies pied and violets blue. His only release, his only *relief*, you might say, has been his love for the boy Hamnet. It's his son's death that brings about the frightful explosion in his own per-sonality and the moment when Rosaline (I have always believed the Dark Lady was a Rosaline) pulls Hamnet's glove on her hand is the climax of the entire action. The physical intrusion and his consent to it brings him to the condition that spewed up Timon of Athens and was seared out of him by his own disgust. I've tried to suggest that for such a man the only possible release is through his work. He would like to be an Antony to Rosaline's Cleopatra, but between himself and that sort of surrender stands his genius. And – inciden-tally – the hard-headed bourgeois of Stratford which, also, he is.'

Peregrine hesitated. Had he said anything? Was it any good try-ing to take it further? No.

'I won't elaborate,' he said. 'I can only hope that we'll find out what it's all about as we work together.' He felt the abrupt upsurge of warmth, that is peculiarly of the theatre.

'I hope, too, very much,' he said, 'that we're going to agree together. It's a great thing to be starting a playhouse on its way. They say dolphins are intelligent and gregarious creatures. Let us be good Dolphins and perform well together. Bless you all.'

They responded at once and all blessed him in return and for the occasion, at least, felt uplifted and stimulated and, in themselves, vaguely noble.

'And now,' he said, 'let's look at Jeremy Jones's sets and then it'll be almost time to drink a health to our enterprise. This is a great day.'

III

Following the reading there was a small party, thrown by the Management and thrown with a good deal of quiet splendour. It was held in the circle foyer with the bar in full array. The barman wore a snowy white shirt, flamboyant waistcoat and gold albert. There was a pot-boy with his sleeves rolled up to his shoulders like the one in *Our Mutual Friend*. The waiters were conventionally dressed but with slightly Victorian emphasis. Champagne in brassbound ice buckets stood along the mahogany bar and the flowers, exclusively, were crimson roses set in fern leaves.

Mr Greenslade was the host. Apart from the Company, Jeremy, Winter Morris, the publicity agents and the stage director and his assistant, there were six personages of startling importance from the worlds of theatre finance, the Press and what Mr Morris, wide-eyed, described as 'the sort you can't, socially speaking, look any higher than.' From a remark let fall by Mr Greenslade, Peregrine was led to suppose that behind their presence could be discerned the figure of Mr Conducis who, of course, did not attend. Indeed it was clear from the conversation of the most exalted of the guests that Mr Conducis was perfectly well-known to be the presiding genius of The Dolphin.

'A new departure for V.M.C.' this personage said. 'We were all astonished,' (who were 'we'?) 'Still, like the rest of us, one supposes, he must have his toys.'

Peregrine wondered if it would have been possible for him to have heard a more innocently offensive comment.

'It's a matter of life and death to us,' he said. The personage looked at him with amusement.

'Is it really?' he said. 'Well, yes. I can see that it is. I hope all goes well. But I am still surprised by the turn of V.M.C.'s fancy. I didn't think he had any fancies.'

'I don't really know him,' said Peregrine.

'Which of us does?' the personage rejoined. 'He's a legend in his own lifetime and the remarkable thing about *that* is: the legend is perfectly accurate.' Well-content with this aphorism he chuckled and passed superbly on leaving an aftermath of cigar, champagne and the very best unguents for the Man.

'If I were to become as fabulously rich as that,' Peregrine wondered, 'would I turn into just such another? Can it be avoided?'

He found himself alongside Emily Dunne who helped in Jeremy's shop and was to play Joan Hart in *The Glove*. She had got the part by audition and on her own performance, which Peregrine had seen, of Hermia in *A Midsummer Night's Dream*. She had a pale face with dark eyes and a welcoming mouth. He thought she looked very intelligent and liked her voice which was deepish.

'Have you got some champagne?' asked Peregrine, 'and would you like something to eat?'

'Yes and no, thank you,' said Emily. 'It's a wonderful play. I can't get over my luck, being in it. And I can't get over The Dolphin either.'

'I thought you looked as if you were quite enjoying it. You read Joan exactly right. One wants to feel it's a pity she's Will's sister because she's the only kind of woman who would ever suit him as a wife.'

'I think before they were both married she probably let him in by the side-window when he came home to Henley Street in the early hours after a night on the tiles.'

'Yes, of course she did. How right you are. Do you like cocktail parties?'

'Not really, but I always hope I will.'

'I've given that up, even.'

'Do you know, when I was playing at The Mermaid over a year ago, I used to look across the river to The Dolphin and then, one day, I walked over Blackfriars Bridge and stood in Wharfingers Lane and stared at it. And then an old, old stagehand I knew told me his father had been on the curtain there in the days of Adolphus Ruby. I got a sort of thing about it. I found a book in a sixpenny rack called *The Buskin and the Boards*. It was published in 1860 and it's all about contemporary theatres and actors. *Terribly* badly written, you know, but there are some good pictures and The Dolphin's one of the best.'

'Do let me see it.'

'Of course.'

'I had a thing about The Dolphin, too. What a pity we didn't meet in Wharfingers Lane,' said Peregrine. 'Do you like Jeremy's models? Let's go and look at them.'

They were placed about the foyer and were tactfully lit. Jeremy had been very intelligent: the sets made single uncomplicated gestures and were light and strong-looking and beautifully balanced. Peregrine and Emily had examined them at some length when it came to him that he should be moving among the guests. Emily seemed to be visited by the same notion. She said: 'I think Marcus Knight is wanting to catch your eye. He looks a bit portentous to me.'

'Gosh! So he does. Thank you.'

As he edged through the party towards Marcus Knight, Peregrine thought: 'That's a pleasing girl.'

Knight received him with an air that seemed to be compounded of graciousness and overtones of huff. He was the centre of a group: Winter Morris, Mrs Greenslade, who acted as hostess and was beautifully dressed and excessively poised, Destiny Meade and one of the personages who wore an expansive air of having acquired her.

'Ah, Perry, dear boy!' Marcus Knight said, raising his glass in salute. 'I wondered if I should manage to have a word with you. Do forgive me,' he said jollily to the group. 'If I don't fasten my hooks in him now he'll escape me altogether.' Somewhat, Peregrine thought, to her astonishment, Knight kissed Mrs Greenslade's hand. 'Lovely, lovely party,' he said and moved away. Peregrine saw Mrs Greenslade open her eyes very widely for a fraction of a second at the personage. 'We're amusing her,' he thought sourly.

'Perry,' Knight said, taking him by the elbow. 'May we have a long, long talk about your wonderful play? And I mean that, dear boy. Your *wonderful* play.'

'Thank you, Marco.'

'Not here, of course,' Knight said waving his disengaged hand, 'not now. But soon. And, in the meantime, a thought.'

'Oops!' Peregrine thought. 'Here we go.'

'Just a thought. I throw it out for what it's worth. Don't you feel – and I'm speaking absolutely disinterestedly – don't you feel that in your Act Two, *dear* Perry, you keep Will Shakespeare offstage for *rather* a long time? I mean, having built up that tremendous tension – '

Peregrine listened to the celebrated voice and as he listened he looked at the really beautiful face with its noble brow and delicate bone structure. He watched the mouth and thought how markedly an exaggerated dip in the bow of the upper lip resembled that of the Droushout engraving and the so-called Grafton portrait. 'I must put up with him,' Peregrine thought. 'He's got the prestige, he's got the looks and his voice is like no other voice. God give me strength.'

'I'll think very carefully about it, Marco,' he said and he knew that Knight knew he was going to do nothing of the sort. Knight, in a grand seigneurial manner, clapped him on the shoulder. 'We shall agree,' he cried, 'like birds in their little nest.'

'I'm sure of it,' said Peregrine.

'One other thing, dear boy, and this is in your private ear.' He steered Peregrine by the elbow into a corridor leading off to the boxes. 'I find with some surprise,' he said, muting the exquisite voice, 'that we are to have W. Hartly Grove in our company.'

'I thought he read Mr W.H. quite well, didn't you?'

'I could scarcely bring myself to listen,' said Knight.

'Oh,' Peregrine said coolly. 'Why?'

'My dear man, do you know anything at all about Mr Harry Grove?'

'Only that he is a reasonably good actor, Marco,' Peregrine said. 'Don't let's start any anti-Grove thing. For your information, and I'd be terribly grateful if you'd treat this as strictly – very strictly, Marco – between ourselves, I've had no hand in this piece of casting. It was done at the desire of the Management. They have been generous to a degree in every other aspect and even if I'd wanted to I couldn't have opposed them.'

'You had this person *thrust* upon you?'

'If you'd like to put it that way.'

'You should have refused.'

'I had no valid reason for doing so. It is a good piece of casting. I beg you, Marco, not to raise a rumpus at the outset. Time enough when anything else happens to justify it.'

For a moment he wondered if Knight was going to produce a temperament then and there and throw in his part. But Peregrine

felt sure Knight had a great desire to play Will Shakespeare and
although, in the shadowy passage, he could see the danger signal of
mounting purple in the oval face, the usual outburst did not follow
this phenomenon.

Instead Knight said: 'Listen. You think I am unreasonable. Allow
me to tell you, Perry – '

'I don't want to listen to gossip, Marco.'

'*Gossip!* My God! Anyone who accuses me of gossip does me an
injury I won't stomach. *Gossip!* Let me tell you I know for a fact that
Harry Grove – ' The carpet was heavy and they had heard no sound
of an approach. The worst would have happened if Peregrine had
not seen a shadow move across the gilt panelling. He closed his hand
round Knight's arm and stopped him.

'What are you two up to, may I ask?' said Harry Grove.
'Scandalmongering?'

He had a light, bantering way with him and a boldish stare that
was somehow very far from being offensive. Perry,' he said, 'this
is an enchanting theatre. I want to explore, I want to see everything. Why don't we have a baccanal and go in Doric procession
through and about the house, tossing down great bumbers of
champagne and chanting some madly improper hymn? Led, of
course, by our great, *great* star. Or should it be by Mr and Mrs
Greensleeves?'

He made his preposterous suggestion so quaintly that in spite of
himself and out of sheer nerves, Peregrine burst out laughing.
Knight said, 'Excuse me,' with a good deal of ostentation and
walked off.

' "It *is offended*,"' Grove said. '"*See, it stalks away.*" It dislikes me,
you know. Intensely.'

'In that case don't exasperate it, Harry.'

'Me? You think better not? Rather tempting though, I must say.
Still, you're quite right, of course. Apart from everything else, I can't
afford to. Mr Greengage might give me the sack,' Grove said with
one of his bold looks at Peregrine.

'If he didn't I might. Do behave prettily, Harry. And I must get
back into the scrum.'

'I shall do everything that is expected of me, Perry dear. I nearly
always do.'

Peregrine wondered if there was a menacing note behind this apparently frank undertaking.

When he returned to the foyer it was to find that the party had attained its apogee. Its component bodies had almost all reached points farthest removed from their normal behaviour. Everybody was now obliged to scream if he or she wished to be heard and almost everybody would have been glad to sit down. The Personages were clustered together in a flushed galaxy and the theatre people excitedly shouted shop. Mrs Greenslade could be seen saying something to her husband and Peregrine was sure it was to the effect that she felt it was time their guests began to go away. It would be better, Peregrine thought, if Destiny Meade and Marcus Knight were to give a lead. They were together on the outskirts and Peregrine knew, as certainly as if he had been beside them, that Knight was angrily telling Destiny how he felt about W. Hartly Grove. She gazed at him with her look of hypersensitive and at the same time sexy understanding but every now and then her eyes swivelled a little and always in the same direction. There was a slightly furtive air about this manoeuvre.

Peregrine turned to discover what could be thus attracting her attention and there, in the entrance to the passage, stood Harry Grove with wide open eyes and a cheerful smile, staring at her. '*Damn*,' thought Peregrine. 'Now what?'

Emily Dunne, Charles Random and Gertie Bracey were all talking to Jeremy Jones. Jeremy's crest of red hair bobbed up and down and he waved his glass recklessly. He threw back his head and his roar of laughter could be heard above the general din. As he always laughed a great deal when he was about to fall in love, Peregrine wondered if he was attracted to Emily and hoped he was not. It could hardly be Gertie. Perhaps he was merely plastered.

But no. Jeremy's green and rather prominent gaze was directed over the heads of his group and was undoubtedly fixed upon Destiny Meade.

'He *couldn't* be such an ass,' Peregrine thought uneasily. 'Or could he?'

His awareness of undefined hazards was not at all abated when he turned his attention to Gertie Bracey. He began, in fact, to feel as if he stood in a field of fiercely concentrated shafts of criss-cross searchlights. Like searchlights, the glances of his company wandered, interlaced, selected and darted. There, for example, was Gertie with her rather hatchet-jawed intensity stabbing her beam at Harry Grove. Peregrine recollected with a jolt that somebody had told him they had been lovers and were now breaking up. He had paid no attention to this rumour. Supposing it was true would this be one more personality problem on his plate?

'Or am I,' he wondered, 'getting some kind of director's neurosis? Do I merely imagine that Jeremy eyes Destiny and Destiny and Harry ogle each other and Gertie glares hell's fury at Harry and Marcus has his paw on Destiny and that's why he resents Harry? Or is it all an unexpected back-kick from the Conducis champagne?'

He edged round to Destiny and suggested that perhaps they ought to make a break and that people were waiting for a lead from her and Marcus. This pleased both of them. They collected themselves as they did offstage before a big entrance and with the expertise of rugby halfbacks took advantage of a gap and swept through it to Mrs Greenslade.

Peregrine ran straight into their child actor, Master Trevor Vere and his mamma who was a dreadful lady called Mrs Blewitt. She had to be asked and it was God's mercy that she seemed to be comparatively sober. She was dressed in a black satin shift with emerald fringe and she wore a very strange green toque on her pale corn hair. Trevor, in the classic tradition of infant phenomena, was youthfully got up in some sort of contemporary equivalent of a Fauntleroy suit. There were overtones of the Ted. His hair was waved back from his rather pretty face and he wore a flowing cravat. Peregrine knew that Trevor was not as old as his manner and his face suggested because he came under the legal restrictions imposed upon child performers. It was therefore lucky in more ways than one that he died early in the first act.

Mrs Blewitt smiled and smiled at Peregrine with the deadly knowingness of the professional mum and Trevor linked his arm in hers and smiled too. There are many extremely nice children in the professional theatre. They have been well brought up by excellent parents. But none of these had been available to play Hamnet Shakespeare and Trevor, it had to be faced, was talented to an unusual degree. He had made a great hit on cinema in a biblical epic as the Infant Samuel.

'Mrs Blewitt,' said Peregrine.

'I was just hoping for a chance to say how much we appreciate the compliment,' said Mrs Blewitt with an air of conspiracy. 'It's not a big role, of course, not like Trev's accustomed to. Trev's accustomed to leading child-juves, Mr Jay. We was offered – '

It went on predictably for some time. Trevor, it appeared, had developed a heart condition. Nothing, Mrs Blewitt hurriedly assured Peregrine, to worry about really because Trev would never let a show down, never, but the doctor under whom Trev was and under whom she herself was – a monstrous picture presented itself – had advised against another big emotionally exhausting role –

'Why bring that up, Mummy?' Trevor piped with one of his atrocious winks at Peregrine. Peregrine excused himself, saying that they must all be getting along, mustn't they, and he wanted to catch Miss Dunne before she left.

This was true. He had thought it would be pleasant to take Emily back to their studio for supper with him and Jeremy. Before he could get to her he was trapped by Gertrude Bracey.

She said: 'Have you seen Harry anywhere?'

'I saw him a minute or two ago. I think perhaps he's gone.'

'I think perhaps you're right,' she said with such venom that Peregrine blinked. He saw that Gertrude's mouth was unsteady. Her eyes were not quite in focus and blurred with tears. 'Shall I see if I can find him?' he offered.

'God, no,' she said. 'I know better than that, I hope, thank you very much.' She seemed to make a painful effort to present a more conventional front. 'It doesn't matter two hoots, darling,' she said. 'It was nothing. Fabulous party. Can't wait to begin work. I see great things in poor Ann, you know.'

She walked over to the balustrade and looked down into the lower foyer which was populous with departing guests. She was not entirely steady on her pins, he thought. The last pair of Personages was going downstairs and of the Company only Charles Random and Gertrude remained. She leant over the balustrade, holding to it with both hands. If she was looking for Harry Grove, Peregrine thought, she hadn't found him. With an uncoordinated swing she turned, flapped a long black glove at Peregrine and plunged downstairs. Almost certainly she had not said goodbye to her host and hostess but, on the whole, perhaps that was just as well. He wondered if he ought to put her in a taxi but heard Charles Random shout: 'Hi, Gertie love. Give you a lift?'

Jeremy was waiting for him but Emily Dunne had gone. Almost everybody had gone. His spirits plummeted abysmally. Unpredictably, his heart was in his boots.

He went up to Mrs Greenslade with extended hand.

'Wonderful,' he said. 'How can we thank you.'

CHAPTER 4

Rehearsal

'*Who is this comes hopping up the lane?*'

'*Hopping? Where? Oh I see. A lady dressed for riding. She's lame, Master Will. She's hurt. She can't put her foot to the ground.*'

'*She makes a grace of her ungainliness, Master Hall. There's a stain across her face. And in her bosom. A raven's feather in a valley of snow.*'

'*Earth. Mire. On her habit, too. She must have fallen.*'

'*Often enough, I dare swear.*'

'*She's coming in at the gate.*'

'*Will! Where* ARE *you,* WILL!'

'We'll have to stop again, I'm afraid,' Peregrine said. 'Gertie! Ask her to come on, will you, Charles?'

Charles Random opened the door on the prompt side. 'Gertie! On dear.'

Gertrude Bracey entered with her jaw set and the light of battle in her eye. Peregrine walked down the centre aisle and put his hands on the rail of the orchestra well.

'Gertie, love,' he said, 'it went back again, didn't it? It was all honey and sweet reasonableness and it wouldn't have risen one solitary hackle. She *must* grate. She *must* be bossy. Shakespeare's looking down the lane at that dark pale creature who comes hopping into his life with such deadly seduction. And while he's quivering, slap bang into this disturbance of – of his whole personality – comes your voice: his *wife's* voice, scolding, demanding, possessive, always too loud. It *must* be like that, Gertie. Don't you *see?* You must hurt. You must jangle.'

He waited. She said nothing.

'I can't have it any other way,' Peregrine said.

Nothing.

'Well. Let's build in again, shall we? Back to *'who is this'* please, Marco. You're off, please, Gertie.'

She walked off.

Marcus Knight cast up his eyes in elaborate resignation, raised his arms and let them flop.

'Very well, dear boy,' he said, 'as often as you like, of course. One grows a little jaded but never mind.'

Marco was not the only one, Peregrine thought, to feel jaded: Gertie was enough to reduce an author-director to despair. She had, after a short tour of the States, become wedded to 'Method' acting. This involved endless huddles with whoever would listen to her and a remorseless scavenging through her emotional past for fragments that could start her off on some astonishing association with her performance.

'It's like a bargain basement,' Harry Grove said to Peregrine. 'The things Gertie digs up and tries on are really *too* rococo. We get a new look every day.'

It was a slow process and the unplotted pauses she took in which to bring the truth to light were utterly destructive to concerted playing. 'If she goes on like this,' Peregrine thought, 'she'll tear herself to tatters and leave the audience merely wishing she wouldn't.'

As for Marcus Knight, the danger signals for a major temperament had already been flown. There was a certain thunderous quietude which Peregrine thought it best to disregard.

Really, for him, Peregrine thought, Marco was behaving rather well and he tried to ignore the little hammer that pounded away under Marco's oval cheek.

'Who is this –'

Again they built up to her line. When it came it was merely shouted offstage without meaning and apparently without intention.

'Great Christ in Heaven!' Marcus Knight suddenly bellowed, 'how long must this endure! What, in the name of all the suffering clans of martyrdom am I expected to *do*? Am I coupled with a harridan or a bloody dove? My author, my producer, my ART tell me that here is a great moment. I should be fed, by Heaven, fed: I should be led up to. I have my line to make. I must show what I am. My whole being should be lacerated. And so, God knows it is, but by what!' He strode to the door and flung it wide. Gertrude Bracey was exposed looking both terrified and determined. 'By a drivelling, piping pea-hen!' He roared, straight into her face. 'What sort of an actress are you, dear? Are you a woman, dear? Has nobody ever slighted you, trifled with you, deserted you? Have you no conception of the gnawing serpent that ravages a woman scorned?'

Somewhere in the front of the house Harry Grove laughed. Unmistakably, it was he. He had a light, mocking, derisive laugh, highly infectious to anybody who had not inspired it. Unhappily both Knight and Gertrude Bracey, for utterly opposed reasons, took it as a direct personal affront. Knight spun round on his heel, advanced to the edge of the stage and roared into the darkness of the auditorium. 'Who is that! Who is it! I demand an answer.'

The laughter ran up to a falsetto climax and somewhere in the shadows Harry Grove said delightedly: 'Oh dear me, dear me, how very entertaining. The King Dolphin in a rage.'

'Harry,' Peregrine said turning his back on the stage and vainly trying to discern the offender. 'You are a professional actor. You know perfectly well that you are behaving inexcusably. I must ask you to apologize to the company.'

'To the *whole* company, Perry dear? Or just to Gertie for laughing about her not being a woman scorned?'

Before Peregrine could reply, Gertrude re-entered, looking wildly about the house. Having at last distinguished Grove in the back stalls, she pointed to him and screamed out with a virtuosity that she had hitherto denied herself: 'This is a deliberate insult.' She then burst into tears.

There followed a phenomenon that would have been incomprehensible to anybody who was not intimately concerned with the professional theatre. Knight and Miss Bracey were suddenly allied. Insults of the immediate past were as if they had never been. They both began acting beautifully for each other: Gertrude making big eloquent piteous gestures and Marcus responding with massive understanding. She wept. He kissed her hand. They turned with the precision of variety artists to the auditorium and simultaneously shaded their eyes like comic sailors. Grove came gaily down the aisle saying: 'I apologize. Marcus and Gerts. Everybody. I really *do* apologize. In seventeen plastic and entirely different positions. I shall go and be devoured backstage by the worm of contrition. What more can I do? I cannot say with even marginal accuracy that it's all a mistake and you're not at all funny. But anything else. Anything else.'

'Be quiet,' Peregrine said, forcing a note of domineering authority which was entirely foreign to him. 'You will certainly go backstage since you are needed. I will see you after we break. In the meantime I wish neither to see nor hear from you until you make your entrance. Is that understood?'

'I'm sorry,' Grove said quietly. 'I really am.' And he went backstage by the pass-door that Mr Conducis used when he pulled Peregrine out of the well.

'Marco and Gertie,' Peregrine said and they turned blackly upon him. 'I hope you'll be very generous and do something nobody has a right to ask you. I hope you'll dismiss the lamentable incident as if it had never happened.'

'It is either that person or me. Never in the entire course of my professional experience – '

The Knight temperament raged on. Gertrude listened with gloomy approval and repaired face. The rest of the company were still as mice. At last Peregrine managed to bring about a truce and eventually they began again at: *'Who is this comes hopping up the lane?'*

The row had had one startling and most desirable effect. Gertrude, perhaps by some process of emotive transference, now gave out her offstage line with all the venom of a fish-wife.

'But *darling*,' reasoned Destiny Meade, a few minutes later, devouring Peregrine with her great black lamps. *'Hopping*. Me? On my first entrance? I mean – actually what an *entrance! Hopping!'*

'Destiny, love, it's like I said. He had a thing about it.'

'Who did?'

'Shakespeare, darling. About a breathless, panting, jigging, hopping woman with a white face and pitchball eyes and blue veins.'

'How peculiar of him.'

'The thing is, for him it was all an expression of sexual attraction.'

'I don't see how I can do a sexy thing if I come on playing hop-scotch and puffing and blowing like a whale. Truly.'

'Destiny: listen to what he wrote. Listen.

> "I *saw her once*
> *Hop forty paces through the public street;*
> *And having lost her breath, she spoke, and panted,*
> *That she did make defect perfection,*
> *And, breathless, power breathe forth."*

'That's why I've made her fall off her horse and come hopping up the lane.'

'Was he sort of kinky?'

'Certainly not,' Marcus interrupted.

'Well, I only wondered. Gloves and everything.'

'Listen, darling. Here you are. Laughing and out of breath – '

'And hopping. *Honestly!*'

'All *right*,' said Marcus. 'We know what you mean but listen. You're marvellous. Your colour's coming and going and your bosom's heaving. He has an entirely normal reaction, Destiny darling. You *send* him. You do see, don't you? *You* send *me*.'

'With my hopping?'

'*Yes*,' he said irritably. 'That and all the rest of it. Come on, darling, do. Make your entrance to me.'

'Yes, Destiny,' Peregrine said. 'Destiny, listen. You're in a velvet habit with your bosom exposed, a little plumed hat and soft little boots and you're lovely, lovely, lovely. And young Dr Hall has gone out to help you and is supporting you. Charles – come and support her. Yes: like that. Leave her as free as possible. Now: the door opens and we see you. Fabulous. You're in a shaft of sunlight. And *he* sees you. Shakespeare does. And you speak. Right? Right, Destiny? You say – Go on, dear.'

'*Here I come upon your privacy, Master Shakespeare, hopping over your doorstep like a starling.*'

'Yes, and at once, at that very moment you know you've limed him.'

'Limed?'

'Caught.'

'Am I keen?'

'Yes. You're pleased. You know he's famous. And you want to show him off to W.H. You come forward, Marco, under compulsion, and offer your help. Staring at her. And you go to him, Destiny, and skip and half-fall and fetch up laughing and clinging to him. He's terribly, terribly still. Oh, *yes*, Marco, yes. Dead right. Wonderful. And Destiny, darling, that's *right*. You know? It's right. It's what we want.'

'Can I sit down or do I keep going indefinitely panting away on his chest?'

'Look into his face. Give him the whole job. Laugh. No, not that sort of laugh, dear. Not loud. Deep down in your throat!'

'More sexy?'

'Yes,' Peregrine said and ran his hands through his hair. *'That's right. More sexy.'*

'And then I sit down?'

'Yes. He helps you down. Centre. Hall pushes the chair forward. Charles?'

'Could it,' Marcus intervened, 'be left-of-centre, dear boy? I mean I only suggest it because it'll be easier for Dessy and I *think* it'll make a better picture,' Marcus said. 'I can then put her down. Like this.' He did so with infinite grace and himself occupied the centre stage.

'I think I like it better the other way, Marco, darling. Could we try it the other way, Perry? This feels false, a bit, to me.'

They jockeyed about for star positions. Peregrine made the final decision in Knight's favour. It really was better that way. Gertrude came on and then Emily: very nice as Joan Hart, and finally Harry Grove, behaving himself and giving a bright, glancing indication of Mr W.H. Peregrine began to feel that perhaps he had not written a bad play and that, given a bit of luck, he might, after all, hold the company together.

He was aware, in the back of his consciousness, that someone had come into the stalls. The actors were all on stage and he supposed it must be Winter Morris or perhaps Jeremy who often looked in, particularly when Destiny was rehearsing.

They ran the whole scene without interruption and followed it with an earlier one between Emily, Marcus and the ineffable Trevor in which the boy Hamnet, on his eleventh birthday, received and wore his grandfather's present of a pair of embroidered cheverel gloves.

Marcus and Peregrine had succeeded in cowing the more offensive exhibitionisms of Trevor and the scene went quite well. They broke for luncheon. Peregrine kept Harry Grove back and gave him a wigging which he took so cheerfully that it lost half its sting. He then left and Peregrine saw with concern that Destiny had waited for him. Where then was Marcus Knight and what had become of his proprietary interest in his leading lady? As if in explanation, Peregrine heard Destiny say: 'Darling, the King Dolphin's got a pompous feast with someone at the Garrick. Where shall we go?'

The new curtain was half-lowered, the working lights went out, the stage-manager left and the stage-door banged distantly.

Peregrine turned to go out by front-of-house.

He came face to face with Mr Conducis.

II

It was exactly as if the clock had been set back a year and three weeks and he again dripped fetid water along the aisle of a bombed theatre. Mr Conducis seemed to wear the same impeccable clothes and to be seized with the same indefinable step backwards, almost as if Peregrine was going to accuse him of something.

'I have watched your practice,' he said as if Peregrine was learning the piano. 'If you have a moment to spare there is a matter I want to discuss with you. Perhaps in your office?'

'Of course, sir,' Peregrine said. 'I'm sorry I didn't see you had come in.'

Mr Conducis paid no attention to this. He was looking, without evidence of any kind of reaction, at the now resplendent auditorium: at the crimson curtain, the chandeliers, the freshly-gilt scrollwork, the shrouded and expectant stalls.

'The restoration is satisfactory?' he asked.

'Entirely so. We shall be ready on time, sir.'

'Will you lead the way?'

Peregrine remembered that on their former encounter Mr Conducis had seemed to dislike being followed. He led the way upstairs to the office, opened the door and found Winter Morris in residence, dictating letters. Peregrine made a complicated but apparently eloquent face and Morris got to his feet in a hurry.

Mr Conducis walked in looking at nothing and nobody.

'This is our manager, sir. Mr Winter Morris, Mr Conducis.'

'Oh, yes. Good morning,' said Mr Conducis. Without giving an impression of discourtesy he turned away. 'Really, old boy,' as Mr Morris afterwards remarked. 'He might have been giving me the chance to follow my own big nose instead of backing out of The Presence.'

In a matter of seconds Mr Morris and the secretary had gone to lunch.

'Will you sit down, sir?'

'No, thank you. I shall not be long. In reference to the glove and documents: I am told that their authenticity is established.'

'Yes.'

'You have based your piece upon these objects?'

'Yes.'

'I have gone into the matter of promotion with Greenslade and with two persons of my acquaintance who are conversant with this type of enterprise.' He mentioned two colossi of the theatre. 'And have given some thought to preliminary treatment. It occurs to me that, properly manipulated, the glove and its discovery and so on, might be introduced as a major theme in promotion.'

'Indeed it might,' Peregrine said fervently.

'You agree with me? I have thought that perhaps some consideration should be given to the possibility of timing the release of the glove-story with the opening of the theatre and of displaying the glove and documents, suitably protected and housed, in the foyer.'

Peregrine said with what he hoped was a show of dispassionate judgement that surely, as a piece of pre-production advertising, this gesture would be unique. Mr Conducis looked quickly at him and away again. Peregrine asked him if he felt happy about the security of the treasure. Mr Conducis replied with a short exegesis upon wall safes of a certain type in which, or so Peregrine confusedly gathered, he held a controlling interest.

'Your public relations and press executive,' Mr Conducis stated in his dead fish voice, is a Mr Conway Boome.'

'Yes. It's his own name,' Peregrine ventured wondering for a moment if he had caught a glint of something that might be sardonic humour but Mr Conducis merely said: 'I daresay. I understand,' he added, 'that he is experienced in theatrical promotion but I have suggested to Greenslade that having regard for the somewhat unusual character of the type of material we propose to use, it might be as well if Mr Boome were to be associated with Maitland Advertising which is one of my subsidiaries. He is agreeable.'

'I'll be bound he is,' Peregrine thought.

'I am also taking advice on the security aspect from an acquaintance at Scotland Yard, a Superintendent Alleyn.'

'Oh, yes.'

'Yes. The matter of insurance is somewhat involved, the commercial worth of the objects being impossible to define. I am informed that as soon as their existence is made known there is likely to be an unprecedented response. Particularly from the United States of America.'

There followed a short silence.

'Mr Conducis,' Peregrine said, 'I can't help asking this. I know it's no business of mine but I really can't help it. Are you – have you – I mean, would you feel at all concerned about whether the letters and gloves stay in the country of their owner or not?'

'In my country?' Mr Conducis asked as if he wasn't sure that he had one.

'I'm sorry – no. I meant the original owner.'

Peregrine hesitated for a moment and then found himself embarked upon an excitable plea for retention of the document and gloves. He felt he was making no impression whatever and wished he could stop. There was some indefinable and faintly disgusting taint in the situation.

With a closed face Mr Conducis waited for Peregrine to stop and then said: 'That is a sentimental approach to what is at this juncture a matter for financial consideration. I cannot speak under any other heading: historical, romantic, nationalistic or sentimental. I know,' Mr Conducis predictably added, 'nothing of such matters.'

He then startled Peregrine quite shockingly by saying with an indefinable change in his voice: 'I dislike pale gloves. Intensely.'

For one moment Peregrine thought he saw something like anguish in this extraordinary man's face and at the next that he had been mad to suppose anything of the sort. Mr Conducis made a slight movement indicating the interview was at an end. Peregrine opened the door, changed his mind and shut it again.

'Sir,' he said. 'One other question. May I tell the company about the letters and glove? The gloves that we use on the stage will be made by the designer, Jeremy Jones – who is an expert in such matters. If we are to show the original in the front of house he should copy it as accurately as possible. He should go to the museum and examine it. And he will be so very much excited by the whole thing that I can't guarantee his keeping quiet about it. In any case, sir, I myself spoke to him about the glove on the day you showed it to me. You will remember you did not impose secrecy at that time. Since the report came through I have not spoken of it to anyone except Morris and Jones.'

Mr Conducis said: 'A certain amount of leakage at this stage is probably inevitable and if correctly handled may do no harm. You may inform your company of all the circumstances. With a strong warning that the information is, for the time being, confidential and with this proviso: I wish to remain completely untroubled by the entire business. I realize that my ownership may well become known: is known in fact, already, to a certain number of people. This is inavoidable. But under no circumstances will I give statements, submit to interviews or be quoted. My staff will see to this at my end. I hope you will observe the same care, here. Mr Boome will be instructed. Good morning. Will you – ?'

He made that slight gesture for Peregrine to precede him. Peregrine did so.

He went out on the circle landing and ran straight into Harry Grove.

'Hall-lo, dear boy,' said Harry, beaming at him. 'I just darted back to use the telephone. Destiny and I – ' He stopped short, bobbed playfully round Peregrine at Mr Conducis and said: '*Now*, see what I've done! A genius for getting myself in wrong. My only talent.'

Mr Conducis said: 'Good morning to you, Grove.' He stood in the doorway looking straight in front of him.

'*And* to you, wonderful fairy godfather, patron, guiding light and all those things,' Harry said. 'Have you come to see your latest off-spring, your very own performing Dolphins?'

'Yes,' said Mr Conducis.

'Look at dear Perry!' Harry said. 'He's stricken dumb at my mis-placed familiarity. Aren't you, Perry?'

'Not for the first time,' Peregrine said and felt himself to be the victim of a situation he should have controlled.

'Well!' Harry said, glancing with evident amusement from one to the other of his hearers. 'I mustn't double-blot my copybook, must I? Nor must I keep lovely ladies waiting.' He turned to Mr Conducis with an air of rueful deference. 'I do hope you'll be pleased with us, sir,' he said. 'It must be wonderful to be the sort of man who uses his power to rescue a drowning theatre instead of slapping it under. All the more wonderful since you have no personal interest in our disreputable trade, have you?'

'I have little knowledge of it.'

'No. Like vinegar, it doesn't readily mix with Oil,' Harry said. 'Or is it Shipping? I always forget. Doing any yachting lately? But I mustn't go on being a nuisance. Goodbye, sir. Do remember me to Mrs G. See you later, Perry, dear boy.'

He ran downstairs and out of the main door. Mr Conducis said: 'I am late. Shall we – ?' They went downstairs and crossed the foyer to the portico. There was the Daimler and, at its door, Peregrine's friend the chauffeur. It gave him quite a shock to see them again and he wondered, for a dotty moment, if he would be hailed away once more to Drury Place.

'Good morning,' Mr Conducis said again. He was driven away and Peregrine joined Jeremy Jones at their habitual chop-house on the Surrey Side.

III

He told the company and Jeremy Jones about the glove before after-noon rehearsal. They all made interested noises. Destiny Meade became very excited and confused on learning that the glove was 'historic' and persisted in thinking they would use it as a prop in the production. Marcus Knight was clearly too angry to pay more than token attention. He had seen Destiny return, five minutes late and in hilarious company with W. Hartly Grove. Gertrude Bracey was equally disgruntled by the same phenomenon.

When Harry Grove heard about the glove he professed the greatest interest and exclaimed, in his skittish manner, 'Someone ought to tell Mrs Constantia Guzman about this.'

'Who on earth,' Peregrine had asked, 'is Mrs Constantia Guzman?'

'Inquire of The King Dolphin,' Harry rejoined. He insisted on referring to Marcus Knight in these terms to the latter's evident annoyance. Peregrine saw Knight turn crimson to the roots of his hair and thought it better to ignore Harry.

The two members of the company who were wholeheartedly moved by Peregrine's announcement were Emily Dunne and Charles Random and their reaction was entirely satisfactory. Random kept saying: 'Not true! Well, of *course*. Now, we know what inspired you. No – it's incredible. It's too much.'

He was agreeably incoherent.

Emily's cheeks were pink and her eyes bright and that too was eminently satisfactory.

Winter Morris, who was invited to the meeting, was in ecstasy.

'So what have we got?' he asked at large. 'We have got a story to make the front pages wish they were double elephants.'

Master Trevor Vere was not present at this rehearsal.

Peregrine promised Jeremy that he would arrange for him to see the glove as often as he wanted to, at the museum. Morris was to get into touch with Mr Greenslade about safe-housing it in the theatre and the actors were warned about secrecy for the time being although the undercover thought had clearly been that a little leakage might be far from undesirable as long as Mr Conducis was not troubled by it.

Stimulated perhaps by the news of the glove the company worked well that afternoon. Peregrine began to block the tricky second act and became excited about the way Marcus Knight approached his part.

Marcus was an actor of whom it was impossible to say where hard-thinking and technique left off and the pulsing glow that actors call star-quality began. At earlier rehearsals he would do extraordinary things: shout, lay violent emphasis on oddly selected words, make strange, almost occult gestures and embarrass his fellow players by speaking with his eyes shut and his hands clasped in front of his mouth as if he prayed. Out of all this inwardness there would occasionally dart a flash of the really staggering element that had placed him, still a young man, so high in his chancy profession. When the period of incubation had gone by the whole performance would step forward into full light. 'And,' Peregrine thought, 'there's going to be much joy about this one.'

Act Two encompassed the giving of the dead child Hamnet's gloves on her demand to the Dark Lady: a black echo, this, of Bertrand and Bassanio's rings and of Berowne's speculation as to the whiteness of his wanton's hand. It continued with the entertainment of the poet by the infamously gloved lady and his emergence from 'the expense of spirit in a waste of shame'. It ended with his savage reading of the sonnet to her and to W.H. Marcus Knight did this superbly.

W. Hartly Grove lounged in a window seat as Mr W.H. and, already mingling glances with Rosaline, played secretly with the gloved hand. The curtain came down on a sudden cascade of his laughter. Peregrine spared a moment to reflect that here, as not infrequently in the theatre, a situation in a play reflected, in a cockeyed fashion, the emotional relationships between the actors themselves. He had a theory that, contrary to popular fancy, this kind of overlap between the reality of their personalities in and out of their roles was an artistic handicap. An actor, he considered, was embarrassed rather than released by unsublimated chunks of raw association. If Marcus Knight was enraged by the successful blandishments of Harry Grove upon Destiny Meade, this reaction would be liable to upset his balance and bedevil his performance as Shakespeare deceived by Rosaline with W.H.

And yet, apparently, it had not done so. They were all going great guns and Destiny, with only the most rudimentary understanding of the scene, distilled an erotic compulsion that would have peeled the gloves off the hands of the dead child as easily as she filched them from his supersensitive father. 'She really is,' Jeremy Jones had said, 'the original overproof *femme fatale*. It's just there. Whether she's a goose or a genius doesn't matter. There's something solemn about that sort of attraction.'

Peregrine had said: 'I wish you'd just try and think of her in twenty years' time with china-boys in her jaws and her chaps hitched up to her ears and her wee token brain shrunk to the size of a pea.'

'Rail on,' Jeremy had said. 'I am unmoved.'

'You don't suppose you'll have any luck?'

'That's right. I don't. She's busily engaged in shuffling off the great star and teaming up with the bounding Grove. Not a nook or cranny left for me.'

'Oh, dear, oh dear, oh dear,' Peregrine had remarked and they let it go at that.

On this particular evening Peregrine himself had at last succeeded, after several rather baffling refusals, in persuading Emily Dunne to come back to supper at the studio. Jeremy, who supervised and took part in the construction and painting of his sets at a warehouse not far away, was to look in at The Dolphin and walk home with them over Blackfriars Bridge. It had appeared to Peregrine that this circumstance, when she heard of it, had been the cause of Emily's acceptance. Indeed, he heard her remark in answer to some question from Charles Random: 'I'm going to Jeremy's.' This annoyed Peregrine extremely.

Jeremy duly appeared five minutes before the rehearsal ended and sat in the front stalls. When they broke, Destiny beckoned to him and he went up to the stage through the pass-door. Peregrine saw her lay her hands on Jeremy's coat and talk into his eyes. He saw Jeremy flush up to the roots of his red hair and glance quickly at him. Then he saw Destiny link her arm in Jeremy's and lead him upstage, talking hard. After a moment or two they parted and Jeremy returned to Peregrine.

'Look,' he said in stage Cockney, 'do me a favour. Be a pal.'

'What's all this?'

'Destiny's got a sudden party and she's asked me. Look, Perry, you don't mind if I go? The food is all right at the studio. You and Emily can do very nicely without me: damn' sight better than with.'

'She'll think you're bloody rude,' Peregrine said angrily, 'and she won't be far wrong, at that.'

'Not at all. She'll be enchanted. It's you she's coming to see.'

'I'm not so sure.'

'Properly speaking, you ought to be jolly grateful.'

'Emily'll think it's a put-up job.'

'So what? She'll be pleased as Punch. Look, Perry, I – I can't wait. Destiny's driving us all and she's ready to go. Look, I'll have a word with Emily.'

'You'd damn' well better though what in decency's name you can find to say!'

'It'll all be as right as a bank. I promise.'

'So *you* say.' Peregrine contemplated his friend whose freckled face was pink, excited and dreadfully vulnerable. 'All right,' he said. 'Make your excuses to Emily. Go to your party. I think you're heading for trouble but that's your business.'

'I only hope I'm heading for *something*,' Jeremy said. 'Fanks, mate. You're a chum.'

'I very much doubt it,' said Peregrine.

He stayed front-of-house and saw Jeremy talk to Emily on stage. Emily's back was towards him and he was unable to gauge her reaction but Jeremy was all smiles. Peregrine had been wondering what on earth he could say to her when it dawned upon him that, come hell or high water, he could not equivocate with Emily.

Destiny was up there acting her boots off with Marcus, Harry Grove, and now Jeremy, for an audience. Marcus maintained a proprietary air to which she responded like a docile concubine, Peregrine thought. But he noticed that she managed quite often to glance at Harry with a slight widening of her eyes and an air of decorum that was rather more provocative than if she'd hung round his neck and said: 'Now.' She also beamed upon poor Jeremy. They all talked excitedly, making plans for their party. Soon they had gone away by the stage door.

Emily was still on stage.

'Well,' Peregrine thought, 'here goes.'

He walked down the aisle and crossed to the pass-door in the box on the prompt side. He never went backstage by this route without a kind of aftertaste of his first visit to The Dolphin. Always, behind the sound of his own footsteps on the uncarpeted stairway, Peregrine caught an echo of Mr Conducis coming invisibly to his rescue.

It was a slight shock now, therefore, to hear, as he shut the pass-door behind him, actual footsteps beyond the turn in this narrow, dark and winding stair.

'Hallo?' he said. 'Who's that?'

The steps halted.

'Coming up,' Peregrine said, not wanting to collide.

He went on up the little stairway and turned the corner.

The door leading to the stage opened slightly admitting a blade of light. He saw that somebody moved uncertainly as if in doubt whether to descend or not and he got the impression that whoever it was had actually been standing in the dark behind the door.

Gertrude Bracey said, 'I was just coming down.'

She pushed open the door and went on-stage to make way for him. As he came up with her, she put her hand on his arm.

'Aren't you going to Destiny's sinister little party?' she asked.

'Not I,' he said.

'Unasked? Like me?'

'That's right,' he said lightly and wished she wouldn't stare at him like that. She leant towards him.

'Do you know what I think of Mr W. Hartly Grove?' she asked quietly. Peregrine shook his head and she then told him. Peregrine was used to uninhibited language in the theatre, but Gertrude Bracey's eight words on Harry Grove made him blink.

'Gertie, *dear!*'

'Oh, yes,' she said. 'Gertie, dear. And Gertie dear knows what she's talking about, don't you worry.'

She turned her back on him and walked away.

IV

'Emily,' Peregrine said as they climbed up Wharfingers Lane, 'I hope you don't mind it just being me. And I hope you don't think there's any skulduggery at work. Such as me getting rid of Jer in order to make a heavy pass at you. Not, mark you, that I wouldn't like to but that I really wouldn't have the nerve to try such an obvious ploy.'

'I should hope not,' said Emily with composure.

'Well, I wouldn't. I suppose you've seen how it is with Jeremy?'

'One could hardly miss it.'

'One couldn't, could one?' he agreed politely.

Suddenly for no particular reason they both burst out laughing and he took her arm.

'Imagine!' he said. 'Here we are on Bankside, not much more than a stone's throw from The Swan and The Rose and The Globe. Shakespeare must have come this way a thousand times after rehearsals had finished for the day. We're doing just what he did and I do wish, Emily, that we could take water for Blackfriars.'

'It's pleasant,' Emily said, 'to be in company that isn't self-conscious about him and doesn't mistake devotion for idolatry.'

'Well, he *is* unique, so what's the matter with being devoted? Have you observed, Emily, that talent only fluctuates about its own middle line whereas genius nearly always makes great walloping bloomers?'

'Like Agnes Pointing Upwards and bits of *Cymbeline?*'

'Yes. I think, perhaps, genius is nearly always slightly lacking in taste.'

'Anyway, without intellectual snobbery?'

'Oh that, certainly.'

'Are you pleased with rehearsals, so far?'

'On the whole.'

'I suppose it's always a bit of a shock bringing something you've written to the melting pot or forge or whatever the theatre is. Particularly when, as producer, you yourself *are* the melting pot.'

'Yes, it is. You see your darling child being processed, being filtered through the personalities of the actors and turning into something different on the way. And you've got to accept all that because a great many of the changes are for the good. I get the oddest sort of feeling sometimes, that, as producer, I've stepped outside myself as playwright. I begin to wonder if I ever knew what the play is about.'

'I can imagine.'

They walked on in companionship: two thinking ants moving eastwards against the evening out-swarm from the City. When they reached Blackfriars it had already grown quiet there and the little street where Jeremy and Peregrine lived was quite deserted. They climbed up to the studio and sat in the window drinking dry martinis and trying to see The Dolphin on the far side of the river.

'We haven't talked about the letter and the glove,' Emily said. 'Why, I wonder, when it's such a tremendous thing. You must have felt like a high-pressure cooker with it all bottled up inside you.'

'Well, there was Jeremy to explode to. And of course the expert.'

'How strange it is,' Emily said. She knelt on the window-seat with her arms folded on the ledge and her chin on her arms. Her heart-shaped face looked very young. Peregrine knew that he must find out about her: about how she thought and what she liked and disliked and where she came from and whether she was or had been in love and if so what she did about it. 'How strange,' she repeated. 'To think of John Shakespeare over in Henley Street making them for his grandson. Would he make them himself or did he have a foreman-glover?'

'He made them himself. The note says "mayde by my father".'

'Is the writing all crabbed and squiggly like his signatures?'

'Yes. But not exactly like any of them. People's writing isn't always like their signatures. The handwriting experts have all found what they call "definitive" points of agreement.'

'*What* will happen to them, Perry? Will he sell to the highest bidder or will he have any ideas about keeping them here? Oh,' Emily cried, 'they *should* be kept here.'

'I tried to say as much but he shut up like a springtrap.'

'Jeremy,' Emily said, 'will probably go stark ravers if they're sold out of the country.'

'Jeremy?'

'Yes. He's got a manic thing about the draining away of national treasures, hasn't he? I wouldn't have been in the least surprised, would you, if it had turned out to be Jeremy who stole the Goya "Wellington". Simply to keep it in England, you know.'

Emily chuckled indulgently and Peregrine thought he detected the proprietary air of romance and was greatly put out. Emily went on and on about Jeremy Jones and his shop and his treasures and how moved and disturbed he was by the new resolution. 'Don't you feel he is perfectly capable,' she said, 'of bearding Mr Conducis in his den and telling him he mustn't let them go?'

'I do hope you're exaggerating.'

'I really don't believe I am. He's a fanatic'

'You know him very well, don't you?'

'Quite well. I help in their shop sometimes. They *are* experts, aren't they, on old costume? Of course, Jeremy has to leave most of it to his partner because of work in the theatre but in between engagements he does quite a lot. I'm learning how to do all kinds of jobs from him like putting old tinsel on pictures and repairing bindings. He's got some wonderful prints and books.'

'I know,' Peregrine said rather shortly. 'I've been there.'

She turned her head and looked thoughtfully at him. 'He's madly excited about making the gloves for the show. He was saying just now he's got a pair of Jacobean gloves, quite small, and he thinks they might be suitable if he took the existing beadwork off and copied the embroidery off Hamnet's glove on to them.'

'I know, he told me.'

'He's letting me help with that, too.'

'Fun for you.'

'Yes. I like him very much. I do hope if he's madly in love with Destiny that it works out but I'm afraid I rather doubt it.'

'Why?'

'He's a darling but he hasn't got anything like enough of what it takes. Well, I wouldn't have thought so.'

'Really?' Peregrine quite shouted in an excess of relief. He began to talk very fast about the glove and the play and what they should have for dinner. He had been wildly extravagant and had bought all the things he himself liked best: smoked salmon with caviare folded inside, cold partridge and the ingredients for two kinds of salad. It was lucky that his choice seemed to coincide with Emily's. They had Bernkastler Docktor with the smoked salmon and it was so good they went on drinking it with the partridge. Because of Jeremy's defection there was rather a lot of everything and they ate and drank it all up.

When they had cleared away they returned to the window-seat and watched the Thames darken and the lights come up on Bankside. Peregrine began to think how much he wanted to make love to Emily. He watched her and talked less and less. Presently he closed his hand over hers. Emily turned her hand, gave his fingers a brief matter-of-fact squeeze and then withdrew.

'I'm having a lovely time,' she said, 'but I'm not going to stay very late. It takes ages to get back to Hampstead.'

'But I'll drive you. Jeremy hasn't taken the car. It lives in a little yard round the corner.'

'Well, that'll be grand. But I still won't stay very late.'

'I'd like you to stay for ever and a day.'

'That sounds like a theme song from a rather twee musical.'

'Emily: have you got a young man?'

'No.'

'Do you have a waiting list, at all?'

'No, Peregrine.'

'No preferential booking?'

'I'm afraid not.'

'Are you ever so non-wanton?'

'Ever so.'

'Well,' he sighed, 'it's original, of course.'

'It's not meant to madden and inflame.'

'That was what I feared. Well, OK. I'll turn up the lights and show you my photographs.'

'You jolly well do,' said Emily.

So they looked at Peregrine's and Jeremy's scrapbooks and talked interminable theatre shop and presently Emily stood up and said: now she must go.

Peregrine helped her into her coat with rather a perfunctory air and banged round the flat getting his own coat and shutting drawers.

When he came back and found Emily with her hands in her pockets looking out of the window he said loudly: 'All the same, it's scarcely fair to have cloudy hair and a husky voice and your sort of face and body and intelligence and not even *think* about being provocative.'

'I do apologize.'

'I suppose I can't just give you "a *single famished kiss*"?'

'All right,' said Emily. 'But not too famished.'

'*Emily!*' Peregrine muttered and became, to his astonishment, breathless.

When they arrived at her flat in Hampstead she thanked him again for her party and he kissed her again but lightly this time. 'For my own peace of mind,' he said. 'Dear Emily, good night.'

'Good night, dear Peregrine.'

'Do you know something?'
'What?'
'We open a fortnight tonight.'

V

BLISS FOR BARDOLATERS
STAGGERING DISCOVERY
ABSOLUTELY PRICELESS SAY EXPERTS

MYSTERY GLOVE
WHO FOUND IT?
DOLPHIN DISCOVERY

FIND OF FOUR CENTURIES
NO FAKING SAY EGG-HEADS
SHAKESPEARE'S DYING SON

IN HIS OWN WRITE
BARD'S HAND AND NO KIDDING
INSPIRES PLAYWRIGHT JAY

Important Discovery
Exhaustive tests have satisfied the most distinguished scholars
and experts of the authenticity –

Glove – Letter – Sensation
'It's the most exciting thing that has ever happened to me,'
says tall, gangling playwright, Peregrine Jay.

WHO OWNS THE DOLPHIN GLOVE?
WE GIVE YOU ONE GUESS
'NO COMMENT' – CONDUCIS

FABULOUS OFFER FROM USA

AMAZING DEVELOPMENTS
DOLPHIN GLOVE MYSTERY

Spokesman for Conducis says No Decision on Sale. May go to States.

Coming Events
The restored Dolphin Theatre on Bankside will open on
Thursday with a new play: *The Glove*, written and directed by
Peregrine Jay and inspired, it is generally understood, by the
momentous discovery of –

Opening Tomorrow
At The Dolphin. Bankside. Under Royal Patronage. *The Glove*
by Peregrine Jay. The Dolphin Glove with Documents will be
on view in the foyer. Completely sold out for the next four
weeks. Waiting list now open.

VI

'You've been so very obliging,' Jeremy Jones said to the learned
young assistant at the museum, 'letting us have access to the glove
and take up so much of your time, that Miss Dunne suggested you
might like to see the finished copies.'

'That's very nice of you. I shall be most interested.'

'They're only stage-props, you know,' Jeremy said, opening a cardboard box. 'But I've taken a little more trouble than usual because the
front row of the stalls will be comparing them to the real thing.'

'*And* because it was a labour of love,' Emily said. 'Mostly that,
Jeremy, now, wasn't it?'

'Well, perhaps. There you are.'

He turned back a piece of old silk and exposed the gloves lying
neatly, side by side. The assistant bent over them. 'I should think the
front row of the stalls will be perfectly satisfied,' he said. 'They are
really *very* good copies. Accurate in the broad essentials and beautifully worked. Where did you get your materials?'

'From stock. A thread of silk here, a seed-pearl there. Most of it's
false, of course. The sequins are Victorian, as you see.'

'They fill the bill quite well, however, at a distance. I hope you
never feel tempted,' the assistant said with pedantic archness, 'to go
in for antiquarian forgery, Mr Jones. You'd be much too successful.'

'To me,' Jeremy said, 'it seems a singularly revolting form of
chicanery.'

'Good. I understand that a car will be sent here to collect the glove tomorrow. I am to deliver it at the theatre and to see it safely housed. I believe you have designed the setting. Perhaps you would call in here and we can go together. I would prefer to have someone with me. Unnecessarily particular, I dare say, but there's been so much publicity.'

'I will be delighted to come,' said Jeremy.

'There is to be an observer at the theatre I understand, to witness the procedure and inspect the safety precautions. Somebody from the police, I think it is.'

'So I hear,' said Jeremy. 'I'm glad to know they are being careful.'

VII

The malaise of First Night Nerves had gripped Peregrine, not tragically and aesthetically by the throat but, as is its habit, shamefully in the guts.

At half past six on Thursday morning, he caught sight of himself in the bathroom shaving-glass. He saw, with revulsion, a long, livid face, pinched up into untimely wrinkles and strange dun-coloured pouches. The stubbled jaw sagged and the lips were pallid. There was a general suggestion of repulsive pig-headedness and a terrible dearth of charm.

The final dress-rehearsal had ended five hours ago. In fourteen hours the curtain would rise and in twenty-four hours he would be quivering under the lash of the morning critics.

'O God, God, why, why have I done this fearful thing!'

Every prospect of the coming day and night was of an excursion with Torquemada; the hours when there was nothing to do were as baleful as those when he would be occupied. He would order flowers, send telegrams, receive telegrams, answer telephone calls. He would prowl to and fro and up and down all alone in his lovely theatre, unable to rest, unable to think coherently and when he met anybody – Winty Morris or the stage director or the SM or some hellish gossip hound – he would be cool and detached. At intervals he would take great nauseating swigs from a bottle of viscous white medicine.

He tried going back to bed but hated it. After a time he got up, shaved his awful face, bathed, dressed, suddenly was invaded by a profound inertia and sleepiness, lay down and was instantly possessed of a compulsion to walk.

He rose, listened at Jeremy's door, heard him snore and stole downstairs. He let himself out into London.

Into the early morning sounds and sights of the river and of the lanes and steps and streets. The day was fresh and sunny and would presently be warm. He walked to the gap where he could look across the Thames to Southwark. The newly-painted stage-house and dome of The Dolphin showed up clearly now and the gilded flagpole glittered so brightly it might have been illuminated.

As he stared at it a bundle ran up and opened out into their new flag: a black dolphin on a gold ground. Jobbins was on his mark in good time. Big Ben and all the clocks in the City struck eight and Peregrine's heart's blood rose and pounded in his ears. The glory of London was upon him. A kind of rarefied joy possessed him, a trembling anticipation of good fortune that he was scared to acknowledge.

He was piercingly happy. He loved all mankind with indiscriminate embracement and more particularly Emily Dunne. He ran back to the flat and sang *Rigoletto* on his way upstairs.

'You look,' Jeremy said, 'like the dog's dinner and you sound like nothing on earth. Can you be joyful?'

'I can and I am.'

'Long may it last.'

'Amen.'

He could eat no breakfast. Even black coffee disgusted him. He went over to the theatre at nine o'clock. Jeremy was to come in at ten with Emily and the assistants from the museum to see the installation of the glove and documents. He, too, crackled like a cat's fur with first night nerves.

When Peregrine arrived at The Dolphin it was alive with cleaners and florists' assistants. As he went upstairs he heard the telephone ring, stop and ring again. The bar was in a state of crates, cartons and men in shirtsleeves, and on the top landing itself two packing cases had been opened and their contents displayed; a pair of wrought-iron pedestals upon which were mounted two bronze dolphins, stylized and sleek. They were a gift from Mr Conducis who had no doubt commissioned Mr Greenslade to go to 'the best man'. This he might be said to have done with the result that while the dolphins were entirely out of style with their company and setting they were good enough to hold their own without causing themselves or their surroundings to become ridiculous.

Peregrine suggested that they should be placed in the circle foyer. One on each side of the steps from the sunken landing.

He crossed the foyer and went into the office.

Winter Morris was behind his desk. He was not alone. A very tall man with an air of elegance and authority stood up as Peregrine entered.

'Oh, lord,' Peregrine thought. 'Another of the Conducis swells or is it somebody to check up on how we behave with the Royals? Or what?'

'Morning, Perry old boy,' said Morris. 'Glad you've come in. Mr Peregrine Jay, Superintendent Alleyn.'

CHAPTER 5

Climax

Alleyn was not altogether unused to the theatrical scene or to theatrical people. He had been concerned in four police investigations in which actors had played – and 'played' had been the operative word – leading roles. As a result of these cases he was sardonically regarded at the Yard as something of an expert on the species.

It was not entirely on this score, however, that he had been sent to The Dolphin. Some five years ago, Mr Vassily Conducis had been burgled in Drury Place. Alleyn had been sent in and had made a smartish catch and recovered the entire haul within twenty-four hours. Mr Conducis was away at the time but on his return had asked Alleyn to call, probably with the idea of making a tangible acknowledgement. Possibly Alleyn's manner had made him change his mind and substitute a number of singularly unsparkling congratulations delivered in a stifled tone from somewhere in the region of his epiglottis. Alleyn had left, uncharmed by Mr Conducis.

Their next encounter was the result of a letter to Alleyn's Great White Chief signed by Mr Conducis and requesting advice and protection for the Shakespeare documents and glove.

'He's asked for you, Rory,' the Great White Chief said. 'No regard for your rank and status, of course. Very cool. In other respects I suppose, you *are* the man for the job: what with your theatrical past and your dotage on the Bard. These damned objects seem to be worth the spoils of the Great Train Robbery. Tell him to buy his protection from a reputable firm and leave us alone, by Heaven.'

'I'd be delighted.'

'No, you wouldn't. You're hell bent on getting a look at the things.'

'I'm not hell bent on getting another look at Conducis.'

'No? What's wrong with him, apart from stinking of money?'

'Nothing, I daresay.'

'Well, you'd better find out when these things are going to be transferred and check up on the security. We don't want another bloody Goya and worse on our hands.'

So Alleyn went to The Dolphin at nine o'clock on the morning of the opening performance.

The housing for the glove and letters was in a cavity made in the auditorium well above the sunken landing which was, itself, three steps below the level of the circle foyer. In this wall was lodged a large steel safe, with convex plate-glass replacing the outward side. The door of the safe, opposite this window, was reached from the back of the circle and concealed by a panel in the wall. Between the window and the exterior face of the wall were sliding steel doors, opened electrically by a switch at the back of the cavity. Concealed lighting came up when the doors were opened. Thus the glove and letters would be exposed to patrons on the stairs, the landing and, more distantly, in the foyer.

The safe was a make well-enough known to Alleyn. It carried a five-figure lock. This combination could be chosen by the purchaser. It was sometimes based on a key word and a very simple code. For instance, the numbers from one to zero might be placed under the letters of the alphabet from A to J and again from K to T and again from U to z. Each number had therefore two and in the case of 1-6, three corresponding letters. Thus, if the key word was 'night' the number of the combination would be 49780.

Jeremy had caused the steel safe to be lined with padded yellow silk. On its floor was a book-hinged unit covered with black velvet, it had a variable tilt, and was large enough to display the glove and two documents. He had made a beautifully lettered legend which had been framed and would be hung below the wall cavity. During performances the sliding doors would be retracted and the plate glass window exposed.

Alleyn made a very thorough inspection and found the precautions rather more efficient than might have been expected. There were not, at large, many criminal virtuosi of the combination lock who would be equal to this one. It would have to be a cracksman's job. An efficient burglar alarm had been installed and would go into action at the first attempt at entry into the theatre. Once the glove and documents were housed the safe would not be re-opened, the interior lighting and sliding doors in front of the glass panel being operated from a switch inside the wall cavity. He pointed out that one man on another man's shoulders could effect a smash, snatch and grab and asked about watchmen. He was told that for as long as the objects were in the theatre, there would be a man on the landing. Jobbins, late Phipps Bros, was revealed in a brand new uniform. He was to be on duty from four up to mid-night when he would be relieved by a trained man from a securi-ty organization. Jobbins would sleep on the premises in an unused dressing-room and could be roused in case of need. A second man already on duty would take over at 8 a.m. and remain in the foyer until Jobbins returned at four. The burglar alarm would be switched on by Jobbins after the show when he locked up for the night.

Alleyn had been fully informed of these arrangements when Peregrine walked into the office. As they shook hands he saw the pallor and the shadows under the eyes and thought: 'First night ter-rors, poor chap.'

'Mr Alleyn's had a look at our security measures,' Morris said, 'and thinks they'll pass muster. He's going to wait and see the treas-ure safely stored.' His telephone rang. 'Excuse me.'

Alleyn said to Peregrine: 'You're all in the throes of every kind of preoccupation. Don't pay any attention to me. If I may: while I'm waiting I'll look at this enchanting theatre. What a superb job you've done.'

This was unlike Peregrine's idea of a plain-clothes policeman. Alleyn had reached the door before he said: 'I'll show you round, sir.'

'I wouldn't dream of it. If I may just wander. You're up to your neck, I'm sure.'

'On the contrary. Morris is, but my problem,' Peregrine said, 'is not having anything real to do. I'd like to show you The Dolphin.'

'Well, in that case – '

It was a comprehensive tour. Alleyn was so clearly interested and so surprisingly well-informed that Peregrine actually enjoyed himself. He found himself talking about the play and what he had tried to do with it and how it had been born of his first sight of Hamnet Shakespeare's glove.

Alleyn knew about the terms of the Will and about Joan Hart getting the wearing apparel. Indeed Peregrine would have betted Alleyn knew as much as he did about Shakespearian scholarship and was as familiar with the plays as he was himself.

For his part, Alleyn liked this strained, intelligent and modest young man. He hoped Peregrine had written and produced a good play. Alleyn asked one or two questions and since he was a trained investigator and was personally attracted by the matter in hand, Peregrine found himself talking about his work with an ease that he would never have thought possible on a ten minutes' acquaintance. He began to speak quickly and excitedly, his words tumbling over each other. His love of The Dolphin welled up into his voice.

'Shall we go backstage?' he said. 'Or – wait a moment. I'll take the Iron up and you can see Jeremy Jones's set for the first act.'

He left Alleyn in the stalls, went through the pass-door, and sent up the elegantly painted fireproof curtain. He then moved onstage and faced the house. He had run up the pass-door passage very quickly and his blood pounded in his ears. Nervous exhaustion, wasn't it called? He even felt a bit dizzy.

The cleaners upstairs had unshuttered a window and a shaft of sunlight struck down upon the stage. It was peopled by dancing motes.

'Is anything the matter?' an unusually deep voice asked quite close at hand. Alleyn had come down the centre aisle. Peregrine, dazzled, thought he was leaning on the rail of the orchestra well.

'No – 1 mean – no nothing. It's just that I was reminded of my first visit to The Dolphin.'

Was it because the reminder had been so abrupt or because over the last week Peregrine had eaten very little and slept hardly at all that he felt so monstrously unsure of himself? Alleyn wouldn't have thought it was possible for a young man to turn any whiter in the face than Peregrine already was but, somehow he now contrived to do so. He sat down on Jeremy's Elizabethan dower chest and wiped his hand across his mouth. When he looked up Alleyn stood in front of him. 'Just where the hole was,' Peregrine thought.

He said: 'Do you know, underneath your feet there's a little stone well with a door. It was there that the trap used to work. Up and down, you know, for Harlequin and Hamlet's Ghost and I dare say for a Lupino or a Lane of that vintage. Or perhaps both. Oh, dear.'

'Stay where you are for the moment. You've been over-doing things.'

'Do you think so? I don't know. But I tell you what. Through all the years after the bomb that well gradually filled with stinking water and then one morning I nearly drowned in it.'

Alleyn listened to Peregrine's voice going on and on and Peregrine listened to it, too, as if it belonged to someone else. He realized with complete detachment that for a year and three months some rather terrible notion about Mr Conducis had been stuffed away at the back of the mind that was Peregrine. It had been and still was, undefined and unacknowledged but because he was so tired and ravaged by anxiety it had almost come out to declare itself. He was very relieved to hear himself telling this unusual policeman exactly what had happened that morning. When he had related everything down to the last detail he said: 'And it was all to be kept quiet, except for Jeremy Jones, so now I've broken faith, I suppose, and I couldn't care, by and large, less. I feel better,' said Peregrine loudly.

'I must say you look several shades less green about the gills. You've half-killed yourself over this production, haven't you?'

'Well, one does, you know.'

'I'm sorry I dragged you up and down all those stairs. Where does that iron curtain work from? The prompt side. Oh, yes I see. Don't move. I'll do it. Dead against the union rules, I expect, but never mind.'

The fire curtain inched its way down. Alleyn glanced at his watch. Any time now the party from the museum should arrive.

He said: 'That was an extraordinary encounter, I must say. But out of it – presumably – has grown all this: the theatre – your play. And now: tonight.'

'And now tonight. Oh, God!'

'Would it be a good idea for you to go home and put your boots up for an hour or two?'

'No, thank you. I'm perfectly all right. Sorry to have behaved so oddly,' Peregrine said, rubbing his head. 'I simply have no notion why I bored you with my saga. You won't, I trust, tell Mr Conducis.'

'I shall,' Alleyn said lightly, 'preserve an absolute silence.'

'I can't begin to explain what an odd man he is.'

'I have met Mr Conducis.'

'Did you think him at all dotty? Or sinister? Or merely plutocratic?'

'I was quite unable to classify him.'

'When I asked him where he found the treasure he said: at sea. Just that: at sea. It sounded rum.'

'Not in the yacht *Kalliope* by any chance?'

'The yacht – *Kalliope*. Wait a moment – what is there about the yacht *Kalliope*?' Peregrine asked. He felt detached from his surroundings, garrulous and in an odd way rather comfortable but not quite sure that if he stood up he might not turn dizzy. 'The yacht *Kalliope*,' he repeated.

'It was his private yacht and it was run down and split in two in a fog off Cape St Vincent.'

'*Now* I remember. Good lord – '

A commotion of voices broke out in the entrance.

'I think,' Alleyn said, 'that the treasure has arrived. Will you stay here for a breather? Or come and receive it?'

'I'll come.'

When they reached the foyer, Emily and Jeremy Jones and the assistant from the museum had arrived. The assistant carried a metal case. Winter Morris had run downstairs to meet them. They all went up to the office and the whole affair became rather formal and portentous. The assistant was introduced to everybody. He laid his metal case on Peregrine's desk, unlocked and opened it and stood back.

'Perhaps,' he said, looking round the little group and settling on Peregrine, 'we should have formal possession taken. If you will just examine the contents and accept them as being in good order.'

'Jeremy's the expert,' Peregrine said. 'He must know every stitch and stain on the glove by this time, I should think.'

'Indeed, yes,' said the assistant warmly. 'Mr Jones, then – will you?'

Jeremy said: 'I'd love to.'

He removed the little desk from the case and laid it on the desk.

Peregrine caught Alleyn's eye. 'Stained, as you see,' he murmured, 'with water. They say: sea-water.'

Jeremy opened the desk. His delicate, nicotine-stained fingers folded back the covering tissues and exposed the little wrinkled glove and two scraps of documents.

'There you are,' he said. 'Shall I?'

'Please do.'

With great delicacy he lifted them from their housing and laid them on the desk.

'And this,' said the assistant pleasantly, 'is when I bow myself out. Here is an official receipt, Mr Morris, if you will be good enough to sign it.'

While Morris was doing this Peregrine said to Alleyn: 'Come and look.'

Alleyn moved forward. He noticed as he did so that Peregrine stationed himself beside Miss Emily Dunne, that there was a glint of fanaticism in the devouring stare that Jeremy Jones bent upon the glove, that Winter Morris expanded as if he had some proprietary rights over it and that Emily Dunne appeared to unfold a little at the approach of Peregrine. Alleyn then stooped over the notes and the glove and wished that he could have been alone. There could, at such a moment, be too much anticipation, too much pumping up of appropriate reactions. The emotion the relics were expected to arouse was delicate, chancy and tenuous. It was not much good thinking: 'But the Hand of Glory moved warmly across that paper and four centuries ago a small boy's sick fist filled out that glove and somewhere between then and now a lady called M.E. wrote a tidy little memorandum for posterity.' Alleyn found himself wishing very heartily that Peregrine's play would perform the miracle of awareness which would take the sense of death away from Shakespeare's note and young Hamnet's glove.

He looked up at Peregrine. 'Thank you for letting me come so close,' he said.

'You must see them safely stowed.'

'If I may.'

Winter Morris became expansive and a little fussy. Jeremy, after a hesitant glance, laid the treasure on Peregrine's blotter. There was a discussion with the museum man about temperature and fire risks and then a procession of sorts formed up and they all went into the back of the circle, Jeremy carrying the blotter.

'On your right,' Morris said unnecessarily.

The panel in the circle was open and so was the door of the safe. Jeremy drew out the black velvet easel-shaped unit, tenderly disposed the glove upon its sloping surface and flanked the glove with the two documents.

'I hope the nap of the velvet will hold them,' he said. 'I've tilted the surface like this to give a good view. Here goes.'

He gently pushed the unit into the safe.

'How do the front doors work?' he asked.

'On your left,' Morris fussed. 'On the inside surface of the wall. Shall I?'

'Please, Winty.'

Morris slipped his fingers between the safe and the circle wall. Concealed lighting appeared and with a very slight whisper the steel panels on the far side slid back.

'Now!' he said. 'Isn't that quite something?'

'We can't *see* from here, though, Winty,' Peregrine said. 'Let's go out and see.'

'I know,' Jeremy agreed. 'Look, would you all go out and tell me if it works or if the background ought to be more tilted? Sort of spread yourselves.'

' *"Some to kill cankers in the moss-rose buds"?'* Alleyn asked mildly.

Jeremy looked at him in a startled manner and then grinned.

'The superintendent,' he said, 'is making a nonsense of us. Emily, would you stay in the doorway, love, and be a liaison between me in the circle and the others outside?'

'Yes. All right.'

The men filed out. Morris crossed the circle foyer. Peregrine stood on the landing and the man from the museum a little below him. Alleyn strolled to the door, passed it and remained in the circle. He was conscious that none of these people except, of course, the museum man, was behaving in his or her customary manner but that each was screwed up to a degree of inward tension over which a stringent self-discipline was imposed. 'And for them,' he thought, 'this sort of thing occurs quite often, it's a regular occupational hazard. They are seasoned troops and about to go into action.'

'It should be more tilted, Jer,' Peregrine's voice was saying. 'And the things'll have to be higher up on the easel.'

The museum assistant, down on the first flight, said something nasal and indistinguishable.

'*What's* he talking about?' Jeremy demanded.

'He says it doesn't show much from down below but he supposes that is unavoidable,' said Emily.

'Wait a bit.' Jeremy reached inside the safe. 'More tilt,' he said. 'Oh, *blast*, it's collapsed.'

'Can I help?' Emily asked.

'Not really. Tell them to stay where they are.'

Alleyn walked over to the safe. Jeremy Jones was on his knees gingerly smoothing out the glove and the documents on the velvet surface. 'I'll have to use *beastly* polythene and I hoped not,' he said crossly. He laid a sheet of it over the treasures and fastened it with black velvet-covered drawing pins. Then he replaced the easel in the safe at an almost vertical angle. There was a general shout of approval from the observers.

'They say: much joy,' Emily told him.

'Shall I shut the doors and all?'

'Yes.'

'Twiddle the thing and all?'

'Winty says yes.'

Jeremy shut the steel door and spun the lock.

'Now let's look.'

He and Emily went out.

Alleyn came from the shadows, opened the wall panel and looked at the safe. It was well and truly locked. He shut the panel and turned to find that at a distance of about thirty feet down the passageway leading to the boxes, a boy stood with his hands in his pockets, watching him: a small boy, he thought at first, of about twelve, dressed in over-smart clothes.

'Hallo,' Alleyn said. 'Where did you spring from?'

'That's my problem,' said the boy. '*Would* you mind.'

Alleyn walked across to him. He was a pretty boy with big eyes and an impertinent, rather vicious mouth. '*Would* you mind!' he said again. 'Who are you staring at? *If* it's not a rude question?'

The consonants and vowels were given full attention.

'At you,' Alleyn said.

Peregrine's voice outside on the landing asked: 'Where's Superintendent Alleyn?'

'Here!' Alleyn called. He turned to go.

'Aeoh, I *beg* pardon, I'm sure,' said Trevor Vere. 'You must be the bogey from the Yard. What could I have been thinking of! Manners.'

Alleyn went out to the front. He found that Marcus Knight and Destiny Meade had arrived and joined the company of viewers.

Above the sunken landing where the two flights of stairs came out was an illuminated peepshow. Yellow and black for the heraldic colours of a gentleman from Warwickshire, two scraps of faded writing and a small boy's glove.

Jeremy fetched his framed legend from the office and fixed it in position underneath.

'Exactly right,' said the man from the museum. 'I congratulate you, Mr Jones. It couldn't be better displayed.'

He put his receipt in his breast pocket and took his leave of them.

'It's perfect, Jer,' said Peregrine.

Trevor Vere strolled across the landing and leant gracefully on the balustrade.

'I reckon,' he observed at large, 'any old duff could crack that peter with his eyes shut. Kid steaks.'

Peregrine said: 'What are you doing here, Trevor? You're not called.'

'I just looked in for my mail, Mr Jay.'

'Why aren't you at school?'

'I took one of my turns last night, Mr Jay. They quite understand at school.'

'You're not needed here. Much better go home and rest.'

'Yes, Mr Jay.' A terribly winning smile illuminated Trevor's photogenic face. 'I wanted to wish you and the play and everybody the most fabulous luck. Mummy joins me.'

'Thank you. The time for that is later. Off you go.'

Trevor, still smiling, drifted downstairs.

'Dear little manikin,' Jeremy said with venom.

Emily said: 'Men and cameras, Winty, in the lane.'

'The Press, darling,' Morris said. 'Shots of people looking at the glove. Destiny and Marcus are going to make a picture.'

'It won't be all that easy to get a shot,' Knight pointed out, 'with the things skied up there.'

'Should we have them down again?'

'I trust,' Jeremy said suddenly, 'that somebody knows how to work the safe. I've locked it, you might remember.'

'Don't worry,' said little Morris whose reaction to opening nights took the form of getting slightly above himself. 'I know. It was all cooked up at the offices and Greenslade, of course, told me. Actually The Great Man himself suggested the type of code. It's all done on a *word*. You see? You think of a *word* of five letters – '

Down below the front doors had opened to admit a number of people and two cameras.

' – and each letter stands for a figure. Mr Conducis said he thought easily the most appropriate word would be – '

'*Mr Morris.*'

Winter Morris stopped short and swung round. Alleyn moved out on the landing.

'Tell me,' he said. 'How long has this safe been in position?'

'Some days. Three or four. Why?'

'Have you discussed the lock mechanism with your colleagues?'

'Well – I – well – I – only vaguely, you know, only vaguely.'

'Don't you think that it might be quite a good idea if you kept your five letter word to yourself?'

'Well, I – well we're all – well – '

'It really is the normal practice, you know.'

'Yes – but we're different. I mean – we're all – '

'Just to persuade you,' Alleyn said, and wrote on the back of an envelope. 'Is the combination one of these?'

Morris looked at the envelope.

'*Christ,*' he said.

Alleyn said: 'If I were you I'd get a less obvious code word and a new combination and keep them strictly under your Elizabethan bonnet. I seriously advise you to do this.' He took the envelope back, blacked out what he had written and put it in his breast pocket.

'You have visitors,' he said, amiably.

He waited while the pictures were taken and was not at all surprised when Trevor Vere reappeared, chatted shyly to the pressman whom he had instinctively recognized as the authority and ended up gravely contemplating the glove with Destiny Meade's arm about him and his cheek against hers while lamps flashed and cameras clicked.

The picture, which was much the best taken that morning, appeared with the caption: 'Child player, Trevor Vere, with Destiny Meade, and the Shakespeare glove. "It makes me feel kinda funny like I want to cry," says young Trevor.'

II

Peregrine answered half a dozen extremely intelligent questions and for the rest of his life would never know in what words. He bowed and stood back. He saw himself doing it in the glass behind the bar: a tall, lank, terrified young man in tails. The doors were swung open and he heard the house rise with a strange composite whispering sound.

Mr Conducis, who wore a number of orders, turned to him.

'I must wish you success,' he said.

'Sir – I can't thank you – '

'Not at all. I must follow.'

Mr Conducis was to sit in the Royal box.

Peregrine made for the left hand doors into the circle.

'Every possible good luck,' a deep voice said.

He looked up and saw a grandee who turned out to be Superintendent Alleyn in a white tie with a lovely lady on his arm.

They had gone.

Peregrine heard the anthem through closed doors. He was the loneliest being on earth.

As the house settled he slipped into the circle and down to the box on the OP side. Jeremy was there.

'Here we go,' he said.

'Here we go.'

III

'Mr Peregrine Jay successfully negotiates the tightrope between Tudor-type schmaltz and unconvincing modernization. His dialogue has an honest sound and constantly surprises by its penetration. Sentimentality is nimbly avoided. The rancour of the insulted sensualist has never been more searchingly displayed since Sonnet cxxix was written.'

'After all the gratuitous build-up and deeply suspect antics of the promotion boys I dreaded this exhibit at the newly tarted-up Dolphin. In the event it gave no offence. It pleased. It even stimulated. Who would have thought – '

'Marcus Knight performs the impossible. He makes a credible being of the Bard.'

'For once phenomenal advance-promotion has not foisted upon us an inferior product. This play may stand on its own merits.'

'Wot, no four letter words? No drag? No kinks? Right. But hold on, mate – '

'Peregrine Jay's sensitive, unfettered and almost clinical examination of Shakespeare is shattering in its dramatic intensity. Disturbing and delightful.'

'Without explicitly declaring itself, the play adds up to a searching attack upon British middle-class mores.'

' – Met in the foyer by Mr Vassily Conducis and escorted to a box stunningly tricked out with lilies of the valley, she wore – '

'It will run.'

IV

Six months later Peregrine put a letter down on the breakfast table and looked across at Jeremy.

'This is it,' he said.

'What?'

'The decision. Conducis is going to sell out. To an American collector.'

'My God!'

'Greenslade, as usual, breaks the news. The negotiations have reached a point when he thinks it appropriate to advise me there is every possibility that they will go through.'

The unbecoming mauvish-pink that belongs to red hair and freckles suffused Jeremy's cheeks and mounted to his brow. 'I tell you what,' he said. 'This can't happen. This can't be allowed to happen. This man's a monster.'

'It appears that the BM and V and A have shot their bolts. So has the British syndicate that was set up.'

Jeremy raised a cry of the passionately committed artist against the rest of the world. 'But *why*! He's lousy with money. He's got so much it must have stopped meaning anything. What'll he *do* with this lot? Look, suppose he gives it away? So what! Let him give William Shakespeare's handwriting and Hamnet Shakespeare's glove away. Let him give them to Stratford or the V and A. Let him give them to the nation. Fine. He'll be made a bloody peer and good luck to him.'

'Let him do this and let him do that. He'll do what he's worked out for himself.'

'*You'll* have to see him, Perry. After all he's got a good thing out of you and The Dolphin. Capacity business for six months and booked out for weeks ahead. Small cast. Massive prestige. The lot.'

'And a company of Kilkenny cats as far as good relations are concerned.'

'What do you mean?'

'You know jolly well. Destiny waltzing over to Harry Grove. Gertrude and Marco reacting like furies.' Peregrine hesitated. 'And so on,' he said.

'You mean me lusting after Destiny and getting nowhere? Don't let it give you a moment's pause. I make no trouble among the giants, I assure you.'

'I'm sorry, Jer.'

'No, no. Forget it. Just you wade in to Conducis.'

'I can't.'

'For God's sake! Why?'

'Jer, I've told you. He gives me the jim-jams. I owe him nothing and I don't want to owe him anything. Still less do I want to go hat in hand asking for anything. *Anything*.'

'Why the hell not?'

'Because I might get it.'

'Well, if he's not an old queer, and you say you don't believe he is, what the hell? You feel like I do about the glove and the letter. You *say* you do. That they ought to be here among Shakespeare's people in his own city or country town – *here*. Well?'

'I can't go pleading again. I did try, remember, when he came to The Dolphin. I made a big song and dance and got slapped right down for my trouble. I won't do it again.'

Jeremy now lost his temper.

'Then, by God, I will,' he shouted.

'You won't get an interview.'

'I'll stage a sit-down on his steps.'

'Shall you carry a banner?'

'If necessary I'll carry a sledge hammer.'

This was so startlingly in accord with Emily's half-joking prediction that Peregrine said loudly: 'For the Lord's sake, pipe down. That's a damn' silly sort of thing to say and you know it.'

They had both lost their tempers and shouted foolishly at each other. An all-day and very superior help was now in their employment and they had to quieten down when she came in. They walked about their refurnished and admirably decorated studio, smoking their pipes and not looking at each other. Peregrine began to feel remorseful. He himself was so far in love with Emily Dunne and had been given such moderate encouragement that he sympathized with Jeremy in his bondage and yet thought what a disaster it was for him to succumb to Destiny. They were, in common with most men of their age, rather owlish in their affairs of the heart and a good deal less sophisticated than their conversation seemed to suggest.

Presently Jeremy halted in his walk and said:

'Hi.'

'Hi.'

'Look. I have been a morsel precipitate.'

Peregrine said: 'Not at all, Jer.'

'Yes. I don't really envisage a sit-down strike.'

'No?'

'No.' Jeremy looked fixedly at his friend. 'On the whole,' he said, and there was a curious undertone in his voice, 'I believe it would be a superfluous exercise.'

'You *do*! But – well really, I do *not* understand you.'

'Think no more of it.'

'Very well,' said the astonished Peregrine. 'I might as well mention that the things are to be removed from the safe on this day week and will be replaced by a blown-up photograph. Greenslade is sending two men from the office to take delivery.'

'Where are they to go?'

'He says for the time being to safe storage at his offices. They'll probably be sold by private treaty but if they are put up at Sotheby's the result will be the same. The customer's hell bent on getting them.'

Jeremy burst out laughing.

'I think you must be mad,' said Peregrine.

V

The night before the Shakespeare relics were to be removed from The Dolphin Theatre was warm and very still with a feeling of thunder in the air which, late in the evening, came to fulfilment. During the third act, at an uncannily appropriate moment a great clap and clatter broke out in the Heavens and directly over the theatre.

'Going too far with the thunder-sheet up there,' Morris said to Peregrine who was having a drink with him in the office.

There were several formidable outbreaks followed by the characteristic downpour. Peregrine went out to the circle foyer. Jobbins was at his post on the half-landing under the treasure.

Peregrine listened at the double doors into the circle and could just hear his own dialogue spoken by strange disembodied voices. He glanced at his watch. Half past ten. On time.

'Good night, Jobbins,' he said and went downstairs. Cars, already waiting in Wharfingers Lane, glistened in the downpour. He could hear the sound of water hitting water on the ebony night tide. The stalls attendant stood by to pen the doors. Peregrine slipped in to the back of the house. There was the man of Stratford, his head bent over his sonnet: sitting in the bow window of a house in Warwickshire. The scratch of his quill on parchment could be clearly heard as the curtain came down.

Seven curtains and they could easily have taken more. One or two women in the back row were crying. They blew their noses, got rid of their handkerchiefs and clapped.

Peregrine went out quickly. The rain stopped as he ran down the side alleyway to the stage-door. A light cue had been missed and he wanted a word with the stage-director.

When he had had it he stood where he was and listened absently to the familiar sounds of voices and movement in the dressing-rooms and front-of-house. Because of the treasure a systematic search of the theatre was conducted after each performance and he had seen to it that this was thoroughly performed. He could hear the staff talking as they moved about the stalls and circle and spread their dust sheets. The assistant stage-manager organized the back-stage procedure. When this was completed he and the stage-crew left. A trickle of back-stage visitors came through and groped their alien way out. How incongruous they always seemed.

Destiny was entertaining in her dressing-room. He could hear Harry Grove's light impertinent laughter and the ejaculations of the guests. Gertrude Bracey and, a little later, Marcus Knight appeared, each of them looking furious. Peregrine advised them to go through the front of the house and thus avoid the puddles and overflowing gutters in the stage-door alleyway.

They edged through the pass-door and down the stairs into the stalls. There seemed to be a kind of wary alliance between them. Peregrine thought they probably went into little indignation huddles over Destiny and Harry Grove.

Charles Random, quiet and detached as usual, left by the stage-door and then Emily came out.

'Hallo,' she said, 'are you benighted?'

'I'm waiting for you. Would you come and have supper at the new bistro near the top of Wharfingers Lane? The Younger Dolphin it's artily called. It's got an extension licence till twelve for its little tiny opening thing and it's asked me to look in. Do come, Emily.'

'Thank you,' she said. 'I'd be proud.'

'How lovely!' Peregrine exclaimed, 'and it's stopped raining, I think. Wait a jiffy and I'll see.'

He ran to the stage-door. Water still dripped from the gutters in the alleyway but the stars shone overhead. Destiny and her smart friends came out, making a great to-do. When she saw Peregrine she stopped them all and introduced him. They said things like: 'Absolutely riveting' and 'Loved your play' and 'Heaven'. They made off, warning each other about the puddles. Harry Grove said: 'I'll go on, then, and fetch it, if you really want me to. See you later, angel.' 'Don't be too long, now,' Destiny called after him. Peregrine heard Harry's sports car start up.

Peregrine told the stage-door keeper he could shut up shop and go. He returned to Emily. As he walked towards the darkened set he was aware of a slight movement and thought it must have been the pass-door into front-of-house. As if somebody had just gone through and softly closed it. A back-stage draught no doubt.

Emily was on the set. It was shut in by the fire-curtain and lit only by a dim infiltration from a working lamp back-stage; a dark, warm, still place.

'I always think it feels so strange,' she said, 'after we've left it to itself. As if it's got a life of its own. Waiting for us.'

'Another kind of reality?'

'Yes. A more impressive kind. You can almost imagine it breathes.'

A soughing movement of air up in the grille gave momentary confirmation of Emily's fancy.

'Come on,' Peregrine said. 'It's a fine starry night and no distance at all to the top of Wharfingers Lane.' He had taken her arm and was guiding her to the pass-door when they both heard a thud.

They stood still and asked each other: 'What was that?'

'Front-of-house?' Emily said.

'Yes. Winty or someone, I suppose.'

'Wouldn't they all have gone?'

'I'd have thought so.'

'What *was* it? The noise?'

Peregrine said: 'It sounded like a seat flapping up.'

'Yes. It did sound like that.'

'Wait a bit.'

'Where are you going?' she said anxiously.

'Not far. Just to have a look.'

'All right.'

He opened the pass-door. The little twisting stair was in darkness but he had a torch in his pocket. Steps led down to the stalls box and up from where he stood, to the box in the circle. He went down and then out into the stalls. They were in darkness. He flapped a seat down and let it spring back. That was the sound.

Peregrine called: 'Hallo. Anyone there?' but his voice fell dead in an upholstered silence.

He flashed his torch across walls and shrouded seats. He walked up the new central aisle and into the foyer. It was deserted and dimly lit and street doors were shut. Peregrine called up the stairs.

'Jobbins.'

'Eh?' Jobbins's voice said. 'That you, guv? Anything up?'

'I heard a seat flap. In front.'

'*Did*jer, guv?'

Jobbins appeared on the stairs. He wore an extremely loud brown, black and white checked overcoat, a woollen cap and carpet slippers.

'Good lord!' Peregrine ejaculated. 'Are you going to the Dogs or Ally Pally or what? Where's your brown bowler?'

'You again, guv?' Jobbins wheezed. 'I'd of 'eld back me quick change if I'd known. Pardon the dishy-bill. Present from a toff this 'ere coat is and very welcome. Gets chilly,' he said descending, 'between nah and the witching ar, when my relief comes in. What's this abaht a seat?'

Peregrine explained. To his astonishment Jobbins pushed the doors open, strode into the auditorium and uttered in a sort of hoarse bellow –

'Nah then. Out of it. Come on. You 'eard.'

Silence.

Then Emily's voice sounded worried and lonely: 'What goes on?' She had groped her way down into the house.

'It's all right,' Peregrine shouted. 'Won't be long.' And to Jobbins: 'What *does* go on? You sound as if you're used to this.'

'*Which* I am,' Jobbins sourly endorsed. 'It's that perishing child-wonder, that's what it is. 'E done it before and 'e'll do it again *and* once too often.'

'Does what?'

"'Angs abaht.'Is mum plays the steel guitar in a caff, see, acrost the river. She knocks off at eleven and 'er 'earts-delight sallies forth to greet 'er at the top of the lane. And 'e fills in the gap, buggering rhand the theyater trying to make out 'e's a robber or a spectrum. 'E knows full well I can't leave me post so 'e 'ides 'isself in various dark regions. "'Ands Up," 'e yells. "Stick 'em up," 'e 'owls, and crawls

under the seats making noises like 'e's bein' strangulated *which* 'e
will be if ever I lay me 'ands on 'im. Innit marvellous?'

From somewhere backstage a single plangent sound rang out and
faded. It was followed by an eldritch screech of laughter, a catcall
and a loud slam.

'There 'e goes,' said Jobbins and flung an ejaculation of startling
obscenity into the auditorium.

'I'll get that little bastard,' Peregrine said. He foolishly made a
dash for the treble-locked doors into the portico.

'You'll never catch 'im, guv,' Jobbins said. His voice had almost
vanished with excessive vocal exercise. ''E'll be 'alf-way up the lane
and going strong. His mum meets 'im at the top when she's sober.'

'I'll have the hide off him tomorrow,' Peregrine said. 'All right,
Jobbins. I'll see you're not pestered again. And anyway as far as the
treasure is concerned this is your last watch.'

'That's right, sir. Positively the last appearance in this epoch-mak-
ing role.'

'Good night again.'

'Good night, guv. Best of British luck.'

Peregrine went into the stalls. 'Emily!' he called. 'Where are you,
my poor girl?'

'Here,' Emily said, coming up the aisle.

'Did you see the little swine?'

'No. I was in front. He came down from the circle. I could hear
him on the steps.'

Peregrine looked at his watch. Five past eleven. He took her arm.
'Let's forget him,' he said, 'and sling our hooks. We've wasted ages.
They shut at midnight. Come on.'

They slammed the stage-door behind them. The night was still
fine and quite warm. They climbed Wharfingers Lane and went in
under the illuminated sign of the new bistro: 'The Younger Dolphin'.

It was crowded, noisy and extremely dark. The two waiters were
dressed as fishermen in tight jeans, striped jumpers and jelly-bag
caps. A bas relief of a dolphin wearing a mortarboard was lit from
below.

As their eyes adjusted to the gloom they saw that Destiny and her
three audience friends were established at a table under the dolphin
and had the air of slumming. Destiny waggled her fingers at them

and made faces to indicate that she couldn't imagine why she was there.

They ate grilled sole, drank lager, danced together on a pocket-handkerchief and greatly enjoyed themselves. Presently Destiny and her friends left. As they passed Emily and Peregrine she said: 'Darlings! We thought we would but oh, no, no.' They went away talking loudly about what they would have to eat when they got to Destiny's flat in Chelsea. At ten to twelve Peregrine said: 'Emily: why are you so stand-offish in the elder Dolphin and so come-toish in the younger one?'

'Partly because of your prestige and anyway I'm not all that oncoming, even here.'

'Yes, you are. You are when we're dancing. Not at first but suddenly, about ten minutes ago.'

'I'm having fun and I'm obliged to you for providing it.'

'Do you at all fancy me?'

'Very much indeed.'

'Don't say it brightly like that: it's insufferable.'

'Sorry.'

'And what do you mean, my prestige. Are you afraid people like Gertie, for example, will say you're having an advantageous carry-on with the author-producer?'

'Yes, I am.'

'How bloody silly. *"They say. What say they? Let them say".*'

'That aphorism was coined by a murdering cad.'

'What of it? Emily: I find you more attractive than any of my former girls. Now, don't flush up and bridle. I know you're not my girl, in actual fact. Emily,' Peregrine shouted against a screaming crescendo from the saxophonist. 'Emily, listen to me. I believe I love you.'

The little band had crashed to its climax and was silent. Peregrine's declaration rang out as a solo performance.

'After that,' Emily said, 'I almost think we had better ask for the bill, don't you?'

Peregrine was so put out that he did so. They left The Younger Dolphin assuring the anxious proprietor that they would certainly return.

Their plan had been to stroll over to Blackfriars, pick up Peregrine and Jeremy's car and drive to Hampstead.

They walked out of The Younger Dolphin into a deluge.

Neither of them had a mackintosh or an umbrella. They huddled in the entrance and discussed the likelihood of raising a cab. Peregrine went back and telephoned a radio taxi number to be told nothing would be available for at least twenty minutes. When he rejoined Emily the rain had eased off a little.

'I tell you what,' he said. 'I've got a gamp and a mac in the office. Let's run down the hill, beat Jobbins up and collect them. Look, it's almost stopped.'

'Come on, then.'

'Mind you don't slip.'

Hand in hand they ran wildly and noisily down Wharfingers Lane. They reached the turning at the bottom, rounded the corner and pulled up outside The Dolphin. They laughed and were exhilarated.

'Listen!' Emily exclaimed, 'Peregrine, listen. Somebody else is running in the rain.'

'It's someone in the stage-door alley.'

'So it is.'

The other runner's footsteps rang out louder and louder on the wet cobblestones. He came out of the alley into the lane and his face was open-mouthed like a gargoyle.

He saw them and he flung himself upon Peregrine, pawed at his coat and jabbered into his face. It was the night-watchman who relieved Jobbins.

'For Gawsake!' he said. 'Oh, my Gawd, Mr Jay, for Gawsake.'

'What the devil's the matter? *What is it? What's happened!*'

'Murder,' the man said, and his lips flabbered over the word. 'That's what's happened, Mr Jay. Murder.'

CHAPTER 6

Disaster

While he let them in at the stage-door the man – he was called Hawkins – said over and over again in a shrill whine that it wasn't his fault if he was late getting down to the theatre. Nobody, he said, could blame him. He turned queer, as was well-known, at the sight of blood. It was as much as Peregrine could do to get the victim's name out of him. He had gone completely to pieces.

They went through the stage-door into the dark house, and up the aisle and so to the foyer. It was as if they had never left the theatre.

Peregrine said to Emily: 'Wait here. By the box-office. Don't come any farther.'

'I'll come if you want me.'

'*O Gawd no. O Gawd no, Miss.*'

'Stay here, Emily. Or wait in front. Yes. Just wait in front.' He opened the doors into the stalls and fastened them back. She went in. 'Now, Hawkins,' Peregrine said.

'You go, Mr Jay. Up there. I don't 'ave to go. I can't do nothing. I'd vomit. Honest I would.'

Peregrine ran up the graceful stairway towards the sunken landing: under the treasure where both flights emerged. It was dark up there but he had a torch and used it. The beam shot out and found an object.

There, on its back in a loud overcoat and slippers lay the shell of Jobbins. The woollen cap had not fallen from the skull but had been stove into it. Out of what had been a face, broken like a crust now, and glistening red, one eye stared at nothing.

Beside this outrage lay a bronze dolphin, grinning away for all it was worth through a wet, unspeakable mask.

Everything round Peregrine seemed to shift a little as if his vision had swivelled like a movie camera. He saw, without comprehension, a square of reflected light on the far wall and its source above the landing. He saw, down below him, the top of Hawkins's head. He moved to the balustrade, held on to it and with difficulty controlled an upsurge of nausea. He fetched a voice out of himself.

'Have you rung the police?'

'I better had, didn't I? I better report, didn't I?' Hawkins gabbled without moving.

'Stay where you are. I'll do it.'

There was a general purposes telephone in the downstairs foyer outside the box-office. He ran down to it and, controlling his hand, dialled the so celebrated number. How instant and how cool the response.

'No possibility of survival, sir?'

'God, no. I told you – '

'Please leave everything as it is. You will be relieved in a few minutes. Which entrance is available? Thank you.'

Peregrine hung up. 'Hawkins,' he said. 'Go back to the stage-door and let the police in. Go on.'

'Yes. OK. Yes, Mr Jay.'

'Well, go *on*, damn you.'

Was there an independent switch anywhere in the foyer for front-of-house lighting or was it all controlled from backstage? Surely not. He couldn't remember. Ridiculous. Emily was out there in the darkened stalls. He went in and found her standing just inside the doors.

'Emily?'

'Yes. All right. Here I am.'

He felt her hands in his. 'This is a bad thing,' he said hurriedly. 'It's a very bad thing, Emily.'

'I heard what you said on the telephone.'

'They'll be here almost at once.'

'I see. Murder,' Emily said, trying the word.

'We can't be sure.'

They spoke aimlessly. Peregrine heard a high-pitched whine inside his own head and felt sickeningly cold. He wondered if he was

going to faint and groped for Emily. They put their arms about each
other. 'We must behave,' Peregrine said, 'in whatever way one is
expected to behave. You know? Calm? Collected? All the things
people like us are meant not to be.'

'That's right. Well, so we will.' He stooped his head to hers. 'Can
this be you?' he said.

A sound crept into their silence: a breathy intermittent sound
with infinitesimal interruptions that seemed to have some sort of
vocal quality. They told each other to listen.

With a thick premonition of what was to come, Peregrine put
Emily away from him.

He switched on his torch and followed its beam down the centre
aisle. He was under the overhang of the dress-circle but moved on
until its rim was above his head. It was here, in the centre aisle of
the stalls and below the circle balustrade, that his torchlight came to
rest on a small, breathing, faintly audible heap which as he knelt
beside it, revealed itself as an unconscious boy.

'Trevor,' Peregrine said. '*Trevor.*'

Emily behind him said, 'Has he been killed? Is he dying?'

'I don't know. What should we do? Ring for the ambulance? Ring
the Yard again? Which?'

'Don't move him. I'll ring Ambulance.'

'Yes.'

'Listen. Sirens.'

'Police.'

Emily said: 'I'll ring, all the same,' and was gone.

There seemed to be no interval of time between this moment and
the occupation of The Dolphin by uniformed policemen with heavy
necks and shoulders and quiet voices. Peregrine met the sergeant.

'Are you in charge? There's something else since I telephoned. A
boy. Hurt but alive. Will you look?'

The sergeant looked. He said: 'This might be serious. You haven't
touched him, sir?'

'No. Emily – Miss Dunne who is with me – is ringing the ambulance.'

'Can we have some light?'

Peregrine, remembering at last where they were, put the house-
lights on. More police were coming in at the stage-door. He rejoined

the sergeant. A constable was told to stay by the boy and report any change.

'I'll take a look at this body, if you please,' the sergeant said.

Emily was at the telephone in the foyer saying: 'It's very urgent. It's really urgent. Please.'

'If you don't mind, Miss,' said the sergeant and took the receiver. 'Police here,' he said and was authoritative. 'They'll be round in five minutes,' he said to Emily.

'Thank God.'

'Now then, Mr Jay.' He'd got Peregrine's name as he came in.

'May I go back to the boy?' Emily asked. 'In case he regains consciousness and is frightened? I know him.'

'Good idea,' said the sergeant with a kind of routine heartiness. 'You just stay there with the boy, Miss – ?'

'Dunne.'

'Miss Dunne. Members of the company here, would it be?'

'Yes,' Peregrine said. 'We were at the new restaurant in Wharfingers Lane and came back to shelter from the rain.'

'Is that so? I see. Well, Miss Dunne, you just stay with the boy and tell the ambulance all you know. Now, Mr Jay.'

A return to the sunken landing was a monstrous thing to contemplate. Peregrine said: 'Yes. I'll show you. If you don't mind I won't – ' and reminded himself of Hawkins. 'It's terrible,' he said. 'I'm sorry to balk. This way.'

'Up the stairs?' The sergeant asked conversationally, as if he inquired his way to the Usual Offices. 'Don't trouble to come up again, Mr Jay. The less traffic, you know, the better we like it.'

'Yes. Of course. I forgot.'

'If you'll just wait down here.'

'Yes. Thank you.'

The sergeant was not long on the landing. Peregrine could not help looking up at him and saw that, like himself, the sergeant did not go beyond the top step. He returned and went to the telephone. As he passed Peregrine he said: 'Very nasty, sir, isn't it,' in a preoccupied voice.

Peregrine couldn't hear much of what the sergeant said into the telephone. 'Some kind of caretaker – Jobbins – and a young lad – looks like it. Very good, sir. Yes. Yes. Very good': and then after a pause and in a mumble of words, one that came through very clearly.

.' – robbery – '

Never in the wide world would Peregrine have believed it of himself that a shock, however acute or a sight however appalling, could have so bludgeoned his wits. There, there on the wall opposite the one in which the treasure was housed, shone the tell-tale square of reflected light and there above his head as he stood on the stairs had been the exposed casket – exposed and brightly lit when it should have been shut off and –

He gave a kind of stifled cry and started up the stairs.

'Just a moment, sir. If you please.'

'The glove,' Peregrine said. 'The letters and the glove. I must see. I must look.'

The sergeant was beside him. A great hand closed without undue force round his upper arm.

'All right, sir. All right. But you can't go up there yet, you know. You join your young lady and the sick kiddy. And if you're referring to the contents of that glassed-in cabinet up there, I can tell you right away. It's been opened from the back and they seem to have gone.'

Peregrine let out an incoherent cry and blundered into the stalls to tell Emily.

For him and for Emily the next half hour was one of frustration, confusion and despair. They had to collect themselves and give statements to the sergeant who entered them at an even pace in his notebook. Peregrine talked about hours and duties and who ought to be informed and Mr Greenslade and Mr Conducis, and he stared at the sergeant's enormous forefinger, flattened across the image of a crown on a blue cover. Peregrine didn't know who Jobbins's next-of-kin might be. He said, as if that would help: 'He was a nice chap. He was a bit of a character. A nice chap.'

The theatre continually acquired more police: plainclothes, unhurried men, the most authoritative of whom was referred to by the sergeant as the Div-Super and addressed as Mr Gibson. Peregrine and Emily heard him taking a statement from Hawkins who cried very much and said it wasn't a fair go.

The ambulance came. Peregrine and Emily stood by while Trevor, the whites of his eyes showing under his heavy lashes and his breathing very heavy, was gently examined. A doctor appeared: the divisional surgeon, Peregrine heard someone say. Mr Gibson asked him if there was any chance of a return to consciousness and he said something about Trevor being deeply concussed.

'He's got broken ribs and a broken right leg,' he said, 'and an unbroken bruise on his jaw. It's a wonder he's alive. We won't know about the extent of internal injuries until we've had a look-see,' said the divisional surgeon. 'Get him into St Terence's at once.' He turned to Peregrine. 'Would you know of the next-of-kin?'

Peregrine was about to say: 'Only too well' but checked himself. 'Yes,' he said, 'his mother.'

'Would you have the address?' asked Mr Gibson. 'And the telephone number.'

'In the office. Upstairs. No, wait a moment. I've a cast list in my pocket-book. Here it is: Mrs Blewitt.'

'Perhaps you'd be so kind as to ring her, Mr Jay. She ought to be told at once. What's the matter, Mr Jay?'

'She meets him, usually. At the top of the lane. I – Oh god, poor Jobbins told me that. I wonder what she did when Trevor didn't turn up. You'd have thought she'd have come to the theatre.'

'Can we get this boy away?' asked the divisional surgeon crisply.

'OK, Doc. You better go with them,' Mr Gibson said to the constable who had stayed by Trevor. 'Keep your ears open. Anything. Whisper. Anything. Don't let some starched battle-axe push you about. We want to know what hit him. Don't leave him, now.'

Mr Gibson had a piece of chalk in his hand. He ran it round Trevor's little heap of a body, grinding it into the carpet. 'OK,' he said and Trevor was taken away.

The divisional surgeon said he'd take a look-see at the body and went off with the sergeant. Superintendent Gibson was about to accompany them when Peregrine and Emily, who had been in consultation, said: 'Er – ' and he turned back.

'Yes, Mr Jay? Miss Dunne? Was there something?'

'It's just,' Emily said, ' – we wondered if you knew that Mr Roderick Alleyn – I mean Superintendent Alleyn – supervised the installation of the things that were in the wall-safe. The things that have been stolen.'

'Rory *Alleyn*!' the superintendent ejaculated. 'Is that so? Now, why was that, I wonder?'

Peregrine explained. 'I think,' he said finally, 'that Mr Vassily Conducis, who owns the things – '

'So I understand.'

' – asked Mr Alleyn to do it as a special favour. Mr Alleyn was very much interested in the things.'

'He would be. Well, thank you,' said Mr Gibson rather heavily. 'And now, if you'd phone this Mrs Blewitt. Lives in my division, I see. Close to our headquarters. If she can't get transport to the hospital tell her, if you please, that we'll lay something on. No, wait. On second thoughts, I'll send a policewoman round from the station if one's available. Less of a shock.'

'Shouldn't we ring her up – just to warn her someone's coming?' Emily asked. 'Should I offer to go?'

Mr Gibson stared at her and said that he thought on the whole it would be better if Peregrine and Emily remained in the theatre a little longer but, yes, they could telephone to Mrs Blewitt after he himself had made one or two little calls. He padded off – not fast, not slow – towards the foyer. Peregrine and Emily talked disjointedly. After some minutes they heard sounds of new arrivals by the main entrance and of Superintendent Gibson greeting them.

'None of this is real,' Emily said presently.

'Are you exhausted?'

'I don't think so.'

'I ought to tell Greenslade,' Peregrine ejaculated. 'He ought to be told, good God!'

'And Mr Conducis? After all it's his affair.'

'Greenslade can tackle that one. Emily, are you in a muddle like me? I can't get on top of this. Jobbins. That appalling kid? Shakespeare's note and the glove. All broken and destroyed or stolen. Isn't it beastly, all of it? What *are* human beings? What's the thing that makes monsters of us all?'

'It's out of our country. We'll have to play it by ear.'

'No, but we *act* it. It's our raw material – Murder. Violence. Theft. Sexual greed. They're commonplace to us. We do our Stanislavsky over them. We search out motives and associated experiences. We try to think our way into Macbeth or Othello or a witch-hunt or an Inquisitor or a killer-doctor at Auschwitz and sometimes we think we've succeeded. But confront us with the thing itself! It's as if a tractor had rolled over us. *We're* nothing. Superintendent Gibson is there instead to put it all on a sensible, factual basis.'

'Good luck to him,' said Emily rather desperately.

'Good luck? You think? All right, if you say so.'

'Perhaps I can now ring up Mrs Blewitt.'

'I'll come with you.'

The foyer was brilliantly lit and there were voices and movement upstairs where Jobbins lay. Cameramen's lamps flashed and grotesquely reminded Peregrine of the opening night of his play. Superintendent Gibson's voice and that of the divisional surgeon were clearly distinguishable. There was also a new rather comfortable voice. Downstairs, a constable stood in front of the main doors. Peregrine told him that Mr Gibson had said they might use the telephone and the constable replied pleasantly that it would be quite all right he was sure.

Peregrine watched Emily dial the number and wait with the receiver to her ear. How pale she was. Her hair was the kind that goes into a mist after it has been out in the rain and her wide mouth drooped at the corners like a child's. He could hear the buzzer ringing, on and on. Emily had just shaken her head at him when the telephone quacked angrily. She spoke for some time, evidently to no avail, and at last hung up.

'A man,' she said. 'A landlord, I should think. He was livid. He says Mrs Blewitt went to a party after her show and didn't meet Trevor tonight. He says she's "flat out to it" and nothing would rouse her. So he hung up.'

'The policewoman will have to cope. I'd better rouse Greenslade, I suppose. He lives at some godawful place in the stockbrokers' belt. Here goes.'

Evidently Mr and Mrs Greenslade had a bedside telephone. She could be heard, querulous and half-asleep, in the background. Mr Greenslade said: 'Shut up, darling. Very well, Jay, I'll come down. Does Alleyn know?'

'I – I don't suppose so. I told the superintendent that Alleyn would be concerned.'

'He should have been told. Find out, will you? I'll come at once.'

'Find out,' Peregrine angrily repeated to Emily. 'I can't go telling the police who they ought to call in, blast it. How can I *find out* if Alleyn's been told?'

'Easily,' Emily rejoined with a flicker of a smile. 'Because, look.'

The constable had opened the pass-door in the main entrance and now admitted Superintendent Alleyn in the nearest he ever got to a filthy temper.

II

Alleyn had worked late and unfruitfully at the Yard in company with Inspector Fox. As he let himself into his own house he heard the telephone ring, swore loudly and got to it just as his wife, Troy, took the receiver off in their bedroom.

It was the Chief Commander who was his immediate senior at the Yard. Alleyn listened with disgust to his story. ' – and so Fred Gibson thought that as you know Conducis and had a hand in the installation, he'd better call us. He just missed you at the Yard. All things considered I think you'd better take over, Rory. It's a big one. Murder. Double, if the boy dies. And robbery of these bloody, fabulous museum pieces.'

'Very good,' Alleyn said. 'All right. Yes.'

'Got your car out or garaged?'

'Thank you. Out.'

It was nothing new to turn round in his tracks after one gruelling day and work through till the next. He took five minutes to have a word with Troy and a rapid shave and was back in the car and heading for the Borough within half an hour of leaving the Yard. The rain had lifted but the empty streets glistened under their lamps.

He could have kicked himself from Whitehall to Bankside. Why, why, why hadn't he put his foot down about the safe and its silly window and bloody futile combination lock? Why hadn't he said that he would on no account recommend it? He reminded himself that he had given sundry warnings but snapped back at himself that he should have gone further. He should have telephoned Conducis and advised him not to go on with the public display of the Shakespeare treasures. He should have insisted on that ass of a business manager scrapping his imbecile code-word, penetrable in five minutes by a certified moron, and should have demanded a new combination. The fact that he had been given no authority to do so and had nevertheless urged precisely this action upon Mr Winter Morris made no difference. He should have thrown his weight about.

And now some poor damned commissionaire had been murdered. Also, quite probably, the unspeakably ghastly little boy who had cheeked him in The Dolphin. And Hamnet Shakespeare's glove and Hamnet's father's message had inspired these atrocities and were gone. Really, Alleyn thought, as he drew up by the portico of The Dolphin Theatre, he hadn't been so disgruntled since he took a trip to Cape Town with a homicidal pervert.

Then he entered the theatre and came face-to-face with Peregrine and Emily and saw how white and desperate they looked and recognized the odd vagueness that so often overcomes people who have been suddenly confronted with a crime of violence. He swallowed his chagrin and summoned up the professionalism that he had once sourly defined as an infinite capacity to notice less and less with more and more accuracy.

He said: 'This is no good at all, is it? What are you two doing here?'

'We got here,' Peregrine said, 'just after.'

'You look as if you'd better go and sit down somewhere. 'Morning, Fred,' Alleyn said, meeting Superintendent Gibson at the foot of the stair. 'What's first?' He looked towards the half-landing and without waiting for an answer walked upstairs followed by Gibson.

Among the group of men and cameras was an elderly thick-set man with a grizzled moustache and bright eyes.

'Hallo,' Alleyn said. 'You again.'

'That's right, Mr Alleyn,' said Inspector Fox. 'Just beat you to it. I was still at the Yard when they rang up so the CC said I might as well join in. Don't quite know why and I daresay Fred doesn't either.'

'More the merrier,' Mr Gibson rejoined gloomily. 'This looks like being an extra curly one.'

'Well,' Alleyn said. 'I'd better see.'

'We covered him,' Gibson said. 'With a dust sheet. It's about as bad as they come. Worst *I've* ever seen. Now!'

'Very nasty,' Fox said. He nodded to one of the men. 'OK, Bailey.'

Detective-Sergeant Bailey, a fingerprint expert, uncovered the body of Jobbins.

It was lying on its back with the glittering mask and single eye appallingly exposed. The loudly checked coat was open and dragged

back into what must be a knotted lump under the small of the back.
Between the coat and the dirty white sweater there was a rather
stylish yellow scarf. The letter H had been embroidered on it. It was
blotted and smeared. The sweater itself was soaked in patches of red
and had ridden up over the chest. There was something almost
homely and normal in the look of a tartan shirt running in sharp
folds under the belted trousers that were strained across the crutch
by spread-eagled legs.

Alleyn looked, waited an appreciable time and then said: 'Has he
been photographed? Printed?'

'The lot,' somebody said.

'I want to take some measurements. Then he can be moved. I see
you've got a mortuary van outside. Get the men up.' The sergeant
moved to the stairhead. 'Just make sure those two young people are
out of the way,' Alleyn said.

He held out his hand and Fox gave him a steel spring-tape. They
measured the distance from that frightful head to the three shallow
steps that led up to the circle foyer and marked the position of the
body. When Jobbins was gone and the divisional surgeon after him,
Alleyn looked at the bronze dolphin, glistening on the carpet.

'There's your weapon,' Gibson said unnecessarily.

The pedestal had been knocked over and lay across the shallow
steps at the left hand corner. The dolphin, detached, lay below it on
the landing, close to a dark blot on the crimson carpet where
Jobbins's head had been. Its companion piece still made an elegant
arc on the top of its own pedestal near the wall. They had stood to
left and right at the head of the stairs in the circle foyer. Four steps
below the landing lay a thick cup in a wet patch and below it another one and a small tin tray.

'His post,' Alleyn said, 'was on this sunken landing under – '

He looked up. There, still brilliantly lit, was the exposed casket,
empty.

'That's correct,' Gibson said. 'He was supposed to stay there until
he was relieved by this chap Hawkins at midnight.'

'Where is this Hawkins?'

'Ah,' Gibson said disgustedly. 'Sobbing his little heart out in the
gents' cloaks. He's gone to pieces.'

Fox said austerely: 'He seems to have acted very foolishly from the start. Comes in late. Walks up here. Sees deceased and goes yelling out of the building.'

'That's right,' Gibson agreed. 'And if he hadn't run into this Mr Jay and his lady friend he might be running still and us none the wiser.'

'So it was Jay who rang the police?' Alleyn interjected.

'That's correct.'

'What about their burglar alarm?'

'Off. The switch is back of the box-office.'

'I know. They showed me. What then, Fred?'

'The sergeant's sent in and gets support. I get the office and I come in and we set up a search. Thought our man might be hiding on the premises but not. Either got out of it before Hawkins arrived or slipped away while he was making an exhibition of himself. The pass-door in the main entrance was shut but not locked. It had *been* locked, they say, so it looked as if that was his way out.'

'And the boy?'

'Yes. Well, now. The boy. Mr Jay says the boy's a bit of a young limb. Got into the habit of hanging around after the show and acting the goat. Jobbins complained of him making spook noises and that. He was at it before Mr Jay and Miss Dunne left the theatre to go out to supper. Mr Jay tried to find him but it was dark and he let out a cat-call or two and then they heard the stage-door slam and reckoned he'd gone. Not, as it turns out.'

'Evidently. I'll see Hawkins now, Fred.'

Hawkins was produced in the downstage foyer. He was a plain man made plainer by bloodshot eyes, a reddened nose and a loose mouth. He gazed lugubriously at Alleyn, spoke of shattered nerves and soon began to cry.

'Who's going to pitch into me next?' he asked. 'I ought to be getting hospital attention, the shock I've had, and not subjected to treatment that'd bring about an inquiry if I made complaints. I ought to be home in bed getting looked after.'

'So you shall be,' Alleyn said. 'We'll send you home in style when you've just told me quietly what happened.'

'I have! I have told. I've told them others.'

'All right. I know you're feeling rotten and it's a damn' shame to keep you but you see you're the chap we're looking to for help.'

'Don't you use that yarn to me. I know what the police mean when they talk about help. Next thing it'll be the Usual Bloody Warning.'

'No, it won't. Look here – I'll say what I think happened and you jump on me if I'm wrong. All right?'

'How do I know if it's right!'

'Nobody suspects you, you silly chap,' Fox said. 'How many more times!'

'Never mind,' Alleyn soothed. 'Now, listen, Hawkins. You came down to the theatre. When? About ten past twelve?'

Hawkins began a great outcry against buses and thunderstorms but was finally induced to say he heard the hour strike as he walked down the lane.

'And you came in by the stage-door. Who let you in?'

Nobody, it appeared. He had a key. He banged it shut and gave a whistle and shouted. Pretty loudly, Alleyn gathered, because Jobbins was always at his post on the half-landing, and he wanted to let him know he'd arrived. He came in, locked the door and shot the bolt. He supposed Jobbins was fed up with him for being late. This account was produced piecemeal and with many lamentable excursions. Hawkins now became extremely agitated and said what followed had probably made a wreck of him for the rest of his life. Alleyn displayed sympathy and interest, however, and was flattering in his encouragement. Hawkins gazed upon him with watering eyes and said that what followed was something chronic. He had seen no light in the property room so had switched his torch on and gone out to front-of-house. As soon as he got there he noticed a dim light in the circle. And there – it had given him a turn – in the front row, looking down at him was Henry Jobbins in his flash new overcoat.

'You never told us this!' Gibson exclaimed.

'You never arst me.'

Fox and Gibson swore quietly together.

'Go on,' Alleyn said.

'I said: "That you, Hen?" and he says "Who d'yer think it is" and I said I was sorry I was late and should I make the tea and he said yes. So I went into the props room and made it.'

'How long would that take?'

'It's an old electric jug. Bit slow.'

'Yes? And then?'

'O Gawd. O Gawd.'

'I know. But go on.'

He had carried the two cups of tea through the house to the front foyer and up the stairs.

Here Hawkins broke down again in a big way but finally divulged that he had seen the body, dropped the tray, tried to claw his way out at front, run by the side aisle through the stalls and pass-door, out of the stage-door and down the alley where he ran into Peregrine and Emily. Alleyn got his address and sent him home.

'What a little beauty,' Fred Gibson said.

'You tell me,' Alleyn observed, 'that you've searched the theatre. What kind of search, Fred?'

'How d'you mean?'

'Well – obviously, as you say, for the killer. But have they looked for the stuff?'

'Stuff – ?'

'For a glove, for instance, and two scraps of writing?'

There was a very short silence and then Gibson said: 'There hasn't really been time. We would, of course.'

Fox said: 'If he was surprised, you mean, and dropped them? Something of that nature?'

'It's a forlorn hope, no doubt,' Alleyn said. He looked at Sergeant Bailey and the cameraman who was Sergeant Thompson: both of the Yard. 'Have you tackled this dolphin?'

'Just going to when you arrived, sir,' Thompson said.

'Take it as it lies before you touch it. It's in a ghastly state but there may be something. And the pedestal, of course. What's the thing weigh?'

He went to the top of the stairs, took the other dolphin from its base, balanced and hefted it. 'A tidy lump,' he said.

'Do you reckon it could have been used as a kind of club?' Fox asked.

'Only by a remarkably well-muscled-up specimen, Br'er Fox.' Alleyn replaced the dolphin and looked at it. 'Nice,' he said. 'He does that sort of thing beautifully.' He turned to Gibson. 'What about routine, Fred?'

'We're putting it round the division. Anybody seen in the precincts of The Dolphin or the Borough or farther out. Might be bloody, might be nervous. That's the story. I'd be just as glad to get back, Rory. We've got a busy night on in my Div as it happens. Bottle fight at the Cat and Crow with a punch-up and knives. Probable fatality and three break-and-enters. *And* a suspected arson. You're fully equipped, aren't you?'

'Yes. All right, Fred, cut away. I'll keep in touch.'

'Good night, then. Thanks.'

When Gibson had gone Alleyn said: 'We'll see where the boy was and then have a word with Peregrine Jay and Miss Dunne. How many chaps have you got here?' he asked the sergeant.

'Four at present, sir. One in the foyer, one at the stage-door, one with Hawkins and another just keeping an eye, like, on Mr Jay and Miss Dunne.'

'Right. Leave the stage-door man and get the others going on a thorough search. Start in the circle. Where was this boy?'

'In the stalls, sir. Centre aisle and just under the edge of the circle.'

'Tell them not to touch the balustrade. Come on, Fox.'

When Alleyn and Fox went into the now fully lit stalls the first thing they noticed was a rather touching group made by Peregrine and Emily. They sat in the back row by the aisle. Peregrine's head had inclined to Emily's shoulder and her arm was about his neck. He was fast asleep. Emily stared at Alleyn who nodded. He and Fox walked down the aisle to the chalk outline of Trevor's body.

'And the doctor says a cut on the head, broken thigh and ribs, a bruise on the jaw and possible internal injuries?'

'That's correct,' Fox agreed.

Alleyn looked at the back of the aisle seat above the trace of the boy's head. 'See here, Fox.'

'Yes. Stain all right. Still damp, isn't it?'

'I think so. Yes.'

They both moved a step or two down the aisle and looked up at the circle. Three policemen and the sergeant with Thompson and Bailey were engaged in a methodical search.

'Bailey,' Alleyn said raising his voice very slightly.

'Sir?'

'Have a look at the balustrade above us here. Look at the pile in the velvet. Use your torch if necessary.'

There was a longish silence broken by Emily saying quietly: 'It's all right. Go to sleep again.'

Bailey moved to one side and looked down into the stalls. 'We've got something here, Mr Alleyn,' he said. 'Two sets of tracks with the pile dragged slantways in a long diagonal line outwards towards the edge. Some of it removed. Looks like fingernails. Trace of something that might be shoe-polish.'

'All right. Deal with it, you and Thompson.'

Fox said: 'Well, well: a fall, eh?'

'Looks that way, doesn't it? A fall from the circle about twenty feet. I suppose nobody looked at the boy's fingernails. Who found him?' Fox, with a jerk of his head indicated Peregrine and Emily. 'They'd been sent in here,' he said, 'to get them out of the way.'

'We'll talk to them now, Fox.'

Peregrine was awake. He and Emily sat hand-in-hand and looked more like displaced persons than anything else, an effect that was heightened by the blueness of Peregrine's jaws and the shadows under their eyes.

Alleyn said: 'I'm sorry you've been kept so long. It's been a beastly business for both of you. Now, I'm going to ask Mr Fox to read over what you have already said to Mr Gibson and his sergeant and you shall tell us if, on consideration, this is a fair statement.'

Fox did this and they nodded and said yes: that was it.

'Good,' Alleyn said. 'Then there's only one other question. Did either of you happen to notice Trevor Vere's fingernails?'

They stared at him and both repeated in pallid voices: 'His fingernails?'

'Yes. You found him and I think you, Miss Dunne, stayed with him until he was taken away.'

Emily rubbed her knuckles in her eyes. 'Oh dear,' she said, 'I *must* pull myself together. Yes. Yes, of course I did. I stayed with him.'

'Perhaps you held his hand as one does with a sick child?'

'It's hard to think of Trevor as a child,' Peregrine said. 'He was born elderly. Sorry.'

'But I did,' Emily exclaimed. 'You're right. I felt his pulse and then, you know, I went on holding his hand.'

'Looking at it?'

'Not specially. Not *glaring* at it. Although – '

'Yes?'

'Well, I remember I did sort of look at it. I moved it between my own hands and I remember noticing how grubby it was which made it childish and – then – there was something – ' She hesitated.

'Yes?'

'I thought he'd got rouge or carmine make-up under his nails and then I saw it wasn't grease. It was fluff.'

'I tell you what,' Alleyn said. 'We'll put you up for the Police Medal, you excellent girl. Fox: get on to St Terence's hospital and tell them it's as much as their life is worth to dig out that boy's nails. Tell our chap there he can clean them himself and put the harvest in an envelope and get a witness to it. Throw your bulk about. Get the top battle-axe and give her fits. Fly.'

Fox went off at a stately double.

'Now,' Alleyn said. 'You may go, both of you. Where do you live?'

They told him Blackfriars and Hampstead respectively.

'We could shake you down, Emily,' Peregrine said. 'Jeremy and I.'

'I'd like to go home, please, Perry. Could you call a taxi?'

'I think we can send you,' Alleyn said. 'I shan't need a car yet awhile and there's a gaggle of them out there.'

Peregrine said: 'I ought to wait for Greenslade, Emily.'

'Yes, of course you ought.'

'Well,' Alleyn said. 'We'll bundle you off to Hampstead, Miss Dunne. Where's the sergeant?'

'Here, sir,' said the sergeant unexpectedly. He had come in from the foyer.

'What's the matter?' Alleyn asked. 'What've you got there?'

The sergeant's enormous hands were clapped together in front of him and arched a little as if they enclosed something that fluttered and might escape.

'Seventh row of the stalls, sir,' he said, 'centre aisle. On the floor about six foot from where the boy lay. There was a black velvet kind of easel affair and a sheet of polythene laying near them.'

He opened his palms like a book and disclosed a little wrinkled glove and two scraps of parchment.

'Would they be what was wanted?' asked the sergeant.

III

'To me,' said Mr Greenslade with palpable self-restraint, 'there can be only one explanation, my dear Alleyn. The boy, who is, as Jay informs us, an unpleasant and mischievous boy, banged the door to suggest he'd gone but actually stayed behind and, having by some means learnt the number of the combination, robbed the safe of its contents. He was caught in the act by Jobbins who must have seen him from his post on the half-landing. As Jobbins made for him the boy, possibly by accident, overturned the pedestal. Jobbins was felled by the dolphin and the boy, terrified, ran into the circle and down the centre aisle. In his panic he ran too fast, stumbled across the balustrade, clutched at the velvet top and fell into the stalls. As he fell he let go the easel with the glove and papers and they dropped, as he did, into the aisle.'

Mr Greenslade, looking, in his unshaven state, strangely unlike himself, spread his hands and threw himself back in Winter Morris's chair. Peregrine sat behind his own desk and Alleyn and Fox in two of the modish seats reserved for visitors. The time was twelve minutes past three and the air stale with the aftermath of managerial cigarettes and drinks.

'You say nothing,' Mr Greenslade observed. 'You disagree?'

Alleyn said: 'As an open-and-shut theory it has its attractions. It's tidy. It's simple. It means that we all sit back and hope for the boy to recover consciousness and health so that we can send him to the Juvenile Court for manslaughter.'

'What I can't quite see – ' Peregrine began and then said, 'Sorry.'

'No. Go on,' Alleyn said.

'I can't see why the boy, having got the documents and glove, should come out to the circle foyer where he'd be sure to be seen by Jobbins on the half-landing. Why didn't he go down through the circle by the box, stairs, and pass-door to the stage and let himself out by the stage-door?'

'He might have wanted to show off. He might have – I am persuaded,' Mr Greenslade said crossly, 'that your objections can be met.'

'There's another thing,' Peregrine said, 'and I should have thought of it before. At midnight, Jobbins had to make a routine report to police and fire-station. He'd do it from the open telephone in the downstairs foyer.'

'Very well,' said Greenslade. 'That would give the boy his opportunity. What do you say, Alleyn?'

'As an investigating officer I'm supposed to say nothing,' Alleyn said lightly. 'But since the people at the bistro up the lane and the wretched Hawkins all put Jay out of the picture as a suspect and you yourself appear to have been some thirty miles away – '

'Well, I must say!'

' – there's no reason why I shouldn't ask you to consider under what circumstances the boy, still clutching his booty, could have fallen from the circle with his face towards the balustrade and as he fell have clawed at the velvet top, palms down in such a posture that he's left nail-tracks almost parallel with the balustrade but slanting towards the outside. There are also traces of boot polish that suggests one of his feet brushed back the pile at the same time. I cannot, myself, reconcile these traces with a nose-dive over the balustrade. I can relate them to a blow to the jaw, a fall across the balustrade, a lift, a sidelong drag and a drop. I also think Jay's objections are very well urged. There may be answers to them but at the moment I can't think of any. What's more, if the boy's the thief and killer, who unshot the bolts and unslipped the iron bar on the little pass-door in the main front entrance? Who left the key in the lock and banged the door shut from outside?'

'*Did* someone do this?'

'That's how things were when the police arrived.'

'I – I didn't notice. I didn't notice that,' Peregrine said, putting his hand to his eyes. 'It was the shock, I suppose.'

'I expect it was.'

'Jobbins would have bolted the little door and dropped the bar when everyone had gone and I think he always hung the key in the corner beyond the box-office.'

'No,' Peregrine said slowly. 'I can't see the boy doing that thing with the door. It doesn't add up.'

'Not really, does it?' Alleyn said mildly.

'What action,' Mr Greenslade asked, 'do you propose to take?'

'The usual routine and a very tedious affair it's likely to prove. There may be useful prints on the pedestal or the dolphin itself but I'm inclined to think that the best we can hope for there is negative evidence. There may be prints on the safe but so far Sergeant Bailey has found none. The injuries to the boy's face are interesting.'

'If he recovers consciousness,' Peregrine said, 'he'll tell the whole story.'

'Not if he's responsible,' Mr Greenslade said obstinately.

'Concussion,' Alleyn said, 'can be extremely tricky. In the meantime, of course, we'll have to find out about all the members of the company and the front-of-house staff and so on.'

'Find out?'

'Their movements for one thing. You may be able to help us here,' Alleyn said to Peregrine. 'It seems that apart from the boy, you and Miss Dunne were the last to leave the theatre. Unless, of course, somebody lay doggo until you'd gone. Which may well be the case. Can you tell us anything about how and when and by what door the other members of the cast went out?'

'I think I can,' Peregrine said. He was now invested with the kind of haggard vivacity that follows emotional exhaustion: a febrile alertness such as he had often felt after some hideously protracted dress-rehearsal. He described the precautions taken at the close of every performance to ensure that nobody was left on the premises. A thorough search of the house was made by backstage and front-of-house staff. He was certain it would have been quite impossible for anybody in the audience to hide anywhere in the theatre.

He related rapidly and accurately how the stage-crew left the theatre in a bunch and how Gertrude Bracey and Marcus Knight went out together through the auditorium to escape the wet. They had been followed by Charles Random, who was alone and used the stage-door and then by Emily who stayed offstage with Peregrine.

'And then,' Peregrine said, 'Destiny Meade and Harry Grove came out with a clutch of friends. They were evidently going on to a party. They went down the stage-door alley and I heard Harry call out that he'd fetch something or another and Destiny tell him not to be too

long. And it was then – I'd come back from having a look at the
weather – it was then that I fancied – ' He stopped.

'Yes?'

'I thought that the pass-door from stage to front-of-house moved.
It was out of the tail of my eye, sort of. If I'm right and I think I am,
it must have been that wretched kid, I suppose.'

'But you never saw him?'

'Never. No. Only heard him.' And Peregrine described how he
had gone out to the front and his subsequent interview with
Jobbins. Alleyn took him over this again because, so he said, he
wanted to make sure he'd got it right. 'You shaped up to chasing the
boy, did you? After you heard him catcall and slam the stage-door?'

'Yes. But Jobbins pointed out he'd be well on his way. So we said
good night and – '

'Yes?'

'I've just remembered. Do you know what we said to each other?
I said: "This is your last watch" and he said: "That's right. Positively
the last appearance." Because the treasure was to be taken away
today, you see. And after that Jobbins wouldn't have had to be glued
to the half-landing.'

Greenslade and Fox made slight appropriate noises. Alleyn waited for a moment and then said: 'And so you said good night and you
and Miss Dunne left? By the stage-door?'

'Yes.'

'Was it locked? Before you left?'

'No. Wait a moment, though. I think the Yale lock was on but
certainly not the bolts. Hawkins came in by the stage-door. He had
a key. He's a responsible man from a good firm though you wouldn't
think it from his behaviour tonight. He let himself in and then shot
the bolts.'

'Yes,' Alleyn said. 'We got that much out of him. Nothing else you
can tell us?'

Peregrine said: 'Not so far as I can think. But all the same I've got
a sort of notion that there's some damn' thing I've forgotten. Some
detail.'

'To do with what? Any idea?'

'To do with – I don't know. The boy, I think.'

'The boy?'

'I fancy I was thinking about a production of *The Cherry Orchard,* but – no, it's gone and I daresay it's of no consequence.'

Mr Greenslade said: 'I know this is not your concern, Alleyn, but I hope you don't mind my raising the point with Jay. I should like to know what happens to the play. Does the season continue? I am unfamiliar with theatrical practice.'

Peregrine said with some acidity: 'Theatrical practice doesn't habitually cover the death by violence of one of its employees.'

'Quite.'

'But all the same,' Peregrine said, 'there *is* a certain attitude – '

'Quite. Yes. The – er – "the show",' quoted Mr Greenslade self-consciously, '"must go on".'

'I *think we should* go on. The boy's understudy's all right. Tomorrow – no, today's Sunday, which gives us a chance to collect ourselves.' Peregrine fetched up short and turned to Alleyn. 'Unless,' he said, 'the police have any objection.'

'It's a bit difficult to say at this juncture, you know, but we should be well out of The Dolphin by Monday night. Tomorrow night, in fact. You want an answer long before that, of course. I think I may suggest that you carry on as if for performance. If anything crops up to change the situation we shall let you know at once.'

With an air of shocked discovery Peregrine said: 'There's a great deal to be done. There's that – that – that – dreadful state of affairs on the half-landing.'

'I'm afraid we shall have to take up a section of the carpet. My chaps will do that. Can you get it replaced in time?'

'I suppose so,' Peregrine said, rubbing his hand across his face. 'Yes. Yes, we can do something about it.'

'We've removed the bronze dolphin.'

Peregrine told himself that he mustn't think about that. He must keep in the right gear and, Oh God, he mustn't be sick.

He muttered: 'Have you? I suppose so. Yes.'

Mr Greenslade said: 'If there's nothing more one can do – ' and stood up. 'One has to inform Mr Conducis,' he sighed and was evidently struck by a deadly thought. 'The Press!' he cried. 'My God, the Press!'

'The Press,' Alleyn rejoined, 'is in full lurk outside the theatre. We have issued a statement to the effect that a night-watchman at The

Dolphin has met with a fatal accident but that there is no further indication at the moment of how this came about.'

'*That* won't last long,' Mr Greenslade grunted as he struggled into his overcoat. He gave Alleyn his telephone number, gloomily told Peregrine he supposed they would be in touch and took his leave.

'I shan't keep you any longer,' Alleyn said to Peregrine. 'But I shall want to talk to all the members of the cast and staff during the day. I see there's a list of addresses and telephone numbers here. If none of them objects I shall ask them to come here to The Dolphin, rather than call on them severally. It will save time.'

'Shall I tell them?'

'That's jolly helpful of you but I think it had better be official.'

'Oh. Oh, yes. Of course.'

'I expect you'll want to tell them what's happened and warn them they'll be needed but we'll organize the actual interviews. Eleven o'clock this morning, perhaps.'

'I must be with them,' Peregrine said. 'If you please.'

'Yes, of course,' Alleyn said. 'Good night.'

Peregrine thought absently that he had never seen a face so transformed by a far from excessive smile. Quite heartened by this phenomenon he held out his hand.

'Good night,' he said, 'there's one saving grace at last in all this horror.'

'Yes?'

'Oh, *yes*,' Peregrine said warmly and looked at a small glove and two scraps of writing that lay before Alleyn on Winter Morris's desk. 'You know,' he said, 'if they had been lost I really think I might have gone completely bonkers. You – you will take care of them?'

'Great care,' Alleyn said.

When Peregrine had gone Alleyn sat motionless and silent for so long that Fox was moved to clear his throat.

Alleyn bent over the treasure. He took a jeweller's eye-glass out of his pocket. He inserted a long index finger in the glove and turned back the gauntlet. He examined the letters HS and then the seams of the glove and then the work on the back.

'What's up, Mr Alleyn?' Fox asked. 'Anything wrong?'

'Oh, my dear Br'er Fox, I'm afraid so. I'm afraid there's no saving grace in this catastrophe, after all, for Peregrine Jay.'

CHAPTER 7

Sunday Morning

'I didn't knock you up when I came in,' Peregrine said. 'There seemed no point. It was getting light. I just thought I'd leave the note to wake me at seven. And oddly enough I did sleep. Heavily.'

Jeremy stood with his back to Peregrine, looking out of the bed-room window. 'Is that all?' he asked.

'All?'

'That happened?'

'I should have thought it was enough, my God!'

'I know,' Jeremy said without turning. 'I only meant: did you look at the glove?'

'I saw it, I told you. The sergeant brought it to Alleyn with the two documents and afterwards Alleyn laid them out on Winty's desk.'

'I wonder if it was damaged.'

'I don't think so. I didn't *examine* it. I wouldn't have been let. Fingerprints and all that. It seems they really do fuss away about fingerprints.'

'What'll they do with the things?'

'I don't know. Lock them up at the Yard, I imagine, until they've finished with them and then return them to Conducis.'

'To Conducis. Yes.'

'I must get up, Jer. I've got to ring Winty and the cast and the understudy and find out about the boy's condition. Look, you know the man who did the carpets. Could you ring him up at wherever he lives and tell him he simply must send men in, first thing tomorrow or if necessary tonight. To replace about two or three square yards of carpet on the half-landing. We'll pay overtime and time again and whatever.'

'The half-landing?'

Peregrine said very rapidly in a high-pitched voice: 'Yes. The carpet. On the half-landing. It's got Jobbins's blood and brains all over it. The carpet.'

Jeremy turned grey and said: 'I'm sorry. I'll do that thing,' and walked out of the room.

When Peregrine had bathed and shaved he swallowed with loathing two raw eggs in Worcester Sauce and addressed himself to the telephone, a task made no easier by a twanging fault on his line. The time was twenty past seven.

On the South Bank in the borough of Southwark, Superintendent Alleyn, having left Inspector Fox to arrange the day's business, drove over Blackfriars Bridge to St Terence's Hospital, and was conducted to a ward where Trevor Vere, screened from general view and deeply sighing, lay absorbed in the enigma of unconsciousness. At his bed-side sat a uniformed constable whose helmet was under his chair and his notebook in his hand. Alleyn was escorted by the ward sister and a house-surgeon.

'As you see, he's deeply concussed,' said the house-surgeon. 'He fell on his feet and drove his spine into the base of his head and probably crashed the back of a seat. As far as we can tell there's no profound injury internally. Right femur and two ribs broken. Extensive bruising. You may be sure he was bloody lucky. A twenty foot fall, I understand.'

'The bruise on his jaw?'

'That's a bit of a puzzle. It doesn't look like the back or arm of a seat. It's got all the characteristics of a nice hook to the jaw. I wouldn't care to say definitely, of course. Sir James has seen him.' (Sir James Curtis was the Home Office pathologist.) '*He* thinks it looks like a punch.'

'Ah. Yes, so he said. It's no use my asking, of course, when the boy may recover consciousness?'

'I'm afraid no use at all. Can't tell.'

'Or how much he will remember?'

'The usual thing is complete loss of memory for events occurring just before the accident.'

'Alas.'

'What? Oh, quite. You must find that sort of thing very frustrating.'

'Very. I wonder if it would be possible to take the boy's height and length of his arms, would it?'

'He can't be disturbed.'

'I know. But if he might be uncovered for a moment. It really is important.'

The young house-surgeon thought for a moment and then nodded to the sister who folded back the bedclothes.

'I'm very much obliged to you,' Alleyn said three minutes later and replaced the clothes.

'Well, if that's all – ?'

'Yes. Thank you very much. I mustn't keep you. Thank you, Sister. I'll just have a word with the constable, here, before I go.'

The constable had withdrawn to the far side of the bed.

'You're the chap who came here with the ambulance, aren't you?' Alleyn asked.

'Yes, sir.'

'You should have been relieved. You heard about instructions from Mr Fox concerning the boy's fingernails?'

'Yes, I did, sir, but only after he'd been cleaned up.'

Alleyn swore in a whisper.

'But I'd happened to notice – ' The constable – wooden-faced – produced from a pocket in his tunic a folded paper. 'It was in the ambulance, sir. While they were putting a blanket over him. They were going to tuck his hands under and I noticed they were a bit dirty like a boy's often are but the fingernails had been manicured. Colourless varnish and all. And then I saw two were broken back and the others kind of choked up with red fluff and I cleaned them out with my penknife.' He modestly proffered his little folded paper.

'What's your name?' Alleyn asked.

'Grantley, sir.'

'Want to move out of the uniformed arm?'

'I'd like to.'

'Yes. Well, come and see me if you apply for a transfer.'

'Thank you, sir.'

Trevor Vere sighed lengthily in his breathing. Alleyn looked at the not-so-closed eyes, the long lashes and the full mouth that had smirked so unpleasingly at him that morning in The Dolphin. It was merely childish now. He touched the forehead which was cool and dampish.

'Where's his mother?' Alleyn asked.

'They say, on her way.'

'She's difficult, I'm told. Don't leave the boy before you're relieved. If he speaks, get it.'

'They say he's not likely to speak, sir.'

'I know. I know.'

A nurse approached with a covered object.

'All right,' Alleyn said, 'I'm off.'

He went to the Yard, treating himself to coffee and bacon and eggs on the way.

Fox, he was told, had come in. He arrived in Alleyn's office looking, as always, neat, reasonable, solid and extremely clean. He made a succinct report. Jobbins appeared to have no near relations but the landlady at The Wharfinger's Friend had heard him mention a cousin who was a lock-keeper near Marlow. The stage-crew and front-of-house people had been checked and were out of the picture. The routine search before locking up seemed to have been extremely thorough.

Bailey and Thompson had finished at the theatre where nothing of much significance had emerged. The dressing-rooms had yielded little beyond a note from Harry Grove that Destiny Meade had carelessly tucked into her make-up box.

'Very frank affair,' Mr Fox said primly.

'Frank about what?'

'Sex.'

'Oh. No joy for us?'

'Not in the way you mean, Mr Alleyn.'

'What about the boy's room?'

'He shares with Mr Charles Random. A lot of horror comics including some of the American type that come within the meaning of the act respecting the importation of juvenile reading. One strip was about a well-developed female character called Slash who's really a vampire. She carves up Olympic athletes and leaves her mark on them – "Slash", in blood. It seems the lad was quite struck with this. He's scrawled "Slash" across the dressing-room looking-glass with red greasepaint and we found the same thing on the front-of-house lavatory mirrors and on the wall of one of the upstairs boxes. The one on the audience's left.'

'Poor little swine.'

'The landlady at The Wharfinger's Friend reckons he'll come to no good and blames the mother who plays the steel guitar at that strip-tease joint behind Magpie Alley. Half the time she doesn't pick the kid up after his show and he gets left, hanging round the place till all hours, Mrs Jancy says.'

'Mrs – ?'

'Jancy. The landlady. Nice woman. The Blewitts don't live far off as it happens. Somewhere behind Tabard Street at the back of the Borough.'

'Anything more?'

'Well – dabs. Nothing very startling. Bailey's been able to pick up some nice, clean, control specimens from the dressing-rooms. The top of the pedestal's a mess of the public's prints, half dusted off by the cleaners.'

'Nothing to the purpose?'

'Not really. And you would expect,' Fox said with his customary air of placid good sense, 'if the boy acted vindictively, to find his dabs – two palms together where he pushed the thing over. Nothing of the kind, however, nice shiny surface and all. The carpet's hopeless, of course. Our chaps have taken up the soiled area. Is anything the matter, Mr Alleyn?'

'Nothing, Br'er Fox, except the word "soiled".'

'It's not too *strong*,' Fox said, contemplating it with surprise.

'No. It's dreadfully moderate.'

'Well,' Fox said, after a moment's consideration, 'you have a feeling for words, of course.'

'Which gives me no excuse to talk like a pompous ass. Can you do some telephoning? And, by the way, have you had any breakfast? Don't tell me. The landlady at The Wharfinger's Friend stuffed you full of newlaid eggs.'

'Mrs Jancy *was* obliging enough to make the offer.'

'In that case here is the cast and management list with telephone numbers. You take the first half and I'll do the rest. Ask them with all your celebrated tact to come to the theatre at eleven. I think we'll find that Peregrine Jay has already warned them.'

But Peregrine had not warned Jeremy because it had not occurred to him that Alleyn would want to see him. When the telephone rang it was Jeremy who answered it. Peregrine saw his face bleach. He thought: 'How extraordinary: I believe his pupils have contracted.' And he felt within himself a cold sliding sensation which he refused to acknowledge.

Jeremy said: 'Yes, of course. Yes,' and put the receiver down. 'It seems they want me to go to the theatre, too,' he said.

'I don't know why. You weren't there last night.'

'No. I was here. Working.'

'Perhaps they want you to check that the glove's all right.'

Jeremy made a slight movement, almost as if a nerve had been flicked. He pursed his lips and raised his sandy brows. 'Perhaps,' he said and returned to his work-table at the far end of the room.

Peregrine, with some difficulty, got Mrs Blewitt on the telephone and was subjected to a tirade in which speculation and avid cupidity were but thinly disguised under a mask of sorrow. She suffered, unmistakably, from a formidable hangover. He arranged for a meeting, told her what the hospital had told him and assured her that everything possible would be done for the boy.

'Will they catch whoever done it?'

'It may have been an accident, Mrs Blewitt.'

'If it was, the Management's responsible,' she said, 'and don't forget it.'

They rang off.

Peregrine turned to Jeremy who was bent over his table but did not seem to be working.

'Are you all right, Jer?'

'All right?'

'I thought you looked a bit poorly.'

'There's nothing the matter with me. You look pretty sickly, yourself.'

'I daresay I do.'

Peregrine waited for a moment and then said: 'When will you go to The Dolphin?'

'I'm commanded for eleven.'

'I thought I'd go over early. Alleyn will use our office and the company can sit about the circle foyer or go to their dressing-rooms.'

'They may be locked up,' Jeremy said.

'Who – the actors?'

'The dressing-rooms, half-wit.'

'I can't imagine why but you may be right. Routine's what they talk about, isn't it?'

Jeremy did not answer. Peregrine saw him wipe his hand across his mouth and briefly close his eyes. Then he stooped over his work: he was shaping a piece of balsa wood with a mounted razor blade. His hand jerked and the blade slipped. Peregrine let out an involuntary ejaculation. Jeremy swung round on his stool and faced him. 'Do me a profound kindness and get the hell out of it, will you, Perry?'

'All right. See you later.'

Peregrine, perturbed and greatly puzzled, went out into the weekend emptiness of Blackfriars. An uncoordinated insistence of church bells jangled across the Sunday quietude.

He had nothing to do between now and eleven o'clock. 'One might go into a church,' he thought, but the idea dropped blankly on a field of inertia. 'I can't imagine why I feel like this,' he thought. 'I'm used to taking decisions, to keeping on top of the situation.' But there were no decisions to take and the situation was out of his control. He couldn't think of Superintendent Alleyn in terms of a recalcitrant actor.

He thought: 'I know what I'll do. I've got two hours. I'll walk, like a character in Fielding or in Dickens. I'll walk northwards, towards Hampstead and Emily. If I get blisters I'll take a bus or a tube and if there's not enough time left for that I'll take a taxi. And Emily and I will go down to The Dolphin together.'

Having come to this decision his spirits lifted. He crossed Blackfriars Bridge and made his way through Bloomsbury towards Marylebone and Maida Vale.

His thoughts were divided between Emily, The Dolphin, and Jeremy Jones.

II

Gertrude Bracey had a mannerism. She would glance pretty sharply at a vis-à-vis but only for a second and would then, with a brusque turn of the head, look away. The effect was disconcerting and suggested, not shiftiness so much as a profound distaste for her company. She smiled readily but with a derisive air and she had a sharp edge to her tongue. Alleyn, who never relied upon first impressions, supposed her to be vindictive.

He found support for this opinion in the demeanour of her associates. They sat round the office in The Dolphin on that Sunday morning, with all the conditioned ease of their training but with restless eyes and overtones of discretion in their beautifully controlled voices. This air of guardedness was most noticeable, because it was least disguised, in Destiny Meade. Sleek with fur, not so much dressed as gloved, she sat back in her chair and looked from time to time at Harry Grove who, on the few occasions when he caught her eye, smiled brilliantly in return. When Alleyn began to question Miss Bracey, Destiny Meade and Harry Grove exchanged one of these glances: on her part with brows raised significantly and on his with an appearance of amusement and anticipation.

Marcus Knight looked as if someone had affronted him and also as if he was afraid Miss Bracey was about to go too far in some unspecified direction.

Charles Random watched her with an expression of nervous distaste and Emily Dunne with evident distress. Winter Morris seemed to be ravaged by anxiety and inward speculation. He looked restlessly at Miss Bracey as if she had interrupted him in some desperate calculation. Peregrine, sitting by Emily, stared at his own clasped hands and occasionally at her. He listened carefully to Alleyn's questions and Miss Bracey's replies. Jeremy Jones, a little removed from the others, sat bolt upright in his chair and stared at Alleyn.

The characteristic that all these people had in common was that of extreme pallor, guessed at in the women and self-evident in the men.

Alleyn had opened with a brief survey of the events in their succession, had checked the order in which the members of the company had left the theatre and was now engaged upon extracting confirmation of their movements from Gertrude Bracey with the reactions among his hearers that have been indicated.

'Miss Bracey, I think you and Mr Knight left the theatre together. Is that right?' They both agreed.

'And you left by the auditorium, not by the stage-door?'

'At Perry's suggestion,' Marcus Knight said.

'To avoid the puddles,' Miss Bracey explained.

'And you went out together through the front doors?'

'No,' they said in unison and she added: 'Mr Knight was calling on the Management.'

She didn't actually sniff over this statement but contrived to suggest that there was something to be sneered at in the circumstance.

'I looked in at the office,' Knight loftily said, 'on a matter of business.'

'This office? And to see Mr Morris?'

'Yes,' Winter Morris said. Knight inclined his head in stately acquiescence.

'So you passed Jobbins on your way upstairs?'

'I – ah – yes. He was on the half-landing under the treasure.'

'I saw him up there,' Miss Bracey said.

'How was he dressed?'

As usual, they said, with evident surprise. In uniform.

'Miss Bracey, how did you leave?'

'By the pass-door in the main entrance. I let myself out and slammed it shut after me.'

'Locking it?'

'No.'

'Are you sure?'

'Yes. As a matter of fact I – I re-opened it.'

'Why?'

'I wanted to see the time,' she said awkwardly, 'by the clock in the foyer.'

'Jobbins,' Winter Morris said, 'barred and bolted this door after everyone had left.'

'When would that be?'

'Not more than ten minutes later. Marco – Mr Knight – and I had a drink and left together. Jobbins came after us and I heard him drop the bar across and shoot the bolts. My God!' Morris suddenly exclaimed.

'Yes?'

'The alarm! The burglar alarm. He'd switch it on when he'd locked up. Why didn't it work?'

'Because somebody had switched it off.'

'My God!'

'May we return to Jobbins? How was he dressed when you left?'

Morris said with an air of patience under trying circumstances: 'I didn't see him as we came down. He may have been in the men's lavatory. I called out good night and he answered from up above. We stood for a moment in the portico and that's when I heard him bolt the door.'

'When you saw him, perhaps ten minutes later, Mr Jay, he was wearing an overcoat and slippers?'

'Yes,' said Peregrine.

'Yes. Thank you. How do you get home, Miss Bracey?'

She had a mini-car, she said, which she parked in the converted bombsite between the pub and the theatre.

'Were there other cars parked in this area belonging to the theatre people?'

'Naturally,' she said again. 'Since I was the first to leave.'

'You noticed and recognized them?'

'Oh, *really,* I *suppose* I noticed them. There were a number of strange cars still there but – yes I saw – ' she looked at Knight. Her manner suggested a grudging alliance, ' – *your* car, Marcus.'

'What make of car is Mr Knight's?'

'I've no idea. What is it, dear?'

'A Jag, dear,' said Knight.

'Any others?' Alleyn persisted.

'I *really* don't know. I think I noticed – yours, Charles,' she said, glancing at Random. 'Yes. I did, because it *is* rather conspicuous.'

'What is it?'

'I've no idea.'

'A very, very old, old, old souped-up Morris sports,' said Random. 'Painted scarlet.'

'And Miss Meade's car?'

Destiny Meade opened her eyes very wide and raised her elegantly gloved and braceleted hands to her furs. She gently shook her head. The gesture suggested utter bewilderment. Before she could speak Gertrude Bracey gave her small, contemptuous laugh.

'Oh, *that,*' she said. 'Yes, indeed. Drawn up in glossy state under the portico. As for Royalty.'

She did not look at Destiny.

Harry Grove said: 'Destiny uses a hire-service, don't you, love?' His manner, gay and proprietary, had an immediate effect upon Marcus Knight and Gertrude Bracey who both stared lividly at nothing.

'Any other cars, Miss Bracey? Mr Morris's?'

'I don't remember. I didn't go peering about for cars. I don't notice them.'

'It was there,' Winter Morris said. 'Parked at the back and rather in the dark.'

'When you left, Mr Morris, were there any cars apart from your own and Mr Knight's?'

'I really don't know. There might have been. Do you remember, Marco?'

'No,' he said, widely and vaguely. 'No, I don't remember. As you say: it was dark.'

'I had an idea I saw your mini, Gertie,' Morris said, 'but I suppose I couldn't have. You'd gone by then, of course.'

Gertrude Bracey darted a glance at Alleyn.

'I can't swear to all this sort of thing,' she said angrily. 'I – I didn't notice the cars and I had – ' she stopped and made a sharp movement with her hands. 'I had other things to think of,' she said.

'I understand,' Alleyn said, 'that Miss Dunne and Mr Jay didn't have cars at the theatre?'

'That's right,' Emily said. 'I haven't got one anyway.'

'I left mine at home,' said Peregrine.

'Where it remained?' Alleyn remarked, 'unless Mr Jones took it out?'

'Which I didn't,' Jeremy said. 'I was at home, working, all the evening.'

'Alone?'

'Entirely.'

'As far as cars are concerned that leaves only Mr Grove. Did you by any chance notice Mr Grove's car in the bombsite, Miss Bracey?'

'Oh, yes!' she said loudly and threw him one of her brief, disfavouring looks. 'I saw *that* one.'

'What is it?'

'A Panther '55,' she said instantly. 'An open sports car.'

'You know it quite well,' Alleyn lightly observed.

'Know it? Oh, yes,' Gertrude Bracey repeated with a sharp cackle. 'I *know* it. Or you may say I used to.'

'You don't think well, perhaps, of Mr Grove's Panther?'

'There's nothing the matter with the *car.*'

Harry Grove said: 'Darling, what an infallible ear you have for inflection. Did you go to RADA?'

Destiny Meade let out half a cascade of her celebrated laughter and then appeared to swallow the remainder. Morris gave a repressed snort.

Marcus Knight said: 'This is the wrong occasion, in my opinion, for mistimed comedy.'

'Of course,' Grove said warmly. 'I do so agree. But when is the right occasion?'

'If I am to be publicly insulted – ' Miss Bracey began on a high note. Peregrine cut in.

'Look,' he said. 'Shouldn't we all remember this is a police inquiry into something that may turn out to be murder?'

They gazed at him as if he'd committed a social enormity.

'Mr Alleyn,' Peregrine went on, 'tells us he's decided to cover the first stages as a sort of company call: everybody who was in the theatre last night and left immediately, or not long before the event. That's right, isn't it?' he asked Alleyn.

'Certainly,' Alleyn agreed and reflected sourly that Peregrine, possibly with the best will in the world, had effectually choked what might have been a useful and revealing dust-up. He must make the best of it.

'This procedure,' he said, 'if satisfactorily conducted, should save a great deal of checking and counter-checking and reduce the amount of your time taken up by the police. The alternative is to ask you all to wait in the foyer while I see each of you separately.'

There was a brief pause broken by Winter Morris.

'Fair enough,' Morris said and there was a slight murmur of agreement from the company. 'Don't let's start throwing temperaments right and left, chaps,' Mr Morris added. 'It's not the time for it.'

Alleyn could have kicked him. 'How right you are,' he said. 'Shall we press on? I'm sure you all see the point of this car business. It's essential that we make out when and in what order you left the theatre and whether any of you could have returned within the crucial time. Yes, Miss Meade?'

'I don't want to interrupt,' Destiny Meade said. She caught her underlip between her teeth and gazed helplessly at Alleyn. 'Only: I don't *quite* understand.'

'Please go on.'

'May I? Well, you see, it's just that everybody says Trevor, who is generally admitted to be rather a beastly little boy, stole the treasure and then killed poor Jobbins. I *do* admit he's got some rather awful ways with him and of course one never knows so one wonders why, that being the case, it matters where we all went or what sort of cars we went in.'

Alleyn said carefully that so far no hard and fast conclusion could be drawn and that he hoped that they would all welcome the opportunity of proving that they were away from the theatre during the crucial period which was between 11 o'clock when Peregrine and Emily left the theatre and about five past twelve when Hawkins came running down the stage-door alleyway and told them of his discovery.

'So far,' Alleyn said, 'we've only got as far as learning that when Miss Bracey left the theatre the rest of you were still inside it.'

'Not I,' Jeremy said. 'I've told you, I think, that I was at home.'

'So you have,' Alleyn agreed. 'It would help if you could substantiate the statement. Did anyone ring you up, for instance?'

'If they did, I don't remember.'

'I see,' said Alleyn.

He plodded back through the order of departure until it was established beyond question, that Gertrude and Marcus had been followed by Charles Random who had driven to a pub on the South Bank where he was living for the duration of the play. He had been given his usual late supper. He was followed by Destiny Meade and her friends, all of whom left by the stage-door and spent about an hour at The Younger Dolphin and then drove to her flat in Cheyne Walk where they were joined, she said, by dozens of vague chums, and by Harry Grove who left the theatre at the same time as they did, fetched his guitar from his own flat in Canonbury and then joined them in Chelsea. It appeared that Harry Grove was celebrated

for a song sequence in which, Destiny said, obviously quoting someone else, he sent the sacred cows up so high that they remained in
orbit forevermore.

'Quite a loss to the nightclubs,' Marcus Knight said to nobody in
particular. 'One wonders why the legitimate theatre should still
attract.'

'I assure you, Marco dear,' Grove rejoined, 'only the Lord
Chamberlain stands between me and untold affluence.'

'Or you might call it dirt-pay,' said Knight. It was Miss Bracey's
turn to laugh very musically.

'Did any of you,' Alleyn went on, 'at any time after the fall of curtain see or speak to Trevor Vere?'

'I did, of course,' Charles Random said. He had an impatient
rather injured manner which it would have been going too far to call
feminine. 'He dresses with me. And without wanting to appear
utterly brutal I must say it would take nothing less than a twenty-
foot drop into the stalls to stop him talking.'

'Does he write on the looking-glass?'

Random looked surprised. 'No,' he said. 'Write what? Graffiti?'

'Not precisely. The word "Slash". In red greasepaint.'

'He's always shrieking "Slash". Making a great mouthful of it.
Something to do with his horror comics, one imagines.'

'Does he ever talk about the treasure?'

'Well, yes,' Random said uneasily. 'He flaunts away about how –
well, about how any fool could pinch it and – and: no, it's of no
importance.'

'Suppose we just hear about it?'

'He was simply putting on his act but he did say anyone with any
sense could guess the combination of the lock.'

'Intimating that he had, in fact, guessed it?'

'Well – actually – yes.'

'And did he divulge what it was?'

Random was of a sanguine complexion. He now lost something
of his colour. 'He did not,' Random said, 'and if he had I should have
paid no attention. I don't believe for a moment he knew the combination.'

'And *you* ought to know, dear, oughtn't you?' Destiny said with
the gracious condescension of stardom to bit-part competence.

'Always doing those ghastly puzzles in your intellectual papers. *Right* up your alleyway.'

This observation brought about its own reaction of discomfort and silence.

Alleyn said to Winter Morris, 'I remember I suggested that you would be well-advised to make the five letter key-group rather less predictable. Was it in fact changed?'

Winter Morris raised his eyebrows, wagged his head and his hands and said: 'I was always going to. And then when we knew they were to go – One of those things.' He covered his face for a moment. 'One of those things,' he repeated and everybody looked deeply uncomfortable.

Alleyn said: 'On that morning, beside yourself and the boy, there were present, I think, everybody who is here now except Miss Bracey, Mr Random and Mr Grove. Is that right, Miss Bracey?'

'Oh, yes,' she said with predictable acidity. 'It was a photograph call, I believe. I was *not* required.'

'It was just for two pictures, dear,' little Morris said. 'Destiny and Marco with the glove. You know?'

'Oh, quite. Quite.'

'And the kid turned up so they used him.'

'I seem to remember,' Harry Grove observed, 'that Trevor was quoted in the daily journals as saying that the glove made him feel kinda funny like he wanted to cry.'

'Am I wrong?' Marcus Knight suddenly demanded of no one in particular, 'in believing that this boy is in a critical condition and may die? Mr – ah – Superintendent – ah – Alleyn?'

'He is still on the danger list,' Alleyn said.

'Thank you. Has anybody else got something funny to say about the boy?' Knight demanded. 'Or has the fount of comedy dried at its source?'

'If,' Grove rejoined, without rancour, 'you mean me, it's dry as a bone. No more jokes.'

Marcus Knight folded his arms.

Alleyn said: 'Miss Meade, Miss Dunne, Mr Knight, Mr Jay and Mr Jones – and the boy of course – were all present when the matter of the lock was discussed. Not for the first time, I understand. The safe had been installed for some days and the locking system had been

widely canvassed among you. You had heard from Mr Morris that it
carried a five-number combination and that this was based on a five
letter key-word and a very commonplace code. Mr Morris also said,
before I stopped him, that an obvious key-word had been suggested
by Mr Conducis. Had any of you already speculated upon what this
word might be? Or discussed the matter?'

There was a longish silence.

Destiny Meade said plaintively: 'Naturally we *discussed* it. The men
seemed to know what it was all about. The alphabet and numbers
and not enough numbers for all the letters or something. And anyway it wasn't as if any of us were going to *do* anything, was it? But
everyone *thought* – '

'What everyone thought – ' Marcus Knight began but she looked
coldly upon him and said: 'Please don't butt in, Marco. You've got
such a way of butting in. Do you mind?'

'By *God!*' he said with all the repose of an unexploded landmine.

'Everyone thought,' Destiny continued, gazing at Alleyn, 'that
this obvious five-letter *word* would be "glove". But as far as I could
see that didn't get one any nearer to a five-figure *number*.'

Harry Grove burst out laughing. 'Darling,' he said, 'I adore you
better than life itself.' He picked up her gloved hand and kissed it,
peeled back the gauntlet, kissed the inside of her wrist and then
remarked to the company in general that he wouldn't exchange her
for a wilderness of monkeys. Gertrude Bracey violently re-crossed
her legs. Marcus Knight rose, turned his face to the wall and with
frightful disengagement made as if to examine a framed drawing of
The Dolphin in the days of Adolphus Ruby. A pulse beat rapidly
under his empurpled cheek.

'Very well,' Alleyn said. 'You all thought that "glove" was a likely word and so indeed it was. Did anyone arrive at the code and produce the combination?'

'Dilly, dilly, dilly come and be killed,' cried Harry.

'Not at all,' Alleyn rejoined. 'Unless (the security aspect of this
affair being evidently laughable), you formed yourselves into a
syndicate for robbery. If anyone did arrive at the combination
it seems highly unlikely that he or she kept it to himself. Yes,
Mr Random?'

Charles Random had made an indeterminate sound. He looked up quickly at Alleyn, hesitated and then said rapidly:

'As a matter of fact, I did. I've always been mildly interested in codes and I heard everybody muttering away about the lock on the safe and how the word might be "glove". I have to do a lot of waiting about in my dressing-room and thought I'd try to work it out. I thought it might be one of the sorts where you write down numerals from 1 to 0 in three rows one under another and put in succession under each row the letters of the alphabet adding an extra A B C D to make up the last line. Then you can read the numbers off from the letters. Each number has three equivalent letters and A B C D have each two equivalent numbers.'

'Quite so. And you got – ? From the word "glove"?'

'72525 or, if the alphabet was written from right to left, 49696.'

'And if the alphabet ran from right to left and then, at K, from left to right and finally at U, from right to left again?'

'42596 which seemed to me more likely as there are no repeated figures.'

'Fancy you *remembering* them like that,' Destiny ejaculated and appealed to the company. 'I mean – *isn't* it? I can't so much as remember anyone's telephone number – scarcely even my own.'

Winter Morris moved his hands, palms up, and looked at Alleyn.

'But, of course,' Random said, 'there are any number of variants in this type of code. I might have been *all* wrong.'

'Tell me,' Alleyn said, 'are you and the boy on the same scenes? I seem to remember that you are.'

'Yes,' Peregrine and Random said together and Random added: 'I didn't leave any notes about that Trevor could have read. He tried to pump me. I thought it would be extremely unwise to tell him.'

'Did you, in fact, tell anybody of your solutions?'

'No,' Random said, looking straight in front of him. 'I discussed the code with nobody.' He looked at his fellow players. 'You can all bear me out in this,' he said.

'Well, I must say!' Gertrude Bracey ejaculated and laughed.

'A wise decision,' Alleyn murmured and Random glanced at him. 'I wonder,' he said fretfully.

'I think there's something else you have to tell me, isn't there?'

In the interval that followed Destiny said with an air of discovery: 'No, but you must all admit it's terribly *clever* of Charles.'

Random said: 'Perhaps it's unnecessary to point out that if I had tried to steal the treasure I would certainly not have told you what I *have* told you; still less what I'm going to tell you.'

Another pause was broken by Inspector Fox who sat by the door and had contrived to be forgotten. 'Fair enough,' he said.

'Thank you,' said Random, startled.

'What *are* you going to tell me, Mr Random?' Alleyn asked him.

'That, whatever the combination may be, Trevor didn't know it. He's not really as sharp as he sounds. It was all bluff. When he kept on about how easy it was I got irritated – I find him extremely tiresome, that boy – and I said I'd give him a pound if he could tell me and he did a sort of "Yah-yah-yah, I'm not going to be caught like that" act.' Random made a slight rather finicky movement of his shoulders and his voice became petulant. 'He'd been helping himself to my make-up and I was livid with him. It blew up into quite a thing and – well, it doesn't matter but in the end I shook him and he blurted out a number – 55531. Then we were called for the opening.'

'When was this?'

'Before last night's show.' Random turned to Miss Bracey. 'Gertrude dresses next door to me,' he said. 'I daresay she heard the ongoings.'

'I certainly *did. Not* very helpful when one is making one's preparation which I, at any rate, like to do.'

'Method in her madness. Or is it,' Harry Grove asked 'madness in her Method?'

'That will do, Harry.'

'Dear Perry. Of course.'

'You told us a moment ago, Mr Random,' Alleyn said, 'that the boy didn't reveal the number.'

'Nor did he. Not the correct number,' Random said quickly.

Destiny Meade said: 'Yes, but why were you so sure it was the wrong number?'

'It's the Dolphin telephone number, darling,' Grove said. 'WAT 55531. Remember?'

'Is it? Oh, yes. Of course it is.'

'First thing to enter his head in his fright, I suppose,' Random said.

'You really frightened him?' asked Alleyn.

'Yes, I did. Little horror. He'd have told me if he'd known.' Random added loudly: 'He didn't know the combination and he couldn't have opened the lock.'

'He was for ever badgering me to drop a hint,' Winter Morris said. 'Needless to say, I didn't.'

'Precisely,' said Random.

Peregrine said: 'I don't see how you can be so sure, Charlie. He might simply have been holding out on you.'

'If he knew the combination and meant to commit the theft,' Knight said, flinging himself down into his chair again, 'he certainly wouldn't tell you what it was.'

There was a general murmur of fervent agreement. 'And after all,' Harry Grove pointed out, 'you couldn't have been absolutely sure, could you, Charles, that you hit on the right number yourself or even the right type of code? Or could you?' He grinned at Random. 'Did you *try?*' he asked. 'Did you *prove* it, Charles? Did you have a little tinker? *Before* the treasure went in?'

For a moment Random looked as if he would like to hit him but he tucked in his lips, gave himself time and then spoke exclusively to Alleyn.

He said: 'I do *not* believe that Trevor opened the safe and consequently I'm absolutely certain he didn't kill Bert Jobbins.' He settled his shoulders and looked defiant.

Winter Morris said: 'I suppose you realize the implication of what you're saying, Charles?'

'I think so.'

'Then I must say you've an odd notion of loyalty to your colleagues.'

'It doesn't arise.'

'*Doesn't* it!' Morris cried and looked restively at Alleyn.

Alleyn made no answer to this. He sat with his long hands linked together on Peregrine's desk.

The superb voice of Marcus Knight broke the silence.

'I may be very dense,' he said, collecting his audience, 'but I cannot see where this pronouncement of Charles's leads us. If, as the investigation seems to establish, the boy never left the theatre and if the theatre was locked up and only Hawkins had the key of the stage-door: then how the hell did a third person get in?'

'Might he have been someone in the audience who stayed behind?' Destiny asked, brightly. 'You know? Lurked?'

Peregrine said: 'The ushers, the commissionaire, Jobbins and the ASM did a thorough search front and back after every performance.'

'Well, then perhaps *Hawkins* is the murderer,' she said exactly as if a mystery-story were under discussion. 'Has anyone thought of *that?*' she appealed to Alleyn, who thought it better to disregard her.

'Well, I don't know,' Destiny rambled on. 'Who *could* it be if it's not Trevor? That's what we've got to ask ourselves. Perhaps, though I'm sure I can't think why, and say what you like motive *is* important – ' She broke off and made an enchanting little grimace at Harry Grove. 'Now don't *you* laugh,' she said. 'But for all that just *suppose*. Just suppose – it was Mr Conducis.'

'*My dear girl* – '

'*Destiny, honestly.*'

'*Oh, for God's sake, darling* – '

'I know it sounds silly,' Destiny said, 'but nobody seems to have any other suggestions and after all he was *there*.'

III

The silence that followed Destiny's remark was so profound that Alleyn heard Fox's pencil skate over a page in his note-book.

He said: 'You mean, Miss Meade, that Mr Conducis was in the audience? Not backstage?'

'That's right. In front. In the upstairs OP box. I noticed him when I made my first entrance. I mentioned it to you, Charles, didn't I, when you were holding me up. "There's God" I said, "in the OP box".'

'Mr Morris, did you know Mr Conducis was in front?'

'No, I didn't. But he's got the OP box for ever,' Morris said. 'It's his whenever he likes to use it. He lends it to friends and for all I know occasionally slips in himself. He doesn't let us know if he's coming. He doesn't like a fuss.'

'Nobody saw him come or go?'

'Not that I know.'

Gertrude Bracey said loudly: 'I thought our mysterious Mr W. H. was supposed to be particularly favoured by Our Patron. Quite a Shakespearian situation or so one hears. Perhaps he can shed light.'

'My dear Gertie,' Harry Grove said cheerfully, 'you really should try to keep a splenetic fancy within reasonable bounds. Miss Bracey,' he said, turning to Alleyn, 'refers, I *think*, to the undoubted fact that Mr Conducis very kindly recommended me to the management. I did him a slight service once upon a time and he is obliging enough to *be* obliged. I had no idea he was in front, Gertie dear, until I heard you hissing away about it as you lay on The King Dolphin's bosom at the end of Act 1.'

'Mr Knight,' Alleyn asked, 'did you know Mr Conducis was there?'

Knight looked straight in front of him and said with exaggerated clarity as if voicing an affront, 'It became evident.'

Destiny Meade, also looking neither to left or right and speaking clearly, remarked: 'The less said about *that* the better.'

'Undoubtedly,' Knight savagely agreed.

She laughed.

Winter Morris said: 'Yes, but – ' and stopped short. 'It's nothing,' he said. 'As you were.'

'But in any case it can be of no conceivable significance,' Jeremy Jones said impatiently. He had been silent for so long that his intervention caused a minor stir.

Alleyn rose to his considerable height and moved out into the room. 'I think,' he said, 'that we've got as far as we can, satisfactorily, in a joint discussion. I'm going to ask Inspector Fox to read over his notes. If there is anything any of you wishes to amend will you say so?'

Fox read his notes in a cosy voice and nobody objected to a word of them. When he had finished Alleyn said to Peregrine: 'I daresay you'll want to make your own arrangements with the company.'

'May I?' said Peregrine. 'Thank you.'

Alleyn and Fox withdrew to the distant end of the office and conferred together. The company, far from concerning themselves with the proximity of the police, orientated as one man upon Peregrine, who explained that Trevor Vere's understudy would carry on and that his scenes would be rehearsed in the morning. 'Everybody concerned, please, at ten o'clock,' Peregrine said. 'And look: about the Press. We've got to be very careful with this one, haven't we, Winty?'

Winter Morris joined him, assuming at once his occupational manner of knowing how to be tactful with actors. They didn't, any of them, did they, he asked, want the wrong kind of stories to get into the Press. There was no doubt they would be badgered. He himself had been rung up repeatedly. The line was regret and no comment. 'You'd all gone,' Morris said. 'You weren't there. You've heard about it, of course, but you've no ideas.' Here everybody looked at Destiny.

He continued in this vein and it became evident that this able, essentially kind little man was at considerable pains to stop short of the suggestion that, properly controlled, the disaster, from a box-office angle, might turn out to be no such thing. 'But we don't *need* it,' he said unguardedly and embarrassed himself and most of his hearers. Harry Grove, however, gave one of his little chuckles.

'Well, that's all perfectly splendid,' he said. 'Everybody happy. We've no need of bloody murder to boost our door-sales and wee Trevor can recover his wits as slowly as he likes. Grand.' He placed his arm about Destiny Meade who gave him a mock-reproachful look, tapped his hand and freed herself. 'Darling, *do* be good,' she said. She moved away from him, caught Gertrude Bracey's baleful eye and said with extreme graciousness: 'Isn't he *too* frightful?' Miss Bracey was speechless.

'I can see I've fallen under the imperial displeasure,' Grove murmured in a too-audible aside. 'The Great King Dolphin looks as if it's going to combust.'

Knight walked across the office and confronted Grove who was some three inches shorter than himself. Alleyn was uncannily reminded of a scene between them in Peregrine's play when the man of Stratford confronted the man of fashion while the Dark Lady, so very much more subtle than the actress who beautifully portrayed her, watched catlike in the shadow.

'You really are,' Marcus Knight announced, magnificently inflecting, 'the most objectionable person – I will not honour you by calling you an actor – with whom it has been my deep, deep misfortune to appear in any production.'

'Well,' Grove remarked with perfect good humour, 'it's nice to head the dishonours list, isn't it? Not having prospects in the other direction. Unlike yourself, Mr Knight. "*Mr*" "Knight",' he continued, beaming at Destiny. 'A contradiction in terms when one comes to think of it. Never mind: it simply *must* turn into Sir M. Knight (Knight) before many *more* New Years have passed.'

Peregrine said: 'I am sick of telling you to apologize, Harry, for grossly unprofessional behaviour and begin to think you must be an amateur, after all. Please wait outside in the foyer until Mr Alleyn wants you. No. Not another word. Out.'

Harry looked at Destiny, made a rueful grimace and walked off.

Peregrine went to Alleyn: 'I'm sorry,' he muttered, 'about that little dust-up. We've finished. What would you like us to do?'

'I'd like the women and Random to take themselves off and the rest of the men to wait outside on the landing.'

'Me included?'

'If you don't mind.'

'Of course not.'

'As a sort of control.'

'In the chemical sense?'

'Well – '

'OK,' Peregrine said. 'What's the form?'

'Just that.' Alleyn returned to the group of players. 'If you wouldn't mind moving out to the circle foyer,' he said. 'Mr Jay will explain the procedure.'

Peregrine marshalled them out.

They stood in a knot in front of the shuttered bar and they tried not to look down in the direction of the half-landing. The lowest of the three steps from the foyer to the half-landing and the area where Jobbins had lain, were stripped of carpet. The police had put down canvas sheeting. The steel doors of the wall safe above the landing were shut. Between the back of the landing and the wall, three steps led up to a narrow strip of floor connecting the two halves of the foyer, each with its own door into the circle.

Destiny Meade said: 'I'm not going down those stairs.'

'We can walk across the back to the other flight,' Emily suggested.

'I'd still have to set foot on the landing. I can't do it. Harry!' She turned with her air of expecting everyone to be where she required them and found that Harry Grove had not heard her. He stood with his hands in his pockets contemplating the shut door of the office.

Marcus Knight, flushed and angry, said: 'Perhaps you'd like me to take you down,' and laughed very unpleasantly.

She looked coolly at him. 'Sweet of you,' she said. 'I wouldn't dream of it,' and turned away to find herself face-to-face with Jeremy Jones. His freckled face was pink and anxious and his manner diffident. 'There's the circle,' he said, 'and the pass-door. Could I – ?'

'Jeremy, *darling*. Yes – please, please. I know I'm a fool but – well, it's just how one's made, isn't it? *Thank* you, my angel.' She slipped her arm into his.

They went into the circle and could be heard moving round the back towards the prompt side box.

Charles Random said: 'Well, I'll be off,' hesitated for a moment, and then ran down the canvas-covered steps, turned on the landing and descended to the ground floor. Gertrude Bracey stood at the top near the remaining bronze dolphin. She looked at it and then at the mark in the carpet where its companion had stood. She compressed her lips, lifted her head and walked down with perfect deliberation.

All this was observed by Peregrine Jay.

He stopped Emily who had made as if to follow. 'Are you all right, Emily?'

'Yes. Quite all right. You?'

'All the better for seeing you. Shall we take lunch together? But I don't know how long I'll be. Were you thinking of lunch later on?'

'I can't say I'm wolfishly ravenous.'

'One must eat.'

Emily said: 'You can't possibly tell when you'll get off. The pub's no good and nor is The Younger Dolphin. They'll both be seething with curiosity and reporters. I'll buy some ham rolls and go down to the wharf below Phipps Passage. There's a bit of a wall one can sit on.'

'I'll join you if I can. Don't bolt your rolls and hurry away. It's a golden day on the river.'

'Look,' Emily said. 'What's Harry up to *now*!'

Harry was tapping on the office door. Apparently in answer to a summons he opened it and went in.

Emily left the theatre by the circle and pass-door. Peregrine joined a smouldering Marcus Knight and an anxious Winter Morris. Presently Jeremy returned, obviously flown with gratification.

On the far side of the office door Harry Grove confronted Alleyn.

His manner had quite changed. He was quiet and direct and spoke without affectation.

'I daresay,' he said, 'I haven't commended myself to you as a maker of statements but a minute or two ago – after I had been sent out in disgrace, you know – I remembered something. It may have no bearing on the case whatever but I think perhaps I ought to leave it to you to decide.'

'That,' Alleyn said, 'by and large, is the general idea we like to establish.'

Harry smiled. 'Well then,' he said, 'here goes. It's rumoured that when the nightwatchman, whatever he's called – '

'Hawkins.'

'That when Hawkins found Jobbins and, I suppose, when you saw him, he was wearing a light overcoat.'

'Yes.'

'Was it a rather large brown and white check with an over-check of black?'

'It was.'

'Loudish, one might say?'

'One might, indeed.'

'Yes. Well, I gave him that coat on Friday evening.'

'Your name is still on the inside pocket tag.'

Harry's jaw dropped. 'The wind,' he said, 'to coin a phrase, has departed from my sails. I'd better chug off under my own steam. I'm sorry, Mr Alleyn. Exit actor, looking crestfallen.'

'No, wait a bit, as you are here. I'd like to know what bearing you think this might have on the case. Sit down. Confide in us.'

'May I?' Harry said, surprised. 'Thank you, I'd like to.'

He sat down and looked fully at Alleyn. 'I don't always mean to behave as badly as in fact I do,' he said and went on quickly: 'About the coat. I don't think I attached any great importance to it. But just now you did rather seem to make a point of what he was wearing. I couldn't quite see what the point *was* but it seemed to me I'd better tell you that until Friday evening the coat had been mine.'

'Why on earth didn't you say so there and then?'

Harry flushed scarlet. His chin lifted and he spoke rapidly as if by compulsion. 'Everybody,' he said, 'was fabulously amusing about my coat. In the OK hearty, public-school manner, you know. Frightfully nice chaps. Jolly good show. I need not, of course, tell you that I am not even a product of one of our dear old minor public schools. Or, if it comes to that, of a dear old minor grammar school like the Great King Dolphin.'

'Knight?'

'That's right but it's slipped his memory.'

'You *do* dislike him, don't you?'

'Not half as heartily as he dislikes me,' Harry said and gave a short laugh. 'I know I sound disagreeable. You see before you, Superintendent, yet another slum kid with a chip like a Yule log on his shoulder. I take it out in clowning.'

'But,' Alleyn said mildly, 'is your profession absolutely riddled with old Etonians?'

Harry grinned. 'Well, no,' he said. 'But I assure you there are enough more striking and less illustrious OB ties to strangle all the extras in the battle scene for Armageddon. As a rank outsider I find the network nauseating. Sorry. No doubt you're a product yourself. Of Eton, I mean.'

'So you're a post-Angry at heart? Is that it?'

'Only sometimes. I compensate. They're afraid of my tongue or I like to think they are.'

He waited for a moment and then said: 'None of this, by the way and for what it's worth, applies to Peregrine Jay. I've no complaints about him: he has not roused my lower-middle-class rancour and I do not try to score off him. He's a gifted playwright, a good producer and a very decent citizen. Perry's all right.'

'Good. Let's get back to the others. They were arrogant about your coat, you considered?'

'The comedy line was relentlessly pursued. Charles affected to have the dazzles. Gertrude, dear girl, shuddered like a castanet. There were lots of asides. And even the lady of my heart professed distaste and begged me to shuffle off my chequered career-coat. So I did. Henry Jobbins was wheezing away at the stage-door saying his chubes were chronic and believe it or not I did a sort of your-need-is-greater-than-mine thing, which I could, of course, perfectly well afford. I took it off there and then and gave it to him. There was,' Harry said loudly, 'and is, absolutely no merit in this gesture. I simply off-loaded an irksome, vulgar, mistaken choice on somebody who happened to find it acceptable. He was a good bloke, was old Harry. A good bloke.'

'Did anyone know of this spontaneous gift?'

'No. Oh, I suppose the man that relieved him did. Hawkins. Henry Jobbins told me this chap had been struck all of a heap by the overcoat when he came in on Friday night.'

'But nobody else, you think, knew of the exchange?'

'I asked Jobbins not to say anything. I really could *not* have stomached the recrudescense of comedy that the incident would have evoked.' Harry looked sidelong at Alleyn. 'You're a dangerous man, Superintendent. You've missed your vocation. You'd have been a wow on the receiving side of the confessional grille.'

'No comment,' said Alleyn and they both laughed.

Alleyn said: 'Look here. Would anyone expect to find *you* in the realm of the front foyer after the show?'

'I suppose so,' he said. 'Immediately after. Winty Morris for one. I've been working in a TV show and there's been a lot of carry-on about calls. In the event of any last minute changes I arranged for them to ring this theatre and I've been looking in at the office after the show in case there was a message.'

'Yes, I see.'

'Last night, though, I didn't go round because the telly thing's finished. And anyway I was bound for Dessy Meade's party. She commanded me, as you've heard, to fetch my guitar and I lit off for Canonbury to get it.'

'Did you arrive at Miss Meade's flat in Cheyne Walk before or after she and her other guests did?'

'Almost a dead heat. I was parking when they arrived. They'd been to the little joint in Wharfingers Lane, I understand.'

'Anyone hear or see you at your own flat in Canonbury?'

'The man in the flat overhead may have heard me. He complains that I wake him up every night. The telephone rang while I was in the loo. That would be round about eleven. Wrong number. I daresay it woke him, but I don't know. I was only there long enough to give myself a drink, have a wash, pick up the guitar and out.'

'What's this other flatter's name?'

Harry gave it. 'Well,' he said cheerfully, 'I hope I *did* wake him, poor bugger.'

'We'll find out, shall we? Fox?'

Mr Fox telephoned Harry's neighbour explaining that he was a telephone operative checking a faulty line. He extracted the information that Harry's telephone had indeed rung just as the neighbour had turned his light off at eleven o'clock.

'Well, God bless him, anyway,' said Harry.

'To go back to your overcoat. Was there a yellow silk scarf in the pocket?'

'There was indeed. With an elegant "H" embroidered by a devoted if slightly witchlike and acquisitive hand. The initial was appropriate at least. Henry J. was as pleased as punch, poor old donkey.'

'You liked him very much, didn't you?'

'As I said, he was a good bloke. We used to have a pint at the pub and he'd talk about his days on the river. Oddly enough I think he rather liked me.'

'Why should that be so odd?'

'Oh,' Harry said. 'I'm hideously unpopular, you know. I really *am* disliked. I have a talent for arousing extremes of antipathy, I promise you. Even Mr Conducis,' Harry said opening his eyes very wide, 'although he feels obliged to be helpful, quite hates my guts, I assure you.'

'Have you seen him lately?'

'Friday afternoon,' Harry said promptly.

'Really?'

'Yes. I call on him from time to time as a matter of duty. After all he got me this job. Did I mention that we are distantly related? Repeat, *distantly:*

'No.'

'No. I don't mention it very much. Even I,' Harry said, 'draw the line somewhere, you know.'

CHAPTER 8

Sunday Afternoon

'What did you think of that little party, Br'er Fox?'

'Odd chap, isn't he? Very different in his manner to when he was annoying his colleagues. One of these inferiority complexes, I suppose. You brought him out, of course.'

'Do you think he's dropped to the obvious speculation?'

'About the coat? I don't fancy he'd thought of that one, Mr Alleyn, and if I've got you right I must say it strikes me as being very far-fetched. You might as well say – well,' Fox said in his scandalized manner, 'you might as well suspect I don't know who. Mr Knight. The sharp-faced lady: Miss Bracey, or even Mr Conducis.'

'Well, Fox, they all come into the field of vision, don't they? Overcoat or no overcoat.'

'That's so,' Fox heavily agreed. 'So they do. So they do.' He sighed and after a moment said majestically, 'D'you reckon he was trying to pull our legs?'

'I wouldn't put it past him. All the same there *is* a point, you know, Fox. The landing was very dim even when the safe was open and lit.'

'How *does* that interior lighting work? I haven't had a look, yet.'

'There's a switch inside the hole in the wall on the circle side. What the thief couldn't have realized is the fact that this switch works the sliding steel front door and that in its turn puts on the light.'

'Like a fridge.'

'Yes. What might have happened is something like this. The doors from the circle into the upper foyer were shut and the auditorium was in darkness. The thief lay doggo in the circle. He heard Jay and Miss Dunne go out and bang the stage-door. He waited until midnight and then crept up to the door nearest the hole in the wall and listened for Jobbins to put through his midnight report to Fire and Police. You've checked that he made this call. We're on firm ground there, at least.'

'And the chap at the Fire Station, which was the second of his two calls, reckons he broke off a bit abruptly.'

'Exactly. Now, if I'm right so far – and I know damn' well I'm going to speculate – our man would choose this moment to open the wall panel – it doesn't lock – and manipulate the combination. He's already cut the burglar alarm off at the main. He must have had a torch, but I wouldn't mind betting that by intention or accident he touched the inner switch button and without knowing he'd done so, rolled back the front door which in its turn, put on the interior lighting. If it was accidental he wouldn't realize what he'd done until he'd opened the back of the safe and removed the black velvet display stand with its contents and found himself looking through a peephole across the upper foyer and sunken landing.'

'With the square of light reflected on the opposite wall.'

'As bright as ninepence. Quite bright enough to attract Jobbins's attention.'

'Now it gets a bit dicey.'

'Don't I know it.'

'What happens? This chap reckons he'd better make a bolt for it. But why does he come out here to the foyer?' Fox placidly regarded his chief. 'This,' he continued, 'would be asking for it. This would be balmy. He knows Jobbins is somewhere out here.'

'I can only cook up one answer to that, Fox. He's got the loot. He intends to shut the safe, fore and aft and spin the lock. He means to remove the loot from the display stand but at this point he's interrupted. He hears a voice, a catcall, a movement. Something. He turns round to find young Trevor Vere watching him. He thinks Jobbins is down below at the telephone. He bolts through the door from the circle to this end of the foyer meaning to duck into the loo before Jobbins gets up. Jobbins would then go into the circle and find young Trevor and assume he was the culprit. But he's too late. Jobbins having seen the open safe comes thundering up from below.

He makes for this chap who gives him a violent shove to the pedestal and the dolphin lays Jobbins flat. Trevor comes out to the foyer and sees this. Our chap goes for him. The boy runs back through the door and down the central aisle with his pursuer hard on his heels. He's caught at the foot of the steps. There's a struggle during which the boy grabs at the display stand. The polythene cover is dislodged, the treasure falls overboard with it. The boy is hit on the face. He falls across the balustrade, face down, clinging to it. He's picked up by the seat of his trousers, swung sideways and heaved over, his nails dragging semi-diagonally across the velvet pile as he goes. At this point Hawkins comes down the stage-door alley.'

'You *are* having yourself a ball,' said Mr Fox, who liked occasionally to employ the contemporary idiom. 'How long does all this take?'

'From the time he works the combination it *needn't* take more than five minutes. If that. Might be less.'

'So the time's now – say – five past midnight.'

'Say between 12 and 12:10.'

'Yerse,' said Fox and a look of mild gratification settled upon his respectable face. 'And at 12:5, or 10 or thereabouts, Hawkins comes in by the stage-door, goes into the stalls and has a little chat with the deceased who is looking over the circle balustrade.

'I see you are in merry pin,' Alleyn remarked. 'Hawkins, Mr Smartypants, has a little chat with somebody wearing Jobbins's new coat which Hawkins is just able to recognize in the scarcely lit circle. This is not, of necessity, Jobbins. So, you see, Harry Grove had a point about the coat.'

'Now then, now then.'

'Going too far, you consider?'

'So do you, Mr Alleyn.'

'Well, of course I do. All this is purest fantasy. If you can think of a better one, have a go yourself.'

'If only,' Fox grumbled, 'that kid could recover his wits, we'd all know where we were.'

'We might.'

'About this howd'yedo with the overcoat. Is your story something to this effect? The killer loses his loot, heaves the kid overboard and hears Hawkins at the stage-door. All right! He bolts back to the circle foyer. Why doesn't he do a bunk by the pass-door in the front entrance?'

'No time. He knows that in a matter of seconds Hawkins will come through the auditorium into the front foyer. Consider the door. A mortice lock with the key kept on a hook behind the office. Two dirty great bolts and an iron bar. No time.'

'So you're making out he grabs the coat off the body, puts it on, all mucky as it is with blood and Gawd knows what – '

'Only on the outside. And I fancy he took the scarf from the over-coat pocket and used it to protect his own clothes.'

'Ah. So you say he dolls himself up, and goes back to the circle and tells Hawkins to make the tea?'

'In a croaking bronchial voice, we must suppose.'

'Then what? Humour me, Mr Alleyn. Don't stop.'

'Hawkins goes off to the property room and makes the tea. This will take at least five minutes. Our customer returns to the body and re-dresses it in the coat and puts the scarf round the neck. You noticed how the coat was: bunched up and stuffed under the small of the back. It couldn't have got like that by him falling in it.'

'Damn, I missed that one. It's an easy one too.'

'Having done this he goes downstairs, gets the key, unlocks the pass-door in the front entrance, pulls the bolt, unslips the iron bar, lets himself out and slams the door. There's a good chance that Hawkins, busily boiling-up on the far side of the iron curtain, won't hear it or, if he does, won't worry. He's a coolish customer, is our customer, but the arrival of Trevor and then Hawkins and still more the knowledge of what he has done – he didn't plan to murder – have rattled him. He can't do one thing.'

'Pick up the swag?'

'Just that. It's gone overboard with Trevor.'

'Maddening for him,' said Mr Fox primly. He contemplated Alleyn for some seconds.

'Mind you,' he said, 'I'll give you this. If it *was* Jobbins and not a murderer rigged out in Jobbins's coat we're left with a crime that took place after Jobbins talked to Hawkins and before Hawkins came round with the tea and found the body.'

'And with a murderer who was close by during the conversation and managed to work the combination, open the safe, extract the loot, kill Jobbins, half kill Trevor, do his stuff with the door and sling his hook – all within five minutes it took Hawkins to boil up.'

'Well,' Fox said after consideration, 'it's impossible, I'll say that for it. It's impossible. And what's *that* look mean, I wonder,' he added.

'Get young Jeremy Jones in and find out,' said Alleyn.

II

When Harry Grove came out of the office he was all smiles. 'I bet you lot wonder if I've been putting your pots on,' he said brightly. 'I haven't really. I mean not beyond mentioning that you all hate my guts, which they could hardly avoid detecting, one would think.'

'They can't detect something that's non-existent,' Peregrine said crisply. 'I don't hate your silly guts, Harry. I think you're a bloody bore when you do your *enfant terrible* stuff. I think you can be quite idiotically mischievous and more than a little spiteful. But I don't hate your guts: I rather like you.'

'Perry: how splendidly detached! And Jeremy?'

Jeremy, looked as if he found the conversation unpalatable, said impatiently: 'Good God, what's it matter! What a lot of balls.'

'And Winty?' Harry said.

Morris looked very coolly at him. 'I should waste my time hating your guts?' He spread his hands. 'What nonsense,' he said. 'I am much too busy.'

'So, in the absence of Charlie and the girls, we find ourselves left with The King Dolphin.'

As soon as Harry had reappeared Marcus Knight had moved to the far end of the circle foyer. He now turned and said with dignity: 'I absolutely refuse to have any part of this,' and ruined everything by shouting: 'And I will not suffer this senseless, this insolent, this insufferable name-coining.'

'Ping!' said Harry. 'Great strength rings the bell. I wonder if the Elegant Rozzer in there heard you. I must be off. Best of British luck – ' He caught himself up on this familiar quotation from Jobbins and looked miserable. 'That,' he said, 'was *not* intentional,' and took himself off.

Marcus Knight at once went into what Peregrine had come to think of as his First Degree of temperament. It took the outward form of sweet reason. He spoke in a deathly quiet voice, used only restrained gestures and, although that nerve jumped up and down under his empurpled cheek, maintained a dreadful show of equanimity.

'This may not be, indeed emphatically is *not*, an appropriate moment to speculate upon the continued employment of this person. One has been given to understand that the policy is adopted at the instigation of The Management. I will be obliged, Winter, if at the first opportunity, you convey to The Management my intention, unless Harry Grove is relieved of his part, of bringing my contract to its earliest possible conclusion. My agents will deal with the formalities.'

At this point, under normal circumstances, he would undoubtedly have effected a smashing exit. He looked restlessly at the doors and stairways and, as an alternative, flung himself into one of the Victorian settees that Jeremy had caused to be placed about the circle foyer. Here he adopted a civilized and faintly Corinthian posture but looked, nevertheless, as if he would sizzle when touched.

'My dear, *dear* Perry and my dear Winty,' he said. 'Please do take this as definite. I am sorry, sorry, sorry that it should be so. But there it is.'

Perry and Morris exchanged wary glances. Jeremy, who had looked utterly miserable from the time he came in, sighed deeply.

Peregrine said, 'Marco, may we, of your charity, discuss this a little later? The horrible thing that happened last night is such a *black* problem for all of us. I concede everything you may say about Harry. He behaves attrociously and under normal circumstances would have been given his marching orders long ago. If there's any more of this sort of thing, I'll speak about it to Greenslade and if he feels he can't take a hand I shall – I'll go to Conducis himself and tell him I can no longer stomach his protégé. But in the meantime – *please* be patient, Marco.'

Marcus waved his hand. The gesture was beautiful and ambiguous. It might have indicated dismissal, magniloquence or implacable fury. He gazed at the ceiling, folded his arms and crossed his legs.

Winter Morris stared at Peregrine and then cast up his eyes and very, very slightly rolled his head.

Inspector Fox came out of the office and said that if Mr Jeremy Jones was free Superintendent Alleyn would be grateful if he could spare him a moment.

Peregrine, watching Jeremy go, suffered pangs of an undefined anxiety.

When Jeremy came into the office he found Alleyn seated at Winter Morris's desk with his investigation kit open before him and, alongside that, a copy of *The Times*. Jeremy stood very still just inside the door. Alleyn asked him to sit down and offered him a cigarette.

'I've changed to a pipe. Thank you, though.'

'So have I. Go ahead, if you want to.'

Jeremy pulled out his pipe and tobacco pouch. His hands were steady but looked self-conscious.

'I've asked you to come in,' Alleyn said, 'on a notion that may quite possibly turn out to be totally irrelevant. If so you'll have to excuse me. You did the decor for this production, didn't you?'

'Yes.'

'If I may say so it seemed to me to be extraordinarily right. It always fascinates me to see the tone and character of a play reflected by its background without the background itself becoming too insistent.'

'It often does.'

'Not in this instance, I thought. You and Jay share a flat, don't you? I suppose you collaborated over the whole job?'

'Oh, yes,' Jeremy said and, as if aware of being unforthcoming, he added: 'It worked all right.'

'They tell me you've got a piece of that nice shop in Walton Street and are an authority on historic costume.'

'That's putting it much too high.'

'Well, anyway, you designed the clothes and props for this show?'

'Yes.'

'The gloves, for instance,' Alleyn said and lifted his copy of *The Times* from the desk. The gloves used in the play lay neatly together on Winter Morris's blotting pad.

Jeremy said nothing.

'Wonderfully accurate copies. And, of course,' Alleyn went on, 'I saw you arranging the real glove and the documents on the velvet easel and putting them in the safe. That morning in the theatre some six months ago. I was there, you may remember.'

Jeremy half rose and then checked himself. 'That's right,' he said.

Alleyn lifted a tissue paper packet out of his open case, put it near to Jeremy on the desk and carefully folded back the wrapping. He exposed a small, wrinkled, stained, embroidered and tasselled glove.

'This would be it?' he said.

'I – yes,' said Jeremy, as white as a sheet.

'The glove you arranged on its velvet background with the two documents and covered with a sheet of polythene fastened with velvet-covered drawing pins?'

'Yes.'

'And then from the panel opening in the circle wall, you put this whole arrangement into the cache that you yourself had lined so prettily with padded gold silk. You used the switch that operates the sliding door in the foyer wall. It opened and the interior lights went on behind the convex plateglass front of the cache. Then you shut the back door and spun the combination lock. And Peregrine Jay, Winter Morris, Marcus Knight, young Trevor Vere, Miss Destiny Meade and Miss Emily Dunne, all stood about, at your suggestion, in the circle foyer or the sunken landing and they all greatly admired the arrangement. That right?'

'You were there, after all.'

'As I reminded you. I stayed in the circle, you know, and joined you when you were re-arranging the exhibits on their background.' He gave Jeremy a moment or two and, as he said nothing, continued.

'Last night the exhibits and their velvet background with their transparent cover were found in the centre aisle of the stalls, not far from where the boy lay. They had become detached from the black velvet display easel. I brought the glove in here and examined it very closely.'

'I know,' Jeremy said, 'what you are going to say.'

'I expect you do. To begin with I was a bit worried about the smell. I've got a keen nose for my job and I seemed to get something foreign to the odour of antiquity, if one may call it that. There was a faint whiff of fishglue and paint which suggested another sort of occupational smell, clinging perhaps to somebody's hands.'

Jeremy's fingers curled. The nails were coloured rather as Trevor's had been but not with velvet pile.

'So this morning I got my lens out and I went over the glove. I turned it inside out. Sacrilege, you may think. Undoubtedly, I thought, it really is a very old glove indeed and seems to have been worked over and redecorated at some time. And then, on the inside of the back where all the embroidery is – look, I'll show you.'

He manipulated the glove, delicately turning it back on itself.

'Can you see? It's been caught down by a stitch and firmly anchored and it's very fine indeed. A single hair, human and – quite distinctly – red.'

He let the glove fall on its tissue paper. 'This is a much better copy than the property ones and they're pretty good. It's a wonderful job and would convince anyone, I'd have thought, from the distance at which it was seen.' He looked up at Jeremy. 'Why did you do it?' asked Alleyn.

III

Jeremy sat with his forearms resting on his thighs and stared at his clasped hands. His carroty head was very conspicuous. Alleyn noticed that one or two hairs had fallen on the shoulders of his suéde jerkin.

He said: 'I swear it's got nothing to do with Jobbins or the boy.'

'That, of course, is our chief concern at the moment.'

'May Perry come in, please?'

Alleyn thought that one over and then nodded to Fox who went out.

'I'd rather he heard now, than any other way,' Jeremy said.

Peregrine came in, looked at Jeremy and went to him.

'What's up?' he said.

'I imagine I'm going to make a statement. I want you to hear it.'

'For God's sake, Jer, don't make a fool of yourself. A statement? What about? Why?'

He saw the crumpled glove lying on the desk and the two prop gloves where Alleyn had displayed them. 'What's all this?' he demanded. 'Who's been manhandling Hamnet's glove?'

'Nobody,' Jeremy said. 'It's not Hamnet's glove. It's a bloody good fake. I did it and I ought to know.' A long silence followed.

'You fool, Jer,' Peregrine said slowly. 'You unspeakable fool.'

'Do you want to tell us about it, Mr Jones?'

'Yes. The whole thing. I'd better.'

'Inspector Fox will take notes and you will be asked to sign them. If in the course of your statement I think you are going to incriminate yourself to the point of an arrest I shall warn you of this.'

'Yes. All right.' Jeremy looked up at Peregrine. 'It's OK,' he said. 'I won't. And don't, for God's sake, gawp at me like that. Go and sit down somewhere. And listen.'

Peregrine sat on the edge of his own desk.

'It began,' Jeremy said, 'when I was going to the Vic and Alb to make drawings of the glove for the two props. Emily Dunne sometimes helps in the shop and she turned out a whole mass of old tatt we've accumulated to see what there was in the way of material. We found that pair over there and a lot of old embroidery silks, and gold wire and some fake jewellery that was near enough for the props. But in the course of the hunt I came across' – he pointed – 'that one. It's genuine as far as age goes and within fifty years of the original. A small woman's hand. It had the gauntlet and tassel but the embroidery was entirely different. I – I suppose I got sort of besotted on the real glove. I made a very, *very* elaborate drawing of it. Almost a *trompe l'oeil* job isn't it, Perry? And all the time I was working on the props there was this talk of Conducis selling the glove to a private collection in the USA.'

Jeremy now spoke rapidly and directly to Alleyn.

'I've got a maggot about historic treasures going out of their native setting. I'd give back the Elgin Marbles to Athens tomorrow if I could. I started on the copy; first of all just for the hell of it. I even thought I might pull Peregrine's leg with it when it was done or try it out on the expert at the Vic and Alb. I was lucky in the hunt for silks and for gold and silver wire and all. The real stuff. I did it almost under your silly great beak, Perry. You nearly caught me at it lots of times. I'd no intention, then, absolutely none, of trying substitution.'

'What *did* you mean to do with it ultimately? Apart from leg-pulling,' said Alleyn.

Jeremy blushed to the roots of his betraying hair. 'I rather thought,' he said, 'of giving it to Destiny Meade.'

Peregrine made a slight moaning sound.

'And what made you change your mind?'

'As you've guessed, I imagine, it was on the morning the original was brought here and they asked me to see it housed. I'd brought my copy with me. I thought I might just try my joke experiment. So I grabbed my chance and did a little sleight-of-hand. It was terribly easy: nobody, not even you, noticed. I was going to display the whole thing and if nobody spotted the fake, take the original out of my pocket, do my funny man ha-ha ever-been-had stuff, re-switch the gloves and give Destiny the copy. I thought it'd be rather diverting to have you and the expert and everybody doting and on-going and the cameramen milling round and Marcus striking wonderful attitudes: all at my fake. You know?'

Peregrine said: 'Very quaint and inventive. You ought to go into business with Harry Grove.'

'Well, then I heard all the chat about whether the cache was really safe and what you, Mr Alleyn, said to Winty about the lock and how you guessed the combination. I thought: but this is terrifying. It's asking for trouble. There'll be another Goya's "Duke" but this time it'll go for keeps. I felt sure Winty wouldn't get round to changing the combination. And then – absolutely on the spur of the moment – it was some kind of compulsive behaviour I suppose – I decided not to tell about my fake. I decided to leave it on show in the theatre and to take charge of the original myself. It's in a safe-deposit and very carefully packed. I promise you, I was going to replace it as soon as the exhibits were to be removed. I knew I'd be put in charge again and I could easily reverse the former procedure and switch back the genuine article. And then: then – there was the abominable bombshell.'

'And I suppose,' Peregrine observed, 'I now understand your extraordinary behaviour on Friday.'

'You may suppose so. On Friday,' Jeremy turned to Alleyn, 'Peregrine informed me that Conducis *had* sold or as good as sold, to a private collector in USA.'

Jeremy got up and walked distractedly about the office. Alleyn rested his chin in his hand, Fox looked over the top of his spectacles and Peregrine ran his hands through his hair.

'You must have been out of your wits,' he said.

'Put it like that if you want to. You don't need to tell me what I've done. Virtually, I've stolen the glove.'

'Virtually?' Alleyn repeated. 'There's no "virtually" about it. That is precisely what you've done. If I understand you, you now decided to keep the real glove and let the collector spend a fortune on a fake.'

Jeremy threw up his hands: 'I don't know,' he said. 'I hadn't decided anything.'

'You don't know what you proposed to do with young Hamnet Shakespeare's glove?'

'Exactly. If this thing hadn't happened to Jobbins and the boy and I'd been responsible for handing over the treasure: I *don't know*, now, what I'd have done. I'd have brought Hamnet's glove with me, I think. But whether I'd have replaced it – I expect I would but – I just *do not know*.'

'Did you seriously consider any other line of action? Suppose you hadn't replaced the real glove – what then? You'd have stuck to it? Hoarded it for the rest of your life?'

'NO!' Jeremy shouted. '*No!* Not that, I wouldn't have done that. I'd have waited to see what happened, I think, and then – and then . . . '

'You realize that if the purchaser had your copy, good as it is, examined by an expert it would be spotted in no time?'

Jeremy actually grinned. 'And I wonder what the Great God Conducis would have done about that one,' he said. 'Return the money or brazen it out that he sold in good faith on the highest authority?'

'What *you* would have done is more to the point.'

'I tell you, I don't know. Would I let it ride? See what happened? Do a kidnap sort of thing perhaps? Phoney voice on the telephone saying if he swore to give it to the Nation it would be returned? Then Conducis could do what he liked about it.'

'Swear, collect and sell,' Peregrine said. 'You must be demented.'

'Where is this safe-deposit?' Alleyn asked. Jeremy told him. Not far from their flat in Blackfriars.

'Tell me,' Alleyn went on, 'how am I to know you've been speaking the truth? After all you've only handed us this rigmarole after I'd discovered the fake. How am I to know you didn't mean to flog the glove on the freak black market? Do you know there is such a market in historic treasures?'

Jeremy said loudly: 'Yes, I do. Perfectly well.'

'For God's sake, Jer, shut up. *Shut up.*'

'No, I won't. Why should I? I'm not the only one in the company to hear of Mrs Constantia Guzman.'

'Mrs Constantia Guzman?' Alleyn repeated.

'She's a slightly mad millionairess with a flair for antiquities.'

'Yes?'

'Yes. Harry Grove knows all about her. So,' added Jeremy defiantly, 'do Marco and Charlie Random.'

'What is the Guzman story?'

'According to Harry,' Jeremy began in a high voice and with what sounded like insecure irony, 'she entertained Marco very lavishly when he had that phenomenal season in New York three years ago. Harry was in the company. It appears that Mrs Guzman, who is fifty-five, as ugly as sin and terrifying, fell madly in love with Marco. Literally – *madly* in love. She's got a famous collection of pictures and objets d'art. Well, she threw a fabulous party – fabulous even for her – and when it was all over she kept Marco back. As a sort of woo she took him into a private room and showed him a collection of treasures that she said nobody else has ever seen.' Jeremy stopped short. The corner of Alleyn's mouth twitched and his right eyebrow rose. Fox cleared his throat. Peregrine said wearily, 'Ah, my God.'

'I mean,' Jeremy said with dignity, 'precisely and literally what I say. Behind locked doors Mrs Guzman showed to Marcus Knight jewels, snuff-boxes, rare books, Fabergé trinkets: all as hot as hell. Every one a historic collector's item. And the whole shooting-match, she confided, bought on a sort of underground international black market. Lots of them had at some time been stolen. She had agents all over Europe and the Far East. She kept all these things simply to gloat over in secret and she told Marco she had shown them to him because she wanted to feel she was in his power. And with that she set upon him in no mean style. She carried the weight and he made his escape, or so he says, by the narrowest of margins and in a cold sweat. He got on quite well with Harry in those days. One evening when he'd had one or two drinks, he told Harry all about this adventure.'

'And how did you hear of it?'

Peregrine ejaculated: 'I remember! When I told the company about the glove!'

'That's right. Harry said Mrs Constantia Guzman ought to know of it. He said it with one of his glances – perhaps they should be called "mocking" – at Marcus who turned purple. Harry and Charlie Random and I had drinks in the pub that evening and he told us the Guzman yarn. I must say he was frightfully funny doing an imitation of Mrs Guzman saying: "But I *vish* to be at your bercy. I log to be in your power. Ach, if you vould only betray be. Ach, but you have so beautiful a botty".'

Peregrine made an exasperated noise.

'Yes,' said Jeremy. 'Well-knowing your views on theatre gossip, I didn't relay the story to you.'

'Have other people in the company heard it?' Alleyn asked.

Jeremy said: 'Oh, yes. I imagine so.'

Peregrine said: 'No doubt, Harry has told Destiny,' and Jeremy looked miserable. 'Yes,' he said. 'At a party.'

Alleyn said: 'You will be required to go to your safe-deposit with two CID officers, uplift the glove and hand it over to them. You will be asked to sign a full statement as to your activities. Whether a charge will be laid I can't at the moment tell you. Your ongoings, in my opinion, fall little short of lunacy. Technically, on your own showing, you're a thief.'

Jeremy, now so white that his freckles looked like brown confetti, turned on Peregrine and stammered: 'I've been so bloody miserable. It was a kind of diversion. I've been so filthily unhappy.'

He made for the door. Fox, a big man who moved quickly, was there before him. 'Just a minute, sir, if you don't mind,' he said mildly.

Alleyn said: 'All right, Fox. Mr Jones: will you go now to the safe-deposit? Two of our men will meet you there, take possession of the glove and ask you to return with them to the Yard. For the moment, that's all that'll happen. Good-day to you.'

Jeremy went out quickly. They heard him cross the foyer and run downstairs.

'Wait a moment, will you, Jay?' Alleyn said. 'Fox, lay that on, please.'

Fox went to the telephone and established a sub-fusc conversation with the Yard.

'That young booby's a close friend of yours, I gather,' Alleyn said.

'Yes, he is. Mr Alleyn, I realize I've no hope of getting anywhere with this but if I may just say one thing – '

'Of course, why not?'

'Well,' Peregrine said, rather surprised, 'thank you. Well, it's two things actually. First: from what Jeremy's told you, there isn't any motive whatever for him to burgle the safe last night. Is there?'

'If everything he has said is true – no. If he has only admitted what we were bound to find out and distorted the rest, it's not difficult to imagine a motive. Motives, however, are a secondary consideration in police work. At the moment, we want a workable assemblage of cogent facts. What's your second observation?'

'Not very compelling, I'm afraid, in the light of what you've just said. He is, as you've noticed, my closest friend and I must therefore be supposed to be prejudiced. But I do, all the same, want to put it on record that he's one of the most non-violent men you could wish to meet. Impulsive. Hot-tempered in a sort of sudden redheaded way. Vulnerable. But essentially gentle. Essentially incapable of the kind of thing that was perpetrated in this theatre last night. I *know* this of Jeremy, as well as I know it of myself. I'm sorry,' Peregrine said rather grandly. 'I realize that kind of reasoning won't make a dent in a police investigation. But if you like to question anyone else who's acquainted with the fool, I'm sure you'll get the same reaction.'

'Speaking as a brutal and hide-bound policeman,' Alleyn said cheerfully, 'I'm much obliged to you. It isn't always the disinterested witness who offers the soundest observations and I'm glad to have your account of Jeremy Jones.'

Peregrine stared at him. 'I beg your pardon,' he said.

'What for? Before we press on, though, I wonder if you'd feel inclined to comment on the Knight-Meade-Bracey-Grove situation. What's it all about? A character actress scorned and a leading gent slighted? A leading lady beguiled and a second juvenile in the ascendant? Or what?'

'I wonder you bother to ask me since you've got it off so pat,' said Peregrine tartly.

'And a brilliant young designer in thrall with no prospect of delight?'

'Yes. Very well.'

'All right,' Alleyn said. 'Let him be for the moment. Have you any idea who the US customer for the treasure might be?'

'No. It wasn't for publication. Or so I understood from Greenslade.'

'Not Mrs Constantia Guzman by any chance?'

'Good God, *I* don't know,' Peregrine said. 'I've no notion. Mr Conducis may not so much as know her. Not that that would signify.'

'I think he does, however. She was one of his guests in the *Kalliope* at the time of the disaster. One of the few to escape if I remember rightly.'

'Wait a bit. There's something. Wait a bit.'

'With pleasure.'

'No, but it's just I've remembered – it might not be of the smallest significance – but I *have* remembered one incident, during rehearsals when Conducis came in to tell me we could use the theatre for publicity. Harry walked in here while we were talking. He was as bright as a button, as usual, and not at all disconcerted. He greeted Mr Conducis like a long lost uncle, asked him if he'd been yachting lately and said something like: remember him to Mrs G. Of course there are a thousand and one Mrs G.'s but when you mentioned the yacht – '

'Yes, indeed. How did Conducis take this?'

'Like he takes everything. Dead pan.'

'Any idea what the obligation was that Grove seems to have laid upon him?'

'Not a notion.'

'Blackmail by any chance, would you think?'

'Ah, *no*! And Conducis is *not* a queer in my opinion if that's what you're working up to. Nor, good lord, is Harry! And nor, I'm quite sure, is Harry a blackmailer. He's a rum customer and he's a bloody nuisance in a company. Like a wasp. But I don't believe he's a bad lot. Not really.'

'Why?'

Peregrine thought for a moment. 'I suppose,' he said at last, with an air of surprise, 'that it must be because, to me, he really *is* funny. When he plays up in the theatre I become furious and go for him like a pick-pocket and then he says something outrageous that catches me on the hop and makes me want to laugh.' He looked from Alleyn to Fox. 'Has either of you,' Peregrine asked, 'ever brought a clown like Harry to book for murder?'

Alleyn and Fox appeared severally to take glimpses into their professional pasts.

'I can't recall,' Fox said, cautiously, 'ever finding much fun in a convicted homicide, can you, Mr Alleyn?'

'Not really,' Alleyn agreed, 'but I hardly think the presence or absence of the Comic Muse can be regarded as an acid test.'

Peregrine, for the first time, looked amused.

'Did you,' Alleyn said, 'know that Mr Grove is distantly related to Mr Conducis?'

'I did NOT,' Peregrine shouted. 'Who told you this?'

'He did.'

'You amaze me. It must be a tarradiddle. Though, of course,' Peregrine said, after a long pause, 'it would account for everything. Or would it?'

'Everything?'

'The mailed fist of management. The recommendation for him to be cast.'

'Ah, yes. What's Grove's background, by the way?'

'He refers to himself as an Old Borstalian but I don't for a moment suppose it's true. He's a bit of an inverted snob, is Harry.'

'Very much so, I'm sure.'

'I rather think he started in the RAF and then drifted on and off the boards until he got a big break in *Cellar Stairs*. He was out of a shop, he once told me, for so long that he got jobs as a lorry-driver, a steward and a waiter in a strip-tease joint. He said he took more in tips than he ever made speaking lines.'

'When was that?'

'Just before his break, he said. About six years ago. He signed off one job and before signing on for another took a trip round the agents and landed star-billing in *Cellar Stairs*. Such is theatre.'

'Yes, indeed.'

'Is that all?' Peregrine asked after a silence.

'I'm going to ask you to do something else for me. I know you've got the change of casting and internal affairs on your hands but as soon as you can manage it I wonder if you'd take an hour to think back over your encounters with Mr Conducis and your adventures of last night, and note down everything you can remember. And any other item, by the way, that you may have overlooked in the excitement.'

'Do you really think Conducis has got anything to do with last night?'

'I've no idea. He occurs. He'll have to be found irrelevant before we may ignore him. Will you do this?'

'I must say it's distasteful.'

'So,' said Alleyn, 'is Jobbins's corpse.'

'Whatever happened,' Peregrine said, looking sick, 'and whoever overturned the bronze dolphin, I don't believe it was deliberate, cold-blooded murder. I believe he saw Jobbins coming at him and overturned the pedestal in a sort of blind attempt to stop him. That's what I think and my God,' Peregrine said, 'I must say I do *not* welcome an invitation to have any part in hunting him down: whoever it was, the boy or anyone else.'

'All right. And if it wasn't the boy, what *about* the boy? How do you fit him in as a useful buffer between your distaste and the protection of the common man? How do you think the boy came to be dropped over the circle? And believe me he was *dropped*. He escaped, by a-hundred-to-one chance, being spilt like an egg over the stalls. Yes,' Alleyn said, watching Peregrine, 'that's a remark in bad taste, isn't it? Murder's a crime in bad taste. You've seen it, now. You ought to know.' He waited for a moment and then said, 'That was cheating and I apologize.'

Peregrine said: 'You needn't be so bloody upright. It's nauseating.'

'All right. Go away and vomit. But if you have second thoughts, sit down and write out every damn' thing you remember of Conducis and all the rest of it. And now, if you want to go – go. Get the hell out of it.'

'Out of my own office, I'd have you remember. To kick my heels on the landing.'

Alleyn broke into laughter. 'You have me there,' he said. 'Never mind. It's better, believe me, than kicking them in a waiting-room at the Yard. But all right, we'll have another go. What can you tell me, if your stomach is equal to it, of the background of the other members of your company?' Alleyn raised a hand. 'I know you have a loyalty to them and I'm not asking you to abuse it. I do remind you, Jay, that suspicion about this crime will fall inside your guild, your mystery, if I may put it like that, and that there's going to be a great deal of talk and speculation. With the exception of yourself and Miss Dunne and Miss Meade, whose alibis seem to us to be satisfactory and possibly Harry Grove, there isn't one of the company, and I'm including Winter Morris and Jeremy Jones, who absolutely could *not* have killed Jobbins and attacked the boy.'

'I can't see how you make it out. They were all, except Trevor, seen to leave. *I* saw them go. The doors were locked and bolted and barred.'

'The stage-door was locked but not bolted and barred. Hawkins unlocked it with his own key. The small pass-door in the front was unlocked when Miss Bracey left and was not bolted and barred until after Morris and Knight left. They heard Jobbins drop the bar.'

'That cuts them out, then, surely.'

'Look,' Alleyn said. 'Put this situation to yourself and see how you like it. Jobbins is still alive. Somebody knocks on the pass-door in the front entrance. He goes down. A recognized voice asks him to open up – an actor has left his money in his dressing-room or some such story. Jobbins lets him in. The visitor goes backstage saying he'll let himself out at the stage-door. Jobbins takes up his post. At midnight he does his routine telephoning and the sequel follows.'

'How do you know all this?'

'God bless my soul, my dear chap, for a brilliant playwright you've a quaint approach to logic. I *don't* know it. I merely advance it as a way in which your lock-up theory could be made to vanish. There is at least one other, even simpler solution which is probably the true one. The only point I'm trying to make is this. If you clamp down on telling me anything at all about any member of your company you may be very fastidious and loyal and you may be protecting the actual butcher but you're not exactly helping to clear the other six – seven if you count Conducis.'

Peregrine thought it over. 'I think,' he said at last, 'that's probably a lot of sophistical hooey but I get your point. But I ought to warn you, you've picked a dud for the job. I've got a notoriously bad memory. There are things,' Peregrine said slowly, 'at the back of my mind that have been worrying me ever since this catastrophe fell upon us. Do you think I can fetch them up? Not I.'

'What do you connect them with?'

'With noises made by Trevor, I think. And then, with Conducis. With the morning when he showed me the treasure. But of course *then* I was drunk so I'm unreliable in any case. However: tell me what you want to know and I'll see about answering.'

'Too kind,' said Alleyn dryly. 'Start with – anyone you like. Marcus Knight. What's his background apart from the Press hand-outs? I know all about his old man's stationer's shop in West Ham and how he rose to fame. Is it true he's temperamental?'

Peregrine looked relieved. 'If it's only *that* sort of thing! He's hell and well-known for it but he's such a superb actor we all do our best to lump the temperament. He's a jolly nice man really, I daresay, and collects stamps but he can't take the lightest criticism without going up like a rocket. An unfavourable notice is death to him and he's as vain as a peacock. But people say he's a sweetie at bottom even if it's a fair way to bottom.'

Alleyn had strolled over to a display of photographs on the far wall: all the members of the cast in character with their signatures appended. Marcus Knight had been treated to a montage with his own image startlingly echoed by the 'Grafton Portrait' and the Droushout engraving. Peregrine joined him.

'Extraordinary,' Alleyn said. 'The likeness. What a piece of luck!' He turned to Peregrine and found him staring, not at the picture but at the signature.

'Bold!' Alleyn said dryly.

'Yes. But it's not that. There's something about it. Damn! I thought so before. Something I've forgotten.'

'You may yet remember. Leave it. Tell me: is the sort of ribbing Knight got from Grove just now their usual form? All the King Dolphin nonsense?'

'Pretty much. It goes on.'

'If he's as touchy as you say, why on earth hasn't Knight shaken the Dolphin dust off his boots? Why does he stand it for one second?'

'I think,' Peregrine said with great simplicity, 'he likes his part. I think that might be it.'

'My dear Jay, I really do apologize: Of course he does. It's no doubt the best role, outside Shakespeare, that he'll ever play.'

'Do you think so? Really?'

'Indeed I do.'

Peregrine suddenly looked deeply happy. 'Now, of course,' he said, 'I'm completely wooed.'

'What can it matter what I think! You must know how good your play is.'

'Yes, but I like to be told. From which,' Peregrine said, 'you may gather that I have a temperamental link with Marco Knight.'

'Were he and Destiny Meade lovers?'

'Oh yes. Going steady, it seemed, until Harry chucked poor Gertie and came rollicking in. We thought the casting was going to work out very cosily with Dessy and Marco as happy as Larry on the one hand and Gertie and Harry nicely fixed on the other. Maddening, this dodging round in a company. It always makes trouble. And with Marco's capacity to cut up plug-ugly at the drop of a hat – anything might happen. We can only keep our fingers crossed.'

'Miss Meade is – she's – I imagine, not an intellectual type.'

'She's *so* stupid,' Peregrine said thoughtfully. 'But so, *so* stupid it's a kind of miracle. Darling Dessy. And yet,' he added, 'there's an element of cunning too. Certainly, there's an element of cunning.'

'What a problem for her director, in such a subtle role!'

'Not really. You just say: "Darling, you're sad. You're heartbroken. You can't bear it" and up come the welling tears. Or: "Darling, you've been clever, don't you see, you've been one too many for them" and she turns as shrewd as a marmoset. Or, simplest of all: "Darling, you're sending him in a big way," and as she never does anything else it works like a charm. *She does* the things: the audience *thinks* them.'

'Temperamental?'

'Only for form's sake when she fancies it's about time she showed up. She's quite good-natured.'

'Did she slap Knight back smartly or gradually?'

'Gradually. You could see it coming at rehearsals. In their love scenes. She began looking at her fingernails over his shoulder and pulling bits of mascara off her eyelashes: And then she took to saying could they just walk it because she was rethinking her approach. She talks like that but of course she never had an approach. Only an instinct backed up by superb techniques and great dollops of star quality.'

'She divorced her second husband, I believe, and lives alone?'

'Well – Yes. Officially.'

'Anything else about her?'

'She's a terrific gambler, is Dessy. On the share-market, with the bookies and everything on the side that offers. That's really what broke up the second marriage. He couldn't do with all the roulette-party and poker-dice carry-on.'

'Is she a successful gambler?'

'I daresay she herself scarcely knows, so vague are her ways.'

'And Miss Bracey?'

'That's a very different story. I don't know anything about Gertie's background but she really does bear out the Woman Scorned crack. She's – she's not all that charitably disposed at any time, perhaps, and this thing's stirred her up like a wasp's nest. She and Marco exhibit the heads-and-tails of despised love. Marco is a sort of walking example of outraged vanity and incredulous mortification. He can't believe it and yet there it is. Rather touchingly, *I* think, he doesn't until today seem to have taken against Dessy. But I've trembled lest he should suddenly rear back and have a wallop at Harry.'

'Hit him?'

'Yes. Bang-bang. Whereas, Gertie doesn't vent all she's got on her rival but hisses and stings away at the faithless one.'

'And so Miss Meade is let off lightly at both ends and Grove is the object of a dual resentment?'

'And that's throwing roses at it,' said Peregrine.

'Knight and Miss Bracey have a real, solid hatred for him? Is that putting it too high?'

'No, it's not but – ' Peregrine said quickly: 'What is all this? What's it matter how Marco and Gertie feel about Harry?'

'Nothing at all, I daresay. What about Random? Any comment on character?'

'Charlie? No trouble to anyone. Not, as you may have discerned, a hundred per cent he-man, but what of that? He doesn't bring it into the theatre. It was quite all right to let him dress with the boy, for instance.'

'Hobbies?'

'Well, as you've heard: Ximenes-class crosswords. Ciphers. And old manuscripts. He's quite an antiquarian, I'm told, is Charles. Jer says he's one of those characters who possess an infallible nose for a rare item. He spends half his time among the sixpenny and shilling bins in Long Acre and the Charing Cross Road. Good, conscientious actor. Minor public school and drama academy.'

'Did all the members of the company know each other before this production?'

'Oh, yes. Except Emily. She's at the beginning,' Peregrine said tenderly, 'and doesn't know many people in the West End yet.'

'Tell me, are you familiar with Harry Grove's overcoats?'

'I caught sight of him going away the other night wearing a contraption that screamed its way up the lane like a fire-engine and heard a lot of carry-on about it among the company.'

'What was it?'

'I wasn't close enough to – ' Peregrine's voice faded. He gaped at Alleyn. 'Oh *no!*' he said. 'It can't be. It's not possible.'

'What?'

'On – on Henry Jobbins?'

'Grove gave his overcoat to Jobbins on Friday evening. He said nobody seemed to like it. Didn't you know?'

Peregrine shook his head.

'I can't imagine,' he said slowly, 'I simply can not imagine why I didn't recognize it on poor Jobbins. I actually cracked a joke about it and he said it was a present.'

'Perhaps the scarf made a difference.'

'Scarf? I don't think he had a scarf on?'

'Did he not? A bright yellow scarf?'

'Wait. Yes,' said Peregrine, looking sick, 'of course. I – I remember. Afterwards.'

'But not before? When you spoke to him?'

'I don't remember it then. It wasn't showing.'

'Please say nothing about the overcoat, Jay. It's of the first importance that you don't. Not even,' Alleyn said with a friendly air, 'to your Emily.'

'Very well. May I know why it matters so much?' Alleyn told him.

'Yes, I see. But it won't really get you much further, will it?'

'If nobody knows of the transfer – '

'Yes, of course. Stupid of me.'

'And that really is all. I'm sorry to have kept you such an unconscionable time.'

Peregrine went to the door, hesitated and turned back.

'I'll do my best,' he said, 'to write down my Conduciae or should it be Conducii?'

'Or Conduciosis? Never mind. I'm glad you've decided to help. Thank you. Could you let me have it as soon as it's ready?'

'Yes. All right. Where will you be?'

'Here for another hour I should think. And then wherever developments send me. We'll leave a PC on duty in the theatre. If I've gone he'll take a message. Do you really mind doing this?'

'No. Not if it's remotely useful.'

'There now!' said Alleyn. 'Goodbye for the moment, then. On your way out, would you ask Mr Knight to come in?'

'Certainly. It's half past twelve,' Peregrine said. 'He'll have got a bit restive, I daresay.'

'Will he indeed?' said Alleyn. 'Send him in.'

CHAPTER 9

Knight Rampant

Marcus Knight was not so much restive as portentous. He had the air of a man who is making enormous concessions. When Alleyn apologized for keeping him waiting so long, he waved his hand as if to say: 'Think no more of it. Nevertheless – '

'One can't tell,' Alleyn said, 'in our job, how long any given interview will last.'

'It didn't escape my notice,' Knight said, 'that you were honoured with an earlier visit.'

'From Hartly Grove? Yes. He had,' Alleyn said, 'thought of something.'

'He thinks of a number of things, most of them highly offensive.'

'Really? This was quite harmless. I wonder if you've noticed his overcoat.'

Mr Knight had noticed Mr Grove's overcoat and said so briefly and with immeasurable distaste. 'One is not surprised however,' he said. 'One recognizes the form. It is entirely consistent. My God, what a garment! How he dares!'

It became evident that he did not know that the coat had been given to Jobbins.

Alleyn briefly re-checked Knight's movements. He had driven his Jaguar from the theatre to his house in Montpelier Square where he was given supper as usual by the Italian couple who looked after him. He thought it was probably about ten past eleven when he got in. He did not go out again but could not absolutely prove it.

Extreme, wholly male beauty is not a commonplace phenomenon. Marcus Knight possessed it to a generous degree. His oval face,
with its subtly turned planes, his delicate nose, slightly tilted eyes
and glossy hair might have been dreamed up by an artist of the
Renaissance or indeed by the unknown painter of that unknown
man whom many observers call the Grafton Shakespeare. He had
the bodily harmony that declares itself through its covering and he
moved like a panther. How old was he? Middle thirties? Younger?
Forty, perhaps? It didn't matter.

Alleyn led him cautiously by way of his own exquisite performance to the work of his fellow players. He uncovered a completely
egotistic but shrewd appreciation of the play and a raw patch of professional jealousy when the work of his associates, particularly of
Harry Grove, came into question. Grove's Mr W. H., it seemed, was
not a true reading. It was showy. It was vulgar. It was even rather
camp, said Marcus Knight.

Alleyn spoke of the theft of the glove and documents. Knight
rejoiced that they had been recovered. He gazed with passionate
concern at Alleyn. Was it certain they were uninjured? Was it quite,
quite certain? Alleyn said it was and began to talk of their
unequalled worth. Knight nodded several times very slowly in that
larger-than life manner that Alleyn associated with persons of his
profession. It was more like a series of bows.

'Unique,' he said, on two mellifluous notes. 'U-nique!'

Alleyn wondered what he would say if he knew of Jeremy's
substitution.

'Well,' he said lightly. 'At least Mr Conducis and the American
purchaser can breathe again. I can't help wondering who she may
be.'

'She?'

'Now, why did I say "she"?' Alleyn ejaculated. 'I suppose I must
have been thinking of Mrs Constantia Guzman?'

It was formidable to see how rapidly, with what virtuosity, Knight
changed colour from deepest plum to parchment and back again. He
drew his brows together. He retracted his upper lip. It crossed
Alleyn's mind that it was a pity the role of William Shakespeare
didn't offer an opportunity for a display of these physical demonstra-
tions of fury.

'What,' he asked, rising and looming over Alleyn, 'has that person – Grove – said to you? I demand an answer. What has he said?'

'About Mrs Constantia Guzman, do you mean? Nothing. Why?'

'You lie!'

'I don't, you know,' Alleyn said composedly. 'Grove didn't mention her to me. Really. She's an extremely well-known collector. What's the matter?'

Knight glowered at him in silence for some time. Fox cleared his throat.

'Do you swear,' Knight began in the lowest register of his voice, building up a crescendo as he went on. 'Do you swear the name of Guzman has not – ah – has not been – ah – mentioned to you in connection with My Own. Here in this room. Today. Do you swear to this? Hah?'

'No, I don't do that, either. It has.'

'*All!*' he bellowed suddenly. '*The whole pack of them!* He's lunched and bloody dined on it. Don't attempt to contradict me. He's betrayed a deeply, *deeply* regretted confidence. A moment of weakness. On my part. Before I knew him for what he is: a false, *false* man.' He pointed at Alleyn. 'Has he – has he told – her, Miss Meade? Destiny? You need not answer. I see it in your face. He has.'

'I've not spoken with Miss Meade,' Alleyn said.

'They've laughed together,' he roared. 'At Me!'

'Perfectly maddening for you if they have,' Alleyn said, 'but, if you'll forgive me, it isn't as far as I know, entirely relevant to the business under discussion.'

'Yes, it is,' Knight passionately contradicted, 'by God it is and I'll tell you why. I've put a restraint upon myself. I have not allowed myself to speak about this man. I have been scrupulous lest I should be thought biased. But now – *now*! I tell you this and I speak from absolute conviction: if as you hold, that appalling boy is not guilty and recovers his wits and if he was attacked by the man who killed Jobbins and if he *remembers who attacked him*, it will be at W. Hartly Grove he points his finger. *Now!*'

Alleyn, who had seen this pronouncement blowing up for the past five minutes, allowed himself as many seconds in which to be dumbfounded and then asked Marcus if he had any reasons, other, he hastily added, than those already adduced, for making this statement about Harry Grove. Nothing very specific emerged. There were dark and vague allusions to reputation and an ambiguous past. As his temper abated, and it did seem to abate gradually, Knight appeared to lose the fine edge of his argument. He talked of Trevor Vere and said he couldn't understand why Alleyn dismissed the possibility of his having been caught out by Jobbins, overturned the dolphin and then run so fast down the circle aisle that he couldn't prevent himself diving over the balustrade. Alleyn once again advanced the logical arguments against this theory.

'And there's no possibility of some member of the public having hidden during performance?'

'Jay assures me not. A thorough routine search is made and the staff on both sides of the curtain confirm this. This is virtually a "new" theatre. There are no stacks of scenery or properties or neglected hiding places.'

'You are saying,' said Knight, beginning portentously to nod again, 'that this thing must have been done by One of Us.'

'That's how it looks.'

'I am faced,' Knight said, 'with a frightful dilemma.' He immediately became a man faced with a frightful dilemma and looked quite haggard. 'Alleyn: what can one do? Idle for me to pretend I don't feel as I do about this man. I *know* him to be a worthless person. I know him – '

'One moment. This is still Harry Grove?'

'Yes.' (Several nods.) 'Yes. I am aware that the personal injuries he has inflicted upon me must be thought to prejudice my opinion.'

'I assure you – '

'And I am assuring *you* – Oh with such deadly certainty – that there is only one among us who is capable of the crime.'

He gazed fixedly into Alleyn's face. 'I studied physiognomy,' he surprisingly said. 'When I was in New York' – for a moment he looked hideously put out but instantly recovered, 'I met a most distinguished authority – Earl P. Van Smidt – and I became seriously interested in the science. I have studied and observed and I have proved my conclusions. Over and again. I have completely satisfied myself – but completely – that when you see a pair of unusually round eyes, rather wide apart, very light blue and without depth – look out. *Look out!*' he repeated and flung himself into the chair he had vacated.

'What for?' Alleyn inquired.

'Treachery. Shiftiness. Utter unscrupulousness. Complete lack of ethical values. I quote from Van Smidt.'

'Dear me.'

'As for Conducis! But no matter. No matter.'

'Do you discover the same traits in Mr Conducis?'

'I – I – am not familiar with Mr Conducis.'

'You have met him, surely?'

'Formal meeting. On the opening night.'

'But never before that?'

'I may have done so. Years ago. I prefer – ' Knight said surprisingly, 'to forget the occurrence.' He swept it away.

'May I ask why?'

There was an appreciable pause before he said: 'I was once his guest, if you can call it that and I was subjected to an insolent disregard which I would have interpreted more readily if I had at that time been acquainted with Smidt. In my opinion,' Knight said, 'Smidt should be compulsory reading for all police forces. You don't mind my saying this?' he added in a casual, lordly manner.

'Indeed no.'

'Good. Want me any more, dear boy?' he asked, suddenly gracious.

'I think not. Unless – and believe me I wouldn't ask if the question was irrelevant to the case – unless you care to tell me if Mrs Constantia Guzman really confided to you that she is a buyer of hot objets d'art on the intercontinental black market.'

It was no good. Back in a flash came the empurpled visage and the flashing eye. Back, too, came an unmistakable background of sheepishness and discomfort.

'No comment,' said Marcus Knight.

'No? Not even a tiny hint?'

'You are mad to expect it,' he said and with that they had to let him go.

II

'Well, Br'er Fox, we've caught a snarled up little job this time, haven't we?'

'We have that,' Fox agreed warmly. 'It'd be nice,' he added wistfully, 'if we could put it down to simple theft, discovery and violence.'

'It'd be lovely but we can't, you know. We can't. For one thing the theft of a famous object is always bedevilled by the circumstance of its being indisposable through the usual channels. No normal high-class fence, unless he's got very special contacts, is going to touch Shakespeare's note or his son's glove.'

'So for a start you've got either a crank who steals and gloats or a crank of the type of young Jones who steals to keep the swag in England or a thorough wised-up, high grade professional in touch with the top international racket. And at the receiving end some-body of the nature of this Mrs Guzman who's a millionaire crank in her own right and doesn't care how she gets her stuff.'

'That's right. Or a kidnapper who holds the stuff for ransom. And you *might* have a non-professional thief who knows all about Mrs G and believes she'll play and he'll make a packet.'

'That seems to take in the entire boiling of this lot, seeing Mr Grove's broadcast the Guzman-Knight anecdote for all it's worth. I tell you what, Mr Alleyn; it wouldn't be the most astonishing event in my working life if Mr Knight took to Mr Grove. Mr Grove's teas-ing ways seem to put him out to a remarkable degree, don't you think?'

'I think,' Alleyn said, 'we'd better, both of us, remind ourselves about actors.'

'You do? What about them?'

'One must always remember that they're trained to convey emo-tion. On or off the stage, they make the most of everything they feel. Now this means they express their feelings up to saturation point. When you and I and all the rest of the non-actors do our damndest to understate and be ironical about our emotional reflexes, the actor, even when he underplays them, does so with such expertise that he convinces us laymen that he's *in extremis*. He isn't. He's only being professionally articulate about something that happens off-stage instead of in front of an official audience.'

'How does all this apply to Mr Knight, then?'

'When he turns purple and roars anathemas against Grove it means, A, that he's hot-tempered, pathologically vain and going through a momentary hell and B, that he's letting you know up to the nth degree just *how* angry and dangerous he's feeling. It doesn't necessarily mean that once his present emotion has subsided he will do anything further about it, and nor does it mean that he's superficial or a hypocrite. It's his job to take the micky out of an audience and even in the throes of a completely genuine emotional crisis, he does just that thing if it's only an audience of one.'

'Is this what they call being an extrovert?'

'Yes, Br'er Fox, I expect it is. But the interesting thing about Knight, I thought, was that when it came to Conducis he turned uncommunicative and cagey.'

'Fancied himself slighted over something, it seemed. Do you reckon Knight believes all that about Grove? Being a homicidal type? All that stuff about pale eyes etcetera. Because,' Fox said with great emphasis, 'it's all poppycock: there aren't any facial characteristics for murder. What's that you're always quoting about there being no art to find the mind's construction in the face? I reckon it's fair enough where homicide's concerned. Although,' Fox added opening his own eyes very wide, 'I always fancy there's a kind of look about sex offenders of a certain type. That I will allow.'

'Be that as it may it doesn't get us much further along our present road. No news from the hospital?'

'No. They'd ring through at once if there was.'

'I know. I know.'

'What do we do about Mr Jeremy Jones?'

'Oh, blast! What indeed! I think we take delivery of the glove and documents, give him hell and go no further. I'll talk to the AC about him and I rather *think* I'll have to tell Conducis as soon as possible. Who've we got left here? Only little Morris. Ask him into his own office, Br'er Fox. We needn't keep him long, I think.'

Winter Morris came in quoting Queen Mary. 'This,' he said wearily, 'is a pretty kettle of fish. This is a carry-on. I'm not complaining, mind, and I'm not blaming anybody but what, oh what, has set Marco off again? Sorry. Not your headache, old boy.'

Alleyn uttered consolatory phrases, sat him at his own desk, checked his alibi which was no better and no worse than anyone else's, in that after he left the theatre with Knight he drove to his house at Golder's Green where his wife and family were all in bed.

When he wound up his watch he noticed it said ten to twelve. He had heard the Knight-Guzman story. 'I thought it bloody sad,' he said. 'Poor woman. Terrible, you know, the problem of the plain highly-sexed woman. Marco ought to have held his tongue. He ought never to have told Harry. Of course Harry made it sound a bit of a yell, but I didn't like Marco telling about it. I don't think that sort of thing's funny.'

'It does appear that on her own admission to Knight, she's a buyer on a colossal scale under the museum-piece counter.'

Winter Morris spread his hands. 'We all have our weaknesses,' he said. 'So she likes nice things and she can pay for them. Marcus Knight should complain!'

'Well!' Alleyn ejaculated. 'That's one way of looking the Big Black Market in the eyes I must say! Have you ever met Mrs Guzman, by the way?'

Winter Morris had rather white eyelids. They now dropped a little. 'No,' he said, 'not in person. Her husband was a most brilliant man. The equal and more of Conducis.'

'Self-made?'

'Shall we say self-created? It was a superb achievement.'

Alleyn looked his enjoyment of this phrase and Morris answered his look with a little sigh. 'Ah yes!' he said. 'These colossi! How marvellous!'

'In your opinion,' Alleyn said, 'without prejudice and within these four walls and all that: how many people in this theatre know the combination of that lock?'

Morris blushed. 'Yes,' he said. 'Well. This is where I don't exactly shine with a clear white radiance, isn't it? Well, as he's told you, Charlie Random for one. Got it right, as you no doubt observed. He says he didn't pass it on and personally I believe that. He's a very quiet type, Charlie. Never opens up about his own or anybody else's business. I'm sure he's dead right about the boy not knowing the combination.'

'You are? Why?'

'Because as I said, the bloody kid was always pestering me about it.'

'And so you would have been pretty sure, would you, that only you yourself and Mr Conducis knew the combination?'

'I don't say that,' Morris said unhappily. 'You see after that morning they did all know about the five-letter word being an obvious one and – and – well Dessy did say one day "Is it 'glove', Winty? We all think it might be? Do you swear it's not 'glove'." Well, you know Dessy. She'd woo the Grand Master to let the goat out of the Lodge. I suppose I boggled a bit and she laughed and kissed me. I know. I know. I ought to have had it changed. I meant to. But – in the theatre we don't go about wondering if someone in the company's a big-time bandit.'

'No, of course you don't. Mr Morris: thank you very much. I think we can now return your office to you. It was more than kind to suggest that we use it.'

'There hasn't been all that much for me to do. The Press is our big worry but we're booked out solid for another four months. Unless people get it into their heads to cancel we *should* make out. You never know, though, which way a thing like this will take the public.'

They left him in a state of controlled preoccupation.

The circle foyer was deserted, now. Alleyn paused for a moment. He looked at the shuttered bar, at the three shallow steps leading on three sides from the top down to the half-landing and the two flights that curved down from there to the main entrance; at the closed safe in the wall above the landing, the solitary bronze dolphin and the two doors into the circle. Everything was quiet, a bit muffled and stuffily chilly.

He and Fox walked down the three canvas-covered steps to the landing. A very slight sound caught Alleyn's ear. Instead of going on down he crossed to the front of the landing, rested his hands on its elegant iron balustrade and looked into the main entrance below.

His gaze lighted on the crown of a smart black hat and the violently foreshortened figure of a thin woman.

For a second or two the figure made no move. Then the hat tipped back, and gave way to a face like a white disc, turned up to his own.

'Do you want to see me, Miss Bracey?'

The face tipped backwards and forwards in assent. The lips moved but if she spoke, her voice was inaudible.

Alleyn motioned to Fox to stay where he was and himself went down the curving right hand stairway.

There she stood, motionless. The fat upside-down cupids over the box-office and blandly helpful caryatids supporting the landing, made an incongruous background for that spare figure and yet, it crossed Alleyn's mind, her general appearance was evocative, in a cockeyed way, of the period: of some repressed female character from a Victorian play or novel. Rosa Dartle, he thought, that was the sort of thing: Rosa Dartle.

'What is it?' Alleyn asked. 'Are you unwell?'

She looked really ill. He wondered if he had imagined that she had swayed very slightly, and then pulled herself together.

'You must sit down,' he said. 'Let me help you.'

When he went up to her he smelt brandy and saw that her eyes were off-focus. She said nothing but let him propel her to Jeremy Jones's plushy settee alongside the wall. She sat bolt upright. One corner of her mouth dropped a little as if pulled down by an invisible hook. She groped in her handbag, fetched up a packet of cigarettes and fumbled one out. Alleyn lit it for her. She made a great business of this. She's had a lot more than's good for her, he thought and wondered where, on a Sunday afternoon, she'd get hold of it. Perhaps Fox's Mrs Jancy at The Wharfinger's Friend had obliged.

'Now,' he said, 'what's the trouble?'

'Trouble? What trouble? I know trouble when I see it,' she said. 'I'm saturated in it.'

'Do you want to tell me about it?'

'Not a question of me telling you. It's what *he* told you. That's what matters.'

'Mr Grove?'

'Mr W. Hartly Grove. You know what? He's a monster. You know? Not a man but a monster. Cruel. My God,' she said and the corner of her mouth jerked again, 'how cruel that man can be!'

Looking at her Alleyn thought there was not much evidence of loving-kindness in her own demeanour.

'What,' she asked with laborious articulation, 'did he say about me? What did he say?'

'Miss Bracey, we didn't speak of you at all.'

'What *did* you speak about? Why did he stay behind to speak to you? He did, didn't he? Why?'

'He told me about his overcoat.'

She glowered at him and sucked at her cigarette as if it was a respirator. 'Did he tell you about his scarf?' she said.

'The yellow one with H on it?'

She gave a sort of laugh. 'Embroidered,' she said. 'By his devoted Gerts. God, what a fool! And he goes on wearing it. Slung round his neck like a halter and I wish it'd throttle him.'

She leant back, rested her head against the crimson plush and shut her eyes. Her left hand slid from her lap and the cigarette fell from her fingers. Alleyn picked it up and threw it into a nearby sand-box. 'Thanks,' she said without opening her eyes.

'Why did you stay behind? What do you want to tell me?'

'Stay behind? When?'

'Now.'

'*Then*, you mean.'

The clock above the box-office ticked. The theatre made a settling noise up in its ceiling. Miss Bracey sighed.

'Did you go back into the theatre?'

'Loo. Downstairs cloaks.'

'Why didn't you tell me this before?'

She said very distinctly: 'Because it didn't matter.'

'Or because it mattered too much?'

'*No.*'

'Did you see or hear anyone while you were in the downstairs foyer?'

'No. Yes, I did. I heard Winty and Marco in the office upstairs. They came out. And I left, then. I went away. Before they saw me.'

'Was there someone else you saw? Jobbins?'

'No,' she said at once.

'There was someone, wasn't there?'

'No. No. *No.*'

'Why does all this distress you so much?'

She opened her mouth and then covered it with her hand. She rose and swayed very slightly. As he put out a hand to steady her she broke from him and ran hazardously to the pass-door. It was unlocked. She pulled it open and left it so. Alleyn stood in the doorway and she backed away from him across the portico. When she realized he wasn't going to follow she flapped her hand in a lunatic fashion and ran towards the car park. He was in time to see her scramble into her mini-car. Someone was sitting in the passenger seat. He caught sight of Alleyn and turned away. It was Charles Random.

'Do you want her held?' Fox said at his elbow.

'No. What for? Let her go.'

III

'I *think* that's the lot,' Peregrine said. He laid down his pen, eased his fingers and looked up at Emily.

The bottom of Phipps Lane having turned out to be windy and rich in dubious smells, they had crossed the bridge and retired to the flat. Emily got their lunch ready while Peregrine laboured to set down everything he could remember of his encounters with Mr Conducis. Of Jeremy there was nothing to be seen.

Emily said: '"What I did in the Hols. Keep it bright, brief and descriptive".'

'I seem to have done an unconscionable lot,' Peregrine rejoined. 'It's far from brief. Look.'

'No doubt Mr Alleyn will mark it for you. "Quite G, but should take more pains with his writing." Are you sure you haven't forgotten the one apparently trifling clue round which the whole mystery revolves?'

'You're very joky, aren't you? I'm far from sure. The near-drowning accident's all complete, I think, but I'm not so sure about the visit to Drury Place. Of course, I was drunk by the time that was over. How *extraordinary* it was,' Peregrine said. 'Really, he *was* rum. Do you know, Emmy, darling, it seems to me now as if he acted throughout on some kind of compulsion. As if it had been he not I who was half-drowned and behaving (to mix my metaphor, you pedantic girl) like a duck that's had its head chopped off. *He* was obsessed while *I* was merely plastered. Or so it seems, now.'

'But what did he *do* that was so odd?'

'Do? He – well, there was an old menu card from the yacht *Kalliope*. It was in the desk and he snatched it up and burnt it.'

'I suppose if your yacht's wrecked under your feet you don't much enjoy being reminded of it.'

'No, but I got the impression it was something *on* the card – '
Peregrine went into a stare and after a long pause said in a rather
glazed manner, 'I think I've remembered.'

'What?'

'On the menu. Signatures: you know? And – Emmy, listen.'

Emily listened. 'Well,' she said. 'For what it's worth: put it in.'

Peregrine put it in. 'There's one other thing,' he said. 'It's about
last night. I think it was when I was in front and you had come
through from backstage. There was the disturbance by the boy – cat-
calls and the door-slamming. Somewhere about then, it was, that I
remember thinking of *The Cherry Orchard*. Not *consciously* but with
one of those sort of momentary, back-of-the-mind things.'

'*The Cherry Orchard?*'

'Yes, and Miss Joan Littlewood.'

'Funny mixture. She's never produced it, has she?'

'I don't think so. Oh, *damn*, I wish I could get it. Yes,' Peregrine said
excitedly. 'And with it there was a floating remembrance, I'm sure – of
what? A quotation: *"Vanished with a –* something *perfume and a – "* that I
think was used somewhere by Walter de la Mare. It was hanging about
like the half-recollection of a dream when we walked up the puddled
alleyway and into Wharfingers Lane. Why? What started it up?'

'It mightn't have anything to do with Trevor or Jobbins.'

'I know. But I've got this silly feeling it has.'

'Don't *try* to remember and then you may.'

'All right. Anyway the end of hols essay's ready for what it's
worth. I wonder if Alleyn's still at the theatre.'

'Ring up.'

'OK. What's that parcel you've been carting about all day?'

'I'll show you when you've rung up.'

A policeman answered from The Dolphin and said that Alleyn
was at the Yard. Peregrine got through with startling promptitude.

'I've done this thing,' he said. 'Would you like me to bring it over
to you?'

'I would indeed. Thank you, Jay. Remembered anything new?'

'Not much, I'm afraid.' The telephone made its complicated
jangling sound.

'What?' Alleyn asked. 'What's that twanging? What did you say?
Nothing new?'

'Yes!' Peregrine suddenly bawled into the receiver. 'Yes. You've done it. I'll put it in. Yes. Yes. Yes.'

'You sound like a pop singer. I'll be here for the next hour or so. Ask at the Yard entrance and they'll send you up. 'Bye.'

'You've remembered?' Emily cried. 'What is it? You've remembered.'

And when Peregrine told her, she remembered, too.

He re-opened his report and wrote feverishly. Emily unwrapped her parcel. When Peregrine had finished his additions and swung round in his chair he found, staring portentously at him, a water-colour drawing of a florid gentleman. His hair was curled into a cockscomb. His whiskers sprang from his jowls like steel wool and his prominent eyes proudly glared from beneath immensely luxuri-ant brows. He wore a frock coat with satin revers, a brilliant waist-coat, three alberts, a diamond tie-pin and any quantity of rings. His pantaloons were strapped under his varnished boots and beneath his elegantly arched arm, his lilac-gloved hand supported a topper with a curly brim. He stood with one leg straight and the other bent. He was superb.

And behind, lightly but unmistakably sketched in, was a familiar, an adorable facade.

'Emily? It isn't – ? It must be – ?'

'Look.'

Peregrine came closer. Yes, scribbled in faded pencil at the bottom of the work: 'Mr Adolphus Ruby of The Dolphin Theatre. "Histrionic Portraits" series, 23 April 1855.'

'It's a present,' Emily said. 'It was meant, under less ghastly circs, to celebrate The Dolphin's first six months. I thought I'd get it suit-ably framed but then I decided to give it to you now to cheer you up a little.'

Peregrine began kissing her very industriously.

'Hi!' she said. 'Steady.'

'Where, you darling love, did you get it?'

'Charlie Random told me about it. He'd seen it on one of his prowls in a print shop off Long Acre. Isn't he odd? He didn't seem to want it himself. He goes in for nothing later than 1815, he said. So, I got it.'

'It's not a print, by Heaven it's an original. It's a Phiz original, Emmy. Oh, we shall frame it so beautifully and hang it – ' He stopped for a second. 'Hang it,' he said, 'in the best possible place. Gosh, won't it send old Jer sky high!'

'Where is he?'

Peregrine said: 'He had a thing to do. He ought to be back by now. Emily, I couldn't have ever imagined myself telling anybody what I'm going to tell you so it's a sort of compliment. Do you know what Jer did?'

And he told Emily about Jeremy and the glove.

'He must have been demented,' she said flatly.

'I know. And what Alleyn's decided to do about him, who can tell? You don't sound as flabbergasted as I expected.'

'Don't I? No, well – I'm not altogether. When we were making the props Jeremy used to talk incessantly about the glove. He's got a real fixation on the ownership business, hasn't he? It really is almost a kink, don't you feel? Harry was saying something the other day about after all the value of those kinds of jobs was purely artificial and fundamentally rather silly. If he was trying to get a rise out of Jeremy, he certainly succeeded. Jeremy was livid. I thought there'd be a punch-up before we were through. Perry, what's the matter? Have I been beastly?'

'No, no. Of course not.'

'I *have*,' she said contritely. 'He's a great friend and I've been talking about him as if he's a specimen. I *am* sorry.'

'You needn't be. I know what he's like. Only I do *wish* he hadn't done this.'

Peregrine walked over to the window and stared across the river towards The Dolphin. Last night, he thought, only sixteen hours ago, in that darkened house, a grotesque overcoat had moved in and out of shadow. Last night – He looked down into the street below. There from the direction of the bridge came a ginger head, thrust forward above heavy shoulders and adorned, like a classic ewer, with a pair of outstanding ears.

'Here he comes,' Peregrine said. 'They haven't run him in as yet it seems.'

'I'll take myself off.'

'No, you don't. I've to drop this stuff at the Yard. Come with me. We'll take the car and I'll run you home.'

'Haven't you got things you ought to do? Telephonings and fussings. What about Trevor?'

'I've done that. No change. Big troubles with Mum. Compensation. It's Greenslade and Winty's headache, thank God. We want to do what's right and a tidy bit more but she's out for the earth.'

'Oh, dear.'

'Here's Jer.'

He came in looking chilled and rather sickly. 'I'm sorry,' he said. 'I didn't know you had – Oh hallo, Em.'

'Hallo, Jer.'

'I've told her,' Peregrine said.

'Thank you very much.'

'There's no need to take it grandly, is there?'

'Jeremy, you needn't mind my knowing. Truly.'

'I don't in the least mind,' he said in a high voice. 'No doubt you'll both be surprised to learn I've been released with a blackguarding that would scour the hide off an alligator.'

'Surprised and delighted,' Peregrine said. 'Where's the loot?'

'At the Yard.'

Jeremy stood with his hands in his pockets as if waiting for something irritating to occur.

'Do you want the car, Jer? I'm going to the Yard now,' Peregrine said and explained why. Jeremy remarked that Peregrine was welcome to the car and added that he was evidently quite the white-haired Trusty of the Establishment. He stood in the middle of the room and watched them go.

'He *is* in a rage,' Emily said as they went to the car.

'I don't know what he's in but he's bloody lucky it's not the lock-up. Come on.'

IV

Alleyn put down Peregrine's report and gave it a definitive slap. 'It's useful, Fox,' he said. 'You'd better read it.'

He dropped it on the desk before his colleague, filled his pipe and strolled over to the window. Like Peregrine Jay, an hour earlier, he looked down at the Thames and he thought how closely this case clung to the river as if it had been washed up by the incoming tide and left high-and-dry for their inspection. Henry

Jobbins of Phipps Passage was a waterside character if ever there was one.

Peregrine Jay and Jeremy Jones were not far east along the Embankment. Opposite them The Dolphin pushed up its stage-house and flagstaff with a traditional flourish on Bankside. Behind Tabard Lane in the Borough lurked Mrs Blewitt while her terrible Trevor, still on the South Bank, languished in St Terence's. And as if to top it off, he thought idly, here *we* are at the Yard, hard by the river.

'But with Conducis,' Alleyn muttered, 'we move West and, I suspect, a good deal further away than Mayfair.'

He looked at Fox who, with eyebrows raised high above his spectacles in his stuffy reading expression, concerned himself with Peregrine's report.

The telephone rang and Fox reached for it. 'Super's room,' he said. 'Yes? I'll just see.'

He laid his great palm across the mouthpiece. 'It's Miss Destiny Meade,' he said, 'for you.'

'Is it, by gum! What's she up to, I wonder. All right. I'd better.'

'Look,' cried Destiny when he had answered. 'I know you're a kind *kind* man.'

'Do you?' Alleyn said. 'How?'

'I have a sixth sense about people. Now, you won't laugh at me will you? Promise.'

'I've no inclination to do so, believe me.'

'And you won't slap me back. You'll come and have a delicious little dinky at six, or even earlier or whenever it suits and tell me I'm being as stupid as an owl. Now, do, do, do, do, do. Please, please, please.'

'Miss Meade,' Alleyn said, 'it's extremely kind of you but I'm on duty and I'm afraid I can't.'

'On duty! But you've been on duty all *day*. That's worse than being an actor and you can't possibly mean it.'

'Have you thought of something that may concern this case?'

'It concerns ME,' she cried and he could imagine how widely her eyes opened at the telephone.

'Perhaps if you would just say what it is,' Alleyn suggested. He looked across at Fox who, with his spectacles half-way down his

nose, blankly contemplated his superior and listened at the other
telephone. Alleyn crossed his eyes and protruded his tongue.

' – I can't really, not on the telephone. It's too complicated. Look –
I'm *sure* you're up to your ears and not for the wide, wide world
would I – ' The lovely voice moved unexpectedly into its higher and
less mellifluous register. 'I'm nervous,' it said rapidly. 'I'm afraid. I'm
terrified. I'm being threatened.' Alleyn heard a distant bang and a
male voice. Destiny Meade whispered in his ear, *'Please come. Please
come.'* Her receiver clicked and the dialling tone set in.

'Now who in Melpomene's dear name,' Alleyn said, 'does that
lovely lady think she's leading down the garden path? Or is she? By
gum, if she *is*,' he said, 'she's going to get such a tap on the temperament as hasn't come her way since she hit the headlines. When are
we due with Conducis? Five o'clock. It's now half past two. Find us
a car, Br'er Fox, we're off to Cheyne Walk.'

Fifteen minutes later they were shown into Miss Destiny Meade's
drawing-room.

It was sumptuous to a degree and in maddeningly good taste: an
affair of mushroom-coloured curtains, dashes of Schiaparelli pink,
dull satin, Sévres plaques and an unusual number of orchids. In the
middle of it all was Destiny wearing a heavy sleeveless sheath with
a mink collar: and not at all pleased to see Inspector Fox.

'Kind, kind,' she said, holding out her hand at her white arm's
length for Alleyn to do what he thought best with. 'Good afternoon,'
she said to Mr Fox.

'Now, Miss Meade,' Alleyn said briskly, 'what's the matter?' He
reminded himself of a mature Hamlet.

'Please sit down. No, please. I've been so terribly distressed and I
need your advice so desperately.'

Alleyn sat, as she had indicated it, in a pink velvet buttoned chair.
Mr Fox took the least luxurious of the other chairs and Miss Meade
herself sank upon a couch, tucked up her feet which were beautiful
and leant superbly over the arm to gaze at Alleyn. Her hair, coloured
raven black for the Dark Lady, hung like a curtain over her right jaw
and half her cheek. She raised a hand to it and then drew the hand
away as if it had hurt her. Her left ear was exposed and embellished
with a massive diamond pendant.

'This is so difficult,' she said.

'Perhaps we could fire point-blank.'

'Fire? Oh, I see. Yes. Yes, I must try, mustn't I?'

'If you please.'

Her eyes never left Alleyn's face. 'It's about – ' she began and her voice resentfully indicated the presence of Mr Fox. 'It's about ME.'

'Yes?'

'Yes. I'm afraid I must be terribly frank. Or no. Why do I say that? To you of all people who, of course, understand – ' she executed a circular movement of her arm – 'everything. I know you do. I wouldn't have asked you if I hadn't known. And you see I have nowhere to turn.'

'Oh, surely!'

'No. I mean that,' she said with great intensity. 'I mean it. Nowhere. No one. It's all so utterly unexpected. Everything seemed to be going along quite naturally and taking the inevitable course. Because – I know you'll agree with this – one shouldn't – indeed one can't resist the inevitable. One is fated and when this new thing came into our lives we both faced up to it, he and I, oh, over and over again. It's like,' she rather surprisingly added, 'Antony and Cleopatra. I forget the exact line. I think, actually, that in the production it was cut but it puts the whole thing in a nutshell, and I told him so. Ah, Cleopatra,' she mused and such was her beauty and professional expertise, that, there and then, lying (advantageously of course) on the sofa she became for a fleeting moment the Serpent of the old Nile. 'But now,' she added crossly as she indicated a box of cigarettes that was not quite within her reach, 'now, with him turning peculiar and violent like this I feel I simply don't *know* him. I can't cope. As I told you on the telephone, I'm terrified.'

When Alleyn leant forward to light her cigarette he fancied that he caught a glint of appraisal and of wariness but she blinked, moved her face nearer to his and gave him a look that was a masterpiece.

'Can you,' Alleyn said, 'perhaps come to the point and tell us precisely why and of whom you are frightened, Miss Meade?'

'Wouldn't one be? It was so utterly beyond the bounds of anything one could possibly anticipate. To come in almost without warning and I must tell you that of course he has his own key and by a hideous chance my married couple are out this afternoon. And then, after all that has passed between us to – to . . .'

She turned her head aside, swept back the heavy wing of her hair and superbly presented herself to Alleyn's gaze.

'Look,' she said.

Unmistakably someone had slapped Miss Meade very smartly indeed across the right-hand rearward aspect of her face. She had removed the diamond ear-ring on this side but its pendant had cut her skin behind the point of the jaw and the red beginnings of a bruise showed across the cheek.

'What do you think of that?' she said.

'Did Grove do this?' Alleyn ejaculated.

She stared at him. An indescribable look of – what?

Pity? Contempt? Mere astonishment? – broke across her face. Her mouth twisted and she began to laugh.

'Oh, you poor darling,' said Destiny Meade. 'Harry? He wouldn't hurt a fly. No, no, no, my dear, this is Mr Marcus Knight. His mark.'

Alleyn digested this information and Miss Meade watched him apparently with some relish.

'Do you mind telling me,' he said at length, 'why all this blew up? I mean, *specifically* why. If, as I understand, you have finally broken with Knight.'

'*I* had,' she said, 'but you see *he* hadn't. Which made things so very tricky. And then he wouldn't give me back the key. He has, now. He threw it at me,' she looked vaguely round the drawing-room. 'It's somewhere about,' she said. 'It might have gone any-where or broken anything. He's so *egotistic.*'

'What had precipitated this final explosion, do you think?'

'Well – ' She dropped the raven wing over her cheek. 'This and that. Harry, of course, has driven him quite frantic. It's very bad of Harry and I never cease telling him so. And then it really was *too* unfortunate last night about the orchids.'

'The orchids?' Alleyn's gaze travelled to a magnificent stand of them in a Venetian goblet.

'Yes, those,' she said. 'Vass had them sent round during the show. I tucked his card in my décolletage like a sort of Victorian courtesan, you know, and in the big love scene Marco spotted it and whipped it out before I could do a thing. It wouldn't have been so bad if they hadn't had that flare-up in the yacht a thousand years ago. He hadn't realized before that I knew Vass so well. Personally, I mean. Vassy has got this thing about no publicity and of course I *respect* it. I understand. We just see each other quietly from time to time. He has a wonderful brain.'

' "Vassy"? "Vass"?'

'Vassily, really. I call him Vass. Mr Conducis.'

CHAPTER 10

Monday

As Fox and Alleyn left the flat in Cheyne Walk they encountered, in the downstairs entrance, a little old man in a fusty overcoat and decrepit bowler. He seemed to be consulting a large envelope.

'Excuse me, gentlemen,' he said, touching the brim of the bowler, 'but can you tell me if a lady be-the-namer Meade resides in these apartments? It seems to be the number but I can't discover a name board or indication of any sort.'

Fox told him and he was much obliged.

When they were in the street Alleyn said: 'Did you recognize him?'

'I had a sort of notion,' Fox said, 'that I ought to. Who is he? He looks like a bum.'

'Which is what he is. He's a Mr Grimball who, twenty years ago and more was the man in possession at the Lampreys.'

'God bless my soul!' Fox said. 'Your memory!'

'Peregrine Jay did tell us that the Meade's a compulsive gambler, didn't he?'

'Well, I'll be blowed! Fancy that! On top of all the other lot – in Queer Street! Wonder if Mr Conducis – '

Fox continued in a series of scandalized ejaculations.

'We're not due with Conducis for another hour and a half,' Alleyn said. 'Stop clucking and get into the car. We'll drive to the nearest box and ring the Yard in case there's anything.'

'About the boy?'

'Yes. Yes. About the boy. Come on.'

Fox returned from the telephone in measured haste.

'Hospital's just rung through,' he said. 'They think he's coming round.'

'Quick as we can,' Alleyn said to the driver and in fifteen minutes, with the sister and house-surgeon in attendance, they walked round the screens that hid Trevor's bed in the children's casualty ward at St Terence's.

PC Grantley had returned to duty. When he saw Alleyn he hurriedly vacated his chair and Alleyn slipped into it.

'Anything?'

Grantley showed his note book.

'It's a pretty glove,' Alleyn read, *'but it doesn't warm my hand. Take it off:*

'He said that?'

'Yes, sir. Nothing else, sir. Just that.'

'It's a quotation from his part.'

Trevor's eyes were closed and he breathed evenly. The sister brushed back his curls.

'He's asleep,' the doctor said. 'We must let him waken in his own time. He'll probably be normal when he does.'

'Except for the blackout period?'

'Quite.'

Ten minutes slipped by in near silence.

'Mum,' Trevor said, 'Hey, Mum.'

He opened his eyes and stared at Alleyn. 'What's up?' he asked and then saw Grantley's tunic. 'That's a rozzer,' he said. 'I haven't done a thing.'

'You're all right,' said the doctor. 'You had a nasty fall and we're looking after you.'

'Oh,' Trevor said profoundly and shut his eyes.

'Gawd, he's off again,' Grantley whispered distractedly. 'Innit marvellous.'

'Now then,' Fox said austerely.

'Pardon, Mr Fox.'

Alleyn said, 'May he be spoken to?'

'He shouldn't be worried. If it's important – '

'It could hardly be more so.'

'Nosy Super,' Trevor said and Alleyn turned back to find himself being stared at.

'That's right,' he said. 'We've met before.'

'Yeah. Where though?'

'In The Dolphin. Upstairs in the circle.'

'Yeah,' Trevor said, wanly tough. A look of doubt came into his eyes. He frowned. 'In the circle,' he repeated uneasily.

'Things happen up there in the circle, don't they?'

Complacently and still with that look of uncertainty: 'You can say that again,' said Trevor. 'All over the house.'

'*Slash?*'

'Yeah. *Slash,*' he agreed and grinned.

'You had old Jobbins guessing?'

'And that's no error.'

'What did you do?'

Trevor stretched his mouth and produced a wailing sound: '*Wheeeee.*'

'Make like spooks,' he said. 'See?'

'Anything else?'

There was a longish pause. Grantley lifted his head. Somewhere beyond the screens a trolley jingled down the ward.

'*Ping.*'

'That must have rocked them,' Alleyn said.

'Can say that again. What a turn-up! Oh, dear!'

'How did you do it? Just like that? With your mouth?'

The house-surgeon stirred restively. The sister gave a starched little cough.

'Do you *mind?*' Trevor said. 'My mum plays the old steely,' he added, and then, with a puzzled look: 'Hey! Was that when I got knocked out or something? Was it?'

'That was a bit later. You had a fall. Can you remember where you went after you banged the stage-door?'

'No,' he said impatiently. He sighed and shut his eyes. 'Do me a favour and pack it up, will you?' he said and went to sleep again.

'I'm afraid that's it,' said the house-surgeon.

Alleyn said: 'May I have a word with you?'

'Oh, certainly. Yes, of course. Carry on, Sister, will you? He's quite all right.'

Alleyn said: 'Stick it out, Grantley.'

The house-surgeon led him into an office at the entrance to the ward. He was a young man and, although he observed a markedly professional attitude, was clearly intrigued by the situation.

'Look here,' Alleyn said, 'I want you to give me your cold-blood-ed, considered opinion. You tell me the boy is unlikely to remember what happened just before he went overboard. I gather he may recall events up to within a few minutes of the fall?'

'He may, yes. The length of the "lost" period can vary.'

'Did you think he was on the edge of remembering a little further just now?'

'One can't say. One got the impression that he hadn't the energy to try and remember.'

'Do you think that if he were faced with the person whom he saw attacking the caretaker, he would recognize him and remember what he saw?'

'I don't know. I'm not a specialist in amnesia or the after effects of cranial injury. You should ask someone who is.' The doctor hesi-tated and then said slowly: 'You mean would the shock of seeing the assailant stimulate the boy's memory?'

'Not of the assault upon himself but of the earlier assault upon Jobbins which may be on the fringe of his recollection: which may lie just this side of the blackout.'

'I can't give you an answer to that one.'

'Will you move the boy into a separate room – say tomorrow – and allow him to see three – perhaps four visitors: one after another? For five minutes each.'

'No. I'm sorry. Not yet.'

'Look,' Alleyn said, 'can it really do any harm? *Really?*'

'I have not the authority.'

'Who has?'

The house-surgeon breathed an Olympian name.

'Is he in the hospital? Now?'

The house-surgeon looked at his watch. 'There's been a board meeting. He may be in his room.'

'I'll beard him there. Where is it?'

'Yes, but look here – '

'God bless my soul,' Alleyn ejaculated. 'I'll rant as well as he. Lead me to him.'

II

'Ten past four,' Alleyn said, checking with Big Ben. 'Let's do a bit of stocktaking.' They had returned to the car.

'You got it fixed up for this show with the boy, Mr Alleyn?'

'Oh, yes. The great panjandrum turned out to be very mild and a former acquaintance. An instance, I'm afraid, of Harry Grove's detested old boymanship. I must say I see Harry's point. We went to the ward and he inspected young Trevor who was awake, as bright as a button, extremely full of himself and demanding a nice dinner. The expert decided in our favour. We may arrange the visits for tomorrow at noon. *Out* of visiting hours. We'll get Peregrine Jay to call the actors and fix up the timetable. I don't want us to come into it at this juncture. We'll just occur at the event. Jay is to tell them the truth: that the boy can't remember what happened and that it's hoped the encounters with the rest of the cast may set up some chain of association that could lead to a recovery of memory.'

'One of them won't fancy *that* idea.'

'No. But it wouldn't do to refuse.'

'The nerve might crack. There might be a bolt. With that sort of temperament,' Fox said, 'you can't tell what may happen. Still we're well provided.'

'If anybody's nerve cracks it won't be Miss Destiny Meade's. What did you make of that scene in her flat, Fox?'

'Well: to begin with, the lady was very much put out by my being there. In my *view,* Mr Alleyn, she didn't fancy police protection within the meaning of the code to anything like the extent that she fancied it coming in a personal way from yourself. Talk about the go-ahead signal! It was hung out like the week's wash,' said Mr Fox.

'Control yourself, Fox.'

'Now, on what she said we only missed Mr Knight by seconds. She makes out he rang up and abused her to such an extent that she decided to call you and that he walked in while she was still talking to you.'

'Yes. And that went bang off into a roaring row which culminated in him handing her a tuppenny one to the jaw, after which he flung out and we, within a couple of minutes, minced in.'

'No thought in her mind, it appears,' Fox suggested, 'of ringing Mr Grove up to come and protect her. Only you.'

'I daresay she's doing that very thing at this moment. I must say, I hope he knows how to cope with her.'

'Only one thing to do with that type of lady,' Fox said, 'and I don't mean a tuppeny one on the jaw. He'll cope.'

'We'll be talking to Conducis in half an hour, Fox, and it's going to be tricky.'

'I should damn' well think so,' Fox warmly agreed. 'What with orchids and her just seeing him quietly from time to time. Hi!' he ejaculated. 'Would Mr Grove know about Mr Conducis and would Mr Conducis know about Mr Grove?'

'Who is, remember, his distant relation. Search me, Fox. The thing at the moment seems to be that Knight knows about them both and acts accordingly. Big stuff.'

'How a gang like this hangs together beats me. You'd think the resignations'd be falling in like autumn leaves. What they always tell you, I suppose,' Fox said. 'The Show Must Go On.'

'And it happens to be a highly successful show with fat parts and much prestige. But I should think that even they won't be able to sustain the racket indefinitely at this pitch.'

'Why are we going to see Mr Conducis, I ask myself. How do we shape up to him? Does he matter, as far as the case is concerned?'

'In so far as he was in the theatre and knows the combination, yes.'

'I suppose so.'

'I thought him an exceedingly rum personage, Fox. A cold fish and yet a far from insensitive fish. No indication of any background other than wealth or of any particular race. He carries a British passport. He inherited one fortune and made lord knows how many more, each about a hundred per cent fatter than the last. He's spent most of his time abroad and a lot of it in the *Kalliope*, until she was cut in half in a heavy fog under his feet. That was six years ago. What did you make of Jay's account of the menu card?'

'Rather surprising if he's right. Rather a coincidence, two of our names cropping up in that direction.'

'We can check the passenger list with the records. But it's not really a coincidence. People in Conducis's world tend to move about expensively in a tight group. There was, of course, an inquiry after the disaster and Conducis was reported to be unable to appear. He was in a nursing home on the Côte d'Azur suffering from exhaustion, exposure and severe shock.'

'Perhaps,' Mr Fox speculated, 'it's left him a bit funny for keeps.'

'Perhaps. He certainly is a rum 'un and no mistake. Jay's account of his behaviour that morning – by *George*, Alleyn said suddenly. 'Hell's boots and gaiters!'

'What's all this, now?' Fox asked placidly.

'So much hokum I daresay, but listen, all the same.'

Fox listened.

'Well,' he said. 'You always say don't conjecture but personally, Mr Alleyn, when you get one of your hunches in this sort of way I reckon it's safe to go nap on it. Not that this one really gets us any nearer an arrest.'

'I wonder if you're right about that. I wonder.'

They talked for another five minutes, going over Peregrine's notes and then Alleyn looked at his watch and said they must be off. When they were half-way to Park Lane he said:

'You went over all the properties in the theatre, didn't you? No musical instruments?'

'None.'

'He might have had Will singing 'Take, oh, take those lips away' to the Dark Lady. Accompanying himself on a lute. But he didn't.'

'Perhaps Mr Knight can't sing.'

'You may be right at that.'

They drove into Park Lane and turned into Drury Place.

'I'm going,' Alleyn said, 'to cling to Peregrine Jay's notes as Mr Conducis was reported to have clung to his raft.'

'I still don't know *exactly* what line we take,' Fox objected.

'We let him dictate it,' Alleyn rejoined. 'At first. Come on.'

Mawson admitted them to that so arrogantly unobtrusive interior and a pale young man advanced to meet them. Alleyn remembered him from his former visit. The secretary.

'Mr Alleyn. And – er?'

'Inspector Fox.'

'Yes. How do you do? Mr Conducis is in the library. He's been very much distressed by this business. Awfully upset. Particularly about the boy. We've sent flowers and all that nonsense, of course, and we're in touch with the theatre people. Mr Conducis is most anxious that everything possible should be done. Well – shall we? You'll find him, perhaps, rather nervous, Mr Alleyn. He has been so very distressed.'

They walked soundlessly to the library door. A clock mellifluously struck six.

'Here is Superintendent Alleyn, sir, and Inspector Fox.'

'Yes. Thank you.'

Mr Conducis was standing at the far end of the library. He had been looking out of the window, it seemed. In the evening light the long room resembled an interior by some defunct academician: Orchardson, perhaps, or The Hon. John Collier. The details were of an undated excellence but the general effect was strangely Edwardian and so was Mr Conducis. He might have been a deliberately understated monument to Affluence.

As he moved towards them Alleyn wondered if Mr Conducis was ill or if his pallor was brought about by some refraction of light from the apple-green walls. He wore a gardenia in his coat and an edge of crimson silk showed above his breast pocket.

'Good evening,' he said. 'I am pleased that you were able to come. Glad to see you again.'

He offered his hand. Large and white, it withdrew itself – it almost snatched itself away – from contact.

Mawson came in with a drinks tray, put it down, hovered, was glanced at and withdrew.

'You will have a drink,' Mr Conducis stated.

'Thank you, but no,' Alleyn said. 'Not on duty, I'm afraid. This won't stop you from having one, of course.'

'I am an abstainer,' said Mr Conducis. 'Shall we sit down?'

They did so. The crimson leather chairs received them like sultans.

Alleyn said: 'You send word you wanted to see us, sir, but we would in any case have asked for an interview! Perhaps the best way of tackling this unhappy business will be for us to hear any questions that it may have occurred to you to ask. We will then, if you please, continue the conversation on what I can only call routine investigation lines.'

Mr Conducis raised his clasped hands to his mouth and glanced briefly over at Alleyn. He then lowered his gaze to his fingers. Alleyn thought: 'I suppose that's how he looks when he's manipulating his gargantuan undertakings.'

Mr Conducis said: 'I am concerned with this affair. The theatre is my property and the enterprise is under my control. I have financed it. The glove and documents are mine. I trust, therefore, that I am entitled to a detailed statement upon the case as it appears to your department. Or rather, since you are in charge of the investigation, as it appears to you.'

This was said with an air of absolute authority. Alleyn was conscious, abruptly, of the extraordinary force that resided in Mr Conducis.

He said very amiably: 'We are not authorized, I'm afraid, to make detailed statements on demand – not even to entrepreneurs of business and owners of property, especially where a fatality has occurred on that property and a crime of violence may be suspected. On the other hand, I will, as I have suggested, be glad to consider any questions you like to put to me.'

And he thought: 'He's like a lizard or a chameleon or whatever the animal is that blinks slowly. It's what people mean when they talk about hooded eyes.'

Mr Conducis did not argue or protest. For all the reaction he gave, he might not have heard what Alleyn said.

'In your opinion,' he said, 'were the fatality and the injury to the boy caused by an act of violence?'

'Yes.'

'Both by the same hand?'

'Yes.'

'Have you formed an opinion on why it was done?'

'We have arrived at a working hypothesis.'

'What is it?'

'I can go so far as to say that I think both were defensive actions.'

'By a person caught in the act of robbery?'

'I believe so, yes.'

'Do you think you know who this person is?'

'I am almost sure that I do. I am not positive.'

'Who?'

'That,' Alleyn said, 'I am not at liberty to tell you. Yet.' Mr Conducis looked fully at him if the fact that those extraordinarily blank eyes were focused on his face could justify this assertion.

'You said you wished to see me. Why?'

'For several reasons. The first concerns your property: the glove and the documents. As you know they have been recovered but I think you should also know by what means.'

He told the story of Jeremy Jones and the substitution and he could have sworn that as he did so the sweet comfort of a reprieve flooded through Conducis. The thick white hands relaxed. He gave an almost inaudible but long sigh.

'Have you arrested him?'

'No. We have, of course, uplifted the glove. It is in a safe at the Yard with the documents.'

'I cannot believe, Superintendent Alleyn, that you give any credence to this story.'

'I am inclined to believe it.'

'Then in my opinion you are either incredibly stupid or needlessly evasive. In either case, incompetent.'

This attack surprised Alleyn. He had not expected this slow-blinking opponent to dart his tongue as soon. As if sensing his reaction Mr Conducis recrossed his legs and said: 'I am too severe. I beg your pardon. Let me explain myself. Can you not see that Jones's story was an impromptu invention? He did not substitute the faked glove for the real glove six months ago. He substituted it last night and was discovered in the act. He killed Jobbins, was seen by the boy and tried to kill him. He left the copy behind, no doubt if he had not been interrupted he would have put it in the safe, and he took the real glove to the safe-deposit.'

'First packing it with most elaborate care in an insulated box with four wrappings, all sealed.'

'Done in the night. Before Jay got home.'

'We can check, you know, with the safe deposit people. He says he had a witness when he deposited the glove six months ago.'

'A witness to a dummy package, no doubt.'

'If you consider,' Alleyn said, 'I'm sure you will come to the conclusion that this theory won't answer. It really won't, you know.'

'Why not?'

'Do you want me to spell it out, sir? If, as he states, he transposed the glove six months ago and intended to maintain the deception, he had no need to do anything further. If the theft was a last minute notion, he could perfectly well have effected the transposition today or tomorrow when he performed his authorized job of removing the treasure from the safe. There was no need for him to sneak back into the theatre at dead of night and risk discovery. Why on earth, six months ago, should he go through an elaborate hocus-pocus of renting a safe deposit and lodging a fake parcel in it?'

'He's a fanatic. He has written to me expostulating about the sale of the items to an American purchaser. He even tried, I am told, to secure an interview. My secretary can show you his letter. It is most extravagant.'

'I shall be interested to see it.'

A brief silence followed this exchange. Alleyn thought: 'He's formidable but he's not as tough as I expected. He's shaken.'

'Have you any other questions?' Alleyn asked.

He wondered if the long unheralded silence was one of Mr Conducis's strategic weapons: whether it was or not, he now employed it and Alleyn with every appearance of tranquillity sat it out. The light had changed in the long green room and the sky outside the far windows had darkened. Beneath them, at the exquisite table, Peregrine Jay had first examined the documents and the glove. And against the left-hand wall under the picture – surely of Kandinsky – stood the bureau, an Oebeu or Rissones perhaps, from which Mr Conducis had withdrawn his treasures. Fox, who in a distant chair had performed his little miracle of self-effacement, gave a slight cough.

Mr Conducis said without moving, 'I would ask for information as to the continued running of the play and the situation of the players.'

'I understand the season will go on: we've taken no action that might prevent it.'

'You will do so if you arrest a member of the company.'

'He or she would be replaced by an understudy.'

'She,' Mr Conducis said in a voice utterly devoid of inflection. 'That, of course, need not be considered.'

He waited but Alleyn thought it was his turn to initiate a silence and made no comment.

'Miss Destiny Meade has spoken to me,' Mr Conducis said. 'She is very much distressed by the whole affair. She tells me you called upon her this afternoon and she finds herself, as a result, quite prostrated. Surely there is no need for her to be pestered like this.'

For a split second Alleyn wondered what on earth Mr Conducis would think if he and Fox went into fits of laughter. He said: 'Miss Meade was extremely helpful and perfectly frank. I am sorry she found the exercise fatiguing.'

'I have no more to say,' Mr Conducis said and stood up. So did Alleyn.

'I'm afraid that I have,' he said. 'I'm on duty, sir, and this *is* an investigation.'

'I have nothing to bring to it.'

'When we are convinced of that we will stop bothering you. I'm sure you'd prefer us to deal with the whole matter here rather than at the Yard. Wouldn't you?'

Mr Conducis went to the drinks tray and poured himself a glass of water. He took a minute gold case from a waistcoat pocket, shook a tablet on his palm, swallowed it and chased it down.

'Excuse me,' he said, 'it was time.'

'Ulcers?' wondered Alleyn.

Mr Conducis returned and faced him. 'By all means,' he said. 'I am perfectly ready to help you and only regret that I am unlikely to be able to do so to any effect. I have, from the time I decided to promote The Dolphin undertaking, acted solely through my executives. Apart from an initial meeting and one brief discussion with Mr Jay I have virtually no personal contact with members of the management and company.'

'With the exception, perhaps, of Miss Meade?'

'Quite so.'

'And Mr Grove?'

'He was already known to me. I except him.'

'I understand you are related?'

'A distant connection.'

'So he said,' Alleyn lightly agreed. 'I understand,' he added, 'that you were formerly acquainted with Mr Marcus Knight.'

'What makes you think so?'

'Peregrine Jay recognized his signature on the menu you destroyed in his presence.'

'Mr Jay was not himself that morning.'

'Do you mean, sir, that he made a mistake and Knight was not a guest in the *Kalliope?*'

After a long pause Mr Conducis said: 'He was a guest. He behaved badly. He took offence at an imagined slight. He left the yacht, at my suggestion, at Villefranche.'

'And so escaped the disaster?'

'Yes.'

Mr Conducis had seated himself again: this time in an upright chair. He sat rigidly erect but as if conscious of this, crossed his legs and put his hands in his trouser pockets. Alleyn stood a short distance from him.

'I am going to ask you,' he said, 'to talk about something that may be painful to you. I want you to tell me about the night of the fancy dress dinner party on board the *Kalliope.*'

Alleyn had seen people sit with the particular kind of stillness that now invested Mr Conducis. They sat like that in the cells underneath the dock while they waited for the jury to come back. In the days of capital punishment, he had been told by a warder that they sat like that while they waited to hear if they were reprieved. He could see a very slight rhythmic movement of the crimson silk handkerchief and he could hear, ever so faintly, the breathing of Mr Conducis.

'It was six years ago, wasn't it?' Alleyn said. 'And the dinner party took place on the night of the disaster?'

Mr Conducis's eyes closed in a momentary assent but he did not speak.

'Was Mrs Constantia Guzman one of your guests in the yacht?'

'Yes,' he said indifferently.

'You told Mr Jay, I believe, that you bought the Shakespeare relics six years ago?'

'That is so.'

'Had you this treasure on board the yacht?'

'Why should you think so?'

'Because Jay found under the glove the menu for a dinner in the *Kalliope* – he thinks it was headed 'Villefranche'. Which you burnt in the fireplace over there.'

'The menu must have been dropped in the desk. It was an unpleasant reminder of a distressing voyage.'

'So the desk and its contents *were* in the yacht?'

'Yes.'

'May I ask why, sir?'

Mr Conducis's lips moved, were compressed and moved again. 'I bought them,' he said, 'from – ' He gave a grotesque little cough, 'from a person in the yacht.'

'Who was this person, if you please?'

'I have forgotten.'

'Forgotten?'

'The name.'

'Was it Knight?'

'*No.*'

'There are maritime records. We shall be able to trace it. Will you go on, please?'

'He was a member of the ship's complement. He asked to see me and showed me the desk which he said he wanted to sell. I understand that it had been given him by the proprietress of a lodging-house. I thought the contents were almost certainly worthless, but I gave him what he asked for them.'

'Which was – ?'

'Thirty pounds.'

'What became of this man?'

'Drowned,' said a voice from somewhere inside Mr Conducis.

'How did it come about that the desk and its contents were saved?'

'I cannot conjecture by what fantastic process of thought you imagine any of this relates to your inquiry.'

'I hope to show that it does. I believe it does.'

'I had the desk on deck. I had shown the contents, as a matter of curiosity, to some of my guests.'

'Did Mrs Guzman see it, perhaps?'

'Perhaps.'

'Was she interested?'

A look which Alleyn afterwards described as being profoundly professional drifted into Mr Conducis's face.

He said, 'She is a collector.'

'Did she make an offer?'

'She did. I was not inclined to sell.'

Alleyn was visited by a strange notion.

'Tell me,' he said, 'were you both in fancy dress?'

Mr Conducis looked at him with an air of wondering contempt. 'Mrs Guzman,' he said, 'was in costume: Andalusian, I understand. I wore a domino over evening dress.'

'Gloved, either of you?'

'No!' he said loudly and added, 'We had been playing bridge.'

'Were any of the others gloved?'

'A ridiculous question. Some may have been.'

'Were the ship's company in fancy dress?'

'Certainly not!'

'The stewards?'

'As eighteenth century flunkeys.'

'Gloved?'

'I do not remember.'

'Why do you dislike pale gloves, Mr Conducis?'

'I have no idea,' he said breathlessly, 'what you mean.'

'You told Peregrine Jay that you dislike them.'

'A personal prejudice. I cannot account for it.'

'Were there gloved hands that disturbed you on the night of the disaster? Mr Conducis, are you ill?'

'I – no. No, I am well. You insist on questioning me about an episode which distressed me, which was painful, tragic, an outrage to one's sensibilities.'

'I would avoid it if I could. I'm afraid I must go further. Will you tell me exactly what happened at the moment of disaster: to you, I mean, and to whoever was near you then or later?'

For a moment Alleyn thought he was going to refuse. He wondered if there would be a sudden outbreak or whether Mr Conducis would merely walk out of the room and leave them to take what action they chose. He did none of these things. He embarked upon a toneless, rapid recital of facts. Of the fact of fog, the sudden looming of the tanker, the breaking apart of the *Kalliope*. Of the fact of fire. Of oil on the water and how he found himself looking down on the wooden raft from the swimming pool and of how the deck turned into a precipice and he slid from it and landed on the raft.

'Still with the little desk?'

Yes. Clutched under his left arm, it seemed, but with no consciousness of this. He had lain across the raft with the desk underneath him. It had bruised him very badly. He gripped a rope loop at the side with his right hand. Mrs Guzman had appeared beside the raft and was clinging to one of the loops. Alleyn had a mental picture of an enormous nose, an open mouth, a mantilla plastered over a big head and a floundering mass of wet black lace and white flesh.

The recital stopped as abruptly as it had begun.

'That is all. We were picked up by the tanker.'

'Were there other people on the raft?'

'I believe so. My memory is not clear. I lost consciousness.'

'Men? Mrs Guzman?'

'I believe so. I was told so.'

'Pretty hazardous, I should have thought. It wouldn't accommodate more than – how many?'

'I don't know. I don't know. I don't know.'

'Mr Conducis, when you saw Peregrine Jay's gloved hands clinging to the edge of that hole in the stage at The Dolphin and heard him call out that he would drown if you didn't save him – were you reminded – '

Mr Conducis had risen and now began to move backwards, like an image in slow motion, towards the bureau. Fox rose too and shifted in front of it. Mr Conducis drew his crimson silk handkerchief from his breast pocket and pressed it against his mouth and above it his upper lip glistened. His brows were defined by beaded margins and the dark skin of his face was stretched too tight and had blanched over the bones.

'Be quiet,' he said. 'No. Be quiet.'

Somebody had come into the house. A distant voice spoke loudly but indistinguishably.

The door opened and the visitor came in.

Mr Conducis screamed: 'You've told them. You've betrayed me. I wish to Christ I'd killed you.'

Fox took him from behind. Almost at once he stopped struggling.

III

Trevor could be, as Alleyn put it, bent at the waist. He had been so bent and was propped up in a sitting position in his private room. A bed-tray on legs was arranged across his stomach, ready for any offerings that might be forthcoming. His condition had markedly improved and he was inclined, though still feebly, to throw his weight about.

The private room was small but there was a hospital screen in one corner of it and behind the screen, secreted there before Trevor was wheeled in, sat Inspector Fox, his large, decent feet concealed by Trevor's suitcase. Alleyn occupied the bedside chair.

On receiving assurances from Alleyn that the police were not on his tracks Trevor repeated, with more fluency, his previous account of his antics in the deserted auditorium, but he would not or could not carry the recital beyond the point when he was in the circle and heard a distant telephone ring. 'I don't remember another thing,' he said importantly. 'I've blacked out. I was concussed. The doc says I was very badly concussed. Here! *Where* did I fall, Super? What's the story?'

'You fell into the stalls.'

'*Would* you mind!'

'True.'

'Into the *stalls*! Cripes! *Why?*'

'That's what I want to find out.'

Trevor looked sideways. 'Did old Henry Jobbins lay into me?' he asked.

'No.'

'Or Chas Random?'

A knowledgeable look: a disfigured look of veiled gratification, perhaps, appeared like a blemish on Trevor's page-boy face. He giggled.

'He was wild with me, Chas was. Listen: Chas had it in for me, Super, really he did. I got that camp's goat, actually, good and proper.'

Alleyn listened and absently noted how underlying cockney seeped up through superimposed drama academy. Behind carefully turned vowel and consonant jibed a Southwark urchin. 'Goo' un' pro-per,' Trevor was really saying, however classy the delivery.

'Some of the company are coming in to see you,' Alleyn said. 'They may only stay for a minute or two but they'd like to say hallo.'

'I'd be pleased,' Trevor graciously admitted. He was extremely complacent.

Alleyn watched him and talked to him for a little while longer and then, conscious of making a decision that might turn out most lamentably, he said:

'Look here, young Trevor, I'm going to ask you to help me in a very tricky and important business. If you don't like the suggestion you needn't have anything to do with it. On the other hand – '

He paused. Trevor gave him a sharp look.

'Nothing comes to the dumb,' he said. 'What seems to be the trouble? Come on and give.'

Ten minutes later his visitors began to arrive, ushered in by Peregrine Jay. 'Just tell them,' Alleyn had said, 'that he'd like to see them for a few minutes and arrange the timetable. You can pen them in the waiting-room at the end of the corridor.'

They brought presents.

Winter Morris came first with a box of crystallized fruit. He put it on the tray and then stood at the foot of the bed wearing his shepherd's plaid suit and his dark red tie. His hair, beautifully cut, waved above and behind the ears. He leaned his head to one side and looked at Trevor.

'Well, well, well,' he said. 'So the great star is receiving. How does it feel to be famous?'

Trevor was languid and gracious but before the prescribed five minutes had elapsed he mentioned that his agent would be waiting upon Mr Morris with reference to the Management, as he put it, seeing him right.

'We don't,' Winter Morris said, eyeing him warily, 'need to worry just yet about that one. Do we?'

'I hope not, Mr Morris,' Trevor said. He leant his head back against the pillows and closed his eyes. 'Funny how faint I appear to get,' he murmured. 'I hope it won't be kind of permanent. My doctors seem to take a grave view. Funny thing.'

Mr Morris said, 'You played that line just like the end of Act I, but I mustn't tire you.'

He tiptoed elaborately away from the bed and as he passed Alleyn, let droop a heavy white eyelid.

Jeremy Jones had made a group of tiny effigies representing the characters in the play and had mounted them on a minute stage. 'Ever so quaint,' Trevor said. 'Ta, Mr Jones. You *have* been busy. Put it on my tray, would you?'

Jeremy put his offering on the tray. Trevor gazed into his face as he did so. 'You *are* clever with your fingers,' he said. 'Aren't you, Mr Jones?'

Jeremy looked suspiciously at him, turned scarlet and said to Alleyn: 'I mustn't stay too long.'

'Don't go,' said Trevor. 'Yet.'

Jeremy lingered, with one eye on Alleyn and awkwardly at a loss for anything to say. Peregrine tapped on the door, looked in, said: 'Oh, sorry,' when he saw his friend and retired.

'I want to see Mr Jay,' Trevor said. 'Here! Call him back.'

Jeremy fetched Peregrine and seized the opportunity after a nod from Alleyn, to make his own escape. Peregrine, having already done his duty in that respect, brought no offering.

'Here!' Trevor said. 'What price that kid? My understudy. Is he going on tonight?'

'Yes. He's all right,' Peregrine said. 'Word perfect and going to give quite a nice show. You needn't worry.'

Trevor glowered at him. 'What about the billing, Mr Jay? What about the programmes?'

'They've been slipped. "During your indisposition the part will be played – " You know?'

'Anything in the Press? They haven't brought me any papers,' the feeble voice grumbled. 'What's my agent doing? My mum says they don't want me to see the papers. Look, Mr Jay – '

Alleyn said: 'You'll see the papers.'

Peregrine waited until Charles Random arrived. 'If you want me,' he then said to Alleyn, 'I'll be in the corridor.'

Random brought a number of dubious-looking comics. 'Knowing your taste in literature,' he said to Trevor. 'Not that I approve.'

Trevor indicated his tray. As Random approached him, he put on a sly look. 'Really,' he said, 'you shouldn't have troubled, Mr Random.'

They stared at each other, their faces quite close together: Random's guarded, shuttered, wary and Trevor's faintly impertinent.

'You've got a bruise on your cheekbone,' Random said.

'That's nothing. You should see the rest.'

'Keep you quiet for a bit.'

'That's right.'

Random turned his head slowly and looked at Alleyn. 'Police taking a great interest, I see,' he said.

'Routine,' Alleyn rejoined. 'Merely routine.'

'At a high level.' Random drew back quickly from Trevor who giggled and opened his bundle of comics. 'Oh, fabulous,' he said. 'It's "Slash" *Z-zzz-yock!*' He became absorbed.

'That being that,' Random said, 'I shall bow myself off. Unless,' he added, 'the Superintendent is going to arrest me.'

Trevor, absorbed in his comic, said: 'You never know, do you? Cheerie-bye and ta.'

Random moved towards the door. 'Get better quick,' he murmured. Trevor looked up and winked. 'What do *you* think?' he said.

Random opened the door and disclosed Miss Bracey on the threshold.

They said: 'Oh, hallo, dear,' simultaneously and Random added: 'This gets more like a French farce every second. Everyone popping in and out. Wonderful timing.'

They both laughed with accomplishment and he went away.

Gertrude behaved as if she and Alleyn had never met. She said good-morning in a poised voice and clearly expected him to leave. He responded politely, indicated the bedside chair, called Trevor's attention to his visitor and himself withdrew to the window.

Miss Bracey said: 'You *have* been in the wars, dear, haven't you?' She advanced to the bedside and placed a small parcel on the table. Trevor lifted his face to hers, inviting an embrace. Their faces came together and parted and Miss Bracey sank into the chair.

'I mustn't stay too long: you're not to be tired,' she said. She was quite composed. Only that occasional drag at the corner of her mouth suggested to Alleyn that she had fortified herself. She made the conventional inquiries as to Trevor's progress and he responded with an enthusiastic account of his condition. The worst case of concussion, he said importantly, that they'd ever seen in the ward.

'Like what you read about,' he said. 'I was – '

He stopped short and for a moment looked puzzled. 'I was having a bit of fun,' he began again. 'You know, Miss Bracey. Just for giggles. I was having old Jobbins on.'

'Yes?' said Miss Bracey. 'That was naughty of you, dear, wasn't it?'

'But,' Trevor said, frowning. 'You know. You were there. Weren't you?' he added doubtfully.

She looked anywhere but at Alleyn. 'You're still confused,' she said. 'You mustn't worry about it.'

'But weren't you, Miss Bracey? Down there? In front? Weren't you?'

'I don't know when you mean, dear.'

'Neither do I. Not quite sure. But you were there.'

'I was in the downstairs foyer on Saturday night for a minute or two,' she said loudly. 'As I told the superintendent.'

'Yeah, I know you were,' Trevor said. 'But where was I?'

'You didn't see me. You weren't there. Don't worry about it.'

'I was. I was.'

'I'd better go,' she said and rose.

'No,' Trevor shouted. He brought his small fist down on the bed tray and Jeremy's microcosms fell on their faces, 'No! You've got to stay till I remember.'

'I think you should stay, Miss Bracey,' Alleyn said. 'Really.'

She backed away from the bed. Trevor gave a little cry. 'There!' he said, 'that's it. That's what you did. And you were looking up – at him. Looking up and backing away and kind of blubbing.'

'Trevor, be quiet. *Be quiet.* You don't know. You've forgotten.'

'Like what you're always doing, Miss Bracey. Chasing him. That's right, isn't it, Miss Bracey? Tagging old Harry. You'd come out of the downstairs lav and you looked up and saw him. And then the office door opened and it was Mr Morris and Mr Knight and you done – you did a quick skarper, Miss Bracey. And so did I! Back into the circle, smartly. I got it, now,' Trevor said with infinite satisfaction. 'I got it.'

'How,' Alleyn said, 'did you know who he was? It must have been dark up there.'

'Him? Harry? By his flash coat. Cripey, what a dazzler!'

'It's not true,' she gabbled and stumbled across the room. She pawed at Alleyn's coat. 'It's not true. He doesn't know what he's saying. It wasn't Harry. Don't listen. I swear it wasn't Harry.'

'You're quite right,' Alleyn said. 'You thought it was Harry Grove but it was Jobbins you saw on the landing. Grove had given Jobbins his overcoat.'

Her hands continued for a second or two to scrabble at his coat and then fell away. She looked into his face and her own crumpled into a weeping mask.

Alleyn said: 'You've been having a bad time. An awful time. But it *will* ease up. It won't always be as bad as this.'

'Let me go. Please let me go.'

'Yes,' he said. 'You may go now.'

And when she had gone, blowing her nose, squaring her shoulders and making, instinctively he supposed, quite an exit, he turned to Trevor and found him, with every sign of gratification, deep in his comics.

'Do I have to see the others?' he asked. 'It's getting a bit of a drag.'

'Are you tired?'

'No. I'm reading.' His eye lit on Gertrude Bracey's parcel. 'Might as well look it over,' he said and unwrapped a tie. 'Where'd she dig that up?' he wondered and returned to his comic.

'You are a young toad, aren't you?' Alleyn remarked. 'How old are you, in heaven's name?'

'Eleven and three months,' Trevor said. He was helping himself to a crystallized plum.

A slight rumpus broke out in the passage. Peregrine put his head round the door. 'Marco and Harry are both here,' he said and cast up his eyes.

When Alleyn joined him at the door he muttered: 'Marco won't wait. He didn't want to come. And Harry says he got here first. He's up to his usual game,' Peregrine said, 'Knight-baiting.'

'Tell him to shut up and wait or I'll run him in.'

'I wish to heaven you would, at that.'

'Ask Knight to come along.'

'Yes. All right.'

'No sign of Conducis as yet?'

'No.'

When Marcus Knight came in he did not exhibit his usual signs of emotional disturbance: the flashing eye, the empurpled cheek, the throbbing pulse and the ringing tone. On the contrary he was pale

and as near to being subdued, Alleyn felt, as he could be. He laid his
offering upon the now filled-to-capacity bed-tray. Fruit: in season
and a gilded basket. He brusquely ran his fingers through Trevor's
curls and Trevor immediately responded with a look that successfully combined Young Hamnet and Paul Dombey.

'Oh, Mr Knight,' he said, 'you honestly shouldn't. You *are* kind.
Grapes! How fab!'

A rather stilted bedside conversation followed during which
Knight gave at least half his uneasy attention to Alleyn. Presently
Trevor complained that he had slipped down in his bed and asked his
illustrious guest to help him up. When Knight with an ill grace bent
over him, Trevor gazed admiringly into his face and wreathed his
arm round his neck. 'Just like the end of Act I come true,' he said,
'isn't it, Mr Knight? I ought to be wearing a glove.'

Knight hurriedly extricated himself. A look of doubt crossed
Trevor's face. *'The glove,'* he repeated. 'There's something about the
real one – isn't there? Something?'

Knight looked a question at Alleyn who said: 'Trevor doesn't
recall the latter part of his adventures in the theatre on Saturday
night. I think Jay has explained that we hope one of you may help
to restore his memory.'

'I *am* remembering more,' Trevor said importantly. 'I remember
hearing Mr Knight in the office with Mr Morris.'

Marcus Knight stiffened. 'I believe you are aware, Alleyn, that I
left with Morris at about eleven.'

'He has told us so,' Alleyn said.

'Very well.' Knight stood over Trevor and imposed upon himself,
evidently with difficulty, an air of sweet reasonableness. 'If,' he said,
'dear boy, you were spying about in front while I was with Mr
Morris in his office, and if you heard our voices, you doubtless also
saw us leave the theatre.'

Trevor nodded.

'Precisely,' Knight said and spread his hands at Alleyn.

'People come back,' said the treble voice. Alleyn turned to find
Trevor, the picture of puzzled innocence, frowning, his fingers at his
lips.

'What the hell do you mean by that!' Knight ejaculated.

'It's part of what I can't remember. Somebody came back.'

'I really cannot imagine, Alleyn – ' Knight began.

'I – *don't – think – I – want – to – remember.*'

'There you are, you see. This is infamous. The boy will be harmed. I absolutely refuse to take part in a dangerous and unwarranted experiment. Don't worry yourself, boy. You are pefectly right. Don't try to remember.'

'Why?'

'BECAUSE I TELL YOU,' Knight roared and strode to the door. Here he paused. 'I am an artist,' he said suddenly adopting a muted voice that was rather more awful than a piercing scream. 'In eight hours' time I appear before the public in a most exhausting role. Moreover I shall be saddled throughout a poignant, delicate and exacting scene with the incompetence of some revolting child-actor of whose excesses I am as yet ignorant. My nerves have been exacerbated. For the past forty-eight hours I have suffered the torments of hell. Slighted. Betrayed. Derided. Threatened. And now – this ludicrous, useless and impertinent summons by the police. Very well, Superintendent Alleyn. There shall be no more of it. I shall lodge a formal complaint. In the meantime – *Goodbye.*'

The door was opened with violence and shut – not slammed – with well-judged temperance.

'Lovely eggzit,' said Trevor yawning and reading his comic.

From outside in the corridor came the sound of applause, an oath, and rapidly retreating footsteps.

Alleyn reopened the door to disclose Harry Grove, gently clapping his hands, and Marcus Knight striding down the corridor.

Harry said, 'Isn't he *superb?* Honestly, you have to hand it to him.' He drew a parcel from his pocket. 'Baby roulette,' he said. 'Trevor can work out systems. Is it true that this is a sort of identification parade?'

'You could put it like that, I suppose,' Alleyn agreed.

'Do you mean,' Harry said, changing colour, 'that this unfortunate but nauseating little boy may suddenly point his finger at one of us and enunciate in ringing tones: "It all comes back to me. He dunnit".'

'That, roughly, is the idea.'

'Then I freely confess it terrifies me.'

'Come inside and get it over.'

'Very well. But I'd have you know that he's quite capable of putting on a false show of recovery smartly followed up by a still falser accusation. Particularly,' Harry said grimly, 'in my case when he knows the act would draw loud cheers and much laughter from all hands and the cook.'

'We'll have to risk it. In you go.'

Alleyn opened the door and followed Harry into the room.

Trevor had slithered down in his bed and had dropped off into a convalescent cat-nap. Harry stopped short and stared at him.

'He looks,' he whispered, 'as if he was quite a nice little boy, doesn't he? You'd say butter wouldn't melt. Is he really asleep or is it an act?'

'He dozes. If you just lean over him he'll wake.'

'It seems a damn' shame, I must say.'

'All the same I'll ask you to do it, if you will. There's a bruise on the cheekbone that mystifies us all. I wonder if you've any ideas. Have a look at it.'

A trolley jingled past the door and down the corridor. Outside on the river a barge hooted. Against the multiple shapeless voice of London, Big Ben struck one o'clock.

Harry put his parcel on the tray.

'Look at the bruise on his face. His hair's fallen across it. Move his hair back and look.'

Harry stooped over the boy and put out his left hand.

From behind the screen in the corner there rang out a single, plangent note. *'Twang.'*

Trevor opened his eyes, looked into Harry's face and screamed.

CHAPTER 11

The Show Will Go On

Harry Grove had given no trouble. When Trevor screamed he stepped back from him. He was sheet-white but he achieved a kind of smile.

'No doubt,' he had said to Alleyn, 'you will now issue the usual warning and invite me to accompany you to the nearest police station. May I suggest that Perry should be informed. He'll want to get hold of my understudy.'

And as this was the normal procedure it had been carried out.

So now, at Alleyn's suggestion, they had returned, not to the Yard but to The Dolphin. Here for the first time Mr Conducis kept company with the actors that he employed. They sat round the circle foyer while, down below, the public began to queue up for the early doors.

Peregrine had called Harry Grove's understudy and he and the new child actor were being rehearsed behind the fire curtain by the stage director.

'I think,' Alleyn said, 'it is only fair to give you all some explanation since each of you has to some extent been involved. These, as I believe, are the facts about Saturday night. I may say that Hartly Grove has admitted to them in substance.

'Grove left the theatre with Miss Meade and her party saying he would go to Canonbury and pick up his guitar. He had in fact brought his guitar to the theatre and had hidden it in a broom cupboard in the property room where it was found in the course of his illicit explorations, by Trevor. Grove got into his open sports car, drove round the block and parked the car in Phipps Passage. He re-entered the theatre by the pass-door while Mr Morris and Mr Knight were in the office. He may have been seen by Jobbins who would think nothing of it as Grove was in the habit of coming round for messages. He was not seen by Miss Bracey who mistook Jobbins for him because of the coat.

'Grove remained hidden throughout the rumpus about Trevor until, as he thought, the theatre was deserted except for Jobbins. At eleven o'clock he dialled his own number and let it ring just long enough for his wakeful neighbour to hear it and suppose it had been answered.

'It must have given him a shock when he heard Trevor, in the course of his fooling, pluck the guitar string. It was that scrap of evidence, by the way, when you remembered it, Jay, that set me wondering if Grove had left his instrument in the theatre and not gone to Canonbury. A moment later he heard the stage-door slam and thought, as Mr Jay and Miss Dunne and Jobbins did, that Trevor had gone. But Trevor had sneaked back and was himself hiding and dodging about the auditorium. He saw Miss Bracey during his activities. Later, he tells us, he caught sight of Harry Grove and began to stalk him like one of his comic-strip heroes. We have the odd picture of Grove stealing to the broom-cupboard to collect his guitar, flitting like a shadow down a side passage, leaving the instrument ready to hand near the front foyer. Inadvertently, perhaps, causing it to emit that twanging sound.'

Peregrine gave a short ejaculation but when Alleyn looked at him said: 'No. Go on. Go on.'

'Having dumped the guitar Grove returns to the stairway from the stage to the circle, climbs it and waits for midnight in the upper box. And, throughout this performance, Trevor peeps, follows, listens, spies.

'At midnight Jobbins leaves his post under the treasure and goes downstairs to ring Police and Fire. Grove darts to the wall panel, opens it, uses his torch and manipulates the combination. There had been a lot of talk about the lock after the safe was installed and before the treasure was put into it. At that time it was not guarded and I think he may have done a bit of experimenting, after hours, on the possible "glove" combination.'

Winter Morris knocked on his forehead and groaned. Marcus Knight said: 'Oh God!'

'He opened the safe, removed the display-stand with its contents and I think only then realized he had engaged the switch that operates the front doors and the interior lighting. At that moment Trevor, who had stolen quite close (just as he did to me when I looked at the safe), said – it is his favourite noise at the moment – "z-z-z-z-yock. Slash."

'It must have given Grove a nightmarish jolt. He turned, saw the boy standing there in the darkened circle and bolted into the foyer clutching his loot. Only to find Jobbins rushing upstairs at him. He pushed the dolphin pedestal over and down. As Jobbins fell, Trevor came out of the circle and saw it all. Trevor is still not quite clear but he thinks he screamed. He knows Grove made for him and he remembers plunging down the central steps in the circle. Grove caught him at the bottom. Trevor says – and this may be true – that he snatched the display-stand and threw it overboard before Grove could recover it. The last thing he remembers now, is Grove's face close to his own. It was the sight of it this morning, near to him, in association with the single twang effected by my colleague, Inspector Fox, who was modestly concealed behind a screen, that bridged the gap in Trevor's memory.'

'"*A faint pefume*",' Peregrine said loudly, '"*and a most melodious twang*".'

'That's Aubrey, isn't it?' Alleyn asked. 'But shouldn't it be a *curious* perfume? Or not?'

Peregrine stared at him. it is,' he said, 'and it should. You're dead right and why the hell it's eluded me I cannot imagine. I heard it, you know, when Jobbins was hunting the boy.'

Emily said: 'And, of course, it's a single plangent note that brings down the curtain on *The Cherry Orchard*.'

'You see, Emily?' said Peregrine.

'I see,' she said.

'What the hell *is* all this?' Knight asked plaintively.

'I'll get on with it,' Alleyn said. 'After a brief struggle Grove, now desperate, rids himself of Trevor by precipitating him into the stalls. He hears Hawkins at the stage-door and once again bolts into the circle foyer. He knows Hawkins will come straight through to the front and he hasn't time to retrieve his guitar, get the key, unlock, unbolt and unbar the pass-door. There lies the body, dressed in his own outlandish coat. He strips off the coat, takes the scarf from the pocket to protect his own clothes and re-enters the darkened circle, to all intents and purposes, Jobbins. Hawkins, now in the stalls, sees him, addresses him as Jobbins, and is told to make the tea. He goes backstage. Grove has time, now, to bundle the body back into the coat, fetch his guitar and let himself out. He drives to Chelsea and gets there fully equipped to be the life and soul of Miss Meade's party.'

'And he *was,* you know,' Destiny said. 'He *was.'*

She clasped her hands, raised them to her face and began to weep. Knight gave an inarticulate cry and went to her.

'Never mind, my darling,' he said. 'Never mind. We must rise above. We must forget.'

Mr Conducis cleared his throat. Destiny threw him a glance that was madly eloquent of some ineffable generalization. He avoided it.

'The motive,' Alleyn said, 'was, of course, theft. Harry Grove knew a great deal about Mrs Constantia Guzman. He knew that if the treasure was stolen she would give a fortune under the counter for it.'

Knight, who was kissing Destiny's hands, groaned slightly and shuddered.

'But I think he knew more about her than that,' Alleyn went on. 'She was a guest of Mr Conducis's six years ago, in the *Kalliope* when the yacht was wrecked off Cape St Vincent. At that time, six years ago, Grove was going through a bad patch and taking any jobs he could get. Lorry driving. Waiter in a strip-joint. And steward.'

He turned to Mr Conducis. 'I was about to ask you yesterday when Grove himself interrupted us: was he a steward on board the *Kalliope?*'

Nobody looked at Mr Conducis.

'Yes,' he said.

'How did that come about?'

'He brought himself to my notice. His father was a distant and unsatisfactory connection of mine. I considered this to be no reason for employing him but he satisfied me of his usefulness.'

'And he sold you the glove and documents?'

'Yes.'

'For thirty pounds?'

'I have already said so.'

Marcus Knight, whose manner towards Mr Conducis had been an extraordinary blend of hauteur and embarrassment now said loudly: 'I don't believe it.'

'You don't believe what, Mr Knight?' Alleyn asked.

'That he was aboard that – vessel.'

'You were scarcely there long enough to notice,' Mr Conducis said coldly.

'I was there long enough – ' Marcus began on a high note and dried. 'But no matter,' he said. 'No matter.'

Alleyn stood up and so did everybody else except Mr Conducis.

'I won't keep you any longer,' Alleyn said. 'I would like to say how sorry I am that this has happened and how much I hope your play and your theatre will ride out the storm. I'm sure they will. I'm taking an unorthodox line when I tell you that Grove has said he will not contest the accusations of assault. He will, he states, admit to taking the treasure, overturning the bronze dolphin and struggling with the boy. He will plead that these were instinctive, self-protective actions committed without intention to kill. This defence, if adhered to, will mean a short trial with little evidence being called and I think, not a great deal of publicity.'

Little Morris said: 'Why's he taking that line? Why isn't he going all out for an acquittal?'

'I asked him that. He said he was suddenly sick of the whole thing. And he added,' Alleyn said with a curious twist in his voice, 'that he thought it would work out better that way for William Shakespeare, Mr Peregrine Jay and The Dolphin.'

He saw then that the eyes of all the company had filled with tears.

When they had gone he turned back to Mr Conducis.

'You said, sir, that you had something you wished to tell me.'

'I have something I wish to ask you. Has he said anything about me?'

'A little. He said you owed each other nothing.'

'I will pay for his defence. Let him know that.'

'Very well.'

'Anything else?'

'He said that as far as he is concerned – this was his phrase – he would keep the glove over his knuckles and I could tell you so. He asked me to give you this.'

Alleyn gave Mr Conducis an envelope. He was about to put it in his pocket but changed his mind, opened it and read the short message it contained. He held out the paper to Alleyn.

'It seems,' Alleyn read, *'that we are both victims of irresistible impulse. Which leads me to the ludicrous notion that you will, as they say, "understand". You needn't worry. I'm bored with it all and intend to drop it.'*

Down below someone whistled, crossed the foyer and slammed the front doors. The Dolphin was very quiet.

'He clung to the raft,' said Mr Conducis, 'and tried to climb aboard it. He would have overturned it. I smashed his knuckles with the writing-desk and thought I'd drowned him. His hands were gloved. They curled and opened and slid away in their own blood. Nobody saw. He has blackmailed me ever since.'

II

'They are not cancelling,' said Winter Morris, giving the box-office plans a smart slap. 'And there's very little publicity. I can't understand it.'

'Could it be the hand of Conducis?'

'Could be, dear boy. Could be. Power,' said little Morris, 'corrupts didn't somebody say? It may do: but it comes in handy, dear boy, it comes in handy.'

He ran upstairs to his office and could be heard singing.

'All the same,' Peregrine said to Emily, 'I hope it's *not* the hand of Conducis. I hope it's The Dolphin. And us. You know,' he went on, 'I'm sure he stayed behind to unburden himself to Alleyn.'

'What of?'

'Who can tell! I've got a feeling it was something to do with his yacht. He's behaved so very oddly whenever it came up.'

'Perhaps,' Emily speculated idly, 'you reminded him of it. That morning.'

'I? How?'

'Oh,' she said vaguely, 'people drowning, you know, or nearly drowning, or hanging on to bits of wreckage. Perhaps he was glad he rescued you. Or something.'

'You never know,' Peregrine said.

He put his arm round her and she leant against him. They had become engaged and were happy.

They looked round them at the upsidedown cupids, the caryatids, the portrait of Mr Adolphus Ruby now prominently displayed and the graceful double flight of stairs. The bronze dolphins were gone and where the safe had been was a montage of the Grafton portrait overlaid by Kean, Garrick, Siddons, Irving and the present great Shakespearians all very excitingly treated by Jeremy Jones.

'If you belong to the theatre,' Peregrine said, 'you belong utterly.'

They went out to the portico.

Here they found an enormous Daimler and a chauffeur. It was like a recurrent symbol in a time play and for a moment Peregrine felt as if Mr Conducis had called again to take him to Drury Place.

'Is that Dessy's car?' Emily said.

But it wasn't Destiny Meade in the back seat. It was an enormous and definitively hideous lady flashing with diamonds, lapped in mink and topped with feathers.

She tapped on the glass and beckoned.

When Peregrine approached she let down the window and, in a deep voice, addressed him.

'You can perhaps assist me. I have this morning arrived from America. I vish to inquire about the Shakespearian Relics. I am Mrs Constantia Guzman.'

The Cupid Mirror

The Cupid Mirror was first published by William Collins in an anthology entitled *The Case of the Vanished Spinster* in 1972.

'Bollinger '21,' said Lord John Challis.

'Thank you, my lord,' said the wine waiter.

He retrieved the wine list, bowed and moved away with soft assurance. Lord John let his eyeglass fall and gave his attention to his guest. She at once wrinkled her nose and parted her sealing-wax lips in an intimate smile. It was a pleasant and flattering grimace and Lord John responded to it. He touched his little beard with a thin hand.

'You look charming,' he said, 'and you dispel all unpleasant thoughts.'

'Were they unpleasant?' asked his guest.

'They were uncomplimentary to myself. I was thinking that Benito – the wine waiter, you know – had grown old.'

'But why – ?'

'I knew him when we were both young.'

The head waiter materialized, waved away his underlings, and himself delicately served the dressed crab. Benito returned with the champagne. He held the bottle before Lord John's eyeglass and received a nod.

'It is sufficiently iced, my lord,' said Benito.

The champagne was opened, tasted, approved, poured out, and the bottle twisted down in the ice. Benito and the head waiter withdrew.

'They know you very well here,' remarked the guest.

'Yes. I dined here first in 1907. We drove from the station in a hansom cab.'

'We?' murmured his guest.

'She, too, was charming. It is extraordinary how like the fashions of today are to those of my day. Those sleeves. And she wore a veil, too, and sat under the china cupid mirror as you do now.'

'And Benito poured out the champagne?'

'And Benito poured out the champagne. He was a rather striking looking fellow in those days. Black eyes, brows that met over his nose. A temper, you'd have said.'

'You seem to have looked carefully at him,' said the guest lightly.

'I had reason to.'

'Come,' said the guest with a smile, 'I know you have a story to tell and I am longing to hear it.'

'Really?'

'Really.'

'Very well, then.'

Lord John leant forward a little in his chair.

'At the table where that solitary lady sits – yes – the table behind me – I am looking at it now in the cupid mirror – there sat in those days an elderly woman who was a devil. She had come for the cure and had brought with her a miserable niece whom she underpaid and bullied and humiliated after the manner of old devils all the world over. The girl might have been a pretty girl, but all the spirit was scared out of her. Or so it seemed to me. There were atrocious scenes. On the third evening – '

'The third?' murmured the guest, raising her thinned eyebrows.

'We stayed a week,' explained Lord John. 'At every meal that dreadful old woman, brandishing a repulsive ear trumpet, would hector and storm. The girl's nerves had gone, and sometimes from sheer fright she was clumsy. Her mistakes were anathematized before the entire dining room. She was reminded of her dependence and constantly of the circumstance of her being a beneficiary under the aunt's will. It was disgusting – abominable. They never sat through a meal without the aunt sending the niece on some errand, so that people began to wait for the moment when the girl, miserable and embarrassed, would rise and walk through the tables, pursued by that voice. I don't suppose that the other guests meant to be unkind but many of them were ill-mannered enough to stare at her and wait for her reappearance with shawl, or coat, or book, or bag, or medicine. She used to come back through the tables with increased gaucherie. Every step was an agony and then, when she was seated, there would be merciless criticism of her walk, her elbows, her colour, her pallor. I saw it all in the little cupid mirror. Benito came in for his share too. That atrocious woman would order her wine, change her mind, order again, say it was corked, not the vintage she ordered, complain to the head waiter – I can't tell you what else. Benito was magnificent. Never by a hairsbreadth did he vary his courtesy.'

'I suppose it is all in their day's work,' said the guest.

'I suppose so. Let us hope there are not many cases as advanced as that harridan's. Once I saw him glance with a sort of compassion at the niece. I mean, I saw his image in the cupid mirror.'

Lord John filled his guest's glass and his own.

'There was also,' he continued, 'her doctor. I indulge my hobby of speaking ill of the dead and confess that I did not like him. He was the local fashionable doctor of those days; a *soi-disant* gentleman with a heavy moustache and clothes that were just a little too immaculate. I was, and still am, a snob. He managed to establish himself in the good graces of the aunt. She left him the greater part of her very considerable fortune. More than she left the girl. There was never any proof that he was aware of this circumstance but I can find no other explanation for his extraordinary forbearance. He prescribed for her, sympathized, visited, agreed, flattered. God knows what he didn't do. And he dined. He dined on the night she died.'

'Oh,' said the guest lifting her glass in both hands, and staring at her lacquered fingertips, 'she died, did she?'

'Yes. She died in the chair occupied at this moment by the middle-aged lady with nervous hands.'

'You are very observant,' remarked his companion.

'Otherwise I should not be here again in such delightful circumstances. I can see the lady with nervous hands in the cupid mirror, just as I could see that hateful old woman. She had been at her worst all day, and at luncheon the niece had been sent on three errands. From the third she returned in tears with the aunt's sleeping tablets. She always took one before her afternoon nap. The wretched girl had forgotten them and on her return must needs spill them all over the carpet. She and Benito scrambled about under the table, retrieving the little tablets, while the old woman gibed at the girl's clumsiness. She then refused to take one at all and the girl was sent off lunchless and in disgrace.'

Lord John touched his beard with his napkin, inspected his half bird, and smiled reminiscently.

'The auguries for dinner were inauspicious. It began badly. The doctor heard of the luncheon disaster. The first dish was sent away with the customary threat of complaint to the manager. However, the doctor succeeded in pouring oil, of which he commanded a great quantity, on the troubled waters. He told her that she must not tire herself, patted her claw with his large white hand, and bullied the waiters on her behalf. He had brought her some new medicine which she was to take after dinner, and he laid the little packet of powder by her plate. It was to replace the stuff she had been taking for some time.'

'How did you know all this?'

'Have I forgotten to say she was deaf? Not the least of that unfortunate girl's ordeals was occasioned by the necessity to shout all her answers down an ear trumpet. The aunt had the deaf person's trick of speaking in a toneless yell. One lost nothing of their conversation. That dinner was quite frightful. I still see and hear it. The little white packet lying on the right of the aunt's plate. The niece nervously crumbling her bread with trembling fingers and eating nothing. The medical feller talking, talking, talking. They drank red wine with their soup and then Benito brought champagne. Veuve Clicquot, it was. He said, as he did a moment ago, "It is sufficiently iced," and poured a little into the aunt's glass. She sipped it and said it was not cold enough. In a second there was another formidable scene. The aunt screamed abuse, the doctor supported and soothed her, another bottle was brought and put in the cooler. Finally Benito gave them their Clicquot. The girl scarcely touched hers, and was asked if she thought the aunt had ordered champagne at thirty shillings a bottle for the amusement of seeing her niece turn up her nose at it. The girl suddenly drank half a glass at one gulp. They all drank. The Clicquot seemed to work its magic even on that appalling woman. She became quieter. I no longer looked into the cupid mirror but rather into the eyes of my vis-à-vis.'

Lord John's guest looked into his tired amused old face and smiled faintly.

'Is that all?' she asked.

'No. When I next watched the party at that table a waiter had brought their coffee. The doctor feller emptied the powder from the packet into the aunt's cup. She drank it and made a great fuss about the taste. It looked as though we were in for another scene when she fell sound asleep.'

'What!' exclaimed the guest.

'She fell into a deep sleep,' said Lord John. 'And died.'

The lady with the nervous hands rose from her table and walked slowly past them out of the dining room.

'Not immediately,' continued Lord John, 'but about two hours later in her room upstairs. Three waiters carried her out of the dining room. Her mouth was open, I remember, and her face was puffy and had reddish-violet spots on it.'

'What killed her?'

'The medical gentleman explained at the inquest that her heart had always been weak.'

'But – you didn't believe that? You think, don't you, that the doctor poisoned her coffee?'

'Oh, no. In his own interest he asked that the coffee and remaining powder in the paper should be analysed. They were found to contain nothing more dangerous than a very mild bromide.'

'Then – ? You suspected something I am sure. Was it the niece? The champagne – ?'

'The doctor was between them. No. I remembered, however, the luncheon incident. The sleeping tablets rolling under the table.'

'And the girl picked them up?'

'Assisted by Benito. During the dispute at dinner over the champagne, Benito filled the glasses. His napkin hid the aunt's glass from her eyes. Not from mine, however. You see, I saw his hand reflected from above in the little cupid mirror.'

There was a long silence.

'Exasperation,' said Lord John, 'may be the motive of many unsolved crimes. By the way I was reminded of this story by the lady with the nervous hands. She has changed a good deal of course, but she still has that trick of crumbling her bread with her fingers.'

The guest stared at him.

'Have we finished?' asked Lord John. 'Shall we go?'

They rose. Benito, bowing, held open the dining room door.

'Good evening, Benito,' said Lord John.

'Good evening, my lord,' said Benito.

NGAIO MARSH

The Inspector Alleyn Mysteries, Volume 1

A MAN LAY DEAD

Sir Hubert Handesley's extravagant weekend house-parties are deservedly famous for his exciting Murder Game. But when the lights go up this time, there is a real corpse with a real dagger in the back. All seven suspects have skilful alibis – so Chief Detective Inspector Roderick Alleyn has to figure out the whodunit...

ENTER A MURDERER

The crime scene was the stage of the Unicorn Theatre, when prop gun fired a very real bullet; the victim was an actor clawing his way to stardom using bribery instead of talent; and the suspects included two unwilling girlfriends and several relieved blackmail victims. The stage is set for one of Roderick Alleyn's most baffling cases...

THE NURSING HOME MURDER

A Harley Street surgeon and his attractive nurse are almost too nervous to operate. Their patient is the Home Secretary – and they both have very good personal reasons to want him dead. The operation is a complete success – but he dies within hours, and Inspector Alleyn must find out why...

'Transforms the detective story from a mere puzzle into a novel.' *Daily Express*

978-0-00-732869-7

NGAIO MARSH

The Inspector Alleyn Mysteries, Volume 2

DEATH IN ECSTASY

Who slipped cyanide into the ceremonial wine of ecstasy at the House of the Sacred Flame? The other initiates and the High Priest claim to be above earthly passions. But Roderick Alleyn discovers that the victim had provoked lust and jealousy, and he suspects that more evil still lurks behind the Sign of the Sacred Flame…

VINTAGE MURDER

New Zealand theatrical manager Alfred Meyer is planning a surprise for his wife's birthday – a jeroboam of champagne descending gently onto the stage after the performance. But, as Roderick Alleyn witnesses, something goes horribly wrong. Is the death the product of Maori superstitions – or something more down to earth?

ARTISTS IN CRIME

It starts as an art exercise – the knife under the drape, the pose outlined in chalk. But when Agatha Troy returns to her class, the scene has been re-enacted: the model is dead, fixed in the most dramatic pose Troy has ever seen. It's a difficult case for Chief Detective Inspector Alleyn. Is the woman he loves really a murderess…?

'As nearly flawless as makes no odds.'   *Sunday Times*

978-0-00-732870-3

NGAIO MARSH

The Inspector Alleyn Mysteries, Volume 3

DEATH IN A WHITE TIE

The season has begun. Débutantes and chaperones are planning their gala dinners – and the blackmailer is planning strategies to stalk his next victim. But Chief Detective Inspector Roderick Alleyn knows that something is up and has already planted his friend Lord Gospell at the dinner. But someone else has got there first...

OVERTURE TO DEATH

It was planned as an act of charity: a new piano for the parish hall, and an amusing evening's entertainment to finance the gift. But all is doomed when Miss Campanula sits down to play. A chord is struck, a shot rings out, and Miss Campanula is dead. It seems to be a case of sinister infatuation for Roderick Alleyn...

DEATH AT THE BAR

A midsummer evening – darts night at *The Plume of Feathers*, a traditional Devonshire public house. A distinguished painter, a celebrated actor, a woman graduate, a plump lady from County Clare and a local farmer all play their parts in a fatal experiment which calls for the investigative expertise of Inspector Alleyn...

'The greatest exponent of the classical English detective story.'
Daily Telegraph

978-0-00-732871-0

NGAIO MARSH

The Inspector Alleyn Mysteries, Volume 4

SURFEIT OF LAMPREYS

The Lampreys were a peculiar family. They entertained their guests with charades – like rich Uncle Gabriel, who was always such a bore. The Lampreys thought if they jollied him up he would bail them out of poverty again. But Uncle Gabriel meets a violent end, and Chief Inspector Alleyn had to work out which of them killed him...

DEATH AND THE DANCING FOOTMAN

It begins as an entertainment: eight people, many of them adversaries, gathered for a winter weekend by a host with a love for theatre. It ends in snowbound disaster. Everyone has an alibi – and a motive as well. But Roderick Alleyn soon realizes that it all hangs on Thomas, the dancing footman...

COLOUR SCHEME

It was a horrible death – lured into a pool of boiling mud and left to die. Roderick Alleyn, far from home on a wartime quest for enemy agents, knows that any number of people could have killed him: the English exiles he'd hated, the New Zealanders he'd despised, or the Maoris he'd insulted. Even the spies he'd thwarted...

'She is astoundingly good.'   *Daily Express*

978-0-00-732872-7

NGAIO MARSH

The Inspector Alleyn Mysteries, Volume 5

DIED IN THE WOOL

One summer evening in 1942 Flossie Rubrick, MP, one of the most formidable women in New Zealand, goes to her husband's wool shed to rehearse a patriotic speech – and disappears. Three weeks later she turns up at an auction – packed inside one of her own bales of wool and very, very dead...

FINAL CURTAIN

Just as Agatha Troy, the world famous painter, completes her portrait of Sir Henry Ancred, the Grand Old Man of the stage, the old actor dies. The dramatic circumstances of his death are such that Scotland Yard is called in – in the person of Troy's long-absent husband, Chief Detective Inspector Roderick Alleyn...

SWING, BROTHER, SWING

The music rises to a climax: Lord Pastern aims his revolver and fires. The figure in the spotlight falls – and the *coup-de-théatre* has become murder... Has the eccentric peer let hatred of his future son-in-law go too far? Or will a tangle of jealousies and blackmail reveal to Inspector Alleyn an altogether different murderer?

'A novelist of glittering accomplishment.'   *Sunday Times*

978-0-00-732873-4

NGAIO MARSH

The Inspector Alleyn Mysteries, Volume 6

OPENING NIGHT

Dreams of stardom lured Martyn Tarne from faraway New Zealand to a soul-destroying round of West End agents and managers in search of work. Now, driven by sheer necessity, she accepts the humble job of dresser to the Vulcan Theatre's leading lady. But the eagerly awaited opening night brings a strange turn of the wheel of fortune – and sudden unforeseen death...

SPINSTERS IN JEOPARDY

High in the mountains stands an historic Saracen fortress, home of the mysterious Mr Oberon, leader of a coven of witches. Roderick Alleyn, on holiday with his family, suspects that a huge drugs ring operates from within the castle. When someone else stumbles upon the secret, Mr Oberon decides his strange rituals require a human sacrifice...

SCALES OF JUSTICE

The inhabitants of Swevenings are stirred only by a fierce competition to catch a monster trout known to dwell in their beautiful stream. Then one of their small community is found brutally murdered; beside him is the freshly killed trout. Chief Detective Inspector Roderick Alleyn's murder investigation seems to be much more interested in the fish...

'A brilliant, vivacious teller of detective novels.'

News Chronicle

978-0-00-732874-1

NGAIO MARSH

The Inspector Alleyn Mysteries, Volume 7

OFF WITH HIS HEAD

When the pesky Anna Bünz arrives at Mardian to investigate local folk-dancing, she quickly antagonizes the villagers. But Mrs Bünz is not the only source of friction. When the sword dancers' traditional mock beheading of the Winter Solstice becomes horribly real, Superintendent Roderick Alleyn finds himself faced with a complex case of gruesome proportions...

SINGING IN THE SHROUDS

On a cold February London night, the police find a corpse on the quayside, her body covered with flower petals and pearls. The killer, who walked away singing, is known to be one of nine passengers on the cargo ship, *Cape Farewell*. Superintendent Roderick Alleyn joins the ship on the most difficult assignment of his career...

FALSE SCENT

Mary Bellamy, darling of the London stage, holds a 50th birthday party, a gala for everyone who loves her and fears her power. Then someone uses a deadly insect spray on Mary instead of the azaleas. The suspects, all very theatrically, are playing the part of mourners. Superintendent Alleyn has to find out which one played the murderer...

'Brilliant – ranks with Agatha Christie and Dorothy Sayers'
Times Literary Supplement

978-0-00-732875-8